FRENCH PRESSED

DECAFFEINATED CORPSE

MURDER MOST FROTHY

"Exciting, delicious fun, with coffee trivia, recipes, a vicarious adventure for those of us at home reading of things we'd rather not face ourselves but understanding Clare Cosi's motives and morals." —*Gumshoe Review*

LATTE TROUBLE

"Anyone who loves coffee and a good mystery will love this story. Rating: Outstanding." —*Mysterious Corner*

THROUGH THE GRINDER

"Coffee lovers and mystery buffs will savor the latest addition to this mystery series . . . Fast-paced action, coffee lore, and incredible culinary recipes . . . All hail the goddess Caffina!" —*The Best Reviews*

ON WHAT GROUNDS

#1 Paperback Bestseller
Independent Mystery Booksellers Association

"A great beginning to a new series . . . *On What Grounds* will convert even the most fervent tea drinker into a coffee lover in the time it takes to draw an espresso." —*The Mystery Reader*

"A hilarious blend of amateur detecting with some romance thrown in the mix . . . I personally adored this book, and can't wait to read the rest of the series!" —*Cozy Library*

Visit Cleo Coyle's virtual Village Blend at
CoffeehouseMystery.com,
where coffee and crime are always brewing . . .

Praise for Cleo Coyle's Coffeehouse Mysteries

ROAST MORTEM

A BookReporter.com Reviewer's Pick
Favorite Book of the Year!

"Coyle incorporates a taste of the real-life bravery of the New York City Fire Department into her brilliantly fast-paced mystery, giving readers a glimpse into the lives of some of the hardest-working men and women in America." —*Fresh Fiction*

"Coyle's strong ninth coffeehouse mystery . . . pays tribute to New York City firefighters . . . Coyle even provides an appendix of useful tips and tempting recipes." —*Publishers Weekly*

"Coyle has an excellent sense of pace . . . Coyle is [also] skilled at defining each character . . . Anyone who isn't already filled with admiration for the heroism of firefighters will certainly come away with appreciation of the bravery of these men and women." —ReviewingTheEvidence.com

"Looking to unwind after a hectic day, sit back with a cup of your favorite coffee and enjoy this entertaining, fast-paced, thrill-a-minute story." —*Chattooga (GA) Press*

HOLIDAY GRIND

"[A] new addition to the coffeehouse mystery series that . . . adds in jolts of souped-up coffee, sweet cooking . . . and super-sleuthing to deliver a fun and gripping fa-la-la-la-latte surprise." —*The Huffington Post*

"The charming eighth coffeehouse mystery . . . will keep readers guessing until the end, while the drink and accompanying treat recipes will send anyone to the kitchen in search of a candy cane brownie and a caffe mocha latte." —*Publishers Weekly*

continued . . . .

"Gives readers . . . many holiday recipes while throwing in a good plot and an in-your-face look at life in the Big Apple for good measure. Fans of culinary cozies by Joanne Fluke and JoAnna Carl will want this." —*Library Journal*

"Coyle's greatest strength is writing characters that feel real. Clare and company are some of the most vibrant characters I've ever read . . . Coyle also is a master of misdirection and red herrings. I challenge any reader to figure out whodunit before Coyle reveals all." —*Mystery Scene*

ESPRESSO SHOT

"Coyle's Coffeehouse books are superb examples of the cozy genre because of their intelligent cast of characters, their subtle wit, and their knowledge of the coffee industry used to add depth and flavor to the stories. Highly recommended for all mystery collections." —*Library Journal* (starred review)

"A realistic depiction of New York City high and low life. The smattering of recipes, romance, and caffeine-fueled detection add up to a lively tale." —*Kirkus Reviews*

"Enjoyable . . . This mellow-paced cozy includes some surprises . . . Recipes and coffee tips are a bonus." —*Publishers Weekly*

"Cleo Coyle's Coffeehouse Mysteries, which are among my favorites, can be counted on for great characters, smooth plotting and pacing that keeps readers engaged . . . *Espresso Shot* is seventh in the series and, in my opinion, it's the best one yet." —*Mystery News*

"Oh, *Espresso Shot* is a fun read! I kept turning the pages long after I should have turned off the light." —*Armchair Interviews*

ROAST MORTEM

CLEO COYLE

BERKLEY PRIME CRIME, NEW YORK

THE BERKLEY PUBLISHING GROUP
Published by the Penguin Group
Penguin Group (USA) LLC
375 Hudson Street, New York, New York 10014

USA • Canada • UK • Ireland • Australia • New Zealand • India • South Africa • China

penguin.com

A Penguin Random House Company

ROAST MORTEM

A Berkley Prime Crime Book / published by arrangement with the author

Berkley Prime Crime Books are published by The Berkley Publishing Group.
BERKLEY® PRIME CRIME and the PRIME CRIME logo
are trademarks of Penguin Group (USA) LLC.
A COFFEEHOUSE MYSTERY is a registered trademark of Penguin Group (USA) LLC.

For information, address: The Berkley Publishing Group,
a division of Penguin Group (USA) LLC,
375 Hudson Street, New York, New York 10014.

ISBN: 978-0-425-24272-8

PUBLISHING HISTORY
Berkley Prime Crime hardcover edition / August 2010
Berkley Prime Crime mass-market edition / August 2011

PRINTED IN THE UNITED STATES OF AMERICA

11 10 9 8 7 6 5 4 3 2

Cover illustration by Cathy Gendron.
Cover design and logo by Rita Frangie.
Interior text design by Kristin del Rosario.

Hero *is not a word one hears in the course of a typical workweek. When it's used at all these days, it generally involves magic wands and superpowers. But if you're a New Yorker who witnessed the events on September 11, 2001, then you know what a hero is. As the FDNY writes in its official description of its symbol, the Maltese Cross: Every firefighter works in courage, a ladder rung away from death, willing to lay down his life for you. This book is dedicated to the firefighters, paramedics, and police officers who lost their lives on 9/11. We will never forget you.*

The Terry Farrell Firefighters Fund was formed in honor of Terry Farrell, a decorated firefighter who perished on September 11, 2001. To find out more, visit the fund's Web site at www.terryfarrellfund.org.

ACKNOWLEDGMENTS

While the characters and events of this book are complete fiction, part of the plotline was initially inspired by a real incident. (More on this in the afterword.) For now, I would like to thank several members of the FDNY who answered my questions (off the record) for background. I would also like to thank author Tom Downey for his excellent insider's look at the New York City Fire Department—*The Last Men Out: Life on the Edge at Rescue 2 Firehouse,* a work I highly recommend to anyone whose interest in New York's Bravest is sparked by this tale. Please note, however, that because this is a light work of amateur sleuth fiction, liberties are sometimes taken with procedure. In the Coffeehouse Mysteries the rules occasionally get bent.

Once again, I thank the excellent Joe the Art of Coffee of New York City (www.JoetheArtofCoffee.com), including its co-owners, Jonathan Rubinstein and his sister Gabrielle Rubinstein. I also owe a big thank-you to their manager and coffee director, Amanda Byron, who shared insights into the world behind her espresso machine, including her recommendation of a true barista bible, *Espresso Coffee* by David C. Schomer.

My second java shout-out goes to the amazing Gimme! Coffee (www.GimmeCoffee.com) as well as its founder and CEO, Kenneth Cuddeback, for taking the time to speak with me about our favorite subject. I must also thank Gimme! for its inspiring handling of the Ethiopian Amaro Gayo, a unique and exotic coffee that also happens to be sold by Asnakech Thomas, the only female coffee miller and exporter in all of Ethiopia. Additional caffeinated hugs to Mary Tracy, a dedicated Coffeehouse Mystery reader, who recommended Gimme! to me.

With epic gratitude, I would like to recognize the intrepid

posse of publishing professionals at Berkley Prime Crime, who shepherded this book from manuscript to printed page. Enormous thanks especially to executive editor Wendy McCurdy for her great goodwill as well as her ingenuity and insight. Props and snaps must also be given to Katherine Pelz for her hard work and gusto.

As always, I thank my husband, Marc, who is my partner in writing not only this Coffeehouse Mystery series but also our Haunted Bookshop Mystery series. (A better partner a girl couldn't ask for.)

Last but far from least, a heartfelt thank-you to our friends and family for their support as well as to our literary agent John Talbot, a premium professional and a darn good joe.

Yours sincerely,
Cleo Coyle

Love is a fire. But whether it is going to warm your hearth or burn down your house, you can never tell.

—Joan Crawford

PROLOGUE

~~~~~~~~~~~~~~~~~~~~~~~~~~~~~~~~~~

COLD here in the alley, but things will get hotter soon . . .

The Arsonist moved deeper into the shadows, orange shopping bag in hand. Back on the busy Queens sidewalk, the day felt bright and balmy. Just a few steps away from humanity, all warmth fled and nearly all light.

Weak shafts of sun barely penetrated the crisscrossing maze of phone wires and fire escapes, coaxial cables and clothing lines. With certain strides, the Arsonist bypassed iron grates and grimy windows, broken crates and dented trash cans. Finally the destination—one particular back door.

Down went the glossy tangerine sack, squatting on the cold concrete. Cloying scents of soy and garlic still haunted its boxy interior, ghosts of last night's Korean takeout. The reinforced bottom and laminated sides made it sturdy enough to carry the necessary items.

Feeling sweaty despite the chill, the Arsonist bent over the shopping bag, grasped two wires from the battery, and fixed them to circuits on the bleach bottle with no bleach inside.

Now it's ready . . .

The Arsonist rose, lifting the bag's handles of nylon rope.

Heavier now, or my imagination?

Nervous fingers tested the shiny brass knob. Unlocked, as promised, the back door swung open on a small utility room. A sink, shelves, supplies neatly stacked.

Male laughter seeped through the brocade curtain. The Arsonist crossed the tight space, teased apart the muffling fabric. An archway framed the caffè's main room. Up front, the elderly owner gabbed with a customer about the rush hour pedestrian parade, mostly about the women.

Stepping back, the Arsonist quickly searched out a spot for the bag. Under the shelf, behind the cleaning products . . .

Perfect.

A stifled sneeze, a few more steps, and the Arsonist was back on the sidewalk. Warmth, pedestrians, unobstructed light. It felt as if nothing had happened—or more like something good had happened.

At 9:25 PM, the caffè would be closed, the old Italian off playing bocce in the park. No one would be in the building. No one would be hurt.

Unless something goes wrong . . .

That prick of a thought had vexed the Arsonist multiple times. This would be the last.

After all, *thought the Arsonist,* it's out of my hands now. The schedule was set for me, and I held up my end. Tonight Caffè Lucia will burn. If people get in the way, it's their own stupid fault.

One

~~~~~~~~~~~~~~~~~~~~~~~~~~~~~~~~~~~~

"**B**oss, I hate to leave you like this, but I have *got* to go."

"Go," I told Esther. "We'll be okay . . ."

At least I hoped we would. I was standing behind my espresso machine, facing a line out my door. The usual Village Blend regulars were here along with a swell of caffeine-deprived commuters grabbing a java hit before heading home. Nothing out of the ordinary, really, and in most respects the day felt like any other. Except it wasn't. This was the day the fires began. When the smoke finally cleared, the fatalities would number two, and they would not be accidents. The deaths would turn out to be murders and I, Clare Cosi, would be the one to prove it.

At this particular moment, however, I wasn't thinking about killers or arsonists, lovesick Italian women or blustery FDNY captains, and I certainly wasn't thinking about a bomb. Mostly what I was thinking about was traffic.

Tucker Burton, my lanky, floppy-haired assistant manager, had arrived on time for his shift and was just tying on his Village Blend apron. A part-time actor-playwright and occasional cabaret director, Tuck loved being a barista in the Italian tradition, which (like a good bartender) had as much to do with convivial customer interaction as it did with temperature and pressure.

"Excuse me, Clare," he said, "but where is Gardner again?"

"Trapped in his car," I replied, "on the New Jersey side of the Holland Tunnel."

Tuck pointed to Esther. "And why can't our resident slam poetess stay and work another hour until he shows? I'll bet my Actors' Equity card she's been late to more than a few of her classes."

Esther's wine-dark fingertips went to her Botticelli waist. "Excuse me, Broadway Boy, but I am not simply taking this class. I am a TA and need to be there on time."

"For what? Introduction to Baggy Pants and Bling 101?"

"Urban Rap's Influence on Mainstream America!"

"Who's the professor? Eminem?"

Esther smirked. "The man has a PhD from Brown in linguistics and is heading my program in the semiotics of urban expression."

"Yeah? And I know what seat he holds: the Snoop Dog Chair."

"Okay, you two, enough!" I turned to Tucker. "Let her off the hook."

"But it's not very fair to you, Clare. You've been here since eight AM."

"And I can't leave you here alone, can I? Traffic is traffic and Esther is a teaching assistant now. Her shift's over and she has to go."

"Thank you!" she said.

I caught her eye. "Just call Vicki Glockner, okay? Tell her I'll give her double time until Gardner can get through that tunnel."

"Will do, boss," Esther promised, and she was gone.

Now my focus was back on that customer line. As Tuck

manned the register and the single-cup Clover machine, I turned out the espresso drink orders: one Skinny Lat (latte with skim milk); one Breve Cap (cappuccino with half-and-half); 3 *doppios* (double espressos); one Cortado (a single shot caressed with steamed milk); two Flat Whites (cappuccinos without foam); one Americano (espresso diluted with hot water); two Thunder Thighs (double-tall mocha lattes with whole milk and extra whipped cream); and a Why Bother (decaf espresso).

When the crush finally eased, I turned to the octogenarian sitting on the other side of my counter. Madame Dreyfus Allegro Dubois was looking as stylish as ever in a springy apricot pantsuit, her silver-gray hair coiffed into a supernaturally smooth twist.

"I'm so sorry," I told her, sliding a *crema*-rich espresso across the blueberry marble.

"Why should you be sorry, dear?"

"Because we're going to be *very* late."

"*C'est dommage,*" Madame said, lifting the demitasse to her peach-glossed lips. "But Enzo will understand. Managerial setbacks are an inescapable aspect of New York's mise-en-scène."

"You mean like bureaucratic bribes and obscene levels of sales tax?"

Madame's reply was an amused little shrug. The woman's Gallic aplomb was admirable, I had to admit, but then what was a minor traffic delay to someone who'd seen Nazi tanks roll down the Champs-Élysées?

Given that I was half her age—with duskier skin, Italian hips, and a preference for discount store jeans—Madame and I made an incongruous pair. At our core, however, we weren't so different, which was why our relationship had survived my late-teen pregnancy and hasty marriage to her wayward son, his drug addiction and recovery, our rocky divorce, and my decade spent in New Jersey exile before returning to Manhattan to run her beloved coffeehouse again.

The latter development was the reason I'd agreed to drive

Madame to Queens today. A valuable piece of Village Blend history was waiting for us at Astoria's Caffè Lucia, and we were both determined to reclaim it.

Just then my thigh vibrated—actually the cell phone in my pocket next to my thigh. I answered without checking the screen.

"Gardner?" I asked, hoping my jazz-musician barista was calling to say he'd finally blown through the Holland Tunnel.

"It's Mike."

As in Mike Quinn, my boyfriend (for lack of a better word). He certainly wasn't a *boy* and he was much more than a *friend*, although that's the way we'd started out. The phrase "Mike is my lover" would have been accurate, but it sounded absurdly decadent to the ears of a girl who was raised by a strict Italian grandmother.

"I'm sorry, Mike, I can't talk—"

"Yes, you can, dear." A hand touched my shoulder. I turned to find Madame behind me, tying on a Blend apron. "Take a break, Clare."

"But—"

"No buts. My hands are clean." With a wink, Madame showed me. "And as you know, I've done this a few times before."

I would have argued, but I really did need to take five, so I pulled off my apron and grabbed her seat on the customer side of the bar.

"Are you still driving to Queens?" Mike asked.

"Slight delay but yes," I said. "Why?"

"I've got another meeting on the undercover operation," he said. "It may run late, but I was still hoping to see you tonight."

"Just come by the duplex," I said, happily accepting the freshly pulled double from my employer. "Use your key. You still have it, right?"

"I still have it." He paused. "So how's your head?"

"Better," I lied, and took a reviving sip of the *doppio*.

In fact, I was still recovering from the Quinn family's St. Patrick's Day bash the night before—"*The* annual event," or so I was told by Mike's clan. He was the only cop among a family of firefighters so he didn't always attend (cops had their own gatherings), but this year Mike wanted to introduce me around.

While the beer flowed like Trevi, I was regaled with heroic stories about the "Mighty Quinn," Mike's late father, a fire captain. Then Mike's mother asked me if I'd be willing to contribute some coffeehouse specialties to the FDNY's upcoming Five-Borough Bake Sale, and she promptly introduced me to the head of the coordinating committee—a lovely (and very sharp) woman named Valerie Noonan.

"And have you made your decision yet?" Mike asked.

I could almost hear him smiling over the cellular line, but I couldn't blame him. I'd called the man three times today, obsessing over what would impress his family more: my cinnamon-sugar doughnut muffins; blueberries 'n' cream coffee cake pie; or honey-glazed peach crostata with fresh ginger-infused whipped cream. There were always my pastry case standbys: caramelized banana bread; almond-roca scones; and mini Italian coffeehouse cakes. (Ricotta cheese was my secret ingredient to making those tasty little loaves tender and delicious.) They were absolutely perfect with coffee, and I topped each with a different glaze inspired by the gourmet syrups of my coffeehouse: chocolate-hazelnut; buttery toffee; candied orange-cinnamon; raspberry–white chocolate; and sugar-kissed lemon, the flavor found in my Romano "sweet," an espresso served in a cup with its rim rubbed by a lemon twist, then dipped in granulated cane—the way the old-timers drank it in the Pennsylvania factory town where I'd grown up.

"I think I should make them all," I said.

"All?"

Am I trying too hard? I thought. *Probably.* Then I remembered tomorrow was March 19, the feast day of St. Joseph (patron saint of pastry chefs). Every year my *nonna* would fry up crunchy sweet bow tie cookies and set them out with hot, fresh, doughy zeppolinis in her little Italian grocery. *That's it!*

"I'll make champagne cream puffs!"

"Champagne cream puffs?"

"Zeppole dough baked in the oven and filled with Asti Spumante–based zabaglione!"

"It's a bake sale, sweetheart, not a four-star dessert cart."

Just then our shop bell rang and a young woman with fluffy, crumpet-colored curls walked across our main floor. "Hey, everyone!" Vicki Glockner waved at me.

"Mike, I've got to go. My relief is here."

"Okay," he said, "but that's why I called. It's my turn to relieve you. Don't worry about cooking tonight. I'll get us takeout."

By the time I drove down the Queensboro Bridge ramp, dusk had fully descended, and streetlights were flickering on, their halogen bulbs pouring pools of blue-tinged light into an ocean of deepening darkness. Madame and I had been late getting started. Then a pileup on the bridge left me inching and lurching my way across the mile-long span. Now we were more than an hour behind schedule.

"Do you want to try calling again?" I asked, swinging my old Honda beneath the subway's elevated tracks.

"It's all right, dear," Madame replied. "I left a message apologizing for our tardiness. Let's hope Enzo picks it up."

Enzo was "Lorenzo" Testa, the owner of Caffè Lucia. He'd called Madame that morning, telling her he'd been cleaning out his basement and came across an old Blend roaster and a photo album with pictures of Madame and her late first husband, Antonio Allegro. While Madame was thrilled about the photos, I was itching to get my paws on the old Probat, a small-batch German coffee roaster, circa 1921. Enzo had bought it used from the Blend in the sixties.

"So this man worked for you and Matt's father," I asked.

Madame nodded. "He came to us fresh off the boat from Italy. An eager aspiring artist."

"Marlon Brando–ish? Isn't that how you described him?"

"More Victor Mature, dear. The young female customers absolutely swooned when they saw him in our shop or Washington Square Park—that's where he liked to set up his painter's easel."

"So he was hot stuff?"

"Oh, yes. Smoldering male charisma, liquid bedroom gaze . . . *Oo-la-la* . . ."

Oo-la-la? I suppressed a smile. "Is that why I'm the one driving you to Astoria to meet with him instead of Otto?"

"My. Don't *you* have a suspicious mind?"

"I think we've already established that."

"Well, the answer to your question is *no*. My Otto would have taken me, but he has a very important business dinner lined up this evening so I'm a free agent."

"Uh-huh." The last time Madame characterized herself as a "free agent" she was in East Hampton, enjoying a fling with a septuagenarian expert on Jackson Pollock.

"And, besides," she added. "I've wanted you to meet Enzo for ages. Given your background, I thought it was about time."

"Whatever became of Enzo's art career, anyway?" (Myself an art school dropout, I couldn't help wondering.) "Did his work ever sell?"

"Oh, yes. Enzo's female admirers bought many of his paintings. Restaurants and caffès hired him, too. At one time, you could see his trompe l'oeil frescos in dozens of pizzerias around town. But most of them are gone now. Irreplaceable because Enzo stopped selling his work."

"Why? What happened?"

Madame shrugged. "Life."

"Life?"

"His lover became pregnant," she said, glancing at the fast-passing rows of storefronts. "The same year her father died. Angela asked Enzo to marry her and take over her family's caffè in Queens, save them from financial ruin." Madame shrugged. "Enzo adored her . . ."

I nodded at Enzo's story (half of it, anyway) because I knew just how many hours it took to run a successful business, and just how much love it took to give up on a dream. Suddenly, without having ever met the man, I liked him, very much.

"Caffè Lucia is a pretty name," I said.

"He renamed the place for his daughter. A lively, outspoken child, as I recall; all grown up by now. And sadly, last year, Angela passed away during their annual visit to Italy . . ."

As I turned onto Steinway Street, I noticed Madame glancing at her watch.

"This trip isn't over yet," I warned.

"I know, dear. I'm looking."

Parking is what we were looking for, and I didn't see a single open spot. Eyeing the crowded curbs, I rolled by cell phone shops, clothing stores, and restaurants with Greek, Italian, Cyrillic, and Naskh signage. Finally I turned onto the tree-lined block where Caffè Lucia was located, and Madame began waving frantically (because attempting to find parking in this town could turn even the most urbane cosmopolitan into a raving maniac).

"There! There! A spot on the right! Get it! Get it!"

"Fire hydrant," I said. "I'll circle again—"

"Look! Look! That car is leaving! Go! Go!"

I zoomed into the spot, right behind a mammoth SUV. As I climbed out from behind the wheel, I could almost feel the adrenaline ebbing from my bloodstream. (Not quite as stressful as driving a golf cart through a war zone, but close.) Unfortunately, I wasn't off the battlefield yet. More trouble was heading our way—in size-twelve Air Jordans.

"Hey, lady!" (The greeting was quintessential Jerry Lewis but the accent was definitely foreign.) "You can't park here!"

A scowling man barreled toward us, gesturing wildly.

"Excuse me?" I said.

"You have to move your car!"

Stone black eyes under tight curls the color of Sicilian licorice; a slate gray leisure suit (sans tie) over incongruous white tube socks. I couldn't place the guy's accent, but that was no surprise. While this area used to be primarily Greek and Italian, more recent arrivals included Brazilians, Bosnians, and natives of Egypt, Yemen, and Morocco.

The guy stopped right in front of us, hands outstretched to keep us from moving down the sidewalk. For a moment, I stared at his day-old jaw stubble. *Another blind follower of Hollywood's derelict chic trend? Or simply a misplaced razor?*

"You have to move that junk heap! I can't have it in front of my club!"

Junk heap? I frowned, scanning the area around my admittedly *non*-late-model Honda. I saw no fire hydrant, construction cones, or city signage.

Madame glanced at me, then back at our human road block. "I don't understand, young man. Are you saying this isn't a legal parking spot?"

"I'm saying you can't park here unless you're going to my club."

"Your club?" I said.

He jerked his head at the shadowy doorway behind him. Under a scarlet neon *Red Mirage* banner, a sign announced: *Happy Hour 5–8 PM. Monday thru Thursday.*

Madame's large, expressive eyes—so intensely blue that tricks of light turned them lavender—displayed gentle crow's feet when she smiled. She wasn't smiling now.

"Listen up, friend—" (Her voice dropped to a serious octave.) "Our parking spot is legal. Your attempt at extortion is not."

Given the level of society to which Madame's late second husband (a French importer) had elevated her, not to mention her Fifth Avenue address, even I sometimes failed to remember that the doyenne of polite society was no cream-filled profiterole. The woman had come to this country as a motherless, penniless refugee. Not long after, she'd found herself alone, a widow in her prime, with a boy to raise and a coffeehouse to run—no mean feat in a city that challenged its shop owners with difficult regulations, sky-high overhead, and a demanding (and occasionally dangerous) customer base.

Of course, Club Guy here didn't know any of that. And when Madame actually took a step *closer*, he froze. A moment later, he began muttering in another language, obviously befuddled by a dignified older lady's willingness to go toe-to-toe with him. Finally, he waved his arms and cried, "I'm a businessman, lady! I'm just trying to keep this spot open for taxis to drop off paying customers!"

Score one for Madame. He was on the defensive. But his Air Jordans had yet to budge. That's when I noticed a flash of headlights. The driver in that mammoth SUV had started his engine.

"There," I said, "why don't you keep *that* spot open for your customers!"

Our human road block instantly raced off to reserve the vacated space.

Madame tapped my shoulder. "Shall we, dear?"

"We shall."

Then I looped my arm through hers, and together we started down the sidewalk toward our hard won destination: Caffè Lucia.

Two

~~~~~~~~~~~~~~~~~~~~~~~~~~~~~~~~~~~~~~

LIKE the accident on the bridge, I approached Enzo Testa's caffè without knowing exactly what lay ahead, although I should have had a clue—not because of the smell of accelerants or the sound of cartoonishly loud ticking, but because of the woman who unlocked the door.

In her early forties, Enzo's daughter Lucia seemed almost storklike in her fashionable gangliness. Her nose was long, her squinting eyes the flat color of sour pickles. Her sleek, short, slicked down hair, which should have echoed the same dark hue as her salon-shaped brows, was striated instead with the sort of shades you'd find in a jar of whole-grain Dijon (or the bottles of an uptown colorist).

Hugging her slim figure was a black designer frock with a high hemline and low neckline, the better to show off the heavy gold bling around her neck and chic gladiator sandals (also gilded) with four-inch heels that added dauntingly unnecessary height to her already lengthy legs. All of this seemed a bit much for shift work in a neighborhood coffeehouse, and I assumed she was dressed for a hot dinner date.

"We're closed," she said, her plum-glossed lips forming a bad-luck horseshoe.

"We have an appointment," I began, all business.

"With Enzo, your father." Madame stepped up, her tone of voice much more placating than mine.

"You're *late*."

"And we do apologize," Madame told the woman. "I did call—"

"It's my fault," I cut in. "I'm very sorry, but I run a coffeehouse, too, and I had trouble getting away. Then we got stuck on the bridge. There was an accident . . ."

Lucia propped a narrow hip, more bling clattering on her narrow wrist. "When isn't there?"

"You're right," I said, biting back a less civil response. "But won't you at least tell your father we made it?"

Lucia's reply was to make a show of looking me up and down. I hadn't changed from my Blend shift so my Italian roast hair was still pulled back in a barista-ready (and now supremely messy) ponytail. My makeup had sweated off in traffic, and my simple cotton Henley was tragically wrinkled.

She squinted with open disgust at my scuffed black boots and economically priced jeans, and in case I missed the squint, she threw in a smirk to go with it.

I was about to say something I'd probably regret when a deep voice boomed from inside the caffè: "Lucia, *che cosa*? Is that Blanche?"

Lucia stepped back—with obvious annoyance—and opened the door all the way. A gentleman in shirtsleeves strode across the spotlessly clean mosaic tile floor. Tall, like his daughter, Enzo was not at all gangly. On the contrary, he appeared especially robust for a man in his seventies. The line of his chin and jaw were giving way, like the inevitable decline of a classic old foundation, but his head was still thick with hair, albeit receding in front, the black pepper copiously sprinkled with gray salt.

When the Italian flung out his arms, Madame stepped

into them, and the man's wide smile tightened the skin at his jaw, restoring for a flickering moment the hallmarks of those Victor Mature looks. Instantly I knew that I was glimpsing a vision of Enzo's earlier self, a long-gone ghost. Like a dying ember, the apparition faded, yet the man continued to give off a color of energy I more commonly saw in the budding green of youth (or diehard romantics)—a color Madame had always embraced.

"*Bella!* Blanche, you are ravishing still. *Bella! Bella!*"

The shop was small, half the size of my Village Blend, with a marble counter the shade of a mature avocado, a restored tin ceiling, and a pair of hanging fans with wooden paddles lazily stirring the air. Large and small tables of sturdy, polished, marble-topped oak crowded the floor. Behind the bar sat a modern, low-slung espresso machine, typical of a New York caffè.

Not at all typical, however, was the sweeping mural on the opposite wall, which stretched the length of the building. The artwork itself contained multiple images, each rendered in a different artistic style.

Is it all Enzo's? I was unable to look away as every thoughtful section of the work evoked either meaningful recognition or absolute astonishment.

Enzo stepped back from hugging Madame, one arm continuing to claim her waist. His free hand reached into a pocket for a large pair of steel-framed glasses.

"Glasses? Oh, no!" Madame laughed. "I doubt I'll look as 'ravishing' now!"

"These old eyes just need a little help for a better view of your beauty." He slipped them on and grinned again. "You haven't aged a day."

Madame glanced back at me and mouthed, *Didn't I tell you? Such a charmer!*

"And *you*, Enzo!" she said. "You're as dashing as the day we first met!"

After more cooing and multiple cheek kisses, Madame stepped away. "There, now that all of those whopping lies are out of the way, we can talk honestly, just like old friends should."

She gestured in my direction. "This is my manager, Clare."

Forcing myself to stop gawking at the finely wrought fresco, I smiled. "So nice to meet you, Signore Testa."

He shook my hand, his grip warm, firm, a little stiff (the beginnings of arthritis?). "At last we meet. I've heard so much about you over the years . . ."

Enzo's stare was as penetrating as his offspring's but held no scorn. I sensed only the painter inside him, evaluating my colors and contours, contemplating depths with his eyes.

"*Bellissima*," he whispered, lifting the back of my hand to his lips. As he held my gaze, he spoke softly to Madame: "Such a jewel, Blanche. Eyes like emeralds set afire. Lady Apples for cheeks, lips full and pillowy, yet the girlish face sits upon a ripened figure. So lush!"

Oh, good God.

"She is another Claudia Cardinale!"

"I always thought so," Madame said.

Lucia made a noise behind me. It sounded like a snort. I didn't blame her. A Fellini leading lady I wasn't. Clearly, the prescription on the man's glasses had expired.

"And you have given Blanche a granddaughter as beautiful?"

"I, uh . . ." The man's aura was so hypnotic I had a hard time finding my tongue. Madame really wasn't kidding about this guy's mojo. "Yes, I have a daughter." I finally replied. "Her name is Joy, and she's—"

"A chef! That's right! Blanche told me this morning in our phone call. She is at work in Paris."

"Not a chef yet. Just a line cook. Of course, in my mind she's still twelve years old, inventing cake-mix biscotti in our New Jersey kitchen."

Enzo's eyes smiled. "Where does the time go, eh?" Then he looked away in what appeared to be a pointedly unhappy frown for his daughter.

"Speaking of *time*," Lucia interrupted. "It's Thursday, and your bocce game is starting *very* soon." She glared at us. "They're expecting my father at the park."

Enzo waved his hand. "Luigi and Thomas can wait."

"But what about *Mrs. Quadrelli*." Lucia's gaze stabbed Madame on that one. "You know she'll be disappointed if you're late."

Enzo folded his arms. "Rita Quadrelli will find some other man's ear to talk off until I get there."

"We always close early on Thursday, just so you can play your weekly game. I don't see why you should let their lateness change your plans."

"That's no way to treat guests!" Enzo replied in Italian. "Show some respect—"

A hesitant knock interrupted. "Yo, Lucy! You in there? I'm double-parked."

A wiry, gum-chewing male about ten years Lucia's junior emerged from the shadows of the sidewalk. His cuffed gabardine slacks, two-toned bowling shirt, and black-and-brown saddle shoes looked like a tribute to the *Happy Days* wardrobe department. Platinum pompadour cocked, he moved to join us.

"Sorry, Glenn," Lucia folded her arms. "I was going to meet you outside, but these *people* came."

Madame shot me a glance.

There's an old Italian saying: "With a contented stomach, your heart is forgiving; with an empty stomach, you forgive nothing." Madame had to be thinking the same thing I was: *Lucia Testa is in sore need of a decent meal.*

Glenn didn't answer his girlfriend. Instead, he put on a warm smile and approached her father, extending a sinewy arm. "Mr. T, how you doin' tonight, sir?"

Enzo shook the man's hand and then gestured toward me and Madame. "This is Glenn Duffy, Lucia's boyfriend—"

"*Fiancé*, Papa, Lucia corrected.

"Yes, yes," Enzo said, but under his breath I heard him mutter. "Who ever heard of an engagement with no ring?"

To this, Glenn made no reply—maybe he hadn't heard Enzo's low remark or maybe he was smart enough to pretend he hadn't. Either way, he turned his full attention to greeting us. As he happily chewed his gum, dimples appeared in his lean cheeks. A bleach-blond Elvis.

"I hope I didn't interrupt anything here," Glenn said.

"You are always welcome," Enzo replied. "How about an espresso?"

"Sure." Glenn shrugged, taking out his gum. "Maybe a few cookies, too?" He smiled a little sheepishly, "I really liked those Italian ones—"

Enzo snorted. "They're all Italian."

Lucia tapped her watch. "No coffee tonight, Glenn! We have to *go*."

"Why?" he asked. "What's the hurry?"

"You said it yourself. You're double-parked! You didn't work for a solid year to restore that car of yours just so some jerk can sideswipe you!"

Glenn put the gum back in his mouth. "The New Jersey Custom Car Show's this weekend," he informed us, jerking his thumb toward the door. "I'm showing my '68 Mustang."

Madame and I moved to the caffè's picture window. The restored coup sported a chassis that gleamed redder than strawberries in a newly glazed tart. The convertible top and leather interior were whiter than castor sugar. Racing stripes ran like Christmas ribbons from bumper to fender, a retro bonnet scoop topped the hood, and the chrome grill was so highly polished it could have been cut from a mirror.

Note to self: Do not, under any circumstances, let Lucia Testa see my *car!*

As Madame and I gushed compliments to Glenn, Enzo turned to his daughter and spoke in Italian. "What's one espresso? What would your mama say about your rude behavior?"

"Well, I don't want *you* to be rude to *Mrs. Quadrelli*," Lucia replied in English.

"*Basta*, child! Blanche and Clare do not have all night to sit here with me! We will drink our coffee, and I will be on the bocce court in less than an hour. Okay? Happy?"

"Okay! That's all I wanted to hear!" Lucia finally looked relieved. "I'll see you on Sunday, Papa. C'mon, Glenn. Don't forget my bag." She pointed to a Pullman in the corner as her gilded gladiators clicked toward the front door.

"Sorry, Mr. T," Glenn shrugged again, grabbed the Pullman's handle. "Maybe next time. Nice to meet you, ladies."

A moment later the door shut, and we heard Lucia struggling to throw the old lock. Silence hovered. Finally, Madame cleared her throat.

"Mr. Duffy seems like a nice young man . . ."

Enzo let out a breath. "He's nice enough, *sì*. And he has a good job working on cars. That is how he met my daughter. Car trouble. Mr. Fix-it comes to the rescue, but Lucia, she is pushing too hard . . ."

He shook his head with that exasperated parent shake (one I knew *oh* so well). "For years, she had offers to marry—plenty. None of them were good enough. Now she is finally feeling the hands of life's clock spinning faster. But Glenn is still a boy. Time passes slower for the young. He is in no hurry. That's why there is no ring!"

Madame and I exchanged glances. *What do you say to that?*

"Well," Madame finally replied, "Lucia wasn't wrong about our tardiness. If you have someplace else to go, perhaps we can reschedule—"

"Nonsense! Sit down!"

We did, taking seats at one of the marble-topped caffè tables.

"I have no intention of playing bocce tonight," he said as he slipped behind the counter and prepared our espressos. "I fibbed to my daughter to send her on her way. Meeting up with that *donna pazzesca*, Mrs. Quadrelli? That's Lucia's idea, not mine."

Donna pazzesca? My eyebrows rose. *Crazy woman?* I mouthed to Madame.

"She's trying to fix you up?" Madame asked, obviously curious.

"I take her to dinner a few times. Nothing special. A movie once or twice. Now the woman stalks me at my game every Thursday, and how she talks my ear off! *Madonna mia!*"

Madame sent me an amused look.

"Knows all the gossip in the neighborhood, that one! And she's always complaining—the daughter-in-law, the store clerk, the upstairs neighbor, eh! Enough already! I told her last week, as clear as I could, that my business was taking too much of my time so she should leave me *alone*."

Enzo crossed the room with a small tray, set the espressos in front of us. "I don't want to hear complaining tonight." He lifted his demitasse and made a toast. "Tonight I am visiting with my ravishing Blanche and her Clare . . ."

TWO hours later, Enzo and Madame were reliving their past via an illustrated narrative of old photo albums. They'd continued toasting, too, only now they'd moved on to grappa.

"It's so quiet down here," Madame declared (because we'd also moved on to the caffè's basement). She proffered her drained glass for a refill.

"I'll put on some records," Enzo said. "Good stuff, too. Not that crap kids listen to today."

He rose, a little wobbly, and crossed to an ancient machine with an actual diamond needle. I checked my watch. Being the designated driver, I'd declined the Italian brandy—no big sacrifice since I was still drying out from last night's green beer—and I was beginning to wonder when this visit was going to end.

As Madame and Enzo fox-trotted around stacks of clutter, I felt my jeans vibrating. Assuming a certain NYPD detective was the reason once more, I dug into my pocket with relish. (Watching these two old friends reflame their affections had me aching for my own man.) But it wasn't

Mike on the line. The cell call came from Dante Silva, one of my baristas.

"Hey, boss. Did you get it? The Blend's old roaster?"

In fact, the vintage German Probat was standing right in front of me. It was about the girth of a small washing machine (only taller) and tarnished with age and neglect—nothing I couldn't remedy with a lot of polish and elbow grease. (Seeing Glenn's restoration job was sufficiently inspiring.)

Of course, I wasn't enough of a mechanic to get the thing up and running again, but that was never my intention. I wanted the antique for display purposes.

"How did you know about the Probat?" I asked Dante, raising my voice over Tony Bennett's dulcet crooning. "You didn't have a shift today."

"I called in to check my schedule and Tuck told me about it. And since I was here in Queens anyway, I thought I'd snap a few pics."

"You're in Queens now? Where?"

"Here. On the sidewalk out in front of Caffè Lucia," he said. "Unless I'm at the wrong Caffè Lucia. The lights are off and the place looks closed."

"We're in the basement. I'll be right up to let you in."

Topside, I spotted Dante's form hovering near the picture window, his trendy chin stubble a textural contrast to the clean geometry of his shaved head. A distressed leather jacket covered the self-designed tattoos on his ropy arms, and around his neck hung a digital camera, which he used for artistic studies, capturing the play of light on urban images from dawn till dusk.

He waved at me as I emerged from the back of the shop. The door's old lock was gluey as Marshmallow Fluff, but I managed to throw the bolt. Then my young, talented barista breezed in, full of beer and good cheer.

"Is that knockwurst on your breath?"

"And sauerkraut. But mostly hops, boss. Lots of hops."

"Where were you, anyway?"

Dante grinned, glassy-eyed. "I helped a buddy install his exhibit at the Socrates Sculpture Park; then I hung at the Bohemian Hall Beer Garden with a bunch of aspiring Jasper Johns."

I almost laughed. Not so long ago someone as terminally hip as Dante Silva wouldn't have been caught dead at an outer-borough beer hall. But that was before the Great Recession completely flipped New York's social scene. These days, slick neon bars with velvet ropes were out. Keggers and kielbasa were in.

Then again, every few years I'd notice my collegiate coffeehouse customers celebrating some kind of music, clothing, food, or art form that had become so outdated and square it went all the way around the wheel to come up hip again: bowling, bacon, sliders, cupcakes, hip-hugger jeans, Tom Jones, Neil Diamond . . . I dreaded the day preground coffee in a can made a comeback.

"So where's this roaster?" Dante asked.

"Let me lock this door and I'll show you."

"Whoa, boss," Dante murmured.

He'd stopped in the middle of the room to stare at Enzo's mural. I walked up to join him. "What do you think?"

"Freakin' awesome."

"That's what I thought."

In a phrase, looking at Enzo's mural was like taking a visual journey through the movements of modern art. The narrative began with impressionism, moved to expressionism, fauvism, cubism, Dadaism, surrealism, and abstract expressionism. Layered in among it all were touches of Iberian art, as well as Japonism and primitivism—all of which influenced twentieth-century artistic developments.

Paul Gauguin's fascination with Polynesian culture and Oceanic art was represented, as well as Parisian fascination with African fetish sculptures. The postmodern movement was explored, with its blurring of high and low cultural lines; the vibrant pop images of spoof and irony were also here, along with the (often misunderstood) reframing of common objects by those visual poets who helped us see with new eyes our cans of soup and boxes of Brillo pads.

Enzo's work served it all up in one continuous masterpiece that felt (like Pollack's best) as if it would go on and on, and yet, this fresco was more than a succession of finely wrought forgeries. He'd stirred the ingredients into an epic stew of modernism, simmering iconic ideas to form a wholly new dish, and while some areas of the mural were no more than well-executed servings of familiar flavors, other sections displayed expressions of color, texture, and imagery that I'd never seen before.

"I've got to get some snaps of this."

"Take your time."

I turned on the lights and Dante clicked away, capturing every foot of the expansive wall art. Then I returned to secure the front door. Unfortunately, the lock began giving me real agita. I jiggled the key several times. No luck. I half opened the door and knelt down to see if I could fix the thing.

"You need help, boss?" Dante turned, took a few steps toward me.

That's when the bomb went off.

THREE

~~~~~~

FIRST came the sound, a monumental *whoosh* followed by a hissing roar. Then the white-hot concussion rippled through the air, the caffè's front window exploded outward and the blast washed over me.

My eyes were at keyhole level while I worked the stupid, stubborn lock, and the force of the firebomb knocked me right through the doorway.

Sprawled on my back on the debris-strewn sidewalk, I turned my head, stared at the carpet of glass shards. Blood was pumping through my system so fast I could barely recognize voices yelling, a car horn beeping. I was unhurt. Small scratches maybe, a few bruises, a little bleeding—*big deal*—I was okay otherwise, and I focused on throwing off the shock.

Smoke rolled out of the caffè, the noxious fog billowing upward in a succession of black, misshapen balloons. Wheezing and coughing, I got back on my feet and scanned the sidewalk for my beer-filled barista.

"Dante!" I shouted, rushing to the caffè entrance. "Dante!"

Flames were repainting the caffè's walls, spilling their

colors onto its tables. The searing light in the urban night would have been beautiful if it weren't so deadly.

"Dante! *Answer* me!"

Smoke stung my eyes. I gritted my teeth, swiped at my cheeks, peered harder into the chaos.

Up front, the heavy marble espresso-bar counter appeared undamaged. But in the rear of the shop, the embroidered fabric that had masked the utility room was a raging curtain of flame. There was no other way out of the cellar. Madame and Enzo were trapped.

I opened my mouth to call out to them but hesitated. The fire door blocking the stairs was so heavy I doubted they could hear me through it. *But will that door be strong enough to keep them safe with an inferno raging above their heads?*

Shoving away the unthinkable, I refocused on Dante and finally spotted him—or, rather, his big black Diesel boots—sticking out amid a cluster of overturned tables. Their heavy marble tops had formed a kind of fortress, shielding him from the dragon, but I knew the protection was only temporary.

Taking a deep breath (and praying to God it wouldn't be my last), I went in. Choking smoke hovered between floor and ceiling, so I dropped to all fours. The bumpy mosaic tiles bruised my hands and knees; the smoke and heat stung my eyes, but I kept on crawling, half feeling, half guessing my way over to Dante's inert form.

I tried to revive him by shaking his shoulders; then I saw the bloody gouge in his head and realized he'd been knocked unconscious by flying debris.

Oh, God . . .

Was he breathing? I couldn't tell. The fire was sucking the oxygen out of the room, replacing it with toxic gasses, and the heat was unbearable. If we didn't get out of this oven, we were going to be baked alive.

I couldn't lift my barista, so I grabbed both of his wrists under his scorched leather jacket and dragged his limp form across the floor. I don't even know where I found the strength, but I was soon hauling him through the narrow doorway and spilling him out onto the sidewalk.

The cold concrete and fresh night air felt like a sweet arctic kiss, but I couldn't enjoy it. I knelt beside Dante, preparing to give him CPR—and saw that I didn't need to. He was breathing on his own.

Thank you, God!

I noticed the sparse crowd then, gathering a few feet away: younger versions of Lucia Testa wearing micro miniskirts, older males behind them with more of that ubiquitous chin scruff, their expressions ranging from blank confusion to morbid excitement—yet no one lifted a spiked heel or over-priced basketball shoe to help!

They're from the Red Mirage, I realized, but I didn't see the owner among them. *Where is that club jerk now? Mr. Guardian of Happy Hour Parking? Isn't he at least worried about his club burning, too? It's right next door!*

Two minutes, maybe three, had passed since the initial blast. It felt like hours. I fumbled for my cell, impatient with my shaking hands and pressed a nine, a one—screaming sirens interrupted me. Flashing lights, nearly the same hues as the caffè's inferno illuminated the shadowy street. The lead fire truck was massive, like a rolling T. rex. One basso blast from its reverberating horn sent tricked-out vans and giant SUVs scampering for the curb.

Seconds later the cavalry pulled up, men bailing out before their ride even stopped. This was an engine, the kind of truck that carried endless canvas hoses folded in its rear. Behind it was a ladder truck, just as big with men leaping off just as quickly. Three police cars and an ambulance rounded out the first responder parade.

With the FDNY here, there was nothing else to do but turn my focus back on the fire and literally begin to pray.

Behind me I was vaguely aware of boots hitting the ground, doors slamming, men yelling, police pushing back onlookers. I stayed on the hard concrete, cradling Dante's head, my eyes fixed on blazing agony.

"Ma'am, are you all right?" (The first person to ask.)

"My friends are trapped!" I pointed, my focus still on those flames. I was shaking pretty badly now and I couldn't keep the hysteria out of my voice—

"My friends! They're in there! I don't know what to do!"

A steady hand squeezed my shoulder. "Slow down, ma'am. Who's trapped? Talk to me."

I glanced up. Under a bulky fire helmet, intelligent eyes were leveled on mine. Wisps of wiry blond hair peeked out from under that Darth Vader headgear. The man's pale skin was smooth. He was on the young side, late twenties maybe, but his voice and expression were cool and composed, his translucent blue eyes like clear beacons in the middle of this searing, dark fog.

"My friend . . . an elderly lady," I said, feeling steadier in the presence of this man's calm. "She's in the basement with the owner of the shop. They're both trapped. There are no windows down there, and the sidewalk chute was bricked up long ago. The only way into or out of that basement is *on fire*. Do you understand what I'm saying?"

"Yes. Anyone else in the upper floors?"

I blanked for a second. "No. There shouldn't be. Enzo— the building's owner—lives alone on the third floor, but he's in the basement now. He mentioned the second floor was being rented, but the business went under a month ago and the space is still vacant."

The fireman nodded, spoke evenly into a radio attached to his coat. "We have two civilians in the basement. The only means of egress is blocked. Fire is doubtful at this time. Repeat. Fire is doubtful at this time—"

"Doubtful!" I cried. "You *doubt* you can save my friends?"

"Easy, ma'am. We'll get 'em out. Try to calm down."

While we spoke, three firemen reached the building, a length of hose unfurling behind them. Another man raised an odd-looking tool—like the long, skinny offspring of a crowbar and a claw hammer. Wielding the thing as confidently as a Yankee all-star, he tore the caffè's front door off its hinges and swept away the jagged remnants of the plate glass window, deftly avoiding the spilling of razor-sharp shards onto the sidewalk's already twinkling concrete.

"Ma'am?"

My fireman again—the one with the reassuring voice. I turned to find he'd waved over a pair of FDNY paramedics.

Two women in dark blue uniforms lifted Dante out of my arms and onto a stretcher. I rose and followed them to the back of their ambulance, watched them take vital signs, cover his mouth with an oxygen mask.

"Will he be okay?"

"He's coming around," one replied. "His vitals are strong, but he'll need a CAT scan . . ."

A paramedic tried to take my pulse, but I waved him off. Knowing Dante was in good hands, I returned to the side-walk to see if there was anything else I could do for Madame and Enzo.

What else can I tell these people to help them?

Another stocky, older fireman approached me. Like the rest, he wore thick, fire-resistant pants under a long, charcoal-colored duster with horizontal stripes of neon yellow, "a turnout coat," that's what the firefighters in Mike's family had called it. *Bunker gear* was the more common term be-cause they once literally stored it beside their bunks.

"We have a three-story attached commercial building," the stocky man recited into a radio, "the fire began on the first floor and is going vertical—"

"Yeah and fast," my fireman added. He must have seen the shock and alarm on my face because he put a hand on my shoulder once more. "Take it easy, okay? The fire is moving up and away from your friends. Right, Lieutenant?"

The lieutenant threw a deadpan glance at my guy, and I finally saw his face full on. The shape, beneath that large helmet, was more oval than square—as if it had once been chiseled quite sharply, but time had added weight, rounding off the angled landscape. His skin texture was craggy, and he had one of those big, red drinker's noses, the kind I'd seen among the crowd in my late father's bookie days. But his celery green eyes were not cloudy or dulled like my dad's old gambling customers. They were as sharp as his voice.

"Two victims are out, two more are trapped behind a fire door to the basement. The fire is confined to the single structure, and there's no shared cockloft with the adjacent building . . ."

After completing his radio report, the lieutenant turned to my fireman. "What the *hell* were those people doing in that basement past Enzo's Thursday night closing time?"

"You know Enzo?" I asked, surprised.

The lieutenant ignored my question. "Is this lady a victim?"

"Yeah, Loo. She got herself and another person out. Shaved-headed guy twice her size. That makes her civilian of the week, right?"

The lieutenant barely glanced my way. "Where's her rescue?"

"He's with the paramedics!" I shouted at the man, barely able to stay sane. "What about my friends? They're trapped in there!"

"We know," my fireman assured me. He was now strapping a bulky oxygen tank onto his back. "But they're safe behind the fire door for the moment. Right now we've got guys on the fire escape. Look—" He pointed. "And they're on the roof doing their thing, too. Right, Loo?"

But the lieutenant was already heading for the caffè's front doorway. I noticed the name *Crowley* printed in yellow across the bottom backside of his turnout coat.

"Okay, get ready with that hose," Lieutenant Crowley bellowed at the nozzle team.

A loud crash sounded over our heads. A spectator cried out as black smoke began to pour off the top of the building's roof.

I pointed. "Is that supposed to happen?"

"They're venting the fire," my guy replied. "That's how we begin to control it, release the heat and smoke, direct it up and out—and away from your friends."

Away from Madame and Enzo, I silently repeated, clinging to that thought.

"Okay," Crowley yelled. "Let's knock this monster down!"

The flat hose swelled like an overstuffed sausage. The men clutching the nozzle released the explosive water stream. Gripping the engorged hose, they moved closer to the blazing shop while more firemen scurried up ladders braced against the walls of the second and third floor. The sound of splintering glass filled the night as they broke windows and climbed through.

"Go, boys!" Crowley cried.

The men gripping the hose advanced through the doorway and vanished into the haze. As the first blast of cold water hit the broiling blaze, a sustained hiss filled the air, and the thick smoke pouring out of the caffè's broken windows quickly faded from black to gray.

The firefighters moved even deeper, directing the stream of water toward the blazing ceiling as they advanced. Smoke billowed, obscuring everything for a minute. Just as the veil lifted, a hanging fan came crashing down, narrowly missing one of them. The firefighters didn't appear to care—they just kept pressing farther into the conflagration.

"What's happening?" I asked my fireman.

"The nozzle team is using the water to cool the combustible gasses at ceiling level. They're cutting a path through the fire to the basement door, then Dino Elfante and Ronny Shaw—that's the man you saw pull the front door off its hinges—those two will get that basement door down and bring your friends out."

But a moment later, one of those firefighter's emerged from the oily smoke with his arms wrapped around the other. Paramedics rushed to the pair.

"Put him in a Stokes basket and strap him down tight! It might be snapneck," Lieutenant Crowley barked to the EMT team. Then he signaled my fireman. "Ronny got clobbered by a chunk of ceiling. We need someone else to go in and make the grab."

"I'm on it," my fireman said. Grinning as if he lived for this, he lowered his Plexiglas face shield.

"Not alone, James—" Crowley warned.

James, I repeated to myself, finally knowing my guy's name.

"Remember: two in, two out," Crowley added then spoke into his radio. "Bigsby, you reading me? You're up."

James ran toward the burning building and another fireman, with *Brewer* stenciled across the back of his coat, paired up with him. Bigsby Brewer was a real colossus, more than a full head taller than my guy, who wasn't exactly a midget. Side by side, the two vanished into the smoke.

As I watched them go, I felt my fragile steadiness going with it. James, like every other firefighter here, seemed almost gleeful about risking his life. But after his kindness toward me I couldn't help feeling I had a third friend in harm's way.

I kept my eyes focused on the building's front door, waiting, hoping, *praying* that those men would emerge with Madame and Enzo safe, ready for more grappa, and foxtrotting.

It was about then I sensed a large presence just behind me. In a deep, vaguely familiar voice, the hovering form spoke—

"Let's have an update, Lieutenant."

"Fire is contained to the single building," Crowley replied. "The adjacent structure has been evacuated as a precaution, but there's no sign of any spread. Right now, the nozzle team's pushing back . . ."

"Anyone hurt?" asked the male voice.

"The lady here says two civilians are trapped in the basement. Ronny Shaw's skull got harassed by a nasty chunk of ceiling and is on his way to the docs. Jim and Bigsie are doin' the snatch and grab on the vics. They should be out any second now."

"It's not like you to miss a rescue, Oat."

Oat Crowley shrugged. "I'm going to Lake George in June, Cap. No time to attend Medal Day."

The man behind me chuckled and I finally glanced over my shoulder. One look at his face confirmed what I'd suspected: the captain and I had met before. In the reflected shadows of the nighttime inferno, his fair complexion had an almost burnt orange cast. Legs braced, one balled hand propped on a hip, Michael Quinn stood like a municipal tower, a full head taller than his lieutenant and most of the men under his command. His substantial chin sported a prominent cleft, and above his upper lip he wore a trimmed handlebar right out of nineteenth-century New York (or a *Lonesome Dove* casting call).

Needless to say, this man was not *my* Mike Quinn. This fire-haired giant was Captain Michael Joseph Quinn of the FDNY—Mike's first cousin. Both were born in the same month and year, and both shared their paternal grandfather's first name, but that's where the solidarity ended.

The captain caught my eye. "You went to an awful lot of trouble to get my attention again, Clare, darlin'. You could have just rung me up for a nice romantic dinner. No need for this elaborate production."

When I didn't immediately reply to the man's stunningly out-of-place innuendo, his hint of a smile blew up into a grin wide enough for his gold tooth to wink at me in the firelight.

"So are you here all alone, then? Where's my cousin Mikey? Spending too much time shaking down parking violators, is he?"

I just kept staring. The last time I saw this character was aboard a fire-rescue boat that had pulled me out of New York Harbor. Even then, surrounded by the men of the marine squad, he was throwing thinly veiled insults at his cop cousin.

The captain grinned wider at my silence, then used a thumb and forefinger to smooth his mustache, more vivid than his flame-colored roof. "Well, the Quinn family black sheep never did know how to treat a lady."

Before my fried brain could even *begin* to formulate a response to that charge, the radio clipped to the man's coat came to life. As if in stereo, the transmission also echoed through Lieutenant Crowley's receiver.

"This is Brewer," the voice said.

"Go ahead, Bigs," Crowley answered.

"Ten forty-five. Repeat. Ten forty-five. Both victims—"

Victims? "What's a ten forty-five?" I shouted. "What's he saying?"

"Take it easy, honey," the captain replied, his monotone maddeningly casual. "They're bringing your friends out right now. Alive and well."

Donning his white helmet, the captain pushed toward the smoldering building. A whoop went up from the firefighters around me as James emerged from the smoking caffè, cradling Madame.

Pristine peach pantsuit blackened, silver hair a sooty tangle, cheeks and chin smudged with grime, my former mother-in-law looked like an elegant, antique doll that some careless child had badly mistreated. One thin arm held on to her rescuer's strong neck, while the other hugged the old photo album from Enzo's basement.

The enormous firefighter named Bigsby appeared next, toting Enzo Testa. As he gently laid the elderly man out on a stretcher, I could see Enzo was in bad shape—conscious but gasping, a long string of dark phlegm under his nose.

In no time, Madame was ringed by a concerned circle of bunker coats. I had to push through the wall of muscle just to get to her.

"Clare!" Tears were in her eyes and mine, too. I moved to hug her, but a female paramedic jumped in first, trying to place an oxygen mask over her mouth. Madame pushed it away.

"Are you insane?" I told her. With her cheeks flushed, I wasn't sure what had affected her more—the ordeal of the fire or all the grappa she'd drunk. "You need oxygen after the smoke you've inhaled!"

"Yes, but"—the octogenarian coughed once then gestured to the army of strapping young firemen surrounding her—"I'd really prefer mouth to mouth."

Four

~~~~~~

THE puddle-strewn pavement gleamed like black onyx. The street was so drenched in places you'd think a cleansing storm had passed. But there was no rain-swept freshness in the evening's air, just a miasma of smoke, creosote, and scorched wood.

Next door, the Red Mirage was vacated and closed. But the continued glow of its neon sign, along with the flashing lights of the emergency vehicles, made the scattered puddles flicker with an almost demonic hue.

Around me, the men of Engine Company 335 were going through the painstaking process of draining and rewrapping the infinite hose. A rookie fireman swept glass off the sidewalk. Others tossed metal tools back into the truck. I'd watched them use those same tools to tear apart the caffè's walls and ceiling.

I would have gone with Madame to Elmhurst Hospital, but she asked me to remain behind and retrieve her handbag from the basement. Because the keys to my car, my apartment, and every single lock in the Village Blend were in my own bag (also in the basement) I decided she was right and I'd better stick around.

Shivering in the cold March night, I peered once more into Enzo's place. The flames were gone now, but his beautiful interior looked like a rest stop on the road to hell. Water had replaced the element of fire, and it was just as damaging.

Though the hydrants were turned off, torrents of gray sludge still poured from the building's upper levels, staining walls and soiling the colorfully tiled floor. The highly polished wooden tables looked like charred kindling. Broken lumber and bent panels of tin dangled from the ceiling like ragged fangs inside the mouth of a dead monster.

Flashlight beams from the fire marshals played across the blackened walls and sodden plaster. Though the stainless steel espresso machine appeared intact behind the thick marble counter, Enzo's breathtaking mural had been burned beyond recognition.

A building could always be restored, new furniture purchased, but that astonishing fresco, completed over decades, could never be replaced. As I surveyed the devastation, tears filled my eyes for the man's lost art.

Something inside the shop crashed to the floor and I started. A moment later, I felt a large body step up behind me and place a blanket over my shoulders.

"You're shiverin', dove."

Captain Michael Quinn turned me around to face him. Hot tears had slipped down my chilled cheeks. I swiped at them.

"I heard you made a save tonight," he said. "The men told me you pulled out a kid twice your size."

"Dante is one of my baristas. I wasn't about to let him burn alive."

"But you could have burned alive tryin' to save him."

"Anyone would have done what I did."

"Oh, sure, any firefighter with a cast-iron pair." He gave me a little smile.

For the first time, I noticed an old burn scar, just under the man's left ear, a patch of flesh blanched pinkish white. His bulky white helmet was tucked under one arm, baring his sweat-slickened hair. The change in light had altered the shade, I realized. At the height of the blaze, it looked fiery orange. Now it seemed more subdued, a deep, muted burgundy, like brandy-soaked cherries.

The man's bunker coat was open and flapped a bit in a sudden March gust. Ignoring his own fluttering clothing, he tucked the blanket more tightly around me.

"I'm surprised you're still here," he said. "Unless you lingered for a reason? To catch a ride home with me, maybe?"

Is he kidding? Laugh lines creased the edges of his smoke-gray eyes, but I wasn't entirely sure he was joking.

"I can't go anywhere, not at the moment. My car keys are in my handbag in the basement, so I'm waiting on a couple of your guys. They volunteered to search for it . . ."

"Then take a load off while you're waiting. After what you went through, you shouldn't be on your feet."

My mouth was dry, my skin was clammy, and my legs were beginning to feel like underchilled aspic. "I'm fine."

"You're *fine*? Right. Sure you are." The captain shook his head. "Come *on* . . ."

His big hand went to my lower back. Too weak to fight the current, I flowed along, letting him propel me toward the back of one of the fire trucks.

He plunked down his helmet on the truck's wide running board, unwrapped another blanket, and placed it on the cold metal. With two heavy hands, he pressed my shoulders until I was sitting on it. Then he grabbed a paper cup and decanted something from a canary yellow barrel strapped to the vehicle's side.

"Drink."

I took the cup, sniffed. It smelled citrusy. *Gatorade*, I realized, and took a sip, followed by a big swallow.

Oh my God . . .

I hadn't realized I was so thirsty, but now my body seemed

to be absorbing the liquid's electrolytes before they even hit my stomach. As I drained the first cup, I realized the captain was already offering me a second. I drained that, too.

"Good girl."

I threw him a look.

"What?"

"I'm not a girl."

"What should I be sayin', then? *Good boy?*" He folded his arms. "Too late, darlin'. I've already glimpsed what's under that blanket and unless I need eye surgery"—he winked—"it's all female."

I exhaled. Dealing with this guy was going to be a challenge, but I shouldn't have been surprised, given our previous meeting . . .

Last December, a not-so-nice person helped me off the Staten Island Ferry (in the middle of New York Bay). Amid my shivering rants to the FDNY marine squad who rescued me was a request that someone contact Mike Quinn. How could I know there was more than one?

The men called the Quinn they knew, this larger-than-life creature of the FDNY. From his blustery entrance on that rescue boat and the flirtation that followed, I got the impression that battling blazes was only one of the captain's burning interests. As usual, the man's suggestive stare was making me feel less than fully dressed (even with this first-responder blanket swathed around me like I'd just taken a seat at his personal powwow).

"Listen, Chief, considering your men just saved my friends' lives, I'm going to cut you some slack—"

"Well, isn't that big of you."

"But I'm not in the mood for games. So would you please drop the retro macho condescension and just call me *Clare*?"

"Whatever you say . . . *darlin'*."

I exhaled. "At least you're true to form."

"How's that?"

"Your attitude comes from the same era as you preferred style of facial hair."

The captain proudly smoothed his trimmed handlebar. "Can't resist the old soot filter, can you?"

"Actually, I can. On the other hand, I wouldn't mind another one of these." I held out my empty cup.

"Women," he grunted, shaking his head. But he refilled it. Then he grabbed a plastic water bottle, chugged half the contents, and gazed at the fire-ravaged coffee shop.

"Hell of a blaze," he said. "Wonder what set it off?"

"What did the fire marshals say?"

"Nothing. They keep their theories to themselves, those boys."

"What do you think happened?"

"When I first rolled up to the scene, I assumed Enzo's espresso machine was the cause—"

"You know Lorenzo Testa?"

"I know every shop owner in this neighborhood. Old Enzo's got the best coffee around. A lot of my men come here for it and his pastries, too."

"What made you think the espresso machine was the cause?"

"The steam pressure, the gas lines, any number of things could go wrong with a mechanism like that. It seemed the most likely culprit for the intensity of the blaze—"

"But that's not what happened. The start of the fire was farther back in the store, near the utility room—"

"That's right, honey. You didn't let me finish. When I saw the actual burn pattern, it was clear the espresso machine wasn't the cause. The mechanism was intact. And the gas line didn't break, even after the fire started—"

"That's because the bomb went off in the back of the store—"

"Whoa there." The captain raised a calloused hand. "Don't be usin' a word like *bomb* so freely."

"I was an eyewitness. I know what I saw."

"And what did you hear then? A loud explosion?"

"No . . ." That made me pause. "There wasn't a loud

noise. No boom; it was more like the sound I hear when the pilot light on my stove is out and I relight it after running the gas."

"So you think the cause was a gas leak?"

"I think it was *arson*, some kind of device rigged to go off at a certain time—"

"Stop. You're back to describing a bomb."

I crossed my arms and met his eyes. "It *was* a bomb. The only questions those fire marshals should be asking now is who set it off and why."

The captain held my eyes a long moment but this time it wasn't a leer. The man was staring into me like a mentalist studying an audience volunteer.

"Oh, no," he finally said, as if he'd just rifled every thought in my brain pan. "No, no, *no* you don't."

"No I don't *what*?"

The captain bent down, moved his face two inches from mine. "I heard about your games, dove—"

"Games?"

"You like to play detective. A bad habit you no doubt picked up from my black sheep cousin. But listen to me now: You're not a fire marshal, and you're not trained to recognize the cause of a fire—"

"But—"

"The real marshals are inside that building." He extended his long arm for a sustained point. "They're taking pictures, evaluating burn patterns, looking for traces of chemical accelerants or electrical damage. They're going to determine how and where the blaze started, and document how my smoke-eaters knocked the monster down, too. They don't need help from an *amateur*."

I met the man's stare. "I may be an amateur, but I'm also an *eyewitness*."

The captain straightened up, moved his hands to his hips. "Now why would you want to worry that lovely head of yours about this, anyway? The marshals will make the final determination on what caused the fire, and they'll do it based on proven investigative techniques, not some womanly hunch."

"I never said anything about a hunch, womanly or otherwise. And this head was there, in that caffè, when the fire started, remember? I only told you what I saw and what I heard."

"What you saw and heard is all you should be telling anyone—without speculation."

"Why?"

"Why . . ." The captain rubbed his eyes, loudly exhaled. Finally, he sat down beside me. When he spoke again, his tone was no longer combative. "Do you know what a fire triangle is, Clare?"

"No."

"Fire is a chemical reaction that occurs when three elements are present: oxygen for the fire to breathe, fuel for it to consume, and heat to ignite the other two in a chain reaction." He ticked off the three points on his fingers. "You followin' me?"

"Three elements. Combustibility."

"Any time these elements are combined, the fire can occur—whether intentionally or accidentally."

"But I witnessed more than the fire itself. I heard a *whoosh,* saw the initial blast. It must have been arson."

"You're so sure, eh? Well, factor this in, darlin'. Of the hundreds of fires I put out last year, there were two that were practically identical. Both started in the kitchen trash can of a row house on a quiet street. In the first fire, a woman lit the end of a cigarette and intentionally tossed it into the can. She was broke, couldn't make the mortgage payment, and needed an insurance pay out to stay afloat."

He paused, met my eyes. "That's arson."

"Yes, obviously."

"In the second fire a man emptied a cigarette ashtray into a closed metal can, not realizing there were still burning ashes. The ashes ignited tissues stuffed into the can.

The fire smoldered, contained and unnoticed, until it reached critical mass and burst out of the metal can, immediately setting the walls and ceiling ablaze. And because an unchallenged fire doubles in size every thirty seconds, the fire spread throughout the house in minutes, destroying everything. You see?"

"No. I'm sorry but you lost me. What's your point?"

"The first fire was arson—obviously, as you say, once the facts were discovered. The second was accidental, but not so obvious. If a witness had been present to hear and see that second fire break loose, he might have sworn that exploding trash can was a bomb, too."

I thought about that. "Okay. I understand. I do. And nothing against your fire triangle, but have you ever heard of the blink theory of trusting your first impressions? As a detective, Mike believes—"

"*Mike?*"

"Yes," I said. "Mike. Your cousin. He believes—"

"To *hell* with what my cousin believes! He's not a fire investigator and neither are you. Stick to the facts, Clare, not what anyone *believes*."

I sat very still for a moment, letting the man's anger dissipate like those black balloons of smoke released by the burning caffè. Then calmly and quietly I asked—

"Why do you care what I think, anyway?"

"Because Enzo's a good man, and I won't have him accused of arson. He's the last person who'd put his own life at risk, or anyone else's, for some lousy insurance money."

"I'm sure Enzo is a good man. My friend Madame has known him for years, decades—"

"But if you start shouting *bomb*, the press may get wind of it, and the marshals will be forced to start treating Enzo as a suspect before they even finish with the forensics."

"Wait a second! I was with Enzo in that basement minutes before the fire started. He could have found an excuse to get out, but he didn't. He was trapped down there, in harm's way. Surely that exonerates him."

"It does not. He may have played a part in the event to throw off suspicion."

"So now you're saying Enzo could be guilty?"

"No! I am not saying that. Listen, Clare, you and I know Enzo's a stand-up guy. To these marshals, Mr. Testa is just another victim, but if this fire is found suspicious and he's the beneficiary of an insurance payout, he'll be their number one suspect. Then they'll tear his life apart looking for evidence of guilt."

I lowered my voice to a whisper. "But what if someone else had a motive to burn Enzo's shop?"

The captain studied me again. He bent his head closer. "Like who? And why?"

Before I could reply, a voice called out: "Ma'am? Are you still here? Ma'am?"

It was my fireman, the one who'd been so kind to me earlier, the one who'd risked his life to rescue Madame and Enzo. He was wandering along the sidewalk, searching for me.

"I'm here, James!" I called. "In back of the fire truck!"

With perceptible reluctance, the captain put distance between his head and mine. A moment later, my young hero firefighter appeared wearing a grin and two handbags.

FIVE

~~~~~~

"**Yo**, ma'am, check it out!" James made a show of point-ing to the women's purses dangling off his broad shoulder. "Can you ID these so I can turn them over to you?"

"Of course. That one's mine and the other is my employ-ers. They're the bags I asked you to look for."

Bigsby Brewer strolled up behind James. His shoulders were so wide, I couldn't imagine the guy going through an average doorway without tilting to one side. Massive mus-cles notwithstanding, Bigsby was far from intimidating. His manner was so happy-go-lucky, his spirit so energetic, he came off about as threatening as an excited puppy.

"So, how do I look, Bigs?" James said, showing off the women's handbags to his friend. "Too last season?"

Shaking his head, Bigsby tugged the bags off James's arm and thrust them into my hands. They reeked of smoke.

"You better take these back, ma'am." Bigs jerked his thumb in James's direction. "Noonan is too dumb to see they clash with his bunker gear!"

The two men laughed.

"Sorry it took so long," James said. "The fire marshals

had to inspect them before we could take them out. They wanted to make sure we weren't removing evidence."

"It's okay. I'm just grateful you located them." I regarded James again. "Did I hear your friend right? Is your last name Noonan?"

James nodded.

"You aren't by any chance related to Valerie Noonan, the banquet manager at Union Square West Hotel?"

James opened his mouth to answer but Bigsby interrupted: "Oh, no, ma'am, you've got that wrong."

"I do?"

"James isn't *related* to Val. It's much worse than that—" As if someone had died, Bigsby took off his helmet and placed it over his heart. "He's *married* to her."

With one sharp, hard thrust, James shot his elbow into his partner's gut. It was a real blow, and Bigs doubled over, gasping and cussing.

"So, you know Val?" James said, ignoring Bigsby's groans while calmly extending his hand. "I'm her husband. Very nice to meet you—"

I stared in horror for a second until Bigs came up again, red-faced but laughing. Apparently, this was business as usual between the two men because James's affecting smile never wavered—as if he hadn't just sucker punched his best buddy right in front of me.

"I, uh . . . I'm Clare Cosi, manager of the Village Blend, and I love Val. I mean, I just met her last night, at the Quinn's St. Patrick's Day party—"

I paused to glance at the captain, wondering why he hadn't shown at the biggest family gathering of the year. He looked away.

"Anyway," I continued, "Val and I are both in the same general trade, so we shared a nice conversation. My boyfriend's mother asked me to help with the Five-Borough Bake Sale, so we had even more to talk over. I understand Val's on the coordinating committee?"

At the mention of the bake sale, the corners of James's

mouth turned down. "If you ask me, she *is* the coordinating committee. Or at least it seems that way from all the hours she's been working on it."

Woops. Obviously a touchy subject. "Well, the sale is for a good cause, right? Scholarships for children of fallen firefighters—and it will all be over in a week or so."

"Just take my wife in stride," James said. "She can turn into a little dictator when it comes to organizing public events."

Bigsby, still nursing his bruised torso, risked a snicker. "Not just public events, brother. From what I've seen, Val is no slouch at ordering you around, either."

Still sitting next to me, the captain finally made a comment: "Women."

It was the second time tonight he'd grunted the single word. I turned on the man. "What is that supposed to mean exactly?"

"You don't know?" he said.

"If I knew, why would I ask?"

The captain glanced at Bigsby. "You want to tell her?"

"Hell no!"

James winked at me. "Don't let them jerk your chain, Ms. Cosi. Two confirmed bachelors—what do they know about women, anyway?"

Bigsby snorted. "We know enough not to hitch our horse to one post, right, Captain?"

"Listen, bro," James replied, "I saw your last one-night stand. She was about as dumb as a post."

"And that would be a problem because . . . ?"

"You guys are terrible," I said.

"They are, aren't they?" James gave an exaggerated nod. "They're really a sad pair. They *wish* they had a beautiful woman in their lives, telling them what she wants."

"On the contrary," the captain replied. "Beautiful women tell me what they want all the time." He threw a suggestive gaze my way. "Even if it's not in so many words . . ."

"Ho!" Bigs nudged James. "Looks like the cap'n's workin' here."

James's brow furrowed. "Working on what?"

"You've been married too long, brother. Four's a crowd." Pulling on James's collar, Bigs headed back to the sidewalk.

"See you at the bake sale, Ms. Cosi," James called as Bigsby dragged him away.

I cleared my throat. Bigsby's joking implication might not have bothered me if the captain's proximity hadn't changed. He was still sitting next to me on the running board, but he'd gradually eased his body closer to mine, so close I could feel the heat from his thigh against my leg.

"You know, darlin', my tour's nearly over." His voice had gone sweeter than maple tree sap. "How 'bout I take you home, make sure you get there safe . . ."

And there's the pitch. "Thanks, Captain, but you know very well I have someone to do that for me. Someone I care for very much."

The captain's little smile twisted into a smirk. "So it's official, then? You're still wasting your time with Mikey—"

"*Mike* is a good guy."

Captain Quinn looked at me as if I'd just declared Adolf Hitler a great humanitarian.

"What's the beef between you two, anyway?"

He folded his arms. "Better you find out from my cousin."

"I asked Mike twice. Both times his answers were so vague I didn't bother asking a third."

"Then do yourself a favor and take the hint."

Touchy, touchy. I studied the man, wondering if I could needle it out of him. "You know what? . . . I'm betting the reason neither of you will answer that question is because neither of you can even remember how the whole thing started. No doubt it was some childish, testosterone-fueled competition back on your parochial school playground."

The captain glared.

"Why two supposedly intelligent men can't work out their differences is beyond me."

"Yeah, honey, it is beyond you. So take my advice and keep it that way."

"Men," I muttered, getting a clue what the captain's single-word epithet was all about. "Well, Michael, it's been a barrel of fun, but now that I have our fire-roasted handbags back, I better get going."

I began to rise, but the captain took hold of my upper arm, pulled me back down. "You're not going anywhere."

"I told you already, I'm not interested—"

"You're not going anywhere until you *give your statement*."

"My statement?"

"Wait here," the captain said. "I'll be back with one of the marshals."

True to his word, the captain returned with one of the FDNY's fire marshals, clipboard in hand. By the newcomer's size, I judged him to be a former firefighter, but there was evidence of more than that here. His nose was mashed a bit, his ears crooked. One was larger than the other, the lobe puffy and swollen into a permanent cauliflower—clearly he'd done some serious boxing. His mind didn't appear to be addled from it, however, because there was astuteness in his gaze; and in the few seconds before he spoke, I could see he was looking me over with a practiced eye, absorbing, evaluating, just like my Mike. Before he even asked a question, this FDNY detective was beginning his interview.

"Are you Miss Cody?"

"*Cosi*," I corrected. "*Ms.* Clare Cosi."

"Spell it for me, please."

I did. Then I smiled and offered him my hand. He shook it but didn't smile back. With every movement his nylon jacket swished, and the array of tech devices on his belt clanked. He flashed the badge clipped onto his jacket.

"I'm a fire marshal, Ms. Cosi; my name is Stuart Rossi. Captain Quinn here tells me you were on premises when the event began?"

"That's right." I felt Captain Michael's intense gaze on us as the marshal asked me a series of standard questions. How did I know they were standard? Because the man made continuous checkmarks on a standardized form.

About five minutes into the interview, Crowley appeared. He signaled the captain, who took a few steps away to speak with his lieutenant. With the man's attention diverted, I lowered my voice to tell Marshal Rossi what I felt in my gut was true.

"I also want to add that I believe this was arson."

"Excuse me?"

I explained how I saw and heard the fire start—with an explosion that I'd witnessed and that felt extremely suspicious. I led the man to the remains of Caffè Lucia. Rossi wouldn't allow me to cross the threshold, so I pointed out the area near the curtain and basement door, where I thought the blaze might have begun. Then I directed his attention to the intact espresso bar and the machines behind it.

"Minimal damage there," I said. "So with the espresso machine and the gas line ruled out as possible culprits, what else could it have been but a bomb?"

"Ms. Cosi, were you a witness to any threats or discussions that involved perpetrating arson on this or any other premises?"

"No. I didn't overhear anything or witness any threats or confessions *directly*, but—"

"So your arson charge is based solely on—"

"What I saw and heard. What I witnessed at the start of the fire."

I left out the part about my gut feelings. Captain Michael made it abundantly clear that these guys wanted hard proof, not guesses, theories, or (God forbid) womanly hunches.

Marshal Rossi went silent as he finished scribbling notes. Finally he slipped the pen into his pocket, tucked the clipboard under his arm, and looked up.

"I want to thank you for your cooperation, Ms. Cosi."

"You're welcome, but won't you tell me what you think about all of this? From what you've seen, what do you think happened here?"

"Thank you again," he said politely. "We have your address and phone number, so if we need to get in touch with you for any reason—"

"Aren't you going to answer my questions?"

"No, Ms. Cosi, I'm not."

"Why?"

"Because it's too early in the investigation to come to any conclusions. Arson is a serious charge with serious consequences. There are tests that have to be done before we'd even consider launching a criminal investigation."

"When will you know?"

"Here's my card. If you think of any other information that you believe is pertinent, give me a call. If I'm not at my desk, leave a message."

The fire marshal gave a polite but final little nod; then, with the swish of his dark blue nylon jacket and the clanking of his gear, he reentered the ruined caffè.

And I thought cops in this town were closemouthed. Compared to New York's Bravest, New York's Finest are downright chatty.

I let the card dangle between my fingertips for a moment and realized my hand was now shaking. My heart was racing, too, and breathing was no picnic. I didn't know if this was some sort of posttraumatic aftershock, exhaustion, hunger, or all three. Maybe it was just plain old ordinary frustration with the bureaucratic wall of silence.

I stuffed the card into my jeans pocket then dug into my bag for my car keys.

"Going somewhere?"

The captain's voice startled me. "Yes. I'm headed for Elmhurst's ER. Now that I have my keys back, I can drive myself. Mike should be at the hospital by now and I've got to meet him—"

"My cousin's meeting you, is he?"

"Yes"—*Didn't I just say that?*—"I called him right after they took my friends to the hospital."

"Good, because a hospital is where you *should* be going, too, and not under your own power."

"I'm fine—"

"Your hands are trembling and you're whiter than a jug of Clorox. Have you eaten anything lately?"

"Uh . . ." Enzo had shared some biscotti and pizzelles with us, but other than the Gatorade, that was it for nutrition. I hadn't had a proper meal since brunch nearly twelve hours earlier.

"Okay," I confessed, "I'm a little shaky and I could use a bite to eat. But I'm certainly capable of driving myself a few miles."

Unfortunately, stating something firmly doesn't make it so. When I took a few steps, my knees refused to go with me.

"Easy, darlin'," the captain said, taking my arm. "An adrenaline crash is catching up to you and your blood sugar's bottoming out."

"I'm fine."

"You should not be driving, and I won't let you." Slipping the keys from my fingers, the captain bellowed to Lieutenant Crowley.

"Oat! Drive Ms. Cosi's car to Elmhurst's ER and park it!"

Crowley frowned. "And how is she getting there?"

"In the captain's car. She's too queasy to drive herself."

"Okay. I'll get Tommy Ennis—"

"No, Oat, I won't be needin' my driver. I'll be takin' her myself. Tommy can hitch a ride home on the engine."

I tensed, not relishing the idea of getting into a car alone with Michael Quinn. Still, he wasn't wrong to take my keys. I was depleted, my brain fuzzy. Driving a car in New York City was no mean feat; doing it at night, in my current condition, approached genuine stupidity.

For some reason Crowley didn't agree. First his gaze ping-ponged back and forth between me and his superior. Then he came right out and said, "Uh, Cap. Not a good idea."

"Why?" the captain replied. "Someone's got to drop by the ER, look in on Ronny Shaw. The poor man may have snapneck."

"Sure," said Crowley, "and that's where I was headed after

we pack up here. Tell you what? Why don't I save you the trouble and drive Ms. Cosi to Elmhurst myself?"

"And why don't you follow orders?"

Silence ensued for a good five seconds. Crowley's cheeks turned the color of pink peppercorns. Then he spoke through a pair of calcified jaws.

"Yes, sir. Meet you at the hospital."

SIX

After I pointed out my car to the lieutenant, Michael Quinn led me to his official vehicle and helped me into the passenger seat. The Chevy Suburban might have been roomy if all kinds of extra gear hadn't been jammed into the compartment—a computer and GPS unit, a radio that constantly crackled with chatter from all over the borough, and a rack between the passenger and driver to hold a shorter version of the claw-topped shaft every fireman seemed to carry.

"It's called a Halligan tool," the captain replied when I asked.

"I see. Why were the firemen tearing out the caffè walls with it, after the flames were out?"

"You mean after the flames *appeared* to be out." The captain tossed his helmet into the backseat. "Fire's a canny beast. She can hide in the walls, the ceilings, the floorboards."

She, I noted. *He thinks of the fire-beast as a she. There must be a story behind that . . .*

The captain leaned over, opened the glove compartment. "Here," he said, handing me a plastic packet of some kind of snack food. "Eat."

I didn't argue—or care, frankly, what the heck it was. There were carbs here and I was light-headed. I ripped it open.

"So what else is the Halligan tool used for? I mean, besides breaking things?" (I said this around a less-than-ladylike mouthful of what tasted like cheddar cheese filled pretzel bites. If it had been royal beluga on a half baguette, I couldn't have shoveled it in any faster.)

"Let me put it to you this way," the captain said, swinging the Suburban around to get clear of the trucks. "King Arthur civilized the British Isles with Excaliber. Babe Ruth broke every record with his Louisville Slugger. And every man jack of us in the FDNY tames the beast with his Halligan tool."

The she-beast? Hmm . . . "I think I'm getting it," I said. *And, brother, does it sound Freudian.*

The captain peered through the windshield. "Now where the hell is Oat and that car of yours?"

My mouth full again, I pointed then swallowed. "Up the block. He's driving the red Honda."

"If that's your clunker, then you *really* shouldn't be behind the wheel right now—or ever."

"You're the second man to insult my car tonight. Not everyone can afford the latest model, you know? It might not look like much, but my Honda's got pep. And it still gets good gas mileage."

"So does a horse. Really, honey. I'm worried about Oat's safety. Running into a fire is one thing, driving that deathtrap is another."

"Why do you call Lieutenant Crowley 'Oat'?"

"You haven't seen him without his bottle top—"

"His what?

"His soup bucket, his umbrella."

"English?"

"His *fire helmet*. You haven't seen him without his head gear."

"Oh."

"He's prematurely gray," the captain explained. "When Crowley was still a probie, someone at breakfast noticed his hair was the same color as the milky oatmeal being served and the name stuck."

"He's named after oatmeal? I'm sure he hates that moniker."

"Trust me, it could have been worse."

As we came to a red light, the Number 7 train rumbled loudly along the elevated train tracks over our heads. When it finally passed, the captain turned toward me.

"Clare . . ." His tone was different, no longer playful. "Earlier you said someone else might have a motive to torch old man Enzo's shop."

"Yes."

"Who exactly were you thinking of accusing?"

I was still tired and feeling a little weak, but a part of me came alert with that question. Maybe it was the way the man asked—as if he were worried that he might know the person. Maybe it was something else. But I went with my gut and held my tongue.

"You were right, Michael," I replied carefully. "It's not my line of work. Forget I said anything."

ELMHURST Hospital was an incongruous sight: a shiny, ultramodern facility planted in the middle of a hardscrabble neighborhood of worn-out storefronts and rundown row houses, most of them packed with recent immigrants from Ecuador, India, Colombia, and Pakistan. By the time we turned onto the hospital's drive, I'd decided that I would put some questions to Enzo Testa. I didn't believe the old coffeehouse owner was responsible for torching his own business. But I was far from convinced that the fire was accidental.

Fire Marshal Rossi had given me his card and told me I could contact him with any further information that I believed was pertinent. As far as I was concerned, that was an invitation to find some.

As I checked my watch again, Captain Michael swung his official vehicle up to the ER entrance and cut the engine.

"You know, darlin'," he said, "it's not too late to forgo the hospital's oxygen for a little mouth to mouth at my place."

Give it up, man. "I don't think so."

"You sure? It's late and you're taking your chances in there. The ER will be packed. You could be here for a long time, only to be seen by an exhausted intern with a funny-sounding name on the unlucky thirteenth hour of a fourteen-hour shift."

I popped the door. "Thanks—but I'll take my chances with the exhausted intern."

My knees nearly gave out as I jumped down from the high vehicle, but I felt a whole lot better a moment later, when Mike Quinn, *my* Mike Quinn, pushed through the ER's exterior doors, his ruddy complexion looking pale in the halogen-flooded entryway.

"You okay, sweetheart?"

I nodded.

Mike's arms went around me. The embrace was much needed, but it came with the slight, familiar stab from the handle of his service weapon, tucked into the holster beneath his sport coat and trench. The momentary prod perfectly summed up our relationship—extraordinarily affectionate, punctuated with the occasional, unexpected jab (metaphorically speaking).

My ex-husband once called the man Dudley Do-Right, but Mike wasn't perfect or even above using a dodgy ploy to get the job done. He hadn't started out as a suit-wearing detective, either. He'd earned his gold shield by coming up in the ranks, which included decorated undercover work as an anticrime street cop, so he was far from naïve or a guy you'd want to cross.

Still my ex was right about one thing: Crime solving wasn't a game to Mike Quinn. It was the fulfillment of what he saw as an almost sacred obligation to remove murderers, rapists, drug dealers, and predators from the rest of the population, which was why I didn't mind the familiar little butt from his weapon. I liked the momentary reminder of my man's place in the world, his dedication to a job that protected the weak, the innocent, the naively trustworthy— which occasionally included yours truly.

When we parted, he held me at arm's length for a cool Mike-like once-over, from the top of my smoke-scented hair to the tips of my soiled, ruined boots.

"I'm fine, Mike, really. How is Madame? And Dante?"

"They're both doing well."

"Thank goodness."

"They'll probably release Mrs. Dubois in the next hour," Mike said. "Dante Silva is awake, with a mighty big headache. He may have a concussion so they're waiting for the results of his tests before they'll release him. And Mr. Testa isn't doing so well . . ."

I tensed. "What's wrong with Enzo?"

"It's his heart they're worried about, but he's in good hands. They're monitoring every beat in the ICU—"

And that's when it came: the *slam*. The driver's side door on the Suburban opened and closed with the force of a rifle shot.

"Hi there, *Mikey*."

Arms folded, Captain Michael Quinn regarded his cousin across the vehicle's hood then flashed him what might have been a grin if it hadn't look more like the baring of gritted teeth.

Crap. I'd held out hope that we'd dodged this bullet, but it came all the same.

"Tore yourself away from doling out traffic tickets to check up on the little lady, eh?"

Mike's eyes went dead cold. "Excuse me a minute, sweetheart," he said with disturbing calm. In a few smooth strides he'd circumvented the front of the Suburban to confront his cousin.

The two were pretty evenly matched, which is to say both were over six feet with wide shoulders, long legs, and prizefighter reaches. Captain Michael may have been a bit taller, but I'd seen Mike power-cuff suspects with the kind of fluid force that I doubted the fireman could counter.

The conversation began with the captain folding his arms and muttering something. Mike's eyes narrowed, and he shoved his finger into the breast of his cousin's bunker coat. His other hand reached backward, toward his belt, as if he were going for his handcuffs. Now the captain's eyes blazed, and I feared a shouting match—or worse—was about to explode.

"Guys, don't fight!" I called.

Without even glancing in my direction, the men stepped farther away, locking themselves in a furious, whispered exchange.

I strained my ears to hear what the two were saying, but the noise of traffic and hospital workers was too loud. Finally, when it looked like fisticuffs were about to break out, a third figure in fireman's gear thrust himself between the men.

"Knock it off!" Oat Crowley barked.

That I heard.

Crowley reached into his pocket and shoved a set of keys into Mike's hand. "Your girlfriend's car is parked down that block." He pointed then shot a naked glare my way before pushing against his boss with both arms. "C'mon, Cap, I'm going inside to check on Ronny Shaw, and you need to go back to the firehouse. There's paperwork waiting."

Captain Michael looked pleased with the scene he'd created, even threw a final, cheeky wink in my direction before turning back to continue arguing with Oat.

My Mike didn't miss the devil's wink. He came back to me in body after that but not in spirit. "Let's go inside," he said, taking my elbow a little too roughly.

"No! What was that all about?"

"Forget it happened," he said with a brusque finality that I rarely heard from him. The retrograde attitude sounded more like his cousin's.

"Sorry. No sale." I planted myself.

"This is not the time or place, Clare." His expression was still rigid, but when he spoke once more, his tone was softer.

"Please." He stepped close, put his hands on my shoulders. "Let's not do this. Let's go check on your friends."

I didn't argue. Not then. Mike wasn't wrong about the timing. So I shelved my questions (for the moment) and let him guide me through the doors of the emergency room.

Seven

~~~~~~~~~~~~~~~~~~~~~~~~~~~~~~~~~~~~~~

"Osso buco is another example," Madame was saying.

"Is that beef? Like the bourguignon?" The voice was gruffly male, its pitch low enough to dub James Earl Jones.

"Veal, dear. The veal hind shank, to be precise, sawed into three-inch-thick pieces . . ."

As I came around the white partitioning curtain in the busy ER, I found Madame regally propped on the pristine sheets of a narrow hospital stretcher. Her silk pantsuit was still smoke stained and wrinkled, but her face was freshly washed, her hair brushed into a sleek silver pageboy.

Relief washed over me—along with fear, anger, gratefulness—the internal emotional swell was nearly as powerful as the moment I'd seen her carried out of that charred caffè.

She hadn't yet noticed me. Her focus was on the man occupying the next stretcher, and I was glad of that. It gave me a few moments to swallow back tears, compose myself.

"So how hard is it to make?" asked Madame's ER neighbor.

The bare-chested guy wore black leather pants and a Vandyke beard long enough to braid. Every inch of skin art along his muscled arms had something to do with Harley Davidson, and if that weren't enough of a giveaway, the flaming hog across his chest expelled scripted exhaust that plainly read *Hells Angels*.

"Osso buco? It's a snap!" Madame chirped. "Salt and pepper the shanks, dredge them in flour, and brown them in a skillet with a bit of olive oil. Then just cover with a mixture of chicken or veal stock, sautéed onions, carrots, and celery and dry white wine—or French vermouth, whichever you prefer."

"I like bourbon. Can I use bourbon?"

"I wouldn't."

"So why put flour on the shanks if you're covering 'em with stock, anyways?"

"As the shanks are braising, flour will thicken the sauce for you. Then there's no need for more difficult measures."

"I get it. Cooking time?"

"Two hours or so. Finish with a sprinkle of gremolata to add a sprightly flavor note."

"Gremo-what-a?"

"It's just a bit of minced garlic with chopped parsley and zest from a lemon."

"Oh, *zest*! I know zest! I seen them make zest on the Food Channel. You grate it off citrus skins with a metal file, right?"

"Almost, dear. That zesting tool is called a Microplane—"

I cleared my throat. Madame turned. "Clare!"

I stepped into her open arms, and the festive aroma of grappa on her breath lifted my spirits. The clashing acridness of smoke in her hair, however, ignited other feelings—ugly ones. I wanted to know who was responsible for putting her here, and I wanted them to pay.

"How are you, Madame?"

"Fit as a Stradivarius."

"Did you call Otto?"

Otto Visser was the "younger man" in Madame's life. (He was only pushing seventy.) The dignified, European-born gallery owner had become smitten with my former mother-in-law after they'd eye-flirted across a semicrowded Manhattan dining room. The two had been a couple ever since.

"I'm not troubling Otto with this," Madame stated.

"That's crazy." I pulled out my cell. "I'll call him."

"Please don't."

"For heaven's sake, why not?"

"Otto's hosting an important dinner between a promising young painter and a very serious Japanese collector. I wouldn't dream of doing anything to hurt the artist's prospects."

Considering what the woman had just gone through, I found that reply frustrating, although I knew where it came from. For decades, Madame had run our Village Blend as a second home for poets, musicians, dramatists, and yes—as cliché as it sounded—struggling fine artists.

Actors, dancers, singers, writers, visual artists, and students burning to prove themselves worthy of said identifiers still frequented our Village coffeehouse. But the neighborhood's skyrocketing real estate values had driven the majority of them to more affordable neighborhoods in Brooklyn, here in Queens, and (in the case of many jazz musicians) North Jersey.

Back in Madame's prime, however, when Greenwich Village was still a "cheap" place to live on Manhattan island, she'd befriended some true legends of the art world (before they'd become legends): Hopper, Pollock, de Kooning, Rauschenberg, Warhol, Lichtenstein, even the graffiti prodigy Jean-Michel Basquiat.

She'd also known artists, just as talented, who'd failed. Not in their art but in their ability to make a passable living at it. What the bottle and needle didn't claim, the demands of day jobs or young families did. So it was no mystery to me why Madame didn't want to feel responsible for interfering with even one aspiring artist's sale.

Still, I had to point out: "When Otto finds out, he'll be extremely upset that you didn't call."

Madame waved her hand. "To tell you the truth, dear, the last time I was in harm's way—you recall, don't you? At Matteo's wedding last year?"

"The shooting?"

"Yes, for weeks after that little incident, Otto was solicitous to the point of annoyance. I'd rather not go through that again. I do adore the man, but a woman needs her space."

Madame glanced up then, beyond me, into the vast fluorescent bustle of the ER's central area. "And where is your knightly young officer?"

Knightly? That's a first. I pointed. "Waiting room."

"I must tell you, Clare, he took excellent care of me, found me a sparkling water, brought me a hairbrush and mirror. Oh!" She pointed to my shoulder. "I see you have my bag. At last, I can do my makeup."

I handed over the recovered booty. As Madame pulled out her compact and lipstick, I heard male laughter and hearty greetings coming through the closed curtain to her right. That patient, whoever he was, had just gotten a visitor. At the same moment, I realized the Biker Guy on the stretcher to the left of Madame was watching us with interest—easy enough to do because the partitioning curtain on his side was pulled completely open.

"Howyadoin'?" he called when he noticed me noticing him.

"Fine," I replied, then gestured to the plastic brace around his neck (the one beneath his narrow version of a ZZ Top beard). "What happened? Traffic accident? Spin out?"

"Slipped in the shower."

"Oh . . ."

"Clare, this is Diggy-Dog Dare." Madame turned to the biker. "Diggy, this is Clare Cosi, my daughter-in-law—"

"Ex," I corrected, and not for the first time.

"Charmed, I'm sure," Diggy replied in basso profundo.

"Before you arrived, we were exchanging recipes," Madame explained. "Diggy gave me his favorite: tequila chicken."

"With tomatillo sauce," Diggy noted.

"And I gave him my bourguignon-style short ribs and—"

"Osso buco," I interjected with a nod. "I overheard."

Madame tapped her chin. "Now that I think of it, dear, didn't you used to make a steak with bourbon sauce? I recall Matt raving about it and Diggy has a proclivity for bourbon. Don't you, Diggy?"

"A proclivity? No. But I do like it a lot."

"Of course, Matt always raved about your cooking," Madame went on. She turned back to Diggy. "Matt's my son. He and Clare have the most beautiful daughter together."

"Is that right?" Diggy scratched the roots of his beard. "I have two myself. Wife number three's got custody of the first. Wife number four's bringing up the second."

"Excuse me, Mr. Dare," I said, moving to the partitioning curtain. "Would you mind very much if I had a private word with my ex-mother-in-law?"

"Naw, no problem. Pull it."

I did, hoping the wall of white on both sides of her would help Madame's grappa-happy mind to focus—on something other than alcohol-soaked meat, anyway.

"What is it, dear? What's wrong?"

"Don't forget!" Diggy-Dog's voice boomed through the drapery. "I sure would like that recipe for bourbon steak!"

"Okay!" I called, then took a breath and approached Madame with my serious face. "Enzo's in the ICU."

"What? Why didn't your young man tell me?"

"For the same reason you didn't call Otto. Mike didn't want to upset you. Enzo's stable now, but they're monitoring him. It's his heart . . ."

Madame closed her eyes. "If anything happens to him, I'll never forgive myself."

"That's absurd. Why would you say that?

"We arrived at the caffè an hour late, Clare. If we'd been on time, we all might have been out of harm's way before the fire started." In a rare show of naked anxiety, Madame wrung her hands. "If only we'd gotten there earlier—"

"Listen to me—" I took hold of her shoulders. "If Enzo dies, the person that killed him is the arsonist who set that blaze."

Madame's hand-wringing stopped. "Arsonist?"

I nodded.

"What are you saying, Clare? Did you see someone set the fire?"

"No. But I witnessed the start. I think someone set off a bomb in Enzo's shop."

"A bomb in Enzo's shop!"

Crap. The laughing voices beyond the curtain fell silent. I waited a few seconds, until the muffled sound of men chatting drifted back through the thin material again. Then I turned back to Madame.

"Try to keep your voice down, okay? Tell me what you remember about the fire."

"There was a *whoosh* at first, that's what I recall, a very loud *whoosh.* Enzo went up the stairs, felt the door, and knew there was a terrible blaze on the other side. Smoke began seeping through the floor." Madame shook her head. "Enzo kept us alive, Clare."

"He did?"

"Yes. He was a rock. We couldn't get out of that basement. But Enzo kept assuring me the basement's metal door was a fire door and we'd be all right as long as we could get fresh air. The man didn't show one moment of panic. I can't say the same for myself."

"Given what was happening, Madame, panic would have been normal." And that thought made me pause . . .

Had Enzo planned, all along, to end up trapped in the building, behind a fire door, to make himself appear innocent?

"And then smoke began to fill the room, and he used all his strength to move some heavy crates. He helped me down onto the floor and made me move my head all the way into an old air vent. The smoke in the room became unbearable. There was only room for one of us to get fresh air. I wanted us to switch off, but he refused. He physically forced me to lie with my face in that vent for fresh outside air . . ."

Madame's voice trailed off as her eyes filled with tears. "And now he's in the ICU . . . he's in there for one reason, Clare, because he did everything he could to make sure I wouldn't be . . ."

I fell silent as Madame composed herself. I grabbed some tissues, handed them to her, one after another. Finally, she wiped her cheeks.

"Thank God those two young men came down when they did to carry us out . . . When they told me you were all right, I nearly fainted. I was so worried about you, Clare . . . You'd gone up there to the caffè to let Dante in, and we didn't know what had happened . . ."

We hugged again and I sat down on the edge of her stretcher. Madame grasped my arm, looked into my eyes. "Who do you think set that bomb? An enemy of Enzo's? Someone with a vendetta?"

"I think it was someone who had something to gain."

"Gain?" Madame frowned. "You're not suggesting Enzo did this?"

"No," I said, thinking *not anymore*. "Enzo put himself in the ICU to save you. That doesn't add up to a snake-blooded arsonist."

"Then who?"

Madame's big, blue-violet eyes were fixed on me. She wasn't making the leap. *Because she doesn't want to . . .*

"I need to speak to Enzo," I said carefully. "I need to find out more about . . ."

"About?" she prompted.

"I just need to speak with him."

"We'll do it together!" Madame announced so loudly the men next to us quieted again.

"Madame, please—"

"If someone deliberately set fire to that beautiful caffè and put all of our lives in danger, we are not going to let that bastard get away with it! Are we, Clare?"

"No, of course not, but please calm down . . ." Not only wasn't the woman calming down, she wasn't staying down. *"Please.* Don't tax your system—"

"What's going on here?" A middle-aged nurse with iron-gray hair instantly materialized. "Where are you going, Mrs. Dubois? You haven't been released yet."

"But I need to speak with my friend—"

"What you *need* to do is get your *butt* back on that stretcher—"

Madame shook her head.

I took firm hold of her upper arms. "Madame, *think.* Enzo is in the ICU. They're not going to let us both in there at the same time, and they're certainly not going to let in another patient."

I felt her muscles relax under my hands. She stopped fighting

"Yes. Of course, of course . . . you're right, dear."

"It's okay," I told the nurse. "She's not going anywhere."

The nurse nodded and hustled away.

"Now rest, okay?" I kept my voice pleasant as I helped Madame return to her hospital sheets, but I really wanted to kick myself. I'd brought up the arsonist to relieve the woman's guilt, not give her a heart attack, too. "Why don't you pass the time by talking to Mr. Dog Dare again?"

I pulled back the curtain to her left.

"Bourbon steak?" Diggy sang in greeting.

"When I come back," I promised.

"Clare," Madame called as I turned to go. "Tell me. Who do you think set that bomb?"

Enzo's bratty little witch of a daughter, who else? And I didn't think she did it alone. But was Glenn her accomplice? Or someone else? How many other lapdog beaus did that woman have on a leash?

I wanted to tell Madame what I thought and what I was beginning to fear—if Lucia had been ruthless enough to torch her father's caffè, what other crimes would she be capable of committing? Would she harm her own father to get her hands on her inheritance faster? Was she capable of setting him up for an "accident"? Poisoning him?

I needed to know more before I started accusing anyone, even through speculation, and as Mike had warned me outside, this was not the time or the place. So my reply to Madame was—

"I have a few people in mind."

"Who?"

"I'll let you know."

I took off fast after that, to avoid any further questions. But after just three steps, I stopped dead.

On the other side of the partitioning curtain, a big man stood, ear cocked against the snowy fabric.

"Oat?"

Lieutenant Oat Crowley had been listening to every word we'd said. Propped up on the stretcher next to him was Ronny Shaw, the firefighter who'd landed in here thanks to a chunk of ceiling.

Crowley and I stood staring at each other. His craggy, roundish face betrayed a mix of embarrassment and annoyance. Finally, beneath the slightly shaggy crown of his oatmeal-colored hair, the man's features hardened into an iron mask. His eyes narrowed like a shooter's gun sight, and I was in his crosshairs.

Crowley opened his mouth to address me, but considering our surroundings and the amount of ears and eyes so close, he appeared to be hamstrung.

Now what?

The lieutenant had shot me some pretty nasty looks outside, as if I'd been the sole cause of the animosity between the Quinn cousins, which was patently ridiculous. Their feud had been going on for years before I'd known either one of them. Still, showing weakness to Crowley would be a mistake (I'd learned a thing or two from Madame by now), and I boldly stepped up to the man.

"Hello," I said.

"Ms. Cosi." The words were more statement than greeting.

"How is your friend doing?"

"Who's this?" Ronny asked from his stretcher, looking a little dazed.

"Nobody," Crowley answered, then stepped toward me—and kept on stepping. He danced me backward, right out of Ronny's designated ER rectangle. "He's going to be fine, Ms. Cosi. How's your old lady?"

"My *employer* is doing all right, *considering . . .*"

"Considering what?"

"Considering someone tried to murder her."

Crowley stopped dancing me backward. "You ought to be careful what you say in a public place."

"Maybe." I folded my arms, finally standing my ground. "But what do you care? You must put out dozens of fires in any given year—"

"*Hundreds.*"

"Exactly. You'll have another fire tomorrow, maybe two. More next week. So what do you care what anyone says about any one of them?"

"I don't."

I studied the man's eyes. *You do. You do care. Why?* I opened my mouth to ask, but Crowley spoke first, his voice so low even I could barely hear him.

"Steer clear of this, missy. For your own good."

"Why? What do you know?"

"I don't know a thing," Crowley said. Then he spun around, walked back to his buddy's bedside, and closed the curtain on our conversation.

Eight

~~~~~~~~~~~~~~~~~~~~~~~~~~~~~~~~~~~~~~~

Seeing Enzo was more difficult than I'd anticipated. For one thing I was tired—emotionally drained over my worries about Madame and Dante, and mentally strained by the absurd scene between Mike and his cousin. The cryptic threat from Oat hadn't helped, and the hospital's critical care facility wasn't exactly a laugh a minute, either.

Laid out like the ER downstairs, the ICU consisted of beds lined up in tidy partitioned rows, but that's where the similarity ended. There was a hypersterile scent to the ICU; no sharp, astringent sting of ER alcohol or bright, clean bleach. There were no grounding smells at all, which only increased the surreal feeling of disconnection, and where the ER was filled with bustle and noise, this unit exhibited the chilling reverence of a funeral home's viewing room.

Male and female nurses in scrubs went about their duties like polite androids, fully aware yet completely detached from ongoing human dramas around them: a young Filipino woman sobbing at the bedside of a comatose grandfather; a Hispanic man mumbling Hail Marys next to a youth swathed in bandages . . .

An RN escorted me through it all, to the bedside of Madame's friend. Enzo's skin appeared fragile as rice paper, his cheeks sunken, his surfaces painted paler than a winter moon. This robust older gentleman, so full of burning energy, now had all the life of one of Mike's postmortems.

I took a breath and closed my eyes, willing myself to toughen up. It wasn't easy. Feelings were washing over me, images from half a lifetime ago: that phone call in the dark morning hours; my frightened little girl crying in her bed; the summons to an ICU like this one to find my dynamic, young husband laid out like a corpse, clinging to life, his strong body brought down by a little white powder.

I thought I'd frozen those memories, left them far away, like ancient snow on a mountain top, but the smells and sounds flash-melted it all, raining it down in a sudden, unavoidable flood.

"Mr. Testa?" The nurse's voice. "Your daughter is here to see you."

"Daughter?" he repeated, voice weak. "Lucia?"

For a few seconds, the steadfast beeping of Enzo's cardiac monitor was the only sound on the planet. Then I silently wished myself luck and stepped up to the bedrail.

"How are you, *Papa?*" I said in clear English, then quickly switched to quiet Italian: "I said you were my father so they would let me in here. Is that all right with you, sir?"

The corners of Enzo's mouth lifted. "Hello, *daughter*," he croaked in English, strong enough for the nurse to hear. Like me (and more than a few Italians) the man obviously believed that rules were made to be broken.

With relief I leaned over the rail and kissed his colorless cheek. Despite the oxygen tube taped under his nose and the IV snaking into the bulging blue vein in his hand, Enzo's eyes appeared clear, a miracle considering everything he'd been through.

He patted me on the cheek, and the nurse walked away. She'd already explained that his lungs were strained from the toxic fumes he'd inhaled, and his heartbeat had become erratic. Further tests were needed to pinpoint the problem.

I knew how important this interview was. None of the fire marshals had come around yet to question Enzo. If he died before they spoke with him, they might just pin the arson on him, which meant the real perpetrator would get away with murder.

"I'm glad you're safe, Clare," Enzo rasped. "When everything went boom, Blanche was worried only about you and your friend. How are they doing?"

"The ER is getting ready to release Madame. How are you feeling?"

"Me? I'm about ready to run the New York City Marathon." Enzo laughed, but it quickly degenerated into a weak cough. "How is your artist friend?"

"Dante was hit on the head, so they're holding him overnight for observation." I summoned a tight smile, still worried about my *artista* barista. "You know, before the fire, he was admiring your mural . . ."

Enzo nodded, eyes glistening as my voice trailed off. "I'm afraid he was the last to admire it . . ." He coughed again. "I still want to meet your friend, see his work maybe?"

"You will, I promise." I touched the man's hand. His graciousness, despite his condition, was moving—and made me all the more determined to nail the monster who'd put him here, destroying his art in the process.

"Has anyone called your daughter yet?"

Enzo shook his head. "No. I don't want that. What happened at the shop is enough of a shock without this, too . . ." He touched the IV tube in his arm. "I feel like a slab of veal."

"Let me call Lucia," I replied, reaching for my cell. "I can do it right now—"

"*No,*" Enzo said. "She looked forward to this weekend for a month. I might be out of here by tomorrow; then *nobody* has to call."

I wasn't comfortable with Enzo's choice, but when I checked my cell phone's screen, I saw there was no reception in the ICU.

"I hate being in this place," Enzo said, eyes spearing the IV bag above. "I want to retire, go back to Italy to be with my two sisters . . . visit my Angela's grave every Sunday . . ."

Retire to Italy? Back at the caffè, Enzo hadn't once mentioned retirement. But then I considered the timing of his call to Madame, unearthing that photo album and wanting to give the Blend back its old roaster. Was that the reason he'd been cleaning out his basement? Had he been planning on moving back to the old country? If Enzo innocently revealed his plans to the fire marshals, what were they going to think?

I leaned closer. "What about the caffè, *signore?* Who is going to run your business?"

"Lucia," Enzo replied. "When I leave this country, I'm signing it all over to my daughter. That was always the plan. Now my daughter's going to have to rebuild . . . if she wants to."

"You sound doubtful. Why is that? Don't you think she'll have the funds to give it a go?"

"It's not the money. There's plenty of insurance coverage on the building—"

(*Exactly what I suspected.*) "So what's the problem, then?"

Enzo sighed, stared off into space. "My Angela . . . she was such a beauty . . ."

"Your *wife*, Angela?"

"We met in the park, in the spring . . ."

Enzo smiled weakly, turned his gaze back to me. "You are like her, Clare . . . like Blanche, too . . . such fire in your spirits yet still so good-natured . . ." He reached out to touch my cheek. "My Angelina came to my loft many times . . . I painted her . . . We made love . . . many times . . . so sweet . . . My best work, those portraits . . . I could not bear to sell them . . ."

Uh-oh, I'm losing him. I tried switching to Italian. "About the caffè, *signore* . . ."

"Angela indulged her, you understand?" he said in English. "Treated her like a baby doll, dressed her up, took her shopping, wherever she wanted to go . . ."

"Lucia? Your daughter? Is that who you mean?"

"If she wanted to stay home from school, she stayed—no questions. Never had to work. Just lessons—dancing, singing, whatever she desired. And then the boys started coming around." He shook his head. "When she was young, Lucia had my Angela's beauty, but not her heart. Her mother could not see it . . . back then, neither could I . . ."

"But now you can?"

"I looked at my daughter through my wife's eyes. Now that Angela is gone, I see with my own eyes: Lucia is not like her mother . . ."

"You don't think Lucia will rebuild the caffè?"

"She talks about marrying Glenn."

The tone was disdainful. "What's the matter with Glenn? You don't approve?"

"What's to approve? Lucia is a grown woman. She can make up her own mind about her life, about this . . . this *boy* . . ."

"A boy? Not a man?"

"You saw how she treats him?"

I nodded.

"Why do you think he puts up with it? He is still a boy. Lucia says they're engaged. *Eh.* She won't go through with it."

"Because?"

"Because there is a man from my daughter's past who still comes sniffing around . . . a real man, a grown one. Lucia has a special smile for this one. Glenn doesn't know it, but she does. Love is a game to my daughter . . . she is not like her mother . . . to Lucia men are playthings . . ."

"And who is this man? The one from her past who still comes around to play with her?"

Enzo shrugged once more. "You don't know him . . ." He looked away again, into space.

"Glenn rebuilds cars, right?" I prodded, trying to keep

the man focused. "With his skills, maybe he can help Lucia rebuild the caffè."

"Glenn Duffy is a *mechanic*, not a carpenter. He has no interest in running a caffè . . ." Enzo paused to cough. "I've heard him talk. He wants to open his own car shop in North Jersey, where he has family."

"It takes money to start your own business," I said. And I was willing to bet ten kilos of Kona Peaberry that a competent car mechanic would possess enough skill to rig a basic incendiary device with a timer.

"Enzo, where do you think Glenn Duffy is going to get the money to—"

"Excuse me." The RN appeared again, a tall, slender woman of East Indian heritage. "How are you feeling?" she asked Enzo, her voice a sweet singsong.

Taking in the nurse's dark, cat-shaped eyes and flawless dusky-skinned face, Enzo immediately perked up. "I died and went to heaven, that's how I feel. Only this can explain the angel I see before me."

The nurse laughed. "You're still here on Earth, I'm glad to say, Mr. Testa."

"You call me Enzo, okay? No more of that Mr. Testa stuff. Mr. Testa was my father."

She arched a pretty eyebrow then turned to face me. "I'm afraid you'll have to wrap up your visit. Mr. Testa has another family member waiting. As soon as you come out, I'll show his sister in . . ."

"Sister?" Enzo and I blurted out at the same time.

"Yes, Mr. Testa, your sister Mrs. Rita Quadrelli."

As the nurse turned and strode away, Enzo's eyes widened in obvious panic. "Clare! A favor, *please*! I beg you."

I already guessed.

"The widow Quadrelli is not my sister. She must have fibbed like you to get in here—"

"And you don't want to see her?"

"When God made that woman, he left out the quiet! Five

minutes with her babbling in my ear, and I'll be pulling these tubes out to get away, even if it means certain death!"

I considered going to the nurse, but that had the potential to turn ugly, especially if Mrs. Quadrelli were confronted. After all, how could I accuse her of not being his sister when I wasn't his daughter?

"I'd better deal with Mrs. Quadrelli directly," I said. "What do you want me to tell her?"

"Tell her I'm sleeping. Tell her I'm drugged. Tell her I'm in a coma!"

I touched his shoulder. "I'll think of something. And I'll keep checking in with your nurse to see how you're doing."

Moments later, I spotted Mrs. Quadrelli just outside the critical-care unit. She was waiting in a small seating area, but the woman wasn't sitting, she was frantically pacing next to the sliding glass doors. And when she saw me walking away from Enzo's station, her expression morphed from impatience to outrage.

"What's this? I was told Enzo was visiting with his daughter. But you're not Enzo's daughter!"

Okay, Clare, come up with something—fast.

NINE

~~~~~~~~~~~~~~~~~~~~~~~~~~~~

ENZO had described Mrs. Quadrelli as a *donna pazzesca*, which is why I'd mentally cast her as a bug-eyed Phyllis Diller with a wild gray 'fro and a voice like Alvin the singing chipmunk.

Way off.

Impeccably tailored in a sleek black pantsuit, Enzo's wannabe love interest was a handsome, slender lady in her midsixties. Her dark hair was cropped short like Lucia's, dead straight, and shiny as a beetle shell with enough shimmering red highlights to have been recently salon-glossed. A cloying cloud of flowery cologne floated around her. Like Lucia, she sported plenty of gold jewelry, which jangled with every fidget, and although she appeared upset to see me, she was far from what I would have described as a *crazy woman*.

"Let me introduce myself," I began, trying to ignore the increasing itch in my nose. *Lord, that cologne. She must have just doused herself!* "My name is—"

"You're not Lucia."

No kidding. "My name is Clare Cosi and—"

"I don't understand! The nurse told me Enzo was visiting with his daughter!"

"And she told me his *sister* was waiting to see him. We both know you're not his sister."

The woman's squinting eyes collapsed another millimeter. "Who *are* you?"

"I told you, my name is Clare—"

"Who are you to *Enzo*?"

"A friend in the coffee business. I went by his place this evening with my employer to look over an antique roaster. We were all caught in the fire."

Mrs. Quadrelli fell silent. Her red lipstick was so boldly applied that when she twisted her mouth into a scowl, I flashed on my years taking Joy to the Big Apple Circus.

Finally she said, "You people shouldn't have been there at all."

"Excuse me?"

"Enzo closes early on Thursdays to play bocce. Everyone knows that." She looked away then, as if a poster on flu prevention were in immediate need of study.

"I don't understand. What does that have to do with—"

She whipped her head back around. "If not for *you* and your *employer*, he'd have been in that park with me. It's *your* fault Enzo is in this hospital."

I studied the woman. "What do you know about the fire, anyway?"

"Me? Nothing! Not a thing!" She threw up her hands. "I wasn't even near Enzo's caffè. It was Mrs. Mercer who told me about it. Dotty saw the whole thing, and she came to the park with her dog, Pinto. Little Pinto is famous in the neighborhood. Do you know about him?"

"No, but if you—"

"He's the dog who rides around in the red wagon. Pinto was featured in the *Daily News* last year. He has cerebral palsy or something and can't walk. Or is Pinto a she? I forget. Anyway, Pinto's vet is that new fellow on Steinway Street—"

"Sorry to interrupt," I said, beginning to get a clue why Enzo was willing to choose a coma over *this* conversation, "but I think we should head downstairs."

The glass ICU doors slid wide just then, and I noticed Enzo's pretty nurse glancing curiously our way.

"Enzo can't see you tonight," I quietly told Mrs. Q.

"And why would that be? He saw *you*, didn't he?"

"The doctors just ordered more tests, so no more visitors, not even family—"

"Tests!" Mrs. Q snorted. "I know all about doctors and their tests! Maria Tobinski, on Thirty-ninth Avenue, she has a husband who's a conductor on the MTA. Works the F train—anyway, Maria went to her gynecologist for a routine checkup and they found—"

"You know what?" I said, cutting her off before I heard every private detail about poor Maria Tobinski's medical history. "Let's you and I go downstairs together—"

I was forming the plan as I said the words. Mrs. Q appeared to know every little happening in Enzo's neighborhood, and Mike's stories of his fieldwork hadn't been lost on me. A source like this one was too good to pass up.

"I need coffee," I said. "Let me buy you a cup . . ." (I had no idea where I'd get one at this late hour, but this was a hospital; they had to have at least four things: doctors, nurses, stethoscopes, and java juice.)

Mrs. Quadrelli frowned at my offer. "Maybe I should double-check with the nurse."

"Don't do that!"

"Why not?"

Why not? "Because, well . . . it's a *secret*." I motioned her closer. "I didn't want to say anything, but . . ."

"What? What?"

The woman's entire body came awake. Her head cocked, even her pupils dilated. *A gossip addict, for sure.*

"The truth is," I continued, snaking my arm around hers, "it's not pretty. Are you sure you want to hear?"

"What? Tell me!"

"Enzo is in trouble," I whispered, guiding her away from the ICU doors, down the hallway, toward the elevators.

"What kind of trouble?"

"Officials are investigating whether or not the fire was deliberately set." *Not a lie!*

Mrs. Quadrelli looked sufficiently horrified. "What makes them think that?"

"I don't know. But Enzo will be their prime suspect."

"Why!"

"Because he's the owner, of course, and the beneficiary of the fire insurance payoff. Did you know he was planning to move back to Italy? It sounds incriminating."

"That's just talk! His daughter will tell you. He's been saying that for years, but he never goes through with it!"

We actually made it to the elevators. I pushed the *down* button. "So you're saying Enzo had no concrete plans to leave the country?"

"None. Not before the fire, at least. Now things have changed though, haven't they? I mean, with the caffè up in smoke."

"I see. So you think he'll bank the insurance money and finally retire to Italy?"

"I certainly hope so because I intend to go with him."

I gaped at her. "You plan to move to Italy? With Enzo?" *This has to be news to him.*

"Don't look so surprised, Miss Cosi, my husband was born in Italy, so I've been there quite a few times already. I just wish it had been more. For years, you see, we ran a restaurant together on Thirtieth Avenue—"

"You're divorced?"

"Bite your tongue! I'm a widow. The restaurant business killed my husband! Put him into an early grave . . . But that's behind me now. And the fire can be behind Enzo soon, too."

She exhaled, gaze turning glassy. "It's been years since I've toured Italy, but it is a beautiful place, and I know I'd love to retire there. Enzo and I could set up a very nice little home near his two sisters."

"You don't sound very broken up about the fire."

"After Enzo gets out of this wretched place and we're all settled in Italy, he'll see it's really a good thing his business went up in flames . . ."

I blinked, recalling the masterpiece of a mural the man had spent half a lifetime creating—not to mention his spotless floor, polished tables, meticulously maintained espresso machine—and wanted to punch this *donna pazzesca* right in the nose.

"Now, Mrs. Quadrelli," I managed through gritted teeth, "why would you say such a thing?"

"The man is over seventy! He should retire already, enjoy his life, not spend every waking hour making silly coffee drinks!"

I had two words for this woman—

Bing! Bing! "Elevator's here!" (Those weren't it.)

Four endless stories of pointless babble later, we reached the hospital's ground floor.

"Come with me to the waiting room," I said, deciding something that very second. "I'll get us coffee and you can talk to the police officer."

"Police officer!"

"Shhhh . . ."

"What's a police officer doing here?"

"That's what I was trying to tell you. I went up to warn Enzo that the officials were looking into the fire being suspicious, so he shouldn't say anything to incriminate himself."

"Oh! I see!"

"And you can help, too."

"How?"

"Well, to start with, you can back me up when I tell this officer that Enzo can't see any more visitors this evening."

Mrs. Quadrelli's head bobbed like an eager parrot. Inside of ten minutes, I'd transformed the woman from suspicious shrew to co-conspirator. Even Mike would be impressed, of that I was certain—what I wasn't so certain about was his reaction to the way I was about to use him.

Ten

~~~~~~~~~~~~~~~~~~~~~~~~~~~~~~~~~~~~

"EXCUSE me, *Officer?*"

Amused blue eyes peeked over newsprint.

I never called Mike *officer.* I sometimes addressed him as detective in a teasing way, which was why I wasn't surprised to see the beginnings of a smile behind the man's *New York Times.*

"This is Mrs. Quadrelli," I quickly added in serious staccato. "I brought her down from the ICU to verify that Enzo is not available for an official interview at this time."

"That's right! Miss Cosi is right!" Mrs. Quadrelli's beetle-brown head began bobbing again. "Lorenzo is undergoing tests. He can have no visitors. None at all, certainly not *you.*"

Mike shifted in his yellow plastic waiting room chair, set the newspaper down, and regarded us, his amused expression fading into one of guarded confusion.

Mrs. Quadrelli frowned at Mike's off-track expression. "You *are* a police officer, aren't you?" She turned to me. "Did he ever show you his identification, Miss Cosi? You can't be too careful these days."

I met Mike's eyes. "Officer, let me explain: This woman is

a friend of Enzo's. As I told you earlier, I don't live in Queens, but Mrs. Quadrelli here might have some ideas about who set that fire because I'm sure it wasn't Enzo."

"That's right," she said. "Enzo would never set fire to that caffè. He was attached to it. *Too* attached if you really want to know."

I cleared my throat. "So, *Officer*, if you'd like to *ask questions* about who might have had a motive to burn the place down, Mrs. Quadrelli here might be able to offer you some leads." *Please follow me, Mike. Please!*

A nano-flash of annoyance crossed Mike's rugged features. It was instantly replaced with his still-as-stone cop mask. Slowly, deliberately, he unfolded his endless form to its full height. With his gaze holding mine, he said, "Have a seat, Mrs. Quadrelli. And talk to me . . ."

Oh, Mike, thank you . . .

"Tell me what you think is relevant," Mike began. "Talk about anything you can think of—"

Anything other than Maria Tobinski's medical history, and the saga of Pinto, the dog who rides around in a little red wagon.

I touched the woman's arm. "Try to stay on the subject of Enzo and his caffè. Police officers don't have a lot of patience." I shot Mike an apologetic look. In my experience, patience was Mike Quinn's defining characteristic—although with Chatty Cathy here, who knew?

Mrs. Quadrelli settled into the plastic chair and looked up (way up) at the broad-shouldered cop now towering over her. Finally, she turned to me.

"He showed you his ID, right, Miss Cosi? You never said."

With a barely perceptible sigh, Mike reached inside his sport coat, pulled out the well-worn leather wallet and flashed his shield.

"That's a *gold* badge!" A scolding finger appeared in my face. "This man's not just an *officer*, Miss Cosi. He's a *detective*."

"Oh?" I said, exchanging another look with Mike. "I'm so sorry, *Detective*. I didn't mean to demote you."

Mike's lips twitched. "No problem." He turned his attention to Mrs. Quadrelli. "Now why don't you start at the beginning . . ."

Contrary to my advice, Mrs. Q began filling Mike in on her relationship with Enzo, starting with their first passing conversation, the weather that day, and what clothes they were wearing.

I am going to need caffeine, I realized, *as soon as possible.*

The only visible source was a bank of machines on the other side of the waiting room.

Vending machine coffee. God help me . . .

Cringing, I crossed over. My handbag smelled of smoke as I opened it and gathered enough change to satisfy the DelishiCo Individual Brew coffee machine—twice. *Oh, sure, each cup was "individually brewed," as promised, but that didn't matter much when the water bin hadn't been flushed in months, and coffee oils had built up along the internal spout.*

I loaded up on the powdered cream, poured in a stack of sugar packets, and returned to Mrs. Quadrelli's side, handing over the cup of coffee I'd promised her.

About then, Mrs. Q's eyes went teary. "And I think maybe it was those men who did it, who set the fire . . ."

"Men?" I echoed. "What men?"

"Theo, the Greek boy, and the other one, Kareem—he's from Morocco or Egypt or something. They run that night-club next to Caffè Lucia—"

"The Red Mirage?" I asked, recalling the scruffy-chinned guy with the foreign accent who'd called my car a junk heap.

"That's the one. Those are the two fellows who manage the place. Theo's been here for years. His family lives by the park. But Kareem is a new émigré, a real shady type."

"What do you mean by shady?" Mike asked. His deep voice remained measured, but his eyes betrayed the tiniest flicker of newly awakened interest.

"Just . . . *shady.*"

"You mean criminal shady?" I pressed.

The woman shrugged. "I wouldn't be surprised."

Mike glanced at me a moment then focused back on Mrs. Quadrelli. "And why do you think these men would want to burn down Enzo's shop?"

"They wanted to buy his place," she explained. "Maybe two months after they opened the club, they began making offers. They were *very* insistent, if you know what I mean—*threatening*, that's what Enzo said. You can ask him; he'll tell you. They kept it up, too, even after Enzo dug in his heels and told them absolutely not."

Mike leaned in a bit. "Why did they want him out so badly?"

"So they could increase the size of that nightclub of theirs. When Enzo wouldn't give in, they expanded in the other direction, after Mr. Ganzano moved his real estate office to that new building on Broadway. I think they forced him out. Did you know he left his wife after thirty-one years of marriage? I hear he has a Dominican floozy stashed in an apartment near LaGuardia Airport—"

"But they stopped bothering Enzo, right?" I said. "It sounds like these men got what they wanted. They were able to expand in the other direction?"

"Yes—and then the club practically doubled in size. Oh, the noise! My goodness the noise on that block was terrible! They kept the music blaring until three in the morning. There were people crowding the sidewalk, fights every night! And the street was always jammed with cars!"

"Did Enzo complain?" I asked. "Get them into trouble?"

"Oh, no. After a time, there was no need to. All that noise and trouble went away."

"Why is that?" Mike asked. "The club's still there, isn't it?"

"Yes, but the crowds aren't. The place used to have lines around the block. But then the economy took a nosedive and a lot of the young people lost their jobs, thank goodness! Now very few of them have money for overpriced nightclubs, so it's a quiet street again."

A dying business, in other words. Mike raised an eyebrow at me. He was thinking the same thing. Here was the perfect motive for a torch job—and what better way to make yourself look innocent than to start the blaze in the business next door?

Mrs. Quadrelli kept talking, but nothing else seemed as promising a lead as these Red Mirage guys. As she chattered on, I continued forcing myself to drink the vending machine coffee.

About a hundred years ago cowboys used to heat ground coffee in a sock placed in a pot of simmering water. When their campfire coffee was ready, they'd pour it into a tin cup. I'd never tasted boiled cowboy sock coffee, but I was absolutely sure it tasted better than *this*.

"So I told him he should call our city councilmen and complain. Those children of hers make such a racket; they should be made to play someplace else, not to mention that barking dog. Don't you agree it's a public nuisance? And what do you think about the lack of response from 311? Isn't that a disgrace, Detective?"

Mike's cop-neutral expression remained as firmly fixed as ever, but I could tell—from the deepening grooves around his eyes and mouth—that even the most patient detective in the NYPD was becoming exasperated.

"I think I got what I need for now, Mrs. Quadrelli . . ." He glanced at me, a trace of pleading on the edge of it. *Are we done now, Detective Cosi?*

With a twinge of guilt, I said. "Just one more thing, Officer—"

"Not officer!" Mrs. Q reminded me with a correcting *tsk-tsk*. "This man is a detective, remember?"

"Yes, of course." I cleared my throat. "*Detective*, weren't you asking me earlier about Lucia? Maybe Mrs. Quadrelli here can help." I turned to her. "How well do you know Enzo's daughter?"

"Oh, very! She and I have so much in common. We just love to shop! She has such a good eye for shoes and jewelry, that one. We also have the same hairdresser—Gustave Flaubert—"

"Flaubert?" I said. "The nineteenth-century novelist?"

"You know him?" She asked. "He works on Fifth at Jean Michel Dubonnet—"

Mike caught my eye. *Dubonnet on the rocks,* he mouthed, and I nearly choked on the last dregs of my coffee (which would have been appropriate since I'd been gagging the stuff down for the past fifteen minutes).

"That's where we met," the woman continued. "It was Lucia who introduced me to her father, said it was time he started dating again—"

"Oh, I almost forgot," I interrupted as I shot Mike a hang-in-there-partner look. "The detective asked me about Lucia's boyfriends. He might want to follow up with them, see if they have anything to add." I lowered my voice. "Their statements could also help clear Enzo of suspicion."

"Of course! She's seeing a younger man now. His name is Glenn Duffy . . . I'll spell it." She stared at Mike. "Aren't you going to write it down?"

Mike gave a little sigh, pulled out his notebook. "Go ahead . . ."

After Mrs. Q gave the background on Duffy, I waited for another name. There was none. Once again, I pressed—

"Enzo mentioned there was another man from Lucia's past who's been coming around lately. Do you know about him?"

"Oh, you mean the fireman?"

Fireman? I glanced at Mike. Even he seemed surprised.

"What fireman would that be?" Mike asked, his pen poised over his notebook with much more readiness.

"I don't know," Mrs. Quadrelli said.

"You don't know?" I couldn't believe it.

She threw up her hands. "I asked, believe me! Enzo mentioned 'the fireman' was back. He said it once, but then he dropped it, refused to say more. And Lucia insists that Glenn is the only man in her life. That's all I know."

She shrugged. "You want more? Go ask Lucia."

ELEVEN

~~~~~~~~~~~~~~~~~~~~~~~~~~~~~~~

"**C**LARE? You okay?"

Two hours after our unorthodox interview with the widow Quadrelli, I was back home in my West Village duplex with a still-empty stomach and a head full of questions.

After we'd dropped Madame off at her Fifth Avenue digs, I ran down my theories with Mike. He agreed with my observations, encouraged me to contact Stuart Rossi, and reminded me that FDNY marshals assigned to a fire were like NYPD detectives working a crime scene.

Fire marshals weren't "just like" law enforcement officers, they *were* officers. They carried guns, interviewed witnesses, and (if warranted) made arrests.

"Just treat the man like a police detective," Mike told me. "Call him first thing in the morning, give him everything you dug up, he'll take it from there."

Now I was descending my apartment's staircase, dragging and tired, until a whiff of smoke hit me. Adrenaline instantly juiced my system.

"Clare? You okay?" Mike was gawking at me. I must have looked ill or gone pale or something until I realized the offending agent was safely contained in my living room fireplace.

"Did you hear me, sweetheart? You okay?"

"I'm okay."

I wasn't. Not really. But I didn't want Mike feeling bad about his cozy fire-building gesture. The lengthening flames would warm the chilly room. Even the disturbing shadows flickering across the polished antiques made me conclude (in a whole new way) how lucky I was to reside in this place.

While this entire Federal-era townhouse was still technically my ex-mother-in-law's, she'd made clear to me that she was legally willing its ownership to me (along with her son), so I felt like a caretaker now as much as a resident—an invaluable bonus that came with managing her coffeehouse two floors below.

As my sock-covered feet slipped across the chilly parquet floor, I noticed Mike's gaze tracking me with unabashed interest. For a second, I couldn't imagine why.

Sexy was not a word I'd use to describe me at the moment. Postshower, I'd dressed for sloppy comfort in a pair of black bike shorts and an oversized T-shirt that warned: *Do Not Give This Woman Decaf!*

The tee—along with an apron that said *I Serve It Up Hot!*—had been a gag gift from my staff last Christmas. But Mike had seen this shirt before. On the other hand, it was the first time I'd gone braless wearing it. (My street clothes, down to my underwear, had reeked of char, and my other bras were still damp from a morning's hand-washing.)

Whatever the reason for the man's open scrutiny, I was happy to return the gesture. With his sport coat tossed off, Mike's muscular shoulders were nicely defined by his dress shirt—spotlessly white yet noticeably wrinkled from hours of wearing his leather holster. Tie well loosened, long, strong form folded into a relaxed crouch, he looked comfortably assured, entrenched in a zone of cool-blue control that was quintessentially Mike.

From our very first meeting, I'd been impressed by the

man's natural confidence, mainly because—unlike my ex-husband—it lacked arrogance. Mike was often wary and sometimes skeptical, but he was never cynical, not in the way some people were, using it as an excuse for complacency or indifference. What attracted me most, I think, was his equilibrium. Mike was as hardened as any cop from the New York streets, yet he'd refused to let the job or the city kill his compassion.

Like a buttoned-down Ivanhoe, he now picked up the black iron poker and stabbed at the heart of the fire he'd built, not to kill the thing but to give it more air. And that's when it hit me just how much Mike Quinn enjoyed igniting blazes in my hearth.

Hmmm . . .

Considering the occupation of the man's cousin and younger brothers, I figured the desire to play with fire was probably a Quinn thing. Or maybe it was just some gene buried deep in the alpha-male string, a primal urge leftover from the DNA of grunting cavemen.

As I settled into the carved rosewood sofa, my gaze caught on his well-worn shoulder holster now hanging off the delicate lyre back of one of Madame's heirloom chairs. Tucked inside the leather was his rather large handgun. *Yet another kind of fire stick . . . ?*

"You look a little funny, sweetheart. Do you need a drink?"

"I need to eat."

I would have chowed down sooner, but I hadn't been able to stand those reeking clothes another minute; so while Mike had taken care of parking my old Honda, I'd headed upstairs for a hot, soapy shower.

I could see from the shopping bag now sitting on the coffee table—not to mention the aromas of cooked meat assaulting my sensory receptors—that Mike had taken care of food, too. But what was it exactly?

The large, glossy bag didn't look like your typical brown paper take-out sack. Vivid orange with a laminated exterior and nylon rope handles, it looked self-consciously hip, which was hardly ever a good thing when it came to authentically tasty takeout.

"UFC?" I said, reading the logo. "KFC I've heard of, but UFC?"

"It's Korean-style fried chicken," Mike said, putting down the poker.

I looked closer at the small print under the large UFC logo. "Unidentified Flying Chickens? I never heard of them."

"There are only three stores in the metro area," Mike said, rising to his full height, "one in Elmhurst, one in Brooklyn, and one in North Jersey. Sully swears by them, says he's addicted. He just dropped it off."

"Sully was here?"

Finbar "Sully" Sullivan worked closely with Mike on the OD Squad, a special task force Mike supervised out of the Sixth Precinct here in Greenwich Village. Sully was one of the nicest men I knew—an openly cheerful forty-something guy with ready quips delivered in a native Queens accent.

"I left my car back in Elmhurst," Mike explained. "I asked Sully and Franco to swing by, bring it back to Manhattan."

"Wait, back up. Did you just say Sully and *Franco*? As in Sergeant Emmanuel Franco?"

Mike nodded and I tensed. Detective Sergeant Franco was the complete opposite of Finbar Sullivan. Edgy and volatile, the man was about as subtle as a ball-peen hammer to the forehead (something I had learned over this past holiday season).

Where Mike and Sully wore suits, ties, and their methodical patience on their sleeves, the younger Franco displayed cocky confidence and a street-tough attitude, with a wardrobe to match: a Yankee jacket, cowboy boots, and an in-your-face red, white, and, blue 'do rag.

Despite the guy's bulldog approach to law enforcement, however, I did not *dislike* him. What concerned me was Franco's interest in my daughter. He'd taken Joy out a number of times while she was visiting me on her last holiday break. But, *thank goodness,* my girl was back in Paris.

I didn't relish the idea of Joy meeting and falling for another French line cook, which could sway her to remain in Europe indefinitely, but I was even less happy with her developing an attachment to a detective whose persona seemed to fall somewhere between Dirty Harry and Rambo.

"I can't believe you're working with Franco," I said.

"Why not?" He crossed his arm. "I needed the manpower."

"The construction site investigation?"

Mike nodded. Over the past two weeks, he'd been following up on recent OD cases, one of which had ended in death. Working closely with the DEA, he and Sully had supervised a covert investigation of a popular nightclub on the Lower East Side, near the Williamsburg Bridge, where both victims had ingested the drugs.

Unfortunately, the place came up clean. No dealing had been uncovered on the premises. Now a source claimed the selling was being done at an adjacent construction site, where someone working on the site itself was dealing recreational drugs like ecstasy and Liquid E to club-goers.

"Well . . ." I tried to focus on the positive. (After all, I could see where a rough-edged guy like Franco would be an asset in working an undercover operation on a construction crew. And when it came to Mike's choice of police personnel, who was I to argue?) "I suppose it was nice of the two of them to bring over dinner, along with your car . . ."

"Yes, it was."

"Unidentified Flying Chickens . . ." I shook my head. "A Queens restaurant with an ironic name."

"Yeah . . ." Mike sat down next to me. "It's way too Manhattan hipster for the geography."

"Have you tried it? What do you think of it?"

Mike arched an eyebrow. "You really care?"

He was right. I didn't. The enticing aromas were making my stomach growl and my mouth salivate. I dug into the bag. The first box I opened was stuffed with warm chicken wings. A second later, my teeth were tearing into skin crispier than a newly fried kettle chip. The caramelized taste of slow-roasted garlic hit my palate first, next came a play of sweet brown sugar, slightly tingly ginger, and under it all, a low, meaty *umami* base note of soy.

"Oh my God," I garbled as I masticated.

"Good?"

"Mm, mm . . . mmmmm . . ."

Mike joined me, opening another box, which was stuffed with fried drumsticks, glistening with a sweet-and-sour glaze. A third held containers of tangy cold slaw with a hint of Chinese mustard; cubes of cold, crunchy Korean radish; and sweet potato matchsticks.

"You know, I could duplicate this," I managed to boast around a mouthful of soy-garlic wing.

"I don't doubt it," Mike said, who'd swooned over my cooking more times than I could count.

"They must fry their chicken twice to get it this crispy . . ." I munched some more, gathering flavor and textural clues, deducing the culinary technique. "Then after they fry it, they must roll it in the sticky glaze and dry it out in a warm oven . . ."

"Sounds like your famous Buffalo wings."

"Except I don't deep-fry those, just crisp them up in a cast-iron skillet. A tempura batter might be interesting to try . . ." I couldn't help channeling one of my old In the Kitchen with Clare columns. "Home cooks tend to use all-purpose flour because it's always in the pantry, but cake flour is the best way to go for frying batters, even for beer-battered onion rings, because it's lower in gluten."

"Well, sweetheart, the day you want to experiment, give me a call. I'll be happy to help with the taste testing."

"I've noticed you're always available for that."

"I'm always available for a lot of things." He threw me his best leering wink. I laughed and leaned back on the sofa, grateful my bike pants had an expanding waistband. "Man, I really needed that . . ."

Mike reached out with a paper napkin, gently wiped at a ruby smear along my cheek. "I'm guessing you liked it . . ."

I did the same for him, rubbing at a smudge on his chin. "I'd say your man Sully's a good guy to trust."

"So am I," Mike said. Then he leaned in and moved his mouth over mine.

That tasted even better.

Mike's mouth was sweet and slightly sticky from the chicken glaze, and (frankly) I would have been happy to gorge myself on nothing but him for the rest of the night. But, after a few blissful minutes, I was the one who broke contact.

"I'm sorry, Mike . . ." I softly pushed on his hard chest. "I'd like to talk a little more . . ."

TWELVE

~~~~~~~~~~~~~~~~~~~~~~~~~~~~~~~~~~~~~~~

As we broke contact, I saw the disappointment in Mike's eyes. I didn't blame him. I needed to talk, and that's not what he needed.

"Everything you did tonight was wonderful," I quickly reassured him, "coming to the hospital, helping with Mrs. Quadrelli, driving us home, arranging the food . . ."

But I wanted one more thing from Mike Quinn: answers about his cousin. And if the lip-lock went on any longer, I wouldn't care about getting them—or anything else apart from the two of us upstairs on my mahogany four-poster.

Mike studied my face. "It's okay," he finally said. "I'm always glad to help . . ."

He sat back on the sofa, stretched out his arm, and gestured for me to move closer. I did, leaning into him.

"I have to admit," he said, gazing at the crackling hearth, "it was nice seeing you with a satisfied expression again. The way you were choking down that vending machine coffee back at the hospital . . ." He shook his head. "I had to bite my tongue to keep from cracking up."

"You had to bite *your* tongue? I thought I was going to

lose it when Mrs. Quadrelli went on about Gustave Flaubert styling her hair."

"Yeah, old Gustave's probably some poor kid from Brooklyn named Gus Flabberson."

"Par for the course on the hustle-a-buck schemes that go on in this town."

"I thought I'd heard every alias in the book," Mike said. "Jacking the name of *Madame Bovary*'s author is more creative than some."

"I'm betting Gustave's boss has an entire list of famous French author names ready to go."

"So you think he's got Stendhal doing the shampooing and Proust on the register?"

"No," I said. "If the man knows his French writers, Dumas is on the register and Stendhal's in charge of color. Proust belongs with the stylists."

Mike laughed. "I actually do follow you, you know?"

"Oh? You mean not all cops are jarheads?"

"Naw. We only *look* like a paramilitary organization."

I smiled. "Well, I'm not in a position to throw stones. I used a false identity to get in to see Enzo."

"And you got some good information, too."

"You think so?"

"Like I told you earlier," he said, "call that fire marshal first thing in the morning. Tell him everything . . ."

The list of suspects wasn't small, but I'd gathered good leads. Only one thing still troubled me: "I can't stop wondering who that fireman is, the mysterious one who's secretly seeing Lucia."

"Me, too," Mike said. "If that woman was looking for expertise in torching her dad's caffè, she couldn't do any better than a fireman."

"You're speaking from experience?"

Mike didn't answer directly. What he said was, "Firefighters are experts in the methods of starting blazes, not just stopping them. It's part of their training . . ."

And there's my opening . . .

"So tell me, Detective, why didn't you ever go through the training? I mean, given your hero father and your younger brothers . . ." *Not to mention your evil twin of a cousin.* "Why aren't you a fireman, too?"

I'd kept the tone light, but my question failed to amuse. Mike's body tensed beside mine; his prolonged silence felt heavy. So I took a guess—and not a very wild one: "Is that the reason why you and your cousin don't get along? Because you didn't follow family tradition and join the FDNY?"

He exhaled. "That's part of it."

I shifted on the sofa, getting some distance so I could see his eyes. This was a situation I'd faced before with this man—*How do you interrogate a trained interrogator?*

Not with tricks. When I wanted answers from Mike, I asked him straight. "I'd like to know what started the beef between you two."

"What *started* it . . ." He let out another audible breath. "I guess you could say it *started* a long time ago . . . when we were in the academy together."

"Police academy?" I assumed.

"Fire academy."

"Fire academy? You went to the fire academy with your cousin?"

Mike nodded.

"What about that story you told me? About always wanting to be a cop? That schoolyard epiphany thing . . ."

Just like me, Mike had gone to Catholic school, where the priests and nuns were big on the idea of vocation. At some point in our lives, they told us, God was supposed to reveal our life's calling.

I'd gotten the cosmic message with the birth of my daughter. According to Mike, he'd picked up the Almighty's voicemail at the age of thirteen during a vicious fight that had broken out between two boys in the school courtyard.

Instead of standing on the sidelines with the others, Mike jumped in to stop it and got a beating for his trouble—from both boys. The Jesuit who finally broke it up told Mike that with his zealousness to leap into human matters and make things right, he was destined to become a priest or a cop.

"I probably could have been a priest," he'd told me when we first started seeing each other. "I just couldn't hack the chastity."

"So how did you end up in the fire academy?"

"My dad wanted it. I respected the man, so I gave it a shot . . ." He shrugged. "It just wasn't for me. After a few weeks, I quit."

"And your cousin Michael couldn't understand?"

Again, Mike shrugged. "He thought we were in it together . . ."

"So he turned on you?"

"Like I said, that's how it *started*. Trust me when I say that my cousin has no love for me, and I'd like you to stay away from him. Can you do that for me, Clare?"

"Yes, of course."

"Thank you."

As we sat gazing at the hearth, I felt Mike's hand brush aside my hair, begin to caress my shoulder. His heavy body leaned into me, and I felt his lips at my nape, applying little kisses.

I knew what the man wanted. (I wanted it, too.) But I couldn't let go. An idea kept banging around my brain, a pithy piece of police wisdom Mike once shared: *If a smart perp wants to dodge an interview, he doesn't clam up or even argue. He keeps feeding the interviewer information—just not any key information . . .*

And that's what Mike had done with me. I was sure of it. Considering the Quinn clan's history with the FDNY, I figured there had to be more to his story. Not that I was some expert on familial expectation.

After my mother left us, my father expressed zero thoughts about my future apart from *I just want you to be happy, cupcake . . .* The equivalent of a "Good girl, Lassie" pat on the head. My old-world grandmother, who'd primarily raised me, never pushed me to be anything—beyond a well-behaved young lady.

It wasn't until college that I realized not everyone was

like me. A number of my classmates were pressured children, saddled with the baggage of parental aspirations. When the stars aligned, they had few issues: *I always wanted to study contract law . . . Electrical engineering works for me . . . Sure, I'm going for the PhD . . .*

But when one future had two different maps, kids got lost.

The strong ones waged external rebellion, raising shields against arrows as they followed the sound of Henry David's drummer. The pragmatic ones chose deafness—*screw the different drummer, he's suspect*—and locked down their spirits to the road often taken.

The ones I worried about lived in the gray purgatory of indecision, giving their families the appearance of going along while quietly burning for another life. These kids saw the lights of an inspiring new highway yet continued to plod along the deadening old one, nurturing quiet resentment with every step. (And I knew from my own lousy marriage that a pretense like that was about as healthy as feeding a piranha in your stomach. Inevitably the thing grew bigger and bigger, gnawing at your insides until it completely hollowed you out.)

Given the Quinn legacy, Mike's father must have been devastated when his eldest quit the fire academy. It couldn't have been the casual decision Mike was now making it out to be.

I cleared my throat: "I noticed you like sharing that story about the schoolyard fight, but there's something more, isn't there? Something you don't want people to know about why you became a cop."

The kisses stopped. The magic fingers quit moving. Mike leaned back, taking his hand and lips with him.

"Mike?"

"It's not a pretty story, Clare."

"I don't care. I'd like to hear it . . ."

For a full minute, he stayed silent, shifting a few times on the sofa. Then just when I thought he would clam up for good, he rubbed his jaw, took a breath, and said—

"When I hit high school, I started dating a classmate.

Leta was her name, Leta Diaz. Bright girl, beautiful smile. She was my lab partner in chemistry, a class we both enjoyed, so we hit it off . . ."

He paused to glance over at me. I nodded. "Go on."

"Leta's family came here from the Dominican Republic. They ran their own little convenience store just off the Brooklyn-Queens Expressway. One afternoon, Leta's dad was robbed at the store. He resisted and was shot to death."

"Oh God, that's awful. Your poor girlfriend."

"Yeah, she took it extremely hard. I tried to be there for her. But I wanted to do more than just hold her hand and watch her cry her heart out, you know? I wanted to do something. So I did."

"What do you mean? You were just a high school kid."

"I had a gut feeling. The week before, at one of the school's basketball games, I noticed the father of a classmate talking to Leta's father. There was something about the way he was chatting up the man—it seemed odd, like a hustle."

"So?"

"So this robbery that happened—it was during a very narrow window of time when Leta's father had a great deal of cash on hand at the store to pay their packaged-food distributor. Once a week they got that delivery, once a week on a certain day, between certain hours."

"And you thought this man, this father of your classmate at school, was the stick-up guy?"

"I knew he'd already done time for mail fraud. My classmate—Pete Hogarth was his name—he'd been complaining that his old man couldn't get any work, also hinted that he had a worsening cocaine habit. So I took matters into my own hands."

"What did you do?"

"I buddied up to Pete, went back to his apartment to hang out. The place was small, no privacy, but when I heard his dad kept pigeons on the roof, I knew that's where I'd find evidence—and I did. The gun and the cash were buried in one of the coops. I called the detectives assigned to the case.

They arrested Pete's father. The ballistics matched up. He was the shooter."

"Leta must have been grateful."

"Honestly, she was too numb to fully understand what I did. Less than a month later, her family was back living in the Dominican Republic."

"So much for young love."

"Don't sweat it, Cosi. My heart survived."

"Those detectives handling the case must have been impressed."

"They were. They checked in on me after that, encouraged me to go to the police academy."

"But your father wanted you to join the FDNY?"

"I was the oldest. Like I said, I respected my dad, wanted to make him proud. But . . ."

"But . . . ?"

Mike turned on the sofa to fully face me. "As it came down, two of the guys in my class at the fire academy—they were relatives of Pete Hogarth's. These guys didn't care that Pete's father was a scumbag killer. They just figured me for a narc, a rat, a guy you could never trust, and they made it a point of spreading the story of what I'd done."

"Is that how your cousin felt about you?"

"No. Michael defended me. But it wasn't enough, and after a few weeks, my reality check kicked in. I knew what I wanted to be doing for the next four decades of my life, and it wasn't fighting fires. I wanted to be hunting down predators, Clare, getting them the hell off the street. Hogarth shot Leta's father in cold blood, and I made sure he couldn't kill again. I *liked* how it felt when I took him down."

My mind flashed on Enzo, pale as a cadaver in the ICU; Madame weak and teary on that stretcher; Dante unconscious on the glass-strewn concrete . . .

I closed my eyes. "Does it always feel good to take them down?"

"For me it does. But you don't always get them, Clare."

I realized something then, something Mike had known all along . . .

"That's why you've never discouraged me, isn't it?" I met his gaze. "You solved your first homicide as a kid, without a badge or a gun. You know what someone like me can do."

"Information and evidence, sweetheart. That's what clears cases. I can flash my shield all day long, but without information and evidence, I can't do my job. That's why we work to develop informants on the street, interview witnesses, run background checks. If you can get those things for an investigator, then you can help him—or her."

I exhaled. Given the fire marshal's brush off earlier in the evening, not to mention Captain Michael's oh-so-subtle warning not to get involved, I hadn't realized how much I needed to hear some encouraging words. Well, I was happy to return the favor.

"I can see why you don't like retelling that story. But it's really something what you did. It took guts . . ."

"Thanks." Mike smiled, but only a little, as if he were flattered by my words but embarrassed, too. Pointing to the take-out bag, he changed the subject. "You want more?"

"Not of that."

"Something else, then?"

I nodded. The flames in the fireplace were at their peak. I could feel their heat against my skin, hear their teasing pops and sparks. Leaning over, I pulled Mike's mouth back onto mine.

He was pleased I'd started the kiss. I could feel it in his tightening arms, his widening smile against my mouth. He tugged me closer, used his tongue to part my lips and deepen our connection. Then his hands slipped under my oversized tee, and his slightly calloused fingers generated something with a whole lot more intensity than what he'd started in my living room hearth.

"C'mon," he whispered, finally breaking away. "Let's go upstairs . . ."

I wasn't about to argue.

ThirteEN

∿∿∿∿∿∿∿∿∿∿∿∿∿∿∿∿∿∿∿∿∿∿∿

I woke the next morning to a pair of cat paws kneading my shoulder. I instinctively reached out for Mike. With a stab of disappointment, I realized the pillow next to mine was empty. That's when I remembered dozing off in his arms. He'd kissed my forehead and whispered something about an early meeting with prosecutors ahead of a grand jury appearance.

Suddenly I felt another kind of stab, a prickly one to my right foot. Java and Frothy were circling me like a pair of miniature *Jurassic Park* raptors.

"Okay, I'm up!"

I threw off the covers. "Happy now?"

Tails raised in feline triumph, the girls bounded off the bed and waited for me at the door. With another yawn, I tied on a robe, thrust my feet into slippers, and followed their proud little forms—one coffee-bean brown, the other latte-foam white—to the kitchen.

Despite that long, steamy shower the night before, I still had a thickness in my throat, a funky odor in my sinuses, and notwithstanding the many splendored moments of

Mike's lovemaking, my subsequent dreams had been filled with images of billowing black smoke, flashing red lights, and glinting razors of splintered glass.

Tucker, my assistant manager, was scheduled to open today, which meant I still had a little time to pull myself together. Thankfully, I felt more human after I fed my tiny, furry raptors a can of furry raptor food and downed a Moka-brewed *doppio* espresso.

Next I phoned Dante at Elmhurst Hospital. He was in good spirits this AM, announcing he was "ready to roll!" His release paperwork was already being prepared, and two friends were waiting in his room to take him home—Kiki and Bahni, the two young women who also shared his apartment.

One for each of his tattooed arms, I thought, relieved to hear some good news.

Next I called Madame, surprised to find her already dressed and on her way out the door. A driver was waiting downstairs, she explained, ready to return her to Queens and the bedside of her old friend.

"You'll need to say you're a family member if you want to see him," I warned.

"Yes, dear, I've already thought of that."

"Well, don't say you're his sister, okay? He may think you're Rita Quadrelli!"

"I plan to inform the nurses that I am his *sister-in-law*. I will be sure to give my name so Enzo knows my true identity."

"Great. Please let me know how he's doing, okay?"

"Of course."

"And there's one more thing . . . Last night, while I was questioning Enzo, he mentioned to me that Lucia was still seeing a fireman."

"Old flame?"

"Very funny."

"Yes, dear, well, it would have to be an old flame, wouldn't it? She described herself as engaged to that other boy, Glenn, didn't she?"

"See if you can get Enzo to tell you who this fireman is. Get a name."

After a pause, Madame said, "Did this fireman have something to do with setting the firebomb, dear?"

"You've certainly had your coffee this morning."

"With or without the java, I'm a lot sharper than you think."

"I think you're *plenty* sharp."

"Don't worry. I'll speak to Enzo."

"Thank you . . ."

By the time I hung up, it was after nine—late for me, but just about the perfect time to contact my favorite FDNY fire marshal. I dug his card out of my charcoal-scented handbag and dialed.

"Rossi."

"Hello," I said, envisioning the big man's slightly mashed nose, blue nylon jacket, and clanking tool belt. "This is the woman you spoke to last night at the Astoria fire. My name is Cla—"

"Clare Cosi. Yes, Ms. Cosi? What can I do for you?"

The speed and clarity of Rossi's response caught me by surprise. Obviously, the man had mainlined his morning joe. "Last night I spoke to the man who owns Caffè Lucia—"

"Lorenzo Testa? You went to the ICU?"

"I did, and I have some information for you. I spoke at length to a friend and neighbor of his, a Rita Quadrelli?"

"Yes."

I took a deep breath, feeling as righteous as Don Quixote—which was apropos. Five minutes from now, Rossi would probably dismiss me as tilting at windmills. But the stakes were too high to be indulging my pride. If I looked like an ass, so be it.

"Let me just say, Marshal, that when you find the evidence that the fire was intentionally set, as I know you will, I'm aware you'll be looking at Enzo as your prime suspect because he's the sole beneficiary of the fire insurance policy. But there are a number of much more viable suspects around Mr. Testa with very strong motives to torch his caffè."

I paused, waited.

"Go on."

"Mr. Testa's adult daughter, Lucia, has no interest in running the business, yet she's set to inherit the store and building when her father finally decides to retire. I think she may have hastened that retirement by having that fire set.

"Then there's the widow Quadrelli. That woman clearly views the caffè as the only thing standing between her and Enzo having some sort of 'happily ever after' scenario.

"And I also think you should look at the two men who run the Red Mirage nightclub: Theo and Kareem. These guys have been losing business since the economy tanked and may have tried to get a fire insurance payout by starting a suspicious fire next door, in Enzo's caffè, hoping it would spread to their property."

I listened for a reaction. But there was none. The line went silent. "Marshal Rossi?"

"Hold on, Ms. Cosi—"

Damn. "I really do think this is *important* information."

"So do I, ma'am. I'm taking notes . . ."

I blinked. *He's actually listening to me?* "So you'll follow up then?"

"That's my job."

"I'm very glad to hear you say that."

"Do you have anything else to add, Ms. Cosi?"

"I do. If Lucia Testa is responsible for setting that blaze—or even if she conspired to do it with Rita Quadrelli—I doubt very much she would have created the actual firebomb herself."

"Why is that?"

"She's a fastidious fashionista, that's why. Building a firebomb set on a timer might ruin her manicure. Ditto for the widow."

"So what's your theory?"

"I think it's possible that Lucia hired an accomplice or persuaded one to help her, either for personal reasons or a monetary payoff."

"And . . . ? Do you have any thoughts on who Ms. Testa or Mrs. Quadrelli may have worked with on that?"

"Yes. I believe there are two strong suspects. The first man is Lucia's boyfriend Glenn Duffy . . ." I told the marshal all I knew about Duffy, including his expertise as a mechanic. "And the second man is . . . actually, I don't have a name, but I know for certain he's a fireman."

"Excuse me?"

"Mr. Testa told me that a fireman's been sniffing around after Lucia. It sounds like a sexual relationship. I would have tried questioning Lucia herself, but she's not in town right now. She went away for the weekend, just a few hours before the bomb went off, which is highly suspicious timing, don't you think? I mean, getting out of town certainly helps her look completely detached from what happened . . ."

Rossi said nothing.

"Anyway," I added. "I think she may have used this fireman and his knowledge to help set off a firebomb and burn down the caffè."

"And you don't have any other information on this man's identity?"

"The only thing I can tell you concerns the firefighters who responded—"

"You're talking about Ladder 189 and Engine 335?"

"If that's who responded."

"It is."

"Well, Enzo confessed to me that his daughter liked to play with men. And the captain of the firehouse that responded told me that a lot of his guys liked to frequent Enzo's caffè, so . . ."

"So you think a member of the FDNY from Ladder 189 or Engine 335 helped Lucia Testa set the fire?"

"It's one theory, but yes, I do . . ."

After another moment of silence, Rossi asked, "Are you sure you can't *get* me a name, Ms. Cosi?"

The question confused me. It took me a moment to process it. "Marshal Rossi, are you saying that you'd like me to investigate further?"

"No comment."

I took a breath. "You can't officially ask me to investigate, can you?"

Rossi didn't answer directly. What he said was: "Like I told you before, Ms. Cosi, if you have *any new information* for me, just give me a call." He lowered his voice. "Call me anytime, okay?"

"I'll see what I can do . . ."

I hung up and stood staring for a moment.

Given Mike's talk with me last night, I shouldn't have been so astonished by Rossi's reaction. The man was a detective, after all, and I was an informant bringing him leads. It was no different from a street cop using snitches. Sure Rossi might have gotten the same leads once he started questioning Enzo, but I'd given him a head start and he knew it.

Obviously, the fire company was another matter. Those guys were tighter than family. James Noonan and Bigsby Brewer even referred to each other as brothers. The second an investigator like Rossi started asking questions, they'd stonewall him, especially if it meant protecting a man in their own firehouse.

And if Lucia has a history of sleeping with more than one of those men, that was just another reason for the entire company to make like irritated oysters and clam up . . .

I dug into the pocket of my robe for an elastic band, scraped my sleep-mussed hair into a taut, work-ready ponytail, and considered my options.

Enzo had been reluctant to give me the name of Lucia's secret fireman lover. Would he give it to Madame? I wasn't so sure.

The strongest connection I had to Ladder 189 and Engine 335 was Captain Michael Quinn. I could talk to him. But Mike specifically asked me to stay away from his cousin.

Just wait, Clare. Calm down and wait . . .

Madame would get a name. That was the easiest solution. And if that failed, there was always next week's Five-Borough Bake Sale to benefit the NYC Fallen Firefighters Fund. I'd have a chance to question some of the guys there, though I had to admit the idea of pressing those men to betray one of their own made me a little queasy.

Now I know how Mike must have felt turning in his classmate's father . . .

Feeling the acute need for some reassuring warmth, I went to the stove, poured filtered water into the lower half of my three-cup Moka Express. I ground the beans fine, piled them into the little filter basket, screwed the two pieces together, and placed them over medium heat.

The shimmering blue flame of the gas burner reminded me of Mike's eyes in the firelight. I chewed my lower lip, still a little swollen from his kisses, and in the quiet of the kitchen, I felt the faintest echoes of his lovemaking still singing through my body—so sweet and slow at first then breathtaking in its intensity. I ached for him now, sorry he'd had to leave so early.

As the express water came to a boil, however, my thoughts began to turn . . .

"Captain Michael," I whispered to the empty air. He truly was my best bet for a source inside that firehouse, which made me reconsider Mike's request to stay away from the man.

Given Mike's fire-academy story, I didn't doubt that things had gone down badly between the two cousins. *But didn't all of that stuff happen more than twenty years ago?*

Last night's Quinn vs. Quinn standoff came to mind—Captain Michael smirking at his cousin in the hospital drive; Mike doing a reach around for his handcuffs.

There must be more to the story. I moved to sit down at the kitchen table and that's when I realized . . .

There is.

A powerful, roasted scent suddenly suffused the air. My espresso was done. I moved to the stove, sloshed the steaming liquor into a demitasse, and sipped it so quickly it burned my tongue. I didn't care.

Quinn was one of the best interrogators in the NYPD. He could effortlessly manipulate any information exchange. I thought I was hot stuff, getting him to spill, but the reverse was true: Mike Quinn had manipulated me.

My fist hit the kitchen table so hard it sent the cats scurrying into the next room.

When I'd asked Mike what had started the beef between him and his cousin, he'd treated the phrasing literally: "What started it," he'd said, emphasizing the *started*. "I guess you could say it started a long time ago . . ."

Then why is it still going on? That's what I should have asked the man!

After downing the hot coffee, I banged open my cupboards and made a hasty breakfast—a giant popover pancake (aka Dutch Baby, Bismarck, poor girl's soufflé): flour, eggs, milk, salt, all whisked up with more fury than Dorothy's tornado.

I poured the batter into a preheated pan and flung it into a blistering oven where it quickly inflated like the puffy exterior of a Navajo bread; but instead of honey, I finished the whole thing in the bracing-sweet style of an espresso Romano, with a quick, tart squeeze from a lemon wedge and a generous dusting of powdered sugar.

My breakfast eaten, I went back to my cupboards and pulled out more ingredients: flour, baking soda, salt . . . I began throwing things together: brown sugar, cocoa powder, leftover espresso . . .

A few minutes later I had a batter for my Magnificent Melt-in-Your-Mouth Mocha Brownies. The manic activity made me feel less like an ineffectual sap, but only a little, so I poured the dark elixir into a square pan, set it aside, and went to the fridge once more . . .

Milk, eggs, butter, and a treasure from the spice rack. Nutmeg? Piquant yet soothing; exotic yet wistfully familiar. The Elizabethans believed it could ward off the plague;

Charlie Parker and Malcolm X used it to get high . . . *Good enough for me!*

I took out my electric hand mixer and assaulted the butter and sugar with glee.

Sell me half a story? Sure! I'll buy it!

I added the eggs, one at a time, ferociously beating between each addition.

Yeah, you're one crack interrogator, Cosi. Homeland Security should put you on speed dial!

Stress always did this to me. I had to bake. At times, nostalgia was the reason. Baking brought me back to those early hours with Nonna in her grocery store's kitchen: hot ovens warming the chilly air; sticky white dough coming together beneath flour-dusted hands; battered sheet pans emerging from their transmuting fire baths heavy with the gold of fresh Italian loaves and crunchy, sweet biscotti.

On a morning like this one, however, other things drove me to the beating of the batter: a sense of reassurance for one, a reclaiming of the feeling I had control over *something*.

Measuring the flour calmed me somewhat (a different part of the brain apparently calculated ounces and grams, sifted out lumps). Then I married the wet and dry ingredients.

"I now pronounce you Doughnut Muffin batter . . ."

In flavor and texture, the resulting muffin would indeed taste like an "old-fashioned" doughnut. It wasn't magic, just a culinary trick. (Most quick-bread batters called for a simple stirring of ingredients, but the dump-and-stir muffin failed to yield an optimal product. Creaming sugar into butter whipped air into the batter's foundation, substantially improving its texture. In this batter, the technique would evoke the same airy tenderness as a classic cake doughnut.)

I filled the paper lined cups, opened the heavy oven door, then slid my pans home with the satisfied sigh of a weary body slipping into a warm bath.

I guess what I most appreciated about baking was its transformative qualities, and not simply because the end product was more than the sum of its parts. The entire process served as a much needed reminder of a simple but profound truth: the fundamentals of cooking never changed.

In a world where firebombs went off in your face and your lover held back on you, just knowing that stirring sugar into liquefied shortening would always give a different result than creaming it into softened butter was an honest-to-God comfort.

I still didn't know how I was going to get the whole truth out of Mike, but I would find a way. In my view, family feuds were ticking time bombs. I'd already had one incendiary device go off in my face. I wasn't about to let it happen again.

WHEN I finally headed upstairs, I felt much calmer—less like a rube of an interrogator than a capable woman back in control. Entering the bedroom, however, my momentary illusion of calm was blown away by a brand-new storm.

The steady sound of beeping may have been weak, but its familiar meaning shot adrenaline through my body as effectively as a blaring ambulance siren.

My cell phone!

I rushed to the dresser and saw the blinking light. Someone had left me an urgent message.

Joy? Madame? Mike? Dante?

I played back the recording, and the frantic voice of my ex-husband assaulted my ear.

"Clare! Where the hell are you?"

I checked the time stamp on the message. Matt had phoned me during my lengthy talk with Rossi.

"I get off my plane at JFK, pass a newsstand, and what do I see? My mother on the front page of two tabloids! Why is she on a stretcher for God's sake? And surrounded by firemen? What the hell happened? I can see *you* standing in the background! Why didn't you call me, Clare? Now I can't reach her! Or you! And my battery is dying. Will you please call me back when—"

Click.

A robotic voice followed. "End of messages."

Fourteen

~~~~~~

THIRTY minutes later, my hair still damp from a quick shower, I descended the back staircase to my coffeehouse. Grabbing a Village Blend apron off a pegboard in the pantry, I peered through the open archway into the main shop.

"Good morning," I called to the lanky back of my assistant manager.

Tucker Burton turned around, tossed his floppy brown mop, and flashed a footlights-worthy grin. "Well, hello, sleepy head! How are you?"

I avoided a direct answer, which might have resulted in a primal scream. Instead I firmly tied my apron strings and pointed to our machine.

"How's she running today?"

"Not bad."

I didn't reply. I didn't have to. Tucker already knew what to do next. He turned back to pull me a test shot, so I could judge how bad "not bad" really was.

The machine itself was a beauty, reliably stable when it came to maintaining temperature and pressure. The espresso was what worried me. Like a gifted but temperamental child, my favorite elixir had easy days and difficult days; days of generous glory with lush, oozing *crema,* and days of stingy infamy with thin, diluted sourness.

The process of coaxing every bit of sweetly caramelized flavor from Matt's superlatively sourced beans was truly a kind of java alchemy. Three solid months of flight time had to be logged by my trainee baristas before they could attempt even one perfect shot for a customer.

What my newbie baristas had to fully understand was the array of variables that could devolve the process; how their perfectly dosed and tamped pulls of sultry-sweet nectar, executed in the exact same manner, with the same equipment and coffee beans, could suddenly turn into acidy slipstreams of espresso hell. Only when the untried learned to get comfortable with confusion, friendly with frustration, would the one-true-God shot be within reach . . .

As Tucker worked on pulling my taste test, I peered over the blueberry marble counter. Our tables were half empty, a normal pattern for a late weekday morning. The occupied seats were recognizable regulars—NYU students with open text books, neighborhood freelancers with open laptops, and a few hospital workers on open cell phones.

Tucker's morning backup, Esther Best (shortened from Bestovasky by her grandfather), appeared to be chatting with a small group of fans. (Yes, I said *fans.* Esther may have been one of my strongest latte artists, but her true renown as a local slam poetess had spread through at least two of the five boroughs. New customers, mostly aspiring "urban poets" and rappers, were showing up every day just to talk to her. Lucky for our bottom line they ordered coffee drinks from her, too.)

I finished scanning the room.

No sign of Matt yet.

After hearing his frantic message, I'd speed-dialed the man. All I got was voicemail (no surprise). So after my shower, I pulled on jeans and a Henley the color of toasted coconut and descended the stairs. I wasn't scheduled for another hour, but

Matt would be bursting in here any minute, and I theorized he'd be more likely to stay calm in a public place.

As the high morning sun broke through the low clouds, it made *me* feel calmer. The dazzling rays gleamed in the sparkling glass of our shop's French doors. The restored wood-plank floor was all waxed and shiny; the twenty marble-topped tables stood reliably in place.

With new eyes, I gazed at the wrought-iron spiral stair-case, soaring like a modern sculpture up to the second floor seating area where my tiny office waited with its shabby familiarity of battered desk and nonswiveling swivel chair.

Not even the relentlessly temperamental espresso-making process, the loudly squeaking back door, or our dangerously low supply of whole milk could shake my (guilty) feeling of thankfulness that it was Caffè Lucia and not my beloved Blend that had gone up in smoke.

"So, anyway, I didn't know what my agent was thinking . . ."

I glanced back to Tucker, who had spoken again but not to me. He was in the middle of a conversation with Barry.

Like many of our regulars, Barry, a sweet doughboy of a guy with a receding hairline and soft brown eyes, was a free-lancer who worked from home and used the Blend as a way to mingle with humanity—or escape from it. Sometimes he brought his laptop, sometimes a paperback; other times, like today, he felt chatty and pulled up a barstool.

"Wait—you mean you don't like the new job?" Barry asked between sips of his latte.

"Well, *now* I like the job. But when she told me about it, I said, 'Honey, the *stage* is the thing for me—'"

"What about that soap you did last year?" Esther interjected from across the room.

"Nobody calls them *soaps*, anymore," Tucker replied. "It's daytime drama."

Esther propped a hand on her ample hip. "Well, whatever you want to call it, that was *not* a 'stage' job!"

Tucker smirked. "You never heard the term *soundstage?*"

"Repeat after me, Broadway Boy: *As the Stomach Turns* ain't *Masterpiece Theatre*."

"Just ignore the Dark Princess," Tucker told Barry, making an insect-shooing motion with his hand.

Esther finally noticed me standing behind the work counter. She lifted her chin. "Oh, hi, boss."

"Hi, Esther."

Tucker had already preheated the portafilter (a required step for maintaining temperature during slow periods). He dosed and leveled off the proper amount of grinds and expertly packed them down with his personal purple tamper. Once more he tempered the group head with a quick flush of water. Then he locked the handle into the machine, positioned a clean shot glass, and hit the go button.

I closely watched the twenty-five-second extraction process. As I teach all of my employees, a barista does not have to taste a shot to know when it's gone bad. The speed of extraction, visual viscosity of the liquor, even the color, are clear indicators of quality.

A full-flavored extraction, for example, has the texture of dripping honey; the color of a deep reddish-brown ale. An espresso with a thinner body and a light golden color might be prettier to look at in the cup, but it was completely sour on the tongue—*not unlike Lucia Testa.*

Hmmm . . .

Conversely black streaks in the *crema* meant there would be a level of bitterness at midtongue.

More of a Mrs. Quadrelli experience . . .

Okay, so I had Rossi's case on the brain. What can I say? Finding solutions to puzzling problems intrigued me, and the puzzle of bad espresso was something I'd already mastered, to wit—

In case number one (the light golden color), there were two possible culprits: either the grind was too coarse or the brewing water not hot enough. In case number two (the black streaks), the grind was either too fine or the water too hot.

Solving bad espresso was usually a matter of testing new

grinds and new water temperatures. The irony did not escape me. When it came to finding out who had torched Enzo's caffè, Rossi would have to test the waters, too . . .

"Anyway," Tucker went on, "I told my agent: 'I will act the lines, I will write the lines, but I *draw* the line at radio announcing. Then she explained that it wasn't radio announcing. This ad agency was looking for 'character' voices to do a series of PSAs—"

"PSAs?" Barry said.

"You're doing PSAs?" Esther asked.

Tucker deadpanned to Barry. "Didn't I just say that?"

Her interest clearly piqued, Esther moved with all speed to join Tucker behind the work counter. "You have any 'ins' at the radio stations?"

"No."

"Boris has a new YouTube upload ready to go. It's called *Strangers on a Train*. He's looking to get some airplay." (Boris was Boris Bokunin, aka BB Gunn, assistant baker by day, urban rapper by night.)

"What is it?" Tuck asked. "A riff on that old switcheroo Hitchcock movie?"

"No," Esther replied. "More of a hookup thing on the midnight A Train."

"Sorry, sweetie," Tuck said. "I'd help your man if I could, but PSAs are prerecorded in studios. I don't have anything to do with FM program directors or their playlists."

"Excuse me," Barry said, "but what's a PSA exactly?"

"It's a public service announcement," Esther said. "You've probably heard a million of them."

"Like?"

"Like . . ." Tucker shrugged. "'If you see something, say something.'"

"Yeah," Esther said, "especially if it's an abandoned backpack in the subway that's ticking real loud."

"'Teachable moments with children . . .'"

Esther nodded. "If Zombie's attack, aim for the head."

"'Just say no,'" Tucker continued.

"Especially to some foreign guy who promises you an exotic vacation in the Middle East."

Tucker raised an eyebrow. "Speaking from experience, are we?"

"No comment."

"You know what my favorite was?" Barry said. "The one with Smokey the Bear. Now how did that one go?"

" 'Only you can prevent wildfires,' " Tucker said.

If only, I thought with a sigh.

"You know what my all-time favorite PSA is?" Esther asked.

Tucker folded his arms. "Do I know or do I care?"

"It's that one where some dude cracks an egg into a sizzling hot pan, and says, 'This is your brain on drugs.' "

"I remember that one!" Barry said. "The egg's a visual metaphor. Like when you're *fried*."

I also recalled that PSA, but a half-assed omelet didn't even begin to cover the extent of the nightmares I'd dealt with when my ex-husband's gray matter had been on cocaine.

Tucker finished pulling my shot and handed it over.

Generally speaking, espresso became more temperamental as the day wore on. The reason (in geek-speak) was the coffee's tendency to be *hygroscopic*, which basically meant that it readily sopped up surrounding air moisture, or in cases of excessively dry conditions, released it. So, in the morning, with lower temperatures and higher humidity, the extractions were magnificently thick and slow—not unlike the start of Mike's lovemaking last night. But as the sun came up and the air dried out, the extractions tended to run fast . . .

Boy did that analogy give me pause.

Tucker's test extraction for me looked pretty darn good. The viscosity was there, the color a deep reddish brown. But as I looked closer, I noticed a marked lack of tiger mottle—the deep brown flecking in a truly great pull.

I sipped.

Tuck fell silent, met my eyes. "What's wrong?"

"There's a slight hint of bitterness . . ."

"I didn't taste it."

"It's there."

Tucker sighed. "The humidity again?"

"I'm not sure . . ." I checked the machine's gauges.

Esther came around the counter. "*This* I want to hear."

"It can't be the humidity!" Tucker protested. "I already went to a finer grind."

"You did?" That surprised me. I turned to Esther. "You better get me the Glass."

Esther showed her palms to the tin ceiling and pumped her arms in a victorious hip-hop club gesture she once told me meant *raise the roof.* "I told you, I told you, now the Best Girl she'll scold you!"

"Oh, don't be a ninny!"

As a gleeful Esther rushed into the back pantry to get the infamous Glass, I grabbed a paper towel, put it under the doser, and ran the grinder. A pile of fine black sand now sat on the flat white background like a negative satellite photo of K2.

"Here you *go-oh!*" Esther sang, setting a Holmes-worthy magnifying glass next to my grind sample. She tossed a smirk at Tucker. "I told you *so-oh!*"

"Tucker's right," I said.

"About what?"

"You're being a ninny."

"I am not!"

"Silenzio!" I picked up The Glass. Tucker and Esther flanked me, wordlessly watching as I spread out the grounds and closely examined them.

"There it is. You see?" I motioned them closer. "Evidence of irregular lumps."

"Not again!" Tucker cried.

"Yes, again," I said.

Coffee properly ground in a burr grinder displayed uniform particles with beautiful lattice networks (at the microscopic level), which properly maximized the area of coffee exposed during the intense espresso extraction process. But the uneven grains I was now studying had clumpish, oafish shapes. They were *almost* as horrific as what a cheap blade grinder would produce.

(Every so often I'd encounter a customer who regularly paid a higher price for our premium coffee beans but balked at investing in a decent burr grinder. Inexpensive blade grinders were fine for chopping spices, I'd always explain, but far too violent for chopping coffee beans. When those suckers started whirring at 20,000 to 30,000 RPMs, they produced enough frictional heat to scorch the beans they were grinding, which was why the coffee ended up tasting bitter. Blade chopping also produced uneven grains, a disaster for getting consistent quality.)

The final coffee might be drinkable, but it was far from achieving its potential. A sad thought because I knew just how much blood, sweat, and tireless tasting went into cultivating, picking, sorting, processing, sourcing, shipping, and finally roasting our premium beans.

My present problem, however, wasn't with the freshness of our roast, the skill of our baristas, or the quality of our appliances. Like any other serious espresso bar, we used a conical burr grinder. The issue today was maintenance.

"Our baby's burrs have gone dull from overuse." I didn't actually need to state this. Tucker had been through this many times before.

"Another teachable moment." Esther smirked at Tucker. "I *told* you it wasn't the weather."

"Don't rub it in. It's bad form."

"I'm just being honest, PSA Boy. You of all people should know the motto I live by."

"Huh?"

"If you see something, say something!"

Tucker's eyes narrowed. "Listen, Clare, I have an idea. Why don't I give the Duchess of High Dudgeon her very own teachable moment, like how to change the grinder's burrs. Then she can start sharing in the fun."

"Good idea," I said.

"But, boss—" Behind her black-framed glasses, Esther's big brown eyes turned pleading. "My friends are here! And I don't really care about learning how to—"

"Good idea," I repeated, cutting her off. "I'll take over the bar. You two take the machine to the worktable downstairs."

We had a backup grinder for situations like this one. I pulled it out as Tucker unplugged the problem appliance. Then off he went, a pouting Esther in tow.

When I glanced up, I found Barry watching all this with a cross between curiosity and amusement. "Wow. I didn't realize so much scientific rigor went into making my latte."

"You have no idea."

I'd once explained it all to Mike, or tried to. When things went wrong in making espresso, any number of variables could be the offending agent—a good barista had to go through each variable, eliminating suspects one by one, until the true offender was found.

Mike replied with one sentence: "Sounds like my job."

I smiled at Barry. "Would you like another latte?"

"Yes, please! You have the best in the city."

"In that case," I told him, "this one's on the house."

Twenty minutes later, Barry was gone, and Tucker and Esther had returned to the espresso bar to help with a brief flurry of prelunch rush customers. I was just finishing the pour on my last order in line—a Hazelnut-Caramel Latte, which I topped with the flourish of a heart-crowned rosetta—when I heard a familiar door slam. *Don't ask how I can recognize one particular man by his door slam. I just can.*

A minute later, our shop's front bell was ringing and so were my eardrums.

"Clare!"

The customers in my half-filled shop came alert at their tables.

"What the hell is going on with my mother!"

My ex-husband had arrived.

Fifteen

〰〰〰〰〰〰〰〰〰〰〰〰〰〰〰〰

Matt dropped his suitcase (loudly) next to a barstool while simultaneously sliding a heavy backpack off his Nautilus-sculpted shoulders. It hit the ground with an equally subtle thud.

"I touched down at JFK an hour ago, after a truly horrendous red-eye out of Charles de Gaulle, and what do I see when I pass the first newsstand?" Matt threw a folded-up *Post* down on the bar. "A front-page photo of my mother being hoisted into an ambulance by a passel of firemen with my ex-wife looking on!" He glared. "What *happened*, Clare?"

I sighed. *So much for my public-place-will-keep-him-calm theory.* "Your mother's fine, Matt. She's perfectly okay."

"She's okay?"

I nodded.

His hard body sagged a moment—until his righteous anger got a second wind. "Why didn't you call me? I mean, last night she wasn't okay, was she?"

Before I could answer, Esther snatched up the paper. "Boss! Front-page news and you didn't mention it! I knew

I should have watched *In the Papers* this morning. I hardly ever miss that segment, but Boris slept over."

"Excuse me," Tucker said, "but why should Boris have anything to do with it?"

"Because he didn't want me to watch New York One first thing in the morning. He wanted to, um . . . I mean, well, he *distracted* me . . ."

"Distracted you?" Tucker folded his arms. "Esther, I'm shocked. A euphemism?"

"A girl has a right to her boudoir privacy."

By now Matt was fairly vibrating with impatience, but he failed to interrupt our baristas, primarily because he was still doing a double-take at Esther. He hadn't seen our most popular employee since she began piling her wild dark hair on top of her head in an ebony half beehive à la torch singer Amy Winehouse.

Tuck, who was familiar with the pop star's unfortunate bouts with alcohol and drugs, had already dubbed it the "Detox Rock look." According to Esther, it was driving her boyfriend mad with desire.

"What's the point of having a news anchor read from the papers, anyway?" Tucker was saying. "Why don't you just read the papers yourself?"

"Because if I watch *In the Papers*, I don't have to read the papers!"

"Okay, Esther. If you don't read the papers, then hand that one over. I'd like to read all about it."

"No!" She clutched the dog-eared tabloid to her Renaissance chest.

"Listen," Tucker said, "I can do New York One's morning anchor in my sleep. I'll read it to you."

"You can do Pat Kiernan?"

"The Clark Kent of local news?" Tucker waved his hand. "He's your basic cross between Mr. Spock and Mr. Rogers."

"Okay." Esther offered up the now substantially wrinkled *Post*. "Do him for me, Tucker!"

"*Clare* . . ."

I glanced over at Matt who was standing stiffer than Oz's Tin Man. His jaw was grinding so visibly, I thought he might actually need the oil can.

"Esther, Tucker," I quickly said before the man blew, "I need to speak with Matt in private. So you two 'read all about it' while you're covering the counter, okay?" I met Tucker's gaze. "Two *doppios*?"

"No problem."

I gestured for my ex to follow me to a corner table. "Like I said, your mother's fine." I kept my voice low as we walked, hoping he'd take the hint.

(He didn't.) "Then why didn't she answer my calls this morning!"

"Please lower your voice. Your mother went to sit with a friend in the Elmhurst ICU. They don't allow cell phones in there. Last night I tried to make a call and I couldn't even get a signal."

"Who's in the ICU, Clare? What friend?"

"Lorenzo Testa."

"Aw, no . . ."

We came to our usual little corner table, which stood next to the line of tall French doors. On days like this I expected a drafty chill, but our old hearth was close by; and even though the fire wasn't what it used to be, the heat was still there for Matt and I, providing just enough warmth to keep us comfortable.

I sat with my back to the smoldering embers and pointed to the chair opposing mine. "Sit. I'll tell you the whole story . . ."

Matt dropped heavily and I talked . . . and talked. Finally, I ran out of words.

"Sorry I blew up," he said.

"It's okay."

Tucker brought over our double espressos. Matt thanked him and bolted his. I sipped mine slowly.

With an agitated hand, he rubbed the back of his short, dark Caesar. Then (at last) my ex relaxed, stretching out his wrinkled khakis until they extended well beyond the table-top's disc of coral-colored marble. His shoes—black high-top sneakers with white laces—were purposefully urban hip. In New York they ran over a hundred dollars. Matt had purchased his in a South American market stall for under two bucks.

Strapped to his right wrist was a glittering Breitling chronometer. Encircling his left was a multicolored tribal bracelet made from braided strips of Ecuadorian leather—and that pretty much summed up the paradox that was Mat-teo Allegro: one part slick international coffee buyer and one part fearless java trekker, lightly folded together in a larger-than-life concoction that I once couldn't get enough of and now sometimes found hard to swallow.

"How's our daughter?" I asked, still savoring my double. (Replacing the grinder had fixed all issues. Tuck's shots were now spot on, the nutty-earthy sweetness of the *crema* drench-ing my tongue in the liquefied aroma of my freshly roasted beans.)

"Joy's doing great," Matt said. "I have pictures to show you once I get this piece of crap recharged."

He threw his latest electronic device onto the cold slab of marble between us—PDA, phone, camera, calculator, mi-crowave oven. I'm not sure what tasks it was supposed to multi.

"Why didn't you just use a regular camera?" I said.

"Joy did. She's going to e-mail you photos of my visit when she can find the time. She's been working extremely hard, but she says she's still loving it."

"Good. I'm glad to hear it. And does she have a new boyfriend?"

"None that she mentioned. But I think she's too busy. Which is more than fine with me." Matt rubbed his eyes. "Frankly, if my baby throws in the towel on this chef thing and decides to join a convent in Lourdes, I'd breathe a whole lot easier."

"Well, I wouldn't. Nothing against the good French sisters, but I want to be a grandmother."

"Bite your tongue!"

"Give it up, Matt. One of these days, Joy is going to settle on a guy, get married, and have kids—and then you'll have to hear it—"

"Don't say it—"

"Grandpa."

Matt visibly cringed.

"Or would you prefer the cheekier 'Gramps'?"

Ribbing the man was just too easy. I'd married him at nineteen. He'd been twenty-two at the time, although in matters sexual he'd been a virtual Methuselah. We'd met one summer in Italy (I'd been staying with relatives while studying art history), and when I'd ended up pregnant, after a blindly blissful summer of love, his mother had pressed him to the altar.

Back then, she was the one who'd wanted a grandchild—a legitimate one. So we never looked back, which is why he was far from the age of your average granddaddy.

Needless to say, our wedding hadn't been the wished-for, dreamed-for event of most young couples, planned down to the last flower petal and Jordan almond. It just happened. And for years I thought that was the reason Matt had gone through such difficulty accepting the ring and the vows and that forsaking-of-all-others-in-short-skirts thing.

I couldn't have been more wrong.

Matt's occupation was partly to blame. I was a needy bride, an uncertain new mother, infatuated with her young handsome groom whose job of sourcing coffee beans took him all over the world, all year long.

Matt had lived for it.

I died a thousand deaths.

Now that we were partners in coffee (instead of matrimony), my feelings about the man's peripatetic gene were completely upended. So go the astonishing ironies of middle age. Live long enough and you come to love the thing you loathed, embrace the thing you dreaded.

These days, I was downright grateful to my ex for trekking the globe, chasing harvest cycles to bring back the world's finest crops. And that's what they were: *crops*. Despite a corner of the industry sealing coffee up in cans with expiration dates implying freshness through a nuclear winter, coffee was seasonal. In Matt's view (and I didn't disagree), it belonged in the produce aisle, right next to the fruits and vegetables.

"How was Ethiopia?"

"Great. Our Amaro Gayo is outstanding, picked at the perfect time and the sorting is good. You should see the first shipment any day."

"I'm looking forward to roasting it."

"And I'm looking forward to tasting your roast." He smiled then, a genuine vote of confidence, which I appreciated.

"Does Breanne know you're back?"

Matt stifled a yawn as he nodded. Annoyed by his own jet lag, he reran a hand over his dark head then waved at Tucker. "Another double!"

"How's Bree been?"

I hadn't seen her since the Blend's holiday party last December. But then Breanne Summour, the ultratrendy, trend-setting editor of *Trend* magazine, traveled in much different circles than *moi*. The woman was a definite trade-up for my ex—in wealth and looks.

Before their marriage last spring, wagging tongues had speculated what a wayward coffee hunter and a socially ambitious fashion maven could possibly share. But I didn't question it.

Despite their wildly different career choices, I knew Matt and Bree weren't so very different under their toned tans. Both enjoyed living large, both craved excitement, and both jetted around the world for their respective careers. Granted, Matt's dusty treks through Nairobi and Bogotá were more exotic than Breanne's glittering tours of Milan and Barcelona, but to someone left behind, globetrotting was globetrotting no matter where your loved one trotted. Conveniently, the Allegro-Summour union left no spouse behind while conveniently providing each nomadic partner with the comforting illusion of a rooted marital home.

"We texted each other before I got on the plane," Matt said. "She's on her way to Milan by now—another trade show. I missed her at JFK by ninety minutes."

"That's too bad."

"Not really." Matt shrugged, a little too casually. "Gives me a little space to relax, kick back, enjoy some time alone in the Big Kumquat . . ."

I frowned. After years stranded on Matteo Island, I'd become way too fluent in Matt-speak. Even his eyes were sparking with that regrettable when-the-cat's-away look.

Before I could challenge the man's wet noodle of a moral code, the Blend's front bell jingled. Glancing up, I saw James Noonan's wife coming through the door.

Valerie Noonan wasn't much taller than I, but the dynamic charge of her fast-clicking heels across my wood-plank floor appeared to lift her to the stature of her firefighter husband.

"Clare!" she called with the burning energy of a Con Ed plant. "We need to talk!"

Sixteen

~~~~~~~~~~~~~~~~~~~~~~~~~~~~~~~~~~~

"How are you?" I asked when Val approached our table.

"Great—now that I know I've caught you!" Val's low, throaty voice belied her bubbly demeanor and freckle-sprinkled nose. What it betrayed was a pack-a-day habit.

I felt for her. I'd smoked a little in high school but quickly kicked it (the kick in the pants from my grandmother had helped). Val said she hated her addiction, had stopped for a few years, but the recent stresses of her job had sent her back.

"You made quite an impression on James last night!"

"Really?" It was the last thing I expected her to say.

"Yes, and let me tell you"—she arched a slender eyebrow—"it's not easy hearing your husband gas on about another woman's heroism before you've even had your coffee!"

"Heroism? Not me. James and his friend Bigsby Brewer were the ones who ran into that burning building. They're the real he—"

"Don't say it." She held up her palm. "James hates the word. He'd say he was just doing his job and that a hero is a sandwich."

Matt coughed—loudly.

Yeah, okay, Matt, keep your pants on. "Val, this is my business partner, Matt Allegro."

As Matt rose to give up his chair, Val cocked her head. "*Allegro?*" She glanced at me then back to Matt. "Clare's daughter's name is Allegro— Oh! You must be Clare's ex—"

"We're still partners," Matt said. "But only in business. Very pleased to meet you, Val. That's a pretty name. Short for Valerie, right?"

Matt took her hand, the simple shake turning into a meaningful squeeze. He moved a little closer, the dilation in his dark pupils as clear a sign of the man's interest as a construction worker's wolf whistle.

If I didn't know Matt better, I might have assumed he was having a simple, Pavlovian reaction to the rich, russet shade of the woman's short, bouncy curls and trim business suit, both of which displayed the exact color of a perfectly pulled shot of espresso *crema.* But I did know Matt, and his reaction had everything to do with woman's curvy figure beneath that stylish suit.

"Val's *husband* is a *firefighter*," I told him with pointed emphasis. *And he'll break your head with his Halligan tool.* "He's also the very same fireman who pulled your mother out of that burning building last night." *So poach elsewhere, please.*

Matt instantly dropped Val's hand. With a weak little smile, he asked her to thank her husband for him then excused himself to "freshen up" in our restroom.

As he sauntered away, I noticed Val considering his well-built back. I shook my head. Matt's Tabasco-colored tee may have appeared to be an easygoing choice, but I knew he'd purposely selected the tighter size to show off his molded pecs. And while his open denim work shirt looked loose and casual, those sleeves had been rolled with strategic precision, giving full exposure to his tanned, sinewy forearms while tempting the ladies with that first teasing curve of his bulging biceps.

Val lowered herself into Matt's chair and leaned toward me. "You actually divorced that hunk?"

"Yes. With relish."

"Do dish."

"It's a lengthy saga."

"Let me guess. He's a womanizer."

"One of his many issues, yes . . ."

"Too bad you handled it by divorcing him. He looks like a real catch . . ." She gazed after Matt once more to connect with him, but he was gone—a succinct description of my young marriage.

"If James ever cheated on me," Val said, "I wouldn't be divorcing him. I'd be dealing with the female involved."

That view surprised me. "Isn't James the one who made you the promise of fidelity?"

"A married man is already taken. The woman is the one who's doing the poaching. She's the one who needs to be dealt with."

"But don't you think your husband owes you—"

"Hey, that's just my view. To each her own." She laughed, but it sounded a little force. "I'd love to hear your side of the story. You and me, after work, over a couple of microbrews, okay?"

"Beer?"

"Oh yeah. That's *my* drink, don't mess with it."

"To each her own, then." I smiled. "Now how about one of mine?"

She nodded, and we moved to the espresso bar where I fixed her up with our latest special, a Belgian Mochaccino (espresso, foamed whole milk, a pump of coffeehouse vanilla, and a half shot of my homemade special syrup, which consisted of imported bittersweet chocolate, cream, sugar, and a pinch of French gray salt).

I leaned on the bar. "So, Val, what is it that you need me to do for you today?"

Val laughed. "How did you know I needed something?"

"The way you came in here. Most of my customers come for a break. You strode in like a general looking for volunteers."

"That's what my husband calls me at home. The Little General." She sighed. "Well, Clare, you're not wrong. I need your help . . ."

She pulled a colorful ad card out of her tote bag. "Can you display this?"

I scanned the sign: *Bake Sale! Union Square! Be There! Live music, hourly raffles, and the best goodies in the five boroughs. Benefits the NYC Fallen Firefighters Fund.*

"Riveting." I smiled. "You wrote the ad?"

"I'm also the gullible chump who had it printed. Tina Wade was supposed to do both, but she crapped out on me—two kids with the flu and a husband pulling 24/7 mutuals. I took care of it. I've got a stack of these going to businesses all over town. I was hoping you could take a few and spread the love."

"Glad to. I'll post ours right now."

I moved to the front window and set the placard beside our own plaque, the one that simply read: *Fresh Roasted Coffee Served Daily.* With the exception of our standing sidewalk chalkboard, the century-old tin was the only sign the Blend had ever displayed—or ever would as long as Madame had anything to say about it.

The bell jingled just then, and I glanced up to find the silver-haired woman herself breezing through the front door, black pants flowing like silk drapery, magenta and lime jacket displaying expressionistic swirls so vibrant they rivaled the feathers of a peacock.

"Clare, we need to talk."

"You're the second person who's said that to me in the last ten minutes."

I was smiling. She was not. *Oh, no.* The news was there in her red-rimmed eyes, the strain around her mouth.

"Enzo?"

"When I got there . . ." She shook her head. "They said he had a stroke very early this morning. He's in a coma. They don't know if he's going to make it."

I was dreading exactly this. My initial shock gave away to sadness, and then I remembered Rossi.

"You weren't able to speak with Enzo?"

"Child, he's in a *coma*."

I closed my eyes. "Sorry."

When I opened my eyes again, I found hers tearing.

"I'm the one who's sorry," she said. "This is my fault."

"No. It's *not*." I took hold of her shoulders. "The person responsible is the monster who set that fire." In my mind, the connection was automatic. "His daughter," I said. "Enzo asked me not to call Lucia unless things got worse. I have her number upstairs—"

"Lucia's already at the hospital. Mrs. Quadrelli called her last night. The child was very upset, of course."

"Did she say anything to you?"

"Very little. I tried speaking with her, but she brushed me off and not very politely. You saw how she acted last evening."

"Sorry to interrupt . . ." It was Val, she had crossed over from the espresso bar. I hadn't noticed her standing right behind us and wondered how long she'd been listening. (I didn't like anyone eavesdropping on me, although, I had to admit, I'd done it myself enough times in the name of snooping.)

"I should be going," Val told me, "but I did have one other thing to discuss with you."

"No problem," I said, "but first let me introduce you to my employer, Mrs. Dubois. Around the Village, everyone knows her as Madame."

"Very nice to meet you," Val said.

"This is Valerie, Madame. The wife of James Noonan, the firefighter who carried you out of that caffè last night."

A moment of blank surprise passed over the older woman's features; then she opened her arms and hugged Val tight. "If there's anything Clare or I can do to thank James for what he's done."

"Actually," said Val, glancing meaningful at me. "I do have an issue you might be able to help me with."

Madame released her and nodded. "Tell us, dear."

"Well, I had planned to use the same beverage vendor for the bake sale that supplies my catering events at the hotel. Unfortunately, they're letting me down. I just got word. I was wondering if you could hook me up with your coffee distributor. I know it's last minute, but . . ."

"The Blend is its own distributor," Madame said, "and we'll be delighted to help."

Val's nutmeg eyes widened. "That's very good of you—"

"Clare, you can set up a kiosk, can't you?" Madame said. "Easy."

"And the Blend will supply a free cup of coffee for anyone who makes a bake sale purchase," Madame declared.

Val's mouth gaped. "That's a lot of coffee!"

"Those young firemen saved my life, and they jeopardize their own health and safety every day. It's the least we can do."

"Thank you both!" Val said, then grabbed her bag and headed for the door. "Sorry I've got to dash. Tons to do yet and only my lunch break to do it!"

Outside, I noticed she stopped abruptly, fished in her handbag, and lit a cigarette. For another moment she stood there, inhaling with visible signs of relief. Then she quickly headed up Hudson.

"Mother!"

I turned from the window to find Matt striding across the floor. Before Madame or I could say a word, my ex had swept his mother up in a hug so enthusiastic her heels took flight.

Seventeen

"**Son!** Put me down! My goodness!"

Matt complied—after a gentle spin and a peck to her cheek. "I was worried about you!"

She glanced at me. "First a troop of doting firefighters, now a public display by a wayward son. Perhaps I should become trapped in burning buildings more often."

"Please don't," I said. "My heart can't take it."

Madame smiled. "I want to show you both something." She motioned us to the espresso bar where she drew a yellowing snapshot out of her bag. "This came from the photo album Enzo gave me last night. There's your father, Matt . . ."

Her expression softened, one wrinkled but beautifully manicured finger caressing the image. "And that bouncing little *bambino* is you as a toddler! Such big brown eyes and thick black hair, just like your daddy . . ."

Tucker peered over Madame's shoulder. "*Bambino* Matteo. *Très* cute, not unlike the big-boy version." He threw Matt a wink.

Matt smirked. "I'm still straight, too, Tuck."

"I know." Tucker waved his hand. "Such a waste."

The shop bell rang again and a customer rushed in. I barely noticed, too distracted by Matt's (admittedly) adorable baby pic (and my own disturbing nanosecond of yearning for one just like it—the baby, not the picture). Too late my peripheral vision registered the fedora coming at me.

"You are no longer *boss* to me!"

Oh, no. Now what?! Looking up, I realized Dante Silva was looming over me. "What's this all about?" Was he angry? Was he quitting?

"I can't call you *boss* anymore, Clare, because you're my *hero*!"

Before I knew what was happening, Dante put his arms around me and lifted me off the floor.

"Hey! Put me down!"

Instead, my crazy barista spun me around. The flight path was much the same as Air Matteo, but with a much higher altitude.

"Did you hear me, Clare? You're my hero!"

"A hero is a sandwich!"

"A hoagie is a sandwich. A hero is my boss!"

Now I knew how James Noonan felt—embarrassed. "Okay, okay, I get the idea! *Down*, please!"

Dante finally obeyed.

"What's with the hat?" Esther asked, pointing to his fedora.

He removed it to show her. His shaved head was swathed in bandages.

"Look, look, everyone!" Esther cried. "It's the Thief of Baghdad! Tell me, oh, genie of the lamp, if I rub you the right way, will you grant me three wishes?"

"Esther, you don't rub anyone the right way," Dante replied, "except maybe your commie ex-pat boyfriend."

"Boris was never a communist. He believes in freedom of expression."

"Okay then. You won't care if I express myself." Dante reached into his backpack's pocket, pulled out a digital camera, and snapped her photo. "That's going on my Facebook page. Amy Winehouse hair and all."

"Good. Link to my page while you're at it. I'm about to post a new poem about a coworker with brain damage."

Dante took another photo. "For Twitter."

That did it. Esther turned on her heel and marched away.

"Well, my friend," Tucker said, gesturing to his swathed head, "my only advice to you is: Do not grow a goatee. Homeland Security might mistake you for Osama bin Laden."

"Oh, yeah? *As-Salamu Alaykum* to you, too, my brother."

"Hey, you said that pretty well." Tuck tapped his chin. "Maybe you *should* grow a goatee. Fox is filming another one of those thriller franchise movies in New York this summer. I think my agent could get you hired as an extra."

"Stop teasing Dante," I shook my finger. "He's lucky to be alive. So is Madame—"

The camera flash went off. I blinked.

"Good one," Dante said, lowering the camera.

"You did *not* just take my picture!" My scolding finger was still hovering in the air. I instantly dropped it.

Matt laughed. "Hey, Dante, do me a favor. E-mail a copy of that one to Joy. If it doesn't keep our daughter in line, I don't know what will."

"Not funny." I folded my arms. "And that blaze last night was no joke, either. But I'm going to nail whoever set it."

Matt cursed.

"What's the matter?" I asked.

"Don't start, Clare."

"Don't start what?"

"I know that look. You're getting all sleuth-y on me."

"I am not getting sleuth-y," I lied.

Madame tilted her head and smiled. "It's like you're both still married, he knows you so well." Then she glanced at the picture in her hand and sighed. "I would so love another grandchild. A little boy this time." She pinned her son with a formidable look. "Perhaps you and Breanne could work on that. She's not menopausal yet, is she?"

Matt paled.

The man was not having a good morning.

LUNCH rush came and went. Madame departed for a date with Otto, and as the pace of the caffè wound down again, Matt pulled up a stool at my espresso bar.

"Tell me the truth," he said. "What's going on with this arson thing you mentioned?"

"I'm determined, Matt, enraged and determined. That's what's going on."

"If you care so much about who started the fire at Enzo's place, why didn't you share your theories with the fire marshal?"

"I did. I called the man this morning."

"And?"

"And Marshal Rossi strongly implied that he wouldn't mind my help as an informant—"

"You've got to be kidding!"

"Keep your voice down."

"Are you telling me that snooping around for the NYPD isn't providing enough of the thrills you missed as a stay-at-home mom? Now you want to play with the FDNY?"

"I am not playing. Rossi is going to find the forensic evidence to prove arson, and I don't want him going after Enzo. I'm certain, down to my bones, that others were responsible. You'd feel the same way if you'd been there. Your own mother was almost burned alive."

"Burned alive!" Matt's olive-skinned face went paler than the cream in my espresso con panna. "I thought you said she was never in any real danger!"

Woops. "Okay, maybe I, uh, downplayed things a little, but you were in a state—"

"And I'm getting there again! Did the marshal at least *say* it was arson?"

"I told you, they won't discuss the case with me—"

"Then drop it, Clare. Let the pros handle it."

"Excuse me," Dante said, interrupting us. "But the pros didn't pull me out of the fire last night. It was Clare who saved my life."

Tucker tapped my shoulder. "Now that you bring it up, sweetie, I think you may be onto something with this arson thing." He slapped Matt's *New York Post* back on the bar top and paged quickly through it. "Look at this." Tuck's finger touched a small square of newsprint deep inside the paper: *Blaze Burns Bensonhurst Beanery*.

"According to the story, there was a coffeehouse fire last night on Avenue O in Bensonhurst, Brooklyn. It started around the same time as your Astoria fire. *Très* coincidental if you ask me."

I frowned, scanned the story. "This is odd."

"Why?" Matt said. "Tucker is right. It's a coincidence, that's all."

Was it? Another one of Mike Quinn's pithy pieces of law enforcement philosophy suddenly came to mind: *In a criminal investigation, there are no coincidences.* I couldn't help wondering what Mike's cynical cousin would say to that.

WITHIN an hour of my thought, the cell in my pocket vibrated. I didn't recognize the number on the screen—a 718 area code, which meant a borough other than Manhattan—so I answered tentatively.

"Hello?"

"Clare Cosi. Guess who it is callin' ya, darlin'?"

Although the man's voice was keyed an octave lower than usual, I would have recognized Captain Michael's roguish lilt even without the played up brogue.

"Don't hang up on me now."

"How did you get this number?"

He didn't tell me. What he said was: "Now I'm *sure* my cousin told you to steer good and clear of me—"

"As a matter of fact he did."

"Well, I can't blame him. But I'm not callin' for my own account. I'm callin' for my guys. They're in trouble."

I bet they are.

I assumed Rossi had started questioning his men, but I couldn't have been more wrong.

"They need help, Clare," the captain went on. "The kind only *you* can provide."

"Me? Why would a crew of New York's Bravest need my help?"

"Simple, dove . . ." I could almost see the man's gold tooth flashing from across the East River. "You know how to make coffee."

Eighteen

~~~~~~

For twenty minutes the Arsonist observed the activity in the slick chain coffeehouse—the customer traffic, the counter service, the café tables—all while nursing the contents of an absurdly large cappuccino . . .

This whole thing should have been over by now. The old man's place was supposed to be empty. It's all because of that *bitch* things got so screwed up . . .

"Excuse me, ma'am."

Across the room, a Latina worker apologized for bumping a female customer and then resumed rolling a stainless steel cart filled with bottles, cleaners, rags, and sponges. She pushed it through the restroom door, and then hung a Closed for Cleaning sign on the knob.

There's my ticket . . .

The Arsonist stayed focused on that closed door, listened to sounds of running water, continued taking hits off the twenty-ounce paper cup. But the dregs of steamed milk tasted cold, the last drops of espresso bitter.

If only I could set off the damn bomb right now . . .

All around the Arsonist, young urban professionals were complaining about stalled careers and condo costs, lost benefits and air-

line delays, needy kids and presumptuous parents—a petty list of privileged problems. A few more minutes of listening to whining in quad and the Arsonist wanted to nuke the place, not just torch it.

Impatient, the Arsonist bent over the orange shopping bag. A small alarm clock sat inside, along with a large battery, a giant jar of high-octane spiked petroleum jelly, and a bleach bottle with no bleach inside. The Clorox bottle had been refilled with a mix of gasoline, naphtha, and benzene—all of it rigged to that clock. When the alarm went off, a quiet spark would awaken the sleeping beast. Then the petroleum jelly would ignite and poof, instant napalm.

Highly destructive, hell to put out . . .

The Arsonist reached into the orange bag, attached two wires sprouting from the battery, fixed them to circuits on the converted bleach bottle.

All ready . . .

The young coffeehouse worker finished cleaning the unisex facility. After tucking her cleaning products back onto her stainless steel cart, she rolled it into a closet adjacent to the restroom.

Time now . . .

The Arsonist rose and walked—easily, casually—to that restroom. Pretending to choose the "wrong" door, the Arsonist opened the closet, quickly slipped the bag onto the bottom shelf of the cart, between two giant bottles of cleaning fluids. The closet door was closed and the restroom door opened.

No one took notice of the Arsonist's "mistake"—not one customer or employee.

After leaving the Long Island City shop, the Arsonist turned for one last look at the posted hours of operation. The timer on the bomb was set for 10 PM, well past the seven o'clock closing. Outside, the day was still pleasant, but the chill was coming.

Another package still had to be delivered—to the Village Blend coffeehouse in Greenwich Village. This one would be for that troublemaking bitch who'd tipped off the fire marshals to look beyond Testa for their torcher . . .

Two firebombs started us down this road. Two more will end it. And if that Cosi bitch doesn't get the message after tonight, we'll just have to end her.

Nineteen

~~~~~~

Locating the captain's firehouse wasn't a problem. Amid a sea of tiny clapboard row houses, Michael Quinn's sovereign domain towered over the landscape like a redbrick citadel.

I parked my near-vintage Honda on the quiet street just off Northern Boulevard. Despite the temperate twilight air, I slipped on my coat and gloves. March was a tricky time in New York. Days might feel bright and balmy, but nightfall could bring the kind of cruel winds that would kill every plant foolish enough to put out its vulnerable buds.

On the face of it, I'd come back to Queens for one reason: Lucia Testa had donated the still-functioning espresso machine from her father's caffè to this firehouse, and the men needed some lessons in how to use it. With Enzo's comatose condition, Lucia was too busy to teach them, so I agreed.

Of course, this was the least I could do to pay these guys back for their rescuing of Madame. But the truth was my little visit this evening would give me the chance to question these guys, find out who among their ranks might be seeing Lucia.

Along the curb I noticed a line of parked cars. Every one

displayed FDNY-related placards or window clings. One of the SUVs had a bumper sticker that caught my eye: *Honk If You're Buffing*.

"Buffing?"

I wondered if it had something to do with weight lifting, that is, *becoming* buff? Maybe it was something one did in the buff? Did that make it a sexual reference? I craned my neck at the towering red challenge in front of me.

The FDNY certainly counted women among its ranks. They drove ambulances and fought fires right alongside the men, but this engine and ladder company didn't have a female among them.

This isn't just a firehouse. It's a Temple of Testosterone.

A granite cornerstone announced the original use for the building as a station for the Queens Company Rail Yard. But the structure's odd Gothic flourishes—including carved stone moldings over the doors and a corner turret with a crenellated roof—gave the impression of a medieval stronghold, complete with castle battlements.

A sudden freezing gust tore at my ponytail. I ignored it, moving with determination into the glowing, cavernous interior of the firehouse garage, the clanking barista supplies in my backpack making me feel like Cervantes's crazy knight again, embarking on a quest in rusty armor.

Amid the industrial tangle of ducts, pipes, and hanging chains, I noticed tire scuffs on the concrete, evidence the fire trucks had been here.

So where are they now?

One thing I knew: Captain Michael absolutely assured me that he would not be here this evening, so there was zero chance of my going back on the promise I'd made to Mike to stay away from his cousin.

I guess a part of me was still curious about the captain (not to mention suspicious), and I wouldn't have minded a crack at interviewing the man. On the other hand, with him out of the firehouse, I could freely question his men without the threat of a red devil looking over my shoulder.

"Ms. Cosi?"

I looked up to search the vast echo chamber for the source of the familiar, upbeat voice.

"James?" I called back.

"Yeah, it's me." James Noonan crossed the track-marked floor to greet me, passing under a high metal catwalk that ran along all four windowless walls. "Sorry the guys are gone. A call came in. But they'll be rolling back soon."

Under the banks of hanging florescent lights, the man I liked to think of as my own personal hero looked like a poster boy for All-American football: glowing skin, close-cropped hair, a dazzling smile. He was as warm and friendly as I remembered, and just about as tall as the two Mike Quinns. By the time he reached my side, I was bending my neck just to meet his translucent blue eyes.

He shook my hand with a wide grin, and then jerked one thumb over his shoulder. "Come on back. I'll show you the espresso machine."

I followed him down an industrial green hallway. At the end he opened a stout wooden door, and the taint of diesel exhaust gave way to a much more appetizing array of aromas—fresh, floral herbs and piquant spices intermingled with the pungent-sweet fragrance of roasting garlic and the heavy but alluring scent of sizzling pork fat.

With quick hands James draped a grease-spattered apron over his gray T-shirt and distressed denims, pulled the strings completely around his lean waist, and tied them at his belt buckle. (The front of the apron assured me the wearer was *Also Good in Bed*.)

I pointed. "Gag gift from the guys, right?"

"You must be psychic," he said flatly.

I smiled. "My staff gave me one of those."

"Oh? So you're also good in bed?"

"No. *I Serve It Up Hot*."

He laughed. "Come on . . ."

James led me around a corner, into a sprawling kitchen area

with two huge refrigerators, a pizza oven, a deep fryer, and a grill-and-gas-range combination under a ventilation funnel.

"Whoa, does every firehouse have such great facilities?"

James snorted. "Are you kidding? I put this place together by my lonesome. Over the past two years I've gone to every restaurant closing and bankruptcy in the five boroughs to gather this stuff."

The savory scent of roasting meat distracted me. I pointed to the oven. "Something in there smells amazing."

"Pork shoulder." James opened the door to display his handiwork.

"¡Hola, pernil!" I admired the beautiful bone-in pork shoulders, four in all, slow-roasting on two cooking racks.

"A PR classic," James noted.

"So you've got Puerto Rican guys in the company?"

"Only one, plus a dude from Cuba and one from the Dominican Republic. All the guys love the *pernil,* though. It's economical, feeds a hungry crew, and leaves enough meat for Cuban sandwiches in the morning."

"And what's in the Dutch oven?" I pointed to the stovetop.

James lifted the lid. "A sweet onion and cheddar casserole."

I sniffed. "Mild cheddar, right? And lots of milk and butter?"

"Yeah. The onions give up a lot of moisture so I use bread crumbs to keep it from getting too watery."

I sniffed again. "A little bland, isn't it? Especially for Latino guys. You should try some dry mustard in there. Maybe a dash of cayenne. I think you'll like the result."

James nodded, gave me a little smile. "Color me impressed."

"Fire's your job, *flavor* is mine."

His smile widened. Then he replaced the lid and closed the oven.

"Do you cook like this at home?" I asked. "Val must appreciate it."

At the mention of his wife, James's good cheer fell away. "We hardly eat together these days."

"I'm sorry to hear that."

He shrugged. "If Val's not working late, I'm on a mutual."

"Mutual? Val used that term. What is it exactly?"

"A 'mutual' is when the guys juggle work schedules so we can do back-to-back shifts."

"Why would you want to do that?"

"If you work twenty-four or forty-eight hours straight, you can get three or even four days off in a row. It's a nice arrangement for guys with kids."

James glanced at his bright orange digital watch. "I don't actually start my mutual for another thirty minutes. I came in early to get some dinner up and running before things got hairy."

"So that's why you're still here while the rest of the guys are off on a call?"

He nodded and turned to take another peek at his pork shoulders. He looked so happy to be here on the job—maybe *too* happy?

Twice now I'd seen the man frown at the mention of his wife. *Why?* Were James and Val just having the typical troubles of a busy married couple? Or were their problems more serious? It wouldn't have been my business, except for the fact that Lucia Testa was fooling around with one of the men of this house. Was James's marriage so unhappy that he'd decided to stray with Lucia?

My God . . . I hope James isn't the fireman I've come here looking for . . .

I cleared my throat, brought up the same question in a new way. "So, I'm sure the guys appreciate having a cook like you in the house, but . . . you must prefer dining with your wife, right?"

"Actually, Val never wants me to go to any trouble. That woman's happy with a cold beer and a couple of sliders."

"Yeah, she mentioned her love of microbrews to me the

other day. I was surprised. Considering her party-planning title, I figured her for a wine-and-brie girl."

James folded his arms. "I'm the guy who won't touch beer, not to save my life. Give me a nice glass of Bordeaux with dinner, a few stinky French cheeses at the end of the meal, and I'm a happy boy."

An electronic crackle interrupted us. James stepped over to a shelf and turned down the volume on what looked like a small, boxy radio receiver.

"Sorry," he said, "I was buffing."

"What is that exactly? I saw a bumper sticker outside— *Honk If You're Buffing!*"

"You saw Oat Crowley's car. That guy buffs in his sleep. When he dies, they'll probably put an FDNY radio in Oat's coffin."

"So buffing has something to do with a *radio?*"

"Buffing is when you listen to FDNY chatter while you're off duty. Even civilians do it, hence the title."

"Oh, buffing is for fire *buffs*. Like fans?" *Or potential arsonists?*

"Bingo," James said. "But lots of firefighters do it, too. You don't climb the ranks without putting in the time, staying on top of what's happening—and I'm taking the lieutenant's exam in a few weeks."

As James turned back to his cooking, I began moving down the counter, checking things out (snooping really). Despite all the appliances, most of the floor space was taken up by a single scuffed table. My gaze ran over some job-related notices on one wall, then snagged on a colorful calendar taped to a cupboard door. The calendar was one of those famous FDNY specials—hunks in fire hats.

"Excuse me, James?" I pointed to the bulging muscles of Mr. March. "Is that who I think it is?"

"Yep," he called from the stove, "that's Bigsie in that cargo net. He's still so proud of being named Mr. March he won't let us take it down."

"Take it down?" I absently repeated, my attention focused on the near-naked, shirtless giant, his arms and chest standing out in bold relief as he clung to a net woven of thick hemp.

Right behind me, I suddenly heard James laughing. "Like every red-blooded American woman who passes through here, you failed to notice that you're gaping at *last year's* calendar."

Woops. I tore my gaze away.

"Don't worry about it," James said. "All the ladies love Bigsie. He's the wildest wolf in this lair, with the possible exception of our captain. But you already know that, right? I mean . . ." He lowered his voice. "That's why you're really here, aren't you?"

"What? No! I'm here to help you and the guys with the donated espresso machine, *that's all.* I hope you're not implying—"

"Sorry." James put up his hands. "Not my business."

I changed the subject (fast) and pointed to the thick, wooden dining table. The circumference looked large enough to accommodate King Arthur's crew. "So how many guys do you cook for on a given day?"

"Twenty or so, I guess, depending on who's doing a mutual and who's coming in for a visit."

"You're the only cook?"

"I'm the only one who actually knows what he's doing. A couple of the guys have tried, but when I'm not around, meals come down to microwave reheats or calls for takeout."

That's when it hit me: all this trouble he'd gone to with the set up, all this passion he put into the firehouse meals . . .

"James, it sure looks like you could manage your own restaurant . . ." *Especially if you had the money to back you—like, say, money from a fire insurance payout?*

"No. Not for me."

"You're that certain?"

"Ms. Cosi, I was raised in my family's diner. Managing a restaurant's all about routine—boring, boring, boring routine. And I like to keep things lively. I'll cook for the guys, sure, but that's it. I'd much rather be running into burning buildings than running a restaurant."

Another danger junkie, just like my ex.

But what James and Matt described as boring, I saw as constancy, dependability—maybe even loyalty.

Sure, my trade demanded that you show up every day and perform the same basic tasks. But the customers I served gave up their hard-earned money in exchange for those tasks, and that wasn't an unworthy thing. To me, maintaining high standards was far from tedious. Every morning, I embarked on my own little war, or at least a series of ongoing battles. Managing the Blend was a continuously renewing challenge.

Of course I didn't articulate any of this. I wasn't here to debate James on my view of the food-and-beverage service trade. I was here to fight another kind of battle . . .

"Excuse me, Ms. Cosi," James said when a kitchen clock pinged. "I'll just need a few minutes . . ."

"Take your time," I said, and went back to looking around. I scanned the various posters on the wall, but they were mostly job related: official announcements, charts, and instructions. Then I spotted a worn wooden closet door across the room. It was covered from top to bottom with personal photographs.

I moved closer. The pictures were all taken at what looked like annual firehouse picnics. Each was hand labeled by year.

"Looks like you guys have a lot of picnics," I called to James.

"Guess so," he replied from the sink. "The guys with families do a thing in August at Six Flags, but our biggest event is the bash right after Medal Day. The captain has a great spot in Flushing Meadow Park on permanent reserve for us."

Medal Day . . . I'd heard all about the tradition at the Quinn's St. Patrick's Day bash. Every June, select firefighters of the FDNY were honored with citations for their bravery and heroism.

As James continued working, I examined the picture gallery. The photos were hung year by year in vertical columns that ran from the top of the door to the bottom. One or two group shots of the company were followed by pictures of the men paired with their wives, families, or significant others.

I noticed an older photo of Captain Michael Quinn and got down on one knee for a closer look. The picture was taken during the 2000 picnic. Captain Michael was grinning like a giddy boy. He looked so relaxed, so lighthearted. He had a woman on his arm. She was nearly as tall as the captain with a voluptuous figure and long, straight raven hair. The photographer caught her in the middle of a laughing fit, and her face was partially hidden by her hand. She was in the 2001 pictures, too—or I was fairly sure it was the same woman. In this photo her beautiful windswept hair was off her face and I got a good look—oval face, long nose, slightly pointy chin, wide, perfect, carefree smile.

In the photos after 2002, the woman was gone. Captain Quinn appeared alone, dateless, and far less lighthearted. In some of these later photos he hadn't even mustered a smile.

My gaze continued moving up through the years of picnic photos—and then it stopped moving. As I stared at one particular photo, taken just three years ago, the tight, forced smile of Lucia Testa stared back at me.

Just then, I heard heavy footsteps walking up behind me.

My gaze still focused on Lucia's face, I tapped the photo.

"James," I said. "Did you know that Lucia Testa is in one of these pictures? She's standing among a group of men. Was she seeing one of these five guys, do you know? I see Oat Crowley is in the group—"

And about fifty pounds lighter . . .

I also recognized Ronny Shaw, the fireman who'd ended up in the ER next to Madame. There were a few other faces I didn't know. One was a Latino man wearing a *Puerto Rican*

Pride T-shirt, and another had a gray flattop—the kind of 'do my Mike called cop hair.

"I see Captain Michael is in this photo. You mentioned what a wolf the man is. Was your captain ever involved with Lucia?"

James didn't answer, but I knew he was there. I could feel the presence of his large body right behind me.

"And while we're on the subject of Michael Quinn's love life, who is that very pretty brunette he's obviously with in the earlier photos? And why isn't she in any of the later ones?"

Again, no answer. A little annoyed by now, I turned around and found myself facing the last man I expected to see this evening.

Michael Quinn's big arms were folded across his white uniform shirt. Beneath his scarlet *Lonesome Dove* mustache, his jaw was working, and the tendons in his neck were stretched as taut as the cables on the GW Bridge. Even the man's burn scar was flushing with fury.

We stared at one another so long I could feel my own cheeks getting warmer than the hot plate of a Mr. Coffee.

Finally James returned, drying wet hands with a towel. "There. All done— Oh, hi, Cap. How's it going?"

"You should be workin' boyo, not gossiping," the captain practically spat, still pinning me with his eyes.

James blinked, obviously confused by his superior's sudden anger. "We were just talking, Cap—"

"Show the lady the espresso machine. That's why she's here, isn't it?"

"Uh . . . yeah, sure," James said. "Right, over here, Ms. Cosi."

I followed James back to the newly installed machine. Captain Michael Quinn remained beside the photo gallery, scowling silently.

Twenty

꩜ꩰꩰꩰꩰꩰꩰꩰꩰꩰꩰꩰꩰꩰꩰꩰꩰꩰ꩜

The espresso maker from Caffè Lucia was a shiny, Italian-made Gaggia with two group heads.

"It's a beauty," I said, stealing uneasy glimpses at the Captain.

"Lucia delivered it . . . uh, not *personally*." Now James was shooting glances at the man. "It was delivered the day after the fire. The Gaggia didn't come with instructions so I downloaded the manual from the manufacturer's Web site and installed it. Oat helped."

"Oat?" I tensed, remembering my unpleasant run-in with the man. "How did he help?"

"He put together the cabinet it's sitting on."

I nodded, trying to concentrate. It wasn't easy. I was too upset by Michael Quinn's unexpected appearance. *Why is he here? Is there an explanation? Or did the man just outright lie to me?*

"So, did I hook this thing up right?" James was asking, face expectant. "Ms. Cosi?"

"Oh . . . right, sorry . . ."

"I've installed a lot of the stuff around here myself, so I'm pretty sure I hooked it up correctly. The metal parts weren't really damaged. I only had to replace some rubber tubes and gaskets that were effected by the heat of the fire."

The fire. Yes, the fire. That hellish inferno came back to me fast, and so did the image of Enzo, fighting for his life in the ICU. I took a breath, refocused.

"I'll check it out," I told James. "Can you hand me my backpack?"

I noticed a commercial burr grinder sitting nearby. It bore the marks of heavy use, but the espresso machine appeared to be relatively new—

Enzo had invested in this thing, I realized. *He wasn't expecting to retire anytime soon. And Lucia had to know that . . .*

Of course I also noted the woman had "donated" this machine to the firehouse in record time. Sure, Enzo had admitted the choice was hers to rebuild or not, but the speed at which she gave up the Gaggia suggested to me that Lucia didn't exactly wrestle with the question. More evidence of motive.

My focus went back to the machine itself. The Gaggia's filtration system and nickel-lined tank were already connected to the water main. According to the gauge, the tank was properly filled. The gas jets appeared to be working, too.

When James returned with my backpack, I fished out one of the Blend's thermometers to check the temperature at the water spout. It was a little high at 205 degrees, and the pressure at the pump was also high. I adjusted both and bled off the excess heat.

Finally I checked the portafilters and the heads. They were spotlessly clean—so clean the heads still needed "seasoning" before a perfect espresso could be pulled. (Like a new pan needing a layer of cooking oil, the heads of an espresso machine required a patina of coffee oil to eliminate the sharp taste of raw metal. A test pull or two at the beginning of each day always solved that problem for me.)

"Good job setting it up," I said at last.

"Thanks."

"The temperature and pressure levels are close to perfect.

You want the temperature at the head around 203.5 degrees, and"—I tapped the pressure meter—"at 8.2 bars for the pressure at the pump. With those settings and the proper grind, you should be able to pull a perfect espresso every time."

"Perfect is good," James said. "In my book if it ain't perfection, it's broke—"

Another ping from the kitchen timer interrupted us.

"I'll be right back," James said with another unhappy glance at his captain, who was still silently standing and staring.

When James was gone, I stuffed the thermometer into my pack and crossed the room. "I want to talk to you," I quietly told the man. "I need to ask you some questions and I want honest answers."

"About my love life?"

"No." I gritted my teeth. "Not about your love life. I don't care about your stupid love life."

He raised a skeptical eyebrow.

What was that? A Quinn family trait? "Okay, *maybe* I'll ask some questions about your love life, but it's not why you *think* I'm asking—"

"You're a terrible liar, darlin'."

"Me! You're the one who said you wouldn't be here!"

The captain smirked. "Now why would I have said a thing like that? This is my firehouse, isn't it?"

I was about to reply (with a string of less-than-ladylike verbiage) when the blare of a truck horn made me jump. A second later I heard rumbling engines, so powerful they reverberated the floor along with the hanging pots and pans.

Captain Michael looked down at me. "Looks like your burnin' questions will have to wait." He unfolded his thickly muscled arms. "My boys are back and you've got some teachin' to do."

A few minutes later, a masculine monsoon swept into the kitchen. For an unnerving second I feared I'd have to teach almost twenty outsized men the art of espresso making—an undertaking I feared would take all night. But after wolfing down plates of James's dinner, the horde vanished into a nearby community room. The entire evening meal took seventeen minutes flat.

Only eight firemen remained in the kitchen, counting James Noonan and his friend Bigsby Brewer (and not counting the unnamed probie who was put to work cleaning the dishes and pans).

While Captain Michael continued his silent watching from the sidelines, the eight arranged folding chairs in a semicircle around the espresso machine.

"So this is everyone?" I asked James.

He nodded. "Yeah, from every shift, too. Some of the guys came in just to learn how to use the Gaggia."

"Great," I said. And I meant it. If these were the core espresso drinkers of this firehouse, they were the most likely to have frequented Caffè Lucia and had continual contact with Enzo's daughter. Scanning the faces, I recognized Oat Crowley and Ronny Shaw. The final three I'd never met. Well, now was the time . . .

"My name is Clare Cosi and—"

A hand shot up. I recognized the lined face under the gray flattop as one of the men in the photos with Lucia.

"No offense, Miss, but I don't know why I'm here. I can't stand coffee. It smells real nice, but most of the time it tastes like brown water."

The speaker leaned back and folded his arms. The kitchen was so quiet I could hear the metal folding chair creak under his weight. Suddenly the group laughed, and I realized I'd missed out on a private joke.

"Dino's just yanking your chain, Ms. Cosi," James informed me from the front row. "Elfante lives on coffee. Like ten or twelve cups a shift."

"Yeah," said Bigs. "We make him kick in extra for beans, the weasel drinks so much—"

"*And* it tastes like brown water. Around here, anyways,"

Dino insisted, and then he continued to rant about their typical firehouse brew until Ronny Shaw beaned him with a balled-up paper napkin.

"Let the lady talk!"

The last time I saw Shaw, he was lying on a stretcher in the ER, Oat Crowley hovering near. Both had eavesdropped on my conversation with Madame, and I still wondered why they seemed so interested. When he raised his left hand to throw the paper ball, I noticed it lacked a wedding band. Then it occurred to me that getting injured in a fire you started yourself is a good way to deflect attention away from your guilt.

"Thank you," I told Ronny. "But Mr. Elfante actually makes a good point—"

"Call me Dino, honey . . ."

"The delicate flavor oils in the bean are volatile," I said, ignoring Dino's wink. "The reason is because if they're released too soon during the brewing process, they go up in steam and you experience them through your nose instead of your palate."

"Told ya," Dino cracked smugly—and got beaned again.

"The purpose of an espresso is to extract the essence of those oils in such a way that the flavor goes into the cup. A perfectly pulled espresso should taste as good as great coffee smells."

As I walked the men through the anatomy of the Gaggia machine, the heads, the control functions, the proper readings for the temperature and pressure, I got to know them a little better.

"Pressure and heat. Like brewing illegal hooch, eh, ma'am?"

This was Ed Schott, the senior member of our class. A pink-skinned man with a bald pate, pug nose, jutting chin, and perpetually clenched fists, he spoke in short, staccato bursts, like a military drill instructor (which he may very well have been, given the Marine Corps' eagle and fouled anchor was tattooed on his meaty forearm).

"Let's move on to the coffee itself. A good espresso starts with a good bean, so—"

"You mean espresso bean, right, ma'am?" said Ronny Shaw. "I've seen them in the grocery store. Is that what we should use?"

"There's no such thing as an espresso *bean*," I explained. "What you saw was an espresso *roast*. Any type of good Arabica bean that's roasted dark can be called an espresso roast."

"What about caffeine, Ms. Cosi?" Bigs said. I noticed he got up to stand beside his chair like a kid in Catholic school called on by his teacher. "Will I get a bigger jolt from espresso than, say, a regular cup of joe?"

"What's the matter, Brewer? Worried you won't be *up* for that hot date after your mutual?" Dino Elfante asked.

Bigsie's smile was lopsided. "It's just that I need a lot of energy. Pep, you know. My lady friends expect it. I got a reputation to uphold."

Bigsby Brewer seemed so guileless it was difficult to see him as a cold-blooded fire bomber. But I had to consider that one of his many "lady friends" could be Lucia Testa. Sweet as he was, Bigs would be an easy mark to manipulate, especially if someone convinced him the fire would end up helping Enzo instead of hurting him.

Alberto Ortiz spoke up just then—I recognized him as Mr. "Puerto Rican Pride" in the Lucia photo.

"If you need pep, Big Boy, try a Red Bull. Or maybe that little blue pill if the situation is code red. But, dude, if you're having *real* trouble with one of those Manhattan fillies, just send her over to me—"

A silver cross hung from Ortiz's neck, and a thin gold band circled his ring finger, but outward symbols aside, Ortiz seemed as randy as the rest of this pack.

"Mr. Ortiz is right," I cut in. "About gulping espressos, I mean. It's not a very efficient way to perk up."

Bigs frowned. "But I thought espressos *had* caffeine."

"Of course there's caffeine in an espresso. But espresso's high-pressure, high-heat extraction process removes more caffeine than regular drip brewing."

"In other words," James said, "if you want a jolt, stick to drip, *drip*."

Bigs poked his friends so hard James tumbled from his folding chair. "Ahhhh!"

"Snots don't know how to behave," muttered Ed Schott.

When things settled down again, I demonstrated the best way to grind the beans for espresso. "If you grind too finely, friction and oxidation from the grinder will ruin your dream of a perfect cup. Grind too coarsely and some of the flavor stays in the portafilter."

I ground enough beans for a few shots and dosed a single into the basket. Then I showed them how to even out the grinds before tamping.

"Grip the portafilter handle with one hand. Using the other, gently sweep the excess grinds away with the edge of your finger. By moving forward, then back, you're evenly distributing the grinds in the basket while you level them. Now it's time to pack."

I rummaged through my bag and produced the brand-new scale from my duplex closet. (Unfortunately, it was pastel blue with pink sea horses—Joy had picked it out a few years ago, and I'd never taken it out of its plastic until now.)

"We don't have to weigh in to make coffee, do we?" Bigs asked.

"I'm not gettin' on that girly scale," Dino said, pointing at the pink seahorses. "It'll make me look fat."

The man laughed.

"What we're going to measure is the amount of pressure applied as we pack coffee into a portafilter. This is the most important step in the espresso pulling process, and the one you're all going to have the most difficulty mastering—"

"Why is that?" asked James.

"The grinds in this filter basket have to be perfectly packed and level when the hot pressurized water streams from the spout, or you're facing disaster."

"Because?"

"Because like all things under pressure, water can turn insidious . . ."

I heard someone shifting uneasily in his chair at that. I looked up to see who, but all the men appeared settled again, gazes expectant.

I cleared my throat. "It's the barista's job to create an even, consistent resistance to that streaming force. If there's even one tiny crack or irregularity in your pack, the pressurized water will find that weakness and exploit it, gush right through, missing the rest of the grinds and completely ruining any chance you had at success."

I handed the tamper to Al Ortiz and placed the full portafilter in the center of my bathroom scale. "I want you to press straight down on the coffee with that, giving the tamper a twist at the end to dislodge any coffee grinds that are sticking to the metal."

"Sure." Ortiz raised his shoulder.

"One more thing," I said. "Watch the scale as you press down, I want you to use about forty pounds of pressure."

"Okay," he said, a little less sure of himself.

It took Ortiz several tries before he got the pressure right, and even his final result was anything but level.

"My turn," Bigs declared. Avoiding the scale, he set the portafilter down on the edge of the espresso cabinet. Gripping the tamper, he pressed until the veins bulged on his sculpted arms.

A tremendous crack boomed as the edge of the particleboard surface broke away. Following a moment of stunned silence, the room exploded with laughter. Even Oat and the captain looked amused.

"Ya stupid mook!" James cried. "Oat just built that!"

Bigsie's cheeks blushed redder than an Anjou pear. "Guess I don't know my own strength."

Ed Schott rubbed his chin. "Maybe you better warn your dates, Hercules."

"My girls work in Manhattan office buildings," Bigs replied with a cocky grin. "Believe me, after ten hours with smooth dudes in penny loafers, most of them are downright desperate for a guy who'll pop their buttons—"

"O-kay," I cut in. "Mr. Brewer, let's give it another try—and this time use the scale."

"Sure, Ms. Cosi, but where's your tampie thing?" Bigs asked.

"It flew off somewhere," Ortiz said.

"Can somebody look for it?" I asked.

"Why don't we improvise?" Bigs suggested. "We can use my roof spike. It's got a flat head like your tampie."

"Tamp*er*, and I don't think your tool—"

But Bigs was already rushing off, retrieving a foot-long piece of stainless steel. "See, Ms. Cosi," he proudly announced upon returning. "This is my roof spike . . ."

I stared at the thing. "Okay, I'll give. What's a roof spike?"

"When we vent the fire, you know, like you saw us do at the caffè the other night?"

I nodded. "You go up to the roof and saw holes in it?"

"Right, well, in case of an emergency, we all carry PSS—personal safety systems. It's a rope with an anchor hook."

"We didn't always carry them." The voice was Oat Crowley's. It was the first time he'd spoken.

I glanced at the man. "Why not?"

"Ask the damn brass," he said. "Back in '05 two good men died because they weren't carrying ropes."

"Well, *now* we carry them," James pointed out.

"And we got these roof spikes, too," Bigsie said. "They're new. We trained on them for two months, but none of us have actually used them in a fire yet."

"Yeah, Big Boy, and you can thank your lucky stars about that," Dino said.

I frowned. "What's it for, exactly?"

"If you're on the roof, venting the fire, and you can't get off again by the fire escape or the building stairs, then you need to attach your escape rope to something to rappel down. But if you end up trapped and there's nothing around to hook onto, then you use the roof spike. Here, Ms. Cosi . . ." Like a student eager to impress his teacher, he grinned with pride. "You want to hold it?"

"Uh . . ."

"It's okay, honey," Dino said. "You don't have to be afraid of handling Bigsie's spike. I hear the ladies all enjoy the experience."

Oh, brother. I took the thing—at the very least to prevent more ribbing. It was heavy in the hand, like an espresso tamper, with a flat head (also like a tamper). Its girth was also the perfect thickness to hold comfortably. But that's where the similarity ended. The spike was a foot long and, well, a *spike*, just as the name suggested.

"So this can save your life?"

Bigs nodded. "See if you were stuck on the roof, you'd drive you ax into the roof itself, then you'd put the spike end into the cut, hammer it down with the back of your ax. It's spring-loaded, like a switchblade, so you can trip these prongs to anchor it." He hit a button and the spring-loaded tool snapped open. "Then you clip your rope to this ring and jump."

"Well . . ." I touched the flat end of the tool. "I'm sorry to tell you. For what I need, this head's too big."

Dino snorted. "That's a first."

"What I mean is we'll need that *tamper* to continue. So why don't we all look for it?" I glanced at the men who just sat staring. "I mean it, guys. Let's get down on our hands and knees and get it done.

"Okay, Ms. Cosi," Ortiz said with a wicked grin. "You go down first and we'll be right behind you."

Now the men glanced at one another with smirks.

"Come on, guys! Give me a break!"

The men burst out laughing—and finally did what I asked. They found the tamper, I washed it, and we began again.

Thirty minutes later, two out of three attempts by each firemen resulted in a decent (if far from perfect) shot. Another

half hour and the guys were producing passable espressos—
far from Village Blend quality but a start.

"I feel like I've mastered something," Ortiz said.

"You know the basics now," I told him. "But you need to
keep practicing. You still have a lot to learn. We've hardly
touched on humidity levels, barometric pressure, heat
or cold weather, the characteristics of different beans and
blends, and the effect these things have on extraction."

Ed Schott laughed. "She sounds like a fire-academy
instructor."

"Espressos, gentlemen, are a lot like life, the more you
learn the less you know—and the quicker you surrender to
not knowing, the faster you will progress."

"*Zen and the Art of Espresso Machine Maintenance* by Clare
Cosi,*" James said with a wink.

"I'll take that as a compliment."

With class dismissed, the men crowded around to thank
me, a few of them asking more questions. I pulled out a
copy of an Espresso-making guide, one I gave to all of my
rookies.

"Damn, even *she's* got a manual!"

The men laughed.

"What's so funny?"

"Are you kidding?" Ortiz gestured to a board filled with
official notices on procedures and new equipment. "Welcome to the FDNY. Manuals 'R' Us!"

I smiled, nodded, then quickly broke away and approached Captain Michael.

"Nice job handling the men," he said softly.

I could tell he meant it. His expression was more relaxed now. Whatever I'd done tonight, it had impressed
(or amused) him. His earlier anger at finding me snooping
around his firehouse was obviously gone.

"Can we talk now?" I whispered. *"Privately."*

"Can't wait to get me alone, eh, darlin'?"

"Cut the crap, will you?"

"What crap?"

"You know what."

"Ah, well, maybe I do . . ." His voice went lower and now his gaze was moving over me. "It's just that when I see a lady such as yourself with so many *feminine charms* . . ." He flashed a grin, his gold tooth winking. "I can't help myself."

"Baloney, Captain, and let me tell you something. I don't like baloney. It's cheap and indigestible."

"You're reading me all wrong, dove. My nature compels me to reveal the truth of my heart. It's just the way the Lord made me."

"The Lord made trees. I sincerely doubt divine inspiration had anything to do with your cheesy pickup lines."

Beneath the crimson trim of his Victorian mustache, the man's patronizing smirk finally vanished. He chucked his thumb toward the heavens. "Upstairs."

Twenty-one

~~~~~~~~~~~~~~~~~~~~~~~~~~~~~~~~~~

STRUGGLING to keep up with the man's long strides, I followed Captain Michael across the kitchen, down a hallway, and into a narrow stairwell. We traveled north a level then moved along another industrial green hallway, passing an office door with a plastic plaque that read *Lieutenant Crowley*. The door was ajar and I heard papers rattling, but I couldn't see the occupant.

The captain's office was no fancier than mine although it was a great deal larger. A battered wooden desk dominated the room. There were two chairs, banks of metal filing cabinets, and an old leather couch. The dark, heavy office felt warm to me. I attributed this not to my hormones (or the captain's, for that matter) but to the clanking, hissing radiator in the corner.

Michael felt the heat, too. He opened the room's only window and gestured to his office door. "Close it if you want privacy."

I did. Then I settled onto a chair opposite his desk. He leaned back on his creaky office throne and cradled his fingers.

"So, I'm guessing you want to know what the fire marshals are sayin', right?"

"That's an ongoing investigation," I said with a straight face. "I'm a civilian, remember? It's none of my business until it's a part of the public record."

Captain Michael blinked, obviously surprised by my answer.

"I have another matter on my mind."

He smirked. "My love life?"

"No. The other fire. The one that happened on the very same night as the fire at Caffè Lucia."

His eyes narrowed. "I wasn't aware there *was* a second fire."

You're lying again. "It made the papers. A privately owned coffee shop in Bensonhurst, Brooklyn. Doesn't that strike you as suspicious? Two coffeehouse fires the same night, at almost the exact same time?"

Captain Michael opened the top button of his pristine white uniform shirt, and then, almost impatiently, he waved the question aside. "This firehouse caught two bakery delivery van fires this morning. Does that strike you as suspicious?"

"No, but—"

"There are just about as many coffee shops in this town as bakery delivery vans. Two vans, two coffee joints. I'd call it a coincidence either way."

"What if both fires turn out to be arson?" I asked. "What then?"

"Then the crimes will be investigated and it's not your business, right? Isn't that what you just said?"

I folded my arms. "Yes. I'm a civilian. But I have a coffeehouse, too. I want to know what you think is causing these fires if it's not arson? I mean, considering the two fires, I'd like your opinion on fire prevention. As a civilian, I think that's a fair question."

We stared at one another for a few silent seconds. He was obviously considering how to handle me.

Your move, chum.

He finally made one—a dodge. "You may be a civilian, Clare, but I'll give you this, you're a big-hearted one. Coming out here tonight after a long day of work, helping out my guys. It was very kind of you."

"I was glad to help." I was, too. Even if I hadn't come to gather information for Fire Marshal Rossi, I would have come to help these men.

A phone trilled just then. It wasn't the land line on the captain's desk. It was a cell phone.

"Excuse me." Michael didn't bother checking the caller ID. He answered quickly, and when the other party spoke, his expression chilled, his lively eyes went dead. With an abrupt lurch, he swung the chair around until all I could see was the starched cotton shirt stretched across his hunching shoulders.

"What do you want?" he said.

He listened for another few seconds, then replied, "No, Josie, and this is the third time you've asked. Three strikes you're out."

Josie? I tucked that name away. I couldn't glean much more from the conversation—just grunts and one word replies. It was also obvious Josie was a woman.

With the captain's back to me, I decided to take advantage of the moment. Rising, I glanced around, looking for any sign the man might be seeing Lucia—a photo of her maybe? Whoever Josie was, she was clearly on the outs, and I found myself curious about the raven-haired woman who'd made the captain so happy in those photos from years ago.

One of the office walls was peppered with framed diplomas, citations, and awards. An "I love me" wall was what they called it in the military because every officer above a lieutenant has one at home or in the office (according to a former U.S. Navy SEAL I'd crossed paths with one summer). But in Captain Michael's case, it was an "I love my little brother" wall. As I moved closer, I realized every single item posted had something to do with Kevin Quinn: from a faded high school newspaper picture in his varsity football uniform to more recent images of Michael bowling with Kevin at Sunnyside Lanes, shooting hoops on a Queens outdoor court, and fishing on the rocky banks of the East River. It was the kind of devotion and pride one usually reserved for a child, not a brother.

I'd heard someone mention Kevin at the Quinn St. Patrick's Day bash. He'd just relocated to Boston this past fall. The most recent photos attested to this, showing Kevin with his family on Boston Commons, at a Yankees–Red Sox game at Fenway Park, hanging out near Plymouth Rock.

The final picture showed Captain Michael standing between Kevin and the man's wife, two smiling preteen daughters on either side. All were bundled in sweaters and coats, and snow dusted the suburban lawn behind them. The handwritten inscription read: "Hey, bro . . . Your visit made our first Thanksgiving in Boston feel like home. Love, Kev, Melody, Melinda, and Megan."

"Look, Josie, I'm on duty. I'm hanging up now."

Michael ended the call. He swung around, noticed me by the Kevin wall and immediately strode across the room.

"Where were we, Clare?"

"I'm a civilian."

"With a big heart, that's right . . ." He relaxed himself, shedding the uneasy business of that call with the ease of a practiced chef crumbling old skin from an onion. "I'd like to thank you for what you've done. I mean it. *Personally* thank you." He smiled down at me, it actually appeared genuine.

"No thanks necessary."

"No baloney now, Clare. It's not every day I meet someone like you. You're something special. All those guts and brains inside that alluring little package—"

"I have some serious questions for you."

"Okay, all right." He showed me his palms. "If that's what it takes. You can go ahead and question my past. I've had my share of women, it's true. At my age, what do you expect? I wasn't exactly a monsignor in my youth."

"Were you ever in a relationship with Lucia Testa?"

The captain's eyebrow arched again. "A gentleman never kisses and tells."

"Tell me anyway."

"Why do you need to know?"

"Were you?"

He took a breath, exhaled it. "No."

I didn't believe him. "Then why is she in a photo on the wall downstairs? Was she seeing one of your men at any time? Maybe a few over a period of years?"

"There are no Firehouse Annies here, and I won't be spreading any gossip. But weren't we talking about you and me, Clare—"

"You're delusional. There is no 'you and me.'"

"But I'd like there to be. You're different. I can see that . . . special."

"I'm involved with your cousin. Is that what you mean?"

"Just give me a chance." He snapped his fingers. "How about a weekend getaway? Maybe Cape May, the Jersey Shore. How about Atlantic City? Dinner. A show. A little Texas Hold 'Em—" His gold tooth flashed.

"Don't hold your breath—"

"I know my cousin, Clare. The guy lives for his job. When was the last time you two went out and had some fun, eh?"

He paused, waiting for my reaction. I didn't offer one.

"Then consider the invitation open-ended. Some weekend when my cop cousin lets you down or ticks you off and you need a nice strong, sympathetic shoulder to lean on, ring me up. Mikey never has to know about it—"

This is a waste of my time.

I wasn't going to get anything more out of this guy. That was obvious. My decision was clear. I would give Rossi all eight names of the men who'd attended my espresso-making lessons this evening: Captain Michael Quinn, Lieutenant Oat Crowley, and firefighters Dino Elfante, Ronny Shaw, Ed Schott, and Alberto Ortiz. Bigsby Brewer and James Noonan would be on that list, too. I hated adding their names. To me, they were heroes who'd risked their safety to carry

Madame and Enzo out of that collapsing caffè—but if there was a chance they were guilty, then I had to tell Rossi, let him investigate, decide for himself.

"Good night, Captain," I said, cutting him off midpass.

"Wait." Michael moved with me, blocking my way. "One more thing, Clare . . ."

"What?"

"I want you to know: Whatever Mikey told you about Kevin"—he lifted his chin toward the I-love-my-brother wall—"it's *his* version of events. Remember that . . ."

Confused for a moment, I turned back to the Kevin Quinn shrine, looked over the photos again. "Your *brother* is the reason you and Mike have been feuding all these years—is that what you're saying? Because that's not what Mike told me . . ."

"What did he tell you?"

I conveyed the story about Mike's old girlfriend Leta, about her dad being shot in cold blood during a bodega robbery, about his classmate Pete Hogarth's father being the killer and Mike's being labeled a narc at the academy because of Hogarth's two relatives being in the same class. "Mike chose to be a cop instead of a firefighter," I finished, "so you felt betrayed, like he let you down and you never got over it."

"My cousin's very good at twisting the truth."

"So are you."

"That's not why we want to take each other's heads off, Clare."

"Okay then. What is it your brother did to Mike?"

"Other way 'round."

I narrowed my eyes at that one. "I'm listening."

"Good. Because you ought to hear this. And once you do, you'll know why he never told you the truth about our feud . . ."

I exhaled. "Never told me *what* exactly?"

"My little brother, Kev, was all set to start at the fire academy. Some of his buddies took him out for a few rounds to help him celebrate. On his way back home, a couple of ex-jarheads in blue pull him over. You know why? Because his SUV had FDNY stickers plastered all over it."

"Why should that matter?"

"The annual FDNY–NYPD football game had just gone down in favor of the fire boys. These cops lost a very juicy bet. So they took it out on Kev. He told them about Mike, said 'Listen, I got a cousin who's a detective, cut me a break.' So they let Kevin call Mike on his cell, and you know what your asshole boyfriend told those cops?"

I stared.

"Mike told those mutts to *arrest* Kevin for DUI. The kid's future was destroyed, Clare. The FDNY wouldn't take him after that. He did jail time. Imagine if it were your little brother—or your child—*for a few beers . . .*"

The man's eyes were flashing. He moved closer, invading my space. "Kevin and I were supposed to be FDNY brothers together. We had wanted that since we were kids, since our dad died. Now Kevin's had to relocate for his civilian job—all the way up to Boston. I hardly see him anymore—my only brother, gone from my life because of my pigheaded cousin's NYPD advancement dreams."

"But . . . aren't you blaming Mike for something that Kevin got himself into . . ."

"Aw, darlin' . . ." He shook his head, looking more heart-broken than angry. "Don't you get it? Mike didn't want to look bad. He didn't want to risk someone finding out that he got the rules bent for a relative. Your precious boyfriend put his police career before helping his own flesh and blood."

My mouth went dry. I wanted to chalk this up to the cap-tain's twisted version of events, but there was such sincerity in his tone, in his eyes . . . I couldn't chalk this one up to baloney. Still, I had to tell him . . .

"That doesn't sound like the man I know."

"You haven't known him long enough, then." His voice went low and soft, like he was doing me a serious favor, warning me of a coming earthquake. "I'm tellin' you, Clare, you should move yourself good and clear of my cousin, for your own well-being . . ."

My reply came, but it was hardly audible. "I don't agree."

"You will, darlin'. Like I told you, my invitation is open-ended. One weekend when you see the jerkoff for what he is and you're cryin' you eyes out, you give me a call . . ."

A loud, throbbing electronic tone interrupted us. A second later, knuckles rapped on the door. The captain held my eyes a long moment then tore himself away, stepped into the hall.

"We got a hot one, Michael . . ."

It was Oat Crowley's muffled voice. On the floor below there were shouts and pounding feet.

"One second, Oat . . ."

The captain ducked back into his office. "Stay here, Clare. I have more to tell you. *Wait* for me to come back."

When he left again, I went to the doorway, watched his broad back moving quickly away.

"What's the job?" the captain asked.

"Long Island City," Oat replied, hurrying to catch up. "It's a two-alarm, going to three . . ."

The heavy bang of the stairwell door cut off their voices. In less than a minute, I felt the massive trucks rumbling under my feet, heard the sirens screaming as the ladder and engine companies raced into the night. When the building was still and quiet again, I headed down to the kitchen to retrieve my backpack. I bundled up tightly—coat, scarf, hat, gloves.

A part of me was curious to hear what else the captain had to say, but I wasn't stupid. Whatever he wanted to tell me was going to come with those increasingly aggressive advances that had nothing to do with my "feminine charms" and everything to do with his vendetta against Mike.

The walk back to my car came with bitterly cold wind gusts. I had expected them, prepared for them, but I shivered just the same. This whole evening had ended badly, and I suddenly knew how those men felt at the end of my espresso lesson. Getting a few answers seldom settled anything, it only confirmed the need to ask more questions.

I didn't want to admit it, but the captain's story had shaken me. I'd always had so much faith in Mike Quinn. We'd been through so much together. But the same had been true with me and Matt—until I'd learned the truth of his behavior during our marriage . . .

When my cell phone vibrated in my front pocket, I was shivering so hard I almost didn't feel it. I tugged off one glove, checked the screen. Who was calling from the Blend?

"It's Tucker. Someone left a package for you."

"What do you mean *someone*?"

"There's no return address."

"Well, didn't you *see* who left it?"

"No, sweetie. Some NYU students noticed a backpack under an empty table. They looked inside and all they found was this brown paper package addressed to you so they brought it to the counter."

It took me a second to add up two and two: abandoned package, nothing else in the backpack, addressed to me, left in our coffeehouse.

Oh my God. "Tucker, clear everyone out of the building! Call 911! Tell them to send the bomb squad! Now!"

Twenty-two

࿐࿐࿐࿐࿐࿐࿐࿐࿐࿐࿐࿐࿐࿐࿐

It was the longest drive of my life—with the possible exception of that predawn cab ride to the ICU all those years ago, when my young, stupid husband had nearly killed himself partying too hard.

Northern Boulevard led straight to the Queensboro, and I ascended the bridge ramp in record time. Just one day ago, shades of magic hour light had gilded this span. Tonight's lonely crossing felt blacker than outer space.

Twice I smacked the button on my car's heater, but the unit was hardly working. It failed to lessen my bone-cold chill, and the dark void between bridge and river only made me shiver harder.

As I hurled my old car toward Manhattan's wall of flickering windows, a distant memory flashed through my mind—the image of a luna moth, throwing herself against the glass of our porch lantern.

"Why is she doing that, Daddy!"

"Just her nature, honey. It's how God made her . . ."

"But she'll burn up!"

"She's not worrying about that part, muffin. She's just trying to get to the light . . ."

Now I knew how that little moth felt. A part of me wanted to soar away, fly off somewhere to get some peace, think everything through. But that's not how I was made. As long as I cared, there was no flying away.

Traffic thickened at the bridge's end and my impatience rose. Spotting an opening, I sped up. Angry horns bleated as I cut off slow-moving bumpers, swung in a careening arc onto the wide, multilaned spectacle of Second Avenue.

Now I was racing south from Fifty-ninth, a straight shot downtown. Green lights tasted sweet, like seedless grapes; red lights were bitter. Yellow felt longer than midsummer days, my excuse to squash down the pedal.

At Fourteenth I turned west, zoomed across the island to Manhattan's West Side, traveled south again and looped around to Hudson. I parked in front of the Blend, cut the engine. The shop's front door was locked but the lights were on. Tucker, Dante, and Matt were standing inside. I rapped on the glass.

"Where is it!" I cried when Tucker threw the bolt.

"Calm down, sweetie." He held up his palms. "Like I told you before you hung up on me, there's no bomb in the package."

"Where!"

"Take it easy, Clare . . ." Matt's face was in front of me now, gaze steady. "I looked the whole package over myself. It's like Tucker told you. There was no need to call the bomb squad. There's no firebomb . . ."

My ex-husband's hands felt firm on my shoulders, but worry lines were creasing his forehead.

"*Show* me," I said.

Matt led me to the marble counter. Dante stood silently behind it, head still bandaged under his fedora, ropey arms folded. I met his eyes.

"That arsonist's ass is mine," he said quietly.

I'd never heard this tone from Dante before. I mean, sure,

he was serious about his painting, but as a barista at the Blend, he was always a carefree dude, as mellow as his ambient playlists.

Not at the moment. The burning demons in Dante's retinas now rivaled Captain Michael's.

"Whenever you nail this asshole, you give him to me."

"She's not nailing anyone," Matt snapped. "Whatever lunatic quest she's been on stops *tonight*."

I still didn't understand what they were talking about—until I moved closer to the counter. A charcoal gray backpack was sitting there with every pocket unzipped and turned out. A small, brown box sat beside it, already opened. Inside was a plain piece of paper displaying three typewritten words.

FOR CLARE COSI

"What's for me?" I whispered.

"A warning," Matt said. He reached in, lifted up the paper.

Beneath it was a box of wooden matches. A single match had been taken out of its box. The slender charred stick had been struck, then blown out, half burned.

Fifteen minutes later I was standing amid a sea of banged up desks in the Sixth Precinct's detective squad room.

"Mike, I'm sorry to bother you," I said above the raised voices and ringing phones.

"It's okay . . ."

Mike Quinn was jacketless, his weapon holstered under his left arm, leather straps making their usual indelible creases in his starched white shirt. Under the harsh fluorescence, his features looked just about as starched. Then his gaze moved over me and his expression softened, his voice melting with it.

"What do you need, sweetheart?"

For you to put your arms around me, that's what I need. For you to explain your cousin's ugly accusations. I need you to make love to me . . .

"Can we talk? Privately."

"Yeah, Quinn." Matt stepped out from behind me. "Make it as soon as possible."

A dunking in liquid nitrogen would have been warmer than the look Quinn gave my ex. His eyes found mine again, as if searching for an explanation. Then he looked back to Matt.

"Give me a second."

"Why's your flatfoot working so late?" Matt loudly asked after Quinn departed.

"Lower your voice," I whispered when a female detective glanced our way. "Mike's launching an undercover investigation. It starts tonight."

My gaze followed Quinn as he strode back over to a cluster of desks in the corner. He spoke for a minute to the tight group of detectives he oversaw, one of whom I recognized immediately by his ruddy face and carrot-colored cop hair: Finbar "Sully" Sullivan.

Sully was wiring up another man for surveillance. (I knew this because when I was helping Quinn on a case a short time ago, Sully had wired *me*.) This second man was also familiar—Sergeant Emmanuel Franco.

Because Sully was still prepping him, Franco's flannel shirt was open, revealing a weight lifter's six-pack and part of a tattoo. A hard hat covered his shaved head and one hand gripped a bright orange vest. The construction-guy costume made sense for his new undercover assignment.

After the trendy Manhattan club near the Williamsburg Bridge was cleared of dealing ecstasy and Liquid E to its clientele, the nearby construction site's workers became the squad's new target.

Matt nudged me, pointed across the room. "That younger guy your flatfoot's talking to, the one in the hard hat with his shirt open, he looks familiar."

"No," I lied, "he doesn't."

"Sure he does. That's the cop who interrogated us last December. Franco was his name. I remember now. Sergeant Emmanuel Franco," Matt spat. "I'll never forget that mook."

I gritted my teeth. Our daughter had failed to inform her father that she'd had several "hot dates" with Sergeant "Mook" after our Christmas party. With Joy back in France, I figured their relationship was over and it didn't matter, anyway. So why bring it up?

Quinn returned and motioned for us to follow him. "I don't have a private office," he said as we crossed the busy floor. "We'll have to talk in an interview room."

"That's fine," I said, expecting as much.

Like the NYPD Bomb Squad, which was also based at the Sixth, the jurisdiction of Mike's OD Squad spanned all five boroughs. With his work mostly in the field, there were no proper offices for his small crew, just that tight cluster of desks in the open squad room.

"I'm not too keen on interview rooms," Matt said as he dodged two suits and a uniformed officer. "You're not planning to chain me to anything, are you, Quinn?"

"I don't know, Allegro. That's entirely up to you."

Mike shut the door and we sat down at a metal table with four equally uncomfortable metal chairs. The interview room's walls were concrete block and the only window had one-way glass.

The space had all the warmth of a closet at the city morgue. But the stifling feeling was exactly the point. Detectives didn't bring suspects in here for tea parties. They brought them here to extract confessions, and the only differences I could see between this airless space and the dimly lit confessional where I'd recited my girlish sins was the kneeler—and the lighting. In Father Pentanni's box, I could hardly see a thing. Here in Quinn's confessional the glare was even harsher than in the squad room.

After we sat, I began to explain the situation.

"Just *show* him," Matt said, cutting me off.

I chafed at my ex's tone, but I didn't say a word. Matt distrusted cops (and all authority figures)—partly because of his run-ins with the NYPD and partly because of his bad experiences with corrupt officials in banana republics. I knew how difficult it was for my ex-husband to come here with me. The last thing I wanted to do was get into an argument.

I set the backpack on the table, pulled out the package.

Quinn almost never showed emotion on the job. But as he studied the box of matches, the single charred stick, and the arsonist's note to me, his features twisted openly with fury, worry, and frustration. When he finally spoke, it was a single, quiet curse.

"That son of a bitch . . ."

Matt folded his arms. "Is that all you've got to say?"

"No . . . I'm going to get this to our people in the Crime Scene Unit, but . . ." Quinn exhaled.

"I know," I said, reading him. "It's been handled to death."

"Who opened it?" Quinn asked.

I turned to Matt. "You explain . . ."

"One of our customers, Barry, first noticed the backpack—"

"Barry?" I interrupted. "Tucker said it was a group of NYU students."

Matt shrugged. "Barry found it first. He went to the students next, asked if it was one of theirs. They all passed it around."

I still didn't like the sound of that. "What was Barry doing in the Blend so late?" For months now, the man had been coming in mornings or early afternoons, never in the evenings.

"Tucker said something about his having a fight with this new boyfriend. The guy's on some anticaffeine or anticoffee kick. I don't know. One of those political food movements. He wanted Barry to give up coffee. Barry said no. They had a fight, and Barry came to the Blend to spite him . . ."

"Excuse me," Quinn said. "But how *many* people handled this thing? An estimate?"

"Ten, maybe twelve," Matt said.

Quinn went silent. The cop curtain finally came down on his emotional show.

"I'm sorry," I said softly. "I know that makes it impossible for your people to find forensic evidence."

"Not impossible. Just harder . . . We'll have detectives from this precinct assigned to your case. After we're done in here, you tell them everything, okay? They can work with the fire marshals investigating the Caffè Lucia fire. You'll also have to get me the names and addresses of everyone who touched this thing. Any fibers, fingerprints, or other DNA evidence we find, we'll have to match against your customers and baristas, and eliminate them one by one."

Matt folded his arms. "How long with *that* take?"

"A while. It's not attached to a homicide—"

"Not yet," I said. "But Enzo is in a coma. He's not expected to live. And if he doesn't, the person or persons who set that fire are going to be—"

"Murderers." Quinn said. "I know."

"What happens in the meantime?" Matt snapped. "While we're waiting for some technician to lift a fiber from the asshole who threatened Clare. We go up in flames?"

Quinn focused on me. "When we're through here, I'll speak to my captain. We'll get you protection."

"It's not me who needs it," I said, meeting his eyes. "I have you, don't I?"

Quinn gave me the sweetest look. I returned it.

"Excuse me!" Matt cried. "What about the *Blend*?"

"I'll take care of it," Quinn said, still holding my gaze.

"Good," Matt grunted.

Quinn reached out then, opening his hand as he moved it across the table. He waited, keeping it there until I put mine in his. Then he gently but firmly closed his fingers.

Matt blew out air. "Are we *done* now?"

"I need to talk to Mike about something else," I said softly. "Privately, if you don't mine."

"Fine. I'll wait for you downstairs." Matt rose, left the room, and shut the door—more of a slam really.

"You okay?" Quinn asked.

I nodded, swallowed the sand in my throat. I wanted to tell him everything then, what I'd learned at the firehouse and not just about possible suspects in the Caffè Lucia fire. I wanted to speak to him about the disturbing story that Captain Michael had told me. But this arid, airless room was so awful—and it was Quinn's turf. If I were going to question the man about his past again, I wanted it to be on mine.

"I need to see you tonight, Mike. My place, okay?"

He arched an eyebrow. "You want me to wake you up at four in the morning?"

"Yes."

The corners of his lips lifted. "Okay then. I will."

I rose. "I'm sorry it isn't easier."

He stood, too, picking up the contaminated evidence. "I'll take this to my captain, explain what you've been up to. We'll get sector cars doing routine checks of the Blend all night, and when you open tomorrow, you'll have at least one plainclothes officer undercover inside throughout the day."

"Thank you, Mike." It was far from the first time I'd said it, but I meant it as much as ever.

"One more thing, Clare."

"Yes?"

"Would you please send Allegro back in here? I'd like a private word with him."

Twenty-three

~~~~~~

"Don't move . . ."

The male voice at my ear was no more than a whisper. I'd been sleeping the sleep of exhaustion, so soundly, so sweetly under a heap of bedcovers. Then came the voice, dragging me back to the land of the conscious, the anxious, the miserably alert.

"Mike?"

"You heard me. Don't move . . ."

I was lying on my side, still groggy and disoriented, when I felt the mattress sinking behind me. Under the blankets, large hands caressed my curves.

"What time is it?"

"All the clocks have stopped, sweetheart. There is no time. Right now there's nothing but you and me . . ."

Soft tugs coaxed off my nightshirt. The touch of slightly calloused fingers were cool at first, but quickly warmed on my naked skin. Tender kisses came next, to the back of my shoulder, along my neck, around my jawline . . .

I smiled in the dark.

A few minutes later, Quinn's long, heavy body was covering mine, and I found my way back to sweet oblivion.

An hour later, we were lying together, still under the covers, my head on his shoulder, his durable arm around me.

"Mike . . . ?"

My voice sounded shamefully hesitant in the shadowy chill of the pre-dawn room. "There's something I didn't tell you earlier . . ."

"That makes two of us."

"Oh?"

"Yes. But you go first."

"No," I said, far from eager to spill. "You."

"All right, well . . . Remember that private word I had with your ex-husband?"

"Yeah, what was that about? Matt wouldn't tell me . . ."

"I asked him to stay here with you."

"You're *kidding* . . ."

Not so long ago, Mike nearly broke up with me because Matt was still making use of this duplex. "I can't believe it," I said. "You asked Matt to stay *here* with me?"

"I didn't want you to be in the building alone. That's all. Matt agreed with me."

"Oh, no, he didn't. I was up here all night alone—until you came."

"You were alone in the duplex, Clare, but not in the building. Allegro spent the night downstairs in the Blend, doing business with Europe and Japan on his PDA. I spoke to him before I came upstairs to you, told him to get home, try to get some rest . . ."

Once again, I was surprised, but only a little. Matteo Allegro's long list of petty vices continued to be trumped by one major virtue: the man had a ferocious protective streak. Whether it was his daughter, his mother, his new wife, or old, my ex-husband refused to accept someone he loved being in harm's way.

"Okay, sweetheart, your turn," Mike said, his voice almost teasing. I felt a soft kiss on my hair. "What didn't you tell me earlier?"

"I went to your cousin's firehouse last night."

Mike's big, warm body froze against mine.

"I'm sorry," I said. "Your cousin swore to me on the phone that he wouldn't be there—"

"But he was anyway."

"Yes."

"I asked you to stay away from him, Clare."

"I thought I was staying away from him. I swear. He lied to me—"

"You *promised* me."

"You're not listening, Mike. Try to understand . . ."

I did my best to explain my side of it. "I needed to do it. I needed to find answers. The problem is . . . I found more questions . . ."

Mike let my final statement hang for a moment. "Okay," he said. "You want to explain what that's supposed to mean?"

"It means your cousin told me about the history between you and his younger brother, Kevin . . ."

Mike exhaled, loud and long. "Let's get this out of the way, all right? I want to know every single thing that son-of-a-bitch cousin of mine told you."

"Fine." I threw off the covers and got up.

"Clare! Where are you going?!"

"I'm not going to discuss your cousin in this bed," I said, grabbing my robe, wrapping it tight. "Are you hungry? I need to cook."

"Oh?" Mike blinked, his tone suddenly more pliable. "What did you have in mind?"

CRAB *cakes.* That's what I had in mind. Mike loved them, and I'd already picked up two pounds of fresh lump crabmeat from the Lobster Place on Bleecker. (Blue, of course. For Maryland-style cakes, the crabs really should be blue.)

So, okay, seafood wasn't your typical breakfast fare. But Mike had been up all night and this was going to be dinner for him.

Now, as the coral glow of dawn lightened the darkness beyond my window, I made a pot of coffee and poured two mugs. Quinn sat at my kitchen table in sweat pants and a faded Rangers T-shirt, his feet bare, his dark blond hair mussed. The man had a strong presence, even when he didn't say a word. With his twilight blue eyes watching my every move over the rim of his coffee mug, I found it difficult to focus on the cooking, but I did my level best.

Back around midnight, I'd already mixed the crabmeat with binders and herbs and formed the small patties. Now I pulled the wax paper covered plates from the fridge, brushed them lightly with an egg wash, and carefully rolled each in a crisp breading of Japanese panko.

The clammy texture of the chilly patties against my fingers and palms reminded me of another dish—my *nonna*'s spinach and ricotta *malfatti*, just one of the daily take-out specialties we made for her grocery.

Malfatti, which translates to "badly formed," were essentially dumplings of ravioli filling (hold the pasta). But the idea I found useful at this very moment was bigger than that. Italian culinary philosophy dictated that you never apologized for your mistake. You just made up a little name for it and moved along.

My malfatti look lumpy? Hey, don't blame me! They're called badly formed, aren't they? Those little meringue-hazelnut cookies of mine resemble toadstool tops? So what! They're called brutti ma buoni, *right? Ugly but good!*

It was exactly the tack I took with Mike, explaining (but never apologizing) for my encounter with his cousin the previous evening.

Laughable, wasn't it? I mean, it wasn't my *fault your cousin was there. Don't blame me!*

(Of course, I was careful to leave out the part about his flame-haired twin inviting me to play Texas Hold 'Em in

Atlantic City.) But then I got to the story of how Mike had put his career ahead of his younger cousin Kevin . . .

When I finished, Mike appeared to come down with a prolonged case of lockjaw. Finally, he let out a harsh laugh.

"He's such a piece of work . . ."

"Kevin?"

"*Michael*. He gave you selected highlights, Clare, a carefully redacted tale of Quinn ancient history . . ."

"You'll have to explain."

"Kevin Quinn was supposed to follow in his late father's footsteps, just like his older brother. But Kevin's partying got out of hand. Underage drinking became a major problem. And then he began to drive drunk."

"So it wasn't just a one time thing?"

"No. When Kevin was pulled over in Manhattan one night, he used my name to get the officers to give him another chance. The pair contacted me themselves—I was on duty so I showed up inside of ten minutes to take my idiot younger cousin off their hands. I drove Kevin straight home, warned the kid to sober the hell up and straighten out. But Kevin blew it."

"What do you mean? He drove drunk again?"

"A few months later, just before he was supposed to start training at the fire academy, the kid was back behind the wheel, loaded up on boilermakers. This time it wasn't just a pull over, it was a traffic accident. He went right through a red light, banged up another vehicle. No one was badly hurt, but a few seconds' difference in that crash and Kevin could have injured or even killed two young women."

"Oh my God . . ."

"The story's not over: this time Michael came to me, hat in hand, asking me to help out his little brother, just like I'd done before. *Make it go away.* Those were his words. But things were different this time. Kevin was falling down drunk when the arresting officers took him in. By the time I heard about it, he was already in the system. I made sure the kid got a good lawyer. I stood up for him in court, vouched for his character. It was all I could do."

"It didn't help?"

"The judge didn't care in the least that Kevin had a relative on the job. She believed he needed a hard lesson. I didn't say so at the time, but so did I. Kevin pleaded guilty and went to jail for a brief time. It killed his chances of becoming a New York City firefighter, and Michael never forgave me for not doing more to help his brother. But, Clare, I swear I did all I could."

I turned back to the stove, considering Mike's words as I slipped six panko-breaded crab cakes into the hot peanut oil. The patties sizzled, the fresh herbs inside giving a hint of floral fragrance to the kitchen, but the primary sensation in the air was heavy and cloying, the kind of feeling you get when you know something is being fried.

"I don't understand why you and your cousin have to be at war over this," I said. "Your actions were obviously reasonable and Kevin was in the wrong. How could anyone trust a kid like that to be a responsible firefighter, for God's sake?"

"Most of the family is on my side, Clare. Kevin even forgave me for not doing more to get him off the hook. But Michael never did."

"Why not? If what you say is true—"

"It is. But my cousin's told his version of that story for so many years now he actually believes it. And that's the tragedy."

I turned back to the burner. Mixing and forming crab cakes was simple enough, but cooking them was not. For one thing, there wasn't much keeping the patties together (not if you wanted to taste crabmeat instead of bread crumbs and binders), so poking them was a bad idea. Flipping should be done only once. And turning them was tricky. Anything held together this precariously had to be handled with finesse.

I glanced over my shoulder at Mike, tried to keep my voice light and casual. "How many years ago did all of that happen, anyway?"

"I don't know. Twelve or so, I guess . . ."

"Is Kevin okay now?"

"Kevin's doing just fine for himself, Clare. He's an engineer, married with two kids, and makes a perfectly good living. Until last summer, he had a great job at a firm in the city."

"But he had to move to Boston, right?"

"That's right . . ."

Mike's voice trailed off, and I let it go, focusing on the completion of his meal. Using a spatula I slipped four of the hot crab cakes onto a large dinner plate, placed three colorful mounds of my homemade condiments around them: lemon-garlic mayo; dill-laced mustard sauce; and avocado, gherkin, and roasted pepper relish. Finally, I piled a generous side of my Thai-style coleslaw into a small salad bowl. (In my opinion, the sweet heat and bright astringency of my Thai slaw was the perfect accompaniment to the unctuous richness of the pan-fried seafood.)

Mike picked up his fork and dug in. "Oh, man, this is good . . ."

I made up my own plate and sat down.

"So . . ." I carefully poked. "Boston?"

"Yeah," Mike said, pausing to chew and swallow. "Kevin was downsized recently—just last year—and he had to relocate for a new job, but I hear he's happy in Massachusetts. And the last time I checked, he no longer touches alcohol."

As Mike inhaled his dinner, I ate my two warm cakes in silence, trying my best to enjoy the freshly fried flavor of lightly breaded seafood, the complementary notes in the tricolored accompaniments. But I still wasn't satisfied.

"Are you sure there isn't anything else between you and your cousin? Just the incident with Kevin?"

Mike looked down, suddenly focusing his attention on the last little bits on his plate. "The thing with Kevin, Clare . . . that's what Michael won't forgive."

"You know, it sounds to me like your choosing your words carefully again. There's more to this story, isn't there?"

"That's all I can tell you . . ."

"You mean that's all you want to tell me."

Mike looked up then, finally met my eyes. "Sweetheart, I'm going to ask you one more time to stay away from my cousin. Will you do that?"

"Yes."

"Promise me, Clare."

"Mike—"

"Promise me."

I sighed. "I promise you, Mike."

"Good, let's change the subject, okay? Mind if I watch the headlines?"

"No . . . I'd like to see them, too."

Mike flipped on the small television in the corner of the counter, turned it to NY1, our local twenty-four-hour news channel.

"I'll make more coffee," I said.

Obviously, Mike was done talking about his cousin, but I couldn't stand having secrets between us, and I was determined to get this one out of him.

As I measured out our Breakfast Blend, I considered how to reopen the subject. For about twenty seconds, the noisy gears of my burr grinder drowned out the dulcet tones of NY1's morning anchor. Then the grinder stopped and Pat Kiernan's voice came back.

". . . a three-alarm fire in Long Island City. The coffee-house was part of a popular international chain . . ."

"Coffeehouse!"

I turned quickly, just in time to see last night's recorded footage. I recognized several members of the fire station I'd just laughed with the night before. Then I recalled what Oat had said to Captain Michael as they strode away from his office—*"Long Island City . . . a two-alarm, going to three . . ."*

". . . and the mayor will make a statement later today about this sad turn of events," Kiernan continued. "The coffeehouse was closed at the time of the blaze and no customers or employees were injured. But one of New York's Bravest lost his life . . ."

I glanced at Mike. We both tensed, waiting. Finally, the still, color photograph came up on the TV screen—a picture of the dead man.

I stumbled backward, fell into a chair.

". . . best known for his appearance as Mr. March in last year's famous FDNY calendar, Bigsby Brewer died instantly after jumping from the building's roof. The cause of the fire is deemed suspicious and is under investigation."

Twenty-Four

～～～～～～～～～～～～～～～～～

THREE days later, a public funeral was held in Queens. Dante, Madame, and I attended. The mayor was there and the city commissioners. The cardinal came, the FDNY Emerald Society Pipes and Drums, the local press, and every member of Bigsby Brewer's beloved firehouse.

The pomp and turnout were overwhelming, the grieving genuine. Thousands of firefighters from every borough showed up in dress blues. The small army couldn't fit inside the church so they lined up in formation on the streets outside, where cops redirected traffic for hours, all the way to the burial ceremony in Calvary Cemetery on Laurel Hill Boulevard.

The younger firefighters looked steely, the older ones visibly haunted, unshed tears glazing their eyes, tense expressions barely masking rekindled memories. Back in fall 2001, this city had seen hundreds of funerals just like this one, final farewells to those who'd answered their last alarms.

Now it was Bigsby's turn. And on the morning of his funeral, that's when it hit me. I'd *heard* his last alarm.

* * *

THE cluster of days that followed blew by like fast-moving storms. Time felt compressed, and so did I. Tensions were so high that most mornings I woke up feeling as though I'd slept with my head inside a panini maker.

The Blend's business went on as usual—morning crush, lunchtime takeouts, evening regulars—but just as Mike promised, detectives from the Sixth took shifts in plain clothes while sector cars drove by so often I was starting to feel like I managed a gangland hangout.

There were no more threats, however, and no more coffee-house fires. My two follow-up calls to Rossi and the precinct detectives handling my case yielded polite but completely fruitless conversations.

Madame continued to spend part of every day at the ICU, reading the newspapers aloud to Enzo. He was still coma-tose, but his condition was stable, at least. Until he woke up—if he ever did—the doctors wouldn't be sure of the ex-tent of his stroke damage.

I met with Valerie Noonan twice (in microbrew bars, her choice) to finalize details for the bake sale. Mike and I man-aged to meet a few times for dinner, too—Cornish hens with coffee glaze and Cumberland sauce; an outstanding recipe for Triple-Threat Firehouse Penne Mac 'n' Cheese (that James shared with me); steak with a Jim Beam reduction; and Korean-style fried wings (my first attempt to identify the ingredients and technique behind those delectable Un-identified Flying Chickens).

As usual, Mike swooned for my cooking, but his under-cover operation near the Williamsburg Bridge sapped so much of his time and energy that we failed to connect be-yond the dinner table.

No more spicy-sweet 4 AM wake up calls. In the wee hours before dawn, Mike would come back to the Blend and relieve Matt from his night vigil of global coffee trading. Then Mike would come up to my bedroom, collapse onto the mattress, and by the time he stirred again I was already at work, pulling espressos . . .

FINALLY, the day of the big bake sale arrived.

Val had chosen the location and it was perfect—Union Square Park, an island of green space ringed by skyscrapers. The park was three city blocks long and the northern perimeter was frequently used to stage open-air farmers' markets. That was the real genius of the location. New Yorkers were already used to stopping by the area for food purchases so the turnout was practically guaranteed.

Early that morning, volunteers from the NYC Fallen Firefighters Fund began setting up their tents and tables. Matt and I spent two hours transporting supplies and erecting our little blue Village Blend stand. Now he was gone—off to catch some sleep since he'd been doing business with Europe and Japan most of the night—while I stayed to man the booth, test our espresso machine, and marshal the troops.

Behind our portable counter, Dante and Esther began unpacking columns of plastic lids and cardboard cups.

Then Tucker arrived, waving the *New York Post* at us like a signal flag. "People, people, did you see this!"

"See what?" Dante asked.

Esther and I stared blankly.

"Oh my *gawd*!" Tucker was close to apoplectic. "There's something in this paper you all *need* to hear!"

"Lottery numbers?" Esther asked.

"Listen!" Tucker cleared his throat and his best PSA announcer voice began to read: "Coffee is a drug. Coffee is toxic to the human body. Coffee is a capitalist tool and should be eradicated from the earth—"

"What is that?" Esther cried.

She reached for the paper, but Tucker pulled it out of reach. "It's a letter from the 'Coffee Shop Arsonist'— according to the headline, that's what the police are calling this Looney Tune. Last week, this letter was sent directly to the *New York Post.* Apparently, they just got the okay from the authorities to publish it."

"*Keep reading*, Tucker," I said quietly.

"Farmers in developing countries should be growing crops, not coffee. Coffee is a threat, a *weapon*! But I have a weapon, too, and I will use it. Close your coffeehouses or suffer the consequences—"

"Toxic?" Esther said. "On what planet? Try reading a Harvard study once in a while, why don't you? And did he say coffee is a *weapon*? That's lunacy. Coffee is the most traded commodity on earth next to oil. And they make *napalm* out of oil. So you tell me—which one is the weapon?"

"Blame it on the writer, Esther. I'm just doing a dramatic read of the lines."

"You'd expect an actual arsonist to know the difference between a thousand-year-old beverage enjoyed around the world and a combustible fluid used to make firebombs. Isn't that his *job*?"

"All I can tell you is that the arsonist's 'job' has got me goosey. And I'm sure I'm not alone. I signed up for mixing espresso drinks, not fielding Molotov cocktails."

Esther shook her head. "Well, I'm not sweating it. This nut job has only burned three coffeehouses. Do you know how many caffès there are in this city? Statistics are on our side."

"Listen, Missy!" Tucker snapped his fingers. "When somebody's out to turn me into a human torch, having the 'odds on my side' is not a comfort! And in case you've forgotten, this firebug already left a warning package in *our* coffeehouse."

"Where's your dramatic spirit? Think *Method*. Can't you see yourself playing Joan of Arc?"

Tuck went quiet a moment. "I realize you're joking, Esther, but that's actually not a bad idea for a black box production—I mean, given that Peter Pan is usually played by an adult woman, I don't see why I couldn't do Joan, although . . ." He flipped his signature floppy 'do. "I'd never want to cut my hair *that* short."

"Either way, you're not in a coffeehouse at the moment," Esther pointed out. "You're outdoors. In a park. And you're surrounded by highly trained members of the New York Fire Department. I really do think you're safe from a fiery death."

Just then a tremendous *whooshing* sound made Tuck and Esther yelp, and me jump. A wave of hot air wafted toward us and we quickly turned our heads. The stand beside ours had erected a banner: *Crème Brûlée! Torched to Order!*

To the enthusiastic applause of a growing group of spectators, two burly firefighters in bunker suits and safety visors proceeded to caramelize the sugar on top of several servings of the classic French egg-custard dessert.

Neither of these guys was using a kitchen salamander; dainty, handheld chef's torch; or even a standard oven broiler (an option I gave my Jersey readers when I was writing my In the Kitchen with Clare column). No, these guys were finishing their crème brûlée with an industrial-sized acetylene torch mounted on a wheeled gurney.

"You're right, Esther," Tucker said, staring. "I feel so much safer with a tank of explosive compressed gas next door!"

"Let's keep it down, guys," Dante told Esther and Tucker. "Remember, these firefighters lost one of their own to this psycho bastard."

"Oh God, you're right," Tuck said, glancing around. "I wasn't thinking."

"Well, I think this letter is absurd," Esther muttered, smacking the newspaper. "And probably a hoax, too."

Tuck clutched his head like the kid in *Home Alone*. "A hoax!"

"Okay, enough," I said in a stern managerial voice. But I shared Tuck's apprehension. Blowtorch aside, this development was a bombshell. *No wonder Rossi and his colleagues were so tight-lipped with me.* If Homeland Security wasn't on board before, they certainly were now.

"Let's get back to work," I said. "Customers are starting to line up."

"Fine with me," Esther said, then she pointed toward the crème brûlée stand. "You know, I've tried making that stuff, but I can never get my custard tops to come out smooth."

"Full of pockmarks?" I assumed.

Esther nodded. "Pothole central."

"You didn't follow the recipe," I stated flatly. "You upped the temperature."

"The lower temperature takes forever!"

"When you turn up the heat, you boil the custard," I said. "Cooking is like a lot of things in life, Esther. Rushing the process only gets you burned . . ."

And speaking of getting burned . . .

I asked Tuck if I could borrow his *New York Post*. Then, letting my capable baristas handle the drink orders, I took the paper to a nearby bench and began reading every story I could find on the Coffee Shop Arsonist. Apparently, the *Post* had received the letter from the alleged bomber the day after Bigsby's death. The *Post's* editors promptly handed it over to the authorities—after copying the text verbatim for today's edition.

Prior to the letter appearing, no one had announced anything connecting the three seemingly separate coffeehouse fires: Enzo's caffè, the shop in Brooklyn that had burned the same night, and this chain store that ended up costing Bigsby's life.

Thus far, the only speculation I'd heard was on the chain store's fire. That particular coffeehouse chain was currently at the center of an ongoing labor dispute over wages and benefits. People assumed the fire was set deliberately by an angry employee.

But this letter changed everything. Now all three fires looked like terrorism, or at the very least a serial arsonist. Its appearance also wreaked havoc on my own suspect list. While I could imagine Lucia Testa or Mrs. Quadrelli torching Enzo's shop for their own selfish reasons, I doubted either woman was capable of burning *two* additional coffeehouses to cover their tracks.

A gust of morning chill swept suddenly across the park, crinkling the tabloid in my hand and stirring the canvas of our nearby Blend tent. In line at our stand, pedestrians shivered inside their light jackets and sweaters. I shivered, too, thinking of the threat I'd received.

But what if the letter isn't real? What if it's a decoy?

Even Esther used the word *hoax*, and the idea stuck with me. The more I thought about it, the more I realized that the pattern of fires made no sense for a political activist. *The authorities have to see that, don't they?*

I glanced up to see our line had gotten even longer. And it appeared there was a problem with the espresso machine. Great.

Break's over . . .

As the sun climbed higher in the cloudless sky, the weather warmed into a perfect day for an outdoor event. The bake sale was soon packed with customers.

"Hey, boss," Esther called after a sudden rush. "The way I'm calculating it, we're going to run out of cups in another two hours."

I glanced at my watch. "Don't worry. Matt wanted a nap and a shower, but he'll be back this afternoon with a van full of supplies—"

My words were drowned out by a sudden cacophony. Pigeons took flight and squirrels escaped into the trees as amplified bagpipes howled from a temporary stage in the middle of Union Square. Over the heads of a hundred off-duty firemen and their families, six men in kilts launched into what would best be described as a *unique* rendition of the Doors' "Light My Fire."

Tucker moaned, his musical aesthetics clearly assaulted. "I hoped to avoid this."

Dante snorted. "Avoid the magnificent sound of the bagpipes? At a fireman's *anything*? What planet are you from?"

"One without men in kilts, apparently," Tuck replied. "Although they do have good legs."

"Look! It's Roger Clark from New York One!" Esther was so excited by the media presence we could actually hear her voice over the racket. "And there's the eleven o'clock news team from WPIX. Looks like the Firefighters Fund will get good publicity."

"Good publicity is an oxymoron," Dante said. "Bad news trumps good news in this town."

"Huh?"

"They're not here for charity. The press came because of Brewer's death and the arsonist's letter." Dante jerked his thumb in the direction of the stage. "See that Asian guy Channel Four is talking to? The dude's name is Jason Wren. He was the owner of Avenue O Joe, that coffeehouse in Brooklyn. The one that burned the same night as the Queens caffè where I almost became human kindling."

Esther shrugged. "So?"

"So the Channel Four news team brought him down here *specifically* so they could interview Wren about the arsonist's letter, using this fireman's event for a backdrop. Tragedy is opportunity to the media." He touched his bandaged head. "They better not stick a mike under my nose and ask for a statement or . . ."

My barista proceeded to describe a use for a handheld microphone that no sound technician would ever consider—not sober, anyway.

While the bagpipers segued into a rendition of Johnny Cash's "Ring of Fire" (I was catching a theme here), my eyes were drawn to a familiar male strut.

The cocky guy approaching us wore a sunny yellow hard-hat over his more typical red, white, and blue 'do-rag, and a dusty flannel shirt over his muscular shoulders, but I instantly recognized the distinctive swagger of Sergeant Emmanuel Franco. Under one arm, he toted a number of pastry boxes and his free hand held a large sandwich cookie.

"I'm still working undercover, Coffee Lady," Franco warned me as he munched the cookie. "So pretend you don't know me."

"My pleasure."

Franco laughed. "You're funny."

"Yeah, I'm a laugh riot. Well, anyway, *stranger*, you look pretty stocked up already, but feel free to peruse our baked good offerings . . ."

I pointed to the table next to our espresso counter. The last few days, I'd been in a lousy mood. Now, amid the sunny sky and cheerful crowds of the charity bake sale, I realized the nicknames I'd given my home-baked treats *might* have been a little dark.

"*Killer* Caramelized Banana Bread?" Franco read, moving down the table. "*Murder by* Mini-Coffeehouse Cake?"

Franco glanced back at me. I shrugged.

"O-kay. What else have we got? *Death by* Double-Sized Double-Chocolate Chip Cookies. Hey, those look tasty, give me six. *Sinful* Salt-Peanut Caramel Shortbread Bars. Oh, yeah, sinful's definitely up my alley, I'll take a dozen of those . . ."

He continued down the table and glanced back at me once more. "*Chokehold* Chocolate Brownies? What are you on, Cosi Lady?"

In my defense, I'd made a half-dozen *normally* named things, too: Blueberries 'n' Cream Coffee Cake Pies (which were—surprise, surprise—a cross between a cake and a pie); Fresh Glazed Strawberry Tarts; Almond-Roca Scones; Star Fruit Upside-Down Cake; and my old standby Cinnamon-Sugar Doughnut Muffins, with a surprise twist this time, a raspberry-flavored heart. I pointed out the muffins to Franco.

"We have jelly doughnut muffins."

Franco just shook his head. "It's a mystery what you have against selling me a good, old-fashioned American jelly doughnut!"

Esther leaned over the counter. "So what are *you* eating, Bob the Builder?"

He held up the cookie. "According to the guys I bought it from, it's a 'Stuck on You' Linzer Heart." Franco winked as he offered her a taste. "Yummy, huh?"

"Peanut butter and marshmallow. Not bad . . ."

"Ladder 219 has a thing for Elvis," Franco said. "All their stuff has the King's theme: Chocolate Hound Dogs, Love Me Tender Blueberry Corn Muffins, Jailhouse Rocky Road Bars, Big Hunk O' Burnin' Fudge. They even dubbed their firehouse 'Graceland.'"

Esther licked some marshmallow off the corner of her darkly glossed lip. "Sticky, but good."

"I wonder if Joy could bake this?" Franco said.

I was about to inform the sergeant that my daughter's interest in Fluffernutters ended when she quit the Girl Scouts. But I bit my tongue. I'd learned a thing or two during Joy's teen years. *Better not encourage their relationship by* discouraging *it.*

"So, Coffee Lady, I heard something about a free cuppa joe with a purchase."

I nodded. "That's right. And for a purchase *that* big he deserves a large."

Esther presented Franco with his coffee—black, no sugar.

"*Mmmm,* hot stuff," he said after a sip. "Kind of like that new batch of digital goodies Joy sent me from France."

When he waggled his eyebrows, I nearly lost it. "Just what kind of photos is my daughter sending you?!"

"Calm down, Momma Hen." Franco laughed over his coffee cup. "They're pictures of some of the dishes Joy's been making. A sweet roasted chicken, some pretty vegetable medleys, a glistening glazed duck, and a *very* sexy puff pastry."

"Oh, thank God," I said, relieved—until I noticed Tucker exchanging a look with Esther.

"Did you know Frenchies eat pigeons?" Franco asked, completely serious.

Esther folded her arms. "You mean *squab*?"

"Squab? Is that what—" Franco suddenly stopped. He seemed to be listening to something that we couldn't—like a micro radio receiver in his ear. "Sorry. I'd love to continue this discussion about what Frenchies call rats with wings, but I gotta go."

"What a relief," I said to Esther when Franco was out of earshot. "I thought my daughter was sending him . . . Well, never mind what I thought."

"Oh, boss . . ." Esther gaped at me with pity. "You are so naïve."

"What do you mean?"

"Franco may come off as a mook, but Joy's really into him. She says he's got these *way* wicked magic hands, and when they're alone together—"

"Stop! I don't want to know!" Now I was the one holding my head like the kid from *Home Alone*.

Tuck put his hand on my shoulder. "Add it up, Clare. Joy's a professional cook. It's her passion. And she's sending Franco pictures of her dishes."

"So?" I said, still feeling clueless.

"Hello!" Esther's eyes bugged. "You never heard of *food porn?*"

The thought of my daughter sending that cocky sergeant *any* form of porn left me sufficiently horrified. For a moment, I was so distracted, I didn't notice what Dante already had.

"Boss . . ." He said, gently tapping me. "James Noonan is here . . ."

Dante lifted his chin and I looked in the direction he'd subtly indicated. The crowd was breaking up after the bagpipers turned the stage over to a local politician. James stood only a few feet away from our tent. He was surrounded by firefighters. I didn't recognize the other men, but it was clear they knew James and were offering their condolences.

"He looks like a freakin' zombie," Dante whispered. "Even worse than at the funeral."

It was true, James seemed to have recovered little since

that heartbreaking day. He'd been inconsolable at the church—so overwhelmed by grief that he'd left the mass early. He never showed up at the wake, either, though his wife made a brief appearance. I'd hoped to see Captain Michael step in and help, but he had his hands full comforting Bigsby's mother and two sisters.

I waited until the other firemen drifted away, and then I brought James a double espresso.

Twenty-Five

~~~~~~~~~~~~~~~~~~~~

"**Hey,** Ms. Cosi."

"Hey to you," I replied, giving him a smile.

He brightened a little when he saw me, but his smile was barely there. In the strong morning sun, James' complexion looked like stale bread dough, his bloodshot eyes were dulled and shadowed, the crimson webs as pronounced as wild mace growing over nutmeg seeds.

I pointed to a bench just vacated by a pair of EMS workers, and we sat down. "So, what do you think of the sale?" I asked, starting with what I hoped was a neutral question.

"It's nice. Real nice. And thank you for the espresso." James sipped once then stared across the park. "Bigs was looking forward to today. All the 'tempting offerings' as he put it."

"He enjoyed home-baked goodies?"

"Yeah . . ." James glanced at me. "Those, too."

He tipped his head and I followed his gaze to a trio of young women—chic, fashionable, and thin as celery stalks— flirting with two young firefighters. The Manhattan girls were shopping for something warm, sweet, and comforting, and it didn't appear to involve chocolate, sugar, or pastry flour . . .

"This town's raining estrogen, you know?" James said. "Ladies in hose and heels. Bigs loved them."

"I noticed. So did Dante. The number of single white roses at Bigsie's funeral was hard to miss . . ." (Not to mention the number of single, well-dressed women.)

"Yeah, Bigs liked to send a white rose to a girl after he had a nice, uh . . . *evening* with her."

James paused and his frown deepened. "You know the worst part of it, Ms. Cosi? My best friend died for nothing. It shouldn't have happened. He did everything right. It was someone else who screwed up . . ."

"I don't want to cause you any more pain," I said as gently as I could, "but I'd like to know more about what happened that night. I'd like to know exactly how your friend died."

James rubbed his neck for a moment then finally spoke. "Two companies were fighting the flames when we got there. It had already spread to the ground floor of the building next door. Oat ordered us up the fire escape to vent the second structure—me, Bigs, Dino Elfante, and Ronny Shaw."

A cloud crossed James's pallid features. "Everything was going okay, by the book. The roof was flat with no apparent hot spots, not much smoke, either. Bigs kind of moved away from the rest of us, poking the roof with his Halligan tool. Then all hell broke loose. There was a blast, and a chunk of the roof flew into the air. It was like a volcano of fire that suddenly just blew."

James paused, gulped at his double.

"The fire marshals said the basement had an illegal conversion. That's what funneled the fire so fast from the coffeehouse to the office building next door. And the second floor of that office structure was undergoing some kind of unlicensed renovation. There were combustibles all over the place. So when the first floor started cooking the second, everything went up without warning."

James drained his cup dry. "We hit the same fire escape

we came up on. Dino and Ronny were long gone when I realized Bigs wasn't behind me."

He crushed the paper cup in his fist.

"I went back up. The roof was still partially intact. There wasn't much smoke, but the heat and fire were unreal. I could see Bigs on the other side of that burning hole. There was no way he could make it back to the fire escape, but he was ready."

"Ready?"

"Bigs had already found a heavy rafter and pounded down his roof spike. He'd hooked the safety line to the spindle, and he was about to jump over the side—"

"Roof spike?" I interrupted. "That's the same tool Bigs had me holding the night I came by the firehouse, right?"

"Yeah," James said.

"So what happened next?"

"Bigs saw me through the flames and he kind of waved. He was even laughing, looking forward to testing out the spike, I think. Then he jumped over the side. That's when the secondary hit—"

"Sorry. What's a secondary?"

"A second explosion. Almost as big as the first. Flames shot up from the lower floors and knocked me on my ass. I hit the fire escape and didn't stop until I kissed the ground."

"Was it the second blast that caused Bigs to fall?"

James stared straight ahead. "That's what Oat said. But that's not the way I see it. I think Bigs was murdered, Ms. Cosi, just like someone shot him with a gun."

I thought I understood. "Don't worry, James. The authorities will catch this arsonist—"

"It wasn't the arsonist." His whisper sounded more like a hiss. "It's worse than that—"

He suddenly stopped talking and his entire body tensed. I followed his stare and realized for the first time that we had an audience. Not far away, Lieutenant Oat Crowley was watching us.

Now I was tensing, too. I noticed Oat take a cigar out of his jacket and light it. Every smoker I knew used lighters. Not Oat. He'd just lit his cigar with a *wooden match*.

Oat wasn't standing alone. Another man was conversing with him—and doing most of the talking. With Oat's gaze still on James and me, he slipped the box of matches back into his hip pocket.

My mind was racing now, but I refocused on James and something significant he'd said: "What did you mean when you said Bigs was murdered? If not by the arsonist, then by whom?"

James had been staring at his lieutenant. With my question, he lowered his eyes. "Forget it, Ms. Cosi. I didn't say a thing, all right?"

"I can't forget it, James. You helped me once, now I want to—"

"Forget it," he repeated.

Oat and the other man were now approaching us. The stranger had a friendly, lopsided smile under shaggy, wheat-colored hair. A crooked line of freckles sprinkled his pug nose and his ears seemed comically large for his head. The awkward boyishness was not without charm, however, and the addition of small round glasses and laugh lines had him coming off more as an absentminded professor than a stand-in for Alfred E. Newman.

Cigar clenched between his teeth, Lieutenant Crowley wore his usual scowl. Blue smoke floated almost satanically around his head. The aroma washed over us. Not the crisp, woody scent of fine tobacco, but the sharp, rank stench of cheap stogies like the ones my bookie father used to hand out to winners, along with their pay out.

I stifled a cough as I rose to greet them.

"What are you two gossiping about?" Oat said around his cigar. The hostility radiating from the lieutenant was nothing new, but there was also *suspicion*.

The boyish bespectacled stranger picked up on the tension and stepped in fast to pump James's hand. "You're Noonan, right? We've met, haven't we? I'm Ryan Lane," he said, flashing a warm smile.

"Hello."

"Oat told me about your loss. I'm really sorry. Brewer was a real hero."

James nodded. "Thanks for that."

"No thanks necessary," Lane replied. "The sacrifice of men like Brewer is what the Fallen Firefighters Fund is all about."

Lane's practiced pitch came as no surprise. I'd noticed the name tag on his camel hair sport coat identifying him as a board member of the firefighters' charity.

"You're the woman responsible for this superb coffee, right?" Lane asked, looking at me now.

"I'm Clare Cosi. Thank you for the compliment."

"The Village Blend is a landmark. I've been there several times," he said.

I forced a smile, trying harder to remember if I'd ever waited on him.

"Excellent coffees, and a nice variety, too. Your espressos are as good as anything I've tasted in Italy. I do a cycling tour every five years." He grinned, adjusted his glasses. "Unfortunately I live and work in North Jersey right now, too far away to be a regular customer. But I buy your whole-bean coffee whenever I'm in town."

"That's nice of you to say."

"Well, I just love coffee, Ms. Cosi! I'd love to tell you about the time I visited a coffee farm—"

This Lane guy was a real talker, but I tuned out on his story the second I noticed Oat speaking to James: "So, kid, you got a shift coming up, right? You heading out soon?"

"Not yet," James replied. "Got stuff to do first."

Oat stared at James for a moment, and then his gaze shifted to me. He took the cigar out of his mouth and flicked the ashes off.

"Like what?" Oat said with a sneer, loudly enough to

make Ryan Lane pause and listen, too. "Like hitting on divorced broads ten years your senior?"

I can't believe he just said that. "Excuse me, Lieutenant?" I said. "But just what are you implying?"

Oat opened his mouth to respond when Mr. Lane (who appeared equally horrified by the man's insult) interceded. "Hey, come on, we should go," he said, touching Oat's arm. "I've got to meet and greet the organizers, you know? And the mayor's entourage is due any second."

"Right," Oat said, still openly glaring at me. Finally he stuck the cigar back in his mouth and walked off, puffing up a cloud like a two-legged dragon.

Ryan hurried to catch up, calling over his shoulder: "A pleasure to meet you, Ms. Cosi."

I waited until James and I were alone before I spoke. "How does that nice guy know Oat?"

"Ryan Lane? He works for Fairfield Equipment."

"What does Fairfield Equipment do?"

"They make rescue gear for firefighters."

"And where does Oat fit into that?"

"Well, as I understand it, Oat's father was a rookie firefighter with Ernest Fairfield back in the 1970s. Fairfield had a nose for business, and Oat's old man was a do-it-yourself type. Together they made a bundle."

"A bundle? How? Gambling?" (Given my father's bookie business, I rarely saw any other way for a working-class man to make real money.)

"Not gambling, Ms. Cosi. Patents."

"Patents?"

"A lot of the old-timers would make their own tools on the job—anything they could think of to make their lives easier. Kind of what I did with our house's kitchen, cobbled together a bunch of appliances."

"Oh, I see . . ."

"So Crowley Senior invented a lot of useful stuff, and Ernest Fairfield quit the department and started a company to manufacture it."

"And Ryan Lane works for Fairfield."

"Yeah. He showed up at our seminar a few months ago when we started training with the roof spikes."

James was shifting impatiently now. It was obvious he didn't like my new line of questioning.

"James, I'm sorry to bring this up again, but when you were talking about your friend's death earlier, you used the word *murdered*—"

"Excuse me, Ms. Cosi. I see my wife heading our way."

A moment later, I heard the fast-clicking heels of Valerie Noonan.

Twenty-six

∿∿∿∿∿∿∿∿∿∿∿∿∿∿∿∿∿∿

"JAMES, I've been looking for you all over!" Val cried, close to breathless. "*Where* did you park our car? I went to the vendors parking area on Sixteenth and—"

"Couldn't find a spot on Sixteenth," James said tightly. "The designated parking area was full."

"Oh, damn." Valerie's shoulders sunk. Her auburn French twist looked a little ragged from the March wind gusts. Her cucumber green linen suit was still crisp, but the name tag on its lapel sat askew.

"So where's the car?" she asked.

"I parked it at the St. James garage on—"

"You paid for parking?" One arm rose and fell, taking her thick clipboard with it. "That's like fifty bucks or more! You know my job situation, James. You know how tight things are going to get for us soon—"

"The fund has an expense account, doesn't it? Take the money from there. You worked hard enough for it. Why do you need the car, anyway?"

"I don't need the car. I left something in the trunk."

James exhaled hard. He took her arm. "Fine. Let's go."

"Oh, forget it now," Val said, pulling away. "I've got a crisis with the sound system on my hands. I've just got to hope that—"

"Sorry," James said, glancing at his watch. "But I ought to get back to the house."

"Oh? Okay. Well, since you're taking the car, could you stop at the store first?" Val said. "I wanted a bowl of cereal this morning and we're out of milk. Paper towels, too, and pick up—"

"I meant the *firehouse*," James said.

Val's mouth closed. Then she reached into her pocket. "You're coming to the party tonight, aren't you?" she asked, fumbling with a pack of cigarettes.

Val was referring to the post–bake sale party. Every borough was having its own for the volunteers, and I'd been invited to the one being held at a Queens pub. Mike was supposed to meet me around eight.

"I'll be there at nine, maybe sooner," James replied, his gaze was unhappily focused on Val's cigarette.

"It's at Saints and Sinners. That's in Woodside—"

"I know where it is," James said. Then he nodded in my direction. "See you tonight, Clare."

Val frowned as she watched her husband's back. I stood and touched her arm. "Are you okay? Would you like to sit down for a few minutes?"

Cigarette between her lips, Val shook her head as she flicked a disposable lighter a half-dozen times in rapid succession without coaxing a flame. She groaned and—in a broad gesture of disgust—tossed the lighter and cigarette into a Parks Department trash can.

"It's been hell since Bigsie died," she said. "James is shutting down. I can't tell his family, his friends. They don't want to hear it."

"What do you mean 'James is shutting down'?"

"He's short with me when I ask questions, he's miserable and pouting all the time, and he won't discuss what's on his mind. Not with me, anyway. He's talking to someone, though, because he disappears once in a while, goes to the garage where he has these long conversations on his cell phone."

Three in the long and tragic list of warning signs your husband is having an affair. Pretty soon he'll be going out with the guys or spending time with a client, or he just won't come home one night.

"Listen, Val, your husband is going through a really bad time, but I think——"

A loud ring tone interrupted us. I'd heard Val's cell go off many times, but I'd never heard it play this set of notes before.

"Sorry, Clare! I have to take this!"

"Sure, of course."

The tinny tune sounded like one of those club hits of the 1980s: "You Spin Me Round (Like a Record)." Val answered the cell without bothering to check the caller ID.

"Dean! I can't believe you called back . . . What? . . . You're *here*? Really?" With her free hand, Val felt the condition of her hair, adjusted her lopsided name tag. "I'm on the north side of the park, across the street from that big Barnes & Noble— Huh? Turn around?"

She did and laughed when she saw a man with sun-bronzed skin in a black leather jacket, standing right behind us, cell phone at his ear.

Val closed her phone and air-kissed the newcomer. "Thank you so much, Dean."

"My guys are at the podium right now, setting things up." Dean's voice was deep, with a slight foreign accent. *Greek?*

"You have a band?" I interrupted.

Val turned to me. "He has a sound system—and that's what I desperately needed. The one I leased for the day cut out, and their so-called technician couldn't fix it. The mayor's coming, so is the fire commissioner and a whole bunch of celebrities. I was in a total panic, so I put in a call to my old friend here . . ." She turned back to the man. "I didn't think you'd get here in time."

"My darling, you sounded so distressed on the phone that I rushed it here from Brooklyn. The nightclub's main system is permanent, you know, so I brought the portable stuff. We use it for live acts, but you're welcome to it for as long as you need it."

"I *so* appreciate this," Val said, again patting her wind-ravaged twist. "Make sure I send you a charitable giving form to fill out. You can declare your labor as a tax deduction."

Dean waved away the thought. "I did this for my dear friend, not for a tax break."

"Clare, I want you to meet the man who saved my life. Clare Cosi. This is Constantine Tassos—Dean for short."

"Nice to meet you," I said. "So you run a club?"

"Oh, yes." Dean nodded, handing over a business card in a smooth, practiced gesture. "The Blue Mirage in Bensonhurst. Actually I own several catering halls in Brooklyn and Queens, and I have two other Mirage clubs. The Purple Mirage in North Jersey—"

"And the Red Mirage in Astoria?" (It was right there on his card.)

Dean nodded. "That's correct."

He was a compact man, a little shorter than Val, with not an ounce of spare weight on his slight form. His eyes were dark and intense under unruly ebony curls. I guessed the man's age around forty, but it was only a guess. His smile looked whiter than bleached sheets, contrasting strikingly with his tanned face. *Florida golf courses or a day spa's tanning booth?* My guess was the latter, given the manicured state of his fingernails when he'd handed over his card.

"Are you a patron of my Queens establishment, Ms. Cosi?"

"I've seen the place," I replied, recalling the garish neon reflected in the wet black pavement the night Caffè Lucia went up in flames. "I met one of your managers." (The jerk who called my car a junk heap.) "And he was kind of . . . pushy."

"Ah, well, the business can do that to you. There's rough

trade around every nightclub and tavern. I'm compelled to operate with managers who know how to handle many situations, some of them ugly." His Clorox smile returned. "I hope the experience wasn't too unpleasant."

"Not at all."

"Listen, Dean," Val said, squeezing his arm. "I need to know how soon we'll have sound."

"It's probably ready," he replied. "Let's go check."

Val turned to me. "Sorry, Clare, I've got to get back to work—"

"I understand. It was a pleasure to meet you, Mr. Tassos."

"The pleasure was mine," he replied, politely shaking my hand.

I watched Val and Dean walk toward the podium. They paused for a moment, while Dean lit a cigarette for Val with a silver Ronson lighter. Then he lit one for himself. Smoking together, they strolled in the direction of the stage. I noticed Dean's hand rest familiarly on Val's waist. She did nothing to shrug him off.

After Val's tirade, I assumed James was having the affair. Now I wondered if my assumptions were misguided. Or maybe it was both partners finding sympathetic ears and arms outside of their unhappy marriage.

How sad it all seemed . . .

On my way back to the Blend's kiosk, prerecorded music blared, signaling the sound system was working again. A moment later the master of ceremonies took to the podium. Corey Parker, action-hero star of *Six Alarm!* a show about the trials and travails of the hunky men on the FDNY, was greeted by applause and whistles from the women—and a few gay men.

Finally I moved on and spied Matt standing at the door of a dingy white rental van that had seen better days.

Dante was just walking away from the truck's open side doors with an arm full of paper products. Matt doublechecked the interior to make sure it was empty.

My ex had changed out of his morning sweats, into blue jeans, retro sneakers, and a black crew-neck sweater. He'd shaved and worked on his hair, too, and as I approached, I detected the musky citrus scent of the latest French cologne—compliments of his new wife, no doubt.

"Thanks for the delivery. I'm sure Esther was frantic," I said.

I think my eyes bugged just then, because Matt stared at me with alarm.

"Clare? What's the matter?"

My attention was fixed on a sleek gold car across the street, and the two people chatting beside it. One was Oat Crowley, still puffing up a storm. The other was a woman with short, slicked-back, salon-blond hair. I felt chilly just looking at her thin capri pants and four-inch metallic gladiator sandals—such was the woman's chosen attire for this blustery March day, along with a silk scarf over a tight blouse with the kind of plunging neckline more appropriate for a night of clubbing than a day in the park. She was laughing, too, which is why it took me a moment to recognize her. The last time I saw this piece of work, she looked like she'd been sucking sour pickles.

"Matt! That's Lucia!"

"Who?"

"Lucia *Testa*, Enzo's daughter, and she's laughing it up with Oat Crowley—oh God, they're getting into her car—"

I opened the door of our rental van and shoved Matt into the driver's seat. I didn't waste time running to the passenger side and going through the door, either. I just climbed right over my ex.

"Clare, what the hell are you—"

"Quick, they're leaving!"

"But—"

"Matt, shut up and drive!"

"Drive where?"

I pointed, my finger tapping the windshield like a mad woodpecker. "Just follow that car!"

Twenty-Seven

~~~~~~~~~~~~~~~~~~~~~~~~~~

Our lumbering, weather-beaten rental van didn't have a lot of pick up—and neither did Matt's reaction time—so Lucia and Oat got a good head start. By the time we pulled away from the curb, their gilded coupe was five vehicles away, all ready to swing onto Fourteenth when the light turned green.

"Who exactly are we following?"

"The people in that car!" I pointed again. "The one with its stupid rear end sticking up!"

"Don't you know anything about cars, Clare? It's shaped that way to reduce resistance to air—"

Not that tone again! "We're too far away."

"It's a *Corvette*, by the way. Looks like a 2009 C6 model. Breanne rented one when we were in Los Angeles. Handles nicely but—"

"Enough with the *Motor Trend* review! You need to get us closer! I want to spy on them!"

"Why?"

I leveled my gaze on the man. "Because these two might be the people who threatened to torch the Village Blend."

Matt's eyes went cold and his smirk vanished. He reached into the sun visor, brought down a pair of Ray-Bans, and slipped them on.

"Buckle your seat belt."

I did. The green light flashed and Lucia's Corvette took off like a Formula One car at the Grand Prix.

"You have to make this light. Pretend you're driving in Zimbabwe."

Matt gunned the engine then slammed the brakes, throwing my torso forward then back.

What the——? In front of us, a yellow taxi stopped moving!

"Do something!" I shouted.

Matt laid on the horn. The cabbie ignored us. Completely. He was picking up a fare.

"Go around! Go around!"

Matt jerked the steering wheel. Our van abruptly nosed into the other lane, rudely cutting off an SUV. The driver blew her horn so loudly I was sure I'd go deaf, but we made it. Matt veered around the taxi and slammed the gas pedal. We sped into the intersection, swinging into the turn so violently that we tipped onto two wheels.

"Holy cats!"

My rear left the seat and my head bounced off the foam ceiling. I dropped down, along with the van, and felt another jolt as Matt hit the brakes, then wrenched the wheel to get around a slow-moving delivery truck. He plowed right through a set of construction cones, bumped us onto a closed sidewalk then off again.

"What are you doing?!"

"Zimbabwe, Clare! Remember?"

Matt made another turn, onto Third Avenue. Now we were heading uptown, our rumbling white antique weaving through traffic at twice the speed of the cars around us. Finally, he slammed the brake for another traffic light.

"And that's how it's done!"

A cocky smile appeared below his Ray-Bans, and I took

my first breath since we'd tipped onto two wheels. A single car now sat between us and Lucia.

"Thank you—"

"You're welcome."

"—for not killing us."

"Have you ever been to Zimbabwe, Clare?"

"Not lately."

"The airport minibus drivers don't like to leave until all of their seats are filled. It can take hours before they depart, then they make up for lost time by racing along lousy roads, shaky bridges, and clogged villages in excess of ninety miles an hour."

"Well, here in New York, we have a little thing called the NYPD. The last thing we need is a pull-over from a sergeant having a bad-cop hair day." I checked the mirror. No sector cars, wailing sirens, or nickel-plated badges—yet.

"Okay, start explaining," Matt said. "Why does Enzo's daughter want to burn down our Village Blend? Something you did, no doubt."

"I'm *this* close to snapping."

The light turned green, and we started uptown again, at a normal speed, thank goodness.

"Clare?" Matt said. *"Explain."*

"This Coffee Shop Arsonist is bogus. I'm sure of it."

"You're sure a terrorist threat is bogus. Right. Uh-huh. And have you told Homeland Security?"

"Matt—"

"The CIA will want to know, too. And don't forget the FBI. They get very testy when they're kept out of the loop."

"Shut up and listen! The pattern of fires makes no sense. Not for a political activist. Terrorists choose targets that have high visibility, targets that will make an impact. Enzo's place is just a small, independently owned caffè. Why would someone with an agenda target it?"

"Because the agenda's crazy—and so is the someone. Maybe this mad bomber lives near Enzo's caffè and found it a convenient target. Come on, Clare, you know very well the chain coffeehouse that burned last week has outspoken detractors all over the world. A few years ago, someone tried to bomb one in Manhattan, don't you remember?"

"Yes, I remember. And I'm sure Oat Crowley did, too."

"I don't follow."

"I think Oat set that third fire to take the heat off the investigation of the arson at Enzo's place. I think he and Lucia sent that letter to the newspaper to mislead the authorities, too."

"What about the other fire, the one in Bensonhurst, Brooklyn?" Matt challenged. "It was set the same night and practically the same time as the fire that almost killed my mother in Queens."

"I don't know about that fire. Oat may have set it as well."

"Why? How could that fire help him?"

"I don't know . . . unless they were planning this coffee shop arson thing from the start to throw off the fire marshals."

"That's a stretch."

I thought it over, glanced out the side window. "It could have been a coincidence."

"Coincidence?" Matt laughed, short and sharp. "Aren't you always quoting your flatfoot back to me when I say that?"

I slumped backward, unable to argue, and reluctant to admit (out loud, anyway) that Matt was right. Mike Quinn would never accept such a lame explanation from a fellow investigating detective. He would probably move forward by reviewing the facts related to that fire, which I didn't have. Still . . .

"I want to start with what's in front of me, okay? Oat has been acting hostile ever since he overheard me vow to find the person who set the Caffè Lucia fire. He used a *wooden match* to light his cigar in the park, a match just like the one I received as a threat. I want to see for myself where exactly Lucia and Oat are going together, what they're up to . . ."

Matt frowned, the quipless quiet an indication the man was at least considering that I might be right. "Maybe I should have brought a weapon."

"I think you've had enough run-ins with the police in this town. And don't get too close to them! They might see us."

"They don't know me, Clare, and I'm wearing shades. As usual, you're the problem. Scrunch down a little and they won't see you."

"Fine. I just don't want to miss anything."

"There's nothing to miss because these two are not lovers."

"How do you know?"

"Watch them," Matt said. "There's no evidence of intimacy that I can see . . ."

"Suddenly you're a relationship expert?" I sat up again and looked for myself. The van was high, the Corvette low, so I could easily peer through its rear window. I watched the pair as Matt eased us into the left lane at Fifty-seventh, then climbed the Queensboro bridge on ramp.

"She's laughing," I said. "She must be having fun with him—"

"She's being polite. See how stiff she is."

"Look there! She's reaching out her hand—"

"To adjust the radio. We're on the bridge now; some stations won't come in."

I folded my arms. "So why are they in a car together?"

"I didn't say there was *nothing* going on between them. The guy's clearly interested. Look at the way he's talking to her, waving his arms. He's fully engaged and really trying to connect. But she ain't buying."

"You're misinterpreting. She's stiff because driving in this city is stressful!"

Through yet another game of urban bumper cars, Matt managed to fend off vehicular interlopers and hang close to Lucia's Corvette from the lower level of the bridge all the way to a tree-lined block in Astoria.

About halfway down the sleepy side street, Lucia swung

into a driveway beside a modest, two-family home. Matt had been hanging back and now stopped the van half a block away. Together Lucia and Oat emerged from the golden coupe and climbed the porch steps. She unlocked the front door, and he followed her inside, still puffing his cigar.

"Look! Lucia let Oat smoke that cheap cigar in her Corvette, and now she's letting him stink up her apartment, too! That's *proof* she's hooking up with him."

"Or she's being polite," Matt said.

"Trust me. Lucia Testa is *not* polite."

Matt bet the pair would be out in minutes. They were in that house for well over an hour. Finally they emerged, strolling casually back onto the porch.

While they were inside, Matt and I had spent the time making up several scenarios for what they might be doing. When Lucia paused to lock her front door, however, the answer was clearer than bottled spring water. Oat stepped close behind Lucia, snaked an arm around her waist, and kissed her neck.

"Matt, look!"

Lucia let the man fondle her for a few seconds then she turned to shake a naughty-boy finger at him. Oat laughed again and lit a new cigar. Then they descended the porch steps and climbed back into her Corvette.

"Where are they going now?" Matt griped as we turned off the side street and onto the main drag of Steinway.

"Admit it, Matt. You were wrong."

He shot me a frown, admitted nothing.

A few minutes later, we were back on Northern Boulevard, then turning onto another shady block.

"I know this street," I said. "They're going to Michael Quinn's firehouse."

Lucia pulled up in front of the redbrick fortress, and Oat emerged from the car, still puffing up a noxious cloud. He walked through the open garage doors, between the two fire trucks, and vanished.

We sat, fifty feet away, waiting for Lucia to leave. But

she remained sitting in her parked vehicle. A few minutes later, Oat appeared again, carrying a bright orange shopping bag.

I sat up straighter. "Matt! Do you see that bag?"

"Yeah."

"It's the same kind of bag that Sully and Franco brought for me and Mike the night of Caffè Lucia's fire."

"What's in it?"

"Well, it's supposed to hold UFC Korean fried chicken. But I doubt very much *that* bag has chicken in it."

"Okay, I'll bite. What does it have inside, Clare?"

"Some kind of bomb-making material."

"And you think that because . . . ?"

"Oat's cigar," I pointed. "It's gone. I'm sure he was afraid to smoke while he was carrying combustible materials."

Matt didn't reply, but he didn't argue, either. He started the van's engine and rolled up behind Lucia as she left the curb.

"So where is she going now?" I said. "Where do you hide a bomb?"

"Drop down in your seat," Matt snapped. "We're right on top of her now."

I scrunched down, staying just high enough to peek over the dashboard. We followed Lucia all the way back to her place again. But she didn't park this time. As soon as we swung onto her quiet street, she suddenly braked her Corvette. We were still a half block away from her place and Matt slowed the van almost to a stop.

"What's she doing?" I whispered.

Lucia's rear lights went on, and her Corvette began backing up until it nearly struck the front of our van. The door opened and Lucia climbed out.

I sank down even farther. "What's happening? I can't see!"

"We're made, Clare. Lucia figured out I was following her."

"Is she angry?"

"No, the opposite. She's coming to my side of the car, shaking her finger and grinning."

"Grinning! Why is she grinning?"

"Because she thinks I'm trying to hit on her. She's got that flirty naughty-boy expression she had on her face with Oat." Matt smirked. "I guess she likes what she sees."

"Can you handle this?"

"Of course."

"*Without* sleeping with her?"

"I'll give it a shot."

But Matt didn't have a chance. As Lucia's metallic sandals teetered closer to our van, she spotted me. Her face flushed and she immediately shifted direction.

"Where is she going now?"

"Your side of the van," Matt said. "I hope you're ready for a cat fight."

Twenty-Eight

~~~~~~~~~~~~~~~~~~~~~~~~~~~~~

My door was yanked open before Matt finished his sentence. Lucia stood glaring. "What the hell are you doing following me?"

I sat up. "We know everything, Lucia. You might as well admit it."

"Admit what?"

"You torched your father's caffè."

"You little bitch! Come down here and say that!"

"My pleasure!"

"Oh crap," Matt muttered as I unbuckled my seat belt. I heard his door opening and closing, but I didn't look back. I jumped right down from the high vehicle, letting my low heeled boots hit the cracked concrete with a satisfying slap.

I'd forgotten how tall Lucia was. For a moment, those four-inch gladiators made me feel like a mud hen next to a flamingo. But I stood firm, leveling my sights on her heavily lined eyes. I was glad it came to this, relieved to confront her at last.

"You and Oat Crowley have been seeing each other secretly," I charged. "You persuaded him to help you set the fire in you father's caffè. I'm sure neither of you expected anyone to get hurt, but people *were* hurt. The investigation got so hot that you tried to cover up the arson by setting another fire—"

"What!"

"This time you and Oat conspired to set the blaze in a chain coffeehouse—one that's been targeted in the past by political activists. Then you sent a fake letter to the newspapers in a pathetic effort to mislead the authorities."

Lucia stood gaping at me. "You've got some imagination."

"I'm not going to let you get away with this! You father's in the hospital, Bigsby Brewer is dead—and someone is going to have to answer for that. So you might as well make it easy on yourself and confess everything to Fire Marshal Rossi. I'm sure he can cut you a deal if you're willing to testify against the man who set the bombs for you."

Lucia's eyes widened. She didn't look outraged anymore. Now she looked scared. "You're crazy!"

"Oh, yeah? Then what's in that orange shopping bag?"

"Shopping bag! What are you talking about?"

"I'll show you!" I pushed past her, went right to her car, and jerked open the passenger side door.

Lucia shouted, waved her hands. "What are you doing?"

"Proving that you were getting rid of evidence!"

"Evidence of what?"

"Of a firebomb!"

"How?"

"With this!" I opened the bag, looked inside.

Matt caught up to me, peered in, too. "Oh, brother."

"I promise you, Ms. Cosi, no one is making a firebomb out of *that*!"

Inside the bag was a smaller bag: silver with pink stripes, the name of an upscale lingerie store splashed across in script. Oat had just given Lucia a white silk-and-lace teddy, white stockings, and two garter belts—clearly a gift that would keep on giving, especially for his next booty call. The fast-food bag had been some kind of foil, probably a way to hide the gift from the guys at the firehouse.

Lucia glared down at me. "What makes you think I'd want to set fire to my father's caffè?"

"Your own father told me that you want nothing to do with it."

"I don't. I'm sorry my father was hurt in that fire—truly sorry. But I don't care a fig about the caffè going up."

"How can you say that! Your father worked his entire lifetime in that caffè. And his wall mural was astonishing!"

"Shows what you know. It was worthless."

"Worthless!"

I couldn't hold back any longer. I launched myself at the woman, ready to shake some sense into her, but a pair of strong arms hooked my waist and yanked me backward.

"Let me go, Matt!"

"Calm down! Both of you!"

Lucia pointed. "Tell *her* to calm down!"

"How can you say that your father's art was worthless?"

"It's not me who said it! I called up an art critic, had the guy come down and check it out. He said it was executed well enough, but he didn't see anything unique about it."

"How long ago was that?"

"I don't know! Five, six years."

"Your father has worked on it since then, Lucia. The new sections were groundbreaking! Don't you have any sense of aesthetics, any appreciation for his use of line, of color!"

"No!"

"No?"

"No!" Lucia shouted. "I'm color-blind!"

I stopped struggling. "What?"

Matt released me. He looked surprised, too. In the awkward silence that followed, Lucia expelled a long, weary breath. All of her fight appeared to go with it.

"My father wanted me to be a painter, Ms. Cosi, an artist like he was." She closed her eyes. "I tried. I *did*. I took the damn classes for him: beginning painting, still life, figure drawing, anatomy—I sucked at it all!"

She threw up her hands. "After that, nothing could make me care about swirls on a wall. *Nothing*. Finally, my father accepted that I wasn't going to be the next Mary Cassatt, but then he started pushing me to try all these other things: dancing, singing, acting. I had no talent for any of it. I just didn't care about that crap! I still don't!"

I exchanged a glance with Matt. This interview wasn't going at all the way I'd imagined. On the other hand, the woman's answers weren't exactly exculpatory.

"Lucia, what you've just said makes you look even more guilty. Like you had a grudge against your father and the caffè . . ."

"You still don't understand! I'm glad the caffè went up in flames because my father hasn't been happy there—not for years, not since my mother died. If it weren't for his obsessive work on that stupid mural, he would have retired, gone back to Italy to be with his sisters. He could have found some peace instead of lying in that hospital bed. God knows if he'll ever wake up again."

The woman's eyes were glistening now, tears spilling down her cheeks. Her charcoal liner began to run. I glanced at Matt again. He stepped up to offer her a handkerchief.

"Thanks."

Lucia sniffled. As she wiped her eyes, her makeup smudged. She looked like a sad raccoon, and I felt like a heel. Still, I had to ask . . .

"How am I supposed to believe anything you say? You lied about Glenn, didn't you? You claimed you were engaged to him."

"Glenn and I *are* engaged."

"Then why are you sleeping with Oat?"

"Not that it's any of your business, but Glenn hasn't given me a ring yet. He keeps saying he wants to find the right one, but I think he's stalling . . . not so sure about me yet."

Lucia shook her head, glanced in the direction of the firehouse. "Oat and I were hot and heavy once. When he started hanging around Dad's caffè again, I decided to have a little fun with him, a last little fling. I needed a break from the hospital today, and Oat's the kind of guy who can make a girl forget her troubles . . ."

"So you have no interest in Oat? You're just leading him on?"

"Oat doesn't want to get married." She waved her French tips. "He's a confirmed bachelor, just like his captain. He knows I'm just playing around, waiting for my stupid boyfriend to get off his ass and marry me. I'm actually hoping Glenn will get wind of what's going on. Nothing like a little jealousy to get a man off his behind and make him commit."

A match made in heaven. "Here." I handed the bag back to her. "If you didn't set the fire, then who do you think did?"

"Some *nut* obviously. Haven't you read the papers?"

Matt tugged my arm. "Let's go, Clare."

"Wait," I said. "One more thing, Lucia."

"What?"

"The arsonist threatened to burn down my coffeehouse. An unmarked package was left for me with a box of wooden matches inside."

I closely watched Lucia's reaction. Her raccoon eyes widened; her glossed lips parted. She looked genuinely surprised.

"I don't know whether you're telling me the truth or not," I said. "But I want you to know: I'm going to *get* this arsonist. I'm going to nail him—or her—right to the wall."

"I hope you do, Ms. Cosi," she said. "As long as you leave *me* alone and stay out of my business. Or I'll nail you to the wall with *real* nails."

"Oh, yeah?"

"Yeah!"

Matt tugged my arm again, harder this time. "Let's *go*, Clare."

As he pulled me away, Lucia returned to her Corvette and slammed the door. I watched her drive away, then I faced my ex.

"I'm not giving up."

I half expected a lecture or at the very least a smirk. Instead, Matt put his hands on my shoulders and said—

"I know you won't."

The guy always did come through when I least expected it.

Twenty-nine

~~~~~~

Hours later, the bake sale over, the Village Blend kiosk packed up and put away, I found myself back in Queens, sitting across from Val Noonan in the shamrock green booth of Saints and Sinners.

The Irish pub had all the traditional trappings: darkly paneled walls, a long bar, authentic Gallic hops on tap, and shiny brass fittings everywhere you looked. (I would have given half my New York lottery winnings for a *doppio* espresso—if I had lottery winnings—but the only coffee this pub served was Irish, so I'd ordered up a Harp.)

Val, who preferred a darker brew, was now nursing a pint of Guinness, eyes riveted on the front door, while I finished up my cell phone conversation.

"Say that again? You're going to be late because of . . . ?"

"A pizza delivery," Mike replied. "We got a last-minute tip. A delivery is scheduled for tonight. The *stuff's* coming in a pizza-delivery car, but it's *not* pizza. You follow me, sweetheart?"

"I do."

I was happy for Mike. I was. Sergeant Franco had ferreted

out a solid lead in their current case. A pizza car was the method of delivering the buffet of club drugs to key players on the construction site—at least Mike thought so. His squad still had to prove it.

"I'm sorry, Clare. I wanted to be there with you tonight, but this is the break we've been waiting for . . ."

I heard the regret in Mike's tone, followed by the barely suppressed excitement. I didn't mind. I knew how he felt—and in more ways than one.

My confrontation with Lucia left me feeling like Don Quixote again, although I wasn't kicking myself for charging a pair of stiletto heels instead of a fire-breathing beast because I'd seen Mike make the same kind of run. He and his squad would spend days, even weeks, racing after some lead only to find their well-meaning lances lodged in a windmill.

"So I won't be seeing you at all tonight?" I said, banishing any timber of disappointment.

"If this turns out to be bogus, I'll be there in an hour or two. But if we make an arrest—"

"I won't see you until morning, I know. Okay, well . . . good luck, Mike. I hope you nail them . . ." I cringed, remembering Lucia's threat to use *actual* nails on me. *Time for a new go-to catch phrase.*

"I'll miss you," I added, "but I understand."

"Thanks, Clare." Mike paused. "You know how much I appreciate what you just said, right?"

"I know . . ."

The man's ex-wife never would have been so understanding (that's what he meant). Every time Mike had to cancel, delay, or let me down because of his job, I always heard the same tension in his voice, as if he were bracing for a Leila-like tongue lashing. But he never got one. Not from me. I wasn't Leila.

"Be careful, okay?" I whispered.

"I always am."

I sighed as I hung up, not because I was left dateless for

this post–bake sale shindig. I'd hoped Mike's skills would help me loosen up James Noonan, get him to explain what he'd meant earlier today when he'd declared Bigsby Brewer was murdered. Now it was up to me alone—if James ever showed.

I glanced around the pub. The place was jammed with firemen and their wives or significant others. I'd already said my hellos to everyone I knew. Many of the faces still packing the place included guys from Michael Quinn's house: Manny Ortiz and the flirtatious Mr. Elfante. The veteran of the company, Ed Schott, was here, too . . . but no James, no Oat. Not even Captain Michael had shown—although for that I was profoundly relieved.

In the corner, an acoustic band played: singer, fiddle, frame drum, tin whistle. The scent of beer saturated the air, the cacophony of laughter and lyrics making it hard to concentrate, which was, of course, the point.

This isn't the time for thinking, Clare. This is the time for drinking . . . (Matt's words from years ago . . .)

We were young then, having a night out downtown, but I couldn't relax. I was too worried about our daughter, our bills, our books, our marriage. Matt couldn't stand that about me, and I'd spent half my life feeling bad about my nature, trying to pretend my mind wasn't working. But that time was good and over: The beverage I pushed was sobering, and I preferred to think . . .

I still suspected Oat Crowley of something here. And the more I considered it, the more I decided I wasn't totally off base with targeting Lucia as the center of the arson spree.

Oh, I believed her claim today—that she was innocent. What I didn't believe was that Oat was a confirmed bachelor. I'd seen the way he looked at her, the way he touched her. And his intimate gift of lingerie looked more romantic than risqué: He'd chosen *white*, hadn't he? Bridal white.

If Mike was sitting across from me instead of Val, he'd probably ask me for a theory on motive. Well . . .

What if Oat wants Lucia for his own, but the young car me-chanic Glenn Duffy stands in the way?

Maybe Oat was trying to do Lucia a favor—without her knowledge. Fire was his business, wasn't it? Burning down the caffè would force Lucia's father to retire and return to Italy, leaving Lucia free. And wouldn't a shocking event like a fire make Lucia see how much she needed a man in her life, a *real* man (as Enzo had referred to Oat) and not a boy like Glenn?

Getting Enzo out of the way—one way or another—already appeared to be working in Oat's favor. Lucia was clearly distressed today, but she hadn't sought out Glenn for comfort, she'd sought out Oat . . .

"What's up?" Val asked when she saw me spacing out. "You okay?"

"Sorry, yeah . . . Looks like I'm on my own."

"You and me both, sister." Val tapped her watch. "James was supposed to be here an hour ago." She pulled an even longer face and drank deeply. Then she put down her Guin-ness and clawed inside her bag for a pack of cigarettes.

"Are you going outside?" I asked. Given my position, I knew chapter and verse of the no-smoking codes of New York's Health Department.

Val closed her eyes, shoved away the pack. "I forgot. I'll go out back later . . ."

I nodded, sipped my Harp, and heard a sudden eruption of voices—

"Hey! There he is!"

"How ya, doin', Cap?"

"Glad you came!"

"Let me buy you one . . ."

The commotion was behind me, near the front door. I turned in the booth but couldn't see—too many giant male bodies.

"What's going on?" I asked Val.

"Michael Quinn is here . . ."

Crap. "Where is he exactly? Can you see?"

She silently tilted her chin. The man was striding past our booth that moment, a crowd of men around him. I couldn't see the guy, but I could almost feel his energy as he passed.

"I'm surprised he came . . ." Val said.

So was I. And I wasn't happy about it. My gaze tracked the mob across the room to the far end of the long bar. A few guys made way so Michael could have a stool. The men shook his hand, pounded his back. The bartender began to pour.

He wore jeans and a knobby fisherman's sweater, both black; *mourning* black, I realized. Behind his flame red handlebar, his complexion looked colorless. A charcoal grayness seemed to surround him now, like the creeping smoke that hissed off the caffè blaze as the engine company doused the life out of the roaring fire.

Michael abruptly glanced up from the bar. I didn't expect it. His eyes locked onto mine. He was surprised to see me here, too. I broke the connection, focused back on Val.

"He looks worn down," I said. "Worse than the last time I saw him."

"When was that?" she asked.

"At Bigsby Brewer's funeral. He's taking Bigs's death hard, isn't he? As hard as James . . ."

Val took a long sip of her dark beer. As she set the glass back down, her hand appeared to be shaking. The Irish band finished its set, and the pub suddenly got quieter, loud voices falling to murmurs and laughter becoming muted. I leaned into the table to hear Valerie's next words—

"Bigs is the first man the captain lost since 9/11. Did you know that?"

"No. I don't know all that much about Michael Quinn."

"He lost every member of his company when the first tower fell. Did you know *that*?"

"No." I risked a second glance at the man. He was knocking back a shot with one of his men. As the bartender refilled their glasses, his eyes found mine again.

"Well, Michael Quinn can be a class A jerk at times, I'll

admit. But I always cut him some slack because of what he lost."

"It must have been hard for him . . ."

"It messed him up. That's what James told me—not that he knew from personal experience. James only joined the FDNY seven years ago. But older guys like Ed Schott and Oat Crowley—they know Michael's whole story—passed it along to the younger guys on the down low."

Val glanced at her watch again, checked the door. "Where *is* James . . ."

"Why don't you try calling him again?" I suggested.

"I left *two* voice mail messages, Clare. He hasn't bothered to return either. What good will a third one do?"

"I'm sorry. I didn't mean to upset you."

She studied the table. "I think he's having an affair."

I tried to sound surprised. "What makes you say that?"

"I just think so."

"With whom?"

Val took another hit of hops, lifted her head, and stared hard at me. "Exactly how long have you known my husband?"

"Not long. The night of the Caffè Lucia fire—that's when we met."

"He talks about you a lot."

"Oh?"

"I heard you went to the firehouse, helped the guys with something?"

"Espresso making. I gave them lessons."

Her eyes narrowed. "And did my husband enjoy it?"

"Excuse me?"

"Forget it . . ." She glanced away.

"Val, look at me." I waited until she did. "I am not having an affair with your husband. I am in a very happy relationship at the moment, and I intend to keep it that way."

"I'm sorry . . ." Despite Val's words, her expression remained stony. "It's just that . . . like I told you at the bake sale, James has been acting so odd since Bigs died. I mean, I expected grief. Those two guys were really tight. But this is something else. He doesn't want comfort from me. He's just snappish and then distant . . . but mostly so angry . . ."

A portrait of James came to me then, a quixotic image of the way he'd looked in the park. A gray fog surrounded him, just like the captain, shrouding his energy. His expression was haggard yet his eyes were wary, continually glancing at Oat Crowley . . . Oat with the wooden matches . . . Oat with his scowls and insults for me . . .

What if James Noonan suspects Oat of setting that second fire to cover up the first one at Caffè Lucia? Is that what James meant when he said Bigsby Brewer was murdered? Does James suspect— or even know for a fact—that Oat is responsible?

I cleared my throat. "Val, I think I might know what's bothering your husband."

"You do?"

"He mentioned something to me at the bake sale. Something that's weighing on his mind. I'd like to talk to him about it. I'd like your help with that. Maybe if we can get him to open up—"

"Ladies! Good evening! How are you doing?"

The overly cheerful greeting was jarring, like a rodeo clown skidding into a morgue. I looked up to find a man standing there—shaggy wheat-colored hair, small round glasses.

"Hello," Val said, obviously forcing her replying smile.

"Just doing the usual rounds," the man told Val. "Two boroughs down, three to go . . ."

She shook the newcomer's hand. "Glad you could make it, Ryan."

Ryan—that's right, Ryan Lane.

I remembered the man now. He served on the board of the Fallen Firefighters Fund, the charity benefiting from today's bake sale.

Lane's camel hair jacket was gone this evening. His simple white dress shirt and sweater vest made him seem more relaxed. He still had those slightly goggle eyes beneath the glasses and ears that were too large for his head, but his

wide, lopsided grin appeared to lacquer over his uneven features with a boyish charm. I'd noticed the same effect in the
park today when he'd been talking with Oat Crowley. My
body stiffened as I realized—

Oat! This man knows Oat!

Thirty

~~~~~~

My mind racing, I vaguely registered Ryan Lane introducing the unsmiling man at his left.

"This is the battalion chief for the entire borough of Queens, Donald O'Shea."

"Good evening, ladies," the chief said, voice gruff, an impatient hand jingling change in his pocket.

O'Shea sported a salt-and-pepper flattop and an expression that appeared equally flat. His outfit reminded me of Fire Marshal Rossi's—pressed dark slacks, nylon jacket, and what looked like a white uniform shirt beneath—which meant he'd just come off duty or was just going on.

Val and I greeted him, and he immediately excused himself. "Some business," he said to Ryan and moved off.

Ryan then gestured to the woman at his right. "And this is my lovely boss, Mrs. Josephine Fairfield. Valerie, you know Josie."

Josie? Now why did that name sound familiar? She was tall and well formed with elegant almond eyes and a long, patrician nose sloped to a wide mouth of glossed cranberry. I'd seen her before. I was sure of it. *Is she a Blend customer?*

Her outfit carried that conflict of classes not uncommon among Manhattan's urban wealthy. The denims appeared stressed and worn, but the sweater was cashmere; her matching scarf—the dazzling color of a dragon fruit cactus—was patterned with front-and-backward *F*s, trumpeting the House of Fen; and her shoulder bag of polished black leather was a cool thousand if it was a penny.

"Good job overall, Valerie," Mrs. Fairfield said, her words clipped. "But the mayor had to wait *fifteen minutes* for the sound system to come online. What was *that* about?"

Val tensed. I felt for her. Over the years, I'd waited on thousands of Mrs. Fairfields, their auras vibrating like crashing cymbals as they worked overtime to advertise how very important they were. Valerie answered the woman with the same tone of pained patience I used on this perpetually displeased Clan of Narcissus.

"The city provided the public address equipment, Mrs. Fairfield. Once I realized the problem, I called my close friend Dean Tassos—he owns the Mirage clubs? Anyway, Dean drove portable equipment all the way from Brooklyn to help us out and that took time."

"Well, *next* time you should test the system out *first*, don't you think?"

Val's fingers tightened around her dark pint. "I assure you, we did test it first. Why don't *you*—"

"Josie," Ryan Lane firmly interrupted, "I'm sure we want to *congratulate* Valerie, too, don't we?"

I had to give it to Lane. He was one good executive. He'd defused Oat the very same way when the guy had been rude to me.

"All of the numbers aren't in yet," said Ryan, "but I can already tell, we had a record take with the bake sale this year."

"It must have been the coffee," Val said.

Ryan nodded. "It was outstanding, wasn't it?"

Val pointed across the booth. "Thanks to Clare."

Ryan looked confused for a second. "Oh, yes! You're the coffee lady. Sorry, I've met so many new people today . . ."

He extended his hand. I shook it.

"No problem," I said. "I'm glad it all worked out."

"Did it ever. You know—"

"I'm moving *on*, Ryan," Mrs. Fairfield announced. She turned and headed straight for the end of the bar where Michael Quinn was perched—and that's when it hit me.

I had seen Josephine Fairfield before, just not in the flesh. She was the mystery woman in those firehouse picnic photos, the ones taped to the door in Michael Quinn's company kitchen.

Mrs. Fairfield was older now, of course, her figure fuller, her free-flowing hair bobbed like a Jazz Age flapper's, but she was just as attractive as her younger self. I could still see her frozen in time with Michael's arm around her. Of course, she hadn't been dressed in designer duds in those old picnic photos, just a simple white cotton sundress. But I remembered Michael's expression—a different man, so buoyant, so carefree . . .

"I'm sorry about Josie." Ryan's voice was low. He had leaned down close to us. "She's easy to misunderstand."

Val shot me a look: *The woman is a be-yotch. How hard is that to understand?*

Ryan straightened. "Anyway, it was good seeing you ladies. Have a nice—"

"Wait!" I lunged for the man's sleeve. "Don't go!"

Ryan was taken aback, but I couldn't let him escape. I needed to question him about Oat!

"Won't you join us, Mr. Lane? For one beer, at least?"

"Uh . . ." Ryan looked worried as he glanced back toward his boss. I didn't blame him: given the level of drinking going on in this working man's bar, if Josie Fairfield treated anyone else like she'd just treated Val, she'd be getting a black shiner to go with that shiny black handbag.

"One drink," he said.

"Great!" I scooted over.

He pointed to our glasses. "But you two need a refill. Allow me—what are you drinking?"

"Let me," Val said. "I have a tab open already. Do you drink beer?"

"Sure do. I'll have what Ms. Cosi's having. Harp, right?"

I nodded. Val got up, and Ryan sat down across from me, fiddled with his cuffs. "Your coffee is quite good, Ms. Cosi, exceptional. Who's your roaster?"

"You're looking at her."

"Is that so?" He considered me with new interest. "I'd enjoy seeing your facilities one day."

"Come by anytime. I do small-batch roasting in our basement."

"You know, I fell in love with coffee years ago . . . on a trip to Nicaragua."

"Oh? I'd really enjoy hearing about it."

Okay, so I wouldn't, but as Mike often said (in a piece of advice that sounded almost culinary), grilling an informant met with much more success if you tenderized him first. So while I half listened to Ryan, I turned my peripheral eye to his boss.

Given Josephine Fairfield's past relationship with Michael Quinn, I was curious to see how he'd react at her approach. But Donald O'Shea had gotten to Michael first. The still unsmiling Queens battalion chief didn't shake Michael's hand or pat his back. They weren't sharing drinks, either. The close conversation looked official—and it didn't look pleasant.

". . . and I ended up in the Samulali region, a rather untamed area," Ryan was saying. "On that first morning, just as dawn was breaking, I drank fresh black coffee in a battered tin cup."

I nodded politely.

"The beans had been dried in the sun and roasted inside a converted oil drum, which was turned by hand over an open fire. It was almost a spiritual experience . . ."

It took me a second to register that Ryan had stopped talking.

"How interesting!" I finally said. "You know, you should

meet my partner, Matt. He's our coffee buyer and travels frequently to South and Central America."

Ryan sighed, his eyes glazing a bit. "Ever since that time, my dream was to buy my own coffee farm."

"It's not an uncommon dream," I conceded. "One of the farms we buy from is run by a former California banker who followed his passion and purchased an estate in Panama after retiring."

"I'm retiring from my job. Very soon."

Finally, an opening. "Speaking of your job, Mr. Lane, you introduced Mrs. Fairfield as your boss?"

"That's right. She is."

"That's unusual, isn't it? For a woman to be in charge of a company that makes rescue gear for firefighters?"

"It was her husband's company. He passed away last year and she took over. But it's just an interim thing. She has no real interest in the business . . ."

"Is that right?"

"Yes, a larger corporation is in the process of evaluating us. In another month or so the purchase of Fairfield Equipment should go through without a hitch."

"Is that a good thing? The company being bought?"

"Oh, yes. It's really just a big infusion of cash and resources. We'll have the opportunity to expand worldwide."

"That's good news, then, but I'm also wondering, Mr. Lane—"

"Ryan."

"Ryan, how well do you know Oat Crowley?"

"Well enough, I guess." He shifted uneasily, scratched the back of his head. "I'm really sorry about the things he said to you today in the park. That was uncalled for. I mean, look at you here. You're obviously friends with James's wife."

"Oat and I aren't exactly on the best of terms, but there's a reason for that and it's not James."

"Oh?"

"I have a female friend named Lucia. She's involved with Oat. Has he ever mentioned Lucia to you?"

Ryan laughed. "Oat and I aren't *that* close."

"I see. Well, Lucia is convinced that Oat's not the marrying kind. That he has no interest in settling down. Would you say that's true?"

"Odd you should ask."

"Why?"

"Any other time, I'd probably say I have no idea. But just today, in the park, when I mentioned retiring, Oat asked after my position. I don't blame him—my job's a lot less hazardous than his." He smiled. "Anyway, I agreed he'd be a good candidate for it, and he confided that he was planning to retire from the department soon. He said he was finally ready to settle down, buy a big house, maybe even start a family."

I knew it.

Crowley was after Lucia for more than the occasional booty call. He wanted to marry her. But with Enzo and Glenn standing in his way, Oat had to find a way to upset the balance in Lucia's life. The caffè fire did that—and if the authorities determined the blaze was random arson (à la some mad coffee shop bomber), then Lucia would also net a portion of a big fire-insurance pay out, a convenient nest egg for a newly married couple to put a down payment for a "nice, big house."

"Here you go, kids!"

Val was back, and in a much brighter mood. She set our topped-off pints in front of us and we toasted the successful bake sale. I was about to question Ryan further when Val waved us closer, hunching down, as if she were going to reveal who stole Salvador Dalí's *Two Balconies* out of Rio's Mansion in the Sky museum.

"So did you notice what's happening at the bar?"

"What?" Ryan and I asked together.

She pointed. "See for yourselves."

We all turned our heads to find Mrs. Josephine Fairfield, affluent owner of Fairfield Equipment, friend of New York City's illustrious mayor, putting her manicured hands all over Michael Quinn. And he did not appear happy about it. Every time she laid a paw on him, he firmly removed it.

"Now that's what I call chutzpah!" Val declared, taking a delighted swig of Guinness.

"Are they a couple again?" I asked.

"No," said Val, eyes bright. "James told me she's been calling him repeatedly, trying to get him back. It's common knowledge at the firehouse. Ever since she dumped him, he can't stand the sight of her!"

My mind flashed back to that night in the captain's office, the same evening I'd discovered his "Kevin wall." Michael had been annoyed by a personal cell call—a call from a woman named *Josie*.

"Look," Val pointed, even more amused, "she's throwing herself at the man!"

Lined up on the bar were a half-dozen shot glasses, sparkling like newly cut diamonds. Standing at the ready was a freshly opened bottle of well-aged, single-malt Irish whiskey (which probably cost as much as your average gemstone).

Josephine knocked back a shot, clearly not her first, and gave up on the patty-cake game. She began wrapping her dragon-flower designer scarf around Michael's neck. She laughed, pretending she was choking him. Then she pulled him forward, expecting a kiss. He pushed her away.

"Son of a *gun*," Ryan Lane spat. "I better get up there . . ."

Val looked surprised by Ryan's disgusted reaction, probably assuming (as I did) that the man would take a *little* delight from his haughty boss's comedown. Then again, if Fairfield Equipment was being evaluated for purchase by a worldwide corporation, seeing your half-drunken boss throw herself at an off-duty member of the FDNY wasn't exactly the optimum public relations moment.

"I'm sorry, Ryan," Val said, quickly sliding across the booth to let him out.

"Don't worry about it," he said, picking up his pint. "Thanks for the beer."

As Ryan moved toward the bar, Val sat back down and leaned across the table. "Josie Fairfield and the captain were supposed to be married. Did you know that?"

I arched an eyebrow. "The leader of the wolf pack was ready to tie the knot? When was this exactly?"

"Oh, like ten years ago," Val said. "Josie broke it off with the captain just a few months after 9/11. According to Ed Schott, she just didn't want to deal with the captain's grief. Six months later she was hooked up with a much older guy who had *a lot* more money and a lot less baggage, the head of Fairfield Equipment—"

"And now that her husband is dead, she has her freedom and her money, so—"

"She wants her first love back. It's a very old song." Val tipped her head toward the bar. "Only it looks like Michael Quinn's not in the mood to be played."

"NO! *YOU'RE* NOT LISTENING!"

Val and I froze, along with every other patron in the pub. Josie Fairfield finally lost it. She was now shouting at the top of her lungs.

Oh God, poor Michael—and poor Ryan. He stood right behind his boss, trying to talk sense into her ear, but she'd belted back too much booze. Her arm windmilled crazily, trying to wave him away.

"NO! I WANT TO KNOW—WHAT DO I HAVE TO DO? START *ANOTHER* FIRE?"

I blanched, looked to Val. *What did that mean?*

Val mouthed something, but I didn't understand her. Then we watched Michael rise from the bar, take Josie by the elbow, and calmly escort her to the pub's front door. He caught my eye as he past our booth, but I couldn't read him.

Ryan trailed behind the two. He also made fleeting eye contact with us and, brother, did he look miserable.

"What a job that guy has," Val said when they were gone. "Now I really need a smoke. You want to come?"

"Sure."

We crossed the crowded room and stepped out the back door, leaving the warm, golden light for the dark, quiet patio. The hulking outline of a large Dumpster sat a few yards away, but the prevailing smell on this dim square of concrete was stale tar. A carpet of butts had been crushed into the ground below my low-heeled boots, and I considered for a moment the hundreds of conversations (drunken and sober) that must have preceded those ends.

A laughing couple rose from a weathered, wrought iron bench, nodding a greeting as they headed inside.

Now Val and I were alone.

She dug into her bag, put a cig between her lips, and snapped her disposable lighter three times. When the tricolored flame kissed the cylinder's tip, she glanced my way.

"Want one?"

I was running on a serious caffeine deficit, so I was sorely tempted. But I'd given up nicotine once in my life, and (like my addiction to a certain ex-husband) I had no intention of fighting that battle again. I thanked her for the offer then said, "So tell me. What did Mrs. Fairfield mean when she shouted that stuff about—"

"Starting *another* fire?"

I nodded.

Val moved to the wrought iron bench and sat down, took long silent drags. "Oh, man, I needed that."

I pulled up a battered garden chair, checked for beer spills, and sat down opposite her. The metal was freezing and the cold seeped through my blue jeans to the backs of my thighs. I ignored it, along with an increasingly edgy feeling that I simply attributed to a creeping jonesing for my own drug of choice.

"So?" I pressed. "Josie Fairfield is an *arsonist*?"

"I always thought that story was just a story. Guess we know the truth—I mean, given her little drunken confession in there. But it's not unheard of, right?"

"What?"

"Come on, Clare, haven't you heard of that game the occasional *whacked-out* New York female plays? Setting a fire to meet a fireman?"

"You've got to be kidding."

Val released a delicate but toxic plume of white into the black night. "James says it probably happens a few times a year."

"And that's how Mrs. Fairfield met Michael?"

"They met when her apartment's kitchen caught fire. That's all I knew . . . before tonight, I mean—"

A muffled ring tone sounded in Val's bag: *You spin me right round, baby, right round . . .*

Val instantly brightened. She hastily dug into her handbag again then silenced the tinny eighties tune as she brought the phone to her ear.

"Hey, what's up?"

As Val chatted, I noticed she was careful not to say the name of the caller. It didn't matter. I already knew she'd set that ring tone for one very special friend.

"Hold on a second," she told Dean Tassos and turned to me. "I'm going to take this in the ladies'. Then I'm heading home. Would you give me a ride, Clare? James obviously isn't showing."

"Of course."

With unexpected relief I watched the shapely outline of Valerie's suit move into the glow of the open doorway. My wool sweater wasn't thick enough for the March night, but I liked the solitude of this smokers' patio so I folded my arms close, leaned back in the battered metal chair, and closed my eyes.

Inside the crowded pub, the band was starting up again. I had no desire to join the party. So much had happened tonight, let alone in the past ten days, that I just wanted a few minutes peace. Too bad I never got it.

"Hello, Clare."

My eyes immediately opened. A wide-shouldered silhouette loomed in the doorway, blocking most of the pub's golden light. Shifting shadows veiled the giant's face but not his identity.

"Hello, Michael."

Thirty-one

~~~~~~

"I hadn't pegged you for a smoker."

"I'm not. I was just leaving." I rose from the chair.

"Don't go. I want to talk to you."

"I don't think that's such a great idea."

"Why not? Is my cousin around? I didn't see him."

"He had to work."

"When doesn't he?"

"Like I said, I should go—"

Michael folded his arms, leaned against the doorframe, effectively blocking my exit.

The closer I stepped toward the man, the more he came out of shadow. His pasty complexion appeared to have more color now, flushed from drink or that little drama queen act with Josie or both.

"That was quite a scene in there," I said.

Michael shrugged. "Josie can't take no for answer. She never could."

"You have zero interest in her, I take it?"

"Let's just say the woman's well-cushioned life hasn't brought out the best in her character."

"I see. Well, I should go back inside . . ." I tried to step around him.

"I saw you at Bigsie's funeral," he said. "It was nice, you comin'. I'm sorry I didn't have a chance to say hello to you at the church."

"You were comforting the man's family. I'm the one who's sorry. I'm sorry for your loss . . ."

He gestured to the empty bench. "Won't you sit down with me? Just for a minute?"

I glanced over his shoulder into the crowded pub. "Val's coming back."

I folded my arms. "What's the matter, dove?" His crow's feet crinkled. "You think I'd stoop to ravishin' you in a bar's back alley?"

"When anything involves you, Michael, I don't know what to think."

"You can trust me." He crossed his heart with two fingers—the good Boy Scout. "Promise."

"I don't know. Seems to me your promises leave something to be desired."

"Maybe they do. But I need to talk to you about something important . . . About the way Bigs died."

Okay, that I didn't expect. "What can you tell me?"

He leaned down, his breath heavy with the smell of alcohol. "He was murdered."

"That's what James said."

Michael straightened. "James shouldn't have shot off his mouth."

"Please," I whispered, "talk to me. Who's responsible?"

"It's complicated . . ."

Somewhere over our heads, an unsettling thunder began. The Number 7 line was just a block away from where we stood. In midtown Manhattan the tracks were buried deep underground, but here in Queens, the subway train was elevated, periodically roaring over neighborhood streets, making quiet talk impossible. (Then again, in my experience, whenever *any* previously buried thing was brought out into the open, polite talk became impossible.)

The captain untangled his arms as he moved around me. With unsteady steps, he went to the bench, sunk heavily down. When the deafening noise finally died out, he spoke again.

"I got the evidence today, put it in a package addressed to you."

"Me?" I sat down next to him on the bench.

"I would have sent the thing to Mike, but one look at the return address and he'd surely toss it in the bin. I want you to give the package to my cousin, explain why it's important. You'll know once you look it over. Mike will listen to you. And after you're done convincin' him, you two call me and we can get this whole thing handled right."

"You want Mike's help?"

"Mikey and I have had our differences. But I know he's a good cop. To a *fault* maybe, but he's still my blood—and he's the only government official in this town I trust."

"What's that supposed to mean?"

"Never let the fire get behind you, darlin', that's what it means."

"English?"

"I can't give the evidence to any of the brass above me. Someone may have been paid off. There's no way I can know . . ."

"What's in the package? Can't you tell me?"

"Not here. Not now." He glanced at the doorway again. Shadows moved past, but none materialized. "I shouldn't even be talkin' to you. But I noticed you came here alone tonight. And you were lookin' my way an awful lot this evening . . . and I thought maybe . . ."

His eyes held mine. As I waited for him to complete his sentence, an icy breeze touched my hair. I tried not to shiver. "Well?"

"I thought maybe you were havin' second thoughts about my offer."

"You mean Atlantic City?"

"I mean me, Clare. You and me."

Oh brother. "There is no you and me. Is there even a package? Or are you playing me again?"

"What I told you in my office, Clare, that was true. I've never met a woman quite like you."

"Stop it. You're still trying to get back at Mike."

"Not this time."

"Listen to me: I've got your number. Mike told me the truth about what happened with your little brother, Kevin. The *whole* truth. You left out enough of the story to make Mike look like a cold-hearted monster. You told me that story to make me doubt him."

"Can you blame me?"

"Yes! I know you've been through terrible things in your life, Michael, terrible things . . . and I'm sorry for that. But it doesn't excuse your treatment of your cousin."

"My little brother would have been my brother in the FDNY if it wasn't for my cousin—"

"Mike had nothing to do with what happened to Kevin! Don't you get it?"

"Get what?"

"Your little brother self-destructed right before he was supposed to enter the fire academy because he was afraid."

"Afraid? Of who?"

"Of you, Michael. I'm a mother! I know!"

He just gawked at me, looking confused.

I sighed. To me it was clear as sunlit glass. Kevin and Lucia had been on the very same unhappy ride, driven by father figures who wanted them to be something they just didn't want to be.

"Kevin didn't want to join the FDNY, but he didn't want to risk your disappointment. He was terrified you'd turn your back on him. So he screwed up royally by driving drunk. He blamed the police, Mike, anyone but himself— and you bought right into it."

"If my little brother had come to me, told me how he felt,

I would have understood. I'd never turn my back on my own flesh and blood."

"You turned on your own cousin, didn't you? You've been treating Mike like the enemy, but he isn't. All you did for all these years was twist the real story until it fit into a bogus 'truth' you could live with."

Michael blinked. He suddenly looked less sure of himself. I could only hope it was because a thin wedge of insight was finally penetrating his thick cranium.

"Come on. Don't you think it's time that you two buried the hatchet?"

"Aw, darlin' . . ." He exhaled hard, rubbed the back of his neck. "There's too much bad blood between us. Years of it. Too much we did to each other. I'd like to be on level ground with my cousin again . . . I would. But Mike won't want to bury the hatchet with me—not unless it's in my skull."

"How can you say that?"

"You don't know everything." He parted his lips, pointed. "You see this gold tooth? That was Mike's right hook . . ."

"What don't I know? Tell me."

"No . . ." He held my eyes. "You tell me. Tell me why you're still sitting here now, talking to me . . . You must feel what's between us, Clare, because I can feel it . . ."

I began to answer, but somewhere above, the Number 7 train was approaching again, the insistent machinery growing louder, drowning out my words.

Michael leaned closer, his breath so saturated with whiskey I could almost feel the burn of the shot. Before I knew what was happening, the man's iron band of an arm was behind my back, crushing me close.

"Michael, no!"

He was half drunk and fumbling, more sad than dangerous. The rough brush of his handlebar mustache moved over my mouth first then down my cheek. I felt his lips at my jaw line, my neck, a hand groping my breast. I squirmed and struggled.

"Stop it right now! Stop!"

The captain froze, finally hearing me above the subway's deafening thunder. His lips moved off of my neck, his hand was no longer groping. He lifted his head and was just beginning to release me when—

"You son of a bitch!"

It was Mike—*my* Mike—standing at the pub's back door. He'd come to Saints and Sinners after all, his shout of outrage half swallowed by the unrelenting movement of the elevated subway. Before I could say a word, he launched, hauling back and punching his cousin in the side of the head.

"Mike, *don't*!"

The fire captain reeled, and Mike punched him again, this time in the gut. The captain's arms remained at his sides. He took the blows, like he knew he had it coming. Michael wasn't even trying to defend himself!

"Stop!" I shouted. "Your cousin's drunk! He didn't mean it!"

Another punch to the face.

"You'll *kill* him! Stop!"

But Mike just kept pummeling his cousin.

I ran to the pub's doorway. "HELP! SOMEONE HELP ME!"

A mob of firefighters rushed out and pulled the cousins apart. A few swings landed on Mike for payback.

"Leave him be," Michael shouted, wiping blood from his nose.

The men complied.

Mike stood there, scowling with fury. The mechanized storm had finally subsided, and the night went deadly quiet as his gaze found mine. We locked eyes—a split second in hell.

"This isn't what it looks like." My voice was raspy and far too weak. "You have to let me explain . . ."

Mike exhaled, glanced at the defensive line of firefighters, most of them his cousin's men. It was the last place he'd want to hear an explanation, and I couldn't blame him. Without a word, he turned and strode down the alley, toward the street.

"Don't leave, Mike. Come back!"

I moved to run after him, but someone caught my arm, held it firm. I turned. It was Val.

"Let him go, Clare. Let him cool off . . ."

I wheeled again, back toward Mike, but he was gone, swallowed up by the city's darkness.

Thirty-two

～～～～～～～～～～～～～～～～～～～

"**Ever** heard of a fire triangle, Clare?"

"Fire triangle?" I said, turning up the car's heater—to little effect.

Val waved her lit cigarette in the air. She'd opened her window to keep the interior from filling up, but the night had gotten colder and my clunker hadn't gotten any newer.

"Fire needs three elements to exist: fuel for it to consume; oxygen for it to breath; and heat to ignite the other two in a chain reaction—"

"Oh, right, I do know this," I said, recalling Captain Michael's little lecture the night Caffè Lucia went up.

"Well, *you*, my friend are in a fire triangle."

"Excuse me?"

"Fuel and oxygen in a room together don't do squat. But introduce heat and . . . *whammo*."

"I am *not* heat. And that wasn't supposed to happen back there. Michael and I were just talking."

Val took a drag. "Timing's like that. You can't always control it. Just like fire . . . or men."

Tell me about it. I'd already tried reaching Mike by cell

phone—*ten* tries in a row. I'd gotten voice mail every time (and I'd left multiple messages). He hadn't bothered to return even one, and my sympathy for the man was slowly turning to impatience. In another hour, it would be full-fledged anger.

"I could understand Mike being upset," I told Val, "but he should have trusted me better than that. He should have waited for an explanation instead of charging in and busting up his cousin!" I struck the steering wheel. "At least Michael didn't fight back. I have to give the man credit for that . . ."

After that one-way boxing match, the captain's men had helped him back inside the pub, where they began to clean him up. That's when Val hustled me outside, saying it was better if I got clear of the place. I didn't argue, and I knew Val's husband would be in much better shape than Michael to discuss Bigsby Brewer's death.

Now I was driving east on Roosevelt, toward the nearby neighborhood of Jackson Heights where Val shared a home with James.

The trip from Saints and Sinners wasn't long, only a few miles. When we turned onto Val's street, she pointed out her address, a redbrick row house three stories high. At the first open spot along the curb, I swerved and parked.

"You have the whole house?" I asked, impressed with the size.

"Just the first two floors," she said. "It's a rental, but we've got a lot of square footage for the money, which is good because I'm probably about four weeks away from losing my job."

"You are?"

"We have a separate garage in back, too. Come on . . ."

As I locked up the car, Val went to the front door. There was still half a cigarette left, but she snuffed it out in the base of a dying potted plant.

"James!" Val called as she strode across the tiled foyer and into the carpeted living room. The lights were blazing all

over the house and somewhere a radio was barking the play-
by-play of a basketball game.

"James!"

No answer.

"Sit down, Clare, relax. He's probably in the upstairs
bathroom. The one down here isn't working."

As Val climbed the stairs, I considered sitting down,
then reconsidered. I really needed a caffeine hit now, and if I
knew James, he had a decent supply of Arabica beans in his
cupboards.

The Noonan kitchen was neat and well appointed. No surprise, considering the way James had manned his firehouse
post. Every pot and pan hung efficiently on its pegboard
hook. A sparkling clean coffeemaker stood at attention on
the counter, its companion grinder on duty beside it. Flour
and sugar canisters were lined up by descending height and
a four-foot tall wine rack stood in the corner, fully stocked—
again, not a surprise given James's preferences.

I half smiled when my eye caught the bright orange of a
shopping bag on the floor near the trash can. *Yet another fan
of UFC Korean Fried Chicken. Val, no doubt . . .*

I was about to check the cupboards for whole bean Arabica when I noticed something on the kitchen table (other
than the lazy Susan of condiments): a single bottle of beer. A
pilsner glass sat next to it. The glass was nearly full, *nearly*
because there was no head, the frothy white bubbles had
died long ago.

But James doesn't like beer . . .

I glanced up and noticed something curious beyond the
back door window. A soft yellow light was glowing between
the cracks in a small wooden shed—the garage Val mentioned. The structure was separated from the main house by
a narrow concrete drive.

I moved to the kitchen's back door and turned the handle. It was unlocked. I exited the house, feeling the chill of
the night once more.

As I crossed the narrow drive, I became aware of a low

rumbling. But this wasn't the Number 7 train. This was the sound of an idling car engine. With every step closer to the shed, the rumbling grew louder. But why would someone want to run a car motor *inside* a garage?

Oh my God!

I lunged the last few feet to the door, tore it open, and gagged on the toxic white fog. A man's body was slumped over the steering wheel.

I stumbled back outside, choking and coughing. Taking a deep breath of fresh air, I charged back in, yanked open the car door, and used every molecule of strength to drag the big, inert body out to the cold concrete.

My heart was pumping, my adrenaline racing. Gasping violently, I turned over the unconscious man, desperate to help.

It was James Noonan, and there was no helping him. He was already dead.

Thirty-three

~~~~~~

METAL clinked against the windshield. I started at the sound. Disoriented, I licked my lips, tasted salt, and realized I'd cried myself to sleep. Then I remembered the reason and my eyes welled up all over again.

My ex-husband rapped the rain-flecked window a second time. To spur me to action, he pointed to the stainless steel thermos in his hand.

Coffee. Oh, thank goodness . . .

I sat up and popped the door lock. Matt climbed into the front passenger seat. His half-porcupine head looked like the before-and-after picture of a men's hair gel commercial; his eyes were bloodshot; and twin emotions warred on his face, an epic struggle between concern and annoyance.

Without a word he unscrewed the thermos lid and poured. I grabbed the metal cup, bolted it, held it out for more, and gulped a second. Now I knew how Val felt, taking those first drags on the smokers' patio.

"Okay, Clare," Matt said, "I'm here. What the hell is going on? You were crying so hard I couldn't understand half of what you were blubbering over the phone."

I spilled the whole awful story: the drunken pass by Mike's cousin, the unholy timing of Mike's seeing it, the ugly bar fight, then my going home with Valerie and discovering her husband's asphyxiated body in their small garage.

My hero firefighter was dead. As I described the baby pink color of James's corpse, I broke down again. Matt handed me a handkerchief then put his arm around me. When I finished getting his leather jacket good and wet, I began telling him what happened after the police arrived.

"An army of them tramped all through the Noonans' home," I said. "Detectives interviewed Val and me in separate rooms, and I told them that I believed James was murdered."

"Murdered? Why?"

"That's what the detectives wanted to know."

"And?"

"James was killed because of what he knew about Bigsby Brewer's death. I'm sure of it."

"What did he know?"

"James wouldn't tell me. That's why I went to see him. He was supposed to be at the pub, but he never showed. So I asked Val to help me try to coax the truth out of him . . . and I *know* there's a truth. Michael Quinn even confirmed it."

Matt looked about as convinced as those guys with the gold shields.

"I told the detectives to speak with the captain. They wrote his name down in their notebooks, assured me they'd follow up in the morning, but I don't know . . ." I shook my head.

"What's the matter, Clare? The cops will follow up."

"It's just that . . . despite my assuring them that James was murdered, they began looking hard for a suicide note, and unfortunately they found one—in Val's e-mail box."

"What did it say?"

"Five words. 'I am so sorry. Good-bye.' It was a text message sent from James's phone earlier in the evening."

"That's it?"

"Anyone could have written it! Especially if James had texted Val in the past. The addresses would be right there, stored inside his phone!"

"Did you tell the cops?"

"Yes," I said, "but I don't think they believed me. Val broke down at the sight of the message, sobbed openly about her husband's depression; his erratic behavior and mood swings; how James was mourning the death of his best friend, Bigsby Brewer; how hard he'd taken the loss . . ."

I met Matt's eyes. "Bigsby was a hero to me, too. He went with James into that collapsing caffè, helped save your mom and Enzo."

I paused to gulp more coffee (and cry a little more).

"Here." Matt pressed a second handkerchief into my hands (the first one he'd given me was already soaked).

With frustration I swiped at my uncontrollable waterfall. "Sorry," I said.

"Don't be. After your call, I laid in a supply." He pulled open the right side of his jacket, the inside pocket was bulging with folded handkerchiefs.

I would have burst out laughing. But it struck me as touching and I started crying all over again.

"Oh, boy . . ." Matt held on to me.

"I don't believe that lame text message," I said against his jacket. "The killer sent it. I'm sure of it."

"I don't know, Clare . . . How can you be?"

"The beer on the kitchen table." I leaned back, finally dried my eyes. "James *hated* beer. If he wanted to get drunk one last time, he had a four-foot rack of good wine he could have guzzled instead."

"People who decide to off themselves do irrational things."

"Right. So if you were going to end it all, you would add arsenic to an espresso made from freshly roasted Yirgacheffe peaberries? Or a cup of green tea brewed from a grocery store box?"

Matt scratched the back of his head. "I see your point."

"And . . . there's something else . . . As I was sitting here, waiting for you, before I nodded off?"

"What?"

"I remembered: At the bake sale in Union Square Park, I met this club guy, Dean Tassos, a 'friend' of Val's, only he was acting like more than a friend: fawning words, lingering touches, sweet looks—"

"Where are you going with this?"

"Just listen: Dean called Val while she and I were at the pub. She didn't want me to hear their conversation so she took the call in the ladies' room."

"And how do you know it was Tassos?" Matt asked.

"The ring tone—'You Spin Me Right Round' . . . Val had it set especially for him, and immediately after Dean calls her, she decides her husband isn't going to show and asks me to give her a ride home."

"So?"

"So what if Dean called Val to tell her the deed was done?"

"Come on, Clare. You're starting to suspect conspiracies 24/7."

"It makes perfect sense: Dean calls Val to tell her that James is dead. She now knows it's safe to come home, and she brings a witness, *me*. One more thing: Dean is part owner of the Mirage clubs." I dug into my bag for the business card the man gave me, handed it to Matt. "Look at the locations."

"North Jersey, Brooklyn, and—"

"Astoria! The Red Mirage club sits right next to Caffè Lucia, and their business has slowed. Before this whole thing started, I even had a run-in with one of Dean's shady managers, an argument over a parking space in front of his club. Yet when this same club was threatened by the caffè fire, this jerk was suddenly nowhere to be seen. Why? Because he knew about—or was involved in—setting the fire and was afraid of being questioned at the scene!"

I took a breath. "I think Dean's dirty. Given Val's *close*

friendship with him and her marriage to a firefighter, she may have been the one to give him the idea to torch the business next to his club so he wouldn't be accused of arson. Then the marshals would pin it on Enzo, and Red Mirage clubs would walk away scot-free with a big fire-insurance paycheck."

"Well, it didn't work out that way," Matt said.

"Yeah, because James's fire company was too good. They stopped the blaze before it spread to the nightclub, and I turned out to be a fly in the ointment, too. I witnessed the start of that fire, gave Marshal Rossi reasons to look beyond Enzo for motive. That's why they threatened me! To get me to butt out. That was the reason they set the second fire, too, the one that killed Bigsby, then sent a fake letter to the newspaper—they needed to throw off the scent."

"So why kill James?"

"Maybe James figured it all out—maybe Val slipped and James overheard a phone call with Dean. Maybe James threatened to go to the authorities unless Dean turned himself in. He and Val could have plotted to kill him to keep him quiet."

Matt rubbed his bloodshot eyes. The midnight rain had stopped by now, but the combination of chilly outside air and steamy coffee had fogged the wet car windows. The effect was far from intimate. It felt almost threatening, as if a gray curtain were closing around us.

"Okay, Clare. If you still feel that strongly in the morning, you can call the police, right? Give them your new theory? So, can we go now? I'm parked behind you. I'll drive you back to the Blend, and we'll come back here tomorrow to get your car."

"I didn't bring you here to be my chauffeur, Matt. I need you to watch my back."

"Excuse me?"

"I'm paying a visit to Mike's cousin—right now."

Matt blinked and stared. "You mean the *drunken* fire captain who felt you up and had a fistfight with your boyfriend?"

"Yes. You don't think I'd be stupid enough to confront him alone?"

"So I'm your muscle again?"

"You don't mind, do you?"

"Me? Why should I mind taking on a giant, inebriated firefighter awakened from a stupor in his own home? Presuming he isn't armed, of course. You do know how to drive to Elmhurst Hospital, right? Because I don't want to bleed to death waiting for an ambulance."

"Things won't go down like that."

"He's a Neanderthal, Clare. And your boyfriend let himself get dragged right down to his level. I see enough of this crap on my buying trips: Family feuds. Tribal wars. Old grudges flaring up into new violence. Why should I let myself get dragged in, too?"

"Because I asked you . . ." I sighed, weary of playing this card again, but . . . "I was always there for you, Matt. Remember? Your addiction, your rehab, your relapses—"

"I know you were. And for *you*, Clare, I would do anything. But this isn't for you. It's for Dudley Do-Right and his hose-wielding cousin."

"Have a heart, okay?" I said. "Someone has to tell the captain he just lost another man in his company. And I need to find out exactly what he knows about Bigsby's death."

"What makes you think he knows anything?"

"Back at the pub, when we were alone together, Michael confided that he put important evidence in a package for me."

"You've got to be kidding."

"What?"

"A minute before the randy fire captain goes octopus on you, he whispers that he has a special *package* for you."

"He didn't mean it like *that*!"

"Clare, you're so gullible. Some guys will spin anything to get you in their bed. I promise you, there's no package."

"And I promise you there is. He even confided he wanted me to show it to Mike—and I was glad to hear it. I thought it might be a way for those two to finally reconcile. I thought Mike would want that, too."

"Who cares what the flatfoot wants?" Matt threw up his hands. "Why do you want to stick your neck out for Mike Quinn anyway?"

"Because I *love* him, that's why!"

My voice sounded almost amplified in the confined space. I'd never said those words out loud before, not even to Mike, and after all I'd been through in my life, I knew Matt understood what it took for me to make that declaration. For a long moment, he fell silent.

"Okay, Clare . . ." he finally said. Lifting his arm, he used his coat sleeve to wipe away the smothering curtain. "Where does Captain O'Lunkhead live?"

"See that redbrick row house three doors down? Val told me he just moved here from Astoria about three weeks ago. He wanted to live closer to work." I pointed farther down the rain-swept street. The captain's fortresslike firehouse was just half a block away.

"And you're sure he's not on duty?" Matt asked.

"Not the way he was drinking."

Matt popped the car door. "Let's hope we can wake this guy up."

"I'll make the man some coffee," I said. "It'll be fine."

I climbed out from behind the wheel and fell into step behind my ex. As he moved to dodge a wide puddle, I caught a striking image in the blue-tinged pool: a perfect reflection of the captain's redbrick row house, only in reverse.

It was exactly how I'd paint the two cousins, I realized, as mirror images; back-to-back monochrome profiles, like Warhol's prints, cool blue and raging red. I'd always seen those men as primary colors. I understood why now. Each was singular in his own characteristics; neither able to change the other . . . *And when they mix, the shade is violence . . .*

"Clare? Are you coming?"

"There's something here . . ."

An object was floating in the puddle. *A ball of cloth?* I

bent down. No, it was a glove. In the uncertain light, it looked black, but when I picked it up, I saw it was cranberry colored. A mirrored *F* pattern was embedded in it . . . *Just like Mrs. Fairfield's House of Fen scarf.*

"What is it?" Matt asked.

"A woman's glove."

"And I care because . . . ?"

"Because"—I tilted my chin toward the second-floor windows—"it may mean we won't find Michael alone in his bed."

"Great," Matt muttered. "Another reason for the guy to be just *thrilled* with out visit."

I tucked the designer glove into the outer pocket of my handbag and followed Matt to the building's front porch. Unlike Val's row house, the three floors had been divided into three separate apartments. New tape over the bell confirmed that Michael Quinn lived on the second floor. Matt touched the button. *Nothing.* We waited and buzzed again.

"He's passed out." Matt glanced at his Breitling. "It's almost three AM and he probably won't wake up until noon."

Matt was ready to leave when I noticed the interior door hadn't closed properly. The last person to leave had left it ajar. I pushed through, entering a narrow hall. "Come on." I hit the carpeted staircase. But when I got to the top, I stopped so abruptly that Matt's nose jammed into the small of my back.

"Clare—"

"The door's open," I whispered.

Matt gripped my arm, holding me back as he stepped around me. He crossed the narrow landing, used one foot to nudge open the door a little wider. I leaned around him, peered inside.

Captain Quinn was lying facedown on the bare hardwood floor. His arms were splayed wide, legs folded over one another. His face was unrecognizable under a scarlet mask of blood. Blood pooled on the floor, too.

"No!"

Matt tried to hold me back again; I broke away hard, rushed to the captain, dropped to my knees. I touched his bloody cheek. It was still warm—and he was breathing!

"He's alive! Call for help!"

Matt pulled out his cell, dialed 911, gave the address. I yanked open Matt's leather jacket, pulled out his stack of handkerchiefs, pressed them against the bleeding wound on Michael's head.

"Your boyfriend's lucky," Matt said as he closed the phone.

"What? What did you say?" Blood was seeping through the thick wad of cloth, staining my fingertips like my oils used to.

"I said your boyfriend didn't kill his cousin. So he's lucky."

"What are you talking about? You can't *think* Mike had anything to do with this!"

Matt didn't reply. He stepped away, found some clean towels, and returned to help me staunch the bleeding.

"Neanderthals . . ." he murmured.

Thirty-Four

∾∾∾∾∾∾∾∾∾∾∾∾∾∾∾∾∾∾

Detective Sergeant Hoyt caught Matt's 911 call. He arrived with a younger, shorter detective named Ramirez and a slew of uniforms, just minutes after the paramedics. The moment the medical team carted the still-unresponsive Michael Quinn off to the ambulance, the two investigators sealed the apartment.

The detectives separated Matt and me for questioning. I remained with Detective Hoyt in the apartment while Ramirez escorted Matt downstairs.

Hoyt was a tall man, about my age with a ruddy complexion and a dramatically receding hairline that made him appear bald (from my angle below him, anyway). His ill-fitting suit was bread-crust brown, and the only design on his pineapple gold tie was a fresh coffee stain. He was thick through the middle yet his craggy face was lean. Given the hour, I half expected him to be as worn out as I was, but Hoyt was wide awake; his eyes giving off an aggressive vitality, like twin flames trapped inside a shrunken pumpkin.

His first question (beyond my name, address, and relationship to Matt) was my connection to Michael Quinn.

"He's my boyfriend's cousin," I said. "We're on friendly terms."

"And why did you pay him a visit so late?"

"One of the men in the captain's firehouse died a few hours ago, under mysterious circumstances. We came here to tell Michael about it."

I told Hoyt everything that happened regarding James Noonan, along with my theory that James's death and the captain's assault were related.

"Come again, Ms. Cosi? The Noonan case sounds like a suicide."

"I think Michael Quinn was attacked because of something he knew or something the attacker thought he might have. He spoke to me earlier this evening about a package—"

"A package? Are you talking about drugs?"

"No, the captain said he had evidence in this package, information about the death of one of the men in his firehouse." I explained about Bigsby Brewer's death, about the Coffee Shop Arsonist. "I'm sure that's why this place was ransacked."

Hoyt glanced around, scratched the back of his head with a pen tip. "Not much to ransack, you have to admit . . ."

That was true. A single recliner, a standing lamp, and a barstool subbing for a table were the extent of Michael Quinn's living room furniture. He'd set a small television on top of a stack of cardboard boxes, but the shattered unit had been knocked down and the contents of those boxes— mostly clothing—were scattered all over the parquet floor.

"Does anything appear missing?" I asked.

"We generally learn that kind of thing from the victim," Hoyt replied in a tone that indicated I'd just asked the stupidest question in the world.

"Okay, well . . . here. You better take this . . ." I dug into my handbag pocket, held out the damp glove.

"And what's this, Ms. Cosi?"

"I found it in the puddle in front of this building. I'm

betting it belongs to Mrs. Josephine Fairfield. She and the captain used to be engaged. There was a scene at the pub. He rejected her pass. I think you should question her."

The detective waved over a uniform officer who bagged the glove for the detective. "Okay, Ms. Cosi, spell that name for me. Fairfield, you said?"

"I *said*: Get the hell out of my way! I want to see my captain!"

The roaring male voice echoed up the staircase, an audio assault on my tired brain. The Bad Lieutenant was here— Oat Crowley. He'd either heard the 911 call while buffing, seen the emergency vehicles down the street, or both.

A few seconds later, Detective Ramirez appeared. He stood on the landing, just beyond the open front door. Oat Crowley loomed behind him—at more than a head taller than the detective, Crowley could easily see into the apartment.

"What the hell is *she* doing here?!" the lieutenant bellowed.

Ramirez jerked a thumb in Oat's direction, announced his name. "This guy claims to know the victim."

"Victim?" Oat said, now looking alarmed. "Where the hell is Michael Quinn?"

Hoyt narrowed his eyes on the blustering firefighter. "By now I'd say he was in the intensive care unit at Elmhurst. Unless he graduated to the morgue."

"It's her fault!" Oat rushed toward me. Hoyt blocked him, the cop in uniform stepped up to help. "I don't know what story she's telling you, but she started this thing, and her cop boyfriend obviously tried to end it—"

"You're crazy!" I shouted.

"Ask her!" he shouted right back, stabbing the air with his finger. "Ask her how she played two men against each other: my captain and Mike Quinn."

"I didn't play anybody!"

Hoyt exchanged a glance with his partner.

"You want them separated, Sarge?" Detective Ramirez asked.

"Not yet. Let's see where this goes . . ." Hoyt turned to Oat. "You clear this up, okay? Mike Quinn is the name of the *victim*."

"It's a family name," Oat said. "Michael Quinn is my captain, Mike Quinn is an NYPD detective with some hotshot squad in Manhattan. The two are first cousins—and *she's* the reason it came down to fists earlier this evening."

"How do you know about that?" I challenged. "You weren't even there."

"Half the firehouse was there, lady! It's all the shift's talking about tonight!"

"Then you haven't heard yet?" I said, hardly able to believe it. "None of you have heard about James?"

"James?" Oat said. "What about James?"

"Quiet! Both of you!" Hoyt said. Now he turned to me. "What was this fistfight about earlier in the evening, Ms. Cosi? You didn't mention it to me."

"It was nothing," I said. "A misunderstanding, that's all."

"That's what you call it?" Oat barked a laugh. "Listen to me, *Sarge*, earlier this evening, in front of a dozen witnesses, her boyfriend—Detective Mike Quinn of the NYPD—worked over his cousin at Saints and Sinners pub in Woodside after he caught her making out with him—"

"I was doing no such thing!"

"Call it what you want, honey, your lousy cop boyfriend obviously came here to *finish* the job he started on his cousin."

"Well, it didn't go down like a fistfight here," Hoyt said. "It appeared the victim was struck from behind with a blunt instrument. The attacker shook down the premises, stole the victim's watch, wallet, rifled his pockets, and then fled with the weapon."

"To make it *look* like a robbery," Oat said. "Quinn's been on the job all his life! He knows how to cover up his own crime!"

"You're wrong!" I said. "Mike might have thrown a punch

in a bar, but he would *never* ambush a man with a club, beat him into a coma."

"Calm down, Ms. Cosi," Hoyt said. "I'm just looking at all the angles, and it sounds like this fight was a heat of the moment thing, except that *you* never mentioned it, which makes it clear to me that you're far from an objective party."

"But that fight has nothing to do with what happened here," I said.

"Bull!" Oat bellowed. "There's been bad blood between the pair of them for years. A real history. Listen to me, Hoyt, you better not try to protect Detective Quinn just because he's another cop, or I'll—"

"You don't want to *threaten* me," Hoyt said, his own threat clear under the tight reply. "Just tell me about the history."

I expected Oat to spill that old Kevin Quinn story or tell Hoyt how betrayed Michael felt about his cousin quitting the fire academy. Instead, he said a name that I never expected to hear.

"Leila Quinn."

"Mike's ex-wife?" I whispered, feeling a creeping sense of dread. "What about her?"

"So your boyfriend never told you?" Surprised by my ignorance, Oat turned disgustingly smug. He played to Hoyt. "About ten years ago, my captain nailed her boyfriend's wife, Leila—a real hot broad, too, former lingerie model. The captain invited Leila down to Atlantic City for a weekend. She took him up on it. Who knows what lie she told her dumb-ass cop husband to get away for the weekend, but off she scampered making herself very available."

I felt cold inside, so cold I shivered. Matt was up the stairs by now, lingering on the landing beside a uniformed officer. Needing a friend, I met his eyes.

"Was there any violence back then?" Hoyt asked.

"Oh yeah," Oat replied. "Detective Quinn didn't find out for months. The wife finally brought it up when they were having some fight, just to stick it to Mikey, and when she

told him the truth"—Oat looked skyward and made a fist—
"*whammo*."

"Define 'whammo' please," Hoyt said.

"Your fellow detective went *nuts*, how's that? The captain's got a gold tooth in his mouth for a reason. Mike Quinn knocked out the real one."

Hoyt exchanged a long glance with Ramirez—and the sight made my stomach turn. *They're making Mike for this.*

Oat folded his arms. "That guy is no damn good. What he did to my cousin Pete, I'll never forget."

"Pete," I said. "Pete who?"

"Pete *Hogarth*," Oat replied. "My mother's family knows all about Mike Quinn. The prick framed Pete's old man on some trumped-up murder charge, planted evidence in his bird coop on the roof of his building."

"That's not true," I said, struggling now to hold my temper. Matt stepped up behind me, put a hand on my shoulder.

"What do you know about it?" Oat spat. "Quinn wasn't even a cop back then, just some rat kid with a Hardy Boys complex. He even got some phony civilian award from the mayor. The jerk was working the angles before he even set foot in the police academy, laying the groundwork to move right up the ladder."

"Pete Hogarth's father was a *killer*!" I shouted, moving fast toward Oat. The man actually took a step back. "He murdered a Dominican bodega owner in cold blood while he was robbing him—"

"Shut your mouth—"

"That's enough," Hoyt said. He turned back to me. "Ms. Cosi, can you account for Detective Quinn's whereabouts after the incident at the pub?"

"Not exactly . . . I mean, Mike left and then . . ." I swallowed. "I called him several times. He hasn't returned my calls yet, but—"

"Then you can't vouch for his whereabouts?"

"No, but I'm sure—"

"Thank you, Ms. Cosi." Hoyt turned to his partner. "Get Detective Quinn's shield number from One Police Plaza and bring him in."

"Wait!" I cried.

"He had motive and opportunity, Ms. Cosi. Unless he can come up with a credible alibi for the last couple of hours, he's going to be a person of interest in this case—"

"What about him!" I pointed at Oat. "He may have had a motive to do this. Let me tell you why—"

"I was *on duty* at the firehouse *all night*," Oat replied levelly. "We had three runs, and every man I worked with is a witness. Go ahead, check me out. Have fun wasting your time."

Oh God. I turned back to Hoyt. "You have to listen to me. Mike didn't do this. The captain had evidence in this apartment—"

"Yes, I already have your statement about that. We'll keep that in mind. Thank you for your help," Hoyt said, waving over a uniformed officer. "You and your business associate are free to go now—"

"But—"

"Now."

The uniform stepped up, hand on the butt of his night stick.

"Come on, Clare," Matt said, tugging my arm. He deliberately moved his body between me and the smirking Oat Crowley. Good thing, too. I was close to ripping the lieutenant's face off.

Outside, several police cars surrounded the apartment building. It was 4 AM, still pitch-dark, but the spectacle had drawn a cluster of gossiping neighbors, coats thrown over robes and pajamas. We stepped clear of it all and headed back to the Honda.

"Now I know why . . ." I said, voice hoarse.

"Why what?"

"I was angry with Mike for reacting so violently behind the pub, but I didn't know about Leila . . . I didn't know what his wife did to him behind his back."

I stopped walking, faced Matt. "I can understand why the captain didn't tell me. He wanted to play me. But why didn't Mike tell me the truth?"

"I'll tell you why. He was ashamed."

"Of what?"

Matt tilted his head back, as if he were going to read me the answer in the stars. "You women talk endlessly about your problems. With your girlfriends, your sisters, your mothers. Talk, talk, talk. But men aren't like that. Mike didn't tell you about his wife going to bed with his cousin because he was ashamed and embarrassed."

"If he had told me, I would have understood."

"Clare . . ." Now Matt was rubbing his neck, as if he were struggling to translate Portuguese into Mandarin. "If I know Dudley Do-Right—and I think I do—whatever he kept from you . . . he did it because he wanted your love, not your pity."

I nodded then whispered, "So now what do I do?"

"Well, Clare, if I know you—and I think I do—you don't give up."

Then my ex-husband, business partner, and oldest friend put his hand against my back and pressed me into forward motion again.

THIRTY-FIVE

~~~~~~

An hour later, dawn broke—although it was hard to tell. Beyond the French doors of my Village Blend, gray buildings met gray clouds in an unending urban haze. Even the sun was too weary to shine.

"How bad is it?" I asked the men sitting across from me. I wasn't due to open for another hour, but I already had two customers: Detective Finbar "Sully" Sullivan, Mike's right-hand man on his OD Squad; and Emmanuel Franco, his younger, street-wise protégé.

"How bad is it?" Franco echoed. "On a scale of one to ten: I'd say a ten."

"The man's not dead," Sully countered. "He's just in custody."

Franco shook his shaved head. "He's charged, which means he's dead to the department, and for a guy like Mike Quinn, when they take away your shield, they might as well put you in the ground."

I closed my eyes, from anguish as much as exhaustion. Matteo was sacked out upstairs. But I couldn't rest, not with Mike in hell. *What awful thoughts must be going through his mind and heart? Is he cursing me now? Sorry he ever met me, ever walked into my coffeehouse?*

"Guys . . ." I said, unable to stop a few tears from spilling out, "isn't there *any* way for me to see Mike? Talk to him?"

Sully reached across the café table, squeezed my hand. "I'm sorry, Clare. We can't even talk to him."

"Or work his case," Franco noted.

"But you can," Sully said.

"His case?" I opened my eyes, wiped my wet cheeks.

Beyond the Blend's windows, a ray of gold had broken through the morning fog, giving Sully's carrot-colored cop hair an almost rousing vibrancy. The man's shared glance with Franco, however, remained darkly pensive.

"You're a civilian," Sully reminded me. "IAB and the Department of Investigations can't sack you for turning up some leads to exonerate him."

"But I already have," I said. "That's why I called you two."

The detectives exchanged glances again, but their expressions were no longer pensive. Now they looked hopeful.

"What have you got?" Sully asked, leaning forward.

"I have three theories," I said.

"Good, let's hear them."

"Okay, but first . . . I need some coffee." I rose from the table. "You guys want some?"

"Are you kidding?" said Franco.

"Please," said Sully.

"A bite to eat would be nice, too," added Franco.

Sully whacked the back of his billiard-ball head. "Don't be an ass."

"Hey, it's not my fault the Coffee Lady makes excellent baked goods! I can see where her daughter gets her, uh"—he waggled his eyebrows—"talent."

I stared at the man. "Detective, you *are* talking about my daughter's *cooking* right?"

"Of course," Franco said, although the wink he threw to Sully gave me pause.

"Well, you're in luck," I called, moving behind the counter. "The pastry delivery just came, and I have some warm pistachio muffins back here. I gave the recipe to my baker for St. Patrick's Day, but the customers liked them so much they asked me to keep them on the menu."

"I'll have three!" Franco said.

"I actually wouldn't mind a couple," Sully added.

Franco snorted. "And I get a head whack? For what?"

"Just for being you."

Ten minutes later, we were sipping hot mugs of my freshly roasted Breakfast Blend, devouring a half-dozen of my warm, green pistachio muffins, and going over my theories on Mike's case.

"Theory number one," I began. "The Crazy Girlfriend. Josephine Fairfield's glove outside the captain's house truly gives me the creeps. The woman already admitted to being an arsonist—in a bar full of firefighters, no less. And she was acting lovesick at the pub. I could easily see her waiting for Michael Quinn at his apartment. Maybe he was harsher with her in his own place, maybe he even slapped her or pushed her, and she retaliated by grabbing an object and braining him with it before running off. What do you think?"

"I think it doesn't answer why the captain's apartment was ransacked," said Sully.

"Yeah," said Franco. "Whoever put down Captain Quinn did it with a cool head."

"And a ruthless one," Sully noted.

Franco agreed. "While the man's lying there, presumably bleeding to death, this scumbag preps the scene to look like a break-in robbery."

"Well, if you want ruthless, I have the perfect candidate," I said. "Theory number two: the Bad Lieutenant."

I told them all about Lucia Testa's secret love affair with Lieutenant Oat Crowley and his possible motive for setting fire to her father's caffè (winning Lucia as his wife along with a fat fire-insurance inheritance that would help feather his retirement nest).

"But why would he attack the captain?" Sully asked.

"Because Michael Quinn had evidence against him," I said. "When James's best friend died during that chain coffeehouse fire, I think James got suspicious of Oat. So he went to the captain with some kind of evidence. Oat got wind of it and eliminated both men. The only problem is Oat's alibi. He claims he was on duty all night and his crew will verify it."

"So how could he have killed James and attacked Michael Quinn?" Sully asked.

"He might have slipped away," I suggested (weakly).

Sully and Franco glanced at each other. *Doubtful.*

"What else have you got?" Sully asked.

"Theory number three: the Fireman's Wife and the Arsonist . . ."

The stars of my third scenario were Valerie Noonan and Dean Tassos. I laid out Dean's motives for arson and Val's desire to see her husband gone. As I talked, Sully and Franco both leaned farther forward in their chairs. The glances they shared felt increasingly energized.

". . . and I think those two set the chain coffeehouse fire and sent a fake letter to the papers to throw off the authorities," I said. "If James Noonan knew about Dean's arson and gave evidence to the captain, Val could have tipped off Dean. She may not have killed her husband with her own hands, but she could have agreed to look the other way while Dean murdered James and made it look like a suicide, then beat down Michael Quinn and made it look like a robbery."

"I think she's got something here," said Sully.

"So do I," said Franco, "and it makes a *helluvalot* more sense than Homeland Security's current theory."

"Is that who's in charge of the arson investigation now?" I asked.

Sully nodded. "They're all over the threat you got here at

the Blend. Word is they're making a case against some anti-caffeine fanatic connected to one of your customers."

"Which customer?"

"Barry something or other."

"You've got to be kidding," I said. "Barry wouldn't hurt a fly. And it's hard for me to believe he'd hook up with a bomb-setting terrorist."

"That's the rumor," said Sully. "This friend of Barry's supposedly has a checkered history and some memberships in activist groups that have gone nuclear in the past. He lives in an apartment near the chain coffeehouse that burned, was seen near Caffè Lucia the day of that fire, and has friends near the coffeehouse in Brooklyn that went up—that's where the backpack was purchased that held the package that threatened you. I'm not supposed to know any of this, of course, and neither are you, Clare."

I blinked. "Who am I going to tell?"

"Your friend Barry for starters," Sully said flatly. "So tell him to get a good lawyer for his boyfriend."

Off my shocked look, Sully simply shrugged. "I'm ready to hang with Mike."

"No!" I said. "I don't want anybody to hang!"

"*Ladies!*" Franco sang. "Before you two get your panties in a twist over Barry and his buddy, can we come up with a strike plan?"

"Yeah . . ." Sully shot him a sour look. "And let's make sure it's better than our last one."

"Hey, Sully, my intel was golden. Last night's op failed because those dealers are smarter than the badges who conducted the stop-and-search. The drugs are *in* that pizza delivery car. I *know* it."

"You know it, but you're the only one," said Sully. "Try, try, again, Detective . . ."

It took me a moment to catch up: These two were talking about their squad's operation last night, the one that went down badly or else Mike would never have shown up at

Saints and Sinners. Val had called it "bad timing." I closed my eyes again, wondering what else it was.

"Clare, you okay?" Sully asked.

"No," I whispered. "I'm thinking about Mike again and what happened last night in Queens . . ."

"Well, don't beat yourself up. After our op went down in flames, Franco was almost made, which meant his life was endangered, not just his cover. Believe me, Clare, by the end of it all, Mike was ready to punch out a choirboy, never mind the cousin who pawed you up."

I opened my eyes. "Do you think Mike knows I never meant for it to happen? Does he know I'm not Leila?"

Sully put a hand on my shoulder. "Of course he does. Mike knows who you are, Clare. And he knows who his cousin is."

"Mike trusts me?"

"Not just trusts, Clare. The man loves you. When he lost it last night at that pub, the reason was his cousin, not you."

"Yeah . . ." Franco shifted, scratched the side of his head. "What he said."

"So have you got anything more on this guy, Tassos?" Sully asked.

"Just his business card." I went to my bag, brought it over.

Franco nodded as soon as he saw it. "I know this club. The Blue Mirage? It's in Bensonhurst, Brooklyn, on the *same block* as the coffeehouse that burned down."

"That's two connections," Sully looked to me. "Right, Clare?"

"That's right." The pieces were falling into place. "Lorenzo Testa was hassled by guys from the Red Mirage club. The neighborhood busybody confirmed that to me the night of the fire."

"How about the coffeehouse owner in Brooklyn?" Franco asked. "Was he hassled by Mirage club goons, too? That'll seal the deal."

"I don't know."

"You have to find out," Sully said. "Do you know the owner's name?"

"Jason Wren. He was at the bake sale yesterday. One of my baristas even pointed him out to me. I could kick myself for not speaking to the man then, finding out more about his fire . . ."

"Take it easy," Sully said. "You didn't have these other leads then. Now you do. Just don't let this guy Wren clam up on you."

Easier said than done. "I don't know anything about this man. I mean, I could confide that my own coffeehouse was threatened, but if he's been threatened in the past, he might ask me why I'm not getting answers from the police, then start to wonder if I'm working for Dean Tassos . . ."

"She's right," said Franco. "We need an angle for her."

"I've seen Wren give interviews on television," I said, thinking it through. "If I could get him to believe I'm a reporter, I could actually get his statements about any threats from Tassos or his people on tape."

"Do you need a video camera?" Franco asked.

"My barista Dante Silva is a serious painter. He has a lot of friends in the art world. He could probably borrow something convincing, act like my cameraman. I just need a credible way to set it up . . ."

We drank more coffee, discussed some options. None seemed very strong. Finally, the shop's front bell jangled.

"Well, hello, gang!" Tucker called, his actor's basso booming through the quiet shop. "What's up? Will I read about it . . . *in the papers?*"

As my assistant manager waved his favorite New York tabloid, he continued talking about the headlines in a perfect Pat Kiernan accent. *Pat Kiernan, the famous local anchorman. Pat Kiernan the well-known voice of NY1.*

Sully and I exchanged glances. Franco smiled.

"Oh, Tucker . . ." I sang. "I need a little favor."

Thirty-Six

~~~~~~~~~~~~~~~~~~~~~~~~~~~~~~~~~~~~~~~

"**Mr.** Wren?" I called. "I'm Clare . . . Clare Stanwyck."

(The alias wasn't my idea. The name came to Tucker as a last minute improvisation. "It's a lock, Clare. I think intrigue and I channel Barbara's performance in *Double Indemnity*." At least Tuck didn't ask me to wear an ankle bracelet—although he did suggest the business suit and stacked heels. I also agreed to the blond wig. A drag queen customer was nice enough to drop it off. It did make me look more "TV polished," and if Dean Tassos saw me on the street, it would cloud immediate recognition.)

"Hey, there!" Jason Wren rose from the floor. He had been using an acetylene torch on the base of a booth in his restored shop. Now he turned off the blue-white flame, yanked off his safety googles, and dropped them next to a box of matches. "You're the people from New York One, right? I spoke with Pat Kiernan this morning about your coming."

Even in my stacked heels, Wren was much taller than I. He pumped my hand, then pulled off his flameproof apron and took his time rolling up the sleeves of a scarlet University of Phoenix tee. His eyes were smoky brown, his hair cut into a spiky mop, and a barbed-wire tattoo ringed one leanly muscled arm.

I placed his biological age at thirty—but when I realized he was watching me for a reaction to his working man's strip-tease, I placed his mental age as much younger.

"Hang on a second," Wren said.

Four flat screens adorned the shop walls. Each was broadcasting the same drag racing sequence from *The Fast and the Furious*. Wren fiddled with a remote control. The screens went blank. He ejected the DVD and tossed it on a pile of films, all of which involved car racing, with the odd exception of the Alfred Hitchcock classic *Strangers on a Train*.

"So, what do you think of Speedway Pizza?" Wren asked as he popped in a new DVD. Now the screens lit up with an animated loop of his logo revving up and driving away.

I glanced around the unfinished interior. The walls were white with red racing stripes, the tiled floor looked like a black-and-white checkerboard flag. In the window, a neon sign welcomed customers: *Speedway Pizza: Home of the Cone*.

I wasn't all that surprised the man's coffeehouse was now a pizzeria. Before Dante and I had driven to Brooklyn, I'd dug up every article I could find on Jason Wren. He never mentioned threats, but he did say that his shop was so badly damaged by the fire he decided to make a "big change."

"You're smart, Mr. Wren," said Dante, who was acting the part of my cameraman. "With the Blue Mirage next door, you should do well. Boozing and raving make people *real* hungry. I worked a pizzeria on club row. We spun dough until five AM."

Wren happily nodded at the comment.

I was glad Dante said something positive. This neighborhood had changed so much since I'd last visited that I had no idea what businesses would work here anymore. Years ago, a little Italian bistro sat on the corner of Avenue P. That bistro was now an Asian karaoke bar. The old-time movie palace was now a Dim Sum Palace Buffet, and the Italian pork store now hawked Chinese herbs.

"So what are you working on today, Mr. Wren?" I asked, warming him up with an easy one.

"Installing booths for my customers," Wren said. "I'm using partial shells of restored classics. That's a Trans Am over there, that's a 'Vette, and over there's a Pontiac Firebird."

"I'm seeing a theme here."

"You're seeing a franchise, Ms. Stanwyck. These booths, this décor, it's all going to be trademarked. This is only the first Speedway Pizza. The first of many."

"Impressive," I said.

He preened. "After I hooked into the cone pizza idea, the rest was easy."

"Cone pizza?" I said. "I assumed you were doing a combo pizza/ice-cream shop thing. You aren't actually going to serve pizza—"

"In a cone?" Dante finished.

"You got it!" Wren fired twin finger guns at us. "The crust is a cone. The cheese, sauce, and toppings are melted inside. I'm putting cone holders in the booths for convenience. They're trademarked, too."

"Cool," Dante said unconvincingly.

"Best of all, no ovens!" Wren grinned.

I blinked. "No—"

"Ovens?" Dante finished.

"All done in a microwave," Wren said with a nod. "In Europe they make cone crust from scratch, but Americans only care about the filling, right? So *my* cones are really more like a cracker than a crust. They come prepackaged, too. No more training baristas for weeks on an espresso machine. A one-armed monkey can learn to make my cone pizza in five minutes!"

Dante and I exchanged looks. *Now there's an inspiring motto.*

Wren paused. "Hey, is this the interview?"

"No, but . . ." I glanced at Dante. "We can get started now."

Dante looked around the shop. "Why don't you stand here, beside your porcelain Godzillas?"

"Dude!" Wren said. "Godzilla is Japanese. Those are Chinese dragons. Nine of them. For luck. My cousin's traditional, says they'll bring fortune to my new business . . ." He waved a dismissive hand. "I'm going to replace them before I open." Wren pointed to a burnt orange chassis. "Shoot me by the Firebird. I'll sit on the hood."

"Sure, okay," Dante said, shouldering the camera again.

"So, Mr. Jason Wren," I said into the microphone, "it looks like you're off to a great start rebuilding after the fire. You must have had lots of help. Did the insurance company jump in for a rescue?"

"Rescue?" Wren laughed. "Dealing with the insurance company involves miles of red tape, but with the arsonist coming forward in the papers, my situation should be resolved pretty quickly now."

"But without an insurance settlement, how could you afford all of this? Were you maybe . . . *forced* to take on business partners?"

"I had some cash saved. Enough to get started."

"What about the other business leaders in the community? Has the owner of the Dim Sum Palace offered to help? How about Mr. Dean Tassos from the Blue Mirage next door? Has he helped you? Or has Mr. Tassos and his club presented a problem for you? Now or in the past?"

"Well . . ." Wren's brows knitted. "I don't know Mr. Tassos, only by name. And the club guys are pretty good neighbors . . ."

Great . . . Now what?

"Mostly I'm doing the work myself," Wren went on. "I used to work in a junkyard and later at an auto-body shop. And some of my friends have helped. One of them was here earlier. He ducked out for lunch."

"I see . . ." *Come on, Clare, another question.* "I, uh, I guess you're eating cone pizza for lunch, then?"

"Soon!" He laughed, pointed to a bright orange shopping bag. "I grabbed some Korean fried chicken on my way to work. That's the way it is when you're trying to get your business started. You work all the time!"

"Let's talk about the arsonist who torched your coffee business." *Okay, here we go . . .* "Any thoughts about who that person might be?"

"None at all. I just hope they get caught. I don't want anyone else hurt."

"Do you think the arsonist was one of your customers, Mr. Wren? Did you get a warning letter or a threatening message? A *package* in a *backpack*, maybe? Another coffeehouse received a threat like that. Did you know?"

Wren's demeanor immediately changed. His open, friendly face went rigid; his smoky brown eyes went cold. "I didn't read about any packages in backpacks or see anything like that on TV. How do you know about it?"

"Surely you read the arsonist's letter. It was published. Do you—"

Wren abruptly stood. "I don't want to talk about the arsonist. I've talked enough about that—with the fire marshals, the insurance people, a whole army of officials. I thought you were here to talk about my *new* business."

"Well, I just wanted to clarify—"

"You know what? I have major work to do today so maybe you better go."

I glanced at Dante. "I think we have enough."

We couldn't gather our stuff together fast enough for Mr. Wren, who looked at his watch three times before he hustled us back onto the sidewalk.

"He made us, right?" Dante said.

"Are you kidding? The guy didn't even ask when his piece would air."

The wind kicked up and I shivered. Dawn's heavy gray clouds had ripened into an afternoon storm front. Holding down my wig, I glanced back through the pizzeria's plate glass window. Jason Wren was making a cell call. *Now who is he contacting so quickly after our interview?*

"There must be some real motor heads around here," Dante said, nudging me. "Check out that sweet number across the street."

The restored Mustang hadn't been parked there when we'd arrived. I would have noticed. The coupe gleamed redder than strawberries in a newly glazed tart. The convertible top and leather interior were white as castor sugar. Racing stripes ran from bumper to fender, and rising on the hood was a classic bonnet scoop.

"Are you okay, boss?" Dante asked. "You look a little pale, or maybe it's the makeup. I'm not used to you wearing any."

"That car," I whispered. "I've seen it before . . ."

"Really?"

"That's Glenn Duffy's car. I'm sure of it."

"That's an odd coincidence—"

"It's not a coincidence." I faced Dante. "I had the right triangle all along—but the wrong guy!"

"What?"

"Listen," I said, excited now. "Wren was using matches to light his torch; Glenn Duffy's car is parked across the street; and that old Hitchcock film that I saw inside? It was completely out of place with those car racing movies."

Dante stared down at me. "Okay. I think you officially lost it."

"No, I found it. I found our arsonists." A chilly drop of rain splashed on the end of my nose. I ignored it. "Have you ever seen *Strangers on a Train?*"

"I'm into David Lynch."

"It's the story of two men who meet during a rail trip. One wants to marry his lover, but he can't get a divorce. The other wants somebody dead so he can inherit a fortune. One suggests they swap murders."

"Boss, maybe I'm slow, but—"

"Jason Wren is friends with Glenn Duffy. Glenn is the

man who stepped out for lunch! Don't you see? The two swapped arson jobs. Jason burned Caffè Lucia. Glenn burned Wren's business."

"How does swapping jobs help them?"

"Alibis, Dante. The day the firebomb was set in Queens, Glenn could have set up an all-day alibi in *Brooklyn*. Then he picks up Lucia in plain sight at the Queens caffè and is off to Jersey. If there's no sign of the guy anywhere near Caffè Lucia that day—even that week—how could he have set the firebomb?"

"And Jason Wren?"

"Same thing, only he sets up an alibi in Queens. Makes it impossible for a Brooklyn fire marshal to pin the firebomb on him."

"What about the threat for you?"

"One of these guys must have set me up with that package the same night the other one set the bomb in the chain coffeehouse. Then they sent a fake letter to the papers to make it all look like some crazed fanatic . . ."

The wind was blowing harder now, the big drops falling faster.

"Okay, boss, you convinced me. So can we go back to the car now?" Dante eyed the violet sky. A white-hot slash seared the dark canvas. "I can't let this camera get drenched. I borrowed it from a friend—"

"Here, take my keys," I said. "Put the camera in the trunk and come right back. I have to see Glenn Duffy for myself. Once I confirm his association with Wren, I can go to Fire Marshal Rossi with it."

Dante took off at a run, shielding the camera with his coat. Unfortunately, we'd parked over three blocks away— so Wren wouldn't see that we'd arrived in my clunker instead of a news van.

I went back to the corner and crossed the street. The water was really coming down now, and I was getting very wet, but I had to get a closer look.

Thunder rumbled a warning. I stepped up to the Mustang anyway, peered into the side window, hoping to spy some identifying item, solve my problems faster. That's when I felt it, hard and cold, pressing into my back.

"It's a nine-millimeter, Ms. Cosi," the man's voice informed me. "That's a gun, in case you didn't know."

"What do you want?"

Glenn Duffy reached around fast, opened the car door. "Get in. Move." I could see the gun in his hand now. He held it low, aimed at my belly. "I said *move!*"

I moved.

"Crawl across. Get behind the wheel."

Oh God. Isn't anyone seeing what's happening to me? I looked up and down the street, but the storm had cleared the sidewalks.

"Buckle up," Glenn insisted, ignoring his own belt.

Everything felt hyper-real. I could smell the dampness of the raindrops, the sharp peppermint scent of the gum Glenn must have discarded before he ambushed me. I forced myself to stop staring at his weapon, lifted my gaze to meet his eyes. The boyish, blond Elvis was gone; the younger man's bland, amiable expression was replaced with a mask of frustrated rage.

"How did you know?" I asked.

"Jason called me. When I saw you staring at my ride across the street, I knew I was made . . . Christ, Jason thinks he's the brains, but he was duped by a reporter act and a bad wig. What a publicity hog."

"Don't do this. You're just making things worse for yourself. Why don't you——"

"Why don't you *shut up?*" He reached over, shoved a key into the ignition and turned it. "Drive. We're going somewhere to talk things over. *Maybe* we can reach an understanding."

I pulled away from the curb, frantically glancing in the rear view mirror, praying I'd see Dante. But there was no sign of him. Was Jason Wren going to take care of my barista while Glenn kidnapped me? *Oh God . . .*

I swallowed hard. "Where to?"

"Stay on Bay Parkway."

I tried again to engage him: "So whose idea was it to copy *Strangers on a Train*?"

Glenn snorted. "That boring movie? That was Jason's idea."

"That's right," I said. "You said *he* was the brains."

"Shut up and drive!"

I counted to three. "It's obvious you burned Jason's business, and he burned Enzo's place. Wren gets to start a cone pizza franchise with his insurance money. What do you get out of it?"

"I get Lucia and her insurance money."

"Lucia Testa? You've got to be kidding. She's Oat Crowley's sex toy. Do you know Crowley? He's a fireman."

Glenn's face flushed. "You think you're telling me something I don't know? I smelled that cheap cigar smoke in Lucy's 'Vette. But that'll change once I get her over to Jersey, away from her sneering old man, away from this city and that fat fireman!"

The low rise buildings were gone now. We were driving through a lonely stretch of two-lane road bordered on either side by rusty chain-link fencing.

Oh God, I know where's he's taking me . . .

The flat, featureless acreage of Washington Cemetery was so isolated it seemed almost rural. The only indication we were driving through one of the world's most populated cities was the elevated subway ahead of us and the Art Deco towers of the Veranzano Narrows looming like pale headstones on the hazy horizon. A lone vehicle rolled maybe five hundred feet in front of us—a city garbage truck.

"Make the next left," Glenn said. "It'll take you right through the cemetery gate. Nice private place for us to have our little talk."

We weren't going to talk and I knew it. Once I pulled into that graveyard, I was never coming out—a sacrifice to the fast-food franchise dreams of Jason Wren and the twisted love of Glenn Duffy.

Do something, Clare . . .

Ahead, the huge garbage truck pulled over to the side of the road. Two men jumped out and flanked a large metal Dumpster. The driver stayed in the cab, began lowering the lift.

"Pass them nice and slow," Glenn warned.

"Slow, okay . . ." At the edge of my vision, I saw Glenn shifting. He was moving the gun from one hand to the other!

NOW, Clare! Do it NOW!

I slammed my foot so hard on the gas pedal I broke my stacked heel. The Mustang shot forward, tires spinning on the wet pavement. We fishtailed into the other lane, then back again.

Duffy shouted obscenities but he didn't shoot (or couldn't). Instead, he threw himself at me, tried to punch the brake. I impaled his foot with my other heel while I pressed the horn and held it.

The impact came in seconds, but at least I was wearing my seat belt. Glenn wasn't so lucky. Like fragile candy the Mustang's front end crumpled against the mammoth truck. The windshield shattered as a large object flew through space—Glenn Duffy's body.

God knows where the gun landed.

The sanitation crew was shouting at me or each other; I couldn't tell. They were speaking English, but nothing registered, just my own hard breathing, the hiss of the shattered radiator, and the occasional moan from Duffy.

I unbuckled my seat belt, stumbled out, and pointed at the groaning hood hanging off the ruined hood.

"Lady, are you okay?" one of the men asked.

"Call the police," I said. "That man is a killer."

Thirty-Seven

∾∾∾∾∾∾∾∾∾∾∾∾∾∾∾∾∾∾∾∾

Clare . . ."

My eyes were happily closed, my body stretched out beneath the warm, soft bedcovers. A man's voice was calling my name. I felt his strong hand on my shoulder. I smiled, waiting to feel more.

"Mmmm . . . Mike?"

"Clare! Wake up!"

I opened my eyes. My ex-husband was shaking my shoulder. He stood beside the bed, holding out my cell. "It's that detective, the one you mentioned before you hit the sack. Sullivan something . . ."

"Sully!" I sat up, grabbed the phone. "What's going on? Is Mike free? Tell me this is over."

"I've got good news and bad news."

"Good news. Please. I could use some."

"You bagged your firebugs, Clare. Much to the dismay of a few smug suits and a whole team of Feds, the case of the Coffee Shop Arsonist is now closed."

"Duffy and Wren confessed?"

"Yeah, those two geniuses broke when the boys in Brooklyn played one against the other. The shields told Jason Wren that Glenn Duffy confessed on his 'deathbed'—that's what they called it, even though the little punk is going to be just fine. Then they turned around and told Duffy that Wren blamed everything on him. Both went for plea deals and signed confessions . . ."

When Sully's positive patter stopped, so did my breathing. "A *but* is coming, right?"

"I'm sorry, Clare. What you accomplished doesn't clear Mike. Neither Wren nor Duffy had anything to do with that midnight assault on Mike's cousin. They both had solid alibis and claimed they had never heard of Captain Michael Quinn—or James Noonan, for that matter."

I glanced at Matt.

"What's wrong?" he whispered and sat down on the edge of the bed.

"What happens now?" I asked Sully.

"My hands are tied. Mike's case is with the DA and the Department of Investigations, which means Franco and I still can't go near it. We were hoping you had another theory."

I closed my eyes, took a deep breath. "I'm going to need a little time—" *And a lot of coffee.* "I'll call you back, okay?"

"That's fine," Sully said, "but listen . . . I've been put in temporary charge of the squad. We're heading over to the construction site for another all-night tour. Franco's still undercover. If you need anything, call *him*, okay? You have the number. I'll be in the surveillance truck and can't use my cell. I'll check in with you again when I get the chance."

"Wait. One more thing . . . what's next for Mike?"

"He's downtown, Clare. They're holding him in the Tombs. And unless something changes, he's going to be arraigned in the morning. The charge is attempted murder."

I think I said good-bye. When Matt called my name again, I was staring at the bedcovers, the phone still in my hand.

"Clare, are you okay? What did the guy say?"

I told him, feeling so numb I hardly even cried. My tear ducts finally went as dry as the Dead Sea.

"Come on," he said. "Get up. You'll want an espresso, right?"

"A double . . ."

An hour later, I was showered, dressed, and sitting at the Blend's bar. In an atypical switch, Matt was behind the espresso machine, pulling shots for me and our last lingering customers.

As Esther ended her shift, she gave me an unexpected hug ("You looked like you needed it, boss.") Then she told me about a roast list Tucker left on the basement work table, wrapped her mile-long black scarf around her neck, and headed into the night with her boyfriend Boris.

By now, Matt and I had gone over my theories twice, but I still couldn't be sure who'd attacked Michael Quinn or why. I considered Oat Crowley again, and I couldn't stop thinking about that House of Fen cranberry glove I found lying in the puddle.

Was it Josephine Fairfield who assaulted the captain? If she didn't, did she see something? Hear something? Know something?

"Tomorrow morning, I'll talk with Mrs. Fairfield," I decided.

"What about that mysterious package," Matt reminded me. "The one Captain Octopus claimed he had for you? Did it ever arrive?"

"No. I rifled the mail before I sacked out. Junk, bills, tax forms from the NYC Fallen Firefighters Fund, and a few invoices addressed to you. Maybe it will come tomorrow."

"Well, don't count on it," said Matt, sliding over another espresso. "Like I said, the whole thing was probably just another ploy to get you into bed—"

"Stop! Please. Let's not speak ill of the comatose, okay?"

I'd called Elmhurst earlier, but the word on Michael

Quinn wasn't good. Just like Enzo, he was in the ICU, his condition touch-and-go.

With a sigh I picked up Matt's demitasse and sipped the burnished *crema*, hoping another golden shot of warmth would revive my weary mind.

"You mentioned invoices for me?" Matt said.

"They're upstairs—check the desk in my office."

"I'll look them over after we close up." He stared at me. "You should move around a little. It'll help you think. Why don't you bake something?"

"I'd rather roast something."

"Okay," Matt said, glancing up at the sound of the front door's bell. A few final customers were just walking in. "I'm giving these orders wings. Then I'm closing up. You go on downstairs."

O︎UR back stairs were narrow but the basement was expansive—and the ambient smells incredible. Generations of coffee roasting permeated these stone walls and thick rafters, and under the overhead lights, my crimson cast-iron Probat gleamed shinier than a ladder truck.

I hit the starter button and turned up the gas, then watched the digital numbers on the infinite temperature control tick upward. A muted roar from the fans filled the enclosed space, and the chilly basement began to warm. Soon the drum would be hot enough to add the first batch of green beans.

But what to roast first?

Tucker had left me a list of the coffees we needed: our signature Espresso Blend, the smooth yet sparkling Tanzanian Peaberry, and the amazing Amaro Gayo from Ethiopia with those exotic berry overtones.

I looked over the line of drums, which held superb Arabicas from around the globe. The right kiss of heat would bring out the absolute best flavors in these green beans—and the wrong would destroy them forever.

Matt was right. The act of roasting (like cooking) held a singular magic for me. Simply warming up the roaster gave me a renewed sense of head-clearing comfort.

I was just reaching for my roasting diary when—

"Clare! Clare!" Matt's voice was so loud I could actually hear him over the roasters' lively hum. Turning, I saw him waving a sheaf of papers.

"What is that?"

"Captain Octopus wasn't playing you! That package came!"

"When? Where?"

"It was upstairs with the mail. That Fallen Firefighters Fund envelope you mentioned? The man used it as a cover. When I looked inside, I didn't find tax forms . . ."

Matt moved over to our wooden work table—the one Tucker and I used to replace coffee grinder burrs. He spread out the pages and we looked them over.

"They're schematics for some kind of tool," Matt said. "But I don't get why the guy sent these to you? Do you even know what this is?"

"It's a roof spike," I said. "I saw one at the captain's firehouse. And look what it says there: 'Property of Fairfield Equipment, Inc.'"

"There's a cover letter from someone named Kevin Quinn."

"That's Michael's brother."

Matt scanned the letter. "Kevin says he hacked into the computers of his old employer and got this evidence of product fraud."

"Old employer? Michael never mentioned his brother worked at Fairfield!" But then I remembered. He didn't— not anymore. Kevin lost his job in New York and was forced to relocate to Boston.

I read the rest of Kevin's long letter side by side with Matt.

"Jesus," Matt said. "Someone at that company replaced

the central titanium core with metal that has all the durability of a cheap furniture rod."

"It was done for profit." I pointed to the end of the letter. "The move cut production costs in half but left the roof spike with a fatal flaw. It couldn't stand up to the high levels of heat the original prototype had been tested under."

"Why would the FDNY approve it?"

"They wouldn't," I said. "I'm sure all the testing and training was done on roof spikes that had been manufactured correctly . . . Oh, Matt, that's what James meant when he said Bigsby Brewer was murdered. When Glenn Duffy and Jason Wren set that final coffeehouse fire, Bigsby was forced to use the roof spike to escape the flames. But the tool failed because someone at Fairfield changed the manufacturing specs."

"Yeah, but who?" Matt asked.

We looked over the papers again. Kevin didn't give any names.

I thought it over. "Do you remember when I found that House of Fen glove in the puddle outside of Captain Michael's apartment?"

Matt nodded.

"I think it was Josephine Fairfield's glove. When her husband died last year, she took over the company. I'll bet she changed the specs on the roof spike and found out the captain was investigating the fraud. Then she paid him a private little visit."

"Yeah." Matt nodded. "Sounds like a strong possibility."

"There's only one problem," I said, pointing to Kevin's documents. "Would a society wife be smart enough to do all this on her own?"

"None that I've ever met," Matt said. "Someone must have helped her."

I considered Oat Crowley or some other member of the FDNY. But it seemed to me the man most likely to help Josephine Fairfield execute this awful scheme was—

"Ryan Lane."

"Who?" Matt asked.

"Ryan works for Mrs. Fairfield," I explained. "He hustled her out of the pub last night when she got drunk and loud. Ryan also talked to me about retiring soon, about giving Oat Crowley his job. And he said Fairfield Equipment was on the verge of a big corporate buyout."

Matt rubbed his chin. "Cutting costs on the roof spike would definitely up the company's profits, make the operation look more valuable to a prospective buyer."

"I'll bet Lane's an officer of the company, in a position to make big money from the sale—except time ran out for him and Josie."

"What do you mean?"

"That buyout isn't final yet," I said. "So I'm guessing he and Josie simply played the odds. The roof spike worked in most situations. They took a chance there wouldn't be any catastrophic failures before they sold the company. But there was—Bigsby Brewer lost his life."

"They must know there's going to be an investigation, right?"

"Yes, but typically something like that will take weeks, maybe even months. James Noonan got suspicious right away and started making waves. He went to the captain, and they bypassed the usual time-consuming bureaucratic process. Michael Quinn used his little brother Kevin to cut to the truth. Ryan and Josie must have found out about it, assaulted Michael, and murdered James—that would buy them enough time to make a clean getaway before the truth comes out."

"But, Clare, does Josephine Fairfield even *know* James Noonan?"

"Ryan Lane does. He spoke to James at the bake sale, and I saw Lane talking to Oat Crowley, too. I'll bet Oat blabbed the whole thing about James's suspicions and the captain's investigation. Lane could have approached James after that, told him he wanted to talk. He could have gone to James's house last night under the pretense of coming clean about the roof spike—but instead Lane killed him."

"Killed him how? You said the police believe Noonan's death was a suicide."

I considered the possibilities, thought again about that glass of untouched beer on James's kitchen table, the Harp that Ryan had enjoyed at the pub. That's when I knew: "James didn't pour that beer for himself! He poured it for his killer!"

"What?"

"James hated beer. I'm sure he poured it for Ryan Lane—and Lane must have found a way to slip a drug into James's wineglass, which he would have taken with him to eliminate any evidence. That would explain the single beer on the table. If Lane was careful not to touch the glass, it would only have James's fingerprints on it. Then James passes out, Ryan hauls him to the garage and stages his suicide. Afterward, he meets up with Josie on her post–bake sale rounds and makes an appearance at Saints and Sinners to establish an alibi."

Matt frowned. "I don't know, Clare, that scenario's a little out there, don't you think? And it's not very smart. Wouldn't a drug be detected in Noonan's autopsy?"

"So what if it was? As long as the cause of death matches the manner of suicide, what difference does it make if James had a drug in his system? The case for murder is pretty thin with Val confirming her husband's depression—not to mention that suicide note." I shook my head. "The scenario I described isn't out there. It's ingenious."

"But what if Ryan Lane isn't the one who helped this Fairfield woman?"

"Well, if he didn't, then I'm sure he won't have any trouble telling a grand jury who did."

Matt thought it over. "Okay, let's do something about this. Get on the phone. Call—"

I heard a meaty smack. Matt's body went limp and fell against me. I stumbled, caught myself, but couldn't stop my ex's heavy form from sagging to the floor.

"Matt!"

"Shut up or I'll hit you, too."

One end of a Halligan tool now loomed in front of my face. I saw dried blood on it, pieces of hair. The other end of that gruesome object was in Ryan Lane's right hand. His left was pointing a gun at me.

I lifted my gaze, met his stare.

Ryan tossed the fireman's tool on the table and threw a bundle of rope at me. "Tie him up."

Thirty-Eight

~~~~~~~~~~~~~~~~~~~~~~~~~~~~~~~~~~~~~

"**He's** bleeding," I said. "He needs a doctor!"

Ryan aimed the gun at Matt's head. "He'll be dead if you don't tie him up. Anyway, I didn't whack him nearly as hard as I hit the captain."

I bit back a curse and began to tie the rope—*loosely*. Ryan caught me. "Tighter, honey. If he gets free before I leave, he's dead. And so are you."

"You're going to kill us anyway."

"Not at all!" Ryan's deceptively boyish face lit up with a grin. "I just want you indisposed while Josie and I get out of the country. After we're gone, I don't care what happens to you."

Ryan sniffed the air. "Mmm . . . coffee. The aroma is magnificent down here"—he took a deep breath—"gives me a jones, you know?"

"Let's go upstairs. I'll pull you a fresh espresso."

Ryan wiggled his gun like a naughty finger. "Nice try, Ms. Cosi, but I'm going to have to wait until I get to Williamsburg. There's a great little all night spot off the bridge. Then I'll pick up Josephine, who thinks we're going on a short business trip, and we're off on a private jet to . . . well, as long as Josie's with me, it'll be paradise . . ."

That's when I knew. "Josephine Fairfield isn't involved in any of this, is she?"

"No. She isn't."

"Then why did I find her glove outside of Michael Quinn's apartment? Did she go there last night to throw herself at him?"

"No. After we left the pub and Josie passed out in her limo, I grabbed her glove and planted it there."

"Why?"

"In case the lady gets homesick. You see, Josie didn't embezzle millions of dollars from her company. That's on me. But if the police suspect she attacked her old lover, well, that's one more nail in her coffin. And once she understands that nothing but prison time awaits her here, she'll be all too happy to keep the bed warm in my new hacienda."

Oh my God . . . This guy is Glenn Duffy in a buttoned-down shirt. Deluded, lovesick, willing to do anything to obtain a woman . . . one who obviously wants someone else.

When I finished tying Matt, Ryan checked the ropes. "Okay, your turn."

I resisted, but Ryan didn't threaten me, he *hit* me with the gun. I bounced off the floor, and he flipped me over like a steer at a rodeo. He placed his foot on the small of my back while he bound my wrists tightly, then roped my ankles together. When he was done, I struggled against the bonds.

"I like to be thorough, Ms. Cosi."

"Were you being thorough when you killed James Noonan?" I spat.

"I thought so."

"What about the captain?"

Lane sighed. "He was my biggest problem. When James told me the captain obtained evidence of my little switch on the production line, I knew I had to pay the man a visit."

"So you broke into his apartment and ambushed Michael with his own Halligan tool."

"The captain didn't have all the documents in his apartment, but—lucky for me—I found a copy of his brother's cover letter stapled to this—"

Ryan leaned over me, displayed a United States Post Office tracking slip.

"I knew the captain sent the package to this address, but I had to wait for it to arrive." He stood up straight again. "You know, a lot of people give the post office a hard time, but their tracking system is really very efficient. I knew it was delivered today, so I stopped in to retrieve it."

Ryan gathered up the letter and schematics, and stuffed them into a backpack. Then he pulled out a strange device. A large battery was connected to an alarm clock and a pair of plastic bottles filled with clear liquid. The whole thing sat on a piece of plywood the size of a small serving tray. He placed the device on the table and set the alarm clock.

"All done," Ryan said, slipping the bag over his shoulders. "In a few minutes the Coffee Shop Arsonist will strike again."

Ryan doesn't know that crime is solved. It hasn't made the news yet! "You won't get away with this! The arsonists have already been caught."

"So?" Ryan smirked. "The police will conclude this is a copycat. Bye, bye, Ms. Cosi."

With the roar of the roaster hammering my ears, I couldn't even hear the jerk's feet on the stairs—but with that bomb ticking away, I didn't bother waiting to make sure he was gone before I began to yell.

"MATT! MATT!" I nudged him with my bound up feet. "WAKE UP!"

Not even a groan. Now I was starting to sweat, from fear as much as the heat radiating from the thrumming Probat. I looked around, searching for something to cut the ropes. A rough edge, a knife, or—

A coffee grinder's burrs!

Tucker had been giving Esther lessons on how to change our burr grinder's parts. One of those parts was sticking out of a vice on the edge of the wooden work table. Was the thing sharp enough to cut through the rope around my arms? Could I even get to it?

One way to find out . . .

I rolled my body across the basement floor. When I felt my torso bump the table, I folded and turned, pressing my back against the leg. When I got my feet under me, I slid up the table leg and moved toward the vice. Balancing on my bound-together feet, I pressed the ropes against the sharp edges of the grinder's burrs and started rubbing.

It took a few minutes—and lots of abrasions to my hands and wrists—but I felt the hemp snap! When it did, I tumbled, falling across Matt's body. He moaned as I worked on my ankles. By the time I got the ropes off my ex, he was awake.

"What hit me?"

"A Halligan tool."

"A *what*?"

"Never mind. There's a bomb down here and it's about to go off."

Matt was on his feet like a shot. He stared at the device. "I don't know what to do to stop it."

"You don't have to! The city's bomb squad is right up the street!" I dug for my cell phone as I ran for the stairs. "Matt, come on!"

"Unlock the front door!" Matt cried.

"What are you going to—"

"Just do it!"

I raced up the steps and across the Blend's main floor. Ryan had left the door unlocked when he fled, and I yanked it open. Matt emerged from the stairway a second later, the bomb cradled in both hands like a harmless tray of cookies.

"Matt, you're crazy!"

"I'm not letting the Blend burn."

He bolted across the street, where a clothing store had gone bankrupt two months before. The space was being gutted and an enormous construction container sat in front of the building. That's where Matt tossed the bomb. Then he turned and ran.

The device exploded, sending an orange and red fireball into the sky, but the core of the blaze (thank goodness) was contained inside the metal box.

In the firebomb's glare, I spotted a black BMW parked down the block. Ryan Lane stood beside it. He'd been waiting to make sure his device went off! Now he was jumping into his car.

"Matt, look!" I pointed. "That guy's the bomber."

My Honda was parked in front of the Blend. I unlocked the door, slid behind the wheel, and started the engine. Matt got in beside me.

"I'm driving," he said.

"No time to switch!" I replied, hitting the gas hard.

"Fine. I'll call the cops." But patting his pockets, Matt realized he'd left his cell in my Blend office.

"Reach into my pocket and take mine," I said.

Ryan was speeding north on Hudson. He hooked a right on Clarkson Street just as the light turned red. I ignored the signal and followed, horns blaring behind me. He made another sharp right, but Matt managed to grab my cell despite the turns.

"Press six three times," I told him.

"Not 911?"

"It's my speed-dial code for Sergeant Franco."

"That jackass!"

"Tell him you're Joy's father."

"Joy? What does our daughter have to do with—"

"Remember last year's Christmas party? Remember when you told Joy to *stay away* from Franco? Bad idea!"

"Franco?" Matt said over the phone. "I'm Joy's father—"

"Tell him we're chasing the guy who assaulted Captain Quinn and murdered James Noonan! Tell him the scumbag tried to kill us and now he's fleeing the country!"

"He heard you," Matt said, and held the phone to my ear.

"He's on Delancey Street and coming your way!" I yelled. "He's heading for the Williamsburg Bridge. Watch for a black BMW!"

"This is Manhattan, Clare," Franco replied. "All the BMWs are black."

"He has a big white NYC Fallen Firefighters Fund sticker on his bumper, and I'll be right behind him in my red clunker. Where are you?"

"I just hijacked a pickup from the construction site. If your perp makes the bridge, we could lose him."

"You have to stop him, Franco! Any way you can!"

I saw the bridge lights ahead. I was closing in on Ryan's BMW, too, until a little green pizza delivery car cut in front of me. I braked to avoid a collision, and Ryan raced toward the ramp.

The delivery car sped up, too. It was hard to see Lane's BMW past the big *Jackrabbit Pizza* sign on top of the little green car, and I looked for a way around him. That's when Franco's dirty yellow pickup shot out from between two other vehicles and T-boned Ryan's BMW!

The delivery car was so close it slammed into the BMW, too. And I ran into both of them. Time crawled as I watched my hood flip open and the safety glass shatter. The shoulder strap bit into my chest, my nose flirted with the steering wheel, and my cell phone flew out of Matt's hand and right through the windshield.

Then everything got very quiet. Matt and I exchanged stunned glances. Finally, we popped our doors.

Franco, in construction clothes, stood next to the BMW, a handgun aimed at a moaning Ryan Lane.

"Are you okay?" he asked, glancing our way.

"I'm fine," I said.

"I *was* fine," Matt replied, "until I found out you're dating our daughter."

"Come again?" Franco said without shifting aim. Suddenly, the door on the pizza car opened and the driver took off at a run.

"Hey, you!" Franco shouted, but didn't try to follow, his aim stayed true.

I pointed to the wrecked pickup. "I'm sorry, Detective. Did I just blow your cover?"

"Yeah," Franco replied. "But you also solved my case."

I didn't understand what the man meant until more police arrived, Sully among them. The older detective eyed my totaled Honda and turned to me. "You have insurance, Clare?"

"Not enough to buy a new car . . ." But Mike was cleared. The cost was more than worth it.

Then Sully joined Franco, who tucked his gun away and pointed to that little pizza delivery car, a green Nissan. The vehicle was shattered in the front and rear. But Franco was more interested in the illuminated *Jackrabbit Pizza* sign on the roof, now broken loose from the car and lying on its side.

"Check it out!" Franco whacked Sully in the arm. "I told you the drugs were in the pizza car!"

A tidy hole had been cut into the Nissan's roof, a cover for the hole now swung loose on its hinges—and stuffed inside that hollow, lighted sign were dozens of plastic bags. Franco began yanking them out and opening them up. They were filled with club drugs.

Sully nodded, looking pretty pleased. "That delivery driver left the construction site when you grabbed the pickup. I think he thought you were chasing *him*."

Franco shrugged. "Hey, man. Whatever works."

Under other circumstances, that kind of slapdash philosophy might have given me pause. But considering the events of the past few days, I had to admit—

"I couldn't agree more."

THIRTY-NINE

~~~~~~~~~~~~~~~~~~~~~~~~~~~~~~~~~~~~~

"**Boy**, oh boy . . ." Michael Quinn lifted a shaky hand and touched his bandaged head. "That expensive whiskey really packs a wallop."

"It wasn't Josie's aged Irish that hit you, Michael. It was her boyfriend. A guy named Ryan Lane."

"Well, can't say as I blame him for it," he said. "Not after the way Josie was goin' on at the pub." He paused. "And I can't say as I blame my cousin for what happened the other night, either."

One of the captain's eyes was covered (the socket required reconstructive surgery), but the other appeared alert behind his bruised flesh. He gazed up at me now through that one good eye, blinking slightly at the bright morning sunlight that washed over the hospital room.

As he stirred and tried to sit up, the IV hose became tangled, and I rose from my chair to help him. "Let me adjust your bed for you," I said. As the head of the mattress elevated, he turned whiter than coconut cake.

"Ouch."

"You okay?

"Yeah, but I think I'll be payin' a little visit to that Ryan fella when I'm out of here."

"If you do, it'll be behind a sheet of Plexiglas." I adjusted his pillows. "The man's in custody—for assaulting you . . . and for killing James Noonan."

Under his scarlet moustache, Michael's lips tightened. "I still can't believe Jimmy's gone."

"I'm so sorry . . . he was a real hero, and his killer will pay. The charges against Lane are piling up. The DA's nailing him on Bigsby Brewer's death, and they're exhuming the body of Josie Fairfield's husband."

"Old man Fairfield?" The captain's one good eye squinted.

"Turns out Lane was originally trained as a pharmaceutical engineer. He whipped up some concoction that knocked James out long enough to fake the suicide, brought it to him in a bottle of wine. Apparently he used a higher dose of the stuff to murder Josie's husband. According to Josie, she and Ryan Lane had been sleeping together behind her husband's back. That's when Lane became obsessed with her. He wanted her for his own, so he killed her husband."

"The poor bastard . . ."

"But then Josie began losing interest in Lane and looking around for a new conquest—you were an oldie but goodie, Michael, and she decided she wanted to rekindle the old passion."

Michael grunted. "She was the only one . . ."

"Unfortunately, Ryan Lane had already decided to force Josie into 'retiring' with him. Given the roof spike fraud and embezzled millions, she looked as guilty as he did. Lane expected an even bigger payday in a few months when the sale of the company went through. He'd planned out his and Josie's getaway, their change of identities, their new life in South America. He'd even purchased an estate with a coffee farm."

"He must have known the roof spike would eventually fail . . ."

"I think he was counting on that. Just one more reason Josie could never return to her old life. But when Bigsby died, Lane knew his time was up. He probably could have gotten away with it—if the wheels of bureaucracy had ground as slowly as usual. But you and James messed that up, jeopardized everything. He killed James and tried to kill you to buy himself enough time to escape with Josie—and the millions he'd already stolen . . ."

I stopped talking when I realized Michael's attention had drifted.

"Noonan . . ." he whispered. "That lad's my last . . ."

"What do you mean?"

"Forget it." He shifted again. "Anyway, Clare, I want you to know . . . I'm not proud of the way I acted the other night. I owe you an apology."

"No, you don't."

"Yes, I do. And you're not the only one—"

The sound of a throat clearing stopped Michael's words. I turned to find a broad-shouldered detective leaning against the doorframe. It appeared he'd been listening a while.

Mike Quinn glanced briefly at his cousin. Then his arctic blue gaze locked onto me.

"Hi, Clare."

I couldn't find my voice.

"Sully gave me a ride over," Mike said. "Filled me in pretty good. Sorry about your car."

"I'm not."

Mike opened his arms and I went into them. When we were through embracing, I noticed Michael on the bed. Despite his pain—and for the first time since I'd arrived—the man was smiling.

Mike released me and approached his cousin. I held my breath, watching the two stare at each other.

Finally, Michael lifted his hand and held it there.

With a silent nod, Mike shook it.

EPILOGUE

~~~~~~

SIX weeks later, Madame and I were heading back over the Queensboro Bridge. This time, I'm happy to say, her art-dealer boyfriend, Otto Visser, was driving.

We were attending the opening of Osso Buco *Pronto!*—a nouvelle Italian restaurant. The location was Long Island City, but the event looked more like a gallery show in SoHo than the launch of an outer-borough eatery (even one with a Manhattan-esque ironic name). Oh, sure, there were trays of samples from the restaurant menu, and a brigade of food writers (online and print) were in attendance, but there were just as many members of the art world here, and for very good reason.

From our corner booth, Madame and I joined the applause when Lorenzo Testa appeared in a wheelchair pushed by his daughter. Grinning tearfully, he joined Dante Silva and the other young artists who had diligently worked to re-create his original mural. (For reference, they'd used blowups of the digital photos that Dante had shot just before Caffè Lucia burned.)

As Enzo rolled by to pose for the press, I caught sight of Lucia's impressive engagement ring, courtesy of Oat Crowley.

According to Madame, Enzo couldn't be happier that his daughter at last had chosen a man over a boy. (Of course, I didn't see that she had much choice, given the third point of that particular fire triangle—Glenn Duffy—was now facing twenty-five years to life.)

"What happened to your man Otto?" I asked Madame, after the restaurant's young chef-owner proposed a toast to Enzo. "I lost track of him . . ."

Madame pointed across the large, crowded space to a tall, dapper fellow, leanly built with thinning but still-golden hair. "He's over there, dear, explaining to that *New York Times* reporter how it took Dante and *six* of his friends an entire month to recreate what my old friend envisioned and painted by himself."

Madame drained her champagne flute and shot me a sly smile. "Of course, what Otto is really doing is laying the foundation for Enzo's public show this summer at his Chelsea gallery."

"Whatever works," I said (my new go-to catch phrase).

The paintings to be shown at the Otto Visser Gallery weren't new. Enzo was still weak and recovering from his stroke; it would take lots of time and therapy before he could paint again. What the world was going to see, for the first time, were the canvases Enzo had painted of his wife—a subject to which he'd lovingly devoted himself for decades. And though the artist himself remained reluctant to part with any of his creations, Enzo at least agreed to a public show, which wasn't bad publicity for Otto, either.

After a few rounds of Prosecco and trays of delightfully seasoned morsels, Madame found me again.

"So where is your noble knight this evening?"

"Another undercover operation," I said. "He phoned to tell me he's running late."

"The wheels of justice perpetually grind, don't they, dear? Well, if he doesn't make it, Otto and I will be happy to give you a lift home."

"Thanks. Matt made the same offer a little while ago—

in front of Breanne, unfortunately. I told them I'd take the subway."

"Well, he knows you don't have that little Honda anymore—"

"Yes and that's fine. I've decided to live without a car for a while. After crashing two of them in one day, I probably couldn't get affordable auto insurance, anyway."

As I sipped my sparkling wine, I noticed Tucker and Esther bantering (or bickering—who could tell?). They shared a booth with Kiki and Bahni, Dante's fawning apartment mates. The girls looked thrilled that their boy was finally getting some critical attention from the press. I was happy for Dante, too, but worried I was about to lose one of my best baristas to the fickle arms of the art world.

"Did you notice that sign across the street when we came in?" Madame asked. "It says the Pink Mirage is coming to Long Island City."

I nodded. "Dean Tassos isn't stupid. He closed the Red Mirage to relocate in this hotter area. Did I tell you that Valerie Noonan is working for him now?"

"That lovely girl from the bake sale?"

"Yes, she's overseeing the activities at all of Dean's catering halls . . ." My eye wandered back to another section of the astounding mural, one of Enzo's later editions to the sprawling piece. Madame noticed my interest.

"That particular image intrigues you, I see."

"Self-portraits always intrigue me." Enzo had painted himself into his mural, a stylized figure peering into a mirror. "But I suppose it's really two self-portraits, if you consider the mirror . . ."

"That's right . . ."

"And the face in the mirror has a different expression than the one looking in—impish, slightly mischievous. More like a dark doppelganger than a reflection."

"Yes, I see that . . . now that you mention it," Madame said, slipping on a delicate pair of glasses. She glanced at me. "So how is that fire captain?"

"The former captain, you mean. I hear he's very happy as a civilian now, up in Boston . . ."

At the urging of his little brother, Michael Quinn resigned from the FDNY and took a job consulting for the company where Kevin Quinn worked. (Now I knew what Michael meant when he'd told me that James Noonan was his last. James was the last man he intended to lose under his command.)

Madame nodded. "Best for everyone, I think, that the man's not going to be tempted to drop by the Blend for your espressos . . ."

"I agree," I said. "And I'm sure Mike would, too."

A short time later, the party wound down and the dining room emptied. I was still alone. No call from Mike, no sign of him, either.

As the lights dimmed, Madame and Otto moved to the back of the restaurant to give their final farewells—and I spotted a familiar trench coat coming through the front.

"Hi, Clare."

"Hi, Mike."

"I'm sorry, sweetheart, I wanted to get here sooner, but . . ."

"That's all right," I said. "You're here now."

Mike sniffed the air, still aromatic with butter and lemon, rosemary and thyme, sizzling seafood and caramelized garlic.

"The party's over, right?" he said.

"Why?" I asked. "You hungry?"

"Starving." He held my eyes. "Feels like I haven't eaten all day."

"I can fix that."

He smiled. "I know you can."

Then Mike reached out his hand, fingers open. I placed mine in his and we found our way home.

AFTERWORD

~~~~~~~~~~~~~~~~~~~~~~~~~~~~~~~~~~

ALTHOUGH the firefighters of New York City use plenty of specialized equipment in the course of their hazardous and heroic work, including personal escape ropes, the spike device in this novel is not one of them. As mentioned in the acknowledgments, however, a very real incident did inspire the creation of this plotline.

On January 23, 2005 (a day known in the FDNY as "Black Sunday"), two members of the department lost their lives in the line of duty—and four more were very badly injured—because they did not have escape ropes. After that terrible day, the FDNY changed its policies and now provides high-heat resistant ropes to their firefighters.

This true, tragic incident left a lasting impression on me and my husband as we began to consider how the life and death of any firefighter may hinge on something as simple as possessing a single piece of reliable equipment.

Like the spike device we invented, the charity in this book is a fictional creation, but there is a very real firefighters' charity that I'm pleased to tell you about right now.

The Terry Farrell Firefighters Fund is a nonprofit organi-

zation dedicated to providing firefighters and their families
with financial assistance for their educational, medical, and
equipment needs. This charity was formed in honor of Terry
Farrell, a decorated firefighter with FDNY Rescue 4 who
perished on September 11, 2001, while fighting fires and
rescuing victims at the World Trade Center.

Originally based in New York, this charity is currently
expanding with chapters in other areas of the country. To
find out more about the Terry Farrell Firefighters Fund,
including how you can help simply by buying a specially
labeled bottle of Jim Beam bourbon or purchasing a *California Firehouse Cookbook*, visit the fund's Web site at www
.terryfarrellfund.org.

Recipes & Tips
From the Village Blend

Visit Cleo Coyle's virtual Village Blend at
www.CoffeehouseMystery.com
for coffee tips, coffee talk, and the following *bonus* recipes:
* Crunchy-Sweet Italian Bow Tie Cookies
* St. Joseph's Day Zeppoles
* *Brutti Ma Buoni* ("Ugly but Good") Italian Cookies
* "Malfatti" (ravioli filling without the dough)
* Dutch Baby Pancake (Bismark)
* Honey-Glazed Peach Crostata with Ginger-Infused
Whipped Cream
* Mini Italian-Style Coffeehouse Cakes
(with Coffeehouse-Inspired Glazes)
* Pistachio Muffins
* "Stuck on You" Linzer Hearts
* Three-Alarm Buffalo Wings with
Extinguisher Gorgonzola Dip
* Puerto Rican-Style *Pernil* (Pork Shoulder)
And more . . .

GUIDE TO ROASTING COFFEE

~~~~~~~~~~~~~~~~~~~~~~~~~~~~~~~~~~~

COFFEE roasting is the culinary art of applying heat to green coffee beans in order to develop their flavor before grinding and brewing. The entire process is highly complex, but this brief guide should give you a helpful overview—as well as something to consider the next time you sit down to enjoy a cup of joe.

Factors of flavor: According to food chemists, roasted coffee has one of the most complicated flavor profiles of all foods and beverages with over eight hundred substances contributing. Many factors influence the taste of the coffee you drink. Coffee beans grown in different microclimates of the world, for example, will display vastly different characteristics with flavors that may range from deep notes of chocolate to bright overtones of lemon.

Botany also plays a role. Coffee comes from a plant (genus *Coffea*) with ninety different species. Only two of those species (*Coffea arabica* and *Coffea robusta*) are primarily grown as cash crops, but different varietals (or cultivars) within those species are cultivated all over the world. Kona, Geisha, Blue Mountain, and Bourbon are just four examples of the many Arabica varietals.

Finally, the journey coffee takes from the seed to your cup will also influence its flavor. Let's begin our coffee trek with . . .

The coffee cherry: Your cup of joe begins its life as a seed or pit within the fruit or "cherry" on a coffee plant. (The coffee plant is often called a tree but is really a shrub.) The cherries on the coffee plant will ripen from green to yellow to red. They are then picked, either by hand or machine.

The coffee bean: Each coffee cherry contains two green coffee beans, which grow with their flat sides facing each other. The exception is the coffee cherry that contains a "peaberry," which is a single, rounded seed. (The peaberry is rarer and for a variety or reasons considered to be of better quality than regular coffee beans.) Once coffee is picked, it must be "processed" as soon as possible to prevent spoilage.

Processing: Most coffee drinkers never consider this unglamorous step in the seed-to-cup journey, but how coffee is processed can greatly affect its final flavor. Before the hard green coffee beans can be roasted (which will turn them brown), they must be extracted from the skin and pulp (or flesh) of the fruit surrounding them. This is usually done by a dry, wet, or semidry processing method.

Dry, natural, or unwashed processing: This method of processing coffee is the oldest and is still used in many countries where water resources are limited. After the cherries are picked, they are spread out to dry in the sun for several weeks. The outer layer of dried skin and pulp is then stripped away, usually by machine. This method is used in Ethiopia, Brazil, Haiti, Paraguay, India, and Ecuador. Because these beans are dried while still in contact with the coffee fruit, they tend to have more exotic flavor profiles than wet processed coffee. They often display more fruity or floral characteristics, for example, and are heavier in body.

Wet or washed processing: Special equipment and large quantities of water are needed to execute this processing method, which gradually strips away the layers of soft fruit that surround the hard coffee beans. The beans are then dried in the sun or machine dried in large tumblers. This processing method, used in major Latin American coffee-growing countries (except Brazil), produces more consistent, cleaner, and brighter flavored coffees than the dry method.

Semidry or pulped processing: This method is a kind of combo of both. Water is used to remove the skin of the fruit but not the pulp (or flesh), which is left on and allowed to dry on the bean. After it is dried, the pulp is removed by machine. This method, which is used in Brazil and (a variation of it) in Indonesia, produces coffee that has the fruity and floral notes of dry processing with the clarity of wet processing.

Home roasting: After green coffee is fully processed, it is ready for roasting. Until the early twentieth century, coffee was primarily roasted in the home, over fires or on stoves, using pans or hand-turned drum appliances. In the eighteenth, nineteenth, and early twentieth centuries, stores and caffès also used small "shop roasters" (also called microroasters) to roast fresh coffee for their customers.

As the twentieth century progressed, however, coffee roasting became a major commercial endeavor. Preground, packaged coffee roasted in factories overwhelmed the market. Home roasting disappeared along with most small shop roasters until late in the twentieth century when coffee drinkers rediscovered the superior quality of freshly roasted coffee. Now the United States and other industrialized countries are enjoying a Renaissance of "small batch" or "boutique" roasting.

These days, a variety of small appliances are available that allow you to roast your own green coffee at home. To learn more, visit the Sweet Maria Web site, which sells home roasting equipment, green beans, and includes information for the home roasting enthusiast: www.sweetmarias.com. Kenneth Davids's excellent book *Home Coffee Roasting* is another great resource.

Roasting Stages

Given all of the factors that can influence a coffee's flavor, roasting has the greatest impact. As Clare well knew from her Village Blend roasting room, "The right kiss of heat would bring out the absolute best flavors in these green beans—and the wrong would destroy them forever."

The roasting itself goes relatively quickly, 11 to 18 minutes. Here is a short list of very basic steps that should give you a general overview of a typical *small-batch* roasting process.

Stage 1—Raw Green Coffee: The green, grassy-smelling beans are released from the roaster's hopper into its large drum. The drum continually turns the beans to keep them from scorching. As the beans dry and cook, they start to turn yellow to yellow-orange in color and give off aromas like toasted bread, popcorn, or buttery vegetables.

Stage 2—Light, Cinnamon, New England–Style: As they continue to roast, sugars start to caramelize and the beans begin to smell more like roasting coffee. At around 400°F, the small, hard green bean doubles in size, becomes a light brown color, and gives off a popping or cracking sound, which is why this stage is called "the first crack" stage. What the master roaster is seeing now is the change in the chemical composition of the bean. (The process is called *pyrolysis* and it includes a release of carbon dioxide.) The acidity or "bright" notes in this coffee will be powerful, and its unique characteristics (based on the origin and processing of the beans) will be pronounced, but the body will be pretty thin. The surface of the light brown bean will be dry because the flavor oils are still inside.

Stage 3—Light-Medium, American Style: The temperature rises to about 415°F and the color of the bean changes from light brown to medium brown. The acidity or "bright" notes are still there but not as strong. The characteristics of the varietals will still be pronounced but the body will be fuller. For residents of the East Coast of America, this is the traditional roasting style.

Stage 4—Medium, City: The temperature rises from 415° to 435°F and the color of the bean is a slightly darker medium brown. The subtle flavor notes in the varietals are not as strong but still quite clear, the acidity or "brightness" is still present, and the body is even fuller. This is the traditional style for the American West.

Stage 5—Dark-Medium, Full City, Viennese Style: Now we are moving toward "the second crack" stage (this stage sounds less like corn popping and more like paper crinkling). This second *pyrolysis* usually happens between 435° and 445° F, the roast color is dark medium brown, and the beans begin to take on a slick sheen as the roasting "sweats out" the oils. The smell in the air is sweeter, the body of this coffee is heavier, the acidity or "brightness" more subdued. Coffees with more pronounced characteristics (such as Kenyan) will retain their strong flavor notes, but those with subtler notes will be lost to the increasing caramelized "dark roast" flavor of the process. Coffee drinkers in the Pacific Northwest, including northern California, traditionally enjoy this style of roast.

Stage 6—Dark, Darker, Darkest: Continuing to roast from this point will yield increasingly darker styles of roasted coffee. (See the basic styles and temperatures below.) Sugars continue to caramelize and more oils will be forced to the surface. The roasting smells turn from sweeter to more pungent and finally smoky. Pushed to the limit, beans will turn very dark and shiny, taking on intense flavors before they become completely black, charred, and worthless.

* **Espresso, European Style:** (445° to 455°F) This style of roast displays a moderately dark-roast flavor.

* **French, Italian:** (455° to 465°F) This style has more of a bittersweet dark-roast taste. While too pungent for some coffee drinkers, these roasts will stand up to mixing with milk and other flavorings to create coffee drinks.

* **Dark French, Spanish:** (465° to 475°F) The more bitter side of the "bittersweet" flavor is displayed here. A smoky taste may also be present. As the beans continue to roast, charred notes will begin to appear, and regardless of their origin all beans will begin to taste about the same.

Stage 7—Cooling: The master roaster will monitor this process by temperature gauges but also by sound (crack or pop), smell, and sight (bean color). When the desired roast style is achieved, the process is stopped by the release of the beans from the heated drum. The still-crackling beans fall into a cooling tray where fans and stirring paddles quickly bring down their temperature. When completely cooled, they are ready for grinding, brewing, and (finally!) drinking.

RECIPES

~~~~~~

With a contented stomach, your heart is forgiving;
with an empty stomach, you forgive nothing.
—Italian proverb

Eat with joy!
—Cleo Coyle

Madame's Osso Buco

See photos of this recipe at www.CoffeehouseMystery.com

Osso Buco (or ossobuco) is an elegant and beloved Italian dish of veal shank braised in wine and herbs. The shank is cut across the bone to a thickness of roughly 3 inches, browned, and then braised. Braising is a very slow cooking process, but preparing the dish itself is relatively simple, and the results pay off with rich, borderline orgasmic flavor. This is the recipe Madame shared with Diggy-Dog Dare in the Elmhurst ER. It was taught to her by Antonio Allegro, her first husband and Matt's late father.

Makes 3–4 servings

3–4 veal shank crosscuts, about 3 inches thick (see your butcher)
½ teaspoon sea salt
½ teaspoon freshly ground black pepper
½ cup all-purpose flour
3 tablespoons olive oil
1 large yellow onion, diced
1 large carrot, diced
4 celery stalks (hearts), sliced
4 garlic cloves, minced
1 cup dry white wine (such as Pinot Grigio)
1–2 cups chicken or veal stock (see note)
1 tablespoon minced fresh rosemary
1 teaspoon minced fresh thyme
Gremolata (a simple garnish; recipe follows)

Step 1—Brown the shanks: Preheat oven to 350° F. Season shanks with salt and pepper, then dredge in flour and set aside. Heat the olive oil in a Dutch oven over medium-high heat until the oil is rippling but not smoking. Place the veal in the hot oil and sear the shanks on both sides, turning once (about 4–5 minutes per side). Remove veal from oil and set aside.

Step 2—Prepare the aromatics: Drain most of the fat and oil from the Dutch oven, leaving just enough to cover the bottom. Add the onion and cook for 6 minutes, until brown. Add the carrot, stirring occasionally, about 3 minutes. Add the celery and garlic, stirring frequently, until they release their flavor and become aromatic, about 2 minutes. (Do not dump everything in at once, the order is important for the best flavor results.)

Step 3—Deglaze and prep the broth: Add the wine to the pan, stirring to incorporate all the ingredients. Simmer for 4–5 minutes, until the wine is reduced by half. Return the veal shanks to the pan, along with all the juice it may have released while sitting. Add enough chicken or veal stock (about 1 to 2 cups) to cover the shanks about two thirds of the way.

Step 4—Simmer and braise the meat: Over a low heat, bring the pot to a gentle simmer, then cover and transfer to hot oven. Braise for 2 hours, turning occasionally. Then add rosemary and thyme, and braise for one more hour, removing the lid during the last 15–20 minutes to cook off excess liquid.

Step 5—Make gravy and garnish: Remove veal shanks. Keep warm and moist before serving by placing in a covered serving dish. Meanwhile, place the Dutch oven on the stovetop again and simmer the cooking liquid over high heat for 5–8 minutes, adding salt and pepper to taste. Now you're ready to serve! Plate your veal shanks, pour a bit of the hot gravy over each shank, and garnish with Gremolata. Eat immediately—you've waited long enough!

GREMOLATA:

Combine 2 tablespoons of finely chopped fresh Italian (flat-leaf) parsley, 1 minced garlic clove, and 1 teaspoon lemon zest (grated lemon peel).

Madame's Note on Veal Stock: If purchasing your veal shanks from a butcher, ask for the top of the shank, which is mostly bone (this is usually discarded) and use it to make your own veal stock. Making stock is a snap. Simply simmer these extra bones in 4 cups of water. Throw in any of your favorite aromatics (1 tablespoon of fresh thyme, rosemary, and parsley, for example), add a bay leaf, a chopped onion, a celery stalk or two, salt and pepper. Simmer for an hour, strain out the liquid, and there is your stock!

Clare Cosi's Jim Beam Bourbon Steak

This outrageous blend of earthy beef with "spirited" brightness makes for a superb gastronomic experience. To help firefighters, Clare happily recommends purchasing a bottle of Jim Beam bourbon with the Terry Farrell Firefighters Fund label. To see what this inspiring label looks like, visit the following Web site, where you can also learn more about the fund, named after one of the fallen heroes of 9/11: www.jimbeam.com/partnerships/terry-farrell-fund

Makes 2 servings

⅓ cup aged bourbon (Jim Beam in the Terry Farrell bottle!)
¼ cup cold strong coffee or espresso
4 tablespoons sesame oil
3 tablespoons Worcestershire sauce
1 teaspoon freshly ground black pepper
2 T-bone, rib-eye, or shell steaks (2–3 pounds total)

Whisk together the bourbon, coffee, oil, Worcestershire sauce, and pepper and pour into a shallow dish or pan that is large enough to hold 2 steaks flat (single layer, no overlapping). Cover the dish, pan, or container with plastic wrap, and marinate the meat for 1 hour in the refrigerator, then flip and marinate for a second hour. Sauté the steaks in a large cast-iron skillet over medium-high heat, about 5 minutes per side for medium rare, or 7–8 minutes per side for medium well. You can also broil or grill them. Eat with joy!

Clare Cosi's Crab Cakes

There are two keys to good crab cakes: (1) keep the binders to a minimum so you can taste the meat, and (2) form the cakes a few hours before cooking so they can be chilled in the fridge, which will help them stay together during the cooking process. As for the meat, fresh lump crab meat from blue crabs will give you an authentic Maryland-style cake. But if you can't get fresh, a good quality canned will certainly work, too. Clare likes to brush the chilled cakes with a beaten egg just before final breading and frying. This is certainly more of an Italian-style method of frying seafood than a traditional Maryland-style, but Clare believes this step adds a delicate layer of flavor while helping to keep the cakes together during cooking. For an accompaniment to this dish, try Clare's Thai-Style Seafood Sauce (page 330) and her Sweet and Tangy Thai-Style Coleslaw (page 331).

Makes 8 crab cakes

5 eggs
1 cup unseasoned bread crumbs (not panko)
½ cup freshly squeezed lemon juice (from about 2 lemons)
½ cup scallions, chopped (white and green parts)
1 teaspoon dry, ground, or powdered mustard (all are the same!)
½ teaspoon Worcestershire sauce
½ teaspoon sea salt
½ teaspoon freshly ground white or black pepper
1 pound Maryland blue crabmeat
(or canned backfin or jumbo lump)
1 cup peanut or canola oil
½ cup panko (Japanese bread crumbs for coating)

Step 1—Mix the crabmeat: Lightly beat 4 of the eggs in a mixing bowl, add the unseasoned bread crumbs, lemon juice, scallions, dry mustard, Worcestershire sauce, salt, and pepper. Mix thoroughly. Separate and flake the crabmeat. If the meat is fresh, make sure you pick through it carefully and remove any shell fragments. Add the crabmeat to your egg mixture and blend thoroughly.

Step 2—Shape into cakes: Shape the crab mixture into 8 equal-sized balls, pat into cakes. Refrigerate uncooked crab cakes between two loose sheets of waxed paper for about 2 hours or up to 8. (The longer they chill, the easier they will be to handle.)

Step 3—Finish with egg wash and breading: Heat the oil in a large frying pan over medium heat. Lightly beat the remaining egg in a small bowl. Remove the crabcakes from the fridge and lightly brush each one with the egg wash. Gently roll each cake lightly in the panko bread crumbs. Do this quickly so they do not lose their chill, and do it carefully so they do not fall apart.

Step 4—Fry the cakes: Gently set each crabcake into the hot oil and cook until golden brown on both sides, about 4 to 5 minutes per side. Turn with care, only once or twice during cooking. Serve with Clare's Thai-Style Seafood Sauce on the side (recipe follows) or your favorite condiments or relishes.

Clare's Thai-Style Seafood Sauce

Makes about 1 cup

1 cup mayonnaise
2 tablespoons Clare's Thai Dipping Sauce (recipe on page 331)

In a small bowl, combine mayonnaise and Clare's Thai Dipping Sauce. Chill and serve with seafood. This is an especially good sauce to serve with boiled shrimp (in place of cocktail sauce). It's also delicious with Clare's Crab Cakes (see previous recipe).

Clare's Sweet and Tangy Thai-Style Coleslaw

Makes about 1 cup

½ medium to large head green cabbage, shredded (about 10 cups)
1 large carrot, peeled into strips (about ½ cup)
½ cup mayonnaise
3 tablespoons Clare's Thai Dipping Sauce, or to taste (recipe follows)
Salt, to taste (optional)

Place shredded cabbage and carrot peels in a large mixing bowl. In a separate bowl, mix the mayonnaise and dipping sauce. Fold the mayonnaise mixture into the bowl of shredded cabbage and blend well. Season with salt to taste. Chill and serve.

Clare's Thai-Style Dipping Sauce

This is the traditional recipe used as a dipping sauce for Thai spring rolls, but this tangy, sweet, and hot sauce is also great on salads, barbecued meats, or vegetable tempura.

Makes about 1 cup

1 cup confectioners' sugar
½ cup water
½ cup white vinegar
3 tablespoons finely chopped garlic (about 9 or 10 cloves)

2 tablespoons Thai fish sauce (or one mashed anchovy fillet or
¼ teaspoon anchovy paste)
2 teaspoons sambal oelek—Indonesian hot chile sauce
(or add more to increase heat)
2 tablespoons lime juice
2 tablespoons finely grated or shredded carrots

Step 1—Combine the sugar, water, and vinegar in a small saucepan. Bring to boil and continue boiling for 5 minutes.

Step 2—Reduce the heat to simmer and stir in the garlic, fish sauce, and *sambal oelek*. Simmer for 2–3 more minutes, remove from heat, and cool.

Step 3—When room temperature, stir in the lime juice and carrots. Store by refrigerating in a plastic container.

Clare Cosi's Korean-Style Sweet and Sticky Soy-Garlic Chicken Wings

An emerging foodie trend these days in New York City is the enjoyment of Korean fried chicken (Yangnyeom Dak)*, which landed on the U.S. East Coast circa 2007 and began to spread. In Korea, this dish is prepared from whole chickens cut up into bite-sized bits, which are then fried for crispy consumption in karaoke bars and pubs with beer or soju. Here in America, Korean fried chicken is prepared with wings or drumsticks, seldom the whole chicken.*

Clare has created a very simple version of Korean fried chicken for the American kitchen, using a technique she honed making Buffalo chicken wings. (You can find Clare's recipe for Buffalo wings at www.coffeehousemysteries.com.) The creation of the glaze came out of Clare's long experience of making homemade syrups for her coffeehouse drinks. (See the Recipes & Tips section of my eighth

Coffeehouse Mystery, Holiday Grind, *for an array of homemade coffeehouse syrup recipes.)*

If you're feeling adventurous (gastronomically speaking) and would like to seek out the authentic Korean ingredients for which Clare has created substitutions, then follow the instructions at the end of the recipe. But remember, the secret to Korean fried chicken is its crunchy crispness, created by the double-frying process. For delicious complements to this dish, try Sweet and Tangy Thai-Style Coleslaw, page 331, or a pile of sweet potato fries.

Makes 24 pieces

> 10–12 chicken wings, cut into thirds, discarding tips
> ½ cup all-purpose flour
> ⅔ cup cornstarch
> Salt and pepper, to taste
> 2 cups water
> 1⅓ cups dark brown sugar, packed
> ½ cup ketchup
> ½ cup soy sauce
> 1 tablespoon Worcestershire sauce
> 4–6 garlic cloves, minced
> Oil, for frying (peanut, canola, or vegetable)

Step 1—Prepare the chicken: Cut the wings into three pieces at the joints and discard the tips (or save and use for making chicken stock). Combine the flour, cornstarch, and salt and pepper in a bowl. Dredge chicken pieces through the mix, coating thoroughly.

Step 2—Make the glaze: Place the water and sugar in a medium saucepan and bring to a boil over medium-high heat. Add ketchup and whisk until the ingredients are blended. Simmer for 15–20 minutes. Mixture should thicken. Finally, add soy sauce, Worcestershire sauce, and garlic and simmer for another 3–5 minutes.

Step 3—Double fry the chicken: In a large skillet, heat the oil until rippling (or until a droplet of water bounces along the surface. In an electric skillet, the oil should be about 350° F). Gently add the wing pieces and cook for 7–9 minutes, turning once. Remove chicken from oil and let cool on a rack for 10 minutes. (Make sure the chicken dries in a single layer—using the rack lets the air circulate around each wing.) Fry a second time for an additional 7–9 minutes, until golden brown and very crisp.

Step 4—Coat the chicken: Drain the refried chicken on a rack over paper towels for a few minutes. Place the prepared glaze in a clean skillet and warm over a low heat. When the glaze begins to bubble, roll the chicken pieces in the mixture until the chicken wings are thoroughly coated.

Note: Right after cooking, the chicken will be delightfully sticky. If you prefer a drier glaze, simply place the wings in a single layer on a foil-covered sheet pan and warm in a preheated 350° F oven for 8–10 minutes.

Authentic Korean Flavor: This recipe is a good copycat of the soy-garlic wings served at the UFC Korean fried chicken stores in New York City. If you're after an even more authentic Korean flavor, substitute 1 tablespoon *myulchi aecjeot* (Korean anchovy sauce) for the tablespoon of Worcestershire sauce. And use Korean brand dark soy sauce.

James Noonan's Firehouse Sweet Onion and Cheddar Bake

This is the recipe that Clare noticed James Noonan cooking in his firehouse kitchen. (She suggested he add a bit of cayenne to kick up the flavor, which you certainly can, too, if you like.)

While Georgia's trademark Vidalia onions are the classic onion to use in this recipe, any sweet onion will work just fine. A sweet onion contains less sulfur and more sugar and water than other onions so it's milder and gentler on the palate. Sweet onions are grown in many places other than the state of Georgia, including Texas (Texas Sweets), California (Imperial), Washington/ Oregon (Walla Walla, by way of seeds from Italy), and Chile/ South America (OsoSweet). One last note from James's recipe file: Caramelized Bacon Bits (page 336) make an outrageously good added topping for this dish, as well as for his Triple-Threat Firehouse Penne Mac 'n' Cheese (page 337).

Makes 6 servings (fills a 2-quart casserole dish)

6 tablespoons butter
5 large sweet onions, thinly sliced
2 tablespoons Wondra flour (see note)
1 tablespoon ground, dry, or powdered mustard
(all three are the same!)
1 cup whole milk
1 cup mild cheddar cheese, grated, plus extra for topping
⅔ cup bread crumbs, plus extra for topping
1 cup Caramelized Bacon Bits (page 336), optional

Step 1—Sauté the onions: Preheat oven to 375° F. Melt 3 tablespoons of the butter in a large shallow pan. Toss in the onions and sauté. When they appear soft and translucent (but not brown), remove the onions from the heat. (This will take roughly 8–10 minutes.)

Step 2—Make an easy cheese sauce: In a small saucepan, melt the remaining 3 tablespoons of butter. Stir in the Wondra flour and mustard. Slowly stir in the milk, *then* add the cheese. (Note: Do not add these two ingredients together—first the milk, then the cheese!). Simmer for 1–2 minutes. When the sauce thickens, it's ready to use. Remove from heat.

Step 3—Assemble and bake: In a 2- or 3-quart casserole or baking dish, layer the onions, cheese sauce, and bread crumbs. (The bread crumbs will help absorb excess moisture released from the onions during baking.) After the final layer of cheese sauce, sprinkle some extra cheese and bread crumbs on top. Bake 30–45 minutes. If using Caramelized Bacon Bits, sprinkle over the top of the casserole before serving.

Clare's Onion Storage Tip: Sweet onions will keep for 4–6 weeks. Because sweet onions will absorb water, don't store them next to potatoes. Store whole, uncut sweet onions in the refrigerator. Place them in a single layer on paper towels in your vegetable bin. For longer storage, wrap them in foil before placing in fridge. To store a cut onion, wrap tightly in plastic and place in fridge.

Clare's Note on Wondra Flour: If you've never used Wondra flour, look for its blue cardboard canister in the same grocery store aisle that shelves all-purpose flour. It's a handy little helper for thickening gravies and making quick sauces.

Caramelized Bacon Bits

These bits of carmelized bacon make a delicious salty-sweet topping for cheesy casseroles. (No kidding. They're a perfect complement for mac 'n' cheese.) Just spread them across the top of the warm casserole before serving or present them on the side to your guests for do-it-yourself sprinkling.

Makes about 1 cup

1 pound bacon (regular cut, not thick), cut into small bite-size pieces
½ cup dark brown sugar, packed

Step 1—Slice and sauté: On medium-high heat, sauté the bacon bits in a large skillet, stirring often, until half cooked (still soft and flexible with fat just beginning to change color) . Drain the rendered fat from pan.

Step 2—Caramelize: Reduce the heat to medium. Add the brown sugar to the pan and stir until dissolved. Continue cooking and stirring until the bacon crisps up. Remove from heat. Drain and cool in a single layer on a sheet pan or another clean, flat surface. (Do not dry bacon bits on paper towels or they will stick! Use paper towels only to dab away the excess grease.) The longer you allow the bacon to cool and dry, the crisper it will become.

James Noonan's Triple-Threat Firehouse Penne Mac 'n' Cheese

This is the best recipe for macaroni and cheese I've ever tasted. It's a "triple threat" of cheeses that work together in delectable harmony to serenade your palate. And forget the typical elbow macaroni, which simply does not hold a candle to the penne macaroni. When cooked to an al dente texture, the larger penne pasta allows this chewy, cheesy casserole to linger on your taste buds that much longer. This one's an absolute joy to eat.

Makes 8 servings (fills a 3-quart casserole dish)

1 pound dry penne macaroni
2 cups grated sharp cheddar cheese
1 cup grated Monterey Jack cheese
1 cup queso blanco or mild cheddar, grated
5⅓ tablespoons butter
1 teaspoon salt
1 teaspoon black pepper

¼ cup all purpose flour
1 teaspoon Worcestershire sauce
2 cups whole milk
Caramelized Bacon Bits (page 336), optional

Step 1—Cook the penne pasta: First, preheat the oven to 375° F. Coat a 3-quart, ovenproof casserole dish (or Dutch oven) with cooking spray. Cook the penne according to directions on the pasta package; do not overcook. You want the penne al dente (still chewy, not soft). Drain the penne well, removing all water, and pour into the casserole dish.

Step 2—Make the cheese sauce: Mix the three cheeses together in a large bowl and set aside. Melt the butter over low heat, in a large saucepan. When butter is completely melted, remove the pan from heat. (Note: To prevent the cheese sauce from breaking on you, make absolutely sure you *remove* the pan from heat before adding these next ingredients!) Stir in the salt, pepper, flour, and the Worcestershire sauce until smooth. Gradually add in the milk. Now return the pan to the stove. Stir constantly over medium heat until the mixture comes to a boil, then reduce heat and simmer until thickened. Add in half of the cheese a little at a time, stirring with each addition.

Step 3—Assemble and bake: After the cheese sauce is warm and well blended, pour it over the macaroni. (Note: Do not mix in the cheese sauce! Just pour it over the top. The sauce will slowly ooze down during cooking. If you mix it in at this stage, too much of the cheese sauce will end up on the bottom of the dish instead of throughout.) Cover with the remaining half of the cheese. Bake for 20–25 minutes. If using Caramelized Bacon Bits, sprinkle them across the top of the casserole just before serving.

James Noonan's Firehouse Non–Beer Batter Onion Rings

Beer is often added to onion ring batter for flavor, lightness, and crispness. But if you're not a fan of beer (like James Noonan) and still want your rings light and crisp, there are two things you can do: (1) use cake flour because it has a lower gluten content, which makes for a crispier fry batter, and (2) substitute cold carbonated water for beer. You'll get all the lightness of the bubbles without the taste of hops.

Makes 4 servings

> 2 large Vidalia onions (or another sweet onion),
> cut into ¼-inch-thick rings
> 1¼ cups cake flour
> (¼ cup for dusting; 1 for the batter—be sure it's cake flour!)
> ¼ teaspoon cayenne pepper
> ½ teaspoon baking powder
> ½ teaspoon garlic salt
> Vegetable, peanut, or canola oil (enough for deep frying)
> 6–8 ounces cold seltzer, club soda, or carbonated water
> (be sure it's cold!)

Step 1—Prepare onions: Toss the raw onion rings in ¼ cup of the cake flour and set aside.

Step 2—Mix dry batter ingredients: Note: For best results, do not make the batter in advance. Finish the batter just before you are ready to fry the onion rings. In a large bowl, mix 1 cup of the cake flour, cayenne pepper, baking powder, and garlic salt. Heat the oil to 350° F. Only when the oil is hot and ready for frying should you move to the next step and finish the batter.

Step 3—Finish the batter and fry: Add enough *cold* carbonated water to the dry ingredients to make a loose batter. Coat your onion rings and cook at once. Fry until golden brown, 2–3 minutes. Serve hot!

Clare Cosi's Doughnut Muffins

Tender and sweet, these muffins taste like an old-fashioned cake doughnut, the kind you'd order at a diner counter with a hot, fresh cuppa joe.

Makes 12 muffins

For the batter:

> 12 tablespoons unsalted butter
> 1 cup granulated sugar
> 2 large eggs, lightly beaten with fork
> 1 cup whole milk
> 2½ cups all-purpose flour
> 2½ teaspoons baking powder
> ¼ teaspoon baking soda
> ¼ teaspoon salt
> ½ teaspoon ground nutmeg

For the cinnamon topping:

> ½ cup granulated sugar
> 1 teaspoon ground cinnamon
> 2 tablespoons butter, melted

Step 1—Prepare the batter: Preheat the oven to 350° F. Using an electric mixer, cream the butter and sugar until fluffy. Add in the eggs and milk and continue mixing. Stop the mixer. Sift in the flour, baking powder, baking soda, salt, and nutmeg, and mix only enough to combine ingredients. Do not overmix at this stage or you will produce gluten in the batter and toughen the muffins.

Step 2—Bake: Line cups in muffin pan with paper holders. Fill each up to the top (you can even mound it a little higher). Bake for 15–25 minutes, or until the muffins are lightly brown and a toothpick inserted comes out clean. Remove muffins quickly from pan and cool on a wire rack. (Muffins that remain in a hot pan may end up steaming, and the bottoms may become tough.)

Step 3—Prepare the topping: Mix together the sugar and cinnamon to create the cinnamon topping. Brush the tops of the warm muffins with the melted butter and dust with the cinnamon topping.

Clare Cosi's Jelly Doughnut Muffins

Clare brought this "jelly doughnut" version of her famous muffins to the Five-Borough Bake Sale. Detective Franco is still waiting for her to make him a plain old American jelly doughnut. He'll have to wait a little longer.

Makes 12 muffins

> 1 recipe Doughnut Muffin batter (page 340)
> ¼ cup raspberry jelly or jam
> 2 tablespoons butter, melted
> ½ cup confectioners' sugar, for dusting

Step 1—Line cups in a muffin pan with paper holders. Fill each cup halfway with the Doughnut Muffin batter. Poke a hole into the thick batter and spoon in 1 teaspoon of raspberry jelly. Top with remaining batter (filling cup about two-thirds full).

Step 2—Bake for 15–25 minutes, or until the muffins are lightly brown. Remove muffins quickly from pan and cool on a wire rack. (Muffins that remain in a hot pan may end up steaming, and the bottoms may become tough.)

Step 3—Brush the tops of the muffins with the melted butter and dust with the sugar.

Clare Cosi's Magnificent Melt-in-Your-Mouth Mocha Brownies

When Clare needs a quick chocolate fix, this is her go-to recipe. She whipped up a pan of these babies after she realized Mike Quinn had played her the previous night by keeping his secrets. On the subject of pastry chef secrets: one way to deepen the rich flavor of chocolate in any recipe is to add coffee. And the trick to keeping these brownies magnificent is (1) allow melted chocolate to cool before adding to the batter, (2) do not over bake. With this recipe, undercooking is better than overcooking. And (3) allow pan of brownies to cool completely before cutting. These moist and tender brownies will drench your taste buds with chocolate flavor, but they need time to cool and harden before they can be cut into bar cookies. (While still warm, these brownies do make an amazing dessert and can be served on a plate with ice cream or whipped cream. Otherwise, give them at least 1 hour out of the oven before cutting.)

Makes one 9-inch square pan of brownies (about 16 bars)

Cooking spray
1 cup good quality semi-sweet chocolate, chopped (or chips)

16 tablespoons (2 sticks) unsalted butter
¾ cup light brown sugar
¾ cup granulated white sugar
2 teaspoons pure vanilla extract
2 teaspoons instant coffee crystals (or 1½ teaspoons instant espresso powder) dissolved into 1 tablespoon hot tap water
3 large eggs
1¼ cups all-purpose flour (measure after sifting)
¼ cup unsweetened cocoa powder, sifted
1 teaspoon baking powder
½ teaspoon salt

Step 1—Melt chocolate and butter: Preheat your oven to 350° F and prepare a 9-inch square pan by spraying bottom and sides with cooking spray (or buttering and lightly dusting with cocoa powder). Melt the chocolate and 4 tablespoons of the butter in a microwave safe bowl. (See note at end of recipe on melting chocolate.) Allow to cool as you make the batter.

Step 2—Create batter: Using an electric mixer, cream the two sugars with your remaining 12 tablespoons of butter until light and fluffy. Blend in vanilla extract, coffee, eggs, and cooled melted chocolate from Step 1. After wet ingredients are blended, add in flour, cocoa powder, baking powder, and salt. (Blend well but do not overmix or you will produce gluten in the flour and toughen the batter.)

Step 3—Bake and cool: Spread the batter into your prepared 9-inch square pan. Bake at 350° F for 30 minutes. Do not over bake these beauties. When are they done? As the batter cooks, you will see the top form a crust and begin to show traditional cracking. Gently shake the pan. If the center appears to jiggle a bit, the brownies are still underdone. Continue cooking five minutes at a time until baked batter feels solid when pan is gently shaken. You can also insert a toothpick into the very center of pan. If batter appears on toothpick, continue cooking and checking. Cool pan on a rack to allow air to properly circulate beneath the hot pan bottom. Do not cut brownies before they are completely cool or they may break apart on you. You can always enjoy still-warm brownie squares on a plate with ice cream or whipped cream. Otherwise, simply wait until cool to the touch (about 1 hour), then cut into bars and eat with joy!

Clare's Note on Melting Chocolate: (1) Make sure bowl and stirring utensils are completely dry. Even a few drops of water can make chocolate seize up. (2) Chocolate burns easily so never heat chocolate until you see it turn completely liquid. Heat in microwave only 15 to 20 seconds to soften. Then remove and stir. Reheat if necessary for 10 seconds at a time and stir again until completely melted. (3) If you do not have a microwave, use a double boiler or create one by placing a dry, heatproof bowl over a saucepan of simmering water. Place chocolate in the bowl or top of double boiler and stir until melted.

Poor Girl's Crème Brûlée

What makes this a "poor girl's" crème brûlée? The lack of a pricey kitchen torch to caramelize the sugar. Clare suggests you do what French housewives have done for years: use the oven broiler. The caramelized crust that forms on top of the dessert will not have the hard shell-like texture that comes from using a professional kitchen torch (or even an industrial model à la the firefighter's bake sale), but the taste of the crunchy, warm sugar atop the creamy silk of the egg custard will be sinfully satisfying. This recipe calls for 6 egg yolks, but do not discard the whites: you can use them to make Nonna's Brutti Ma Buoni ("Ugly but Good") Italian Cookies. (See the recipe at www.CoffeehouseMystery.com.)

Makes 4 to 8 servings (depending on ramekin size)

6 large egg yolks
⅔ cup confectioners' sugar
1⅓ cups whole milk
1⅓ cups light cream
2 teaspoons pure vanilla extract
For topping: ⅓ cup turbinado sugar or "sugar in the raw" (Do not substitute granulated white sugar. If you can't find raw sugar, use light brown sugar.)

Step 1—Make the custard: Preheat oven to 300° F. Using an electric mixer, beat the egg yolks with the sugar until smooth. Mix in the milk, cream, and vanilla. Pour the mixture evenly into four individual 7–8-ounce size ramekins (or eight 4-ounce size ramekins). Set ramekins in a shallow roasting or baking pan and create a water bath by pouring water into the pan until it reaches halfway up the outside of the ramekins.

Step 2—Bake the custard: Bake until set, about 1 hour. Cooking time may be longer or shorter based on your oven and the size of your ramekins. So when is it done? You are looking for the top to set. The custard may still jiggle slightly, but the top should no longer be liquid. It should feel firm (spongy but set) when lightly touched, and when a toothpick or skewer is inserted down into the custard at the edge of the cup, it should come out clean. Otherwise, keep baking and checking.

Step 3—Chill it, baby: Remove from oven and cool to room temperature. Cover each ramekin tightly with plastic wrap and chill completely in fridge for 4 hours or overnight. (Note: Covering with plastic will keep a skin from forming, but be sure to allow the custard to cool completely before covering.)

Step 4—Caramelize the top: Okay, here's the "poor girl" part. If you do not have a kitchen torch to caramelize the sugar, then take Clare's advice. Before serving, sprinkle turbinado sugar over the top, set ramekins in a shallow pan filled with ice (to keep custard cool), and place under your oven broiler for a few minutes to caramelize. Check often. Do not let sugar burn. Serve immediately. (Note: If substituting light brown sugar, re-chill in fridge to harden top.)

Clare Cosi's Blueberries 'N' Cream Coffee Cake Pie

See photos of this recipe at www.CoffeehouseMystery.com

Mix, pour, bake, eat. Given the flour and eggs on the ingredient list, this supremely easy batter filling gives you a unique cross between a dense coffee cake and a fruit pie. Blueberries are truly the star of this confection, and their fresh, sweet, slightly tart flavor bursts brightly in your mouth with every delicious bite (and it's just as good, if not better, right out of the refrigerator the next day).

Makes one 8- or 9-inch pie

2 pints fresh blueberries
1¼ cups all-purpose flour
1 cup granulated sugar
⅛ teaspoon salt
⅔ cup half-and-half
2 large eggs
1 teaspoon cinnamon
1 Clare's Cinnamon Graham Cracker Crust (recipe follows) or
prebaked 8- or 9-inch graham cracker or shortbread crust

Step 1—Toss blueberries with flour: Rinse and dry your blueberries. Toss with 2 tablespoons of the flour. (You are coating the berries with flour to soak up excess liquid during baking.)

Step 2—Make batter: Preheat oven to 375° F. Using a simple hand whisk, gently blend the flour, sugar, salt, half-and-half, eggs, and cinnamon. Do not overmix or you'll toughen the batter. Carefully fold in the flour-tossed blueberries. You are not crushing the berries, just gently folding.)

Step 3–Bake: Pour the batter into your pie shell. If using an 8-inch crust, there may be a bit too much batter, that's okay, just hold it back. (See my crust tips below.) Bake about 1 hour. When is it done? The trick here is not to undercook the pie. You want the batter to firm up completely. The pie is done when a knife or skewer inserted down into the pie at the center comes up with little to no loose *batter* sticking to it. (You will always see some blueberry juice smeared on the knife or skewer when you insert it.) After 1 hour, check your pie. If not done, keep returning to the oven for 5-minute intervals until the pie is fully baked. (Depending on your oven, it may take 5–15 extra minutes beyond the initial hour.) Remove from oven and cool on a rack for at least 30 minutes before cutting. Enjoy plain or with sweetened whipped cream or ice cream.

Pie Crust Tip #1—Store-Bought: When I have no time to make a homemade crust, I simply purchase a prebaked graham cracker pie shell from my local grocery. I know that sounds odd. Premade crusts are primarily used for unbaked cream or pudding pies, but they work very well in this recipe! As the blueberry batter bakes, it caramelizes the graham cracker crumbs in the prebaked shell, giving a wonderfully sweet, satisfyingly al dente texture to your final pie crust, a nice contrast with the soft, slightly tart filling. An important point to remember if you do this: before pouring the batter into your store-bought pie shell, set the shell, aluminum pan and all, into a standard, empty metal pie pan. This added sturdiness will make the pie much easier to handle as you transfer it to the oven and finally cut and serve the pie. Final note: the store-bought crusts come with the aluminum pan's edges folded down. Before baking the pie, be sure to

unfold these edges, opening them up completely. This wi
make cutting the pie and removing the slices much easier!

Pie Crust Tip #2—Homemade: Press-in graham cracker (or cooki
crusts are very easy to make. If you have time for this extra ste
see Clare's Cinnamon Graham Cracker Crust below.

CLARE'S CINNAMON GRAHAM CRACKER CRUST

Makes one 8- or 9-inch press-in pie crust

Nine 2½ × 5-inch square cinnamon-flavored graham crackers
½ cup butter, melted

Pulverize the graham crackers into crumbs using a food proce
sor, blender, rolling pin, or another fun smashing device. Th
should give you about 1¼ cups of crumbs. Mix the crumb
with the melted butter. Press into an 8- or 9-inch pie pan.

For Clare's Blueberries 'N' Cream Coffee Cake Pie: Chill for 2
minutes before filling and baking. There's no need to pre
bake for my blueberry pie recipe—just chill and fill.

For no-bake pie recipes: If you'd like to use this crust recipe fe
a cream, pudding, or other no-bake pie recipe, then you wi
need to bake this crust before filling. Preheat oven to 350°
and bake for 8 to 10 minutes, depending on your oven. D
not over bake or it may turn out too hard!

Final Note: If you prefer regular graham crackers to t
cinnamon-flavored variety, be sure to add 2 tablespoons
sugar to this recipe.

Joy's Mini Cake-Mix Biscotti

*"Hey, Mom, I just added butter and eggs to a cake mix and made
kind of biscotti dough out of it. What do you think?" Joy came*

with this one when she was twelve. Clare used it for one of her In the Kitchen with Clare columns—and began to get a clue that her daughter might have a future in the world of food.

Makes 24 to 28 cookies

For Chocolate-Hazelnut Biscotti:

> *1 package chocolate cake mix*
> *3 large eggs, 1 separated*
> *8 tablespoons butter, melted*
> *1 cup all-purpose flour*
> *2/3 cup hazlenuts, toasted and chopped (see note)*
> *White or semisweet chocolate chips (for dipping), optional*

For Vanilla-Almond Biscotti:

> *1 package yellow cake mix*
> *3 large eggs, 1 separated*
> *8 tablespoons butter, melted*
> *1 cup all-purpose flour*
> *1 cup slivered almonds, toasted (see note)*
> *White or semisweet chocolate chips (for dipping), optional*

Step 1—Form the dough: Preheat the oven to 350° F. Line a large baking sheet with parchment paper. Using an electric mixer, blend the cake mix, 2 eggs and 1 egg yolk, butter, flour, and nuts. When a dough forms, turn off the mixer. Using your hands, form a dough ball in the bowl. Turn the ball onto the lined baking sheet. Work the dough until smooth and shape into two cylinders of about 1½ inches in diameter and 10-inches long. There should be a few inches of space on the baking sheet between the two logs. (They will expand during baking.) Now generously brush the top, sides, and ends of each log with the egg white (no need to brush the bottom and no need to use all of the egg white). This brushing will help keep the baked log together when you slice it later.

Step 2—Bake and slice the logs: Bake for about 25–30 minutes. The dough logs are finished when they are cracking on the surface, fairly firm to the touch, and a toothpick inserted in the centers comes up clean. Remove the hot pan from the oven. The logs are very fragile at this point so do not move them or they will break apart. Simply cool them on the pan for 2 to 3 hours. The pan should be placed on a rack to allow air to circulate beneath the pan bottom. Note: If you try to cut the logs while they are still the least bit warm, you will see the cookies crumbling as you cut. This is heartbreaking! Let the logs cool completely before cutting. Using a sharp, serrated knife, cut the log into slices on the diagonal. Slices should be about ¾- to 1-inch thick.

Step 3—Biscotti means baked again: Lay the biscotti slices flat on a sheet pan and bake for 8–10 minutes on one side. Then turn them over carefully. Don't burn your fingers and don't allow cookies to break apart! Bake on the flip side for 6–8 minutes. (You are literally toasting the cookies to give them more flavor and make them harder.) Remove from the oven and allow to cool completely before handling or storing.

Step 4—Optional chocolate dip: If desired, melt a cup or two of white or semisweet chocolate chips. Dip the top edge of the cooled biscotti slices into the warm chocolate and set on wax paper. (Or dip half the cookie into the chocolate—your call.) Serve after chocolate has hardened. (For tips on melting chocolate, see Clare's Magnificent Melt-in-Your-Mouth Mocha Brownies recipe on page 342.)

How to Toast Nuts: Spread nuts in a single later on a cookie sheet and bake in a preheated 350° F for 8–10 minutes. Stir once or twice during toasting to prevent scorching.

Cleo Coyle is the pseudonym for a multipublished author who collaborates with her husband to write the *New York Times* bestselling Coffeehouse Mysteries. Although they did not meet until adulthood, Cleo and her husband had very similar upbringings. Both were children of food-loving Italian immigrants, and both grew up in working-class neighborhoods outside of Pittsburgh, Pennsylvania, before moving to the Big Apple to begin their postcollege careers: Cleo as a journalist, and children's book and media tie-in author; and her husband as a magazine editor and writer. After finally meeting and falling in love, they married at the Little Church of the West in Las Vegas. Now they live and work in New York City, where they write books independently and together, cook like crazy, haunt local coffeehouses, and drink a *lot* of joe. Among their many coauthored projects are the Haunted Bookshop Mysteries, written under the pseudonym Alice Kimberly.

Cleo enjoys hearing from readers. Visit the virtual Village Blend coffeehouse at CoffeehouseMystery.com, where she also posts recipes and coffee industry news.

Don't Miss the Next
Coffeehouse Mystery by Cleo Coyle

MURDER BY MOCHA
Can chocolate and coffee heat up your love life?
For Clare Cosi, the answer will be murder.
Includes chocolate recipes!

For more information about the
Coffeehouse Mysteries,
and what's next for Clare Cosi
and her baristas at the Village Blend,
visit Cleo Coyle's Web site at
CoffeehouseMystery.com.

From National Bestselling Author
CLEO COYLE

Murder by Mocha

A Coffeehouse Mystery

Clare's Village Blend beans are being used to create a new java love potion: a "Mocha Magic Coffee" billed as an aphrodisiac. Clare may even try some on her boyfriend, NYPD detective Mike Quinn—when he's off duty, of course.

The product, expected to rake in millions, will be sold exclusively on Aphrodite's Village, one of the Web's most popular online communities for women. But the launch party ends on a sour note when one of the Web site's editors is found dead.

When more of the Web site's Sisters of Aphrodite start to die, Clare is convinced someone wants the coffee's secret formula—and is willing to kill to get it. Clare isn't about to spill the beans, but will she be next on the hit list?

Includes recipes and coffee-making tips!

penguin.com

Praise for Christine Feehan's Dark Carpathian novels . . .

DARK PERIL

"An . . . intoxicating series of love, adventure and vampires."
—Examiner.com

DARK SLAYER

"Fresh and gender-bending." —*Midwest Book Review*

DARK CURSE

"A very intense book." —*The Best Reviews*

DARK POSSESSION

"Steamy . . . danger, fantasy and wild, uninhibited romance."
—*Publishers Weekly*

DARK CELEBRATION

"[A] sex-and-magic-filled treat." —*Publishers Weekly*

DARK DEMON

"A terrific, action-packed romantic thriller." —*The Best Reviews*

DARK SECRET

"The erotic heat . . . turns scorching." —*Booklist*

DARK DESTINY

"Deeply sensuous." —*Booklist*

DARK MELODY

"A richly evocative fantasy world . . . [the] love scenes . . . sizzle." —*Publishers Weekly*

continued . . .

DARK SYMPHONY

"Feehan's followers will be well sated." —*Publishers Weekly*

DARK GUARDIAN

"A skillful blend of supernatural thrills and romance that is sure to entice readers." —*Publishers Weekly*

DARK LEGEND

"Vampire romance at its best!" —*Romantic Times*

DARK FIRE

"If you are looking for something that is fun and different, pick up a copy of this book." —*All About Romance*

DARK CHALLENGE

"[An] exciting and multifaceted world . . . [Feehan] is setting the stage for more exhilarating adventures to come."
—*Romantic Times*

DARK MAGIC

"With each book Ms. Feehan continues to build a complex society that makes for mesmerizing reading." —*Romantic Times*

DARK GOLD

"Wish I had written it!" —Amanda Ashley

DARK DESIRE

"A very well-written, entertaining story that I highly recommend." —*The Best Reviews*

DARK PRINCE

"For lovers of vampire novels, this one is a keeper!"
—*New-Age Bookshelf*

DARK PERIL

A CARPATHIAN NOVEL

CHRISTINE FEEHAN

JOVE BOOKS, NEW YORK

THE BERKLEY PUBLISHING GROUP
Published by the Penguin Group
Penguin Group (USA) Inc.
375 Hudson Street, New York, New York 10014, USA
Penguin Group (Canada), 90 Eglinton Avenue East, Suite 700, Toronto, Ontario M4P 2Y3, Canada
(a division of Pearson Penguin Canada Inc.)
Penguin Books Ltd., 80 Strand, London WC2R 0RL, England
Penguin Group Ireland, 25 St. Stephen's Green, Dublin 2, Ireland (a division of Penguin Books Ltd.)
Penguin Group (Australia), 250 Camberwell Road, Camberwell, Victoria 3124, Australia
(a division of Pearson Australia Group Pty. Ltd.)
Penguin Books India Pvt. Ltd., 11 Community Centre, Panchsheel Park, New Delhi—110 017, India
Penguin Group (NZ), 67 Apollo Drive, Rosedale, Auckland 0632, New Zealand
(a division of Pearson New Zealand Ltd.)
Penguin Books (South Africa) (Pty.) Ltd., 24 Sturdee Avenue, Rosebank, Johannesburg 2196,
South Africa

Penguin Books Ltd., Registered Offices: 80 Strand, London WC2R 0RL, England

DARK PERIL

A Jove Book / published by arrangement with the author

PRINTING HISTORY
Berkley hardcover edition / September 2010
Jove mass-market edition / October 2011

ISBN: 978-0-515-14999-9

JOVE®
Jove Books are published by The Berkley Publishing Group,
a division of Penguin Group (USA) Inc.,
375 Hudson Street, New York, New York 10014.
JOVE® is a registered trademark of Penguin Group (USA) Inc.
The "J" design is a trademark of Penguin Group (USA) Inc.

PRINTED IN THE UNITED STATES OF AMERICA

10 9 8 7 6 5 4 3 2 1

For Alexa Bridges,
with much love

FOR MY READERS

Be sure to go to http://www.christinefeehan.com/members/ to sign up for my PRIVATE book announcement list and download the FREE e-book of *Dark Desserts*. Join my community and get firsthand news, enter the book discussions, ask your questions and chat with me. Please feel free to email me at Christine@christinefeehan.com. I would love to hear from you.

ACKNOWLEDGMENTS

I could never have written this book without the help of two wonderful men. Dr. Christopher Tong is always amazing with his continual support. His song is beautiful and perfect for Dominic and Solange. As always, thank you for your help with the language; thank heavens you always find a way to get things done.

Brian Feehan really came through in my hour of need, as he always does, working late with me to map out our destruction of the vampire stronghold.

Thanks to both Cheryl Wilson and Kathie Firzlaff, who gave me invaluable feedback at literally the eleventh hour and without whom I wouldn't have been able to finish the book.

And Domini, what can I say. You work long hours and far into the weekends to make the book the best that it can be. I appreciate you so much!

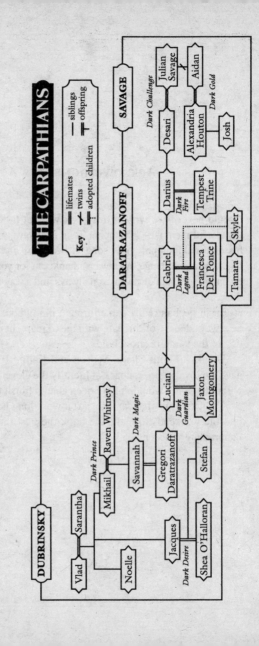

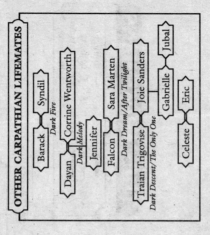

OTHER CARPATHIAN LIFEMATES

Barack ⬦—⬦ Syndil
Dark Fire

Dayan ⬦—⬦ Corrine Wentworth
Dark Melody

Jennifer

Falcon ⬦—⬦ Sara Marten
Dark Dream/After Twilight

Traian Trigovise ⬦—⬦ Joie Sanders
Dark Descent/The Only One

Gabrielle ⬦—⬦ Jubal

Celeste ⬦—⬦ Eric

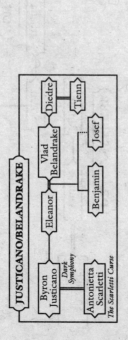

JUSTICANO/BELANDRAKE

Diedre ⬦—⬦ Tienn

Vlad Belandrake

Eleanor

Byron Justicano ⬦—⬦
Dark Symphony

Antonietta Scarletti
The Scarletti Curse

Benjamin

Josef

THE CARPATHIANS

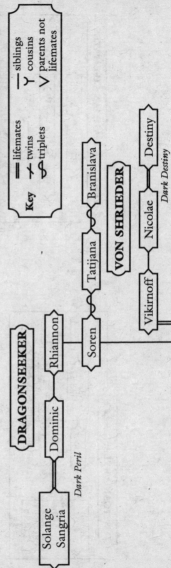

Key
— lifemates
⌣ twins
⌢ triplets

⎤ siblings
Y cousins
V parents not lifemates

DRAGONSEEKER

Solange Sangria

Dark Peril

Dominic — Rhiannon

Soren — Tatijana

Branislava

VON SHRIEDER

Vikirnoff — Nicolae — Destiny

Dark Destiny

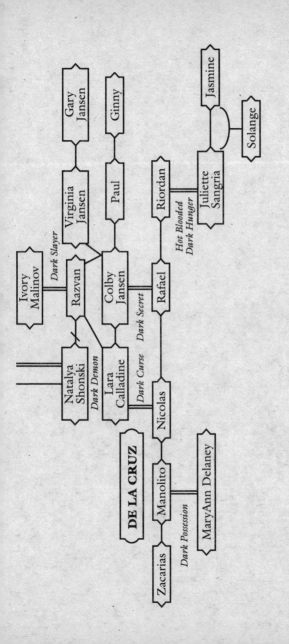

DARK PERIL

1

I was half-alive for a thousand years.
I'd given up hope that we'd meet in this time.
Too many the centuries. All disappears
As time and the darkness steal color and rhyme.

DOMINIC TO SOLANGE

Carpathian males without a lifemate didn't dream. They didn't see in color and they certainly didn't feel emotion. Pain, yes, but not emotion. So why had he been reaching for a dream for the past few years? He was an ancient, an experienced warrior. He had no time for fantasy, or for imagination. His world was stark and barren, a necessity for battling an enemy who, inevitably, had been a friend or family member.

Over the first hundred or so years after losing his emotions, he had held out hope. As centuries passed, the hope of finding his lifemate had faded. He had accepted he would find her in the next life and he was carrying out his resolve to do his last duty to his people. Yet here he was, an ancient of great experience, Dominic of the Dragonseeker line, a lineage as old as time itself, a man of wisdom, a warrior renowned and feared—lying awake beneath the rich soil, dreaming.

Dreams should have felt insubstantial—and at first his had been. A woman. Just a vague idea of her appearance. So young in comparison to him, but a warrior in her own right. She hadn't been his concept of the woman who would partner him, yet as she grew in substance over the years, he realized how perfect she was for him. He had fought far too long to ever lay down his sword. He knew no other way of life. Duty and sacrifice were bred into his very bones and he needed a woman who could understand him.

Perhaps that was what dreams were. He'd never dreamt until a few years ago. Never. Dreams were emotions, and he'd long ago lost those. Dreams were color, although not his. But they felt like color as the years shaped the woman. She was a mystery, sheer confidence when she fought. She often had fresh bruises and wounds that left scars on her soft skin. He'd taken to examining her carefully each time they met—healing her had become a traditional greeting. He found himself smiling inside, thinking how she was entirely the opposite of confident when it came to viewing herself as a woman.

For a few moments he contemplated why he should be smiling inside. Smiling was equated with happiness, and he had no emotions to feel such things, but his memories of emotions were sharpening as he moved toward the end of his life, instead of dimming as he had expected. Because when he summoned the dream, he felt a sense of comfort, of well-being and happiness.

Over the years she had become clearer to him. A jaguar-woman. A fierce warrior with exactly the same values he held on loyalty and family and duty. He would never forget

the night, only a week ago, when he saw her eyes in color.
For a moment he couldn't breathe, looking at her in wonder, shocked that he could remember colors so vividly that
he could attribute an actual color to her cat's eyes.

Her eyes were beautiful, glowing green with faint hints
of gold and amber that darkened when he managed to elicit
a laugh from her. She didn't laugh often or easily, and when
she did, he felt it was more of a victory than any of the battles
he'd won.

As dreams went—and they only occurred when he was
awake—they always seemed a bit out of focus. But he looked
forward to seeing her. He felt protective toward her, as if
his allegiance had already swung toward his dream woman.
He wrote to her, songs of love, saying all the things he wished
to tell his lifemate. And when she refused to rest, he'd lay
her down, her head in his lap, stroking her thick mane of
hair and singing to her in his language. He'd never felt more
content—or more complete.

He stirred, disturbing the rich soil surrounding him. The
moment he moved, the pain took him, thousands of knives
ripping from the inside out. The tainted vampire blood he'd
deliberately swallowed had been thick with parasites, and
they moved in him, replicating, seeking to take over his body,
to invade every cell, every organ. And as often as he purged
some to keep the numbers down, they seemed to work harder
to multiply.

Dominic hissed out his breath between his teeth as he
forced his rising. It was not yet fully night and he was an
ancient Carpathian with many battles and kills to his name.
As a rule ancients didn't rise before the sun had set, but he
needed the extra time to scout his enemy and get his bear-
ings in this land of walking myths and legends.

Deep within the cave he'd chosen in the Amazon forest,
he moved the earth gently, allowing it to settle around him as

he awakened, wanting to keep the area as undisturbed as possible. He traveled only at night, as his kind did, listening to the whisper of evil, on the trail of a master vampire, one he was certain had knowledge of the plans to destroy the Carpathian species once and for all. His people knew that the vampires were coming together under the rule of the five. At first the groups had been small and scattered, the attacks easily fended off, but lately the whisper of conspiracy had grown into a roar, and the groups were larger and more organized and widespread than first thought. He was certain the parasites in the tainted blood were the key to identifying all those forging an allegiance to the five *masters*.

He'd gleaned that much over his days of traveling. He had tested the theory several times, coming across three vampires. Two were relatively new, and neither had the parasites and were easy for an experienced hunter to kill. But the third had satisfied his questions. The moment he came into close proximity, the parasites had gone into a frenzy of recognition. He had listened to the vampire bragging for most of the night, telling him of their growing legions and how emissaries were meeting in the Amazon, where they had allies in the jaguar-men and a human society that had no idea they were in bed with the very ones they sought to destroy. The *masters* were using both humans and jaguar-men to hunt and kill Carpathians. Dominic had killed the vampire, a quick extraction of the heart, and, calling down the lightning, incinerated him. Before leaving the area, he had taken great care to remove any trace of his presence.

He knew time was running out fast. The parasites were hard at work, whispering to him, murmuring evil enticements, unrelenting in their quest for him to join with the *masters*. He was an ancient without a lifemate and the darkness was strong in him already. His beloved sister had disappeared hundreds of years earlier—he now knew she was dead and her children safe with the Carpathian people. He could do this one last task and end his barren existence with honor.

He rose from the rich soil, as rejuvenated as one with parasites in his blood could possibly be. The cave deep beneath the earth kept the sun from touching his skin, but he felt it anyway, knowing it was just outside the darkness, waiting to scorch him. His skin prickled and burned in anticipation. He strode through the cave with absolute confidence. He moved with the easy self-assurance of a warrior, flowing over the uneven ground in the darkness.

As he began the climb to the surface, he thought of her—his lifemate, the woman in his dreams. She wasn't his true lifemate of course, because if she were he would be seeing colors vividly, not just her eyes. He would see the various shades of green in the rain forest, but everything around him remained gray hued. Was finding solace with her cheating? Was singing to her about his love of his lifemate cheating? He longed for her, needing to conjure her up at times to get through the night when his blood was on fire and he was being eaten alive from the inside out. He thought of her soft skin, a sensation that seemed amazing when he was like an oak tree, hard iron, his skin as tough as leather.

As he neared the exit of the cave, he could see light spilling into the tunnel and his body cringed, an automatic reaction after centuries of living in the night. He loved the night, no matter where he was or what continent he was on. The moon was a friend, the stars often guiding lights he navigated by. He was in unfamiliar territory, but he knew the De La Cruz brothers patrolled the rain forest, although there were five of them to cover a very large territory and they were spread thin. He had a feeling the five who were recruiting the lesser vampires against the Carpathians had deliberately chosen the De La Cruz territory as their headquarters.

The Malinov brothers and the De La Cruz brothers had

grown up together, more than friends, claiming a kinship. They'd been regarded by the Carpathian people as two of the most powerful families, warriors unsurpassed by many. Dominic thought about their personalities, and the camaraderie that had turned into a rivalry. It made sense that the Malinov brothers would choose to set their headquarters right under the noses of the very ones who had plotted theoretical ways to remove the Dubrinsky line as rulers of the Carpathian people and then, in the end, had sworn their allegiance to the prince. The Malinov brothers would become the De La Cruz brothers' most bitter and unrelenting enemies.

Dominic's logical line of reasoning had been confirmed by the vampire he had killed in the Carpathian Mountains, a very talkative lesser vampire who wanted to brag about all he knew. Dominic had made his way, taking no prisoners, so to speak, surprised at how the parasites were such a fantastic warning system. It had never occurred to the Malinov brothers that any Carpathian would dare to ingest the blood and invade their very camp.

Going closer to the cave entrance, he was hit by the noise first, the sounds of birds and monkeys and the incessant hum of insects in spite of the steady rain. It was hot, and steam actually rose from the floor just outside the cave as the moisture poured down from the skies. Trees hung over the swollen banks of the river, their root systems great gnarled cages, the thick tendrils snaking over the ground to create waves of wooden fins.

Dominic was impervious to rain or heat; he could regulate his own temperature to stay comfortable. But those thirty feet or so from the entrance of his cave to the relative safety under the thick canopy were going to be hell, and he wasn't looking forward to it. Traveling in the sun, even in another form, was painful, and with the sensation of glass shards ripping his insides to shreds, he had enough to contend with.

It was difficult not to reach for the dream. In her company, the pain eased and the whispering in his head ceased. The constant murmurs, the parasites working on his acceptance of the *masters* and their plan, were wearying. The dream gave him solace in spite of knowing his lifemate wasn't real.

He knew he had slowly built up his lifemate in his mind—not her looks, but her characteristics, the traits that were important to him. He needed a woman who was loyal beyond all else, a woman who would guard their children fiercely, who would stand with him no matter what came at them, one he would know was at his side, and he wouldn't have to worry that she couldn't protect herself or their children.

He needed a woman who, when it was just the two of them, would follow his lead, who would be feminine and fragile and all the things she couldn't be during the times they would have to fight. And he wanted that side of her completely to himself. It was selfish, maybe, but he had never had anything for himself, and his woman was for him alone. He didn't want other men to see her the way he did. He didn't want her to look at other men. She was for him alone, and maybe that was what a dream really was—building the perfect woman in your mind when you knew you'd never have one.

He was well aware of her fighting skills. He saw the battle scars. He respected and admired her when he walked with her, yet he couldn't really hold her image for long. In dreams she came to him, shielded by a heavy veil, their exchanges in images more than words. It had taken a long time for either to reveal any part of themselves other than the warrior. They'd built trust between them slowly—and he liked that about her. She didn't give her allegiance easily, but when she did, she gave it wholly. And it was to him.

Again he found himself smiling inside at such a ridiculous fantasy at his age. It must be a sign of his mind deteriorating. Senility had set in. But how he missed her when he couldn't bring her to him. She seemed closer there in the heat of the forest, with the rain coming down in silvery sheets. The veil of moisture reminded him of the first time he'd managed to peer through that haze in his dream and see her face so clearly. She'd stolen his breath. She'd looked so frightened, as if she'd deliberately revealed herself—finally taken a chance, but stood trembling, waiting for him to pass judgment on her.

At that moment he'd felt closer to actual love than he ever had before. He tried to compare the feeling with what he'd felt for his sister, Rhiannon, in the early days when they'd all been happy and he still had his emotions. He'd held on to the memory of love all those centuries, yet now, when he needed the feeling to complete his dream, before he went out fighting, the feeling was entirely different.

Feeling. He turned the word over and over in his mind. What did it mean? Memories? Or reality? And why would his memories be so sharp all of a sudden, here in the forest? He smelled the rain, inhaled the scent of it, and there was an edge of pleasure in the sensation. It was frustrating, to almost catch the feeling, and yet it eluded him. It wasn't simply a by-product of ingesting the vampire blood—he'd begun "dreaming" much earlier. And the dreams took place while he was awake.

He was suspicious of all things that didn't make sense. He wasn't a man prone to dreams or fantasies, and this mythical woman was becoming too much a part of his life—of him. She was tricking him into thinking she was a true lifemate—a reality instead of a myth—yet here in the land where myths and legends came to life, he could almost convince himself she was real. But even if she was, it was far too late. The continual pain clawing at his belly told him his time had run its course and he had to carry out his plan to infiltrate the enemy camp, gain their plans, send the information to Zacarias De La Cruz and then kill as many vampires as he could before he went down. He chose to go out fighting for his people.

He shifted, taking the form of the lord of the skies—the harpy eagle. The bird was larger than normal, and the harpies were already large birds. His wingspan was a good seven feet, his talons enormous. The form would help to protect him as he went into the sunlight before reaching the relative shelter of the canopy. He hopped on the ground and into the light. In spite of the heavy rain, the light burst over him. Smoke rose from the dark feathers, pouring off the bird's form. He'd suffered burns and his body remained ravaged with the scars, although they'd eased over time, but he would never forget that pain. It was branded into his very bones.

Sharply sucking in his breath, he forced himself to spread his wings and rise toward that hideous burning mass of heat. The rain sizzled over him, spitting and hissing like an angry cat as the large bird took flight, wings flapping hard to get height to take him into the trees. The light nearly blinded him, and inside the eagle, he shrank away from the rays, no matter how diffused by the rain. It seemed to take forever to cross the thirty feet, although the bird was in the trees almost immediately. It just took a few moments to realize the sun was no longer directly on his feathers. The sounds of hissing and spitting gave way once again to the calling of the birds and monkeys, this time in sharp alarm.

Below him, a porcupine dropped the figs he'd been dining on as the shadow of the eagle passed overhead. Two female spider monkeys, drunk on fermented fruit, stared up at him.

The Amazon rain forest passed through eight borders, extending through the countries with its own diverse life-forms. A silky anteater climbing in the branches of a tree paused to gaze at him with a wary eye. Bright red and blue macaws called warnings as he flew above them, but he ignored them, expanding his circle ever wider to take in more and more territory.

The eagle moved noiselessly through the forest, as high as the canopy would allow, without emerging above it, covering miles. He needed the shelter of the twisted limbs and heavy foliage to block the light. With the eyes of the harpy eagle he could see something as small as an inch from more than two hundred yards. He could fly at speeds of up to fifty miles per hour if he was in open territory, and drop with dizzying speed if needed.

Now, eyesight was the primary reason for having chosen the eagle's form. He spotted hundreds of frogs and lizards dotting the branches and trunks as he swept by. Snakes coiled along twisted limbs, hiding among blossoms drenched in rain. A margay shrank deeper into the foliage of a tall Kapok tree, its large eyes fixed on prey. The eagle dipped lower, inspecting the overgrown vegetation. Limestone blocks lay half buried in debris, strewn about as if by a willful hand. A sinkhole shimmered with blue water, testifying to the presence of an underground river.

The eagle continued to expand his circle, covering more and more miles, until he found what he was looking for. The bird settled high in the branches of tall tree on the edge of a man-made clearing. A large building made of steel and bolts had been brought in piece by piece and constructed sometime in the last year. Growth around it had been encouraged, presumably with an eye to hiding it, but there hadn't been enough time for the forest to reclaim lost terrain.

Something had blown a hole through the metal from the

outside, and a fire had started. The smell of smoke couldn't mask the stench of rotting flesh rising to make his skin crawl even deep within the form of the bird. *Vampire*. The scent was there, although faded, as if many risings had gone by since the undead had visited this place. Still, the wail of the dead rose from the surrounding ground.

The right side of the building was blackened and the hole gave glimpses of the interior. A very recent battle, perhaps in the last couple of hours, had taken place here. The sharp eyes of the eagle could see the furniture overturned inside, a desk and two cages. A body lay on the floor, unmoving.

Two men—human, he was certain—stood outside the building in combat gear, large guns strapped to their shoulders. One tipped a bottle of water to his mouth and then stepped back into the relative shelter of the doorway, trying to avoid the steady rain. The second stood stoically, the water drenching him, as he said a few words to the first guard before moving on to circle the building. Both watched vigilantly, and the guard in the doorway favored his left leg, as though he'd been injured.

The eagle watched, motionless, hidden in the thick, twisted branches and umbrella leaves up above the clearing. It wasn't long before a third man appeared, coming out of the forest. Naked, he was thick-chested with stocky legs and heavily muscled arms. He carried another man over his shoulder. Blood streamed down his shoulder and back, although it was impossible to tell if it was from the unconscious man or him. He staggered just before he reached the door, but the guard didn't move to help him. Instead, he stood to one side, the muzzle of his gun barely raised, but enough to cover the newcomers.

Jaguar-men. Shapeshifters. There was no doubt in Dominic's mind. Someone had attacked this facility and done a considerable amount of damage. Obviously the human guard was leery of the jaguar-men, but he allowed them into the building. The second guard had hung back and covered the two shapeshifters, his finger on the trigger. Clearly it was an uneasy truce between the two species.

Dominic knew the jaguar-men were on the verge of extinction. He had seen the decline a few hundred years earlier and knew it was inevitable. At that time, the Carpathians had tried to warn them of what was coming. Times changed and a species had to evolve in order to survive, but the jaguar-men had refused the advice. They wanted to stick to the old ways, living deep in the forests, finding a mate, impregnating her and moving on. They were wild and bad-tempered, never able to settle.

The few jaguar-men Dominic had spent any time with had tremendous feelings of entitlement and superiority. They viewed all other species as inferior, and their women were seen as little more than a vessel to carry offspring. The royal family had a long history of cruelty and abuse toward their women and female children, a practice the other males viewed as example and followed. There were a few rare jaguar-men who had tried to convince the others that they needed to value their women and children, rather than treating them as property, but they were considered traitors and were shunned and ridiculed—or worse, killed.

In the end the Carpathians had left the jaguar-men to their own devices, knowing the species was ultimately doomed. Brodrick the Tenth, a rare black jaguar, led the males just as his father and his ancestors before him had done. He was considered a difficult, brutal man, responsible for the slaughter of entire villages, of the half-breeds he deemed unfit to live. It was rumored he had made an alliance with the Malinov brothers as well as the society of humans dedicated to wiping out vampires.

Dominic shook his head at the irony. Humans couldn't

distinguish between a Carpathian and a vampire, and their secret society had been infiltrated by the very ones they were trying to destroy. The Malinovs were using both species in their war against the Carpathians. So far, the werewolves hadn't come down on either side, instead staying strictly neutral, but they existed, as Manolito De La Cruz had found with his lifemate.

Dominic spread his wings and moved closer, tuning his hearing to catch the conversation inside the building.

"The woman is dead, Brodrick. She went over the cliff. We couldn't stop her." There was weariness and distaste in the voice.

A second voice, one filled with pain, added, "We can't afford the loss of any more of our women."

The third voice was lower, a growl of sheer power, stunning in the absolute authority it carried. "What did you say, Brad?" The voice conveyed a distinct threat, as if the very idea of any of his subjects having a thought of his own in some way made him a traitor.

"He needs a doctor, Brodrick," the first voice hastily intervened.

Dominic watched as a large man dressed in loose jeans and an open shirt emerged from the house. His hair was long, shaggy and very thick. Dominic knew instantly he was looking at Brodrick, the ruler of the jaguar-men. His prince had decreed the Carpathians should leave the species to its own fate, otherwise Dominic would have been tempted to kill the man where he stood. Brodrick was directly responsible for the deaths of countless men, women and children. He was consumed with evil, drunk on his own power and the belief that he was superior to all others.

Brodrick looked at the two guards contemptuously. "What the hell are you doing hanging out in the doorway? You're supposed to be doing a job."

The second guard kept his gun pointed in Brodrick's direction even as the two human men moved in opposite circles, the one who'd been sheltering in the doorway limping badly, confirming Dominic's belief that he'd been wounded. Brodrick scowled up at the rain, allowing it to pour onto his face. He spat in disgust and stalked around to the side of the building where the fire had been. Crouching, he searched the ground. He was thorough about it, leaning down to sniff, using all senses to pick up the trail of his enemy.

Suddenly he sat back on his heels, stiffening. "Kevin, get out here," he called.

The jaguar-man who had carried the wounded one hurried out, barefoot, but in jeans and pulling on a T-shirt that strained across his chest. "What is it?"

"Did you get a good look at whoever broke in and freed Annabelle?"

Kevin shook his head. "He's a hell of a shot. He took out two guards, the bullets so close together everyone thought only one shot had been fired."

"There aren't any tracks. None. Where the hell was he? And how did he know the precise place to blow the building to free Annabelle? There were no windows."

Kevin glanced in the direction of the guards. "You think someone helped him?"

"What happened out there?" Brodrick gestured toward the forest.

Kevin shrugged. "We went after Annabelle. She ran through the forest toward the river. We thought maybe it was her man, the human she spoke of, coming to try to save her. We didn't need weapons to fight him, so we both shifted. We'd be faster traveling through the forest than Annabelle, even if she shifted."

It had been logical thinking, Dominic conceded from his lofty perch above them, but they'd lost the woman.

Brodrick shook his head. "How did Brad get shot? And where's Tonio?"

Kevin sighed. "We found his body just on the other side of the caves. He'd tangled with another cat. Brad was kneeling beside him, and the next thing I knew, he was on the ground and we were pinned down. I had no weapon and I shifted to try to circle around and find the shooter, but I couldn't find any tracks."

Brodrick swore. "It's her. *She* did this. I know it was her. That's why you didn't find any tracks. She took to the trees."

Neither said who *she* was. Dominic wanted to know who the mysterious woman they obviously hated—and feared— could be. Someone he wouldn't mind meeting. Four of the five De La Cruz brothers had lifemates. Could the elusive woman be one of their lifemates? It was possible, but he doubted it. The De La Cruz brothers would not want their women in battle. They were men with fiercely protective natures, and coming to this part of the world had only increased their dominant tendencies. They had eight countries to patrol, and the Malinov brothers would know how impossible it was to cover every inch of the rain forest. They would never, under any circumstances, send their women out alone. No, this had to be someone else.

The eagle spread its massive wings and took to the air. The sun was beginning to fade, making him a little more comfortable, but the whisper of the parasites grew louder, tempting, pushing his hunger to a ravenous level, until he could barely think straight. It was only the bird's form that kept his sanity as he tried to adjust to the rising level of torment. As the night grew closer, the parasites went from sluggish to active, stabbing at his internal organs while the vampire blood burned like acid. He needed to feed, but he was becoming more and more worried that insanity was grabbing hold and he wouldn't find the strength to resist the temptation of a kill while feeding.

Each rising he'd woken voraciously hungry, and each time he fed, the parasites grew louder, pushing for a kill, demanding he feel the rush of power, the rightful rush of power, promising sweet coolness in his blood, a feeling of euphoria that would remove every pain from his weary body.

He kept to the shade of the canopy as he expanded his exploration, heading for the site of the battle, hoping the eagle could spot something the men hadn't. He found the cave entrances, very small and made of limestone, but these didn't seem to curve back underground to form the labyrinth of tunnels as the cave system miles away had done. There were only three small chambers and in each he found Mayan art on the walls. All three caves showed evidence of occupation, however brief, but violent in some way. There were dried spots of blood in all of them.

He took to the sky again, a vague uneasiness in his gut. That bothered him. He had seen horrific sites of battle, torture and death. He was a Carpathian warrior, and his lack of emotion served him well. Without a lifemate to balance the darkness in him, he needed the lack of emotion to stay sane over a thousand years of seeing cruelty and depravity. Yet the sight of the blood in that cave, and the knowledge that women had been brought there by the jaguar-men to be used as they wished, sickened him. And that should *never* happen. Intellectually, perhaps. An intellectual reaction was acceptable, and the honor in him would rise up to abhor such behavior. But a physical reaction was completely unacceptable—and impossible. Yet . . .

Unsettled, Dominic expanded his search to include the cliffs above the river. The rain continued, increasing in strength, turning the world a silvery gray. Even with the clouds as cover, he felt the bright heat invading as he burst into the open over the river. A body lay crumpled and lifeless in the water, caught on the rocks, battered and forgotten. Long, thick hair lay spread out like seaweed, and one arm was wedged in the crevice two large boulders made. She was faceup, her dead eyes staring at the sky, the rain pouring over her and running down her face like a flood of tears.

Cursing, Dominic circled and then dropped. He couldn't leave her like that. He just couldn't. It didn't matter how many people he'd seen dead. He would not leave her, a broken doll with no honor or respect for the woman she'd been. From what he'd gleaned from the conversation between Brodrick and Kevin, she had a family, a husband who loved her. She—and they—deserved more than her body battered by water, left to swell and decompose and be fodder for the fish and carnivores that would feast on her.

The bird settled on the boulder just above her body, and he shifted, covering his skin with a heavy cloak, the hood helping to protect his neck and face as he crouched low and caught her wrist. He was strong and had no trouble pulling her from the water and into his arms. Her head lolled back on her neck, and he saw the bruises marring her skin and the prints around her neck. There were circles, black and blue around her wrists and ankles. Again he was shaken by his reaction. Sorrow mixed with rage. Sorrow was so heavy in his heart that it slowly blotted out the rage.

He took a breath and let it out. Was he feeling someone else's emotions? Did the parasites amplify emotions around him, adding to the high the vampire received from the terror his victim felt—from the adrenaline-laced blood provided? That was a possibility, but he couldn't imagine that a vampire could feel sorrow.

Dominic carried the woman into the forest, every step increasing the heartache. The moment he entered the trees, he scented blood. This had to have been where the second battle had taken place and Brad had been wounded. He found where the third jaguar-man had shed his clothes and gone on the hunt, hoping to circle around and take the shooter.

There were few tracks to show the jaguar's passing, a small bit of fur and a partial track the rain had filled, but it wasn't long before he found the body of the cat. There had been a battle here, one between two cats. The dead cat's prints had been heavier, and spread farther apart, indicating he was larger. But the smaller cat had obviously been a veteran fighter; it had killed with a bite to the skull after a fierce struggle. The foliage was soaked in blood and there was more on the ground.

Dominic knew the jaguars would return to burn the fallen cat, so after carefully studying the ground to commit the victorious jaguar's prints to memory, he carried the woman to the most lush spot he could find. A grotto of limestone covered in tangled vines of flowers would be her only marker, but he opened the earth deep and gave her a place to rest. As the soil closed over the woman, he murmured the death prayer in his native language, asking for peace and for her soul to be welcomed into the next life, as well as asking that the earth receive her body and welcome her flesh and bones.

He stayed a moment while the rays of the sun sought him out through the cover of the canopy and rain, burning through his heavy cloak to raise blisters on his skin. The parasites reacted, twisting and shrieking in his head, his insides a mass of cuts that caused him to spit blood. He pushed some of them from his body through his pores. He found that if he didn't decrease the number, the whispers grew louder and the torment impossible to ignore. He had to incinerate the writhing mutated leeches before they slipped into the ground and tried to find a way back to their masters.

He moved the vegetation on the ground to cover all signs of the grave. The jaguar-men would come back to remove all traces of their species, but they wouldn't find her. She would rest far from their reach. It was all he could give her. With a small sigh, Dominic checked one last time, making certain his chosen spot looked pristine, and then he shifted once more, taking the shape of the eagle. He needed to find where the victorious jaguar had gone.

It didn't take long for the sharp eyes of the eagle to spot his quarry several miles from the site of the battle. He simply followed the sounds of the forest, the creatures warning one another of a predator close by. The eagle slid noiselessly through the tree branches and settled on a broad limb high above the forest floor. The monkeys howled and shrieked warnings, calling to one another, occasionally throwing twigs down at the large spotted cat weaving its way through the brush toward some unknown destination.

The jaguar was female, her thick fur spotted with dark rosettes and, in spite of the rain, blood. She limped, slightly dragging her back leg where the worst of the lacerations seemed to be. Her head was down, but she looked lethal, a flow of spots sliding in and out of the foliage so stealthily that at times, even with the eagle's extraordinary eyesight, it was difficult to spot her against the vegetation of the forest floor.

She moved in complete silence, ignoring the monkeys and birds, padding along at a steady pace, her muscles flowing beneath the thick fur. So intrigued was Dominic by her dogged persistence in traveling in spite of her severe injuries, it took several minutes before he realized the hideous whispers in his mind had eased significantly. All the times he had drained off the parasites to give himself some relief, he had never had them cease their continual assault on his brain; yet now, they were nearly silent.

Curious, he took to the skies, circling overhead, staying within the canopy to keep out the last rays of the sun. He noted that the farther he was from the jaguar, the louder the whispers became. The parasites ceased activity the closer he got to her, so that the stabbing shards of glass cutting his insides remained still, and for a short time he had a respite from the brutal pain.

The jaguar continued to move steadily into deeper forest, away from the river and into the interior. Night fell and still she traveled. He found that he couldn't leave her, that he had no wish to leave her. He began to equate the strange calming of the parasites with her, as well as the even stranger emotions. The rage had subsided into an unrelenting sorrow and anguish. His heart was so heavy of a burden he could barely function as he moved overhead.

Below, large limestone blocks appeared, half buried in the soil. The remnants of a great Mayan temple lay cracked and broken, trees and vines nearly obliterating what was left of the once-impressive structure. Scattered over the next few miles were the remains of an ancient civilization. The Mayans had been farmers, growing their golden corn in the middle of the rain forest, whispering with reverence of the jaguar and building temples to bring sky, earth and the underworld together.

He spotted the sinkhole, and beneath it the cool waters of the underground river he'd noted earlier in the evening. The jaguar continued without pause until she came to another Mayan site, although this one had been used more recently. The thick growth of tangled vines and trees put the date nearly twenty years earlier, but clearly there had been more modern houses here. A generator, long since rusted and wrapped with thick lianas and shoots of green, lay on its side. The ground wept with the memories of battle and the slaughters that had taken place here. The sorrow was so heavy now,

Dominic needed to ease the burden. The harpy eagle flew through the canopy a distance away from the jaguar and remained motionless, just watching, as the jaguar made her way through the long-ago battlefield, as if she were connected to the dead who wailed there.

2

My life was an anguish, my family ripped from me.
My rage had sustained me. I'd given up hope.
Tears fell in rain forest, heart bled in the blood-ground.
My father betrayed me. I barely could cope.

SOLANGE TO DOMINIC

The rain fell steadily, making the miserable heat worse, a relentless downpour, no light drizzle, but sheets of blinding, endless rain. Birds hid among the thick, twisted branches, high up in the canopy in hopes of relief. Tree frogs dotted the trunks and branches while lizards used leaves for umbrellas. The air remained still and stifling on the forest floor but up above in the canopy, the rain seemed bent on drenching the many creatures living there.

Through the gray rain and the humid heat, the jaguar padded silently over the rotting vegetation and the fallen trees and through the varieties of lacy giant ferns sprouting from every conceivable crack or crevice. The small stream she followed led from the wide, fast-moving river on the outer edges of the rain forest into the deep interior. She had trod this path twice a year for the last twenty years, making her way back to where it had all begun, a pilgrimage when she was weary and needed to remember why she did what she did. No matter how the forest changed, no matter how much new growth had emerged, she knew the way unerringly.

Flowers burst into bright color, winding up the great trunks, curling around limbs, petals drenched and dripping, alive with vivid beauty through the various shades of green that made up the rain forest. Buttress roots of the emergents—giant trees that pierced the canopy—dominated the forest floor. The twisted, elaborate shapes provided sustenance as well as support to the largest trees in the rain forest. The root systems were massive and came in all shapes, fins and cages and dark, twisted labyrinths providing shelter for creatures desperate enough to brave the insects carpeting the layers of leaves and decay, sharing the space with the small dawn bats that made homes in the huge network of roots of the impressive Kapok tree.

High above the jaguar, following her progress, flew a great harpy eagle, much larger than normal, the dark wings spread wide, a good seven feet. He moved in silence, keeping pace in the sky, winding through the labyrinth of branches with ease. With two predators on the prowl, the animals hunkered down, shivering miserably. The eagle peered down, ignoring the tempting sight of a sloth and band of monkeys to examine the jaguar's progress through the tangle of vegetation on the forest floor far below.

Roots snaked across the floor, seeking nutrients and causing the ground to be a mass of sometimes impenetrable obstacles. Coiled around the massive trunks were thousands of climbing plants of various nature, using the trees as ladders to the sun. Woody lianas, stems and even roots of climbing plants hung like massive ropes or twisted together, tree to tree, providing an aerial highway for animals. Lianas, looped and twisted into tangles, were full of crevices and grooves, ideal hiding places for the animals taking shelter up and down the trunks and in the branches.

The jaguar hesitated, aware of the large raptor traveling with her. Night was falling fast and yet the great bird continued to trail her progress, sometimes gliding in lazy circles overhead and other times diving through the trees, stirring up the wildlife until the din was frenzied and so loud the jaguar considered roaring a warning. She decided to ignore the bird and follow her instincts, moving on toward her goal.

Hills and slopes were riddled with freshwater streams and creeks flowing over rocks and vegetation as they rushed toward the larger rivers. White-water rivers, heavy with sediment, appeared the color of creamy coffee. Rich with life, the waters were home to the rare river dolphins. The blackwater rivers looked clear and perhaps more inviting, as they were sediment free, but were almost lifeless, unnaturally clear, tinted reddish-brown and poisoned by the tannins seeping into the ground from the rotting vegetation. The jaguar knew to hunt in the rich waters of the white-water rivers, easily flipping the fish onto the banks when she was hungry.

Ticks and leeches swarmed up, meeting the heat and rain with a frenzy and in need of blood, searching for any warm-blooded prey. The jaguar ignored the tiresome bloodsuckers, which were attracted by her warmth and the open wound on her left flank. Thunder boomed, shaking the trees, an ominous portent of trouble. A sloth moved with infinite slowness, its algae-covered fur green, helping it to blend into the leaves of the tree it was currently dining in. But the jaguar was very aware of it above her head, as she was aware of all things in the forest—aware the harpy eagle continued to dog her every move, high in the sky, in spite of night stirring. Instead of bothering her, the unusual presence soothed her, quieted the growing dread and the utter weariness as the jaguar plodded steadily through the maze of vegetation.

The tangle of lianas grew thicker as the jaguar padded silently through the growth, over fallen logs and through umbrella-like leaves dripping with water. She moved with complete assurance, a sea of spots flowing through heavy brush in spite of her obvious limp. The sound of water was deafening as she approached the slopes where water burst through the bank and tumbled to the river below.

As the great cat moved through the forest and the raptor floated in the sky, monkeys and birds called a warning to the peccaries, deer, tapir and paca that either predator might consider a meal. The howlers shrieked fearfully, calling to one another. A jaguar's bite could crack their skulls like a nut. Able to climb trees or swim with equal ability, she could hunt on land, in trees or in the water. The harpy eagle could easily rip prey from a branch, dropping silently from a lookout perch to snatch an unwary victim.

Ropes of muscle rippled beneath the jaguar's sleek, spotted fur. Her rosettes held more spots than those of a leopard, and her pelt was the color of both night and day shadows, allowing her to move like a silent phantom through the forest. Golden sable marked with rosettes, some considered her fur a map of the night sky and hunted her for the treasure.

She moved with nobility in spite of her obvious injury, prowling her domain, commanding respect from all the other occupants of the forest. Built for stealth and ambush, she had retractable claws and vision six times better than a human's. The animals shivered as she passed, called warnings and watched with wary eyes, but she kept climbing, skirting the thin strip of land that barely covered the top of the waterfall, knowing from past trips that the plant-covered slim bridge was a treacherous hazard waiting for the unwary to place a wrong step. She went the more circuitous route, pushing her way through the dark ropy tangle of vines and roots, into the darker interior.

Slate black feathers covered the wings and back of the harpy eagle. The white mantle was striped with the same black, and a black band collared the powerful raptor so that the gray head stood out with the double plume cresting it. The black and white striped leggings led to enormous talons nearly the size of a grizzly bear's claws. With his wings spread wide, it seemed impossible for the powerful predator to maneuver the tight passageways of the canopy, with the knotted and twisted branches and the hanging lianas, but the eagle did so with majestic ease, keeping pace with the predator on the ground.

The jaguar continued through the forest, and her limp became more pronounced as she tried easing the weight from the wounds on her left flank. Caked blood began to run with the infusion of water on her pelt, down her leg, to drip onto the forest floor. The jaguar kept the same steady pace, head down, her sides heaving as she moved with growing pain through the twisted web of roots and vines, determined to reach her goal. The sky above the canopy turned dark and the rain eventually lessened.

Bats took to the air and the forest floor came alive with millions of insects. She kept moving, weaving her way through the trees. Twice she had to take to the aerial highway, using the branches to pass over fast-moving water. She could swim, but she was exhausted and the rain had swollen the banks of even the smallest streams, so the entire forest floor seemed bursting with water. All the while, the eagle kept her company, giving her the strength to continue her journey.

She walked most of the night until she came to the first marker she recognized, a broken remnant of an ancient temple, an impressive structure in spite of the ruins joining sky, earth and the underworld together. The jaguar statue guarding the remains, made of limestone, snarled at her, eyes wide open and staring, judging her worth. Right now, exhausted and far too weary, she didn't feel very worthy.

She put her head down and slunk past the statue, for the first time dropping her chin, avoiding the staring eyes as she padded silently over the ancient stones and pushed deeper into the overgrown brush. A few more miles and the night seemed darker, the trees closer together. Vegetation coiled along every trunk and took up every available space, crowding so close it took effort to push through to the broken limestone blocks that were strewn about and half buried in the thick vegetation covering what once had been a clearing.

Trees had long since overtaken the spot where the land had been cleared to make way for a small village and farm. The corn was long gone, but the jaguar remembered it, the rows of bright green stalks lifting their heads to the sun and the rain in the midst of the surrounding forest. Squash and beans lined the rows, as her people had returned to the old ways, using the same mixture of maize, limestone powder and water for their flour as their ancestors once had done here, in this very same place.

She could feel the blood, running like the great underwater river beneath her feet, flowing, soaked permanently into the ground. Her ancestors had died here—and then, twenty years ago, her family and friends. She would forever hear the sounds of their screams, would know the terror and fear of true evil.

Overhead, the cry of the harpy eagle sent the sleeping
monkeys into a wave of howling, the sound swelling through
the forest, yet the noise reassured her. The eagle, lord of the
sky, landed in the canopy, folded its wings and peered down
at the jaguar. She acknowledged its presence with a lift of her
head, peering upward into the thick canopy. It was unusual
for the great predator to hunt at night, and should have been
unsettling. Anything out of the ordinary in this forest where
legends and nightmares came to life and walked the night
made her uneasy, yet she felt a strange companionship with
the bird.

The jaguar and eagle stared at one another a long time,
neither blinking, neither giving ground. The jaguar studied
the sky predator, vaguely wondering what it meant when a
daytime hunter was moving about at night in the tapering
rain. She was too weary to have much interest in the answer,
and was the first to break eye contact. Here, in the ruins of
two villages slaughtered, where wailing ghosts howled for
revenge, was not the place to find the rest she so badly needed.
She continued her journey, picking her way through the
broken stones and half-buried foundations to the tall Kapok
tree where the eagle perched.

Majestically the bird rose into the air, circled the Mayan
ruins and dropped lower to peer at what was left of the
foundations of more recent destruction. The sharp eyes
examined the ground as it flew overhead, then it dipped even
lower, nearly skimming the jaguar before rising abruptly,
the giant wingspan taking the large raptor back into the
cover of the canopy.

The jaguar felt the beat of those powerful wings as it
passed so close to her. She raised her head and watched until
the eagle was out of sight, her only reaction before she took
to the tree, using her claws to aid her ascent. She stood for a
moment looking at the empty sky, feeling absolutely and

utterly alone, her sorrow a heavy burden. She couldn't afford to feel sorrow. She needed this trip to dredge up anger; no, not anger—that wasn't enough to sustain her when she was alone and exhausted and wounded. She needed a well of rage, a weapon honed by years of fighting evil, fighting for women who couldn't fight for themselves.

She found a comfortable crook in a wide limb and settled her aching body, sheltered from the endless rain, and tucked her head on her paws, looking down at the wreckage of her village. The ruins receded and she stared at the destruction of what had once been her home. The overgrown brush disappeared in her mind, and the sacred spot was no longer a blood-soaked graveyard but a place of the living with four small houses and a cornfield and vegetable garden.

At once she could hear the sound of laughter, of children playing on the cleared ground, kicking a ball around. Her younger brothers, Avery and Adam, both looked so much like her beloved stepfather. He'd been so tall and handsome, his face always smiling, lifting her high in the air and spinning her like a top, making her feel like a princess there in the midst of the rain forest. There was her best friend, Marcy, as well as Marcy's brother, Phin, a tall, serious boy who loved to read. Marcy could always get him to play their games with her winning smile and big green eyes. Their parents . . .

The jaguar blinked, trying to remember the names of Marcy and Phin's parents. How could she forget? She would never forget these people. She was the only person left to mark their existence. Agitated, she rose, her sides heaving, panting, tongue lolling as she struggled with her sluggish brain to recall the two people who had been so good to everyone in the small homestead. *Annika and Joseph.*

Breathing heavily, she settled once more on the branch. The third house belonged to Aunt Audrey, her mother's younger sister, with her daughters Juliette and little Jasmine, her newest cousin. She was very close to Juliette, as they were less than a year apart in age and went between the two houses all the time. The fourth structure held the majority of the children—four boys and two girls, all orphans the couple, Benet and Rachel, had taken in and parented.

They lived and worked and played deep in the forest, far from other civilizations, and they were taught to secrete themselves in nearby caverns and underground tunnels. Unfortunately the caves were often under water, and they had to be careful never to be trapped inside when the tunnels flooded. But still, every few days their parents would conduct drills, running fast, not looking back, going through water to leave no tracks.

Phin was the oldest of them, and she often followed him, peppering him with questions about the outside world and why, at times, they had to hide so quietly. He looked sad, and he'd drop his hand on the top of her head and tell her how special she was. And that they all had to watch over her.

The jaguar sighed. The rain fell down and she lifted her face, allowing the drops to wash the tears from her muzzle. It did no good to weep for the past. She couldn't change what had happened; she could only try to prevent others from feeling her pain and loss.

As she looked down on the ruins, the laughter of the children turned to screams as men poured from the jungle, and with them, great cats, claws rending and tearing, ripping out the throats of the boys. Adam and Avery were caught in the middle of the cornfield. The three of them were playing hide-and-seek and suddenly the great jaguar-men were surrounding them. They bashed in the heads of her brothers without mercy, spilling brains and blood on the ground and trampling the cornfield. She tried to run, but she was snatched up by one of the great brutes and taken into the clearing where Phin and her father fought, back-to-back, trying to prevent the men from dragging her mother from the house.

A sob welled up, a strangled wail the throat of the jaguar couldn't quite handle. She panted, her face to the sky, tears burning, mingling with the drops of the rain. Adam and Avery were gone from her, brutally thrown aside, their bodies tossed like garbage. She remembered the dizzying ride as she was tucked under an arm and rushed through the field, the corn hitting her face, blood spatter everywhere. She saw a man with a machete kill Benet and then the four boys behind his fallen body, even the youngest: little Jake, who was only two. Rachel fought them back using a gun, firing at the men to keep them away from the three little girls. One of the men used a shotgun, and Rachel lay broken and bleeding in the doorway of her house. The men trampled her body while they pulled the screaming girls from inside.

There was so much blood. So much. It ran red and then black and shiny when the moon came out. Someone started a fire, burning their homes and gardens to the ground around them. Phin turned his head and looked directly at her as one of the jaguar-men thrust a knife into his kidney. They stared at one another, his mouth open in a silent scream, matching her mouth. Her captor threw her on the ground beside Phin's crumpling body and she watched in horror as the life drained out of his eyes.

Her stepfather fought valiantly, trying to protect her mother. She lost track of the stab wounds in his chest and back. A great big man cut his throat, ending the fight, and her mother was dragged from the house by the same man, the blood of her husband covering his hands. He hit her mother repeatedly in the face and shoved her at the men before going to each body to make sure no man or male child remained alive. And then he turned toward the girls.

Inside the jaguar, her heart pounded, and she tasted fear and the beginnings of rage. Rage. She reached for it. Needed it. Tried desperately to let it pool inside her as the horrible man caught her thick mane of hair and dragged her across the blood and into the house where they brought each of the young girls.

They must have scouted the small village because the men went looking for Audrey, Juliette and Jasmine. Thankfully, the three were gone, off getting supplies, hiking to the river to meet the supply boat when the attackers had struck. Their attackers were jaguar-men—shapeshifters looking for women who could still shift into animal form. So many had done as her mother had done, found a human man who would stay and love them—raise a family with them. But that had weakened the shapeshifter species, and now fewer and fewer females could provide a shifter. Some of the men, led by a rare black jaguar, had begun forcing the women into servitude, essentially using them as breeders. Any children not capable of shifting were purged.

Solange Sangria stared down at the ground soaked with the blood of her ancestors—and the blood of her family. She could return here only in the form of the jaguar, unable to face the loss in human form. She could weep, with the rain soaking her face and her heart shredded, remembering looking into the eyes of that great black beast, great yellow-green eyes weighing her worth. Her father—*Brodrick the Terrible*. The man who had forcefully mated her mother because of her pure blood and then, when she escaped, had relentlessly hunted her. He had finally found her and slaughtered her husband and sons and the rest of those residing in their small village, children of parents he deemed unfit to walk the earth.

She would forever remember that unblinking stare. Cold. Ruthless. A man who should have loved her as his daughter, but who only saw her worth if she could successfully breed a shapeshifter.

The girls had been tied down and then the torture began. One by one. The girls were forced to watch as each was slashed with small cuts and then larger ones, over and over, in an effort to provoke a jaguar into emerging to protect the child. One by one, when no cat emerged, in front of the others, the leader—her father—declared them worthless. The girl was murdered and her body thrown out of the house into the clearing with the others.

Then it was her turn—the last girl. The man who had sired her worked on her meticulously, using a large blade, his icy fury growing as he. tried to provoke her cat into revealing itself. The pain was excruciating. He slashed her legs until she bled, until her mother pleaded and struggled and finally shifted into the form of a female jaguar only to be knocked out and restrained by the men. They'd taken her mother away, leaving Solange facing her steely eyed, merciless father. He was called Brodrick the Terrible for a reason.

He had spent hours torturing her, certain she could shift, as both her mother and he were from the most powerful line of jaguar-men. A lineage revered by the others. She had steadfastly hidden her cat from him, obeying her mother, knowing her father was evil. To survive the pain she had filled her young mind with childish thoughts of revenge. She lay for hours—days. The nights and days ran together, and the man who had fathered her had been patient, uncaring of her discomfort, making tiny cuts into her skin, poking, as if with his knife he could peel back her human skin and find her jaguar form.

She had said nothing. In the end, she hadn't cried. Not even when he grabbed her matted, bloody hair and threw her from the bed to the floor, shaking his head in disgust.

"A child I sired and she's no good to anyone," he pronounced. "Truly worthless."

She saw the great claw coming at her throat to tear her open, and she hadn't flinched, hadn't tried to move out of the way, staring straight into his eyes defiantly. She would never forget the horrific pain tearing through her, the blood gushing as he tossed her body carelessly aside to lie among the dead on the blood-soaked ground.

Solange had no idea how long she lay unconscious, but when she woke, it was daylight. She was thirsty and every bone in her body felt as if it had been broken. The jaguarmen were gone and all around her were the bodies of her friends and family. She stumbled to her feet and wandered through what looked like a slaughterhouse. The ground was red and damp, and already insects swarmed over the bodies.

She had no idea why she was still alive when her throat gaped open and blood clotted, sticky and wet. She went to each body, trying to awaken them, an eight-year-old girl alone in the forest with everyone she knew and loved dead—slaughtered. Thirst drove her to the sinkhole where the underground river beneath the limestone ran. She drank and once again lay down to allow the darkness to take her. She woke to the sounds of screaming. Her heart slammed hard in her chest and terror held her frozen. Had they returned? That horrible man with his cold, dead eyes judging her worthless?

Aunt Audrey burst through the jungle, Juliette at her side, following the blood trail to the sinkhole. Tears ran down Audrey's face and Jasmine cried in her arms. She fell to her knees beside Solange, pulling her niece into her embrace, and the four of them wept endlessly for everyone they loved.

The jaguar stretched, easing her weight from the injured leg, blinking while her eyes ached and her heart twisted with terrible pain. So many more deaths she couldn't prevent, and she was so tired. So very tired. How did one keep hate alive? And how could she continue to fuel the rage so that she could continue with her mission? Most of all, how did one remain completely, utterly alone?

Her cousin Jasmine was pregnant, and Juliette was mated to a Carpathian male. She might say those men were the scourge of the earth, but in truth, she was happy for Juliette. And Jasmine was now in their care. She loved Juliette and Jasmine as sisters and didn't want this life for them, yet someone had to rescue women from the monsters preying on them in the forest.

She rested her muzzle on her paws and allowed her eyes to close, summoning her only companion. A myth. A dream. Juliette and Jasmine would laugh if they knew how man-hating Solange really survived the terrors of her life. She reached for her dream lover, the one man who got her through every horrific event. And God knew, tonight she needed him desperately. She reached in her mind, knowing the dream so intimately now. His voice first—so gentle and compelling. How many nights had he sung her to sleep? She loved his song, that haunting melody she would never forget as long as she lived.

The Amazon was a place where legends and myths came to life, where reality and dream met. Where sky, earth and the underworld were joined by the great temples of her ancestors. Throughout history, the shamans had revered the spirit of the jaguar, knowing the shifters hunted as both man and animal, day or night, taking command of the unknown. Long ago, when she was deep in a limestone cave, her wounds severe, hopes fading, she had conjured up a companion—a legend come to life in her mind. Maybe she'd been delirious, and maybe, like now when she needed him, she still was.

He had to be a warrior, of course. She needed to be able to respect him. She'd dreamt of him, sometimes at night, sometimes during the day, slowly allowing him to take shape in her mind. He was tall, with flowing black hair, broad shoulders, strong arms and a man's face. He'd fought many battles and, like her, was weary of being alone, but knew he would only have her in his dreams. He would come to her after his battles and he would lay down his arms and find solace in her.

She could never quite decide on the color of his eyes. She loved making them intensely blue, but then at times they would be like the green of the emerald. She was always fascinated by her dream lover's eyes. Never the same, always unpredictable, they mirrored the mystery of the man. He had a poet's soul. He was very gentle, his voice mesmerizing, melodic and quite beautiful. He often sang her to sleep when pain clouded her mind and she lay alone in the dark with her heart pounding and the taste of fear in her mouth.

She dared not dream of him when she was in human form, or around anyone else. He was hers alone, and she needed to protect him, so she only allowed him to invade her dreams when she was in the shape of a jaguar. Deep inside the animal's body, she couldn't murmur aloud where another might hear of him. He was her secret weakness—or strength—however she was in the mood to view her dream life.

She made certain he had all the attributes of a noble man, someone like her stepfather, who took on a wife and child and loved them with everything in him. She'd never been treated differently by him, not even when his sons were born. He'd loved her and treated her like a princess, even spoiled her. She'd loved him so much, and if she ever had a man of her own, which she knew was impossible, he would have to have that generous, loyal, giving spirit.

Some small part of her smiled. She'd given those attributes to her dream man. And she needed him now, when the past was too close and everything had gone so wrong. When she'd failed and a woman had died.

I need you. Come to me tonight. I'm so tired. I couldn't save the woman before they got to her and she killed herself, threw herself into the river. I tracked them for four weeks and fought to get her back, but I was too late. Sometimes it feels like I'm always too late.

She visualized him, building him inch by inch in her mind. The strong thighs, narrow waist and burning eyes, very green tonight. Lately, when she'd called him to her, he bore new scars, a strange thing in a dream where she was the conjurer and yet she couldn't remember attributing new scars to him. A few burn marks on the left side of his face and neck, spreading down his shoulder, worsening along his arm. Maybe, because she'd sustained wounds, her dream lover did as well.

She chose a limestone cave deep beneath the ground to meet him—a safe place where the jaguar-men wouldn't be able to find them even if they were searching. She pulled the cozy cavern, a place she often chose in which to recuperate, from her memory, and added a warm fire and a few soft chairs. In her dream, she could afford to be feminine, although she wasn't beautiful like Juliette or Jasmine; her body bore too many scars and she'd long ago forgotten how to smile—unless she was with him. Even though she wanted to see herself as beautiful in her dream world, it was impossible. She couldn't imagine smooth, flawless skin or a willowy body.

The nice part about her dream man was he didn't mind

that she wasn't perfect or not feminine enough. He didn't mind that she sometimes wept, or showed to him what she couldn't show to the rest of the world. And he would never betray her, never disappoint her; she could whisper her deepest fears and worst secrets and he would still accept her. He knew things about her no one else did.

She pictured the cavern, the Mayan artwork decorating the walls, stories of lives long gone, a world in the distant past where the moon and stars were close and jaguars walked the night upright—men to respect and revere, not shun and despise. A much happier time. She couldn't imagine herself in a dress, a soft feminine outfit like Juliette often wore, but she made certain she appeared as nice as she could. Her favorite top, soft and clingy, which sometimes made her feel a bit of a fool. She never wore it in public, not even around her cousins, but when she wanted to feel feminine and maybe a little pretty, she put it on—just for a moment.

Of course she wore jeans, never a full skirt, because he'd see the scars up and down her legs. She knew he wouldn't care, but she wanted to appear her best for him. She'd considered trying earrings, and once, MaryAnn, a woman she knew and admired, had painted her nails, which for some strange reason made her feel more feminine, yet she was too embarrassed to try to conjure that detail up in her dreams as well.

She sat by the fire, barefoot, looking as nice as she could, her heart pounding, waiting for him. It was silly really, that she had so much invested in a man who wasn't real, but she had no one else. She ran a hand through her thick mane of hair. It was more the color of the dark rosettes in the jaguar's fur than the golden tawny color of her pelt. Almost a sable, it was nearly unmanageable the way it grew.

There wasn't much time left. It was impossible to keep

fighting and not end up dead. A few more inches and her latest wound would have killed her. And life in the jaguar camp was far worse than dying. If they succeeded in their attempts to capture her—and they knew her now and were actively seeking her—she would find a way to take her own life.

Do not say that. Do not even think it. I would come to you. Sustain you. And I would find a way to free you.

The jaguar closed her eyes tighter, as if that could keep him with her. She saw him coming toward her, emerging out of the shadows thrown by the edges of the fire. She loved the way he moved, that sure confidence, those long strides. He was always like that, so confident in himself that he never raised his voice or appeared to be upset, even when he was reprimanding her for cowardice.

Not cowardice, he objected, flowing across the room with his usual grace until he loomed in front of her, towering over her, making her feel small and feminine instead of an Amazon woman. She wasn't tall by any means; she was compact, certainly not fashionably slender. It was a strange thing to have such complete and utter confidence in herself as a warrior, and yet none at all as a woman.

You are tired, csitri, *that is all. Come lie down in my arms and let me hold you while you rest. But first, I must see to your injury.*

He had often called her *csitri,* his tongue caressing the word. She had no idea what it meant, but that single word made a swarm of butterflies take flight in her stomach. She stared up at him, afraid to move or blink, terrified he would disappear, that her perfect dream would shatter. She didn't want him to see her injury. In her dream she wasn't supposed to have an injury. She'd always been able to control her dream, but lately, reality had crept in a little too much.

He gripped her chin in his hand and turned her face

toward the light of the flickering fire, a small frown settling over his rugged features. *Your face is bruised.*

Those bruises shouldn't have been there. What was wrong that she couldn't keep her wounds out of her dreams anymore? Was she that tired? Reading her thoughts, as he always did, her warrior swept her hair from her face with gentle fingers.

You never say my name. Even as he pushed the words into her mind, his fingers moved to the bruises.

At once Solange felt the ache in her bruised face recede. She hesitated. How to explain without hurting his feelings. *This is a dream. I made you up. I don't have a name for you that feels right.*

He smiled at her, his eyes now very, very blue. *Have you ever considered that maybe I made you up? That you are my dream?*

She would love to be someone's dream, but doubted seriously if that would ever be so. In real life she was abrasive, her only protection when she felt too much. Sometimes it seemed as if she went around with her heart shredded all the time. *Somehow I think someone like you could have come up with a better dream.*

Someone like me? I am a warrior who has spent a thousand years looking for my lifemate. I know exactly who she is and what qualities she has.

Solange sighed. This conversation skated too close to having to admit her shortcomings. She didn't want to remind him of all the times she whined about being alone and afraid and tired. *I made you Carpathian. I didn't mean to, you know. I respect Juliette and MaryAnn's husbands.*

Lifemate, he corrected gently. *When we are bound, soul to soul, we are called lifemates. That binding goes from one life to the next.*

She smiled at him and sank down beside the fire. He

filled the cavern with his masculine strength. *That's a beautiful concept. Juliette is very happy with Riordan, her lifemate. He's bossy, but really, after watching them, I can see he does everything to make her happy.*

As I would you. I have waited too many years, csitri, *and my time on this earth draws to an end. I have ingested vampire blood in the hopes of entering the camp of our greatest enemy and spying on them. I will be unable to come to you. Already the blood is consuming me, perhaps faster than I believed it could. I will have only a few risings to complete my task before I must seek the dawn, or go down fighting. I could not find you in this life, but hold hope for the next.*

Her heart nearly stopped beating. Panic set in. Full-blown panic. Dreams didn't end like this. Nightmares did. He wasn't real, but he was the only reality for her when life closed in and she had nowhere else to go. She'd fallen in love with him, as silly as that sounded. This man with his warrior's scars, the face of an angel and demon, all in one, this man with the soul of a poet.

No. I refuse to let you go. I won't. You're all I have. You can't leave me alone.

He touched her hair, rubbing the silky strands between his fingers. *Believe me, little one, I would prefer to stay with you in our dream world. You have so many times gotten me through moments I found not a little troubling. But I have a duty to my people.*

Her throat clogged with unexpected tears. *If I am the lifemate you talk of, isn't your first duty to me?*

His smile was sad. *Had you truly been my lifemate, when I heard your voice, you would have restored colors and emotions to me.*

You're feeling sad. I can see it in your eyes and hear it in your voice.

Merely a trick, csitri. *I wish for these emotions and*

*draw from memories. You have sustained me these last few
years, and I thank you for that.*

No! I won't give you up. It was selfish of her. He had a
right to his nobility and sacrifice. Hadn't she sacrificed her
entire life for the women of her species? But to give him to
the vampires . . .

In desperation, without truly thinking her decision
through, Solange shifted, right there in the crook of the
Kapok tree, and, clinging to the branch, called out to the
only man who mattered to her. Solange Sangria, the woman
who had never needed—or wanted—any man, of royal
blood, powerful in her own right. A warrior renowned and
feared.

In her human form, in her own voice, born of desperation and need, terrified that her dream lover might be real
and going into danger to sacrifice his life for his people,
she lifted her voice to the heavens, allowed the skies to
carry it far and wide. She humbled herself before the forest
dwellers to save him—to save herself.

"Don't leave me!" The cry was torn from her throat,
from her soul, her anguish spilling like the blood of her
family onto the ground where everyone she loved had been
slaughtered and she'd been left alone—the last hope of justice for the women and children of her species.

The sound of her voice lifted the birds from the canopy
and spread through the forest like the wind, filling every
empty space, her sorrow so acute the very trees shivered
and the animals wept with the rain.

3

But then beyond hope, you came into my dream . . .
Glowing eyes like a cat, but fierce need like a child.
Your warrior heart, loyal. Your anguished, "Don't leave me."
Your head in my lap: Csitri! *Strong and wild.*

DOMINIC TO SOLANGE

The birds went quiet. The monkeys ceased all sound.
Even the insects held their breath. Everything in the
forest stilled. Color burst behind Dominic's eyes, blinded
him, even within the body of the eagle, so that for a moment
all he could see was vivid, acute colors, every shade of green,
dazzling reds and violets, the flowers on the trees drenched
in water and bright beyond all imagination. His stomach
clenched and shifted, nausea rising like a tidal wave, the
colors so bright they beat at his mind after centuries of seeing in shades of gray.

He thought the eagle would be a protection, but the colors

had nowhere to go, no way to disperse behind the eyes of the bird, beating at him, filling his mind, overwhelming him with the various shades of brightness. The macaws stood out on the branches, staring at him curiously as he sailed to the ground and shifted into his own form. Dominic staggered, pressing one hand to his roiling stomach and the other up to shield his eyes. There was no way to stop the colors—it was as if a dam had burst in his brain and every conceivable shade and tint, every hue, mingled and fought for supremacy.

Sorrow lived in him, breathed in him. Regret. Fear. Shock. Every emotion that could be felt hit him in the next wave of attack. He went to one knee, trying to process, to sort out what he was feeling and what *she* was feeling, the emotions so overwhelming they left him disoriented and vulnerable. His lifemate was alive—was here in this rain forest somewhere close. His dream woman, the woman he had courted so slowly, building trust between them, was real, not the insubstantial myth he thought her.

No. His denial was low, his shattered call back to her.

This couldn't be happening. Not now. Not after so many centuries. Not when he'd given up and committed to a path that would destroy them both. She couldn't be real. This couldn't be happening. He had only days to live. If he touched her, claimed her, bound them together, she would be locked to his fate.

I am destroyed if you leave me. Her voice filled his mind, the tones soft and so achingly familiar. Why hadn't he considered that she was real? She'd been in front of him the entire time and he hadn't realized it.

A thousand years he'd walked the earth looking for her. *Lifemate.* He could taste the word in his mouth, feel it in his soul. He'd been alone for so long, walking an honorable path, one he had chosen, but he had wanted her—no, *needed* her. The darkness called to his soul. A thousand men, many his friends and kin, had seen their death at his hands. There had been no solace, nowhere to turn, only the memory of honor and the fading hope that she would come to him.

How many times had he walked the night in need? *Save me.* He had thought himself insane at times. The haunting loneliness, the call of evil always pulling at him, that need to feel *something*—anything—was so overwhelming as the endless years stretched out in relentless isolation.

I need you. The anguish in her voice tore at him.

What had he done? *Given up.* He'd lost all hope and he'd taken steps to leave the world while his honor was still intact. The decision had been couched in nobility, a fitting way for a Dragonseeker to end his existence, but it was still an act of cowardice. He had reached a point when he knew he was far too close to the darkness, the need for feeling so strong it was taking root even in his strong bloodline. He didn't want to risk being the first Dragonseeker to ever succumb to the call of the vampire. He had refused to take the chance of giving up his soul, and in doing so, when the risk was becoming sharp and agonizing, he had made the decision to end his days.

Stay. Stay with me. Her anguish clawed at him.

How did he tell her it was too late? He covered his face with his hand, wept bloodred tears. His decision to ingest the vampire blood and end his life had cost him this one last shred of a dream. Worse, it had cost her. His woman. So strong, yet so fragile. What had he done? He had betrayed her as every other male had done in her life.

He knew her—he knew her most intimate fears. Her thoughts. She had told him, but he hadn't listened, not as a lifemate. He should have known, but he'd given up, despaired, turned his back on the most important person in his life.

It was not betrayal.

Resignation tinged her tone. Acceptance. That hurt almost as much as knowing he had given up on finding her. The moment he had the first strange dream, a waking dream, he should have renewed his efforts to find her. Unlike the younger Carpathians, he had heard the strange tales some of the elders had told of how the call of lifemates could be heard over great distances and could manifest itself in a variety of strange ways. He had fallen into the trap so many of his kind had without realizing it. He had lost hope, and that had left him open and vulnerable to the temptation of the vampire. She didn't call it betrayal, but to him, a man of honor, when honor was all he had, it was the worst sin he could have committed.

Perhaps another could not understand. I have given up hope many times. When all we have is honor, when we stand alone against such horrors as we've seen, sometimes despair is all that is left to us.

She shamed him and yet made him proud. A woman to stand by his side. She knew what he had done. He had told her. She knew what a Carpathian was, what could happen should he stray, even for a moment, from the path. And she had to know what it meant when he'd informed her that he'd ingested the vampire blood and was going into their very camp to spy.

Around him, the rain forest had become another world. The sound of the rain was a soft rhythm, music that drummed in time to his heartbeat. Gray had become a silvery mist, incredibly beautiful, each drop a shimmering crystal prism. He felt the individual beads on his skin, and for the first time, the sensation was sensual. He opened his mouth and tasted rain, looking around him in wonder even as he opened his mind to share the precious gift she'd given him. He heard her gasp as she comprehended the enormity of their bonding. It was a sharing he had never expected to experience, and her presence heightened his body's reaction.

He breathed deep as blood rushed to his groin, as every nerve ending in his body went on alert and his skin seemed to sizzle just with the touch of the rain. Strangely, the parasites were quiet, almost as if they'd been as mesmerized by her presence as he was. The hideous whispers in his mind ceased completely.

He allowed himself to just feel, to drink in her presence, to enjoy that moment of not being alone. They shared the same mind, and for that time, everything in him settled, was at peace. He could sense the rightness in her as well, although he knew she was horrified at the things she'd revealed to him about herself in their shared dreams. She was embarrassed that she'd been so vulnerable, that he'd seen that one side of herself she kept hidden from every other person in the world.

I feel both honored and privileged to know you so completely—to know the woman, not just the warrior.

A very male part of him rose up, dominant, protective, a hint of jealousy at the idea of another man uncovering her vulnerability. The woman belonged to him alone—as he did to her. The world could see the warrior in them both, but the man and the woman were an intimacy no other needed to know.

Above, the last of the light faded away to shadow the land in complete darkness. Everything stilled—the rain forest holding its breath. There was no wind, yet a dark cloud moved fast through the canopy, the flutter of wings loud in the stillness of the descending night.

Bats. Dominic hissed the warning in his mind. *The undead are rising.*

From the tangled caverns formed by the finlike roots of the Kapok tree streamed thousands of tiny bats, answering the call of the *masters*. The ground erupted with ticks and armies of ants, swarming up the trees and over rocks.

They will be hungry. Shift and hide, get to safety. It is unsafe to communicate this way. Any surge in power will alert them.

He was on his feet, already moving fast, sliding into the familiar persona of a warrior unsurpassed. Being a lifemate was new to him, but this—this he knew how to do. He took to the air, streaking across the sky, a dark cloud among the dark clouds, the form of a thousand bats, all with fangs and claws, all ravenously hungry—as he was. He let his hunger amplify, heard the howling wind high above the canopy, protesting the unnatural things traveling across the sky. Any in their path would be destroyed. The animals went silent, the night predators slinking under cover. Lightning forked in the night sky, splitting it with whips of white-hot electricity. Thunder boomed, shaking the ground.

Come to me, Dominic. There was a command in the male voice.

A deep, strong voice of authority—a man used to instant obedience. Dominic recognized the voice. It had been so long ago. They had been friends of sorts, warriors together in the old days. He had much respect for the man and his amazing fighting skills.

Zacarias. Leave this place.

I will aid you. Word was sent of what you have done. You will need every aid possible for such a task. I am to the south, an old man walking alone by the river.

Dominic felt the old camaraderie welling out of nowhere. He would die on this rising or the next and yet his lifemate had given him this powerful gift of emotion. He could feel, not just remember, how much he had enjoyed Zacarias with his quick intelligence and fierce fighting skills. He didn't question that any vampire might mimic the oldest De La

Cruz brother's voice, the resonance was too perfect—no one could adequately portray the power of the man with just his voice alone.

It would be good to see you, old friend, but dangerous. If the five could get their hands on you, they would probably be happier than if they managed to capture the prince. Dominic sent the warning, certain Zacarias was well aware the ones leading the vampire rising were the Malinov brothers. Once, the De La Cruz brothers and the Malinovs had been as close as family; now the Malinovs hated the De La Cruz brothers with every bit of malice and treachery their black souls could conjure up.

Do you know if the remaining brothers are here? Dominic turned south. He did so more to protect Zacarias than for any other reason. If one of the undead spotted him, a fight would ensue. He had no doubt of Zacarias's capabilities in a fight, but the undead seemed to be in significant numbers, and even a warrior of Zacarias's skill could be defeated.

I have hunted them. There seem to be several lesser of the undead, newly recruited, and a few more with greater experience. I have spotted two masters, but neither are the Malinovs. They have targeted my brothers, Dominic. I have no choice but to hunt them.

That was Zacarias. His brothers would always come first. He cared little for his own life, but he would survive to remove any threat to his younger brothers. Which was laughable. The other four De La Cruz brothers were more than capable warriors, each highly skilled, trained by Zacarias, with the experience of thousands of battles.

The bats wheeled in the sky, a black flutter of wings as he circled closer to get a better look at the ground. Far below, walking through the trees, was an old man, bent over, using a tall walking stick, looking very vulnerable, an enticement for any self-respecting vampire. Dominic smiled to himself. Zacarias wasn't prone to a lot of talking. He drew his enemy to him and disposed of him without fanfare or bravado.

He came to earth at a safe distance, just because prudence dictated caution in the midst of enemy territory. The old man remained a few yards from him. They studied one another. Zacarias kept the aged appearance, but there was no mistaking those piercing steel eyes. The shaggy hair was streaked with gray, but Dominic knew it was as black as a raven's wing without the disguise.

"*Arwa-arvod mäne me ködak*—may your honor hold back the dark," Dominic greeted, striding forward. He clasped Zacarias's forearms in the age-old greeting of the highest respect between two warriors.

Zacarias gripped him hard, with remembered affection. "*Arwa-arvo olen isäntä, ekäm*—honor keep you, my brother," he returned formally. "It has been long since I heard our language. We speak Portuguese or Spanish as a rule. Sometimes Dutch. We have to adapt to whichever country we are sweeping for vampires. It is a big continent for the five of us to patrol and the Malinovs know this."

They stepped apart and regarded one another. Dominic smiled. "It has been too long, Zacarias."

Zacarias nodded. "Long have I been fighting, holding on to honor. My brothers have found their lifemates and my job is nearly done."

Dominic looked at him sharply. "You have given up all hope of a lifemate of your own."

"I am weary of this life, Dominic," Zacarias agreed. "And I no longer can change to suit the times. Women are different, have grown beyond all that we knew. I have lived too long as a dominant man, my word law, everything my way. The women I have observed would not be happy living under such restraints as I would put on them, nor can I be other than who I am." He shook his head. "I cannot regret what I do not know. I am not suited to be a lifemate. Those days are long gone."

"Do not be so hasty, old friend," Dominic said, shaking his head. "I gave up hope and chose to give up my life for my people. It is too late, I have taken the blood and it eats me from the inside out. Soon my brain will rot, and I will have no option but to reveal myself to those I would spy upon. I will go down fighting, but I leave behind my lifemate. I found her at long last, in my last hour. Do not betray your woman as I have mine."

There was a long silence. Zacarias's gaze never wavered from Dominic's face.

Dominic nodded. "I see in colors. I feel emotion."

"And you go to the very heart of the enemy's lair."

"That is so. Sorrow is a heavy stone to carry," Dominic admitted. "And guilt. I found her, yet I must leave her alone. If I claim her, she will follow me."

Never once did Zacarias's appearance falter. His impression of an older human was impeccable. He looked and smelled and even kept his brain, should a vampire scan, with the thoughts of a man setting up night cameras. Yet behind the façade, he was the man Dominic had known from so long ago.

"We must find a way to switch places. Infect me and then take yourself to the healers to see if they can save you."

Dominic wanted to smile at the demand in Zacarias's voice. Perhaps the man was right in saying he had too long been a dominant predator. There was no going backward. Their experiences shaped who and what they were and what they became. Zacarias did not belong with a modern woman. A lifemate was dedicated to making his or her other half happy. He knew only his way.

Sorrow for the man and his many lifetimes of service pressed hard on Dominic. Zacarias, as if reading Dominic's thoughts, shrugged.

"There is no need to feel emotion for me, Dominic, as I cannot feel for myself. I am here first to retrieve a wayward family member, and second, to uncover just where the Malinovs are. Word came to me that you might need aid in your plan. My taking your place makes sense if it is indeed possible."

Dominic frowned. "Wayward family member?" He couldn't imagine any member of Zacarias's family not submitting to his rule.

Zacarias inclined his head. "Solange Sangria. She is jaguar. Her cousin Juliette is lifemate to Riordan, and Juliette's sister, Jasmine, is under the care and protection of our family. Solange is a problem, a little cat running wild. I have to admit—reluctantly—that she has my respect as a warrior, but she will be killed if she continues along the path she has chosen. Both of her cousins grieve for her and fear, as they should, for her life."

Dominic felt his heart twist. *Solange Sangria.* The name was beautiful. The sound resonated in his soul. She was *his.* Not Zacarias's, not his family's; she belonged solely to Dominic. Solange Sangria was the only person—the only thing—in the entire world he wanted for himself. He held the name to him, knowing with absolute certainty that Solange was the name of his lifemate. It rang true, the heart of a warrior, her femininity hidden from the world, but there for him alone.

"She is mine."

Zacarias's eyes flickered. "I should have known it would be Solange. The woman is as cunning and as wild as the cats in the rain forest. For all that, Dominic, she is a woman worth the world and a worthy match for a warrior such as yourself. She has seen far too much horror and slaughter. She lives only for battle. I fear she will not retreat from this fight. She will need care, Dominic. All the more reason for me to take your place."

"It was my decision to ingest the blood and make my way into the enemy camp," Dominic replied. "This is my battle, Zacarias. It was my choice and I have no honorable option but to see this burden through to the end."

"Your lifemate may feel differently."

"If she is my true lifemate, she will understand that I can do no other than continue on this course. I would not expect another, no matter how generous the offer, to take my place. It would be a disservice both to him and to his lifemate. You cannot fail your own woman, Zacarias, by giving her up too soon."

A faint smile touched Zacarias's mouth, but it failed to soften his rugged features or reach the cool steel of his eyes. "I failed her a long time ago, my friend. I cannot change. I cannot be what this century dictates is proper, nor do I want to. I cannot demand a woman live within my rules." He shrugged. "I came to terms with this long ago."

"Perhaps she would choose to do so, given her free will."

"My point. What free will would she have with me? You and I both know she would have none."

"You cannot know until it happens," Dominic said. "The world changes. You feel nothing now, but should a woman restore your emotions . . ."

"I would hold her too tightly. I am too old, Dominic, too set in my ways. My demands would be absolute."

"Then your lifemate would have to be an extraordinary woman who will find her way in dealing with you," Dominic predicted. "Do not be so eager to throw away hope just yet. Lifemates are destined, Zacarias. We do not just find them anywhere. There is only one to complete us, and while

I do not believe it is always easy, I do believe the binding can only take place with the one who is the other half of our soul."

Zacarias shrugged, unconvinced. Without further pre-amble, he ripped his wrist with his teeth and held out the offering to Dominic. "You will need strong blood to do this thing, my brother. Take what I freely offer. I will come at your call and sustain you throughout this trial."

Dominic raised the wrist to his mouth and drank, the rush of strong, ancient blood hitting like a fireball, rushing through his system to soak into infected organs. The para-sites reacted with a frenzy of stabbing pain. He could feel them in his veins, crawling under his skin, ripping and clawing at his gut. He closed the wound on Zacarias's wrist and immediately pushed as many of the parasites through his pores as possible, bleeding them off to keep the damage to his system as minimal as possible.

Zacarias regarded the wigging mutations with interest. "Riordan told me of such things. This is how they identify the ones who work with the Malinovs?"

Dominic raised his hand to call down the lightning, incinerating the vile creatures. "Yes. I must keep them inside of me and they multiply very fast. Gregori first brought these to our attention when he found them in Destiny, Nicolae's lifemate. Gary, a human male who works closely with him, compared those parasites with the ones I have since ingested and found the newer ones to be far stronger. He is not certain what that means, only that Xavier mutated them further. I think they drive those who host them to insanity. They whis-per continually . . ." His voice trailed off and his eyes met Zacarias's.

"When I was close to the jaguar, the voices ceased. The parasites stopped moving within me, almost as if they were afraid, as if they were hiding."

"From what?" Zacarias asked. "Your woman?"

"If they fear a female, they could not have infected Destiny," Dominic pointed out.

"Perhaps, with Solange close, the pain simply was easier to ignore."

Dominic shook his head. Zacarias's eyebrow shot up. "While I appreciate your current disguise as a vampire, parasites wiggling near your eye are a bit much."

Dominic flicked the offending creature off and watched it incinerate. Lightning forked overhead and the trees shivered.

"They are drawing closer, Zacarias."

Zacarias regarded him with his cool eyes. "Did you think I have traveled all this way to run when the enemy approaches? I will stay here and play my part as the researcher bent on installing these night cameras to catch sight of the elusive jaguar. I even have a proper permit for my work and credentials. I have found it is a good lure for the evil ones."

"Are your brothers close?"

"I do not stay near them. Their happiness is all I have sought to secure, yet being near them is unsettling in ways I cannot say." He flashed another humorless smile. "I irritate their lifemates with my demands. It seems I have not the right way of asking for their safety."

Dominic laughed, uncaring that his vampire pointed teeth gleamed black and atrocious in the night. "I can imagine how you would sound to those women."

Zacarias shrugged. "None of them should be allowed to do what they do. Even Rafael has gone soft."

An army of ants swarmed up and over the fallen trunk just behind Zacarias. One moment the truck was covered in moss and fungus and the next a moving carpet of black and red poured over it. Dominic jerked Zacarias away from the trunk, throwing him behind him, an instinctive reaction to protect the other man. Even as he did so, he threw one hand up toward the sky, bringing down several forks of lightning.

The white light, hot and bright, slammed into the fallen tree. The ants burst into flame, snapping and sizzling, some leaping into the air, others crawling through the vegetation on the forest floor, breaking around Dominic's booted feet to get to Zacarias.

Dominic's breath hissed out between his teeth. *Vampire. He is coming at you.*

Then surely I must hide behind you in cowardice. There was nearly an edge of rough humor to Zacarias's voice, as if he remembered irony and humor just barely.

Lightning followed the swarm of ants, several strikes, but the massive numbers spread out across the ground to surround Zacarias. The two warriors went back-to-back, sweeping the ground around them with fire to clear the debris.

"*Muonìak te avoisz te*—I command you to reveal yourself," Dominic ordered, his voice low, but the tone one of absolute authority.

The ancient words used with the power of the ancient warrior carried every bit as much strength as the bolt of lightning.

The mass of insects undulated, a living carpet that began to reluctantly weave itself into a dark shadow creeping along the ground. Obviously trying to resist, the shadow transformed back and forth between insubstantial shadow and thousands of ants.

"*Veriak ot en Karpatiiak, muonìak te avoisz agbaainad és avoisz te ete kadiket*—by the blood of the prince I command you to take your true form and reveal yourself before the instruments of justice," Dominic demanded.

A shrieking wail, much like nails on a chalkboard, reverberated through the trees. The forest responded with painful cries. Monkeys whimpered, tails tucked, heads down, hands over their ears.

The insubstantial shadow grew into an elongated body, the vampire's arms stretched toward Zacarias, the fingers of his hands bony and gnarled, the nails sharp and slightly curled like claws. The vampire raised its head in defiance, revealing skin pulled tight over bone, worn thin in places, so that he appeared scraped raw, maggots pouring from the gaping holes. He spat at Dominic.

"Traitor. You are one of us. Share this fool." The vampire dug his nails into the ground and dragged himself closer to Zacarias, his attention centered on the "human researcher." He made growling noises as he spoke, his vocal cords rusty and strained. He sounded more animal than man. His bony knees dug deep into the dirt, and beneath his body the earth groaned and small ugly white maggots writhed and wiggled as he dropped them. His body was long rotted, indicating he had been a vampire for many years, possibly centuries, yet he was no *master*.

Dominic struck fast, as was his way. He had long ago given up bravado or talking. He was there for only one purpose—to destroy the undead. There was no reason to talk to them unless he was extracting information, and he knew there were more in the area. This one was too close to Zacarias and might carry tales.

He struck while the vampire was still crawling on his belly toward Zacarias, who remained utterly motionless, the perfect picture of a human man shocked by a nightmare come to life. Dominic's fist slammed through the vampire's back, ripping through muscles and bone, penetrating deep, reaching for the heart.

Vampire blood spewed over his hand and his arm, black and shiny in the dark of the forest. It burned through his skin. All the while the parasites inside Dominic shrieked and screamed helplessly in protest, stabbing his insides so he felt as if he'd swallowed glass. Hot fire closed around his wrist and arm, as the undead's leeches tried to protect him, wrapping around Dominic's flesh and chewing fast. Dominic pushed deeper, ignoring the pain.

Sensing the hunter was nearing his heart, the desperate vampire rolled fast, howling, his serrated teeth snapping at Dominic even while his other hand reached for Zacarias's ankle. Dominic went to the ground beneath the rotting walking corpse, his hand unerringly shoving through attacking parasites even while those in his own body reacted with agitation, stabbing and clawing, tearing at his organs to control him.

Zacarias eluded the searching hand of the vampire, melting away to reappear a few feet away, his cool eyes studying the sky and ground rather than the struggle between hunter and prey. A few yards away, sap ran like black blood, oozing from the trunk of a fig tree. The leaves shriveled and drops of the sap hit the ground in a slow drip, sizzling and burning a hole in the thick vegetation surrounding the tree. A small porcupine shot its quills into an erect position, scurrying away from the tree, dropping the fruit from its paws.

A monkey screamed and leapt, as if burned, from the lower branches to the next tree over. Several birds took flight and a snake lifted its head, forked tongue reaching toward the dark, seeping sap. Abruptly it uncoiled, reaching out for an interlocking branch from the neighboring tree. Frogs and lizards abandoned the branches, and insects made a mass exodus.

Zacarias moved closer, flowing over the ground, moving fast, reaching the tree just as the massive trunk broke open and expelled the foul creature poisoning it. At once the stench of rotting eggs mixed with decomposing flesh spewed into the still air. Leaves on the surrounding trees and shrubbery withered. Flowers closed petals and shrank away from the abomination.

"Drago, old friend. I see you have come to visit me," Zacarias said gently. "Long have I issued you an invitation, but you refused. It is good that you finally have opted for justice. It is long overdue."

Drago snarled, pulling back his lips in a snarl to reveal hideous teeth, pointed and black, stained with the blood of the many lives he had taken. He stroked the air beneath his hands, as if petting an invisible creature, his nails dagger-like, each stroke precise.

"Foolish upstarts. They are so busy fighting over the scrap of a meal, they failed to notice the prize they had." When he spoke, Drago growled each word, just as precisely as the movements of his hand.

"But you did," Zacarias said gently. His cool eyes continued to sweep their surroundings. Drago would never confront him so calmly unless he thought he had the advantage.

Behind them, Dominic was very aware of the second vampire on the scene, but around him, tentacles burst through the ground, running along the floor of the forest, seeking prey. He heaved the vampire off him, rolling on top, slamming the rotting face into the ground among the tentacles, even as his fist pushed through the mass of writhing parasites to get at the heart.

Tentacles immediately circled the vampire's neck and skull; more pulled at his legs and arms in an attempt to drag him underground. Dominic's fingertips reached the cold, withered heart. The undead shrieked and redoubled his efforts to throw Dominic off him. The absolute silence of the hunter was unnerving. The vampire had no idea whether Dominic was one of his fellow recruits for the *masters*, as his parasitic blood indicated, or whether he was a highly-skilled hunter, as his earlier commands indicated. Dominic had invoked the name of the prince, something no vampire would ever do.

Dominic's fingers burrowed around the blackened organ, feeling more parasites wriggle against his palm as he enclosed the prize in his fist and began to extract it from the vampire's body. The tentacles fought him for possession. Overhead, lightning forked in readiness. Thunder rolled ominously. The sound was horrendous, the sucking of the undead's acid blood trying desperately to hold on to the heart, the high-pitched shrieking of the vampire and the wail of the parasites already spilling out of the body, abandoning their host.

The tentacles frantically jerked at the undead in an effort to draw him beneath the earth, out of Dominic's reach, but Dominic rose, the heart in his fist, dripping parasites and acid onto the ground as he leapt away, commanding the lightning. The bolt slammed into the body before the tentacles could save it. He tossed the heart into the white-hot blaze and directed the energy across the blackened ground until every tentacle and every parasite was incinerated. His arm and hand burned, the flesh nearly eaten away down to the bone. He rinsed his flesh in the edges of the light to take off the blood and kill any remaining parasites that might have gotten on his skin.

Deep inside his body, in the veins and organs, the parasites rushed to hide from the blinding heat, giving him, for one moment, a reprieve from the constant agonizing torture. Never once did he allow his appearance to change from his vampire persona to that of a Carpathian hunter. Only when he was finished did he look up to meet Drago's eyes. He snarled, pulling back thin lips to reveal serrated, bloodstained teeth, his growl a challenge.

"That is my food you are toying with," he snapped, then strode through the trees to put his body between Zacarias and the new threat.

He knows who I am, Zacarias warned. *He would never openly challenge me if he did not have some nasty little surprise up his sleeve.*

"You have no idea who this is," Drago snarled. "He is a prize beyond compare."

"I remember you from the old days," Dominic prodded. "Drago, a whining, sniveling coward. You always disappeared in a battle."

Drago smirked. "I managed to live another day while so many others fell."

Dominic studied his enemy. Drago's hand continued those precise strokes, down low, close to his hip, as if he might be petting a dog. His tone had a strange cadence, each word separate, almost as if he punctuated each with a stop after it. Dominic had seen many traps in his centuries of battling the vampire, but he was in new territory here.

He took another step closer to the undead in an effort to get into a position to close the gap quickly and finish the vampire before the trap could be sprung.

Drago shook his head. "You are one of us, sworn to the five *masters*. This is Zacarias De La Cruz, sworn enemy of our leaders. They will want him alive."

Dominic shrugged. "You cannot take credit for my having found him."

Zacarias flexed his shoulders, regarding them both with cool eyes. "I am not captured yet, nor do I think either one of you has the ability to defeat me in battle, alone or together, but you are welcome to try."

Dominic sneered. "Hunter, stay quiet while I deal with this fool." He allowed his gaze to sweep the surrounding forest, paying attention to the trees closest to them.

Drago had evidently traveled through the ground and entered the fig tree via the roots, emerging from the trunk when he thought it safe. If he was traveling with others— and from his confidence, Dominic was certain that he was—they could be using the trees to hide.

Stay away from the trees, he cautioned Zacarias.

Zacarias must have had the same thought as Dominic, because he was already shifting position, trying to secure a spot where he could keep an eye on the surrounding trees. Dominic was grateful he had the hunter at his back. They might look like predator and prey, but they had battled together many times in the past, in the old days, hunting vampire and the enemies of both humans and Carpathians. There was no other he would have chosen to fight with him.

Drago's fingers rose and fell over his invisible companion. "This hunter will be turned over to the *masters*."

Dominic risked a glance at Zacarias. He was every inch the Carpathian hunter, broad shoulders, long flowing hair and eyes cool under fire, yet minutes earlier he had been an older man, bent over, fumbling with his cameras in the trees. *How did he know who you were?* Zacarias's disguise had been faultless.

I have no idea.

"*I* am a *master*," Dominic growled at Drago, staying in role as a braggart and bully, as so many of the undead were. "You cannot tell me what I must do with my prey. Stand away or you will meet the same fate as that fool who challenged me."

Drago spat on the forest floor, and small parasites wiggled obscenely in the dried and decaying leaves. His eyes glowed a deep red, and he threw back his head and howled. A tree to the left of Dominic shivered. A large snake that was twisted around the branches lifted its head and slithered along the trunk, uncoiling its long body as it descended to the ground and slithered almost to Drago's feet. Its long tongue tested the air and then flicked over the parasites before he rose, taking his hideous true form, to stand a few feet from his companion.

Drago's fingers continued to stroke the air under his palm as the ground just behind Zacarias split open and spewed a third vampire. A fourth emerged from the twisted branches of the blackened fig tree that Drago had come from, and Dominic automatically put him down as the weakest link. His face was still half recognizable, the flesh still covering the shrinking bones. Dominic had encountered him when he was still a hunter, not even an ancient, yet he had been unable to control his desire for emotion and had obviously capitulated to the whisper of darkness. His name had been Robert, but Dominic thought of him as a worm.

Zacarias looked around at the four vampires surrounding them. *We could be in a little trouble here.*

Dominic sent the impression of a smug smirk. *Just like in the old days. The way I like it.*

You always were a little crazy. You love the battle. Zacarias's tone was wry.

And you do not? There was laughter in the question.

4

But then beyond hope, you came into my dream . . .
Your melody haunting, your gentle voice healing.
The soul of a poet, great heart of a warrior.
You gave all for your people. Let me give you feeling!

SOLANGE TO DOMINIC

What had she done? Solange stood in the rain, hands covering her face, throat aching, her heart thundering in her chest. She'd told him every secret thing about her. She'd thought herself safe, that he wasn't real. She had exposed her every weakness. Had the dreams been some kind of trick? She groaned and stroked a hand over her throat to try to ease the terrible pain. Her vocal cords felt shredded—just like her heart.

A Carpathian warrior. She had made him up. Built his image detail by detail—hadn't she? She had known back then, when she first began to daydream, that she had given up all hope and was coming to the end of her days. Her warrior had been the only thing keeping her going through all the battles and all the horrific slaughters she had encountered. Brodrick the Terrible had been determined that he would purge every diluted strain of jaguar he could find. Only those who could shift were spared—male and female.

There was no way to stop the evil inside of her father. The sickness had begun hundreds of years earlier, treating the women like slaves, like breeders, the men following the suit of the royal family. They had been self-indulgent, depraved, craving the power and building upon it, encouraging the worst traits of their species rather than attempting to become something different. Brodrick *enjoyed* killing. He surrounded himself with men just like him.

The familiar rain felt like a seductive stranger, teasing her senses, running between the valley of her breasts and down her belly to the junction between her legs. Strangely aroused by the sensation, Solange lifted her face to the rain, capturing a few drops in her mouth, allowing it to run down her throat to ease the ache. There was no easing the ache between her legs.

Colors as bright as the sun swirled in front of her eyes, nearly blinding her. Every emotion was magnified a thousand times. Humiliation. Embarrassment. Sorrow. Rage. A terrible sexual hunger, raw and volatile, a craving she'd never experienced. The rain dripped from the tips of her breasts, now tight, blossoming into twin hard peaks. She looked down at her body, and tears burned behind her eyes.

This need, this craving, was stronger than any heat she'd ever experienced. It took her breath and stole her sanity. The passion didn't just involve her body—every single part of her, heart and soul, seemed to have an overwhelming desire to be with him. Lifemates. She had seen the devotion her cousin Juliette's lifemate had to her. He paid attention to the smallest thing, seemed completely focused on her every moment—and that kind of concentration would make Solange crazy. She'd been alone too long. She went weeks without seeing or talking to another person. How could she possibly be in a relationship? She didn't know how. She didn't know the first thing about sharing her life or—or *anything*.

Panicked, she could barely breathe, her lungs burning for air. She could never go to him. *Never.* There was hardly a place on her body that wasn't scarred. She had no smooth skin to offer, no soft side to the hard-edged woman who had become nothing more than a fighting machine. The dream woman had been an illusion. MaryAnn, Manolito's lifemate, was as close to a friend as she had, and even MaryAnn had chided her for her wild hair and lack of femininity. She had pretended it didn't matter that she wasn't womanly, and it hadn't then. But now—now that he was in her life, now that he had come, this man among men, this warrior who stood head and shoulders above the rest . . .

She moaned and pressed her fists into her eyes. She wasn't a woman to cry. Or to crave a man. Or to need him. Yet somehow, over the course of the last few months, that had all changed. *She* had changed—driven to the brink of destruction by the endless horror of her chosen life. There had been no respite—but him. The Carpathian. *Her* Carpathian.

She inhaled sharply and silently admitted that she needed the Carpathian, even if it was just to share his last days. He would never flinch from what he perceived as his duty to his people any more than she would. This was a terrible mess and it came at the worst possible time. She had finally found Brodrick. She knew where he was, but she also knew he would never stay there long. And he usually traveled with his most violent soldiers.

Around her the air stilled. All noise ceased in the forest.

Her jaguar froze, shoved close to her skin as if to protect her. The hair on her arms stood up and a frisson of fear slid down her spine. Insects poured over the ground, ants and beetles swarming, covering everything in their path. She saw them flowing like a black river over the fallen trunks, moving toward her. Overhead, the sky filled with bats, moving fast through the canopy, an ominous black cloud, dark portents of things to come.

The vampires had risen. She shifted quickly, letting the change take her. The undead would rise hungry and looking for prey. In her human form she would easily attract them. Her jaguar form could get into the canopy and wait until they passed.

Bats. Her dream lover's voice hissed the warning in her mind. *The undead are rising.*

She was already back in the trees, the jaguar climbing into the crook of a branch, high up beneath an umbrella of thick leaves. She stayed very still.

They will be hungry. Shift and hide, get to safety. It is unsafe to communicate this way. Any surge in power will alert them.

Her tail twitched in annoyance. Did he think she wasn't aware of what to do? She wasn't stupid. Manolito and Riordan had taught her, Juliette and Jasmine how to kill a vampire should the need arise. Lately, in the last several weeks, their training had saved her life numerous times. She was a warrior first. Always. She didn't take the chance of responding because she knew her Carpathian was right, and the undead might feel the surge in power it took to communicate telepathically. It probably could be done without them knowing, but she wasn't experienced enough and Solange never took unnecessary chances.

She kept her head on her paws and pushed everything from her mind as the bats wheeled and dipped in the air, some consuming flying insects while others settled on the fruit in the trees. She could see others crawling along the ground in search of warm prey. She remained very still, even keeping the tip of her tail still until, slowly, the bats moved on to new territory. Only then did she rise and stretch with a cat's languid manner.

She had a job. She'd set a trap and she knew Brodrick and his men would fall into it. They would never be expecting her to return. By now they would know she was wounded. They would think themselves safe from her. And Brodrick had formed an uneasy alliance with the vampires. The undead could control the minds of the jaguars with diluted blood and even pure blood, but certainly not a royal. As long as Brodrick got what he wanted from the vampires, he would continue to have a relationship with them. It was a pact made in hell as far as she was concerned. Brodrick was set on a path of destroying any jaguar unable to shift. The vampires had vowed to help him reach his goal so he was fine with helping them.

The huge laboratory built by the human society—a group of people dedicated to hunting and killing vampires—was used supposedly just for research, but she'd been inside and knew the building was used for much more nefarious purposes. Enemies were held and tortured there. Jaguar-women were often taken there to be used by Brodrick and his men. But the real purpose for the building was much more bizarre. She'd seen the banks of computers. Vampires didn't have the ability to sit for hours at a computer compiling data, but both humans and jaguar-men could do so, and the vampires needed them to carry out the task of building a database of psychic women around the world for them.

Brodrick's men seemed to handle most of the details, and she was certain they were compiling a hit list of people— particularly women—who carried the jaguar blood. She hadn't been able to confirm that, but she often lay in the branches of the trees for hours watching over the facility—a terrible risk certainly, yet one she hoped would yield even a single piece of important information.

Certain now that the vampires had moved on through in search of blood, Solange began to make her way back toward the bluff overlooking the river where the woman, Annabelle, had thrown herself onto the rocks below rather than be recaptured by the men who hunted her. She tried to push the face of the desperate woman from her mind. Solange had shifted and called to her, exposed herself in order to stop her, but Annabelle had been so desperate, she refused to take a risk when the men began firing guns at Solange.

The jaguar shook its head. The dead often rose up to taunt her. Sometimes she thought she might drown in their screams, in the terrible cruelty done to them. Solange knew human trafficking had become a major problem in other places, but here, in her world, it had been going on for centuries, thanks to the leaders of her people. Women were objects, nothing more. Vessels and possessions. The men had such entitlement, believing themselves above all laws, even the laws of common decency. The women were put there simply to serve their brutish sexual needs and give them children.

Solange padded softly along the labyrinth of interlocking branches forming the arboreal highway. The animals and birds, still cowed by the passing of evil, simply shivered as she moved past them toward her destination. She went fast—she'd covered many miles throughout the day to get to the site of her childhood home, and now had a long way to go in return. It was faster using the canopy to travel, but several times she was forced to go to the forest floor.

The wound on her hip broke open, seeping more blood.

She couldn't afford the scent in the air. With a sniff of impatience, she made her way to one of her many stashes throughout the forest. Deep inside a cage of roots she had hidden a small waterproof box. A set of clothing, weapons, ammunition, dried food, clean water and a medical kit waited for her. She had to shift and sew up the wound.

It was always important in the rain forest to cleanse and close a wound, applying an antibiotic cream—and this was no exception. Infections were rampant, easy to get and easy to die from. As a rule she was meticulous with wounds, and the fact that she'd traveled all the way to the place of her family's slaughter without caring for the lacerations told her a lot about her mental state. She needed to find a way out or she was going to die soon. She had nothing left to give—and that shamed her.

She shifted back into her jaguar form. It was easier to handle the deep emotion threatening her sanity when buffered by her animal, especially at the realization that there would be no end to Brodrick's depravities. There were so few women in the rain forest, or even living on the edge of it, that Brodrick had resorted to using the vampire database to find jaguar-women in other countries. He had them kidnapped and brought to him. That was how Annabelle had been taken. Her husband was human, from what Solange had understood, but that hadn't stopped the men Brodrick had hired from kidnapping her.

The human society was in close league with Brodrick, although she'd noticed that all the men guarding the laboratory were afraid of him. As they should be. Brodrick was as cruel and depraved as any vampire, and just as cunning. He knew the rain forest—it was his home turf. Her reputation had grown over the years, and by now, he would know there was a pureblood female shifter wreaking havoc with his plans. He despised disobedience, and his punishments were swift and brutal. He demanded complete submission, especially from a female. He would want her alive—her one advantage. The males she encountered would be handicapped by trying to bring her to Brodrick still breathing.

She hurried now, loping occasionally. They would burn the body of the jaguar male she'd killed tonight to keep their presence hidden. They would want Annabelle's body to burn as well. Hopefully Brodrick would be there to direct the operation personally, but if not, and she managed to send him another body or two, he would stay to hunt her. He would never be able to take a slap in the face like that from a female. He would move heaven and earth to find her. She would let him and she would kill him. She expected to die, but she wasn't going alone. She would rid the remaining jaguar-women of his evil presence even if it meant paying with her death.

She could hear the roar of the river and she went to her belly, listening, sniffing the air, looking for signs in the animals as well. She scented the presence of at least two males, jaguar-men, but not in their animal forms. Their senses would be a little duller, their hearing less acute. She worked her way south of them until she came to another of her small stashes, again sheltered from the elements by the roots of a tree. This box was longer and held her weapons, carefully cleaned, with a wealth of ammunition. She shifted and dressed quickly, strapped on a knife, a crossbow, extra arrows and her rifle. She wasn't the best with a handgun, although she wasn't bad, but at a distance she was a damned good shot with both a rifle and crossbow.

She made her way through the forest, keeping to the animal trails. She had the advantage of being small and compact, allowing her into spaces the larger jaguar males might not go to pick up her scent. She crawled on her hands and knees some of the time and other times she slid on her belly to get to the site she'd chosen for her attack.

She took a good careful look around, scent-testing the air, before she went up the tree. It was much more difficult to go half human, half cat, but she'd used the technique often over the years so she could climb to the canopy fast and yet bring the weapons and clothing she might need.

She settled into the crook of the tree, listening to the sounds coming from the river's edge. A lot of swearing. Muttering. She narrowed her vision, peering through the leaves to survey the rocks. From that angle, she couldn't see a body. They had to have moved it, or perhaps the body had come off the rocks into the water and had been swept downstream. Evidently that was the conclusion the two men had come to.

"You should have hauled her up onto the bank, Kevin," one complained.

She recognized the speaker. She'd wounded him. She'd hoped she'd done a better job, but he was walking on his own now.

"I was too busy hauling your ass back to the lab to stop the bleeding. You would have died out here if I hadn't, Brad," Kevin snapped.

The jaguar-men were famous for their ugly tempers. Neither wanted to follow the river for miles in the hopes of finding the body, but they had no choice. It was a law they all lived by, to destroy all evidence of their species. The two men stood looking down over the bank, and then spat, almost simultaneously, their disgust evident. Solange bit her lip hard, furious that they would show such disrespect to the woman they had so brutally used—the woman they'd driven to suicide. She put the rifle to her shoulder, took a breath, finger on the trigger, and put Kevin squarely in her sights.

There was always that moment when she wondered if she could do this—if she would hesitate and alert them to her presence, allowing them to kill her first. She'd never be taken alive. She'd rescued too many women and seen close-up what they did to their victims, and would never allow herself to fall into their hands. Jasmine, her cousin, had been taken by these same men. Solange detested them. They deserved to die. Every one of them had committed murder, killing men, women and children. Yet . . . She felt that horrible moment stretch out in front of her. Could she do this again? How much of herself would she lose regardless of whether it was justice? The cost of taking lives had gone so high she was no longer certain that she was willing to pay.

She squeezed the trigger. Kevin jerked, and the sound of the shot reverberated through the forest as the body slowly crumpled, a hole blossoming in the back of his head. Brad twisted around, leaping into the air as he tried to locate the source of the sound even as she squeezed off the second shot. The bullet caught him in his shoulder, spinning him as he began his fall from the cliff's edge to the raging river below. He shifted in midair, frantically trying to tear at his clothes as he plummeted into the roaring water.

Bile churned in her stomach, rising to her throat as she wiped sweat from her face. The second man would probably live, but he would be out of commission for a while. She'd have to hunt him later. And she could never stake out another body again; they'd be waiting for her. Already she was automatically putting weapons in the proper place for a descent, trembling the entire time but moving out of pure experience and reflex. She had to move fast and get out of

the area. Brodrick traveled with a group of fighters and she
wasn't in any shape to fend them off. Sound traveled at
night and they would have heard the gunshots.

A bird shrieked. She leapt from the branch, hand outstretched, catching at the thick, woody liana vines hanging
from all the trees and swinging hard, using her forward momentum to drive her across to the next vine. Her arms were
nearly yanked out of their sockets as she hurled her body
across open space toward the next tree. She managed to
pull herself onto a branch, shifting her weight to give herself the best leap toward the vines hanging between the
next two trees.

She glanced over her shoulder as she jumped, and saw
the huge black jaguar running along the branches of the tree
she'd vacated. Her heart slammed hard in her chest, her
breath exploding out of her lungs. *Brodrick the Terrible.* For
a moment she was a terrified child again. The eight-year-old
girl with her family dead around her and the man, larger
than life, staring at her with flat, dead eyes, driving the point
of his knife into her skin to try to provoke her cat into revealing itself.

Don't panic, she chided herself, forcing her brain to
work as she moved between the trees. She changed her
course subtly, always one step ahead of that fierce, angry
cat. He was too heavy to use the vines, forced to run along
the branches. Her advantage was the air, and she went for
the trees without interlocking branches, forcing him to slow
in his chase, making him go to the forest floor to follow her
progress. Below her, he raged, running, snarling, his roar
filling the night.

After that first initial shock, Solange held her terror in
check. She knew this part of the rain forest, probably better
than Brodrick did. He had no idea she was his daughter, the
one he thought he'd murdered and thrown away as garbage

years earlier. She had a few advantages if she kept her head. She caught the vine that would take her into the tree nearest the fast-flowing river. Swollen from the endless rain, the water flooded the banks on either side and churned and rolled over the rocks, creating a series of rapids. She moved through the trees overlooking the river.

Brodrick roared again and leapt at the thick liana just as she grasped it, her momentum swinging the wooden rope toward her destination. She felt the jerk and her heart jumped in her throat. Her body slammed into the branch hard, hands reaching desperately for a purchase. She missed with her left hand but her right caught the gnarled branch firmly. She managed to grip with her left and kept moving, using her weight as a pendulum to swing herself onto the branch.

She ran along the branches, fitting an arrow into her crossbow. Brodrick scrambled up the trunk and landed behind her, hard enough to shake the tree. She faced him, standing her ground, looking into those evil yellow eyes. He stared at her, motionless, in a crouch, prepared for a rush. She felt the pull of his mesmerizing power, those eyes burning over her, marking her as prey.

She held the crossbow at her hip, loosely aimed, and stared into his eyes. She let him see her loathing. She despised him. There would be no respect. No give to this monster. And no fear. She would *never* show him fear again. His lip curled at her insubordination. Grown jaguar-men, experienced fighters, bowed before him, but here she was, a lowly woman, meeting his stare, not looking away—daring to *challenge* his authority.

Solange made certain that he could see her contempt. Her defiance. Her complete revulsion of everything he was. Taunting him. She knew him. She'd studied him. He demanded complete reverence, and he got it through intimidation and cruelty. All must bow before him, especially women. He hated the women who carried life in their bodies but refused to follow his will. They were put on earth to serve their men, to be used in whatever way the men saw fit, and yet they'd fled the rain forest and his authority to find human males. It was a slap in his face and he despised them. Every chance he got he punished them in demeaning and brutal ways. She knew her defiance would enrage him—and she wanted him enraged.

They stared at one another for a long time, neither blinking. She saw the power gathering in his muscles, the fierce directness in his stare.

"It's been a long time—Father." She spat the word.

The jaguar stilled, muscles going rigid. She'd thrown him off his attack. She kept his gaze, playing the life-and-death game with him.

"You wanted royal blood. Am I the only one you didn't manage to destroy?"

She saw the hesitation—the puzzlement. He wanted a female shifter of pure blood, but where had she come from? And *royal* blood? In all the hundreds of female children he'd destroyed, he wouldn't remember one. He would want her alive. He knew she was a shifter and that she was fast at it. There were so few women left who could shift.

She waited patiently, breathing. In. Out. Waiting for him to hear what she said. Not pure. Royal. She saw the moment he understood. *Father. Royal.* Yeah, he put it together. He shook his head, clearly shocked, his eyes never leaving her face.

She flashed her teeth. "Aren't you going to say welcome home—*Daddy*?"

It was a taunt. A dare. A female challenging him.

He snarled and began to shift—as she knew he would. She had only seconds. He was fast—faster than she'd imagined he could be. She brought up the crossbow and shot an arrow straight into his shifting throat. Turning, she leapt into the next tree, moving fast, knowing if she hadn't killed him, he would come after her.

She heard the roar, caught the spatter of blood on the leaves around her and kept going. The jaguar was enraged, and a wounded cat was doubly dangerous. Something big crashed onto the tree behind her and the entire tree shook, nearly dislodging her. She threw herself precariously onto the next branch, scrambling to get across the shaking limb. Tree frogs jumped out of her way. A lizard burst out from under leaves and ran. She caught the movement out of the corner of her eye but didn't slow, leaping to the next tree, landing in a crouch to whirl around and let fly a second arrow.

The black jaguar looked hideous, all teeth, blood running down its neck to the broad chest. There in the darkness his eyes glowed red, fixed on her, angry and determined, his ears going flat when he saw the loaded crossbow. The arrow took him high in the shoulder and he roared his anger, the sound reverberating through the forest.

Birds shrieked, rising from the canopy in spite of the darkness, taking to the skies to avoid the vengeance of an enraged jaguar. Solange knew better than most just what force a large cat could hit with, and as Brodrick sprang at her, she dove to the next tree. Her hands missed the branch and her heart somersaulted. Her outstretched arms slammed into a thin branch. The crack was audible, but she grabbed out of sheer desperation. Her fingers wrapped around the limb and the jaguar landed hard on her back, claws ripping flesh.

Hot breath poured over her neck as the jaguar tried to bite down on her shoulder. The limb broke and they fell together. Solange tried to turn enough to jam the crossbow against the cat's heaving sides, but it was impossible. His spine was too flexible and he turned with her, preventing her from dislodging him. Her body hit a branch and broke it in half, sending the heavy jaguar careening against the trunk and finally off of her.

Solange looked down at the churning water and then up at the jaguar gathering itself for another spring. Head down, she somersaulted off the branch and into the raging water. The bellow of the jaguar followed her down. She tried to enter the water straight, feet first. The cold was shocking to her body as the dark waters closed over her head and threw her tumbling downstream. She rolled over and over, lungs burning. She lost the rifle and crossbow immediately, the weapons ripped from her hands as the vicious current took her.

Exhausted, her body numb, Solange fought her way to the surface to grab a lungful of air before the current rolled her under again. She tucked her legs into her chest and tried to ride it out, no longer fighting the pull, just allowing the strength of the river to carry her far from her enemy. She had to grab air when she could, and twice she slammed into rocks. Their surface was too slippery for her to hold on to, so she went spinning down river again.

In the inky darkness she caught sight of a tawny jaguar lying on the bank, stretched out, and she swept by so fast she couldn't tell if he was dead or alive. She tried to stay quiet, to suppress her gasps for air, the sobs trying to escape her burning lungs. She was so exhausted it was becoming difficult to move her arms or try to keep her body straight, feet pointed ahead of her. She couldn't see rocks until she was on them, and had no chance to pull herself out of the water.

For just one moment it crossed her mind to let the water take her. She was tired of fighting and her body was battered and bruised. She could barely move her arms, let alone find the strength to pull herself out of the water. And she was bleeding from several punctures and bite wounds. She couldn't swim, she couldn't see, and her clothes were

weighing her down. She could just let go . . . but there was
the problem of her Carpathian.

The water shot her around a bend and something large
loomed in front of her. Her heart leapt. A fallen tree lay partially across the river, branches sweeping out. If she didn't
kill herself by knocking her head on the trunk, she might
have a chance. She gathered herself as she neared the outer
branches. She hit harder than she expected, the solid wood
driving her knees into her chest, robbing her of the small
amount of air in her lungs. As the river sucked her under,
she threw her hands out and managed to hook her arm
around a branch. Sending up a silent prayer that the branch
was strong enough to hold against the pull of the water, she
gathered her strength for the next step.

Before she could drag herself onto the branches, she
heard a chilling noise. She barely caught the sound above
the roar of the river and her own heartbeat thundering in
her head, but there was a distinctive voice, a mixture of
growling and human vocals. For one terrible moment she
nearly lost her grip on the branch, shocked that she wasn't
alone and that the voice was distinctly jaguar. Shivering
continually, she held herself still, trying not to allow her
ragged breath to escape.

"She can't be alive," the voice snarled as it came closer.
"He's out of his mind."

She tried to pull herself into the tangle of branches. She
didn't want to let go. She knew she'd drown. As she inched
her way inside the labyrinth of branches, her shin hit a
thick limb beneath the water line and she quickly wrapped
her legs around it. She had to let go of the death grip she
had on the higher branch. It was terrifying to even consider
such a folly, and it took several seconds to force herself to
allow her fingers to slide along the branch until her body
was no longer stretched out in plain sight. She closed her

eyes and let go, using every bit of strength she possessed to hang on with her legs.

The current dragged at her, a powerful force intent on ripping her free to send her careening down the river. But she fought back, slowly pressing her upper body back toward her legs. Her fingertips brushed leaves and small twigs. She strained harder and managed to curl her fingers around the underwater branch. Fighting not to breathe loudly, she tried to stay calm. She was in a precarious position, her strength gone. The tree shook and she knew something heavy had leapt onto it. Her heartbeat thundered louder than the roaring of the river.

"He's got two arrows in him," a second voice said. "If we go back without her, he's liable to kill us both."

"Maybe we should take off for a while, search downriver and not make it back for a few days. He's going to get those lazy guards to search the banks and he'll take out his frustration on them."

"She killed Kevin."

Solange closed her eyes and tried not to shake. He was right above her. He was in human form, but he smelled like wet cat. She wondered if she smelled the same way. Probably more like drowned rat.

"She's killed a lot of us, Brett," the second voice continued from the bank. "And if we don't get to her, she'll kill a few more."

"Yeah," Brett answered with a little sigh. "I got that."

"Brad's a mess. He can barely drag himself back to the lab. He said Brodrick used them as bait. He guessed the woman might try for them when they went back to burn the bodies, but Brodrick didn't warn either of them that she might ambush them."

"Brodrick's insane," Brett said under his breath.

"What?" the other voice hissed out in a soft stream of fear.

"He's never going to rest until he finds her—or her body, Steve," Brett said. "He'll be obsessed."

Steve came closer, stepping onto the massive downed tree. Solange felt the vibration under the water. She shivered continually now. If they didn't leave soon, she was going to lose her ability to hold on to branches. She couldn't feel her fingers anymore, but the knife was a reassuring weight at her side, not that she could ever get to it.

"This used to be fun. We could have all the women we wanted, any way we wanted them," Steve said. "It will be hard to find somewhere else to do whatever we want, take whoever we want. But maybe we should leave, Brett. Get out of here. We could go to Costa Rica, somewhere else."

Brett walked toward Steve, picking his way over the tree trunk. Solange held her breath. He was right above her. She could smell him. The dark fur that was just under his skin, the depravity and violence in him.

"I wouldn't mind leaving, but if we do, I'd like to find that sweet little virgin we had. We could take her with us for the long nights." He laughed softly. "She was a little fighter."

"All teeth and claws," Steve added. "Yeah, she stuck in my head, too, but there's no way I'm going anywhere near her. Brodrick said she's under the protection of the De La Cruz brothers. We'd never get near her." There was speculation in his voice.

"Probably suicide," Brett agreed. "I fed off of her fear. That was such a turn-on. I'm getting hard just thinking about it."

"You're hard all the time," Steve snickered.

Solange knew exactly who they were talking about. Her

cousin Jasmine had been taken prisoner by the jaguar-men. Solange and Juliette had managed to get her back with the help of Riordan. The rescue had nearly cost Juliette her life. Riordan had converted Juliette to Carpathian to save her. But they had been too late to keep Jasmine out of the hands of the jaguar-men and she carried a child.

Solange clenched her teeth together to try to keep them from chattering. Rage replaced her weariness. She wanted to rise up out of the water and shove her knife into Brett's throat. She remembered Jasmine's face, bruised and battered, her eyes wide with shock. She would never be that same carefree girl. There were shadows now where she'd been bright. Hate lived and breathed in Solange, and she despised being weak and helpless, cowering in a swollen river, clinging like a child to the tree branches. But she was wounded and exhausted. It was impossible to fight either of the men right then, let alone both together.

Steve jumped from the tree back to the bank. "I say we get out before Brodrick kills us all. I can't take the idiot humans he works with."

"They've found women for us," Brett said. He followed Steve, landing on the bank in a crouch, staring out over the river. "We should find a little island no one knows about and start a collection. We could train them to do whatever we wanted."

Steve licked his lips. "Sex slaves. Brodrick had a room full of them until he got so brutal he killed them one by one. Damn maniac. I spent a lot of time with his little slaves."

"He didn't mind?"

Steve shook his head. "He didn't give a damn about them. He liked to watch, especially if I hurt them. He gets off on hurting them."

Brett smiled. "I like it, too."

Steve laughed. "You're so messed up."

"I don't hear you complaining when we're sharing a little hot bitch."

"Hell, I don't care if you like to mark them up. All I care about is fucking them." He cupped his groin obscenely. "They were put here for one thing."

"That's where Brodrick went wrong. He wants cubs. Forget that," Brett snarled. "Use 'em and abuse 'em. Half the fun is finding them, stalking them and taking them away from their safe little lives. I love watching a woman dancing in a bar, knowing I can take her any time I want right out from under the nose of anyone she loves. I can kill her boyfriend or lover or husband and take her right there next to the body." He flashed another grin. "It's even better when I force the man to watch. I like to make the bitch beg me to take her in every way possible right in front of him, show her how utterly worthless he is and show him what a whore she is."

"You're so screwed up." Steve snorted with laughter.

"Let's get the hell out of here," Brett said. "Far away from this place. But I'm telling you, Steve, I want that little one. I want her in our collection."

Jasmine. Solange felt the tears burning behind her eyes and clamped down hard on her emotions. She couldn't afford emotions. She would somehow find the strength to hunt these two. Anyone threatening her cousin was going to die. It was just a matter of time. But she was so tired. She ruthlessly pushed weariness away.

She had weak moments—that was allowed. Pity wasn't. She'd *chosen* this life. She had trained for it. She knew there was no going back once she'd set her foot on the path. There was too much evil and it couldn't be ignored. The law of civilization hadn't come to the rain forest yet, and until it did, there were only a handful standing between the predators and their prey.

The voices faded into the night. She waited as long as

she dared and then began to try to make her way to shore. Again she feared releasing her grip, but she was in a better position in the mass of branches beneath the water to climb, if she could make her leaden body move.

She loosened her hand first, flexing her fingers beneath the water before she reached for one of the branches just above the surface. She grasped the branch tightly and let go with her other hand. Very slowly she counted to three, marshaling every bit of strength she had left. She let go with her legs and kicked strongly to propel herself upward. She dragged her head and chest completely out of the water to lie across the bed of branches.

She had no idea how long she lay there, but other than the constant roar of the river, it was quiet in the forest. By the time she was able to find the strength to lift her head again and crawl the rest of the way onto the maze of branches to the solid trunk, the insects were once again humming, frogs were croaking and the rain had let up to a fine silvery mist.

5

When you meet me,
You complete me.
You bring me back to life again.

DOMINIC TO SOLANGE

Dominic took another slow look at the other four vampires surrounding them. To say it was unusual to have so many of the undead gathered would be putting it mildly. There was still the matter of whatever Drago was fawning over. Dominic didn't so much as glance at Zacarias, but the other Carpathian had nerves of steel. He could feel the hunger pouring off the vampires. They had arisen with voracious appetites and he presumed the humans at the laboratory were strictly off limits if they wanted to keep up the façade that they were helping to track and kill vampires—the Carpathians being the supposed vampires. That meant Zacarias was food for all of them.

Drago smirked. "I think you are outnumbered."

Dominic's eyebrow shot up. "Really?" He flexed his shoulders. "The prize is mine. I claimed him and no one—*no one*—will take him from me."

A snarl went up around the loose circle. Dominic gave a little ground, mostly so he and Zacarias could fight back-to-back. Normally Dominic preferred to simply strike without any foreplay, but he suspected there was one other that hadn't yet joined the party, and that meant continuing his outraged vampire act.

"You think that traveling with this pack will intimidate me, Drago? That one"—Dominic indicated the vampire of slight stature he'd encountered on the battlefields—"is a worm, crawling on his belly from every battle. He will be of no use to you." His voice was filled with contempt. "And then there is this one." Dominic indicated the best dressed of the group. He was taller and more filled out, his form kept tidy, the serrated teeth barely blackened. "Jason, a fop who prefers colorful clothes to getting the job done. You amuse me, Drago, with your choice of warriors. You cannot fight yourself and you have no eye for those who will aid you in battle."

A murmur of protest went up, but none of them dared to attack, not without permission, and not when Dominic appeared so confident. Spittle burst from Drago's mouth as he shrieked a protest. His hand gripped something hard at mid hip, his sharp, pointed nails digging deep into whatever he had been stroking.

Smoke and flames burst out from under his fist, and Drago screamed and pulled his hand away. Blistered and raw, the flesh fell away from the bones. A shadow took substance. Drago scrambled back, moaning, holding his hand to his chest. The other three vampires put distance between them and the developing apparition, gliding, trying to be subtle about it. Dominic and Zacarias remained unmoving.

The man emerging from the shadows was tall with broad shoulders and long flowing hair, his skin flawless, his clothes immaculate. His dark eyes rested on Dominic for a brief moment, slid over Zacarias and then went back to Dominic. The imposing figure of power, clearly a *master*, was not one of the Malinov brothers. Somehow, against every odd, the twisted brothers had managed to recruit other *masters* to serve them.

Demyan of the Tiranul lineage. Dimitri's brother. We thought him dead these years. Dominic identified the *master* to Zacarias. *We grew up with him. He is a master at battle.*

New emotions were difficult to control; he had been friends with Demyan. They had traveled for a time together, battling the enemy, slaying any vampires they came across. Sorrow welled up, intense, shaking him for a moment. The Tiranul family had been famous as master swordsmen, and he was certain Demyan would never give up his love of the blade. The undead inclined his head.

"I see you are in disguise and these imbeciles did not recognize you." The voice was mesmerizing. Pitched low.

Dominic had forgotten the power in that ensnaring voice. He shifted his features, hiding every scar so that he looked as Demyan remembered him. Dominic knew he had been a handsome man by any standards, long before he had been burned in the fight to save the prince. He allowed his long black hair to flow neatly down his back in a pony-tail, tied with the thin leather cord, always a weapon should one need it.

"Much better. Dominic Dragonseeker."

Dominic inclined his head regally. "These . . ." He swept his hand in a contemptuous circle to indicate the vampires surrounding him. He didn't bother to look at the offenders, his gesture and tone said it all. "Interrupted my evening."

"Silly of them. But then, you didn't allow them to know who you truly are."

Dominic shrugged. "I do not find my identity necessary to intimidate ones such as these."

Drago snarled, but subsided when Demyan shot him a cold glare. "I have not heard the news that a Dragonseeker has joined our ranks—and it would be huge news—yet your blood calls to mine."

Dominic sent him an enigmatic smile. "I can walk among the Carpathians without fear of their suspicion. It is useful, although tedious at times. This one"—he indicated Zacarias, with an indolent gesture—"recognized my intentions before I could slay him." He inhaled deeply, drawing the tantalizing scent of powerful blood into his lungs, and sent Zacarias a smirk, allowing, just for a few seconds, his eyes to glow ruby red as he turned back to Demyan. "His blood is . . . powerful."

For a moment Demyan lost his composure, the lure of the ancient blood a temptation beyond his control. The skin stretched and frayed, and then split in places, revealing masses of writhing worms. His lips thinned, drew back to reveal his pointed teeth, hideous blackened needles set in a sunken gaping mouth. The skull caved in, the bones sticking through flesh, as warped and twisted as the blackened heart. The master vampire sniffed the air, a dog on the hunt, desperate for the rich, powerful blood of the ancient.

The lesser vampires reacted, salivating, hissing, moving closer to Zacarias. Dominic lifted his hands toward the sky and they immediately subsided.

"You do not understand," Demyan said, his voice raspy now, but he managed to regain his composure, his illusion of beauty settling over him. "This one must be taken to the laboratory. You can use him as often as you want for sustenance, but you cannot kill him."

Dominic slowly allowed his hands to drop once more to his sides, as if the master vampire was lulling him with his voice. "I can use him here without sharing him," Dominic pointed out. He glided one small step closer to Demyan, Zacarias moving with him so that the action was so subtle those around them missed it.

"He is the most hated enemy of our leaders. They will reward all of us greatly for his capture."

"You mean I am the most feared." For the first time Zacarias spoke, a whip of contempt. "He fears me, they all do." He paused. "As they should."

Demyan hissed. "You are fodder for the five. You will be made to crawl before them."

Zacarias's eyes were very black. "I believe they are no longer five. A couple of them sought and found justice."

"You think to mock them? To taunt them? You will suffer greatly before they allow you death."

Zacarias spread his arms out. "They have sent many after me, century after century I have been hunted, yet I still live."

"I am the one who fooled Zacarias." Dominic declared ownership. "No one else."

"A Dragonseeker." Zacarias spat his disgust. "You have no right to use that title. You dishonor it. *Te kalma, te jama ńiŋkval, te apitäsz arwa-arvo*—You are nothing but a walking maggot-infected corpse, without honor." He inclined his head regally toward Dominic. "I know you seek the justice you deserve, and once these worms you travel with have gone, we will finish our little dance."

Drago couldn't contain himself. He flew at Zacarias, his teeth exposed, growling and spitting. Demyan and Dominic both whirled toward him, holding up a hand. The lesser vampire slammed into an invisible barrier and bounced back.

Dominic gave a short, humorless laugh. "I see your beast needs a little more training, Demyan. He is not quite up to your standards."

Demyan shrugged. "It is difficult to get decent help these days. They believe they know more than they do. No patience to learn how to kill a hunter."

"Why do you bother? You do not need one such as this." Dominic gestured toward Drago, his contempt obvious.

Demyan, like most vampires, preened under praise. "They are useful, as you will find. You are used to working alone, but you will find having worms to serve you will be advantageous, especially in a position such as this one. Join with us."

"Yes, *hän ku lejkka wäke-sarnat*—traitor, liar. Crawl to your new master," Zacarias urged.

Demyan whirled to face him. "You can crow all you like, but your blood will soon feed our ranks."

Dominic cleared his throat. "One small detail, Demyan." He waited until the master vampire turned to face him. "His blood belongs to me, and I have never believed in sharing." He smiled and there was a clear challenge in his smile.

～

Solange pushed herself to her hands and knees and took a careful look around. She inhaled the scent of the two jaguar-men. She wanted to remember them, to be able to know them anywhere, know the men responsible for taking the light from her beloved cousin's eyes.

Mustering as much strength as she could, she crawled

along the trunk to the bank and let herself fall onto the ground, into the mud and grass. Giant root cages made a bizarre-looking jungle, dark and mysterious, where creatures could watch her with fear-filled—or hungry—eyes. She got to her feet and fell twice, so she dragged herself into deeper forest. She could shift, but she had so many injuries, she doubted if the jaguar would be better off than the human was.

She used a hanging liana to pull herself up again and, stumbling, took off in the direction of five small limestone caves. They each appeared to be small single chambers, but she had discovered years earlier, in one of them, an entrance that led to the honeycomb of caverns much deeper beneath the earth. More than once, she'd retreated to them when she needed to heal wounds and be safe. It never occurred to her to go to her cousins, or to anyone else. She was wounded and vulnerable. She would never take the chance of leading an enemy to her family's door. It simply wasn't in her code.

She wrapped her arms around her middle and continued her journey. It was dangerous moving through the rain forest at night, bleeding from a half dozen wounds, but she didn't dare try to examine her body. She burned with every jarring step, and she knew from past experience the damage claws and teeth could do, but as a rule she healed fast. Brodrick could have killed her, but he hadn't. He'd been angry, but he wanted her royal blood and ability to shift. He was depraved enough to think she might give him a royal son.

She pushed her hand through her matted, stringy hair. She often chopped it off when it got out of control. Her hair was thick, as it was with most jaguar-people, and it grew fast. The more she cut it off, the faster it seemed to grow. The color was dark sable, much like her jaguar fur, with a few golden streaks. If there was any one feature that might be considered beautiful on her, it would have been her hair. Not so much now.

Her cat's eyes allowed her to see in the dark as she made her way through the trees and brush, the forest of giant ferns and the tangle of roots snaking across the ground. She simply put one foot in front of the other. She had been here before, wounded, weary, heartsick, and she would be again. Sometimes, like tonight, there was no win for anyone. Annabelle had died; she wouldn't be going home to her husband. Annabelle probably hadn't even known why the men had kidnapped her from her home in France.

Solange closed her eyes briefly and then snapped them open, taking a deep breath, aware of the silence of the insects. The hum was continual as a rule, a background noise that never ceased, yet this part of the forest was abnormally still. Something dangerous lurked here. Something unnatural. This was no jaguar. No predator that walked the night familiar to the rain forest inhabitants. The danger had to be the undead.

She melted into the trees, her body close to the trunk. Drawing on her jaguar, she tested the night. Her heart began to pound. Not one but several, just ahead. She felt the familiar and very strange reaction in her veins. Adrenaline coursed through her body. She turned to slip away and caught a familiar scent.

De La Cruz.

She would recognize that scent anywhere. Juliette wore it all over her, as did MaryAnn. She swore under her breath. She was exhausted, but he was family and family was sacred. She tried to clear her brain and think straight. Right now she was fuzzy, off balance, and she couldn't go into battle with vampires without a plan or a clear head. Somewhere close she had a cache, but . . . She turned in each direction, trying to throw off the exhaustion in preparation for battle.

Vampires were difficult to kill. She could rip out their hearts as a jaguar, but she couldn't incinerate them. The undead called for special weapons. Riordan and Manolito had worked with her, perfecting her skills, and, she had to admit, coming up with specialized weapons for her to give her a little edge, which was needed. They were monstrous creatures.

She made her way a few yards to the north, jogging, ignoring the pain in her body now. Nothing mattered but to give aid to whichever brother was in trouble. She found her cache just off the trail leading to the first limestone cave. She never cached inside a cave, aware that vampires and Carpathians went underground to rest. She pulled out the weapons she needed, chewed several leaves that would help numb the burning pain in her body but not fog her mind, and jogged back toward the battleground.

She came in downwind, drawing on her jaguar's strength when she feared she couldn't keep going. When her legs felt too rubbery to support her, she went to her belly and slithered through the vegetation, ignoring the swarm of insects drawn by her wounds. Using toes and elbows, she inched closer to the group of men gathered under the trees.

She could hear the moan of the trees and the wail of the grass as the undead trampled ferns and brush, withered flowers and leaves, poisoning everything they touched. The De La Cruz brother was easily recognizable. They all had that impressive stamp of absolute authority, the broad shoulders and handsome face. This had to be the elusive Zacarias, the eldest of the five brothers. She'd once caught a glimpse of Nicolas, and she knew Riordan, Rafael and Manolito. Zacarias looked calm and confident and not in the least bit concerned that he was surrounded by vampires.

She gasped when the man standing in front of him

turned slightly and she glimpsed him. *Her* Carpathian—the man in her dreams. He had no scars, but it was definitely the one who came to her in her worst moments. The one she'd so happily—and stupidly—spilled her guts to and cried like a whiny baby in front of. He was even more handsome in real life than he was in her imagination, which made it all the worse that she'd told him her darkest secrets.

She let her breath out slowly, cursing herself for reacting like a woman instead of a warrior. He didn't need a woman now; he needed her fighting skills—and *that* she could give him. That might be the only gift she ever had for him, but she would fight with every breath in her body to save him from the circle of rotting flesh surrounding him.

She inched closer, and stopped abruptly when she caught the flash of the tall Carpathian's eyes. His gaze moved over her—he knew she was there. She was certain that he did. He gave a small shake of his head, which she had every intention of ignoring. Zacarias glanced her way, and she felt the weight of his disapproval. That lightened her mood considerably. He'd always disapproved of her, and that constant in her life gave her another boost of energy. She really did find secret delight in annoying authoritative men.

She pushed away the somewhat satisfying thoughts and drew on her last reserves of strength.

~

Dominic felt the sudden shift in his blood—everything went quiet and still. The parasites had been on a rampage, trying to kill him from the inside out, but now they retreated as if from a deadly foe. Every nerve ending in his body went on alert. He scented the air, but there was no telltale fragrance. That didn't matter. He knew. His lifemate was close. Too close.

Zacarias's head suddenly came up alertly, his dark gaze sweeping the surrounding forest before touching Dominic's face.

We have company.

Power flared all around them as Demyan kept the lesser vampires under control. There was no way for them to tell the two Carpathians were communicating.

My lifemate.

Warn her off.

Dominic never changed expression. He merely glanced at Zacarias, keeping his attention directed toward Demyan. *You would never abandon your lifemate, Zacarias, not in a fight. You are not capable of that, nor is she.*

She is a woman.

She is my *woman and she is a warrior as is befitting my needs.*

Zacarias made a single sound that meant many things. Outrage. Disapproval. Disagreement. Solange was under his protection, but lifemates took precedence over everything else. In any case, he knew the woman by reputation. She was as stubborn as a mule.

And what happens if they kill her? You will suicide.

I am on a suicide mission, Dominic responded. *I am already dead.*

Zacarias sighed. *So be it, old friend.*

The lesser vampires swayed, their feet moving in a pattern much like the drumbeat in a ceremonial ritual. Power crackled in the air. Thunder rolled in the distance. A whip of lightning cracked overhead.

"I see you grow impatient, Demyan," Dominic said.

"I am not used to interference," he snapped. He knew as well as Dominic that the delay only made him look weak in the eyes of his followers, but he was reluctant to attack a Dragonseeker.

"I have never had anyone stupid enough to come between me and what is clearly mine."

"You think to stop us from taking this traitor to the *masters*?" Demyan snarled. Once again his lips drew back and the blackened, needlelike teeth were a mockery against his handsome image.

Hideous growls and murmurs of protest came from the four lesser vampires. They separated, taking up positions in a loose semicircle around Dominic. Insects swarmed up the tree trunks and over fallen logs. Bats dipped and wheeled in the air above them. A snake slithered along the nearest tree branch and tiny bright frogs stared with round dark eyes. Demyan had marshaled his army.

Dominic paced a little away from Zacarias to give the Carpathian room to fight. Dominic would go for Demyan, the biggest threat. He would have to trust Zacarias to keep the others off him. It wouldn't be easy, but it could be done.

"Perhaps *you* will call another *master*, Demyan, but I will not."

Drago let out a shriek of outrage. "He is sworn. His blood calls."

"I do what suits me. It does not suit me to hand my prize over to all of you and then see the *three* feed off blood that belongs to me." Deliberately Demyan reminded them that five Malinov brothers had begun the campaign to destroy the Carpathian people, but now only three remained alive. Zacarias's brothers had been a large part of destroying the master vampires.

"The sun is near rising and I tire of this little game. Who will start this dance then, Dominic?" Demyan asked quietly.

Silence fell. The forest held its breath. The vampires swayed back and forth.

Solange emerged from the shadows, her weapon held

down low, already aimed at the vampire dressed in fashionable clothes. She'd marked him as an easy kill, and God knew she needed an easy one.

Dominic didn't turn or look at her. Zacarias's gaze was cool, without recognition. The vampires' swaying stopped for a moment, murmuring and showing black teeth. Demyan's elegant eyebrow shot up and then he smiled, a slow, evil smirk.

"I like to dance," she announced and shot the arrow straight toward Jason, the colorfully dressed vampire, aiming for the perfect spot on his silk-covered chest. The arrow ignited just before it tore through flesh to find the wizened heart, incinerating it with the white-hot flame.

Jason had no time to react, no time to scream or retaliate. He imploded, fire bursting through skin and bone, spraying fiery blood and blackened worms onto the ground.

Zacarias whirled around to slam his fist deep into the chest of the nearest vampire, driving straight to the heart. He ripped it away, the action happening so fast, the well-dressed undead hadn't yet managed to fall to the ground. Zacarias called the lightning down to incinerate the heart even as he turned to face his next opponent. Drago was Demyan's disciple, the lesser vampire a pawn for the *master*, but as long as Drago lived, Demyan would stand and fight, believing he had a better chance of survival against one hunter. It was imperative to keep Drago occupied and stall killing him until Dominic maneuvered Demyan into a kill position.

Dominic was on Demyan before the master vampire could react, leaping across the distance in an effort to end the battle before it actually started. Such a vampire had been centuries in the making, perfecting skills and acquiring knowledge, growing more powerful each century until he could appear beautiful and clean, holding other vampires in his thrall. Carpathians aged in the same way, but the cunning guile came only when they were close to turning themselves. Dominic wanted to stop the fight before it got started.

Demyan's eyes went wide in shock. It was clear he had believed the parasites in Dominic's blood would control him, prevent him from attacking one of their own, as they should have. He whirled out of reach just before Dominic's fist penetrated his chest, seeking his heart. His eyes went feral and Dominic managed to snatch his hand back as knives spun around Demyan, creating a moving suit of armor.

"I should have known you would use your family's expertise," Dominic said, studying the spinning knives.

He'd never come across anything like it before in all his fights with undead. There seemed to be no noticeable pattern that he could detect, the spinning blades moving around Demyan at varying rates of speed, so that it would be impossible to slam his fist through the armor without getting his arm cut off.

"You should have known better than to challenge me," Demyan corrected.

Dominic filed the hint of the vampire's ego away for future use. The blades whirled and swayed, flashing silver in the dark night. Dominic caught the gleam of a long blade, just a quick flash, his only warning. He just managed to form his own sword to meet the swing of Demyan's blade. Sparks rained around them as metal came together with such force the forest shook. The sound reverberated through the trees. Birds shrieked. A mass exodus followed as the clashing swords slammed into one another over and over.

Demyan's sword came down in a straight slice right over Dominic's head. He barely managed to get his blade up to parry the strike away from him, arms up, head level to prevent the sword from falling on the top of his head. The moment his arms went up, the smaller whirling blades burst toward him, as if fired from a gun, a hundred knives thrown simultaneously. Dominic swept his sword across his body, knocking most of them away, but one lodged in his thigh and another in his chest.

The blades were fashioned with Carpathian skill, forged by a master, and they sliced clean through flesh and muscle, burying deep. Dominic had no choice but to dissolve into vapor in order to rid himself of the metal. The blades dropped to earth, but Demyan was too experienced to allow that brief respite to stop him. He followed the droplets of blood, the scent in his nostrils, and like a bloodhound, he drove through the cloud of vapor, slashing with his sword.

Dominic materialized, countering, pushing pain to the back of his mind while he met each of Demyan's moves, his brain working to find the pattern of the swirling knives as well. He needed to anticipate each of Demyan's moves and get ahead of him.

As Dominic sprang to attack Demyan, Solange turned and shot Robert the worm in one smooth motion. The arrow flew true, slamming through the chest to pierce the heart, exploding into the same white-hot heat that incinerated everything on contact. Exhaustion was something even her willpower couldn't overcome. Her legs went out from under her and she found herself sitting on the undulating ground. Around her the ground groaned. Wide cracks began to weave across the forest floor, hairline fractures that slowly widened until debris began to fall into them.

"Get off the ground," Zacarias yelled as he rushed toward Drago. "Get to safety."

She sent a smoldering glare. Did she look stupid? She had already scrambled to her feet and leapt for the lower branches of a young tree. As a shelter, it didn't offer much, bending under her weight, but it got her away from the splintering ground.

She heard the clash of metal against metal and turned her head to see sparks raining down. Her heart jumped to her throat. She nearly stood up on the flimsy tree branch, fear for her Carpathian crashing through her unexpectedly. She'd had no idea how much she had invested in a man she'd made up. She watched him flowing like water over the uneven ground, avoiding tree roots as he danced around the master vampire. The spinning blades were mesmerizing, and she was forced to turn her attention back to Zacarias. There was no way that she could see to help her Carpathian, but if Zacarias could defeat Drago, he would be able to help defeat the powerful vampire.

Zacarias and Drago came together, two fierce fighters, going up off the ground, hovering in midair for just a moment. Zacarias slammed his fist into the chest wall and instantly thousands of bats dropped from the sky to cover his body, teeth sawing flesh, driving him away from the lesser vampire. He stumbled under the weight, falling to earth where the bats carried him to the ground.

Solange let go a third arrow as Drago rushed into the feeding frenzy of the bats, obviously intending to kill Zacarias while the night creatures had him trapped. The arrow sank into Drago's shoulder, bursting into flame as it hit the flesh. The vampire's shoulder exploded from the inside out. His shoulder, his arm and the side of his neck turned black and fell into ashes. Drago screamed, his head snapping around, those pitted red eyes finding her in the precarious shelter of the tree.

Her heart slammed hard in her chest. She crouched, preparing to leap, even as she fitted another arrow into the crossbow. Howling, Drago threw his good arm toward the sky so that the dark clouds boiled and lightning forked along the edges. The bolt slammed into the tree as she jumped into the branches of the next tree, landing hard, catching with one hand, claws bursting through her left hand to grip the trunk while her right hand clutched her weapon. Few of her kind could perform such a difficult feat in the midst of a battle, utilizing one body part in jaguar form and the other in human form.

She dragged herself onto the branch, lifting her bow to get another shot off. Zacarias was back on his feet, whirling so fast his large frame seemed to blur, flinging off the bats, leaving his clothing shredded and bloody. He bowed slightly as he moved to his right, forcing Drago to move as well.

"I see you learned a trick or two from your master."

Drago drew back his lips to show his hideous teeth. "You will regret your contempt."

Zacarias smiled. "I think not." The two opponents rushed forward again, two gladiators crashing into one another while the thunder rolled over their heads.

Around Solange trees groaned and tilted as the massive upheaval continued. From her position she could see the center of the web, with the cracks spreading out, reaching like silken threads, searching . . .

She gasped. This was an attack against a specific person. *Her* Carpathian. The ground swells and cracks were reaching to find him. She could see the gaping lines in the earth switching directions, away from Zacarias and the vampire he was fighting with.

The blades spun too fast, making a shot with her arrow nearly impossible. She was good, but the timing was out of the question. Her heart in her throat, she watched her Carpathian. He seemed to be anticipating every move the vampire made, his sword meeting with crash after fiery crash. From her vantage point she could see the vampire trying to maneuver him into a position, but the Carpathian seemed able to avoid traps. Twice she saw his blade penetrate the whirling knives, a slash that swept cleanly through the armor and bit deep into the vampire.

Black blood sprayed across the whirling blades, hissing as the acid hit the ground. Demyan spat blood at her Carpathian and touched his head in a mock salute. Her Carpathian sliced a second time, striking through the armor, and Demyan's eyes went mad, the red killing haze reflected there. He attacked hard, driving her Carpathian back, fearful now of allowing him the offense, as he had somehow figured out how to time the spinning of the blades.

The cracks widened, drawing Solange's attention again, now several feet long, the ground opening a good inch across. It was impossible to see how deep each crack went.

Look out! It sucked that she didn't even know his name. *On the ground, a trap.* She didn't know what kind of trap, but it was closing in on him, ring after ring of spiderweb cracks. She sent the detailed image into his mind.

Dominic. The name was given to her in a calm, detached tone, even as his sword parried thrust after thrust, the vampire clearly trying to maneuver him toward the widening, gaping holes in the forest floor. *I am Dragonseeker.*

Solange frowned, the adrenaline running wild, the blood in her veins pumping in a ferocious, almost violent reaction to the parasites in the vampire's blood. She actually could feel the reaction inside of her, as if her blood rose up to fight the blood of the vampire in complete revulsion. Everything inside of her felt feral and uncontrollable, yet he was the exact opposite. Dominic. That was all. As if he was strolling through a meadow of wildflowers, not in the fight of his life.

She took a breath, watching the way the master vampire maneuvered him, stepping back, drawing him in, turning left, then right, attacking, retreating, but keeping Dominic's attention on him as he expertly wielded his sword.

That terrible razor-sharp blade sliced into Dominic's chest, shredding elegant clothes and leaving deep slashes across his skin.

The master vampire and Dominic anticipated one another's moves, a very violent ballet that was terrifying yet so mesmerizing, she couldn't look away. All the while those rings kept circling Dominic, coming closer and closer. To her horror, spiders began to pour out of the cracks. She recognized them immediately. Brazilian wandering spiders were highly venomous and aggressive. The spindly legs spanned a good five inches, and they seemed to pause, rearing back to stare at Dominic with their eight eyes, the two largest glowing with the same ruby-red maniacal hatred Demyan's eyes held. They displayed red jaws, a signal of anger, evidence of their readiness to attack.

Solange knew from experience that Carpathians could push deadly venom from their system, but with multiple, excruciatingly painful bites, Dominic would have problems fighting the master vampire. She couldn't spray the ground with fire to incinerate them, but she could perhaps disrupt Demyan's battle plan. She had no idea how to get through those spinning blades but she was willing to try. Before she had a chance to let him know, she felt the stirring in her mind.

Distract him with your arrows and I will call down the lightning to burn these creatures. Watch for the faint blurring just below his heart. I will attack hard. He will be hard put to keep the knives in various patterns. That is his vulnerable spot.

She should have known he would have the same plan as she did. In her dreams, they often discussed the battles they'd been in and they definitely thought alike. She took careful aim, breathing deep for calm, her eyes on the spot just below Demyan's heart. The knives were terrible, glinting, silvery bursts that never seemed to show an opening. She waited with complete faith that Dominic would maneuver the master vampire into her line of fire. She'd get one, maybe two arrows off and he'd attack her. She had to be ready to abandon her perch, but she wasn't going to ground, not with those spiders everywhere. She didn't have the Carpathian ability to remove the venom from her system.

Dominic, as calm as ever, ignored the thousands of eyes staring at him and glided close to Demyan, coming in at an angle and forcing Demyan to sidestep or go backward. For one tiny second his armor faltered, repeating the pattern, and Solange let the arrow fly. It wasn't even close to a kill shot, but it sank into the spot just below the heart and exploded. The air charged fast, her hair standing on end. She leapt.

Instantly, the world around her exploded with heat and a great burst of light. The force knocked her backward in the air. She used her flexible cat spine to turn, hands seeking a branch. She had no choice but to drop her crossbow to save herself. She needed both claws to catch what surface she could to keep from hitting the ground, now on fire, the spiders burning and popping with hideous shrieks, a foul stench permeating the air, making her cough.

She dragged her body up into the tree, her strength waning. She saw Zacarias glance at Dominic, who gave an imperceptible nod. Her heart jumped. They were in communication and they were planning on an all-out attack. Zacarias drove through Drago's defenses with an ease that made her realize he'd been deliberately keeping the lesser vampire alive for some reason she couldn't fathom. He slammed his fist through the chest wall, nearly lifting the undead into the air with the force.

There was a horrible sucking sound as he extracted the heart and flung it into the fiery blaze Dominic called down.

At the same time, Dominic timed his throw, slamming his blade straight through the knives. Sparks became fireworks, the blades grinding to a halt, shattering and dropping to reveal Demyan's blood-streaked body.

The master vampire roared his hatred, taking in Drago's body as it turned to ashes, his gaze leaping to Zacarias. The knowledge that the two hunters were working in conjunction hit him. Solange saw the shock on his face. Instantly lianas dropped from the trees, coiling like living snakes around Dominic as he thrust his fist toward Demyan's chest. Solange shed her clothes hastily, tearing off her blouse and shoving her jeans aside. She leapt from the tree to the rolling ground, shifting with practiced speed. The vines wrapped Dominic tight, pinning one arm and covering his mouth and nose. One looped around his neck, drawing tight around his neck as another grew the head of a viper and reared back, teeth exposed to strike at his eye.

The jaguar rode out the sudden upheaval of ground beneath it, setting itself, waiting. The moment the swell subsided, she charged Demyan, rushing at him from behind. His attention was on Dominic, directing the vines that were imprisoning him. The jaguar hit the master vampire full force, teeth sinking into the back of his head. Powerful jaws clamped down on his skull as the momentum of the jaguar's attack drove him forward to impale his chest on Dominic's outstretched fist.

As Solange jumped back, Zacarias picked up Dominic's discarded sword and, with a fierce swing, cut the blade through Demyan's neck. His head went flying and Solange turned away, unable to look at the sight of a head rolling across the ground, right into the fire. His screams raked at her insides, and even in her jaguar form, she felt bile rising. Dominic tossed the heart into the blaze and the two

Carpathians stood, heads down, breathing hard, while around them the ground blazed with fire and the vampire blood burned through skin to bone.

Solange made her way to the tree where she'd left her ragged clothes, not looking back. She knew the two Carpathian males were seeing to their wounds, healing themselves as best they could before trying to clean up the area and remove all the vampire blood as well as parasites to aid the forest recovery.

She dressed behind some brush, considering making a run for it, but she was too tired to even try it. She couldn't help with the cleanup. She'd be lucky to find a safe place to sleep. Steeling herself, she squared her shoulders and turned, nearly bumping into—*him.*

6

My dream lover and lifemate,
You know every part of me.

SOLANGE TO DOMINIC

Solange stared up—and up. Dominic was far taller and larger in life than he seemed in her dream. This was no shadowy figure, but a real man, flesh and blood standing before her. He was an imposing figure, his shoulders wider, his chest more muscular, everything just *more*. Her gaze traveled up his body, noting every wound, noting the narrow hips, the tapered waist and the ripples of muscle over the flat belly. Her lungs refused to draw air. She literally had no idea how to react to him.

Her gaze got stuck on his mouth. He had a beautiful mouth, his lips very sculpted. She just stood there, her heart pounding, her mind screaming, staring at his mouth, unable to look away or look farther up his face. She felt small and insubstantial beside him. She felt feminine. Like a girl. A young, silly girl who had no idea of the world between man and woman. She was at such a disadvantage.

She was likely to blurt out something insulting. She pushed people away when she felt vulnerable, and she'd never felt more vulnerable in her entire life. This man could break her heart. She knew that just by standing in his presence, and when her heart was involved, she was at her most lethal. Her claws were tipped with venom. She could be very mean, capable of cutting him into little pieces with insulting words. She had perfected her sarcastic, uncaring attitude until it was an art form.

She'd already lost him and she hadn't even opened her mouth. She couldn't do this. She could fight any battle asked of her, walk unafraid into the heart of the enemy's camp and steal a woman out from under them to set her free, but she couldn't do this. She pressed her lips together tightly, legs trembling, turning to jelly, wanting to run. She tasted fear in her mouth. *Fear.* Her. Solange Sangria, afraid of a man. She detested the feeling.

Solange with a man. For the first time in her adult life, she was terrified. Absolutely terrified. She couldn't do this. She couldn't face this—the one person on earth she had given her soul to. She had opened her soul to him, told him every secret desire, every fear, *everything*. Jaguar-women were naturally submissive to their males. They fought until the strongest, most aggressive dared to mate with them, and they submitted to the male. She was preprogrammed for that fight/submit dance between male and female, and it terrified her. She could never acknowledge that side of her personality. She could never submit, yet that part of her wanted to, so she pushed it deep, submerged it totally beneath the fighter, hidden from all eyes—all but his.

She shivered—or trembled; she honestly didn't know

which. He caught her chin between his thumb and finger in a firm grip. Birds took wing in her stomach. His touch was just as she imagined, gentle but impossibly firm, the touch of a man in complete command of himself—and of her.

"Look at me, Solange."

His voice was every bit as gentle as his touch. A low caress, like velvet against skin. Tender, but a command nevertheless.

She struggled with her nature, with the heat between them, the need in her for a soul mate, for someone to share her lonely life, a need so strong she could barely think with wanting to be everything he desired. Someone like her might get lost in someone like him. Another man, one less—just less—and she would be able to save herself. The other side of her, fierce and proud—the side she was most familiar with, the one she took refuge and comfort in—would never respect a lesser man.

Silence stretched between them. It was sheer agony to obey. It was worse not to. He left the decision completely up to her, but the force of his personality was daunting.

"Does it require courage, then, to look at me, *kessake*— little cat?" That soft voice that stroked over nerve endings shook her.

He sounded so deceptively gentle, yet she'd seen him rip the heart from a master vampire. She actually trembled.

"I believe, if there is one woman with courage on this earth—it is my lifemate."

Her gaze jumped to his. Locked with those cool green eyes. No, they were slowly going as blue as the deepest water, changing color as the warrior in him gave way to the man. Her stomach somersaulted. Her heart contracted.

He smiled at her, a slow, sexy smile that took her breath. His teeth flashed at her, perfect and straight. His straight aristocratic nose, even his scars belonged—enhanced rather than detracted from his potent masculine aura. Everything about him seemed so perfect. She stood there soaked to the skin, shivering, her hair hanging in damp trails, wild and out of control, her body covered in scars, bruises and lacerations, streaked with blood and reeking of sweat instead of perfume.

His thumb slid over her lips, the softest of brushes. His palm framed the side of her face. He looked at her as if there were no other woman in the world. An illusion, but it warmed her when she was cold inside.

"Hello."

That simple greeting accompanied by that intense blue gaze burning over her, that slow, sexy smile and the dark, melting voice, turned her inside out. She moistened her lips, wanting to answer, but no sound would come out. She could only stand there helplessly looking up at him, wishing she was Juliette or Jasmine. Anyone but Solange Sangria.

"I need to inspect you, *sívamet*—my heart."

Her heart jumped again. *Inspect her?* For what? To see if she was good enough for a man like him? A thousand ugly smart-ass comments welled up, but she couldn't utter a word, she couldn't even look at him. Mutely, she shook her head. Tears burned behind her eyes. She wouldn't hold up to any inspection if he was looking for the perfect woman.

Her hair was all over the place, muddy and straggly. She was covered in river water and blood. She tried to imagine what her body would look like to him. She was *not* removing her clothes. Jaguars were not modest, but in front of *him*? No way! It wasn't happening. For one horrible moment she pictured herself standing in front of him, nude, hands behind her head, presenting herself to him. She had thunder thighs. She didn't want to think about her hips or her butt. Okay, she did have nice breasts, and a narrow waist, but she had ropes of muscle everywhere. She was too heavy . . .

Panic took over. She nearly hyperventilated. His hands were gentle on her skin and she closed her eyes, shoving down a sob. She would not run from him like a coward. She was royalty, although Juliette often said she was a royal pain in the butt—which was true. How did other women handle this?

His fingers skimmed down her arms and then settled. Her heart jumped. He turned her around and bent his head to the bite on her shoulder, the one still oozing blood. He inhaled, taking the scent into his lungs so he would recognize anywhere the man who had assaulted her, simply by smell. "Hold still, *kessake*."

She couldn't have moved if she wanted to. She felt much like a wild animal cornered with nowhere to run. His tongue moved over the puncture wounds with healing saliva. The feeling of that velvet rasp against her bare skin robbed her of breath. He pushed her shirt out of the way and followed the wounds down her back.

Of course he hadn't wanted to inspect her body to see what his lifemate looked like. She felt embarrassed all over again, praying he hadn't read her wayward mind. It shocked her that he would take the time to see to her relatively minor wounds when his had been major. He even took the sting out of most of the bruises. She'd never really had a sensual experience, but the feeling of his fingers and mouth on her skin turned her body into a bundle of raw, throbbing nerve endings.

"You need blood."

The voice startled her and she jerked away from Dominic, dragging down her shirt. Zacarias. How had she forgotten him? She'd almost—Well, okay, she had been thinking erotic thoughts, forgetting they weren't alone. What was wrong with her? She'd never blushed before, but he'd witnessed her total humiliation and she could feel color turning her face an ugly red. She blinked rapidly, trying to break the spell Dominic had woven around her.

It took her a moment to realize Dominic's larger frame had blocked Zacarias's view of her. For some idiotic reason the knowledge that Dominic had protected her in her moment of weakness from prying eyes made her feel warm and comforted.

"As do you," Dominic responded. He turned then, keeping Solange close to him, his hand on her arm.

Both men looked at her. Her heart pounded frantically. She'd seen Juliette giving Riordan blood. Zacarias was torn to shreds and he was family. He was her family, whether extended or not, and therefore under her protection. But this . . . She'd never considered that she would ever have to give a man her very blood.

"It is our way, *kessake*." Dominic's voice was pitched low, but the sound moved inside her, that soft, velvet caress, snaking its way seductively into her mind.

She bit her lip hard, trembling, wanting to do this for him, such a small request, but enormous in her mind. Why did it matter whether she pleased him? She had never cared what anyone thought of her, yet she stood there like a mute imbecile, unable to say no when everything in her demanded that she run. She stood trembling, desperate to get away, yet she couldn't move, at war with her own nature.

Dominic was her chosen one. It mattered little if she'd thought he wasn't real. He was there now, more of a man than any she knew, more respected and more powerful. She wanted to be that woman he needed, and he needed this from her.

Hardly daring to breathe, she watched Zacarias approach, his body bleeding from a thousand tears from the vampire bats, their teeth and claws stripping his body of flesh at the command of Drago. Her stomach churned. Bile rose. He was going to sink his teeth into her skin and she was going to stand there, shuddering with distaste, caught in Dominic's spell. She had to find the strength to resist the madness that had settled around her, turning her body to lead.

She swallowed hard and looked up at Dominic. At once his blue eyes trapped her gaze and held her captive. His smile was tender, only for her, as if he were reading her mind and knew her abhorrence of this act, knew she was on the verge of fleeing and that it was only the sheer power of his personality that kept her there. He drew her body against his, her back to him, one arm just under her heaving breasts, his hold so gentle she didn't realize at first that she was locked to him with his enormous strength, unable to break away if she wanted to. His other hand slowly but inexorably stretched her arm out toward Zacarias in invitation.

"From her wrist, and be gentle," he cautioned.

She shuddered again as the Carpathian male drew near. Dominic bent his head and whispered softly to her in his own language. "*Solange. Eŋnim. Tõdak pitäsz wäke bekimet mekesz kaiket. Te magköszunam näŋamaŋ kaćʒ taka arvo.* Solange. My woman. I knew you had courage to face anything. Thank you for this gift beyond price."

His breath was warm on her neck, and he pressed his lips over her frantic pulse. His teeth scraped back and forth, gentle, more than seductive, so that her heart beat fast and her breathing turned ragged. She was aware of him with every single cell in her body.

She closed her eyes and absorbed the sound of his voice, the pleasure in it, the way he made her feel as if he knew she was feeding the other male just for him—only for him. She could never have done it without his seductive voice in her ear, or his hard body against hers. It felt as if she were giving herself to him, giving him everything she was, and yet it was another man who took her wrist.

At the last second, as that hot breath touched her skin and she saw the length of those fangs, she felt panic and nearly jerked her arm away. Before she could move, Dominic bit down into her neck and the crashing pain turned instantly to a pleasure so intense she cried out, her body reacting with a tidal wave of pure fire. She had experienced the heat of her cat many times, a purely physical drive that didn't touch her beyond the abstract. But this—this was all encompassing. Every nerve ending felt raw with desire.

Her womb spasmed. Heat rose between her legs and her nipples tightened into hard, desperate peaks. The fire burned her skin, her insides, poured like molten gold through her body until she writhed against him, unable to control herself. Solange, who had so much control. Solange, who despised men, was giving herself body and soul to this man and his needs—not just his needs, his every desire. A small sob escaped.

Dominic had never imagined that anything could have been so erotic as taking his lifemate's blood. To him, the act of taking or giving blood had always been mundane, a necessity with no particular feeling attached to it, not even before he'd lost his emotions. He was unprepared for the need slamming wicked and low, a hard punch of arousal that shook his deadly calm as nothing else ever had. He was disciplined and controlled. It had never occurred to him that once he held Solange in his arms and his teeth connected them, the act of taking her blood would be as intimate as taking her body or her mind.

He was in such a state of arousal, it felt to him as if he was sharing her with another man in an extremely intimate act—something he would never do. She was his to protect, to love and cherish. He didn't want another man to see her vulnerable or afraid or sexy, and right at that moment, he found her the most sensual being on earth. That part of her belonged solely to him. Had he realized what taking her blood would be like, he would never, under any circumstances, have forced her to give Zacarias blood.

And he had forced her—or at least coerced her. He knew she found the idea repugnant, yet Zacarias was family to her. She lived by her sense of code, her honor, her duty. She would not have forgiven herself for denying him in his moment of need. She would have dwelt on her refusal in the long hours of the day when Dominic couldn't comfort her. He had a code, too, and that code was to provide his lifemate with everything she needed, even if that meant stretching her limits beyond what she thought she could handle.

But this might be stretching his limits beyond what he could handle. She had been a warrior to Zacarias, but Dominic had seen her vulnerable. Her vulnerability was beautiful to him and that she would show it to him was an honor. It brought out his every protective instinct, and the beast prowling inside of him roared for her. Not simply the physical mating, but the completeness of what a lifemate was. She needed. He provided. He needed. She provided. Each was dedicated solely to the other.

But this—this shocking reaction of body and mind—was nearly his undoing. Her blood swept into his body and the parasites cowered before it, more than they had with Zacarias's pure Carpathian blood. They retreated, became quiet, hiding from the royal jaguar blood as if afraid of the fierce fighting cat. As her blood spread through his system, the internal fire started, a great sweeping storm that burned hot and fast and out of control.

Her body moved against his, inflaming his already rock-hard groin. He didn't want to stop; his hand stroked the underside of her breast, although what he wanted—no, *needed*—was to feel her silken skin against his. Her small sob brought him up short. Restored control. Order. An awareness of where he was and what was happening around him. He'd been so far into the throes of madness, he was astonished as he took a slow lick across the pinprick holes and followed the ruby-red drops of blood down her shoulder. He straightened slowly, breathing her in, absorbing the feel of her small, curvy body tight against him. Nothing had ever felt so right to him.

Aware of her growing fear, he pressed his mouth to her pulse, wanting only to calm and comfort her. His little wildcat had a feminine side she considered submissive, and it terrified her. It was up to him to show her that part of her was every bit as important as her warrior persona and that being a woman didn't in any way take away from who she was.

"*Pesäd te engemal*—You are safe with me." He whispered the words against the frantic pulse, his tongue swirling there, holding her while she calmed.

Her wild nature was evident. Solange had lived her life on the fringes of society, never in the midst of it. Laws didn't apply in her world. She didn't need to learn the niceties of city life, or even life within a community. Her world was survival only—very much like his world had been.

Zacarias went to slide his tongue over the laceration to politely close it, but Dominic pulled her wrist to his mouth. He took one drink, felt the fireball rolling through his body and then he closed the wound himself.

"Thank you," Zacarias said.

Dominic knew the Carpathian hunter was thanking him, not Solange. In ancient times, lifemates were sacred and others didn't speak to them without express permission. Zacarias was of that old school, and perhaps, if he was entirely truthful with himself, Dominic was, too.

He lifted his head to meet Zacarias's gaze. "The dawn approaches."

Zacarias nodded. "*Kolasz arwa-arvoval*—may you die with honor." He stood for a moment. "It is long since I have heard our own language spoken. For a moment, I felt the call of our homeland."

"*Veri olen piros, ekäm*—blood be red, my brother," Dominic answered. The meaning was clear. Find your lifemate.

Zacarias looked from him to Solange, her clothes and skin stained with blood. He shook his head. "My time is past for that. The world has changed and left me behind. I will aid you when you call, old friend."

He simply vanished, the vapor merging with the smoke from the dying fire. There was silence. Solange didn't turn her head to look over her shoulder at Dominic, she simply stood waiting for his direction, holding herself very still, although he could feel the tremors running down her spine.

Above her head, he smiled, the tension easing from his body now that there were no males near her and they were alone. He gathered her to him. "I will take us to a safe place where we can bathe and rest."

She wanted to just let go of him and drop to earth and shatter. Did other women feel this way? Wanting to please him, to do what he asked and yet feeling so terrified she couldn't breathe? And what was he asking? A simple thing. Bathe and rest. He hadn't said anything else. She could never, *ever* give her body to him. Not him. A shudder went through her body. Mutely, she shook her head.

He heard the quick intake of her breath as he lifted her. "Courage," he whispered against the nape of her neck.

She didn't fear the method of travel he chose, he knew that. He also knew she didn't fear him—not Dominic the warrior. She trusted him or she never would have entered into battle with him. It was Dominic the man she feared, and he was the one who needed to earn her trust. More than anything else, he wanted all of her. He knew his need was selfish, but he'd had very little brightness in his life, and Solange shone like the brightest of stars. He took her into the skies, her body locked to his.

Solange jammed her fist into her mouth to keep from protesting. She didn't want to do anything wrong, but if she didn't have an idea of how to act, she was bound to make a mistake. Her cat prowled back and forth, one moment purring contentedly and the next hissing and growling as she sensed Solange's growing terror.

How was she going to shed her clothes in front of him? Why hadn't she listened to MaryAnn when she was trying to help Solange learn to be more girly?

He leaned into her and stroked his tongue over the exact spot where he'd taken her blood. Her mind lost its train of thought. Heat flooded between her legs. Her stomach muscles bunched beneath his palm and her breasts suddenly felt full and aching. On top of everything else, she was going to react to him like a cat in heat. Except . . . she could never lay with him, never give herself to him because he would swallow her up, leave her with nothing.

He nuzzled her neck. *Stop thinking and just let yourself enjoy what is left of the night. Relax into me.*

She was holding herself stiffly, terrified of feeling his immense strength, petrified of the commitment just accompanying him meant. How much further would she go to please him? Would she lose her sense of herself?

Is it so difficult, kessa ku toro—*my little wildcat, to relax for me?*

Was it? She was being silly. She took a deep breath and let it out. She forced her eyes open and looked up at the night. They were out of the heavy canopy in open sky. High.

Higher than she'd ever been before. She'd never been out of the rain forest. She'd never flown in a plane. For a moment she was frightened and she clutched at him.

Spread your arms out, minan—*my own.*

She swallowed hard. There was that low purr in his voice, as if all she had to do was stretch her arms out like wings and she'd please him beyond anything else. Was it so simple? She had to trust him to keep her from falling. She'd trusted him in battle implicitly. Of course he would keep her safe. It was ridiculous to think that he wouldn't. And she would have the experience of flying, for maybe the only time in her life.

She let out her breath and pried each finger from his arm. Only then did she realize she was hanging on to his forearms with her claws. She gave a soft inarticulate cry, ashamed.

No worries, little cat. Just let go and fly with me.

It was a seductive whisper. She felt the warmth of his breath on her neck somehow giving her reassurance. To please him—to say she was sorry for inadvertently hurting him—she let go and spread her arms to the wind as if she were a great bird. The wind touched her face and ruffled her hair. Above her was a sea of clouds, rolling and turbulent, but so beautiful. Around her was open sky. Below her were the tops of the trees, some shooting past the thick cover to emerge triumphantly from the crowd. The earth below dazzled her eyes. She'd never felt so free in her life.

His mouth nuzzled her neck, a whisper really, yet she felt his touch like a brand. No one had ever made her feel like that—dizzy, important, his entire focus on her. With just one touch. And he'd asked. He could easily merge his mind with hers, Carpathians did it all the time—an invasion, she'd always thought. *Wrong.* No one should have access to one's private thoughts. And yet . . .

It is not necessary.

She couldn't detect disappointment, but still, why couldn't she just say yes? He was giving her such a beautiful experience, one she doubted very many people would ever have the chance to have. Was it such a big thing to let him see how much she appreciated this moment? He wasn't making her feel guilty; that was all her own. Was she really such a coward? What could happen if just for this moment she said yes?

She took a breath, knew his hands felt it, that swift intake of breath, so raw and ragged. *I don't mind.*

You honor me.

And then he was inside her mind, a slow penetration that sent a thousand darts of fire burning over her skin and deep *inside* of her, sending a slow burn through her stomach to her most feminine core. She felt him in her, just as if they were sharing the same skin, merged together so deep she didn't know where he started and she left off.

She realized her insecurities were displayed for him, her fragile hold on her courage, the terrible need she had for him, the horrendous, almost insurmountable fear of letting him down.

Shh, minan, *see the night with me. That is all. Just share the night.*

His soothing murmur, almost a caress, calmed her wild thoughts and she turned her attention to the spectacular sensation of soaring through the air. She found the miracle so much more special when shared. He took them in a large circle over the river and she spotted the rare pink dolphins. Of course she'd seen them before, but not like this, where she could see their amazing speed in the water. She laughed. With their minds merged together, his burst of happiness elated her. He was like a child experiencing everything for the first time after hundreds of years without emotion, and that enhanced her enjoyment.

She turned her head toward him and found herself wanting to nuzzle his neck in a rare display of shy affection, but she couldn't quite dare to touch him so she just inhaled his scent, took his masculine essence into her lungs and held it there, as if she were hugging it to her.

I will link my hands around your waist, Solange. Lean out and let me take your weight so you feel the actual flight.

Her heart stuttered at the idea. He was really pushing her limits of trust, yet he seemed unaware of it. Or was he? He couldn't be. He was inside her mind. He knew her fears. She moistened her lips, her pounding pulse thundering in her ears. As before he remained silent, he did not repeat the request. He simply waited for her choice.

She licked her suddenly dry lips. Her life would be in his hands. Arms outstretched, her body falling forward as if she were really flying, she wouldn't have the opportunity to hang on to him. She doubted she was fast enough at shifting to turn and latch on with claws should he drop her. Could she do it? Would it displease him if she didn't? Would it matter? She tried to touch his mind, but he simply waited.

She could feel the weight of his gaze on her. That single-minded focus. His complete concentration on her alone. She felt tears burning behind her eyes. She wanted to give this to him. It was all she could give him. Moments like this one. She knew there was no other woman for him. It wasn't that he loved her. Or wanted her. He had no choice, yet he was willing to give her choices. It was just that his personality was so overpowering.

She closed her eyes and nodded.

He brushed a kiss over the top of her head, setting off a peculiar fluttering in the pit of her stomach. She held her breath as his mouth drifted to her temple and then pressed his cool, firm lips to her ear.

My woman.

Her heart contracted. Her womb clenched and she felt a

flood of damp heat between her legs. Two words and she melted. What did that say about her? Was she so desperate for his approval that all he had to do was sound happy with her and she would do anything he wanted?

He waited for her to shift position on her own. She almost wished he'd moved her first, but he didn't. She slowly, with caution, began to lean into his palms, so that she swung out, away from the solid comfort of his body. The wind increased and she couldn't stop her hands from grabbing his wrists. Instantly he brought her back against him and . . . waited.

She knew he was waiting for her to gather her courage and put her trust in him. There was no pretending she was too exhausted—he had her entire weight. All she had to do was hang there in the sky while the magic of the night surrounded her. He was giving her a gift of such importance. There had been no gifts since her family had been slaughtered, until now, until this moment. He seemed a dark sorcerer she couldn't resist—especially when he offered her such a rare, phenomenal experience.

Time slowed down. She could feel her heart pounding. He made her feel important when she'd never felt so before, not to anyone. The air seemed crisp and fresh, the night a cool blanket. She closed her eyes, took a deep breath and let go. She brought her arms straight out away from her body. He removed his hands from her and she knew this was the moment, now or never. She would never summon this kind of courage—or trust—again. She let herself fall forward. The sensation took her stomach and for a moment she was afraid he wouldn't catch her, but there his palms were, and she found herself suspended in the air with nothing but his hands under her.

Very slowly she opened her eyes. Her breath caught in her throat as she soared and dipped and wheeled with the freedom of the birds. Again she experienced that dizzying rapture that was physical, the adrenaline pouring into her bloodstream like dark gold, thickening her blood, spreading heat through her. She felt Dominic with her—in her—sharing the dazzling moments. It was pure magic—*he* was pure magic.

The wind tore tears from her eyes. After one of the worst days of her life, losing Annabelle, killing two men and nearly getting captured or killed by her own father, fighting vampires and having to face her lifemate, she was overwhelmed by sheer joy as she flew through the air. It was too much and yet she didn't want it to end.

Dominic drew her in, turning her so that her face was pressed over his heart. The rock-steady beat comforted her, helping her to keep from sobbing aloud. She wept quietly, her fingers buried in the front of his shirt. She just didn't care about anything in that moment. Not where they were going or what would happen when they got there. He had a destination in mind and it was evident he wouldn't drop her, so she just gave herself up to his care.

Dominic felt the exact moment she let go and gave herself over to him. His arms tightened around her, holding her close to him. She was very fragile, and so vulnerable. Not simply her physical self, but the woman she hid from the rest of the world. She was exhausted and she would have gone off to a damp retreat to lick her wounds alone and try to recover before she took on the enemy again.

Not this time, my little cat. This time I will see to your care.

She didn't answer, but her weeping, the tears tearing at his heart, lessened. He meticulously scanned the area for signs of the undead before he took her down to the forest floor, to the entrance of her favorite retreat. He'd seen it a dozen times, that small, snug cave deep in the recesses of the limestone labyrinth, when they met in her mind. The images were very detailed. She had no idea how much information he could pull from her mind in seconds when needed. And both of them needed this.

He found the entrance too small to carry her through, and reluctantly let her feet drop, his arm firmly anchoring her to him.

"How did you know . . . ?" Solange looked around her, lashes wet, her eyes bright and slightly shocked.

"I am your lifemate," he pointed out, his voice gentle. "This place brings you comfort."

She turned away from him and ducked inside, blinking back tears. He doubted if anyone had seen to her comfort in years. He followed her, noting the fluid movement of her body, just like the cat that was so much a part of her. She had a wild, untamed scent that appealed to him more than any other perfume he'd ever smelled. She belonged in the forest, and she moved with silent stealth, even in human form in the dark.

The tunnel led downward, deep under the earth. She stopped at what appeared to be a dead end and reached down to work at several large stones. Dominic gently moved her out of his way and simply levitated the large blocks of limestone and set them aside, and with a low bow gestured for her to precede him.

She hesitated, standing very close to him in the small confines of the tunnel. He could hear her heart, the rhythm too loud. She was frightened, but she was still putting herself in his hands; her courage humbled him. To encourage her, he took her hand and brought it to his mouth. He stroked long fingers over her wrist, the one Zacarias had drawn blood from, as he pressed a kiss into the exact center of her palm.

Solange's breath hitched, her gaze jumped to his face and then quickly skittered away. "You have to crawl to get into the chamber, and your shoulders . . ."

He kept possession of her hand, her fingers against his mouth. "I can turn to vapor," he reminded, a smile in his voice.

He felt her acute embarrassment that she hadn't remembered. Her body flooded with heat and immediately tensed. She started to pull her hand away, but he refused to relinquish control back to her. Instead, he drew her fingers into the warmth of his mouth and sucked on them. A shiver of awareness went through her body as he then drew her fingers to his lips and bit softly on the tips. "You are very tired, Solange. I thank you for your concern."

Once again her gaze flicked to his. She looked so uncertain he wanted to crush her to him. Instead, he released her hand and dropped his hand to her shoulders, silently guiding her to her knees. For a moment, he savored the feel of her warm breath on his rock-hard cock right through the material of his trousers. It would be so easy to remove them. The idea of her mouth on him shook him, but he didn't allow his own pleasures to be put before her care. He pressed gently until she was on all fours and crawling into the narrow, tight tunnel leading to the chamber.

The channel reminded him of a rabbit warren. He flowed through it easily, following his woman into the cave. She had made it somewhat of a home and his heart stilled in his chest when he realized she had never shared this sacred place, her only true refuge, with anyone else. She went to the north wall to find her lantern, but he lit the candles with a wave of his hand. Immediately the soft light threw shadows over everything.

He was grateful for the rich dirt floor. In one corner there was a hand-woven rug and a few wooden bowls. The sound of water was background music as it trickled steadily from the wall on the east side to fill the basin so a wide pool took up one corner of the chamber. The ceiling was high, giving the illusion of space when actually the cavern was snug.

He noted that she stayed a good distance from him, silent, her green cat's eyes watching his every move as he explored. He took his time, allowing the silence to stretch out, listening to the beat of her heart, waiting for her to calm. He saw books and picked up several to study the titles. Most were on making weapons and the plants of the Amazon. He thumbed through one of the volumes and found many of the healing plants highlighted.

When he moved closer to Solange, she reacted the way a cornered wildcat might, retreating, her eyes wide, almost mesmerized by him. She kept her head down, face slightly averted, but she was watching him the entire time. He went to a small pile of articles carefully placed on a rock shelf inside a small alcove, and the tension seemed to ease out of her just a little bit more. Her heart rate slowed nearly to normal.

There was a ragged blanket, very old, that someone had lovingly made for a child. Not hers, he guessed by the blue color. A boy. Someone she loved, by the look of it. A faded picture of a woman in a wooden handmade frame, a woman who must have been her mother, sat on a shelf. She had the same amazing eyes. A hand-carved comb of the finest wood. He touched each item. Read the memories imprinted there. A brother—no, two brothers. The comb had been made by her father. He frowned. Not her birth father. The man she loved as a father. All gone. Every one of them.

He lifted his head and looked at her, his gaze colliding with hers. "Come here to me, Solange. Right here." He pointed to a spot right in front of him.

She looked startled. Her eyes went dark. Her heart began pounding again, filling the small chamber with its frantic beat.

7

Can you come to trust a man once again?
Can you come to love an old one like me?
Let my strong arms protect you, let me sing you to sleep.
Let my song bring you healing, like the earth and the sea.

DOMINIC TO SOLANGE

Solange's heart nearly burst out of her chest. Tremors ran up and down her body, and icy fingers of fear slid down her spin. Dominic filled the room with his power. She couldn't look at his face, not those piercing eyes that could change color like a storm. She actually wrung her hands together. The distance between them seemed to be miles, although it was only a few steps. It might as well have been miles. Men weren't supposed to be like him—except in dreams. She could handle him in dreams, but this was crazy. What did he want from her?

He waited. He always seemed to be waiting so patiently

for her to make up her mind. He never raised his voice, his tone soft and compelling. She stared at his chest for a long time before she could make her frozen foot step forward. One. She counted to herself. Two. He seemed to loom larger than ever. Three. She could see the muscles ripple beneath his shirt. Four. Head down, refusing to meet his eyes, she took the last step to stand in the exact spot he'd indicated. It was the best she could do for him.

"The dawn is approaching fast, *päläfertiil*—lifemate. I need to make certain I have adequately taken care of you."

Her stomach somersaulted. What did that mean, "Taken care of you"? She licked her lips, trying to get enough moisture to do more than squeak. She was perfectly capable of taking care of herself if she could find a way to move. She felt paralyzed.

He caught the hem of her shirt and simply pulled it over her head before she had a chance to stop him. She gasped and covered her generous breasts with her hands, her face going from bright red to nearly a translucent white.

"Your bath, Solange," he reminded.

She swallowed twice. "I can undress," she blurted. It was a blatant lie. She couldn't take off her clothes in front of him to save her life.

"And deny me the pleasure of doing it for you?"

She stared mutely at his chest. He would *see* her. There was nowhere to hide in the small cavern. He took her wrists gently, and pulled her arms down and away from her body. A blush spread from her toes all the way to her face. She could feel warmth running under her skin, and worse, moisture gathering between her legs. The cool air in the cave teased her bare breasts, so that her nipples reacted, forming hard nubs that drew his attention.

He took a breath, his gaze drifting over her with a hint

of possession. "Why would you hide your breasts from me? Are they not part of my woman? Do they not belong to me just as she does? Is my body not yours?"

She heard a strangled sound emerge from her throat, but it was the only sound she could get out. She felt mesmerized by him, standing there trembling while he stepped close, so close she felt the brush of his chest against her sensitive nipples. With every breath she drew the scent of him into her lungs. If she raised her head, she knew she would see those fierce green eyes instead of his calming blue ones. He was every bit as aroused as she was, his heat setting her on fire. She closed her eyes when his hands dropped to the front of her jeans.

"I'm not beautiful," she managed to warn him, hoping that if she said it first, he wouldn't be too disappointed.

His hands stopped. "Solange."

She winced. His voice was stern. Still pitched low, but very stern.

"Look at me."

She wanted to look anywhere but at him, but she couldn't stop herself from raising her eyes to his. It was pure compulsion. Her entire being crumpled at the displeasure plain on his face.

"This is a very important rule, Solange. My lifemate is the most beautiful woman on this earth to me. Anyone who says differently insults her, which is a capital offense and insults me. I do not think you want to do that, do you?"

She shook her head. To her horror tears burned behind her eyes. She could *not* do this. She hated disappointing him, but what would be worse? Letting him discover on his own, or trying to tell him? "I was trying to be honest."

His hand cupped the side of her face, his gentleness nearly her undoing. His thumb caressed her cheek and jaw.

"*Kessake*—my little cat. Do not look so distressed. When a man has waited a thousand years for the one woman who is his alone, she is the very definition of beauty to him. What others see cannot matter. Only what I see matters. And I want you to see yourself through my eyes. You should see the woman I see."

His fingers trailed down her throat to her collarbone and then down to the swell of her breasts. "Look at you. The very epitome of a woman." His fingers touched her nipples.

She drew in her breath, held it, shocked at the electricity sizzling between her breasts and belly, moving lower still to tease her thighs with arousal and catch fire to the very center of her core.

Abruptly his hands dropped to her jeans again, to push them down over her hips. Solange caught her breath again, closing her eyes as she obeyed the pressure of his hand to step out of her clothes. Jaguars couldn't wear underwear as a rule because they couldn't get out of their clothes fast enough when they shifted. She stood absolutely naked in front of him, grateful for the softening effect of the candles, unable to look at him. She kept her arms where he'd positioned them and bit down hard on her lip to keep from blurting out anything else that might disappoint him.

No matter what he said about being beautiful, she didn't feel that way. And she wanted to be beautiful for him. She was going to die soon. There was no way to live in a fight with Brodrick; he was too strong. She'd accepted that she had limited time left, and in a way, she was grateful. She was so weary of days like this one, days of failure, of killing. Of not having anyone . . .

She wanted these last moments with Dominic. She respected him above all other men. She would never have been able to accept another man. But she wanted so much, for once in her life, to belong. To be cared for. To be a woman, not a warrior. This was her chance, now at the end of her days . . . if she could stand him looking at her scarred, repulsive body.

"Solange."

She winced. He was definitely reading her mind.

He shook his head. "Not your mind. Your expression." He traveled in a slow circle around her. She had a strong urge to shift into her jaguar, but now it was somewhat of a challenge. Did he tell the truth? Was he an honorable man? She needed to know. He was the first person she'd trusted enough to allow him to lead. She'd never even allowed her beloved cousins to do that.

He returned to stand in front of her and her legs nearly went out from under her. He was naked. Magnificently so. There was no way to breathe. Her mind came crashing to a halt. There was nothing small about Dominic, and right now, there was no doubt that he was aroused—for her. He drew a deep breath and she knew he could smell her own arousal. His eyes went darker green.

"I love the way you blush," he said. "So enticing. I had no idea my little wildcat would be so sexy."

She felt light-headed. Dizzy. Faint. The room tilted.

He swept her up into his arms, cradling her against his chest. "You forgot to breathe, *kessake*. It helps."

She was fairly certain *nothing* was going to help, but she took a breath anyway. "I can't . . ." She gestured vaguely. There was not going to be sex. She couldn't go that far, could she?

"I can't either," he replied, amusement in his voice.

She relaxed a little, comforted by his humor. He was much like the man she had conjured up. Patient. Relaxed. Content with who he was and who she was.

"You look like you could," she pointed out.

His gaze flicked over her and there was definite amusement. "I *feel* like I could. You are not ready, no matter what your body says. And I have vile parasites in my body. I cannot take a chance that I would pass them to you." He stepped into the basin of water.

She caught at him. "The water's cold."

His eyes went deep emerald. "Would I allow my lifemate to be cold when she is exhausted and wounded? I see to your needs, *minan*, at all times."

They sank into the blessedly hot water. She didn't care how he'd managed it, but every cell in her body thanked him. The heat surrounded her, easing the terrible strain on her muscles that the physical exertion of the day had brought, as well as the tension of meeting the man she believed she'd made up. She ducked her head under the water, but when she emerged and reached for the shampoo she kept tucked into a small rock ledge, his hand was there before hers.

"Let me. It gives me pleasure."

Maybe if he didn't sound so completely sexy all the time she could handle being with him. It was the tone of his voice. His choice of words. *Pleasure.* She could see his hands, big and strong like the rest of him. He dealt in death, just as she did, but there was knowledge in his eyes— knowledge of her, of what she craved and never believed she would have.

He just took up so much room. He filled the entire chamber with his presence. She felt petite beside him, and she was a sturdy woman. He made her curves seem lush and sexy instead of too much. Everything he did was deliberate and precise. He positioned her exactly as he wanted her, turning her back to him, fitting her snugly in his lap so that her head could rest against his chest. She could feel him, hard as a rock, long and thick, unashamed against her buttocks.

She desperately tried not to think about sex. Her cat wasn't close to heat, and she *never* thought about a man touching her. It would be unthinkable to allow a man's hands on her body after all the terrible things she'd seen that men did. Yet, lying in the water, her body warm and surrounded by liquid heat, her head back, her breasts floating and his obvious erection in mind, she had to struggle to keep erotic thoughts from her mind.

He gently rubbed shampoo in her hair. His fingers settled into her scalp, beginning a slow, magical massage that sent her body into a near hypnotic state of relaxation. She felt the tingling in her scalp spread through her, a pleasant sensation that grew into pure pleasure. He took his time rinsing her hair thoroughly before his hands dropped to her neck, those strong, marvelous fingers massaging every knot and tight muscle.

Solange sighed, shocked at how good she felt. The hot water, his hands and feeling clean eased most of the tension out of her.

"Aside from the entire naked thing, why is it so difficult to talk to you?" She heard her own voice musing aloud, and was slightly shocked at herself. It was his magical hands, now working on her shoulders, that seemed to make her less inhibited. "I talked to you all the time before."

"You were safe. The man you believed you conjured up couldn't expect anything from you."

That made her seem such a coward. Was she a coward? She didn't think so. But she was afraid. He lifted her arm out of the water to begin using his strong fingers to ease the tension from those muscles as well. Defined muscles. Ropes of muscle beneath her scarred skin. She could see the hundreds of white indentations, tiny ones that reminded her of the painful stabs from her father's knife as he worked over her entire body in his determination to provoke her cat into revealing itself.

She hated looking at her body. She hated those polka-dot scars marring her skin. She couldn't look at herself without remembering the slaughter. If she closed her eyes she could smell the blood running through the house and outside into the ground. Her brothers' bodies thrown carelessly aside, arms and legs sprawled out, little Avery lying partially across Adam as if in a garbage dump. Bile rose and she fought not to be sick. Her friends. Her family. She made a single sound, inarticulate, and tried to jerk her arm away from him.

He didn't let go. His gaze leapt to her face. "Do not turn away from me, Solange. We share this. The slaughter of your family. The slaughter of mine."

His soft words allowed her to breathe away the images.

"Do you wish to remove the evidence from your skin?"

He asked the question quietly, his voice so gentle she looked away because she couldn't stop the tears from welling up. She'd never been so emotional. Or maybe she had when she'd talked to him, thinking he wasn't real. She'd felt safe enough to cry in front of him. He had been her only outlet. Juliette and Jasmine had often helped her with the rescues, Juliette more than Jasmine, as they both tried to protect her. But they relied on Solange and she looked after them with fierce protectiveness. She blamed herself that she had been away when the jaguar-men found her aunt Audrey and dragged her away. They'd mounted a rescue but . . . The damage had been done. Just as with Jasmine.

She tried desperately to stop her thoughts. She was in a hot bath with a shockingly handsome man—larger than life—and she was so emotional she'd nearly forgotten that small detail.

"Solange?" His fingers continued to work their magic down her arm. "Would you do it if you could? Remove these tributes?"

She closed her eyes and allowed him to draw her head back until it rested against his chest as he lifted her other arm and began that slow, soothing massage. She'd never thought of the scars as badges or a tribute. Were they? She'd thought of the scars with hatred and anger, a reminder of who her father was, of what blood ran in her veins. She'd never once considered the small white dots as something beautiful—a tribute to her love of her mother, her family.

"Could you remove them?" Was that even possible?

"Perhaps." His tone was noncommittal.

Solange didn't try to look up at him; she merely relaxed, her head resting on his chest as he massaged her arm, knowing he would wait with infinite patience for her answer. She loved that calmness in him, the lack of anger and need for revenge. She was driven by both destructive emotions, and desperately needed that calm in the midst of the wild fury that drove her so hard. When she was close to him like this, she felt steadier. Safe. Comforted. She might be off balance, but as long as she wasn't thinking in terms of man and woman, she could lay down the fight and just be still.

He brought his mouth to her shoulder where the puncture wounds had been. "He nearly got you today."

She nodded. "I was terrified. I never want him to get his hands on me again. I went into the river, just as poor Annabelle did." She pressed her fingers to her temple and shook her head. "I left her there. In the river. To bait them. I don't care about the jaguar-man, he can rot there. But I can't get her out of my mind. I should have tried to find her body."

"I found her body and I buried her deep where no human, no animal and no jaguar will ever find her. I removed all scent from the area. She is safe from them."

The relief was overwhelming. Solange leaned back and rested her head on his chest once more. "Thank you. I've never left a woman alone in her death. I do my best to do right by them, even if I can't save them. It would have haunted me that she wasn't buried or burned properly."

His arms circled her, just under her breasts, and held her close. "It is done, *sívamet*—my heart. You can rest now."

She felt relaxed, the tension at last completely gone from her. His arms felt safe, and when she closed her eyes she allowed herself to drift a little and just enjoy the feel of him surrounding her. This, then, was what other women felt. Part of someone else. Cared for.

"I wouldn't," she murmured.

"Wouldn't?" he echoed.

"Remove my scars. They're part of me, part of who I am now. I don't like being angry, and killing makes me sick. After a while I wonder if I'm as bad as they are, but in a way, you're right about the scars. I didn't break. I didn't let him use me and turn me into something weak and helpless. I honored my mother and stepfather's memories, as well as those of our friends and my two younger brothers." She ran her fingers over her arms, for the first time seeing her skin differently. A tribute, not something so ugly.

"You are a gift, Solange. An amazing, priceless gift." He swept her wet hair aside and brushed a kiss along her neck.

Without another word he lifted her into his arms and stepped out of the basin. She opened her mouth to protest. The water had been a cocoon of heat. For the first time that she could remember, she had been sheltered and comforted, and she didn't want it to end. But there was something implacable about his expression. The lines were etched deep. His eyes were again a deep blue, and there was a hint of possession there she felt secretly thrilled about.

The cavern should have been cold, and Solange was prepared to shiver, but the air was warm. He had seen to her comfort once again. He set her on her feet in front of him, produced a soft towel out of the air, in the strange way Carpathians could produce clothing, and began to gently rub the droplets of water from her body. She found herself unbearably shy all over again.

He stood so close, his body heat enveloping her, his gaze drifting over her body as though it belonged to him. Hadn't he actually used those words? He was slow and methodical, taking his time, using the corner of the towel to rub her arms dry, but then he suddenly leaned in and flicked a drop of water from the tip of her breast with his tongue. She jumped as streaks of fire rushed to her feminine channel, setting off a spasm of need. His mouth moved to the bite mark he'd previously healed. The punctures were sealed, but this time he lapped at the damaged tissue until she no longer even felt the mark on her.

"You don't have to do that." She shivered, not from the cold, but from his sensuous touch.

"You are wrong, *kessake*," he corrected. "No other man can put his mark on my woman. He cannot harm her in any way. I *have* to heal you or I cannot live with myself."

She let him. She didn't know why she let him. His touch should have been disturbing, and perhaps, because it was arousing, it was—but she didn't care. She had never experienced anyone's attention before, let alone that of a man who focused so completely on her well-being. He made her feel special and beautiful, almost like a fragile flower there in the rain forest. She wasn't, and they both knew it, but for those few minutes when he was lavishing such care on her, she didn't want the moment to end.

A fairy tale. She closed her eyes and gave herself up to the experience. The perfect man, a warrior with changing eyes, the absolute calm in the center of a storm. He thought her beautiful when she was a perfect, dreadful mess. But he made it so. Somehow, Dominic made it so.

He paid attention to detail, and each time he found a bruise or an angry scratch, he bent his head and used his mouth to heal it. The act was erotic, although she guessed he didn't intend it that way. He was focused on her health, not on her shape. His tongue found a puncture wound on the small of her back, several more near her buttocks. His hands held her hips motionless as he attended to each separate wound.

Solange worked hard to control her breathing. She was grateful he had moved behind her so she didn't have to admire his physique, because, to her, he was perfection. She had no idea what could possibly happen after this encounter with him, but she'd take this moment and keep it in her heart forever. He made a complete circle until he was standing in front of her again. This time he leaned down and brushed a kiss on her trembling mouth.

Abruptly he went to his knees in front of her. She couldn't move. Couldn't find breath. What was a man like Dominic doing on his knees in front of her? It was so wrong. She could fight side by side with him, and she would consider herself his equal, no matter that he was a warrior unsurpassed. But she wasn't his equal here. Not when they were alone. She wanted to protest, to back away, to serve him, but she had no idea how.

"I can't do this," she managed to get out. Her voice wasn't

her own, just a thread of shivery sound that could have been taken for fear.

He looked up at her with eyes darkened with desire. Her heart clenched hard in her chest. There was something so compelling in the way he looked at her. She was jaguar, used to direct stares—but that was the locked-on gaze of a predator. Dominic looked at her as if she were the most desirable woman in the world—and she was his. She shook her head, biting down hard on her lip to keep from upsetting him again by blurting out that she wasn't.

"You deserve . . ." Her fingers tentatively touched the silky strands of that hair, so black, like the wing of a great bird shining in the sky. ". . . so much more. I can't be what you need."

"I deserve you," he said, his voice as gentle as ever. "I need this." He leaned forward and captured droplets of water running down her hip right over the jagged, ugly wound.

She cried out, the shock of his mouth on her sending waves of heat through her body. The brush of his hair against her thighs sent a thousand streaks of arousal burning through her legs so that she might have fallen if she hadn't gripped his shoulders. He felt solid, like a rock, someone she could lean on if she just let herself break. And maybe that was what he had been after all along.

His hands spread her thighs. He didn't say a word, simply positioned her with his hands. His breath touched her first. The sound of her heart echoed through the cavern. He carefully lapped at every single laceration, every scratch, and when he once again found the puncture wounds on her back and buttocks, she wanted to weep with the care he took.

"What happened?"

She had to search to find her vocal cords. He hadn't

touched her sexually, not really, yet her body was no longer hers. Pliant and soft, it belonged to him—she belonged to him. She didn't know what kind of claiming the Carpathians did with their lifemates, but she felt claimed. She felt as if he cared for her like a rare and precious jewel. Nothing had ever come close to such a feeling before.

"I set a trap and he was waiting for me. He sacrificed his men, left them out in the open, and I took the shots. I was about to run when he dropped down out of nowhere. It's difficult to fool my jaguar. She's very alert, especially to any male in the area. She's had to be. But he was there and now he has the scent of my blood."

"Who is he?" Dominic bent his head forward to place a kiss on the puncture wounds, his hair making her shiver as it brushed against her skin.

"He's called Brodrick. Brodrick the Terrible. He's my father."

Dominic was silent a moment, taking his time rising. He enveloped her body in the warm towel and drew her into his arms. "Tell me about him."

Solange rested her head against his chest and allowed herself the pleasure of circling his waist with her arms. She could hear the steady rhythm of his heart, a reassuring beat. Where had all the men like Dominic gone? She doubted that she deserved such a man, not when she didn't even know how to be a woman. But there were so many other women, good and loving, who would care and nurture and partner a man in the world. How had this happened? A mistake? Perhaps, but she was willing to accept the gift she had been given. Her time was past and maybe his was as well.

"He killed every person my cousins and I loved. He kills any woman or child who can't shift. He kills every male jaguar child who has human blood in their veins. The men who follow him are not royals, but they all shift and they help him slaughter our people."

"Why is he working with the humans if he despises them so much?"

"He's made an alliance with the vampires as well. I think they're compiling a database of women with psychic ability. He targets women he believes have jaguar blood. They're kidnapped from all over the world and brought here. If she can shift, they try to impregnate her; if she can't, she's raped, tortured and killed. The entire alliance is built on a web of deceit. The humans don't realize they're working with vampires who are using them to kill the very people who protect them. Brodrick can't be influenced by vampires, so he believes himself safe from them. And the vampires are trying to use everyone to build their numbers to defeat the Carpathians. They want all the women killed so there can be no lifemates for the Carpathians. At least, that's what I believe."

"How in the world did you learn all that?" His hand came up to bunch in her hair.

"I only recently managed to get inside, so some of what I just told you is guesswork. I spend a lot of time gathering information before I make a strike. I don't have any help, and to plan a rescue with only one person is extremely difficult."

"I thought your cousins . . ."

"They have lifemates. Their men don't want them in jeopardy. In truth, neither do I. Jasmine is pregnant, and Juliette is too soft for this kind of life." She sighed and looked up at him. "That's not right, Dominic. She's too good for this. There's a brightness in her and I don't want that to ever go away. At first I was terrified for her when she met Riordan, but I can see that he makes her happy. I'm grateful for him. He'll take care of both of them."

His eyes darkened. "You intend to kill Brodrick." He made it a statement, neither good nor bad, no judgment in his tone, just a fact.

"Yes." There was nothing else to say. She had no choice. He would never stop. Without him, the other men would scatter. They weren't good men, and they would cause problems, but without direction, they would be manageable. If they went out of the rain forest, the law would eventually find them.

Dominic handed her a glass of water. "Drink."

Where he got it, she had no idea, but she took it without protest and as she drank, he opened up the ground.

"I will need the soil to heal my wounds completely," he said. "I have placed safeguards all around your cave and nothing will disturb us while we sleep."

Solange looked down into the deep pit. A good ten feet down. Her cat could perhaps jump out if needed, but sleeping in the dirt? She wanted to be close to him, but . . .

He smiled at her, that slow, sexy smile that somehow turned her entire insides to a melted pool of acquiescing heat. How did he do that?

"You need to trust me."

Trust. He was a respected warrior. He had lived a thousand years with absolute honor. His word *was* his honor. If he said she was his, that she was beautiful to him, that she was the one he wanted, she should be able to accept that without all the self-doubts. And most of all, she should trust in him.

"I think trust is a gift," she said in a low voice. "A beautiful gift so many women have naturally. I want it, Dominic. More than anything, I want that gift, but . . ." She trailed off. Was she even capable of trust anymore?

His fingers settled around the nape of her neck. "Your trust in me runs deep, Solange. You do not trust in yourself, the woman. You see yourself as two beings. One, the warrior: confident, incredible in her resolve, uncaring how the world views her as long as she can save the women of her species from the brutality of the men. You live in a world of deceit and violence and you understand and accept those rules. The other being is this one, the one who shares herself with me—her true lifemate. You are the other half of my soul. You are the light to my darkness. You cannot see yourself that way, because you have to live in darkness. You buried her deep, my woman, but what you do not understand, *sívamet*, is that I appreciate that in you. I do not wish others to see you as I do. I do not want to share this woman with anyone else, male or female. This side of Solange is mine alone."

She shook her head, but took every word into her heart and held each close to her.

"Make no mistake, the warrior and the woman are not two separate entities. You are both, and I see you clearly. I know I have to share the warrior. That trait is strong, and there is no denying you. Events shaped what was already a fighter's spirit, honed and perfected in the fires of agony. In order to survive and ensure the safety of women you love, the women only you stand for who survived, you had to suppress the light in you. But that light is there, and I can see it. If I am the only one who does, that is all that matters."

God help her, every word touched her soul. He saw her. He knew her. He knew her better than she knew herself. She wanted to be everything for him, that woman who lived in the light, at least during the moments she actually could spend with him. She wanted to give him whatever he wanted.

They both had so little time left. She accepted that and so did he. They were committed on their individual paths. But this was their time—maybe their only time. She lifted her hand to his face, tracing those lines etched so deep, lines that made him look like such a tough, ruthless man. There was no boyish trait anywhere. He was all man. He didn't move away from her tentative exploration, nor did he hurry her decision to get into that pit of dark, rich soil with him. He stood beneath her fingers and let her commit his face to memory.

"You want me to sleep beside you?"

"I do not want you even inches from me, *minan*. I need you this day."

She swallowed every fear and lifted her chin. "How will you know I'm there?" She was going to give him this small thing. What did it matter? It was all he would allow her to give him. She couldn't touch his body, couldn't relieve that fierce arousal. He gave and gave, and she . . .

"I receive pleasure from giving you pleasure, Solange. And you are always gracious enough to share each moment with me, even though allowing me into your mind is terrifying to you. I will know you are with me."

"I don't understand why you won't let me . . ." She couldn't articulate what she wanted so she simply dropped her hand around his thick, rock-hard erection.

The breath hissed out of him. "It is not safe." Very gently he removed her fingers and pulled her palm to his heart. "It is enough that I share your pleasure."

She doubted that, but she was too unsure of herself at the moment to pursue it. She would have to think about his statement for a while. The vampire blood? He might lose control and convert her? She knew, from talking to Juliette, that the drive was fierce and unrelenting in the male to bind his lifemate to him, yet Dominic had shown no signs of needing to bind her to him, or wanting to convert her. What did that mean? If she took him at his word that she was everything he wanted, then there was another reason.

He swept his arm around her waist and took them over the edge of the deep pit. Just before her feet settled into the soil, a small, thin comforter covered one side of the dirt floor. Her bare feet landed on the material. He sank into the soil and let out a sigh.

"Juliette tried to describe to me what it was like to be rejuvenated by the earth, but I couldn't get the concept."

"You would like me to share the experience with you, *kessake*?" He settled into the cradle of dark, rich loam and held out his hand to her.

She took his hand and allowed him to pull her down to his side. She settled against him, curling like the cat she was, one hand flung boldly across his chest. "Yes." She wanted every experience with him that she could have.

No one would probably ever know about Dominic, her dream lover. He was hers alone, and maybe it was the way it was supposed to be. She'd done a lot of terrible things in her life, committed a lot of sins. In the rain forest, she told herself it was kill or be killed, but the truth was, she was the one who determined who lived and who died. If she had two jaguar-men in her sights, she tried for both of them, but the first was always the one she considered the most dangerous and violent. These stolen moments of happiness with Dominic made up for a lifetime without.

He brushed a kiss on top of her head and then waved his hand. Another quilt settled over her. "While I sleep, should you wake, I do not want you cold."

She touched the exquisite quilt with the symbols woven into it. The material was soft, dark greens, like her forest, with animals embroidered into squares beside the symbols. She found herself tracing each one with a light finger. "This is beautiful."

"Gabriel's woman makes them for us. She weaves in

whatever is needed. I wanted one to comfort you and bring you peace of mind. I will appear dead, Solange, with no breath or heartbeat. You cannot panic."

She smiled at the command in his voice. "I don't easily panic. Well, not as a rule. You definitely shocked me."

"By being real?"

"Yes."

He laughed softly. "You shocked me as well. We have bad timing, *päläfertiil*. Maybe the worst timing of any couple in history."

She turned his words over in his mind. "I needed time to grow, Dominic. There was so much anger in me, so much hatred for the men who slaughtered my family, who have been systematically committing genocide on our own people because they believe the bloodlines need to be pure. I hated for so long and I couldn't distinguish between those men who have destroyed our species and other men. It wasn't until Juliette met her lifemate, and I saw the honor in him, that I came to terms with my rage."

He brushed the hair from her face with gentle fingers. She remembered those same tender caresses from her dream man and her heart fluttered in her chest. He was so much like the image she'd conjured up, and yet a little frightening. Mostly because she wanted to bring him the same peace and joy he brought her.

He nuzzled the top of her head, and at the same time merged his mind with hers, catching the next, not-so-altruistic thoughts, the need to give him the same release he had given her.

Dominic sighed inwardly. *I will not take the chance with you.*

He could feel the need clawing at her, saw the erotic images in his mind, but he would never have been able to find the control to keep from claiming her both with his body and his soul. He craved her. A dark need that grew the longer he spent time with her.

His first duty was to protect her, even from himself. He had the blood of a vampire running in his veins, and with that acidic poison were thousands of greedy parasites working to consume him from the inside out—although . . . the vile creatures had gone still. None of them moved in him. There were no whispered commands, and there was no stabbing, relentless pain, not since he had been near his lifemate. Why was that? How could it be? Could lifemates provide such solace even for one already lost?

He took a deep breath. The night was gone. The sun rose steadily in the sky. He was deep beneath the earth, but he could still feel the effects on his body. Soon he would be a leaden weight and his heart would cease to beat. He felt Solange's sharp intake of breath and knew she was experiencing the prickly sensation on her skin, the scorched feeling that lived right under his skin in all the nerves.

He relaxed into the richness of the soil bed. The earth welcomed him, whispered to him, the abundance of minerals immediately seeping into his pores, enriching his body, speeding the healing of every wound, the long slices caused by the sword that had bit deep into his flesh. Zacarias had helped to speed the healing, but it was here in the earth where he would find the natural medicine for his kind.

Solange's wonder delighted him. She put her hand in the soil between them and allowed it to slip through her fingers. "I had no idea. All this time I've walked on it and yet didn't feel it alive, living and breathing with cures. Even if they aren't for my kind, it's a miracle what the earth does for yours."

"She welcomes us as her children." He tried to put it in

words she might understand, although he could feel her acceptance.

He would cover them with dirt, but not their faces. Unlike him, Solange would need the air to breathe. He moved, and the aching demands of his body moved with him.

"I could . . ." She stopped when he put his hand on her head and held her to his chest.

"You cannot tempt me, Solange. I battle with my honor. Honor is important to me. And you—you are my most precious gift. I could never live with myself if my selfishness placed you in danger. Go to sleep and it will be enough to hold you in my arms."

He had sung to her in their shared dream, and he did so now, his song to her, the haunting melody, all the things he'd always wanted to say to his lifemate.

I was half-alive for a thousand years.
I'd given up hope that we'd meet in this time.
Too many the centuries. All disappears
As time and the darkness steal color and rhyme.

8

Can you find beauty in this rough-hewn woman?
Can you come to love a shapeshifter like me?

SOLANGE TO DOMINIC

The female jaguar smelled blood. The scent was in her nostrils and she quickened her pace, working her way along the branches, careful not to slip. She ignored the animals scrambling to get out of her way. She had no time to hunt them, all she cared about was getting to her mother. She had finally picked up the trail after four long years. Aunt Audrey was with her, and Juliette followed, keeping her eye on Jasmine, still so young.

Solange had argued with her aunt for hours, but after all, she was only twelve, and Audrey the adult. She knew they shouldn't have brought Jasmine on the rescue mission, but they had nowhere safe to leave her. Audrey was right about that, but the cub's presence doubled the danger to them all.

Already, Solange's jaguar was a fierce fighter and she had learned to handle weapons, particularly guns. She practiced night and day. She went through hundreds of rounds of ammunition, which was difficult to get. She threw knives when she wasn't shooting guns. And she practiced in the forest, stealth and tracking, sometimes coming so close to a male jaguar, she could have reached out and touched him, but he never knew she was there. Audrey often punished her for that, but Solange didn't care. It was all for this reason. This moment. Getting her mother back.

Solange leapt from one branch to the next, and finally to the forest floor. The scent of the male jaguar was strong throughout the entire area. Her heart beat so fast. Her mother. Solange loved her fiercely and she had sworn, standing over her stepfather and brothers, that she would get her back. She'd snuck out so many times, disappearing into the interior of the rain forest for days, tracking the jaguar-men. They moved constantly, and she knew that once she'd picked up her mother's scent, if she missed this opportunity, they would never recover her.

Audrey had been torn between protecting the children and getting her sister back. In the end, Juliette and Solange had persuaded her, or perhaps it had been the knowledge that Solange would have gone by herself. Her childhood had ended there in the clearing with the bodies of her loved ones surrounding her. She never went to sleep without hearing the cries of the dead and dying, or the sound of her mother's anguish as the jaguar-men tore her daughter out of her arms and dragged her into the house to torture her.

She knew where the trail led now. The men moved prisoners often, but they used existing structures when they were on the move. Nearby was an old hut built into the trees, off the forest floor. It was rarely used, but the jaguars would know about it and they were most likely using it.

Her jaguar was small still, moving through the forest along the game trails, slipping beneath large umbrella leaves as she unerringly moved close to the two trees supporting the structure.

Somewhere behind her was her aunt Audrey, ready to protect them if Solange were right and her mother was held captive in that house. Her heart beat loud, too loud, as she left the safety of the foliage and took to the trees once more. She spotted a sentry in the branches high above the wooden shelter. A jaguar lay in the shadows of the canopy, sleepy, nearly dozing, only the tip of his tail occasionally twitching.

Solange kept a wary eye on him as she crawled along the twisted limb. She was shaking with fear and anticipation. She had dreamt of this moment, prayed for it, spent the last four years preparing for it. Now that the moment was at hand, she could barely control herself. She needed every ounce of stealth she'd worked on to maintain the slow, inch-by-inch freeze-frame of her kind to keep from drawing the eye of the sentry. The closer she got to that tiny house, the more the scent of her mother filled her lungs.

She dragged herself across the two feet of sparse cover to gain the porch. She was now out of the sentry's sight. She pulled herself up and peered into the dirty window. A woman half sat, half sprawled on the floor, a collar around her neck, her hands tied behind her. Her face was swollen, one eye closed. A cut on her lip oozed blood and there were bruises on her face and neck and down her arms.

Solange didn't recognize her for a moment. She was thin, like a skeleton, her once glorious hair hanging in matted dreads. She raised her head slowly and opened her one good eye. They stared at one another, Solange afraid her heart would shatter. The fire was long gone from her mother, leaving a broken shell of a woman.

Solange looked around the room. Her mother was alone. It was now or never. She slipped inside and rushed across the space. She used her teeth on the ropes binding her mother. Sabine Sangria shook her head, tears leaking from her eyes.

"You shouldn't have come, baby," she whispered.

Solange thrust her head against her mother, the only way she could convey her deep love. They had to hurry. There was no time to throw herself into her mother's arms. They had to go before the others returned. She watched her mother struggle to her feet and limp slowly across the floor to the door. They both peered out. Solange started to push her way out of the room, but her mother dropped a restraining hand on her shoulder. Solange paused and looked up.

"*Never* let them take you alive, Solange. Do you understand me? They are worse than monsters, and you can't let them get their hands on you."

Solange nodded. She'd seen them. She had seen too many women after the jaguar-men had gotten their hands on them to not realize the brutality of these men.

"Audrey? The girls?" There was anxiety in Sabine's voice.

Solange indicated with her head they were waiting outside. Sabine nodded and Solange slipped out the door, her heart nearly bursting with joy. She couldn't wait to put her arms around her mother and just hold her close. Four years of working toward this one moment and she was so close. She forced herself to go slow across that open space.

She turned back to watch as her mother shifted. She could hardly bear to take her eyes off her mother. It was shocking to see the effort it took to shift, the gasping pain for both the human and animal. Did her mother have internal damage? Broken bones? Only that kind of pain could affect the cat. Solange tried to keep an eye on her mother as they carefully crossed that nearly open space on the branch together and made their way stealthily through the canopy toward freedom.

As they put a good mile between them and the jaguar sentry, Solange allowed joy to burst through her. They'd done it. They had finally brought her mother home. She wanted to weep with happiness. The little cub suddenly squawked and shifted into human form, and Jasmine nearly fell from the canopy. She didn't make a sound, a child already well versed in the need for absolute silence. She had never been able to hold the jaguar form for long. Her father had been human. Had she been in the village the day Brodrick had come, she would have been killed with the others.

They waited while she awkwardly crawled onto her sister's back and, because she was in human form and it was too dangerous to continue moving through the canopy, they made their way to the forest floor. Audrey had the weapons stashed in a bag slung around her neck, but still, they moved fast. Every step lightened Solange's heart more. Her mother. She'd dreamt of it at night, waking more than once calling for her mother. She could barely believe they'd actually managed to find her.

A sudden silence in the canopy froze her. A sentry monkey called a warning. A bird shrieked. Her heart nearly stopped. She reacted immediately, still the child but already the one most skilled. She shifted immediately and snatched the bag of weapons from around Audrey's neck and signaled Juliette to run with Jasmine. Juliette would take to the water to keep from leaving tracks. Audrey and Solange would delay those following to give Juliette the best chance with little Jasmine to escape.

She sank onto the ground and quickly reached into the bag to pull out a gun. Her mother's hand on her wrist stilled her. She, too, had shifted to human form. Very gently she tugged at the weapon in Solange's hand. Solange shook her head stubbornly, holding on.

"Give it to me, baby," Sabine said.

Solange looked at her mother, taking in the bruises and scars, the misshapen rib cage, the signs of the brutality she had endured these last four years. "Go with your aunt now."

"No. You go with her. I'm a good shot."

"You can't get all of them. Do as I tell you." Sabine hugged her hard for the briefest of seconds. "*Never* let them take you alive, Solange," she whispered. "I love you, baby. Go with your aunt now." She shoved Solange at her sister. "Thank you, all of you."

Knowledge burst through Solange. Her mother was going to fight the attackers off to allow the rest of them to get away. And she would die here. She shook her head, opened her mouth to scream a protest, but Audrey, with surprising strength, clapped her palm over Solange's mouth, wrapped an arm around her waist and turned and ran with her.

Solange screamed and screamed. No sound came from her throat. She heard the shots of the rifle and then the horrible sound of jaguars fighting. She screamed again, called to her mother. Again there was no sound, nothing. She couldn't cry. She couldn't look at anyone. The pain had gone so deep there was no adequate way to express it.

Solange found herself rocking back and forth, holding the comforter to her, the memories refusing to recede as they always did when she recalled them. *Mama,* she whispered softly, *I wish I had gone with you.*

Coldhearted Solange had been born that day. Her mother's daughter was dead. She had never been able to hold her mother close again, not even her body. They had burned it and left no trace for Solange to even mark. She realized something inside her had died that day, something she could never get back. She trained daily after that to become what she was now—a killer. She had fueled her rage to keep herself going every single day.

But Solange was no more. They had killed her that hot afternoon, just as surely as they killed her mother. She was alone. No one could possibly understand the change that had taken place in her that day. She had made a vow, sworn over the blood of her mother and then again, when she'd made her pilgrimage back to her village, sworn over the rest of her family—she would not turn her back on the other women who needed her. She would remain alone.

Fél ku kuuluaak sívam belső—*beloved.* The voice moved in her head. Soft. Tender even. *You are not alone anymore. I see you. I hear your screams and I share your anguish.*

Solange heard the ring of truth in Dominic's voice. He had shared her memories. As violent and vivid as they were, every detail etched forever into her mind, she had disturbed his sleep, pressing those memories into him without her knowledge. His own beloved sister and her lifemate had been ripped from him. He had spent several lifetimes trying to find her, only to discover she had long ago been tortured and killed. Yes, he did know the anguish and sorrow inside of her, the slow death of everything good.

She pushed the comforter against her mouth, still rocking slowly. If she looked there in the darkness, she would see him with her cat's eyes, but she didn't want to look at death, see him lying so still without a heartbeat, without breath, not when the death of her mother was so close. She couldn't bear to see him that way. Not now. Not with the past so near and her life closing in around her.

Not death, avio päläfertiil—*lifemate. The earth holds me in her arms and heals me. She gives me sustenance in her way. This is life, just a different version than you know.*

"I have to go outside and just breathe." She couldn't

sleep. She needed to lose herself in her cat, to prowl the rain forest and look for—*him*.

I do not think so, little cat. If you must shift, of course you should do so, particularly if it eases your mind, but you cannot go out hunting him in your present state of mind. You would be killed. You are seeking death.

"That might be true," she said, willing only to admit the possibility that he might be right about her seeking death. "But sadly for you, you're lying there dead or not dead, and can do nothing to stop me."

Amusement filled her mind. *I am an ancient Carpathian,* minan, *and far more powerful than you can conceive. I am your lifemate and it is my duty to see to your health. Do not think because I am gentle with you, that I do not have the ability to take care of your needs.*

Had anyone else said those words to her, Solange would have scoffed at them, but Dominic was Carpathian, and she had seen and felt his power. And he had some sort of power over her. One she didn't quite understand.

You may of course try, Solange, but your doing so would be going against my wishes and you would disappoint me. Again there was no judgment in his voice, no anger. He simply waited for her to make her decision.

Her heart clenched hard in her chest. The pain was so real she pressed the comforter clutched tightly in her fists to her aching heart and then dropped her face into the soothing material. She wasn't weeping. She was in human form.

His arm moved. She felt it. He touched her hair and she sensed the tremendous effort he made. *I have never had the pleasure of lying beside a jaguar.*

That was all. A simple sentence, but Solange closed her eyes, grateful for something—anything—she could do to push the memories further away. She took a breath and forced herself to look at him.

He was so beautiful. Every muscle carefully crafted, and the thickness of his arms and chest made her feel small in comparison—almost feminine. She leaned over him, her breasts brushing his chest, nearly crawling on him in order to study his face. His eyes were closed, but she sensed that he saw her. Maybe he was only in her mind, but it didn't feel that way. It felt to her as if his power filled the chamber and surrounded her with warmth, with acceptance.

He didn't think less of her because she wept. Or raged. Or killed. He accepted everything about her. She doubted he would think less of her if she tried to leave, and there was no doubt in her mind that neither she nor her jaguar would find a way out of the chamber. She wasn't going to waste her strength trying. *You don't want to disappoint him,* her warrior self taunted.

She straddled him and bent down, her hands framing his face. He was so incredible, this one man she'd thought never to find. She didn't know one such as he could exist. She was in his mind, knew him to be a man who would protect a woman, would fight to the death for her. She brushed her fingers lightly over his tough features. He was no boy. A strong face, for a strong man. He had chosen duty to his people, the one thing she understood. He thought to die.

"There are so many terrible men in the world, Dominic, men who do horrible things to those weaker just because they can. I don't understand anymore. Why are you chosen for such a terrible mission, and not one of them?"

I chose, fél ku kuuluaak sívam belső—*beloved. I did not know you were in this world. I was going to the next in hopes of finding you.*

Of course he was aware of her hands on him. She sighed

and rolled off of him, afraid she was too needy for his touch, for his wisdom. For his company. "Would you have chosen not to go on this mission then? Had you known about me, would you have allowed another to take your place?"

An image of Zacarias came into her mind. *He offered. He wanted me to go to a healer and try to remove the blood. He said he would go in my place.*

Her heart contracted as he replayed the exchange in his head. "Because I am his family? I despised him. He is so . . . overbearing." She was ashamed. "I had no idea he would do such a thing for a woman he has never met."

He loves his brothers. His memory of that love and of his honor have kept him going all these long endless years, Solange. He believes he cannot live with a woman who would resent his dominance. He has little left but service to those he loves.

She pressed the heels of her hands to her eyes hard. "Why didn't you say yes?" Her heart pounded, waiting for the answer.

I have the best chance to fight the pull of the bloodlust call. I am Dragonseeker. I will not, for my own pleasure, turn this job over to someone else. I set my foot on this path and I must follow it.

She let her breath out. Of course he would do the right thing. He had honor. "When Juliette found Riordan in their laboratory, Jasmine was taken. They managed to get their hands on my mother, my aunt and little Jasmine, although I had taken an oath to protect them—especially her. There was a jaguar who could partially shift. I'd never seen anything like that. None of us could do that, not my mother, and not Aunt Audrey. I knew how strong they were when I saw that."

She was silent and he simply waited for her to continue. The silence stretched a long time, but he never stirred, not even in her mind. She could feel his presence there, but he didn't push her. If she wanted to share, he would listen, but he wouldn't force her confidence.

Solange sighed. She'd never needed anyone, and to tell him her secrets was frightening and yet liberating. She respected his abilities as a warrior. She wanted to succeed in killing Brodrick. She didn't want to die in vain and leave her birth father behind to continue his despicable purging of any jaguar strain that wasn't pure.

"I began to practice. Running and shifting. Leaping from trees and shifting. Most of all partially shifting, and I've gotten very good at it. Purebloods can do things other jaguars can't do. My blood is pure, Dominic, but it's also royal. As far as I know there are only two people left on earth with my blood type."

She reached back and touched the bite marks nearly gone from her shoulder, thanks to Dominic's ministrations. "I'm far faster than he knows. Maybe as fast as or faster than he is."

So your plan is to confront him.

She listened for the censure in his voice, but as always he sounded strictly neutral. "It's the last thing he'll expect. And he knows I'm his daughter now, that I carry the royal blood. As vile as it sounds, he will believe I'm his chance for an heir. He isn't the kind of man to allow a little thing like incest to stop him."

You believe he will hesitate to kill you, that he will seek to incapacitate you in some manner.

"Which will be another advantage."

He put his teeth into you, his claws.

"But his bite was to my shoulder, not my neck."

Her hand crept up to stroke the scars there, where, so long ago, Brodrick's claws had bitten into her neck in an effort to kill her. Had she moved just enough that he'd gone much shallower than intended? She had no idea what had saved her. She remembered his face, twisted with disgust, blood spattered across him, and those evil eyes staring down at her. He'd jerked her up by her hair and swept his claw across her neck and then, as he had the girls before her, thrown her outside the cabin into the clearing with the other bodies he considered rubbish.

So he will try to keep you alive. And if you do not succeed in killing him and he captures you, he will force you to bear his child, just as the mage forced my sister to bear his.

Her heart ached for him. She hadn't considered how similar the scenario was to his past. His tone of voice gave nothing away, but still, there was censure there in his words. She wished she could give him reassurance, but she wouldn't lie to him. "I will find a way to commit suicide before that happens."

You know that is unacceptable.

She snorted and slowly stretched, the languorous stretch of a lazy cat. "You should know. Your plan is equally stupid."

You are very brave when I cannot move.

She found herself smiling. This was what she was most familiar with. In the dark, she could pretend he was a dream man rather than a real flesh and blood one. She had no inhibitions with this man. They could play their verbal chess match long into the night and she was absolutely safe. She shifted into her jaguar form and the cat curled around him, guarding him, daring anyone or anything to try to harm him.

Absolutely, she agreed, safe in the large cat's form. *But it doesn't make anything I say less reasonable. You plan to go into the camp of the enemy, hear their plans, relay them to Zacarias and go out fighting. Isn't that the same thing?*

He was silent for a moment, and deep inside the jaguar's

body, Solange smirked. She felt just fine now. He had kept her off balance with his absolute masculinity and his blatant sexuality, but now she was back on her game. Equals.

It is not the same thing. I did not know you were in this world when I ingested the vampire blood. You, however, know I exist.

That brought her up short. *Are you planning to die because of the vampire blood? Is that why you aren't going to try to leave the camp without them suspecting you of spying?* She hadn't considered that. She should have. Of course he would think the blood would eventually turn him into the very thing he was fighting against.

No healer will be able to remove all the parasites from my body. There was a young woman who lived with them for years, but they were not mutated into this form as they are now. They are strong and multiply fast.

She couldn't hear regret in his voice, and that was one of the things she admired most about him. He didn't waste time on regret. He'd stepped onto a path and intended to see it through in spite of the circumstances that had changed everything.

She took a breath and revealed the truth, safe inside the body of her cat. Her most terrible and wonderful secret. The secret she knew would bring every vampire down upon her, as well as every member of the Carpathian race.

My blood kills the parasites.

She gave him the truth as a gift. Only Dominic would realize the enormity of the cost that admission was to her. She had never trusted anyone, not even Juliette, with that accidental knowledge she'd discovered. Her blood resisted the vampire's lure, their hypnotic suggestions. She knew there was something about it that drew mages as well. It wasn't about being a pureblood jaguar; it was her royal lineage, the lineage her father had managed to destroy. She knew if anyone found out about her, they would lock her in a laboratory and she'd never get out.

Brodrick hadn't yet realized the significance of what the mages, vampires and even the humans were looking for. He was very single-minded in his quest to destroy all those of his species who couldn't shift, who he deemed impure.

How could you know this?

Even within the jaguar's body her heart pounded in alarm. There was no difference in his voice, but something . . .

I gather information all the time. I sit in the trees outside the laboratory and I listen to the guards, to the jaguar-men, the mages, even to the vampires. They are never aware of my presence. I noticed they rarely were aware of Brodrick until he showed himself, yet the vampires and most mages always seemed to know when the other jaguar-men were close. So something had to be different about Brodrick and me.

Dominic stirred in her mind, flooding her with warmth as he often did in their exchanges when she found it difficult to tell him something. A small nudge of encouragement. But this—this was monumental and she knew it.

A few weeks ago, I broke into their laboratory. I heard Annabelle had been taken and they often bring prisoners there now. They have tight security and few prisoners ever manage to escape. I needed to know the layout of the building. And I wanted to take a look at the computers.

She'd had to go alone. Juliette was helping her less and less, and only if Riordan was with them. Too many women were slipping through the cracks. She couldn't blame Riordan. He and his brothers had so much territory to protect that he couldn't be in all places at one time, any more than she could be.

She had gone without telling Juliette or Jasmine. More and more she went off for long periods, avoiding the De La Cruz ranches and their many homes scattered throughout the countries bordering the rain forest. She'd had to learn to rely solely on herself. She had become very good at secreting herself right under the noses of the humans and even jaguar-men. The mages and vampires had terrified her until she realized they couldn't sense her presence.

I managed to get into the laboratory through a window they had barred, but the bars weren't welded very well. I was able to pry them loose and then make it look as if they were intact. I checked their security cameras and found the rooms where they held prisoners. The computers were difficult—I don't really know a lot about them—but I found a spot in the room where I could hide. I stayed for hours.

Dominic remained silent, but inside he could feel the beast rising, a Carpathian male viewing his mate in extreme danger. She didn't tell him how she had made herself as small as possible and stayed absolutely still, her muscles cramping until she was afraid she wouldn't be able to walk again, but he caught the images and the very real fear of getting caught pouring off her. Shifting, she had no clothes, a lone woman naked in the very heart of the enemy camp.

Her courage terrified him and yet his pride and respect for her grew even more. She had nerves of steel, yet when she came to him, she was open and vulnerable. He hadn't expected to love her. Respect, admire, protect and care for, yes; even lust after. But to see that image of her, nearly bent in half, huddled, yet forcing herself to gather needed information to help the women of her species, brought an overwhelming emotion that burst through him like a volcano. He couldn't hold her while she told him, but he could surround her with warmth and he did, enveloping her in his love.

I heard the techs talking back and forth. At first I didn't really understand, but eventually I realized they were researching genetics, searching for psychic women. Jaguars have psychic abilities, so I knew that was how they were finding the ones in other countries and targeting them for kidnapping. Some went on a hit list and others were put on a list to bring back to the laboratory.

That made sense. Dominic had to get his hands on those lists. He would be walking into the laboratory and extracting the lists before destroying those computers.

A mage came in while I was there and he wanted them to pull up the jaguar lineages. He said his master needed a particular bloodline. He wasn't making sense. When they asked him what he was looking for, he muttered something about a sacred book and blood. I got chills down my spine, something that happens when I've stumbled across something important.

Of course. Jaguars were psychic. She had radar. Dominic knew about the book, stolen from Xavier, the mage who had first started the war with the Carpathian people. He had been the one to kidnap, use and eventually kill Dominic's sister. The book was now safely in the hands of the prince. Dominic had heard the book couldn't be opened, but needed to be destroyed. No one knew how. This news was unexpected, and like Solange, he felt instantly that it was important.

How close did the mage get to you? He shouldn't ask. He was already shaking inside. He wanted to be the man to protect her from everything, any harm, any pain, especially the torment of her past, but he could only lie helplessly as if dead while she told him what she had done. He couldn't even hold her close to him, shelter her in his arms.

Dominic couldn't imagine what it was like for her, knowing one of power had walked into the room and she'd had no weapons, no defense, if they found her. They would chain her up in one of their cells and the jaguar-men would have her whenever they wanted.

You must have been terrified of being caught. And if she hadn't been, he was terrified for her.

Fear has an odor. I told myself I am invisible. In the rain forest, I often tell myself that when a jaguar male gets too close. Sometimes I believe that I am. The mage was so close to me that I could have reached out and touched him. Controlling my breathing was actually the most difficult task. He was angry that he couldn't find what he was looking for. He wanted someone from Brodrick's line, but Brodrick's blood was tainted somehow for their purpose. His depravities, the mage said. But they found no one else.

Because you're dead. Dominic realized it was the truth. Brodrick had killed his useless female child. Sabine and Audrey had carried the same royal blood, the last of their lineage. Both had mated with humans and their children had diluted that pure strain.

Your mother had never become pregnant again, in all the years of captivity. Surely Brodrick tried with her.

Aunt Audrey, too. He captured her a couple of years later. They held her about two years before we found her and she was pregnant. She and the baby both died in childbirth. I think, for a jaguar, the stress of captivity was too much for them. He beat them regularly, and viciously. I think he hates women.

Dominic turned the information over and over in his mind. *So Brodrick has believed you to be dead all these years, so you were never entered into their database. The mages, the vampires, even the jaguars never knew your true identity.*

He knows now. I've set things in motion. Brodrick will come after me now.

His instinctive reaction was one of violent protest, but he remained quiet, willing her to talk about the properties of her blood.

I got to thinking about how the vampires and the mages couldn't sense me. What was different about me and

Brodrick? I'm a woman, he's a man; we're both jaguar, but different sexes. But then it occurred to me that everything with both the vampires and the mages comes down to blood—at least, she qualified, *the mages who follow Xavier.*

He is dead. The news reached me a week ago.

Xavier? So that's what shook everyone up. I knew something big had happened. There was a frenzy of activity around here.

How did you find out about the parasites? he prompted, almost afraid to ask. Because she'd done something very, very dangerous.

He had known she was an amazing woman from the first time he'd begun to talk to her in his dreams, but then, like now, when she was in jaguar form, he didn't actually hear her voice. He should have known she was his lifemate because he had begun to feel emotion, a slow emerging rather than the usual burst. He hadn't recognized what was happening because it was so out of the realm of possibility.

He had thought the woman he'd conjured up to talk to had been a fearless warrior because only another warrior could understand him. Now he knew she was real. She did feel fear—she simply dealt with it because she had no other choice if she wanted to succeed. Just like she was dealing with her fear of giving herself wholly to him. He knew she was probably more terrified of him than she was a vampire.

I fought a couple of vampires with Riordan when they came up on us unexpectedly. He said they were lesser, or newer vampires and were not yet in full control of their powers. He had been working with all of us on how to kill one, so while he was occupied . . .

He told you to stay back. No De La Cruz would ever want a female member of his family in danger. Even the youngest would be influenced by their brother, the most dominant male Dominic had ever known.

Solange gave the mental equivalent of a shrug. *He may have said something like that. Who listens when they are throwing out orders all the time? He is not my lifemate.*

No, Dominic was her lifemate, and he had to bind her to him in such a way that she would choose to follow his dictates. It had to be her choice. Solange would fight a cage. She needed the freedom of being who she truly was, and they had to find a balance between his instincts and hers. It took a moment for him to realize he was thinking in terms of remaining alive.

He went very still. He believed her; her blood was valuable to his entire species and she could stop the spreading infestation of the parasites already running rampant in his body. He had a chance to live—with her. For one moment, despite the time of day, his heart fluttered, the sound loud in the chamber. He felt her startle. The cat stirred and lifted its head, looking around warily.

What is it?

He heard the courage in her voice. The determination to protect him. She would risk her life for him. But when she fully realized that neither of them was going to die, she would fear his hold on her. It was a tenuous thread that could be broken so easily. She didn't give herself easily, and it was one of the things he most admired about her.

All is well. No vampire would be out this time of day, and I do not feel a jaguar near. Tell me about the parasites. Show me. He needed to see the battle, see how she had handled her first solo fight with a vampire.

He felt her hesitation and knew she was afraid of his disapproval. He felt some satisfaction in that. Clearly, Solange didn't care what anyone else thought—except him.

I am not critiquing you, kessake. It is essential for me to understand how you think in battle.

Honesty was crucial in his every encounter with his lifemate. If they were to have a future, she needed to know him just as well as he knew her, and for the first time, he believed they might really have a future.

Two vampires attacked Riordan. He's fast. Really fast. I watched how they tried to ensnare him with a hypnotic pattern, Juliette had to look away, but it didn't seem to affect Riordan, or me for that matter. He whirled around and went after the largest and most aggressive. The vampire maneuvered Riordan so that his back was to the second vampire.

He could see the entire battle in her mind. She had an eye for details. He could see the river shining through the trees, even hear the flow of it. There was no rain, but fog hung heavy through the trees. Riordan fought fiercely, circling around the larger vampire, flowing like the De La Cruz brothers seemed to do when in battle. His long hair cascaded down past his shoulders and his eyes were fierce pinpoints of steel.

He saw the second vampire step into position and knew immediately that the two undead had fought battles together before. He recognized the maneuver as one the Malinovs favored. Riordan recognized it as well. He'd fought side by side with the Malinovs for centuries. These two lesser vampires were students of one of the brothers.

Solange burst from the trees, running straight at the vampire, intercepting him before he could slam his fist into Riordan's back. Riordan had already vanished, moving in the fog, reappearing behind the larger vampire. Solange obviously used the speed and muscle of her jaguar, hitting the vampire with the force of the large cat. He saw the vampire grunt and howl, and then his talons ripped at her shoulder and neck.

She leapt away, her arm covered up to her shoulder with black acidic blood, her own body bleeding red blood. In her claw, she held the wizened, blackened heart.

"Riordan!" she called his name and tossed the dead organ toward him.

Lightning lit up the sky and a bolt hit the heart directly, and then jumped to the vampire already crumbling into the ground. Solange didn't have the luxury of removing the vampire blood by bathing in the white-hot energy; it would have killed her.

She raced to the river and plunged her arm into the water, rinsing. He saw the parasites exiting the wounds the vampire had torn in her skin. They should have burrowed into the lacerations, but instead they appeared to be fleeing with all possible haste. They dropped to the ground, her blood dripping over the top of them. Dominic could clearly see the tiny worms writhing, and then slowly they began to disappear, those ruby-red drops consuming them.

9

Can you come to trust a man once again?
Can you come to love an old one like me?

DOMINIC TO SOLANGE

Dominic knew the exact moment the sun set. He'd spent centuries beneath the ground waiting for that moment when his body came to life and the soil released him back into the world. He had waited impatiently for his time to rise. Solange had turned inward, silent after her revelation. He knew she felt she had given him too much information, and more important, that she had given him a way for both of them to survive.

Solange was very intelligent. She had to have known she was handing him a key to a future, and then she'd disappeared, deep inside her jaguar, hiding from him, hiding from herself and most of all, hiding from the repercussions of her admission. Trust was balanced on the edge of a very sharp blade. If he made the wrong move, he would lose everything. Solange was too great a prize to lose through careless handling.

Solange Sangria was a miracle in more ways than Dominic had thought. He replayed the image of her fight with the vampire over and over in his head. She might not have noticed so small a thing, but he stared for a long time at the ground where so many of the parasites had dropped when fleeing her bloodstream. Unbeknownst to her, she reached with her other hand to scrub at the vampire blood, scattering more of her own over the top of the black acid burning through her skin—or it should have been.

The acidic blood had burned through flesh, but the moment it came into contact with her veins, the vampire blood had dried and fallen from her flesh. She was busy washing it off in the river, and she hadn't noticed. What was in her blood? Was she the one Xavier had been hunting for her blood? And if so, what did she have to do with the book the prince guarded so carefully?

The sound of his heart beating filled the cavern. His eyes snapped open. The jaguar lay across his body, obviously on guard. He buried one hand in the thick fur. It was silky, like Solange's soft hair, the dark strands streaked with that soft, tawny color that seemed to melt into swirls in her hair. He stroked his fingers through the fur and up to her head.

The jaguar yawned lazily.

"You stayed up all day. I had strong safeguards surrounding us." He sat up. "Shift."

You guarded against the undead and mages. Your safeguards would work on humans and other animals as well, but I'm not certain they would work on Brodrick. I don't want him to find you unable to defend yourself because he's hunting me.

He waited. He had endless patience. She didn't want to face him, but the longer she stayed in the cat's form, the more terrifying facing him would become. He had been in her mind many times now. The information flooded from one to the other and he was beginning to know how she thought. If he wasn't very careful, she would run, more afraid of their connection, growing as fast as it was, than she would be of any battle.

It took her a few minutes. The cat sighed, the hot breath blasting his chest. *I would like clothes, please. It would be . . . easier.*

"Of course." Although he rather preferred her naked. Unfortunately she was a temptation that would be difficult to continue to resist. Passion ran deep in her. How could it not? She was passionate about her cause, passionate about her family, and she would be passionate with her lifemate in bed. Mix that fire with her sheer vulnerability to him and it made for a fairly heady aphrodisiac. She sounded sleepy. He knew she'd stayed awake most of the day, worried Brodrick would find his resting place. He rubbed his fingers through the thick fur, massaging those strong muscles.

"Stay as you are and I will return in a short time. You can sleep while I hunt."

Mmmmm.

The drowsy note in her voice was more Solange than jaguar, and his body tightened instantly. The soft sound produced a hard punch to his groin, and that was as expected. But the beast rising ferociously, demanding he claim his mate, was not only shocking but unsettling. It wasn't the vampire blood in his veins; it was his Carpathian blood. He had found his lifemate after waiting centuries, and there was a chance for a future with her. His soul called to hers, and all of a sudden the darkness was far thicker and much uglier. His barren existence grew unbearable now that he had been in her mind—now that he could feel again.

He waved his hand and the blanket of soil he'd allowed himself dropped away as he carefully extracted his body out from under the sleepy jaguar. As he did so, he murmured a command, gently pushing her toward sleep.

He felt her languid stirring in his mind. *That won't work on me.*

He laughed out loud, startling himself. The sound filled the cavern with happiness. "Just testing, *kessake*, to see if you were paying attention."

For the first time he felt the brush of her amusement, and the heady feeling burst over him. She had relaxed enough to respond to his teasing. It wasn't much, but it was a start. She'd handed herself to him with her revelation, and she was terrified of the consequences, but he'd still managed to slip past her guard and make her laugh.

"This will not take long," he promised and because he loved the feel of all that soft, silky fur and knew she was hiding deep in the cat's form, he deliberately ran his fingers down her entire spine.

He felt her shiver in reaction, but the jaguar didn't lift her head and eye him with her piercing stare. She kept her head on her paws. He floated to the surface of the cave and poured through the tunnel as vapor, scanning the area surrounding their resting place before unraveling the safeguards. He would replace them, but if she was right about Brodrick, he couldn't guarantee her safety from the male jaguar. That meant he couldn't travel too far from her and he would have to be especially alert for the predator.

The moment he was a good distance from Solange, the parasites began their whispers, calling to him to feel the rush of the kill. They weren't as active, her blood still subduing them, but the farther he moved from his lifemate, the more the mutated worms awoke, raking and clawing at his insides, demanding he remove all traces of Carpathian and royal jaguar blood and replace it with the acidic blood of the vampire, the environment where the creatures thrived.

Ignoring them, he continued out of the caves. Vapor poured across the open ground, low, parallel to the floor, climbing higher once it gained deeper forest. The gray mist shifted until it stacked itself, taking the form of the harpy eagle, circling high above the area while he fastened safeguards around the series of cliffs that hid the limestone caves, all the while using sharp eyes to detect any movement on the ground that would indicate the jaguar male was on their trail.

The rain forest burst with color, flowers winding up the tree trunks, great splashes of brilliant purples and pinks and bright ruby reds. He noted each and every one, savoring the beautiful colors he hadn't seen in centuries. He could once again appreciate the beauty of the world instead of simply remembering it. Truthfully, even his memories had faded in the last century. Now he could look down from his ever-expanding circle and drink in the sight of the flower-covered trees, the explosion of colors, the vivid greens of the trees and the brilliant hues of the fungus. The waterfalls and pools dotting the landscape along with the swollen river winding in and out of the forest, carving its way through the rugged terrain, were beautiful to him.

He found no evidence of Brodrick anywhere. Relieved, he doubled back toward the spot where they had battled the vampires. He knew Zacarias would meet him there if at all possible. Below him, he spotted the laboratory. Someone had already begun repairs on the side of the building. He circled overhead, trying to pick up Brodrick's scent. If he found the man, he would kill him. He knew Solange intended to face her birth father, but all that really mattered was that he was rendered incapable of continuing his slaughter of those he deemed impure and his kidnapping and brutal assault on women.

A sudden charge built in the surrounding air and Dominic settled in the trees, folding the expansion of wings and watching as a tall, impressive figure emerged from the knee-high fog rolling across the ground. The man stood for a moment, silver hair hanging down his back, his build fit and muscular. He turned, and Dominic recognized him from the old days. Giles. An old friend. His family had been craftsmen. Dominic had always admired Giles. He was smooth and controlled in battle, a good man to have at one's back in a fight. He had never expected to see Giles as a vampire.

He looked good, his face impeccable, his teeth white and his charm noticeable even from the distance between them. He had to have been a vampire a long, long time to acquire the necessary skill to cover all evidence of the rotting flesh and blackened soul. Giles tapped his foot, the only movement indicating he might be annoyed. He was obviously waiting for something and impatient that anything or anyone would make him late. And that said everything Dominic needed to know. Giles was a master vampire, experienced in the dark arts as well as battles. He was used to being at the top of the food chain. And if he was involved in the Malinovs' conspiracy to take down the prince, there was far more danger than anyone had ever conceived of. No *master* of Giles's caliber would bind himself to serve beneath another. The vampires were evolving. Somehow the Malinovs had managed to find a way to bring the vampire's vanity and need for reckless destruction under some semblance of control.

Two more figures wavered, transparent for a few moments before revealing themselves fully, an occurrence that usually happened when someone had transported quickly. Both were disheveled, although as they emerged fully under the moon, they pulled themselves back together. Giles was already frowning at their lack of ability to maintain their appearances at all times. The newcomers weren't lesser vampires, another mark for Giles. Most *masters* could keep only the newest close to them, to serve as pawns as they learned the ways of the vampire, but both men had obvious skills.

"You are both late," Giles accused. He narrowed his gaze, fixing that ruby-red stare on the man to his left. "You were to escort Demyan and his followers to this location. I do not see them. I hope you have a good explanation, Beau." He turned his head slowly, a reptilian movement that had the second man taking a step back. "And you, Fabron, I do not see them with you either."

A shudder went through Beau. "We went to the appointed spot to meet them, Giles, but they weren't there. We searched the area. A few miles to the east, there were signs of a battle. I believe the oldest De La Cruz brother is in this area and he attacked them."

Gile's breath hissed out between his teeth. "That maggot human we tortured lied to us. I should have kept him alive longer. You said you scanned his brain . . ."

"The brothers protect those who serve them," Fabron reminded.

Instantly the air sizzled and something snapped hard against Fabron's cheek. Sparks rained down, a dazzling display. Giles hadn't appeared to so much as lift his hand. Dominic studied the vampire more closely. He was smooth. Very fast, the action too quick to follow with the human eye, but Dominic had seen the action as a blur. For a moment he thought he'd blinked, but Giles had actually moved, used a wave of his hand to push the electrical charge toward his followers. It was no wonder he cowed them. He must appear to them as a mage might, able to do things no other could.

"You believe Zacarias has destroyed Demyan and his followers?"

Fabron and Beau both nodded vigorously. "There was a battle. We could not read the ground. Already, the rain forest is fighting back."

Deep inside the body of the harpy eagle, Dominic smiled. He and Zacarias had made certain to remove every trace of vampire blood from the ground and trees so the rain forest could repair itself. Dominic had even remembered to stimulate the forest growth before he'd allowed himself to look upon his lifemate. She had been so beautiful to him, standing there like a fierce warrior who had battled side by side with him, looking at him with the eyes of a vulnerable woman.

He hadn't expected the flood of overwhelming emotion. He'd felt protective of her. He'd wanted so much to gather her into his arms and hold her close. Trust was everything with a woman such as Solange. He had to earn her loyalty and respect, and most of all her love. He understood what a gift it was and he valued her all the more for her reserve. He was not a man to ever share his woman, and that side of her, soft and vulnerable, belonged to him alone.

He studied his enemy. He had expected to go into that camp and eventually die. Now, a miracle had happened. He could rid his body of the parasites and claim his lifemate. There was a future for him—for both of them—and that changed everything. He would have to be much more careful. He had everything to live for now. Before when he went into battle there was nothing to lose. Life changed dramatically when one found the other half of his soul. He wanted to live. He wanted to spend time with her. He could rise every evening for the rest of his existence, looking into her eyes.

Giles suddenly lifted his head and took a quick look around. A quick, piercing probe struck at Dominic, a fast, hard attack directed at the surroundings, a push to draw out the enemy. Dominic felt the stabbing pain, dismissing it, calming the bird, keeping the brain patterns the same so as not to alert the enemy to his presence. The probe passed slowly, but he remained deep within the eagle, holding himself still. The bird was hungry, looking for food, sharp eyes watching for prey before it settled down for the night. The probe came again, harder, deeper, the shaft painful and precise. The bird spread its wings and then resettled as Giles moved on, satisfied there were no enemies around.

"Where is Etienne?" Giles demanded.

"He was searching for tracks, hoping to find out where Zacarias might have gone."

"Stupide! Imbécillité!" Giles hissed his displeasure. "He has no hope of killing Zacarias. He is already destroyed." With a wave of disgust, Giles spat on the ground. Tiny white parasites wiggled and writhed.

"The others should be here in a few days," Beau said, clearly hoping Giles would allow a change of subject.

"If we have lost Demyan and his followers, we have few to spread the plans. I am representing the *masters*. We need to get our people organized for a telling strike against the prince. He must be brought to his knees."

The three men moved toward the laboratory. As they approached the human guards, Giles held his hand up to the others and whispered a command. "Leave them. You are human."

Dominic was shocked at the way the vampires immediately assumed the demeanor of a human, keeping their eyes on the ground rather than looking at the temptation of human flesh and blood. They felt utter contempt for and

despised the human men they were working with, yet they
didn't fall on them and feast on them as they normally would
have. Dominic felt the voracious hunger, the call to blood,
the parasites shrieking with desire for the rich hot temptation, even the need just to show those so inferior to them
who they were. Yet the vampires simply ignored the call.

The *masters* had done a good job forcing their wills on
the lesser vampires. That alone represented a danger. The
behavior had evolved into actual intelligence. Vampires
had always been cunning and lethal, but a coordinated
group with intelligence and strategy behind them, with the
ability to control those deadly, powerful creatures, was
shocking and even frightening.

The Malinov brothers had amassed an army consisting
of jaguars, humans and vampires. They had a plan and
they had a semblance of discipline. To Dominic, it was the
discipline that was most troublesome. He watched the
vampires disappear inside the building before he spread
his wings and took to the sky to find Etienne. The vampire wouldn't be returning to his master, but it would
be Dominic who would contribute to Zacarias's fierce
reputation.

The harpy eagle cut through the canopy with astonishing speed, moving fast to cover the distance before Etienne
found the resting place of Zacarias. Dominic knew the
hunter had actual homes in the area. It was possible he'd
gone to one of them. The De La Cruz brothers had, centuries earlier, established a relationship with a human family
who guarded them during the day, watched over their lands
and helped to maintain the illusion that they were human.
They had built an empire, their cattle ranches renowned,
but their enemies often went after their family members as
well. Zacarias would have strong safeguards, but if the

vampire tracked him to his home, the humans would be in danger. At this hour, Zacarias would be out hunting.

He spotted the place where their fight with Demyan and his lesser vampires had taken place. The area at first glance appeared undisturbed, but as he swooped lower, he could see the withered vegetation where it had shrunk from the unnatural abomination treading upon the ground as Etienne and the other vampires had searched for Demyan. Some of the brush had shriveled where the undead had passed.

The harpy eagle flew toward the river, taking a direct route. Dominic was suddenly worried about what he might find. On the edge of the trees, the De La Cruz's sprawling ranch was nestled into the valley between the rolling hills. It was surrounded by forest, but meticulously maintained, so the cattle could roam freely in the lush grasses. The house, Spanish style, with thick walls and cool verandahs, was shaped like a U with a courtyard in the center. The green of the courtyard provided an oasis of sorts, colors rioting with one another from the various flowers and bushes.

Along the stone walkway, the sharp eyes of the eagle spotted bright red blood. The small stream was narrow and slowly moved along the stones in a thin crimson line. Dominic dropped down, shifting to his human form as he bent over the fallen man. He had fought, but the vampire had nearly ripped out his throat. He was already dead, and Dominic left him, striding into the house. The door had been left open, providing him with a good view of the long, shaded room.

He heard a snarl and a hard slap coming from another room.

"Where is he?" Etienne demanded, his voice spitting and hissing, alerting Dominic that he was fast losing control.

"I'll *never* tell you."

A female voice. Fairly young. Terrified. Just the way the vampire liked them. The rush of adrenaline in the blood would serve as a drug flooding the system.

"So you would die for him."

"Yes." The voice trembled, but the word was firm.

Dominic burst through the door as dramatically as possible, hoping to throw the vampire's timing off. Etienne spun even as he delivered the killing blow, swiping at the woman's throat, tearing through arteries and vocal cords and flesh. Blood sprayed across the room. The woman clamped both hands to her throat and went to her knees even as Dominic leapt the distance, slamming hard into the undead, driving him away from the woman.

A roar announced the arrival of Zacarias. He burst through the window, shattering glass and adobe. Debris rained down on them as Dominic seized the vampire with one hand and drove into his chest with the other. Etienne dissolved, trying to stream from the room through the open window. Droplets of blood trailed after him, giving him away in the bank of mist.

Zacarias dropped to his knees and gently removed the woman's hands from her throat. She was young, even for human years, perhaps in her early twenties. Her eyes were dark brown, very large, framed with long black lashes. He could see the light receding from her eyes, but she looked glad to see him alive. For some reason, that little flutter of recognition moved him after so many centuries of emptiness. Her family had given his family service generation after generation. Her father lay dead in his courtyard and this young woman was dying on her bedroom floor, obviously trying to protect his resting place.

He wrapped his hands around her throat and pressed heat into her skin, bright and hot and painful for her, he knew. He couldn't prevent the pain, not with the life draining from her body so fast. Her throat was crushed. He sent himself outside his body and into hers, working as fast as possible to repair the damage to the artery, to stem the flow of precious blood. Trusting Dominic to keep the undead from him while he worked on the woman, he left his body vulnerable to attack while he meticulously cauterized the artery, closing and sealing the gaping wound.

Without thought of the consequences, Zacarias slit his wrist and dripped blood into her mouth, stroking until her reflex allowed her to swallow. He had to guide the blood through her torn throat to allow it to soak through her veins and into every cell of her body. He replaced what she'd lost, giving no thought to leaving himself too weak to move. There was no blood supply for him, not with Dominic's blood so contaminated. Right at that moment it didn't matter to him.

This woman's family had done so much for the De La Cruz family, and he wasn't going to lose her. He'd seen her a couple of times moving through his house, cleaning, always in the distance. He rarely went near anyone these days. The call of the darkness had become strong in him these last years and he spent most of his time alone, far from temptation. He rarely used this house, until these last few weeks. His brothers had lifemates, and that only increased the darkness in him as he felt separated from them, so long alone. He didn't know any other way of life, so he had come here to put distance between him and his brothers. But in doing so, he had endangered those people who were under his protection.

Zacarias managed to get his feet under himself and, bending, took the woman's slight weight in his arms, cradling her close to his chest. He was strong, but he had awakened ravenous and the scent of blood only increased his need. Giving her blood had weakened him further. He carried her through the house to the master bedroom, the one situated over his lair. Her braid was long and thick, a mass of blue-black hair, now stained with blood. He had no idea if she would live or die, but he'd done what he could. He laid her on the bed and covered her body with a blanket before turning back toward the sound of the battle.

Hideous growls erupted, as Etienne fought the trap Dominic had encased him in, making it impossible to stay in the form of vapor. Blood streaked Dominic's face and shoulder. Savage claw marks slashed through two places in his chest, ripping through clothes as the vampire had tried to get to the hunter's heart. Etienne was no amateur at battle, and he fought with magic and skill, knowing he was facing an ancient adept at destroying the undead.

Etienne looked worse than Dominic, black blood streaking his body. He had lost his ability to keep his appearance, his skin tight against his skull, so that he looked like a walking skeleton. His once dark hair was muddy gray, long tufts of it, like tails sticking out over a mostly bald skull. His eyes were sunken pits of hate, and his teeth had taken their serrated, pointed shape, coated with the blood of his many victims.

Dominic rushed in, gripped the head in his large hands and wrenched, diving away as Etienne raked again with bloody, sharp talons. There was an audible crack and Etienne shrieked, whirling so fast he was a blur, leaping on Dominic, driving him to the ground, his face elongating into a muzzle with dripping fangs. He opened his jaws wide and drove hard at Dominic's neck.

Zacarias's foreman, Cesaro Santos, ran into the yard with three of his men behind him, all carrying rifles. They skidded to a halt when they saw the undead tearing at Dominic, half-skeleton and half-animal. Before anyone could move, a jaguar rushed past the three men to slam at

full force into the back of the undead, knocking him over
so that he somersaulted and landed hard several feet away.

Dominic had already dissolved out from under him,
sliding around with the intention of taking the vampire's
heart, but he was no longer in position. The jaguar's next
bound took her right onto the vampire's back. Her teeth
crunched down on the head and she shook it like a rag doll.
The skull cracked like a nut, the bones crushing the brain.
One of the men beside Cesaro lifted his rifle to his shoulder, but Zacarias was there before he could pull the trigger,
pushing the muzzle toward the ground. Cesaro ripped open
his shirt, exposing his neck to Zacarias.

"Take what you need," he offered.

Zacarias could hear his heart pounding. The temptation
was too much. He'd never be able to stop, not in the heat of
battle when he was so ravenous. He shook his head and
stepped away, his fangs bursting into his mouth. He would
not endanger those who served him, those under his protection. Better to meet the dawn than to succumb now.

I'm sorry. Realizing her mistake, Solange apologized to
Dominic, as she tried to back away from the undead.

Etienne ripped at her, a lucky swipe tearing through the
fur at her belly. He caught her in the air, tossing the large
cat with his enormous strength. She landed hard a distance
from him. He crawled toward her, his head wobbling, the
insides spilling out.

No problem, Dominic answered with his unfailing calm.
*We will learn to coordinate our attacks in time. Move to your
right just a little, slow enough that he thinks he can get to
you, but that you are circling for another try. When I move,
leap away fast.*

Dominic felt her calm assurance. She knew how to fight,
and with a vampire, he was the acknowledged master. She
was too intelligent and too experienced not to recognize

that. Had she not interfered, he would have already had the undead's heart. It was a lesson and she learned fast. He respected the fact that she didn't beat herself up for mistakes. She simply did what had to be done.

The female jaguar began her circle, her green eyes glowing as she fixed on her prey. Head down, ears rotated backward, indicating aggression without fear, she began a slow stalk, never taking her eyes from her prey.

The humans stepped back, loathing in their eyes as they watched the jaguar circle the vampire, rifles at the ready. The only thing holding them back from firing was the will of their *Chefe* or *Jefe*, depending on which language they were thinking in. They detested both species. For too long they had endured the jaguar-men abusing their women. They had to guard the women carefully at all times, curtailing their freedom near the forest. The vampire was an ever-present threat that hung over their heads and threatened their boss as well as their families. Well versed in the ways to kill a vampire, each of them was armed with a stake, a torch and a cross as well as their rifles.

Zacarias didn't dare move away from them, knowing it was only his presence that prevented them from shooting the cat, and that if they did, Dominic would slaughter everyone in sight. The Dragonseeker was in motion, a thing of beauty, his body fluid and graceful, so fast he was a blur, slamming hard into Etienne even as the jaguar jumped back out of reach.

Etienne shrieked, a bizarre animalistic sound that startled the sleeping cattle in the distance. The herd came to its feet, mooing and stomping restlessly. Cesaro jerked his hand back, gesturing toward the rolling hills, and his men took off at a run. Others poured from homes scattered around the hills, leaping on horses, racing to calm the frightened cattle.

The vampire spun, moving fast like a twister, whirling

and spinning, trying to use his feet like a drill bit, digging
into the earth, hoping to escape the relentless hunter. Dominic spun with him, lost to sight in the debris, drawn into the
tornado reaching from earth to sky. He flowed with the turbulent winds, implacable in his resolve to destroy the undead.

The air began to charge. The hair on their arms stood
up. Zacarias called a warning to Solange as he took Cesaro
to the ground, covering his body with his own. Solange
leapt away from the charging air and nearly landed in a
fountain. She flattened herself as close to the ground as
possible just as lightning struck, the bolt going from earth
to sky and back to earth again. Etienne shrieked hideously.
The smell of decomposed, rotting flesh turned to smoke,
permeating the air with a foul stench.

Zacarias could only smell the blood around him as he lay
over the top of his foreman. The scent was everywhere,
heavy in his lungs. His fangs refused to retract. The sound of
hearts beating became a drum of desire pounding through
his skull. Warm flesh beckoned, the lure of hot blood strong,
the pulse right beneath his mouth. So close. So tempting.
The whisper was insidious in his ear. *Just this once.*

His mouth nearly touched that strumming pulse. His
ears filled with the sound, the ebb and flow of the life force
in Cesaro's body. His mind refused to work, flooded now
with need. *Just this once.* He could smell the delicious fear.
The adrenaline racing through veins. He moved his head
back, his sight narrowed to that temptation.

The jaguar hit him full force, knocking him off Cesaro's body. He rolled and came up on his feet, his mind a red
haze of need and anger. Ruby-red eyes fixed on Solange,
furious that she had stolen his prey. She prowled back and
forth between Zacarias and Cesaro, keeping him from the
hot, spicy blood his body needed so desperately. He hissed

his anger, the two predators locked in a stare, each waiting for the other to attack.

Cesaro moved slowly, carefully, trying not to draw the attention of the large cat. His fingers inched their way to his rifle and, increment by increment, drew it to him. *Don* Zacarias needed and he provided, just as his family had done century after century. If it was his blood Zacarias needed, Cesaro would give it. His fingers drew the rifle into his hand and his fist closed around it. He took a deep breath and surged to his feet, the butt of the weapon fitting snugly into his shoulder, his sights on the cat. Very slowly his finger found the trigger and he began to squeeze.

Behind them, bloody, his shirt and chest shredded, Dominic roared a challenge to Zacarias even as he ripped the rifle from Cesaro with one hand and slapped him away with the other. The strike was casual, but so hard the force sent Cesaro flying through the air to land hard against the house.

"See to the woman," Dominic ordered, his voice a low command that brooked no argument. He pointed and the man slowly got to his feet, looking dazed, his eyes showing his confusion.

Cesaro was protected from compulsion, so it was only the sheer force of Dominic's personality that overrode the loyalty ingrained in the foreman to protect Zacarias.

"She's in the bedroom and needs immediate medical attention."

That spurred the man into action. He hurried into the house, leaving the two Carpathians facing one another. Dominic held his hands out to his sides. "Zacarias." Just the name. A calling.

Zacarias shook his head. The whispers refused to stop, pounding like a drumbeat deep in his veins, in his mind, until he was consumed with the dark desire for blood. "Go. Go while you can, old friend. Save yourself."

"*Ekam*. My brother. *Anaakfel*. Old friend." There was anguish in Dominic's voice—in his heart and mind. "This is not your choice. Your choice is to serve your people. I need you. The prince needs you. We have to get this information to him." Even as he spoke, Dominic glided into position, his heart so heavy he could barely keep the burning tears from moving past his throat. There was a ball of them lodged there. Zacarias. A man noble beyond anyone's imagining. To kill him felt like a sacrilege.

I'm going to shift, Dominic. I need clothes.

Solange's voice startled him. She was so calm. Her utter composure surprised him. He felt her in his mind, knew she felt his love for Zacarias. They were ancients. They had been childhood friends. They'd spent centuries fighting the same enemy, sometimes side by side, other times alone, but they'd always been in the world sharing the same fate. His heart would shatter when he killed Zacarias—but he would kill him. He would spare Zacarias the humiliation of losing his honor. The Carpathian people would remember him as the hero he truly was.

Leave us, Solange.

Dominic flexed his fingers. He'd taken a beating killing Etienne. The ancient had been a skilled fighter and he'd sustained several injuries. Zacarias was one of the best, most experienced warriors he'd ever encountered. Dominic's love for him, his respect, would be difficult to overcome. He didn't want Solange anywhere near this battle. He had no doubt that he would kill his friend, but there was every possibility that Zacarias would kill him, too.

There's a chance to save him.

His first reaction was to order her away, but the absolute belief in her voice swayed him. More than anything, he wanted her protected. Yet Zacarias was as close as he was ever going to get to a real friend, and Dominic didn't want to have to kill him.

She didn't wait for him to make up his mind, but shifted just to the left of him. He clothed her in her normal clothes, the faded jeans and thin tee that worked best when she was moving through the forest. She had emerged closer to Zacarias than he liked, and he knew it was deliberate.

"I am family to you, Zacarias," she said, addressing the Carpathian hunter.

Centuries old, Zacarias was more than intimidating under normal circumstances. But he was so close to turning, he was growling, his eyes already changing, revealing the red haze of the vampire already trying to possess his mind.

Dominic moved into position to strike. He would need every ounce of speed and strength he possessed to drive through the wall of Zacarias's chest and extract the heart before Zacarias could retaliate. The attack would have to come as a complete shock if he had any chance at all to end it fast. The idea sickened him, but he meticulously went over each move in his head. Solange had merged her mind with his. He knew she saw the attack in his mind, but she continued to try, taking another step toward the hunter.

Even as Dominic reached out a hand to stop her, Zacarias stepped out of reach and shook his head. "Take her and go while you can, Dominic." His voice was little more than a growl.

"Look at me," Solange persisted. "I am your family. Sister to you. Would you really destroy the one you have long protected? The scent of blood, so much death, it's calling to you, but I'm offering you freely, as your sister, as one under your protection . . ."

Dominic's breath hissed out between his teeth, his heart

pounding. She was reading his mind, seeing the traditional and very formal Carpathian ways. Her life for his. *No, Solange. I will not accept that.*

For you, not for him. This is a gift to you. I want to love him and see him as you do. You see honor and I want to see that as well. Let me give you what I can of myself. This is for you.

Not at the risk of your life.

You risk yours to kill him. Let me risk mine to save him.

If he hadn't loved her before, he did now. The force of the emotion shook him as Solange extended her wrist toward Dominic. All the while he watched Zacarias watching them. Zacarias was more predator than hunter. Perhaps both of them were in that moment. Both dangerous beings. But then Solange had faced danger unflinchingly before. He took a breath and allowed one nail to slide over her skin, opening the vein. Bright ruby droplets welled up, small, beautiful gems, glittering like jewels.

"Come, brother," she said softly. "Feed and then go to ground. This will pass. It has happened before. You're strong and we need you."

Zacarias couldn't tear his eyes from the blood. "Not like this. Never like this. It is too dangerous, Dominic. Send her far from me."

"I will honor your wishes should you go too far," Dominic promised, his heart in his throat along with the ball of unshed tears. "You are my brother. *Our* brother. Drink. You will stay in control." He tried a little push to aid Zacarias, but ultimately, it was his choice. He had to fight the beast, find the last bit of strength to get him through this foul crisis.

Solange stood her ground. Of all of them, she was the most calm. She held her wrist out to Zacarias. If he stepped forward to take the offering, he would be fully exposed to Dominic. She had placed herself as bait. All three knew it.

Life or death.

Choose life, Dominic pleaded silently.

Zacarias glided across the space between them, taking the offered wrist, his chest and heart completely exposed and vulnerable to Dominic. Deliberately he kept one arm out away from his body while with the other hand he took Solange's wrist.

She couldn't stop the shudder running through her mind—or her body—but she stood her ground as Zacarias's mouth covered her wrist and he drank.

10

Let my soft arms caress you, let our songs blend together.
Let me stand by your side—let me set your heart free!

SOLANGE TO DOMINIC

Dominic inched closer to Zacarias, knowing how fast the other Carpathian was. He'd fought beside Zacarias in countless battles and knew his every move. Like shadow dancers, they eyed one another, Zacarias bent over Solange's wrist. Zacarias appeared vulnerable, but Dominic wasn't deceived. Solange was Dominic's lifemate, and she was the most vulnerable of all. Zacarias could kill her in seconds. That alone would shake Dominic enough to give Zacarias a little edge.

The tension heightened. Solange stood very still, her eyes on Dominic's face. She didn't so much as glance at Zacarias as he drew the precious blood from her body. She pulled out of Dominic's mind, but he slipped into hers, hearing her silent screams, seeing the fear amounting to terror. Yet astonishingly, none of it showed on her face, not even in her eyes. Had he not been connected with her, Dominic would never have known how frightened she was.

His woman. His lifemate. Her courage terrifying to him. He wanted to jerk Zacarias away from her. He could see the greed there, the desperate need, the mounting danger. Time stretched out. The sound of Zacarias taking her blood was hideous, the sight intolerable—yet he forced himself to stand as still as Solange and endure. Sweat beaded on his body, trickled down his chest to mix with the ragged tears in his flesh. For a Carpathian to know his lifemate was not only in danger but was suffering was one of the worst things possible.

Dominic started to stir, but he felt Solange's resistance.

Please give him time to recover. He's trying to pull back.

She would know. Zacarias's mouth was sealed to her vein, drawing heavily on it. She was pale, clammy, but she didn't resist. Dominic realized that was what kept Zacarias in check—her lack of resistance. She had offered her life. She was his family, under his protection, and Zacarias was all about honor. She made him remember. She forced him to choose honor. There would be no escape for Zacarias this night. His life would continue, barren and ugly and without hope.

When I say enough, you do not argue, you run. His voice was implacable.

If you believe it is too late, I'll respect your decision, she agreed.

The tension stretched to a breaking point. Dominic fought with his instincts, trying to give his friend the time he needed to pull back from the precipice himself, but seeing the mouth gulping at his lifemate's blood was worse than just about anything he had ever endured. She was stoic, but she was frightened, and his own discipline was close to the edge.

It seemed a lifetime before Zacarias managed to conquer the beast growing in him. He swept his tongue across Solange's wrist and he bowed low, a gesture of his deepest respect. He had to have known how frightened she was as well. Her blood had been laced with adrenaline, giving him a rush, a fireball burning through his veins, but her courage had defied all logic, her sacrifice great for a warrior so close to turning. He seemed ashamed to be in Dominic's company, and more ashamed to be in hers.

Dominic let out his breath, emotion shaking him, knowing the cost to his friend and to his lifemate. "I apologize, Zacarias. I could not let you go. I know it is difficult, but I cannot yet give you up. Solange knew that. It is my weakness, not yours."

He reached out and gripped Zacarias by his forearms, warrior to warrior, staring into his eyes. They both knew the gesture was brotherhood, respect, and to check that Zacarias had conquered their enemy one more time. The ruby red in Zacarias's eyes had receded along with the haze. His fangs slowly retracted. It took a moment before he responded, clasping Dominic's forearms in a firm grip.

"There is nothing weak about you, Dragonseeker. You hide your fierce nature under that calm charm but those of us who know you are fully aware of the power you wield. I will wait for your call. I go to ground now to keep my people safe."

"Should you need blood," Solange said, "call to us."

Dominic didn't protest, but he was *never* going to allow such a risk to her again. Fighting vampires was one thing, but walking into the very fangs of a Carpathian on the verge of turning was something altogether different. His heart was still pounding, the sound drumming in his veins. He looked at her, this woman who was such a miracle to him.

Solange seemed so young, yet so intensely vital. Her sable hair was thick and streaked with red and gold, as if the sun had kissed her. The streaks of red represented the fire and passion running so deep in her. And that thick dark hair, gleaming in the moonlight, was her courage, sharp and terrible and so endless, like the rivers cutting through the forest. He needed her, needed to bind them together, hold her close, claim her for his own.

He wanted to drag her into his arms and kiss her forever. He wanted to turn her over his knees and punish her for scaring him. He didn't know what to do with her, but they were going to resolve this one way or the other, because he couldn't go through such an ordeal again. With centuries of facing the undead, the experience of countless battles, facing death every day, nothing had prepared him for the sight of his lifemate offering up her life.

For him. In his name. Her gift to him. A single sound emerged from deep within his throat and he spun on his heel and pointed toward the dwelling, needing to get her away from the other Carpathian. Zacarias would be able to find her, call to her, perhaps make her an unwitting victim. He would always be a threat to her as long as he was unmated. "We must see if we can help the young woman."

Zacarias inclined his head. "Thank you. Try to save her for me, Dominic. I would consider it a great favor. I would go myself, but I no longer trust myself to be near my people. They would sacrifice themselves for me." He bowed again toward Solange. "The infusion of your lifemate's blood has quieted the dark whispers, but I must take myself away from here."

"You will await my call?"

Zacarias nodded. "I will hear when you call or should you need blood. You can trust me to send the information on." He melted into vapor and streamed away.

Heart heavy, Dominic gestured for Solange to precede him into the house. She took a cautious step, as if testing her legs. She appeared a little dizzy, but he didn't touch her, watching Zacarias instead. He wanted her away from the Carpathian hunter as quickly as possible, and he needed to stay alert.

Zacarias was so close to turning and both knew there was little time left for him. The danger was twofold now. Once Zacarias determined he was no longer needed, after this crisis, he would either choose the dawn or he would succumb to the darkness. The loss of such a friend was nearly unthinkable, a stone in Dominic's chest weighing him down, but he wasn't risking Solange any further. They had done what they could for Zacarias. It was up to him now.

Beside Dominic, Solange moved a little closer, as if to console him, but she didn't touch him. When she glanced at him and saw his gaze on her, her eyes shifted from his. She was still uncomfortable around him in any other guise than that of a warrior. He didn't speak, allowing the silence to stretch between them. He was proud of her, yet he was troubled. Upset. His stomach muscles had knotted tight. He had the urge to shake her, or fold her close and hold on so tight she couldn't breathe. He felt as if he were coming down from an adrenaline high that left him edgy and out of sorts—conditions he was unfamiliar with.

Dominic swept Solange behind him, uncaring that she might be upset that he was protecting her, but he was done with her putting her body in harm's way. Zacarias had taken enough blood that she was feeling weak, and because of the parasites, he couldn't even provide for her. She'd stumbled twice and tried to cover it, but he couldn't fail to notice. He knocked politely on the open door leading to the master bedroom. Below, he was certain, Zacarias had a lair, but he wouldn't be using it, wouldn't risk his close proximity to his people, not with his strength waning. He would never knowingly endanger them.

"Zacarias wanted me to see if I could help," Dominic greeted as Cesaro spun around. The man looked disheveled. His face was twisted with grief.

"I don't know what you can do for her," he replied, stepping away from the bed to give Dominic room. "She's alive, but her throat . . ." He trailed off.

Dominic took his place, noting that rather than rushing to the young woman's side, Solange went to the windows, moving like a silent shadow through the room, checking the outside.

"Her father is dead. Out in the courtyard. She has no mother. No other family."

"She has Zacarias and his brothers, and she has you," Dominic said. "Zacarias wants everything possible to be done, and for this home to be considered her home."

Cesaro nodded. "He is like that. Always he looks after us."

"What's her name?" Dominic asked. He needed a moment to breathe his way through the sight of the young woman, so small and helpless, barely making a ripple in the large comforter, torn as she was, her dark, thick braid bloody and her face nearly gray. The reminder of the destruction a vampire could cause in seconds only added to his resolve to curb Solange's courage just a little—enough that he could live with.

"Marguarita," Cesaro answered. He wiped his hand over his face. "I don't know what I'm going to tell the others."

Dominic leaned over the young woman. Her breath was barely moving through her lungs. *Have him leave the room, Solange.*

Solange didn't hesitate. "We need you to patrol the grounds with your men. If you need to remove her father's body from the courtyard, do so, but there could be another attack. They were after Zacarias. He's a huge threat to them."

She said the right thing. Cesaro hurried to guard his boss's estate and left the dying woman to them. Dominic trusted Solange to watch over his vulnerable body while he went outside himself and sent his energy into Marguarita.

At once he could see that Zacarias had worked a miracle in the short time he had. The Carpathian had awoken ravenous, but he'd still given his blood and what energy he had to try to save one of those loyal to him. Had he known she'd been attacked because she refused to give up his resting place? Her mind had been protected and the vampire had been unable to break through the safeguards Zacarias had woven for each of those working for him.

The Carpathian blood rushed to every cell, trying to repair the terrible damage. Her vocal cords were nearly destroyed. Dominic took up the repairs where Zacarias had left off, striving to make certain she could both breathe and swallow properly. The torn muscles were reattached. Thankfully Zacarias had given her the blood she needed. Dominic couldn't supply her, and there was no way of knowing if Solange's blood was compatible. He did the best he could, realizing that he hadn't fed when he came back to his body weak and swaying.

"You've been working a long time," Solange said, holding out her wrist. "You need . . ."

"Do not!" He held up his hand. "I think I have had enough of your sacrifices to last a lifetime. I will hunt while you watch over her."

Solange winced, but she dropped her wrist to her side without protest. Her face flushed and she averted her face.

His words were sharper than he intended, the need for blood—hers—riding him hard. He wanted more than her blood. The beast was still too close, needing to carry her off, keep her safe. He had every intention of laying down the law in a way his lifemate could understand, but right now, when his entire body was still in shock from the terror of those teeth in her veins and the ruby-red eyes of the near-vampire marking her as prey right under his nose, he couldn't find it in him to be gentle with her.

"Is she going to live?"

Was there a tremor in her voice? He caught her chin and lifted her head until her eyes met his. She was trembling like a little bird. The pad of his thumb strummed across her soft lips.

"She will live. Her people will take care of her. I am the only one taking care of you, and I am not doing a very good job of it."

She frowned, her lashes fluttering. She looked confused, the color rushing into her face. "Why would you need to take care of me? I did make the one mistake, but I realized it immediately. There is no need to worry about me. I'm sorry I knocked the vampire off you. I should have known you had a plan." Her words tumbled out, a breathless explanation, almost painfully delivered. She could barely force herself to look at him.

"You are a warrior of great skill and I have no quarrel with the way you helped this rising. You kept Cesaro from being killed and Zacarias from dishonoring himself while I was slaying the vampire." He gave credit where it was due. "I was proud of you."

She swallowed hard, her eyes a deep green, almost emerald. The long lashes fluttered and she looked away. She wasn't used to compliments—or attention. Dominic turned away from the sheer vulnerability on her transparent face. She gave that only to him. It was a privilege, a treasure, and yet, a great responsibility.

"You're upset with me." She made it a statement.

"Not with you, *kessake*. I am upset with myself. Stay alert. The undead are traveling in packs. I have not had the time yet to remove all evidence of his presence."

She opened her mouth and then as abruptly closed it, nodding once before turning her attention to Marguarita.

Dominic didn't touch Solange as he wanted. He strode from the room and went into the smaller bedroom where Etienne first had questioned Marguarita. This was her room. She kept the house for the absent owner while her father and Cesaro ran the large cattle ranch. She'd probably never met Zacarias, but loyalty was so ingrained in the families—from birth, the secret of the Carpathians entrusted to their lineage—and all of them would rather die than betray their honor.

He sighed as he meticulously repaired the damage to the structure and removed all evidence of the attack. Etienne's master would know he was dead and he would want to know where it had happened and how. If he came looking, he would find no evidence of Zacarias or Etienne in this place. He would remind Cesaro to exercise caution with the body of Marguarita's father. It would be best to incinerate it. The undead riddled with parasites often left them behind in the ragged wounds and they would call to their masters. Marguarita had none in her bloodstream, but Dominic had interrupted the attack so that the vampire hadn't had the time to inject his passengers into her.

He glanced around the room. A woman's room. Did Solange have a woman's room hidden away somewhere? He doubted it. She would be ashamed to acknowledge that side of herself. She considered the warrior strong and the woman weak. She would hide the softer side from everyone who knew her. His body reacted to that thought. She wouldn't hide it from him. He would peel back the layers until the woman was exposed and given exclusively to him. *His*. Like Solange, he'd never had anyone of his own. He'd never belonged to anyone. The idea that she was his and his alone and would never want to be anyone else's was an intriguing thought.

As he worked fast in the room, he noted everything: the brushes, the mirrors and the perfume bottles. Everything in the room suggested Marguarita was ultrafeminine, and yet she'd had a backbone of steel, refusing to give up her employer in the face of certain death. The hideous, vile creature tormenting her hadn't broken her. Women could be many things. They came in all shapes and sizes with vastly different personalities, but no matter what was on the surface, it was what lay beneath that counted to him—as it did for all Carpathians. They could see into the mind, and what lay there, along with the heart and soul of the women, was what made them beautiful, not that outside package.

He knew Solange well enough now that if he should tell her the outside package didn't matter at all to a Carpathian, she would take it wrong. She would feel that was his way of politely saying he saw her body as she did—unattractive—and that was far from the truth. He retraced Etienne's steps, destroying all evidence of his passing. He found himself in the courtyard. The body had been removed, but the blood remained, staining the flower beds, the slabs of stepping stones and the dark, rich soil. Several plants had withered, the effects of nature coming into contact with the abomination of the undead. Vampires would easily spot that telltale sign from the sky.

Again, he was meticulous in removing all traces of the undead's presence and the fight that had taken place here. If it was known that Zacarias had been here, this ranch and everyone in it would be targeted. Things had to appear mundane—as if no one had any idea of the presence of vampires. He was ravenous by the time he had finished. He knew the moment Cesaro approached, coming slowly, almost reluctantly, up behind him.

Dominic turned. "You have questions?"

Cesaro shook his head. "*Don* Zacarias sent word to me that you may need blood. He asked, as a favor to him, that I supply your needs. I gave him my word. He asked me to follow any instructions you might give."

"Did he assure you that I would not harm you?" There was no making it easy with Zacarias's safeguards on the man. He would know Dominic was taking his blood, and yet, courageously, he had followed orders. No, not orders; a request.

"This has been a traumatic evening for all of you," Dominic said with a small sigh. "I do not wish to make it worse. Unfortunately the body of the young lady's father must be incinerated. The undead leave behind small parasites that will call to their masters and draw them to this place. I am removing all evidence of the battle, but you cannot allow anyone to speak of this night, or even mention Marguarita's injuries. It is for the safety of everyone here."

Cesaro inclined his head. "We have been well trained in what to do. We are preparing the body now."

"I know you would prefer to burn it yourselves out of respect, but my way will be faster, cleaner and will ensure no parasites escape. It will also not provide a beacon for the undead."

"This is a bad night." Cesaro sighed. "Tell me honestly if Marguarita will live."

"She will live. I do not know if she will speak again. We did our best, but her throat was very torn. She will have this place and all Carpathians will honor her for her sacrifice."

Cesaro rubbed his temple, as if trying to ease a nagging

headache. "Our people have always been De La Cruz. We fight for them, guard them and are honored to die in their service. Marguarita is no different. We will take care of her." He took a breath, let it out. "It would be an honor to carry out *Jefe's* wishes."

"You are certain," Dominic asked, liking the man more and more.

"I believe so."

Dominic didn't waste time. Every cell in his body was crying out for sustenance. He'd been using so much energy to heal Marguarita and to remove all signs of the battle that he'd grown pale. He moved toward the man rather than force Cesaro to walk to him.

"My people exist on blood, just as you exist on the meat of animals. We do not kill. Only the vampire does that."

Cesaro's swallow was audible. He nodded his head. "*Don* Zacarias has explained this to us. It is . . . difficult, but I wish to do this for you."

"If you allow me to, I will help you not to feel anything. You will retain the memory without fear."

Cesaro frowned, but shook his head. "I want to know what it feels like to serve those who have been so good to our families these long years."

Dominic preferred to take the blood from the neck, as did all Carpathians, but he didn't want this man's heart to explode. He could hear the trepidation in his brave request, and the strong heart accelerating. It was all he could do to respect the man's wishes and not calm him.

He swept his tongue over the offered wrist to numb the skin and then sank his fangs deep into the vein, almost in one continuous movement. Cesaro made a single sound, but he didn't flinch or try to pull his arm away. Dominic understood why the De La Cruz family believed in these humans. They were loyal to a fault and just as courageous. Hot blood flowed into his body, soaking into cells, muscles and tissue, instantly providing strength, replenishing his energy.

He was careful not to take too much, but when he swept his tongue over the twin holes, closing them, Cesaro swayed and Dominic helped him to sit.

"It didn't hurt like I thought it would," Cesaro murmured. He gave Dominic a small smile. "One builds it up in his head until he is afraid, but there was little pain."

"It can be dangerous," Dominic reminded. "When we have lived too long and killed too many times, there is no longer feeling."

"*Don* Zacarias told me that. He said you and your woman saved me. And saved him."

Dominic shook his head. "Perhaps we made his choice easier. I will clean up the battlefield while you drink plenty of fluids. Then you must take me to the body and send everyone else away."

~

Solange brushed back the stray trendrils of hair from Marguarita's face. She looked like a beautiful broken doll lying there so still and pale. There were dark circles under her eyes, and two thick crescents of dark lashes fanned her cheeks. She had been a beautiful, vital woman just hours before. Solange sighed softly. There was so much violence in the world, especially, it seemed to her, against women. What had this woman done to anyone? She'd been living her life, happy. Now, her father lay dead and her throat was crushed. It all seemed so senseless to Solange. She'd spent nearly every day of her life working to prevent just such atrocities, and yet she seemed to fail at every turn.

"I'm sorry I wasn't here," she murmured softly. Sometimes it felt as though she was always late, always just a little short, and the last couple of days had been bad ones.

She removed Marguarita's shoes and socks and drew a blanket over her. It would be up to the people on the ranch to see to her care now. "How are they going to explain all this?"

"They have doctors in the family," Dominic said from behind her.

She whirled around, a growl emerging. No one snuck up on her. She was cat. She scented the presence of others, yet there he stood, taking up the room with his wide shoulders and powerful frame.

"How did you get in here?"

"I used another form. It seemed easier than trying to remain unseen by the workers. Are you ready to go?"

He spoke in that same gentle voice, but she knew there was an edge to him. There had been ever since she'd given her blood to Zacarias. She tried to figure out what she'd done wrong. It had been a long while since she'd spent so much time in anyone's company, and especially the company of a man. How could she be what he wanted when she could barely force herself to speak to him? Was a relationship supposed to be so difficult, or was she making it that way? She had no idea how to act. What to feel or think. Or say. Especially say.

Solange wanted to tell him she knew she could be all he could ever need, but she didn't believe it. She didn't want another woman touching him, sharing his time, his life, even his laughter or conversation. She knew she had somehow taken an irreversible step when she'd told him the truth about her blood. She'd opened the door for the possibility of a future. She was terrified of the consequences. She didn't give her heart into a man's keeping, it just wasn't done. Yet she couldn't stop herself from wanting him.

He took away the utter loneliness she'd endured for most of her life. She told herself it wasn't real, that he'd been her dream and she'd given the real man her dream man's characteristics, but she knew better. Dominic was—Dominic. He was also Dragonseeker, and that gave her more pause than him being male.

She'd heard the name *Dragonseeker*. The title had been whispered, a legend. A terrifying myth. Even the De La Cruz brothers inadvertently lowered their voices when speaking of the Dragonseeker. She hadn't thought him real, more a story told in Carpathian society, a great warrior, a fierce fighter, so strong no one in his lineage had ever turned vampire. She had seen the respect Zacarias gave him, and Zacarias respected few. She knew Zacarias had a fierce reputation as well, yet he had definitely stepped back from Dominic.

It was difficult to equate the man who treated her so gently with the whispered legend. She took a quick look up at his face. She could see the stamp of ruthlessness there in those lines etched so deep. He had given her the best moments of her life in the short time they'd been together, but at what price? He was not someone she could ever push around, and she had a fiery temperament. What would happen when she opened her mouth and the wrong thing came out?

"Solange?" he prompted. "Are you ready?" He held out his hand to her.

Her heart jumped into her throat. She could never take his hand publicly. What if someone saw her? She would look girly . . . weak. Her pulse went wild. Frantic. He simply looked at her, his ever-changing eyes on her face, compelling her to step forward and put her hand in his. Women did it all the time, held hands with their man. She rubbed her palms along her thighs in agitation.

He didn't drop his hand, only continued to look at her. She scented the air and licked her suddenly dry lips, her gaze flicking toward the door, checking for anyone close.

"Look at me," Dominic instructed. "Only at me. It does not matter what anyone else thinks or feels. Only me."

"It's just that . . ." She trailed off under his burning gaze.

Why couldn't she just do such a simple thing? What was wrong with her? She found herself shaking her head, stepping back away from him, knowing she was blowing the only chance she had at happiness, but unable to reach for his hand.

He didn't waver. Didn't drop his arm. He crooked his finger at her. "I am aware of the location of every person on this ranch, and aware of your fears. Do you not trust me to look out for you?"

She wanted to sob at the look in those piercing blue eyes. Of course he knew where everyone was. He shouldn't have had to remind her. She knew he wouldn't take the step to her. She was going to have to do it. She glanced at the woman so silent and pale on the bed. Marguarita could have done it and she wouldn't have thought twice about it.

Was pride getting in the way? Her pride was already in tatters. She closed her eyes, took a breath and stepped forward, placing her hand in Dominic's. At once his fingers closed around hers, making her feel small and far too vulnerable. He drew her to him, close so that her body was nearly touching his. So she could feel the heat radiating from him.

"That's my little cat."

The approval in his voice warmed her and that frightened her. She'd never needed or sought anyone's approval. Why was it so important to her? She was upset with herself that she'd never asked Juliette or MaryAnn about how they felt when their men were upset or happy with them. Was she normal? Who was she kidding? There was nothing normal about her.

He brought her hand to his mouth. She could feel the warmth of his breath, see warmth in his eyes, although she could barely look at him. She was *so* going to blow this. Her stomach flipped and her womb spasmed when he nibbled on the ends of her fingers.

"Are you ready?" he asked again.

Ready to be alone with him again? Was she ready for that? She doubted it, but what was she going to do? It was better to just not say anything. She nodded her head.

He let go of her and a part of her was grateful while another idiotic part wished he was still holding her close. He bent over Marguarita and she tasted bitterness in her mouth. Her cat slammed hard against her skin and, glancing in the mirror, she saw her eyes had gone completely jaguar. She turned away from that display of female jealousy. She was sad for poor Marguarita, her life changed for all time, yet she was anxious that Dominic might compare them. Marguarita was a beautiful woman, slender, with curves and flawless skin, while she was . . . all sinewy muscle and padding.

Dominic turned, and this time he was frowning. "I do not like your unflattering comparison of my woman to another."

Her heart did that now familiar jump. She sighed. *Maybe you shouldn't be reading my thoughts without my knowledge.* She couldn't help the thought from popping into her head and she winced, hoping he didn't hear that. She squashed every snippy thing she wanted to say and bit down hard on her lip. She couldn't imagine what he would do when she gave him attitude—which was inevitable. Even her younger cousin Jasmine, who loved her very much, said she had a major attitude problem.

"You seem to be having problems censoring what you are thinking." There was amusement in his voice. He didn't wait for her reply, but led the way out into the yard.

Cesaro sat in a chair on the front verandah. He looked tired and worn, but he managed a small smile. "I will send my wife in to Marguarita. She'll stay with her until the doctor gets here. The doctor is my brother, so have no fear, there will be no one speaking of this terrible night. And thank you for killing that monster."

Dominic gave a small, formal bow and continued striding away from the ranch into the trees. Solange lifted her hand, and without speaking, followed Dominic until the forest swallowed them completely. They walked in silence for a few minutes, Solange staying a few steps behind and to his left, giving him plenty of room to maneuver should they run into an enemy.

"How far are we walking?" she asked.

He stopped and turned, his gaze thoughtful as it drifted over her. "It is a distance to our lair," he acknowledged. And waited.

Her breath hissed out between her teeth. Instinctively she knew what he wanted from her, and that stubborn part of her just didn't want to go there. She was *not* going to ask to be carried. What was she? A child? She could walk. She could walk all night if she had to. Maybe she'd just shift into her cat and make it easier . . .

"No." His eyes stayed locked with hers, refusing to allow her to look away.

She bit her lip hard. "What do you want?"

"I think you should answer that question."

"You don't understand. Really. You don't." Frustrated, Solange shoved her fingers through her hair, making more of a mess out of the thick mass than it had already been. "You think you know me, but you don't. If I open my mouth I'm going to ruin all this."

A slow, sexy smile softened the hard edge to his mouth and set the butterflies free in her stomach. "I doubt that very much, Solange. You are my lifemate. It does not work that way at all. You cannot ruin it, nor can I. We will find our way with each other. You just have not chosen to commit to our relationship yet."

She shook her head. "I have. I told you about my blood, that it could get rid of the parasites. I didn't go after Brodrick while you were gone. That's commitment."

"Then why do you find it so difficult to ask such a simple thing from me as to transport us back to our lair?"

When he put it like that, it did sound silly. But she wasn't in the habit of asking favors. She was more honest with herself than that. Okay. It wasn't about favors. She didn't want to show weakness. Or ask him for anything. She hated that he was right. It was about trust, but how did one become different? She *wanted* to be different. She just couldn't get past that terrible wall she'd built around herself in order to survive.

"I don't know how to do this, Dominic." There was despair in her voice. "I can't talk to you." She was beginning to have the urge to run—and she'd never run from anything in her life.

"You had no trouble talking to me in our dreams."

He was relentless. And calm. She had the urge to smack him. This wasn't about a dream. "You weren't real then. I could tell you anything and there weren't . . ." She trailed off trying to find the right word. "Repercussions. You have to know it's different. Doesn't it feel different to you?" She couldn't get the pleading tone out of her voice. She wanted him to understand.

"Completely different," he agreed. "Better. I feel emotions I have not felt in hundreds of years. I know what love is. I know what it is to be jealous and to be happy. I can look at my woman and feel the demands of my body. I welcome even the possibility of heartache. I know what it is to *not* feel, Solange, and I will take emotion and the risks that come with that ability."

She lifted her chin. She knew her eyes had gone cat, but she couldn't help the stir of anger at the implied reprimand. "I've felt too much all my life, Dominic. Sorrow. Heartache. Rage. Whether you want to admit it or not, it's a risk."

He held his arms out to his sides, his gaze steady. "Then you have to decide for yourself whether I am worth the risk."

Her breath came out in a long hiss. "You're backing me into a corner. I'm a fighter. I don't like being cornered."

Those brilliant eyes never left her face. He shook his head. "You are trying to find a reason to run because you're afraid, Solange. Why would you be afraid of me?"

"Because," she said, feeling desperate. "I don't know what to do." The moment the words were out, she wanted to take them back. She sounded so silly. She was a grown woman and she should be able to handle a simple conversation with a man, but that was the trouble. She'd never been a woman. She didn't know how to be. She knew she could not be the woman he wanted and sooner or later he'd walk away from her.

She would be shattered. Completely and utterly broken. It was too much of a risk. She could be a coward in this one instance, because it was self-preservation. She waited for his disgust, for him to simply disappear as Carpathians could.

Dominic stepped forward and framed her face, forcing her gaze to meet his. "All you have to do, *kessake*, is ask me to take us back to our lair—our home. Is that really so difficult?"

He used that voice, the one that crept inside and wrapped around her heart, squeezing until she wanted to cry. She wanted him so much. She wanted to belong to him. How could she ever believe she was worthy of him? That he would really choose her over all the women he could have? How could he love a woman like her?

He didn't prompt her again and she knew he wouldn't. He would just stand there until she acquiesced. She knew he could hear her heart pounding. She tasted fear in her mouth. Why wasn't this easy? She took a breath. Let it out.

"Will you take us home, Dominic?" With that one sentence, she risked everything she was or would ever be.

The approval in his eyes sent heat rushing through her body. She was so lost in him already. It didn't matter what happened in the future. It was already too late for her, she could tell by her reaction to that look on his face. She wanted to please him when she'd never cared about pleasing anyone. And that told her it was far too late for her.

11

When you meet me,
You complete me.
You bring me back to life again.

DOMINIC TO SOLANGE

The cavern was lit with torches, sending a soft glow dancing over the ceiling. Spiderwebs of glittering silver
adorned the walls in various patterns. Woven rugs lay on the
floor and two high-backed, overstuffed armchairs sat on
either side of a small table. A basket of fresh fruit looked
inviting on the table beside a platter with cheese and bread
on it. Solange looked around at the small enhancements
Dominic had added to her sanctuary. The food made her
stomach growl, but she was too busy looking at the shimmering pool of water in the rock basin.

The water glowed in the middle with a flickering oranged-
red flame. The colors made the water seem even more

inviting, and she walked over to the pool to give herself time to collect her thoughts. She had made the decision to see this through, now she just had to figure out how to maneuver her way through the pitfalls. If only he weren't so sexy. Or such a good warrior. If she could find a balance with him she could handle this.

"Do you like the changes?" he asked.

She nodded. "Very much." He hadn't touched anything of hers, simply added to what she already had, and that made her feel a little better. She wanted him to like the few things she'd gathered over the years.

"How in the world do you make the water look like there's a flame inside of it?" She turned to face him and jumped when her body nearly bumped against his.

He was so close. Silent. And his scent didn't reach her until he chose. She took a breath and breathed him into her lungs. His body heat surrounded her. He was close enough that the heavy erection brushed her stomach. She could barely force herself to look up his tall body, her gaze resting on his tempting mouth, not daring to go any higher to see the look in his eyes.

Her body reacted to him, going soft and pliant, her nerve endings close to the surface. She *never* reacted physically to men, not even when her cat was in heat. The need rode her hard, her cat feeding her drive to procreate, but the moment she was near a man, she just couldn't feel physically ready. Not even her snarling, edgy cat could overcome her distaste for males. But with Dominic, she couldn't seem to keep her raging hormones under control.

She knew he was aware of her body's reaction, just as she was aware of his, but somehow her lack of control embarrassed her. Wanting a mate was perfectly natural, yet . . .

"You are so hard on yourself," he said.

His voice was that sexy blend that only added to her growing desire. She swallowed hard. "I just don't know what I'm doing."

"Is that really so bad?" His fingers skimmed down her hair, tucked a strand behind her ear with exquisite gentleness. "Do you have to be perfect at all times? I would imagine that would be rather wearying."

The pad of his finger traced over her mouth, brushed back and forth until she parted her lips. He pushed inside her mouth and instinctively she closed her lips around his finger, her tongue flicking over it, sucking before she could stop herself. Hot color swept into her face and she tried to turn her head, but his hand spanned her throat, holding her still, his head slightly thrown back as if he was enjoying the sensation of her mouth around his finger. She stroked along his knuckle with her tongue, and followed as he slowly withdrew, so that she nibbled at the pad of his finger before he went back to tracing her lips.

"Do you, Solange? Do you have to be perfect all the time?"

"Of course not." She could barely speak.

"Only with me then." He bent his head and brushed his mouth across hers.

The shocking jolt slammed through her body with the force of a lightning bolt. His touch had been so light, yet a fireball shot through her to settle deep in her core.

"You want to please me." He made it a statement.

She nodded, afraid to speak. Afraid he would move. Afraid he wouldn't move.

"That is as it should be. Has it occurred to you that I wish to please you?"

She glanced up, her gaze colliding with his. He looked

so powerful. A predator looming over prey. She was jaguar and not afraid of anything—with the exception of her lifemate—and wasn't that insane?

Lifemate. She tasted the word.

"Solange." He refused to allow her to look away from him. "When I ask a question, I require an answer."

The color in her face went from pink to crimson. "Yes, I'm sorry. It has occurred to me. It's just difficult to believe. I'll get used to it, though." *Maybe.* "I just need a little time."

He smiled at her, that slow, sexy, heart-melting smile that she seemed to feel all the way to her toes. She loved to see that look on his face. The light in his eyes.

"That was not so difficult, was it? To tell me how you feel? How will I please you if you do not tell me the things you need?"

He brushed a kiss over her mouth again. Her lips trembled in response. The fireball in her core radiated so much heat she was afraid she might spontaneously combust. Her feminine channel burned for him, and between her legs she could feel the hot dampness spreading.

"I have put several items of clothing in the small alcove for you. It would please me greatly if, when we are alone, you would wear one for me."

All over again her heart began to accelerate. Her pulse beat frantically, drawing his attention. He swept the hair from her neck and leaned toward her. She went absolutely still. His breath was warm against her skin. A shudder of desire started a wave of tremors. She rubbed her hands down her jean-clad thighs—her armor.

Solange had to moisten her lips twice before she could get a word out and then it was a croak. "Where?"

He turned and gestured toward the little alcove where she had stashed extra clothes and weapons. Needing to put space between them, she forced her trembling legs to walk across to the small grotto arched with rock where she could hide her burning face from him. There was a full-length mirror that hadn't been there before. She could see the shock and excitement on her face. Her eyes were bright, almost emerald green. Her breath was ragged, drawing attention to her full breasts—more than full. She wasn't fashionably lean, for all the exercise she got. She was built—sturdy. Compact and sturdy.

Solange was grateful he hadn't followed her. She felt overwhelmed by him. Somehow he had managed to put a small closet together to hang several items in a corner. She touched the fabric of the nearest long dress. At least she thought it was a dress or some kind of gown. It was long, and she bet it fit perfectly, but it was a dress—and she didn't even own dresses. Made of black stretch lace, it was formfitting at the top, with spaghetti straps. The front dropped scandalously short, just barely covering the vee between her legs, and the back was a long train that reached her ankles. The lace was utterly sheer. Transparent. Only a few darker webs of fabric tried to hide anything, and it was more teasing than hiding. If she put the thing on, her curvy body would be on display. There were no panties or bra.

She cleared her throat. "You want me to wear this?"

"When we are alone together."

That same soft, compelling voice. No demands. It would be her decision. But he had said this would please him. Did she want to do this for him? Could she? Her fingers touched the lace with a kind of reverence. She wasn't the kind of woman who could pull it off, but . . .

Solange pulled the next one out to see if maybe that one would give her more confidence. This was a duster, a shimmering metallic red that fell all the way to the floor. At first she breathed a sigh of relief, but as she studied it, she realized the fabric stretched and would fit like a glove over her

breasts, would cinch tightly at her waist and flare to the
floor with the front completely open from the waist down.
A generous portion of her breasts would be revealed by the
V-neck. She stepped back, swallowing hard.

"Have you heard of underwear?" She dared to ask because she couldn't see him.

"I would like my woman available to me when we are
alone," he replied in that same calm voice. But the way his
tone lowered when he said *available to me* sent another
wave of arousal crashing through her.

She took a breath and looked at the next dress. This time
she was more prepared, but still shocked when she saw the
dress—if it could be called that. This was nothing but film
and straps, a micromini halter dress with a see-through
front just barely there and the back was nothing but pieces
of thin strips all the way down, hugging the form so the
very edges of her bottom would peek out with every step.
There was more skin than material down the back.

"I've never worn anything like this in my life. I've never
even seen such a thing."

"You are not comfortable with your body, *kessake*.
Dressing this way will not only please me, but it will make
you very aware of how sexy you really are."

She swallowed hard and forced herself to look at the
emerald green dress. Again, it was very short. Made to hug
her curvy figure and show it off, the material stretched over
and clung to skin. This one also had spaghetti straps,
scooped low in the front. A vee of straps laddered down the
dress both in the front and back, revealing bare skin. Most
of her chest would be bare, and what was covered could be
clearly seen through the thin fabric. Due to the straps the
dress was as open in the front as it was in the back.

She frowned at herself in the mirror. "I've been in a
battle. I need to . . ."

"Bathe? The water is hot. And then you can put on your choice and come eat."

She shivered. Another bath in front of him. But if she could do that, then surely she could wear one of his dresses.

She forced herself to pull off her shirt. At once she caught sight of herself in the large, full-length mirror. Her breasts were full, high, and her nipples peaked in the cool of the cavern. Her hair was wild and with her tilted cat's eyes, she looked . . . exotic . . . if she didn't look too harshly at herself. She'd never been so aware of herself as a female—and that was it, that was the problem, she realized with a gasp. Dominic Dragonseeker made her *feel* completely, utterly, absolutely feminine when she was alone with him.

She peeled off her jeans and stared at her body. She was short, but she had an hourglass figure. Juliette had once described her as a "pocket Venus" and she'd looked it up. To her shock, the description had been one of a voluptuous, beautiful woman. Well, she wasn't beautiful, but she was definitely voluptuous.

"I don't have a razor." She didn't want to walk out nude in front of him and she couldn't find much to wrap around her. "And I need a robe." The moment the words were out of her mouth, she bit down hard on her lip. He'd asked her not to cover up her body and that was the first thing she was looking to do. But honestly, did women just walk around naked in front of their men? *Without shaving their legs first?* She should have asked Juliette or MaryAnn that question, too.

Dominic suddenly appeared behind her in the mirror, a good foot taller than she was. He seemed to dominate the small space and it wasn't just his physical frame, but the power emanating from him. He held power in his eyes and voice, compelling her without physical force to do as he wished. Or maybe it was really her, so desperate to keep that look she loved so much on his face.

Out of reflex, she tried to cover her breasts with her hands, but he caught her wrists and held her arms outstretched, away from her body.

"Look how beautiful you are. For me alone. Do you have any idea how appealing that is to a man who has had no one of his own for centuries? You are my other half and I find you incredibly sexy."

She met his eyes in the glass. There was a dark lust there, a glimpse of a stark, raw hunger that made her shiver in anticipation. His heavy erection, the evidence of the truth that he found her sexy, lay hot against the small of her bare back through the thin fabric of his trousers. There was something very decadent about being nude, staring at herself in the mirror, arms outstretched, with Dominic fully clothed, watching her with a predator's stare and standing so close just behind her.

His arms wrapped around her even as his hands came up to cup the weight of her full breasts in his palms. He watched her in the mirror. She could see her eyes go cat, slumberous, her lashes falling as his hair brushed her bare shoulder.

"Stay this way for me," he murmured softly as he lowered his head to the pulse beating so frantically in her neck. "Open and giving. *My* woman."

She felt the rasp of tongue, a stroke of velvet that sent a tremor through her body.

"You are my woman?"

It was a question. When he asked a question, he required an answer, no matter how difficult it was. She was trembling, her body in need just from the way his hands lifted her breasts so possessively. "Yes." It was barely a whisper, but she managed.

"Your skin is so soft, my little cat. Like the fur of your jaguar, only better. Silky soft."

His teeth scraped along her pulse and the breath left her lungs in a rush. Her breasts heaved, nipples so hard they were small beads. His thumbs brushed against her, feather-light, and then his fingernails sent a fire bolt careening from her nipples and through her belly to lodge with white-hot heat in her core.

"Tell me you want this," he whispered. A temptation. "Say *please*. Ask me for this."

She swallowed the lump in her throat. Her mind was already accepting—no, not accepting, *craving*—the erotic bite. His fingers stroked over her breasts, then rolled and tugged her nipples until she thought she might fall. She couldn't look away from the sight of him. So handsome. All that black hair falling like a shimmering deep waterfall on the darkest night. His eyes burning with passion, with desire, his arms so strong around her. She'd never seen a more erotic sight than the two of them in the mirror.

"Ask me," he prompted. His teeth took a small nip, sending streaks of fire through her veins.

She could barely breathe, let alone talk, but she wanted this moment for herself as much as for him. "I want you to take my blood," she whispered.

He waited. One heartbeat. Two.

Her womb clenched. Her feminine channel spasmed. For one moment she thought she was on the verge of an orgasm. She was so close, riding the edge, and he had done no more than touch her breasts and take tiny nips over her pulse. She was wet and needy, the pressure building at an alarming rate, pushing her further and faster than she'd ever gone. Her cat had always driven her sexual needs, and this craving was frightening but impossible to ignore.

"Please take my blood," she whispered, knowing her need was as great as his.

His teeth sank deep and she cried out as pleasure and

pain merged together, bursting through her body like a star exploding. White lights danced behind her eyelids. Her body went boneless, so she felt as if she'd melted into him. His fingers were on her breasts, yet she felt them between her legs, stroking, penetrating deep. Or was that his tongue stroking deep inside of her? The pressure built and built while the white-hot heat consumed her.

She didn't want him ever to stop. Fire roared in her womb and spread through her body. Her brain seemed to seize, until there was nothing in her mind but pure pleasure. Every thought disappeared, every embarrassment. There was only Dominic and his magic mouth and hands. There was only the fire burning through her body. She felt the first ripples of an orgasm and gasped, no sound coming out. The rush was strong, ripples swelling in strength, gathering speed and momentum, tearing through her body like a massive quake. She heard her own strangled sob of pleasure as if from far away. Her legs went weak, but Dominic's strength kept her up.

Open your eyes for me.

The soft command was a sinful whisper impossible to ignore. Her lashes fluttered once before she managed to find the ability to lift them. She found herself staring into the mirror. Her body was flushed with pleasure. Her mouth was open, her eyes glazed and bright, her breasts swollen, cupped in his big hands. Behind her, he loomed large and powerful, surrounding her with his arms, his mouth against her neck while his long hair fell in a shimmering cascade of silk.

Was that her? Sexy and uninhibited with the most sensual man on earth? She could feel his heavy erection pressed tightly against her. Had she done that? Brought his body to such a state? Her womb nearly convulsed at the erotic sight. She'd never considered herself a sensual being, but Dominic saw her that way, and looking into the mirror, she had no choice but to see herself the same way.

His tongue slid over the small pinpricks, closing them. He rested his chin on top of her head and just watched her in the mirror, holding her while the tremors eased in her body.

"Look how beautiful you are, Solange."

"That's how you see me."

"This is how you are. I see true."

She couldn't bring herself to ask aloud, but she wanted to give him the same kind of pleasure. Dropping her gaze from his in the mirror, she managed to use the more intimate means of communication. *I have no idea how to take care of your needs the way you have mine, but I'd like to try . . . please.*

He gave a soft groan and brushed a kiss over her hair. "This is your time, *kessake*. When you reach the point where my need is your need, I will teach you all you need to know. The beauty is in the giving. You need this right now, becoming comfortable with who you really are, not in pleasuring me. That is only an added complication for you and one more thing for you to be nervous over. I do not wish you to be afraid of who you are, not when you are with me."

"Who do you think I am?"

He smiled and her world tilted.

"You are a sensual, passionate woman in every sense. You just need time to discover that."

She wasn't certain how she felt, both a mixture of disappointment and relief. He'd effectively allowed her to relax a little now that she knew nothing was expected of her, but still there was the continual relentless aching pressure and welcoming dampness that didn't seem to go away. And, if she was being honest, the desire to explore his body. She wanted to be the woman who could give him pleasure.

Dominic held out one hand, still retaining possession of her left breast with the other, his thumb almost lazily brushing her nipple. While she shivered against him, and aftershocks rippled through her body, a long robe appeared across his palm. "For you, Solange."

She loved his voice, that low, sexy tone that made her feel so special. She looked up at him as he enveloped her in the soft folds. The robe draped over her body. Sensuous. Filmy. Barely there. She could see her body, every curve, through the midnight blue of the fabric in spite of the silver dragon star constellation scattered across the material. The robe enhanced and emphasized her curves rather than hid them.

"Thank you, Dominic," she whispered, running her hand over her thigh.

She felt shy. A little embarrassed at her wanton behavior. Again, she had a difficult time looking him in the eye. Jaguars had no problem holding a stare, and all her life no one, male or female, had been able to lock eyes with her and not look away first. With Dominic, she couldn't seem to meet his direct gaze.

She didn't know what to think about her appearance. He made her feel so different about herself. It was difficult not to get caught up in the spell he wove. She felt not only feminine, but sensual. Her body was very sensitive, every nerve ending alive, raw and focused on him.

"You are very welcome."

Dominic stepped back, allowing her to slip past him. It was strange walking in the transparent robe, the dancing light spilling over the constellation so that the dragon gleamed as if in the night sky. She could feel his eyes on her and every single step she took sent more heat rushing through her body. She was so damp she knew the evidence of her need gleamed between her legs. He was Carpathian; he couldn't fail to scent her arousal.

She forced herself to keep walking, and if there was an added sway to her hips she couldn't quite stop, she was going to blame it on the robe. Who could wear such a thing and not feel particularly sexy, especially under his burning stare, and with his compliments spinning around and around in her mind?

She reached the edge of the basin and shrugged out of the robe almost reluctantly. Just as her jeans and tees were her fighting armor, the sensual lingerie made her feel feminine and attractive. The material seemed to hide as much as it revealed. She felt flawless in it, yet the moment she shed it, she felt strangely exposed.

His hand reached over her shoulder for the robe and she relinquished it, knowing that garment would always be a particular favorite no matter what happened. While wearing the robe, for the first time in her life she felt wanted as a woman. She felt sexy and even beautiful. The robe was as magical as Dominic. Standing so close, with him behind her, she was conscious of his heat, of the absolute control he seemed to have over both of them, and of his enormous strength. As a female jaguar, she looked for those qualities in a mate, and he had them in abundance.

She slipped into the steamy water and gratefully sank deep. The heat eased the soreness in her muscles. "Dominic, this feels so good."

He moved into the shadows, sitting in one of the two armchairs, almost hidden from her. One candle flickered with just enough flame to occasionally throw light across his face. A warrior's face. Dark. Mysterious. So tough. He was beautiful to her. She ducked her head under the water and rinsed out her hair. Strangely, even that familiar action seemed sensuous.

Solange allowed her head to rest against the side of the rock pool. She knew Dominic was watching her. The light spilled directly across her, probably spotlighting her breasts under the transparent water. The flame turned the water into prisms of color, drawing the eye, but with Dominic in the shadows, it was almost like her dreams when he would come to talk with her.

"I am glad you are enjoying your bath. I could tell you were still sore from your wounds."

She flashed a small, tentative smile. "You actually healed the worst of them. I just have a few aches and pains. Nothing serious." She hesitated.

He waited.

She cupped a handful of water and watched it run through her fingers. "You made me feel cared for."

"You are cared for."

Her gaze jumped to his. Her stomach fluttered at the impact of meeting those dark, mysterious eyes. "Thank you."

"If you could live anywhere in the world, where would it be?"

She frowned. "I've never been anywhere. Never. I've only lived here in the rain forest, but I used to dream of traveling. I would have loved to see all the different rain forests in the world. My aunt sometimes talked of far-off places. I used to pretend I was a princess, like in the stories she read to us, and a prince would come along and rescue me." She shrugged her shoulders. "I stopped needing to be rescued a long time ago."

"Perhaps," he murmured. "Or perhaps you simply stopped dreaming."

"What about you? Where would you want to live if you could live anywhere?"

She heard the chair move slightly, as if he had shifted

positions. She glanced up and saw his hooded eyes drift over her. Instantly she was aware of her body again. It was the look in his eyes, she decided, that made her feel so sexual. Her cat wasn't in heat, yet she was. The burning between her legs just kept growing as if her body would never quite be sated. The craving for him seemed endless.

He wanted her to know herself as a woman and for his needs to become hers. She was fast approaching the point of needing him. She thought she'd been relieved when he'd told her that he expected nothing of her, but now her palms itched to touch his skin. She found herself sitting in the heated bath and fantasizing a little about taking him into her mouth, just to see what he tasted like, and most of all, what it would feel like to have him inside her, relieving the relentless ache.

"I have traveled all over the world and gone to the highest peaks, and the densest jungles. The Carpathian Mountains will always be my homeland, but my home is a woman. Solange Sangria. *You* are home to me. Your body is my home. Your mind. Your heart and soul. It matters little to me where we are."

She inhaled sharply. Now she wished she could see his face more clearly. "Are you saying we could live anywhere in the world that I wanted?"

"You have only to wish it."

There was no way to hide the shock on her face, and she knew he saw it by his sigh.

"Do you think yourself less than me?"

"No!" She absolutely didn't but . . .

He nodded his head. "I see. You thought *I* would think you were less than me."

She was ashamed. "I'm sorry." She sensed his disappointment in her for her lack of faith in him, and that hurt more than if he'd yelled at her. Dominic had never given her reason to think that he would ever think her less. "I think most men . . ." She trailed off when he lifted his hand to stop her.

"There is only one man in your life, Solange. You have only to worry yourself with what I think and feel, not other men."

His voice, as always, was utterly calm, but she sensed the edge to it and she pulled her knees to her and wrapped her arms around them, under the water where she felt warm and safe.

"Do you understand?"

She nodded her head. He waited.

"Yes," she said aloud, almost stammering. "I really didn't mean to accuse you of . . ." What had she been accusing him of? What was wrong with her? Why did it matter so much that she might have hurt him?

"You thought I would dictate to you," he finished for her. "We are partners—equal, Solange, in every sense of the word. As your lifemate, your happiness and health matter more to me than my own, but lifemates are in one another's mind. I know what you need. I think some things are difficult for you to see or admit about yourself, and it is my job to make certain you get all that you need."

She lowered her eyes. "What about your needs?"

"We will see to them in time. I have waited centuries to find you. In that time I have learned patience. Before anything else, I need your trust. Your absolute trust in me—and in yourself. You have to know you are the only woman I will ever want or need. You have to know that it is in you to meet my every desire, just as I will meet yours."

"What if I'm no good at sex?" She voiced the question most on her mind and blushed a deep crimson while she did. Her body went hot and she was very grateful for the steamy water that helped to disguise her embarrassment.

"Then your teacher will have failed and we will begin again."

She swallowed hard. "Is that what you're doing? Teaching me about sex?"

His white teeth flashed briefly in the flickering candle-light and then he was completely in the shadows. "We have not yet begun your instruction on sex."

"Oh." Her heart jumped and then beat wildly in her chest.

"Lift your leg out of the water for me."

Her gaze widened as he stood up and glided over to the edge of the basin. His movements were so fluid she knew there was no other way to describe him. He loomed over her, his shoulders wide and his dark hair flowing. She hesitated, uncertain what he wanted of her. If she scooted close to the edge so her leg would be out of the water, she'd have to lean back and she'd probably go underwater. He said nothing at all, simply waited.

Solange scooted forward as far as she could and took a deep breath, leaning back as she obediently lifted her leg out of the water. To her shock, her back and head were instantly supported.

Dominic took her ankle in his hands, his touch gentle. He smiled at her. "That's my *kessake*. Your trust in me is growing."

She wasn't certain it was her trust in him so much as her desire to please him. She wanted that smile and the look of approval in his eyes.

She couldn't look away from him, aware of how she must appear, only the steaming water for a cover. The water lapped at her breasts, teasing at the soft, feminine curves. One leg was bent, her foot on the floor of the basin while his hands shackled the ankle of the other. He moved his palms up her calf to her knee, a long, slow, very even stroke. Her body felt the touch deep inside. If it was possible to grow even wetter and more welcoming there in the water, she managed to do so. It took a moment to realize he had removed the short stubbles of hair on her leg.

His hands continued up her thigh. A small whimper escaped. She bit down hard on her lip to prevent any more sounds. His fingers brushed over her entrance, teased at her lips for a few moments before his palm covered her mound, shocking her. She nearly pulled away, but his eyes held her still.

She swallowed hard as his fingers moved over her body, exploring every shadow, every hollow, until she couldn't stop squirming, her body no longer her own.

"I don't understand what you're doing." She gasped the words, feeling a little desperate. She'd never even dreamt a woman could want a man so much.

"There will be nothing between my mouth and your body. I want you to feel everything I do to you."

She was already feeling it. How was she going to feel any more without it killing her? He replaced her leg gently and crooked a finger at her. Solange gave him her left leg and closed her eyes, trying to breathe through the exquisite pleasure. Could a woman just have orgasms over and over without her man actually entering her? Evidently Solange could, because she was on the brink of one. His hands worked their magic, and when he was finished, he lowered her leg carefully, as if she were made of the finest porcelain.

This time, rather than ask her to lift her leg, he reached into the water and secured her right ankle, pulling her leg to him. She was grateful. She felt almost weak, unable to move, mesmerized by the look on his face. The lines were etched deep. His eyes were dark with lust. He appeared so focused on her she was almost afraid to breathe.

Small droplets of water ran down her leg, revealing the

silky smooth skin. He bent his head and licked the drops of water off her thigh.

Solange's breath hissed out of her. "Dominic!"

He smiled and released her leg just as gently as he lifted it. "I think you are beginning to understand."

The only thing she understood was that he was the most amazing man in the world. This time when he held out his hand, she didn't hesitate in taking it. He drew her up out of the water and she stood, totally exposed to him. This time, as his gaze moved over her, she stood still for him, not attempting to cover up.

"You look beautiful." The warmth in his voice made her flush.

"You make me feel beautiful," she replied. And he did. The look in his eyes made her feel as if she were the most wanted woman in the world.

What would it be like to have the love and respect of a man like Dominic? To be in his care? She was a woman who had answered only to herself.

Dominic enfolded her in a warm towel and dried her off. He took his time, paying attention to detail, making certain to catch every drop of water. He rubbed her breasts, down her belly and even in between her legs. He nudged her knees apart and made certain her thighs and buttocks were completely free of moisture. He wasn't in the least impersonal as she'd hoped. His strokes were deliberately provocative, making her squirm. She could hear her own breathing change as his hands lingered. Once he bent his head and caught a drop of water that ran down her thigh.

Her entire body was flushed and alive, acutely aware of him. He slipped the sleeves of the dragon robe over her arms and tied the cinch at the waist. The spidery fabric slid over her bare skin like living silk. She stood still while he towel dried her hair. To her amazement, he began to blow warm air over it as he used his fingers to encourage the unruly waves. Only when he was finished did he indicate the chair.

She smiled up at him, dazed by his care. "My aunt took me in when I was eight years old, Dominic, but we were always on the run. She homeschooled us, and we learned weapons and fighting, but there was . . ." She looked around at the snug room. He had done all this for her. "I was responsible for my cousins by the time I was fourteen. I don't know how to do this back for you."

His hand curled around the nape of her neck and he drew her close to him, bending his head to hers. Her breath caught in her throat when his lips brushed hers. She was stunned at the impact of that slight touch. Electricity sparked over and through her skin, sending a hot, sizzling rush through her veins. Her breasts swelled, nipples sensitive and aching for attention. The fire burned lower still, deep in her sex, so that she throbbed and pulsed with need.

He straightened, took her by the shoulders and led her to the chair. "You need to eat."

"Eat?" She looked up at him. "I can't even breathe."

He laughed softly, the sound filling her with unexpected joy. She hadn't known joy. She hadn't known a man could be like Dominic.

"Then I will breathe for you."

He probably would, too. She picked up an orange, too awed by him to wonder where he got it. "I'm so afraid of disappointing you. I'm not very good at relationships. Ask my cousin. She only puts up with me because we're related."

"She puts up with you because she loves you," he corrected, and took the orange from her trembling hands to peel it himself.

12

You reveal me. Then you heal me
Of all the scars and strife.
And when my life was spinning downward,
You caught me.
I'd forgotten how to smile, but
You re-taught me.

SOLANGE TO DOMINIC

Solange tried to slow her breathing, knowing he was watching her closely. She cleared her throat and tried to sound calm. "I don't think I've spent this much time with another person in years."

Minan—*my own.* The words were a soft, gentle whisper in her mind. Aloud, in his calm tone, he added, "Neither have I." He didn't hand her the peeled orange, but instead took a section and held it to her lips. "We make this journey together."

Everything in Solange settled. Her mind calmed and she found she could breathe. She simply had to match the basic rhythm of his lungs. In and out. It wasn't really that difficult. They were in this together, for better or worse. He didn't seem to mind that she floundered with her words, that she had no idea what she was doing. He seemed to accept her with all of her failings.

She opened her mouth and accepted the cool fruit. It was bursting with flavor. The orange was one of her favorites and difficult to get. She knew he had created it especially for her. He seemed thoughtful that way, finding the things she loved the most in some little corner of her mind and providing them for her. She ran her hand over the exquisite robe. She could see her silky skin, smooth in spite of the small white scars, those little dots she'd always detested and hidden, revealed now as if they didn't matter. A little subconsciously, she rubbed at them through the lacy material.

"When the candlelight plays over the dots, they look as if they are alive, dancing their way up your thigh. It is a highly erotic sight, Solange, and makes me want to follow them with my tongue. I will taste every inch of you, and those delightful dots lead the way to the feast."

She blushed again. There was no way to control the sweeping color so she opened her mouth as he slipped another orange slice against her lips. His words had once again called her attention to her body, to the way she looked, her voluptuous curves emphasized by the stretchy lace of her robe. The scattered stars did nothing to hide the swell of her breasts or her flared hips. She squirmed a little, wishing her chair was more in the shadows as his was. She crossed her legs.

"I would prefer you were open to me."

His voice was so soft. It was no command, just a simple

statement. She hadn't meant to close herself off to him . . . She glanced up at his face. God, but he was beautiful. "Wouldn't you prefer I was a little modest?" Which, when one thought about it, was hilarious. Cats were *not* modest as a rule. When she shifted, she was nude. That was all there was to it, yet this seemed so different.

"I would hope the woman is for me alone and that you are comfortable enough—and trust me enough—to take delight in your sexuality. You are naturally passionate and sensual. I love to look at you, to see you wanting me. When I feel your eyes moving over my body, and when I can look so openly on what is mine, it gives me great pleasure."

It sounded so simple, but it took great effort on her part to uncross her legs to give him the view of a wanton, needy woman. She couldn't help but feel sexy and a little wicked, but it was still one of the most difficult things she'd done. Worse, it sent another rush of heat that glistened between her legs. He inhaled, drawing the scent of her arousal into his lungs.

Solange knew her reaction to his request was only encouraging him in drawing her out of her shell—and she was a little afraid of where that might lead. That simple smile of appreciation, for her, was the greatest praise he could give her. It was shocking how satisfying it was to please him, when she'd never sought to please anyone.

"That's my woman."

He gave her a small, courtly bow that sent a ripple of pleasure through her. His manners were so Old World, as was his formal speech, but it seemed to suit him and make him, for her, all the more alluring.

"What's your plan?"

His eyebrow shot up and she blushed. "Not *that*," she qualified. "The vampire camp. You told me you'd ingested vampire blood so they would recognize you as part of their conspiracy. Do you think the parasites in your blood alone will gain you acceptance?"

"The vampires I have met so far have believed the call of the parasites, but they are never active with you around. I also took your blood a little while ago." He held another orange slice to her lips and waited until Solange bit into it. "So if you are thinking you will accompany me in some way, it will not work."

She frowned at him. "Of course I'm going to have your back. I can't imagine that you aren't already thinking of ways to kill Brodrick."

"Naturally."

She forgot all about not wearing her warrior armor. Her green eyes went cat and she frowned at him. "Don't ever make the mistake of thinking I don't know what I'm doing. If you meant what you said about partners and respect and being equal, and knowing who I really am, then you have to know I'm going to be guarding your back."

She pushed out of the chair, forgetting the gossamer robe as she paced restlessly across the floor of the cavern, her cat prowling close to the surface. "You either accept me as I am, or you don't. You can't have it both ways. I would *never* be able to stay safe waiting while you're in danger."

Only the sound of water falling into the basin filled the room. She became aware of her harsh, agitated breathing, her accelerated heartbeat, the rush of adrenaline in her body. His silence stretched out until the tension was nearly unbearable. He simply looked at her with that dark, unfathomable, very direct stare that spoke volumes.

She raised her chin and stared right back. Protecting those she loved was her fundamental core. If he thought he could shape her into something or someone else with a few sexy outfits, he was very wrong. She wasn't good at this kind of crap anyway. She'd just go back to being a jaguar and find her place in the forest. She felt the familiar itch run under her skin and the call of the wild raged inside of her. Escape . . . it was the only way.

"You are a fierce fighter, Solange. When you cannot win a battle, what do you do?"

She fought back her cat to try to make her vocal cords work. "Retreat and plan a different way."

"You cannot win a battle with me. Not you. Not your cat. We both would lose if you insisted on such an action."

"What *exactly* are you saying to me? Because you are *not* going to dictate to me."

"You are looking for a fight and I refuse to join you. You have a very bad habit of jumping to conclusions and putting me in the worst light possible."

She opened her mouth and closed it again, forcing herself to breathe away panic. And she was panicking. She *wanted*, even *needed* to run before he took this any further. Until she wanted him with every cell in her body and she would do anything to keep him. She had more self-respect than that.

He stepped close to her, ignoring the warning look in her eyes, one hand spanning her throat, letting her feel his immense strength. More than physical strength, she could see the power and confidence the centuries had given him. The look in his eyes shook her. Censure. Pure, unadulterated censure. And it hurt. Maybe she deserved it, but it really hurt.

"You cannot lie to me or yourself, Solange. I will not allow that. You want to run from me, not out of self-respect but out of cowardice. You do not want to trust me with your body or your heart, and I am getting too close to both."

"I would shatter into a million pieces," she defended. "Don't you see? I'm not this woman you want."

"How do you know what I want when you refuse to look—or listen? You were waiting for your opportunity and you thought you found it. Did I not tell you that I respected you as a warrior? That I believed you to be my equal and a partner? Do you think that I would lie to you? I am Dominic Dragonseeker, and the Dragonseeker honor has never been called into question, not once in thousands of years." There was an edge now to that normally calm voice.

Solange felt the tears gathering behind her eyes. Of course she'd screwed things up. It was all too good to be true. Or maybe she just couldn't handle being happy after so many years of rage and sorrow.

His hand moved to the nape of her neck, and suddenly his fingers were doing a soothing massage. "Breathe, Solange. Just take a breath."

Her lungs *were* burning for air and she hadn't even realized it. Real shame, an emotion she hadn't known until then, was more bitter than rage. Dominic had put himself on the line. She hadn't really given him a chance, not in her heart. Her mind had tried, and her body certainly wanted him, but there was so much fear of having her heart torn out that she hadn't really committed to him. She was ready to run at the first sign of danger with him.

"Don't you see? I can't do this," she said. "I'm going to keep hurting you. I've never even lived in a house with people. We lived in camps and learned to defend ourselves. I haven't had a home since I was eight years old." She didn't know if she was pleading for understanding or pleading with him to let her go.

His fingers continued that slow, seductive massage. "Then perhaps it is time you had a home, Solange. *I* want to be your home. Give me your trust. I know we can do this."

"We'd need a miracle," Solange said, shaking her head. "I want to do this, Dominic, I really do, but I just don't think

I'm capable. I look into your eyes and a part of me knows I'll be safe if I give myself to you, but I'm holding on to safety so tightly that I don't think I can let go and fall. You're like this amazing, larger-than-life hero who has swept into my personal nightmare, and I've just never believed in heroes."

He brushed at the tears in her eyes with his fingers, caught them in his hand and applied pressure. She drew in her breath when he opened his hands. Sparkling gems of red and green strung together with links of gold lay in the palm of his hand. "Green for your eyes and red for your temper, both of which I am very partial to."

Solange would have backed away from him if he hadn't held her in place. "You have too much power for anyone, Dominic." She couldn't keep the tremors out of her voice.

"You said we needed a miracle." He nudged her hand until she opened it. He dropped the bracelet into her palm. "We have a miracle, Solange. You and I together can be a miracle. What are the odds after so many centuries of being alone that I would find you here in this place where I came for my final battle?"

Her fingers closed around the gems and she held them to her. "I want to be the woman you need, Dominic, but I'm too afraid of losing myself."

"How would you do that?"

"You asked me what I do when I can't win a battle. How could I ever win with you? You're too strong. Not just physical strength; I might be able to fight that. It's not even your gifts. It's the power in you. The absolute power I feel radiating from you."

He smiled at her and brushed back the fall of soft waves around her face. "That power belongs to you, Solange. It is there for your protection. For your happiness. For your use. It belongs to you. You have not figured it out yet, but you are both intelligent and a fighter. Do not fight me. Fight *for* us. Fight for me. Without you, I cannot survive. Can you do that?" He leaned down and brushed a soft kiss across her lips. "You are a strong woman, Solange. Will you save me? You are the only one who can."

Her heart contracted. "You don't need me, Dominic. You're so—so absolute. You could have any woman you wanted. This has to be some bizarre mistake."

He shook his head. "In many ways Carpathians look to be a superior species, and it is true we have many gifts, but in truth, like every species, we have weaknesses. Jaguars and humans can mate with anyone, and they often mistake physical attraction for a lasting relationship. For Carpathians there is only one. You are the other half of me. There is no getting it wrong, Solange. You were meant for me. If you choose not to commit to me, I will be lost."

Solange blinked back tears and opened her hand to look down at the bracelet, at the fiery red gems nestled in her palm. "I have a really, really bad temper," she warned. "And a very mean mouth."

Very gently he took the bracelet from her hand and fastened it around her wrist. He leaned down and brushed another kiss across her upturned lips before very gently slipping the robe from her body. "Then we will have to teach you other uses for your mouth. I dream of it often."

Her body reacted, flooding with heat. He leaned his head toward her, a slow, steady movement that only seemed to heighten her anticipation. Her legs trembled and turned to jelly. She gasped when he lifted her into his arms and when they turned, there was a thick, handwoven rug carpeting the bench. She had time for one brief thought—*How does he do that?*

"I think you need to relax. You are shaking again."

He placed her faceup on the padded table. She stared up at the ceiling of the cave. It was as if he'd thrown her midnight blue robe up above her and scattered amazing silvery stars across the night sky. She recognized the dragon constellation. This dragon was blazing, as if the stars hadn't faded with time and still had the wings.

"I am going to give you a scalp massage. You do not have to worry about anything, Solange. I am not expecting or asking anything of you at this time. Only to relax."

His fingers were strong, yet so very gentle. The mesmerizing soft voice stroked like velvet over her skin while his fingers worked their magic.

"I want you to feel warm, *kessake*. And safe. Because you are always safe in my care. Do you know what the binding ritual is? Has your cousin talked to you about it?"

His voice had dropped an octave lower. Solange listened for the sound of it, concentrating on every cadence and rhythm of his tone as she looked up at the burning eyes and sharp teeth of the dragon overhead.

"Not really. I didn't understand what she did say." Her mind was a little hazy from the absolute pleasure his hands were inducing. There was no way she could fail to relax, not with his large hands drawing the tension out of her.

"The male of our species is imprinted with the binding words before birth. Once we say them to our lifemate, she is bound, soul to soul, to us. We believe the soul was split. The male is the darkness and she is the light."

In spite of the sheer magic of his fingers, she winced. "Surely mistakes are made. I've told you before, there is little light left in me. I kill, Dominic. I plan an attack and I carry it out with precision and no hesitation."

He waited in silence, and Solange bit her lip and then lifted her left hand into the air so she could look at the bracelet. The light from the candles caught the rubies and emeralds, and they blazed to life. "Maybe that's not exactly the truth. Lately, I've been hesitating." The confession came out in a soft little rush. She didn't want to lie to him. "The last few times I've known I'm going to kill someone, I feel sick inside. But if I don't do it, I know they'll harm another woman sometime, someplace, and there is no one else to stop them."

"I know that was difficult to admit to yourself, let alone to me."

The approval in his voice warmed her. She was startled to see him looming above her, but his hands began to work on her shoulders, those strong fingers digging into every tense muscle, and she subsided under his magic.

"There can be no mistake. When I heard your voice, my emotions returned. After centuries of living on memories, it was a little difficult not to be overwhelmed. My first thought was to find you and carry you off, as I believe my ancestors would have done. I see color. Your hair, all that soft, silky hair with so many colors blended together." He rubbed the strands between his fingers. "So beautiful."

She tried to stifle the little moan of pleasure his compliments elicited. She tried concentrating on the mouth of the dragon as those magic hands continued her massage right along her collarbone. The feeling was bone-melting. Her body began a delicious tingle, as if her nerve endings had begun to awaken all over again. That should have been alarming, but she was too relaxed under his ministrations to protest. He made her feel beautiful and cared for. He made her feel as if she really were his protected and safe lifemate.

"Why haven't you carried me off?" she asked. Her voice sounded faraway, drowsy. Maybe even a little sexy. Certainly not really her.

His hands cupped her breasts. Her stomach muscles bunched as he began a slow, gentle massage, and this time there was oil on his hands. Her heart pounded, drawing his attention to her accelerated pulse. "Carrying you off would not be right for you. For some women, yes, but you, my *kessake*, my little cat—you require seduction. Finesse. *Loving.* I have to earn your trust, and I would not want it any other way."

Her gaze jumped to his face when he tugged and rolled her nipples between his finger and thumb. He left behind a minty oil that began generating heat at the very tips of her breasts.

"Does that feel good, Solange? Your body is sexy, a temptation that is getting more difficult to resist. You are very responsive, and that is so seductive to me."

He bent his head and the long fall of silky midnight black hair spilled over her chest, teasing her senses as he sucked her nipple deep into his mouth and stroked with his tongue. She heard herself whimper, a soft, breathy sound that came close to a plea. He cupped both breasts, turned his head and found her other, woefully neglected nipple and drew it into his mouth, giving her left breast the same, unhurried loving attention. Pleasure was so intense she shook, her hips moving restlessly.

His hands stroked down her rib cage and over her belly. He found the tight little muscles and began his slow, leisurely massage. "Do you see, Solange, that you are the only woman in my world? The one woman who can choose life or death for me. You are the center of my world and you always will be. When I tell you that your pleasure is mine, I mean that literally. I can feel your body's response. I can feel your mind relax just as your muscles do, and it pleases me that I am the one, the only one, who can do that for you. I am the man your body responds to and your mind accepts."

His fingers slipped lower to her mound, massaged ever so gently, stroked lightly over her damp sex and moved to her inner thighs. Her breath exploded in a ragged rush as his hands continued that bone-melting kneading of her tight muscles. All the way down her calves to her feet, he kept kneading and stroking until she simply melted there on the table.

His hand on her shoulder urged her to turn over. She could barely summon the strength, already drifting in a state of arousal and relaxation. She turned her head to one side as he stretched out her arms by her sides and began work on her shoulders with his clever fingers.

"Why did you say I can't accompany you when you go to the gathering of the vampires, when you know I won't be able to stay away?" She murmured the words, her lashes falling as his hands went to her back.

He was using an oil of some sort. It smelled a little minty, and as he applied it, rubbing it into her muscles, heat spread. She wasn't certain if it was the oil, his hands or her body's response, but deep inside her core, her temperature soared. He worked down each arm and then down her lower back until she was nearly purring. A pure jaguar couldn't purr, but her species could, thankfully, and right now would be an appropriate moment.

"You cannot be close to me—or to them. The moment the parasites sense you they will go quiet and they'll know either you or Brodrick is near. We will need a good plan."

She rubbed her cheek against the soft padding of the table. "That's what you were trying to tell me, but I jumped to conclusions."

"I have given some thought to how I phrased it. Perhaps I could have chosen my words more carefully."

His hands on the small of her back felt wonderful. "I think you were being who you are, Dominic. You were named well. You have dominant tendencies. Unfortunately, although I doubt I was born with them, I've developed them."

"Your fighting skills are extraordinary, as is your courage in battle," he acknowledged.

His praise sent a warm glow through her. His hands moved lower, to her buttocks, working deep in the muscle, kneading thoroughly until her body was limp. He took a few moments to stroke gentle caresses over her lush curves before his hands moved her thighs apart. She thought of protesting; she was already aroused beyond what she thought she could bear. But this time he started with her feet, so she submitted, thinking herself safe.

How many times had she limped her way back to this cave, cold and bloody and sore, and wished just for this one thing—a massage. She remembered telling her dream man how she often fantasized about a massage. It warmed her that he remembered and cared enough to give her this amazing experience. She'd never felt so pampered in her life.

His hands worked their way steadily up her legs and her breath caught in her throat as he began pressing and rubbing above her knees. The strokes moved up higher, toward the junction of her legs, and she couldn't stop the flood of telltale damp heat. She actually could feel her sheath pulsing, empty and in need. A small sound escaped and she jammed her fist into her mouth. She should have told him to stop, but it felt like heaven.

"So what do you think we should do?" She tried to keep her mind on battle, on any distraction, but she was so aware of those strong fingers moving closer and closer to the place where she needed him most.

"I think we have a couple of days before the big meeting takes place. More vampires are in the area. I want to make certain they stay away from Zacarias's people."

She frowned. "Can you do that?"

"I am going to try. It will be a difficult safeguard to cast, and I will need blood to do it."

"I don't mind you taking mine," Solange said, and realized it was true. She would rather provide for him than have anyone else do so. In the end, when she'd gotten past her fear of being conquered, she'd found it an erotic experience.

His finger moved down her bottom, tracing the firm flesh and sliding across her very wet sex. She inhaled sharply and rolled over. She couldn't take one more moment of his hands on her. She'd never felt so needy in her life.

He stepped back and helped her to sit. She was too limp to stand. "I do not know if it is safe for me to take your blood, for either of us. Not until we get the information needed from the vampires."

"For either of us?" Solange found it hard to look at him. He was so gorgeous and she was so naked, her skin flushed, her breathing almost harsh. Hadn't he been as affected by touching her as she was by his touch?

"Your blood may be killing the parasites, and I need them," he explained. "As for you, the act of taking your blood is very sensual, and I dare not lose control and convert you. How are you feeling now?"

"I feel better. Thank you."

"More relaxed?"

She bit her lip. She didn't want to lie to him. He'd gone to a lot of trouble for her.

Two fingers lifted her chin. "What is it, *kessake ku toro sívamak*—beloved little wildcat? I thought we had established that when I ask a question, I require an answer. Is that not easy?"

She shook her head and attempted a smile. "Not as easy as you make it sound."

"What would you be afraid of telling me?"

Now she was embarrassed to sit in front of him completely naked, her body so unbearably aroused she could barely think straight, let alone find the right words to tell him. She felt vulnerable all over again. Why should it be so difficult to voice her sexual needs? What more did she want from him? The way he'd said that taking her blood was sensual, and the tone of his voice when he'd uttered *conversion* had sent her already aroused body into a shocking frenzy of need. She stilled; in spite of her raging body, desperate for release, she wasn't certain her brain would allow her to receive him without a fight. So classic jaguar and so difficult to explain.

"It's embarrassing and I don't want to disappoint you." There. She'd told him the truth. Okay. Maybe she'd whispered, but she managed to say the words without stammering.

"You only disappoint me when you do not trust me enough to share your needs."

How could she possibly describe the slow-building, burning, relentless ache that refused to give her rest? The silence stretched between them. He didn't move, his body still, his eyes on hers, refusing to allow her to look away.

"I'm very . . ." Her voice trailed off and she shook her head. "I feel as if I'm burning alive. I ache."

A slow smile briefly teased his mouth. His eyes warmed. "For me? Did I put that ache here?" His fingers slid down her bare stomach to the smooth mound. The pads of his fingers did a slow massage "Do I make you this way? Is all the wetness a welcome for me?"

She closed her eyes, her head falling back at his touch. Deep inside, her body began to pulse. "Of course for you. I didn't know I could feel this way."

"You should never hide from who you are, Solange. Or hide from your needs. Certainly you should never try to hide them from me. I am the only one to give you satisfaction. Do you understand what I am telling you? Only me. I want you to embrace yourself as a woman, as *my* woman. I have never understood why a woman should be unfulfilled sexually, or in any other way. Partners should trust one another enough to share their needs."

Very gently, he pressed his hand against her shoulder, forcing her to lie back down on the bench. "Just relax again and let me put you where I want you."

She swallowed her apprehension and let him shift her body so her bottom was at the end of the bench and her legs straddled the end of it. He opened her thighs, draping her there, her feet flat on the floor.

Her first instinct was to close her legs, but his hand rested on the inside of her knees so very gently, and she found she couldn't move. She tried to breathe evenly. He wasn't physically preventing her, but still, the power of his mind did. She didn't want him to stop, yet she felt so completely vulnerable. Her body was open to him, her most private center. She was a woman and she would have to accept invasion.

A small sob escaped. *Invasion.* Was that how she viewed sex? Making love? What was wrong with her? And how could he put up with her being so absolutely terrified of such a natural act? She wanted him. She needed him. She was extremely aroused, so much so that she knew her scent was pervading the air. But she didn't move. She *couldn't* move.

Dominic loomed over her nude body, completely clothed, and she found the situation even more arousing, especially when his heavy-lidded gaze drifted so possessively over her. She could see he was hard and thick and ready for her. *She* had done that. Solange Sangria, with her not-so-perfect body and her idiotic stammering ways and the millions of mistakes she made in a relationship. She had been the one to put that tremendous erection on such an amazing, powerful, very sensual man.

"When you let out those little breathy sobs, Solange, it should be out of pleasure, not because you are upset with your thoughts. You are not ready for joining with me yet.

When you are, you will want to take care of my needs. That will be the only thing on your mind. You will cease to exist other than to please me, as I do for you now. That is how it should be."

His fingers traced over her breasts and then he simply bent his head and took possession of her mouth. The shock of pleasure sent a current of electricity straight to her core. She moaned as his tongue tangled and dueled with hers. She'd never kissed a man this way. Not once. Nothing had prepared her for Dominic sweeping her into a sensual, dazzling world where her body refused to be her own. His claiming was the most dominating thing she'd ever experienced.

His mouth took command of hers and insisted on her compliance. She couldn't have stopped herself if she wanted to. Besides his compelling, seductive nature, she could taste the dark lust in him, the passion that welled up for her, so strong, like a raging river. He seemed to feed at her mouth, kissing her again and again, his strong hands framing her face while he devoured her.

Just when her arms began to circle his neck, he bit at her lower lip with just enough force to sting her, sending a jolt of fire darting from her breasts to her sex. She moaned again as he kissed his way down to the swell of her breasts. He nuzzled there for a moment while her heart jumped and her hips grew even more restless.

"I love how you sound. So sexy," he murmured against her nipple.

Before she could reply he drew her breast inside that scalding-hot cauldron of his mouth, sucking strongly, his tongue flicking and licking, alternating with his fingers as they tugged and rolled her nipple. She heard her own broken cry and her hips bucked. She hadn't known she could be so sensitive. She arched her back, giving him better access, compulsively circling his head with her arms. She tried to stifle the small sobs of need as all discipline and thought deserted her. Small lights burst behind her eyes, and sensation overwhelmed her.

He lavished attention on her breasts. She felt the scrape of his teeth and heard the change in his breathing—for her. All for her. He was in her mind, heightening her pleasure, showing her his. He loved her breasts. He could spend hours suckling there, feasting, teasing and tormenting. Some of the images in his head were shocking, but still very erotic, and she was willing, in that moment, to give him anything if he would just relieve the terrible building pressure in her body.

His hair swept her stomach as he kissed his way down, pausing for a just a moment to tease her belly button before he moved lower still. "This is why," he murmured against her bare mound, "I do not want anything between my mouth and your skin. I want you to feel everything I can give you."

His hands cupped her bottom and he lifted her hips to his mouth, his tongue sweeping over her in a languid, almost lazy lick. She jumped, her cry shocking her. That desperate, needy sound couldn't have been her.

"Mmm. Delicious. You taste like nectar to me. I hope you enjoy yourself, *kessake*, because I have the feeling this will be a favorite pastime."

He took his time at first, a gentle, slow torment while he kissed and licked and explored until she was writhing under his mouth. His tongue plunged deep and the breath hissed out of her. And then he stroked that hard little button where every nerve ending centered. She nearly convulsed with rapture.

Dominic feasted, exactly as if this were his favorite pastime. His expert tongue never stopped, and when he flicked and then suckled her clit, her shattered cries became pleas.

He took his time, his fingers plunging deep while he lapped at her cream. Tremors rolled through her as she moaned brokenly, desperate for release. Her heart raced so fast, almost in time to the pulsing in her womb. Her body wound tighter and tighter until the sensation was nearly unbearable. She tried to push herself onto his mouth; her hips bucked uncontrollably. The hunger in her built and built with no end in sight. She was afraid she was going insane, thrashing on the table, her cries and pleas filling the room.

His relentless mouth didn't stop, his tongue flicking her small, inflamed button, fast and slow, then plunging deep to draw out more nectar, pushing her beyond every limit she'd ever considered, beyond any imagining. She sobbed, begged and promised him anything if he would just allow her release. Her hips rose pushing into his mouth helplessly. His torment was exquisite, a pleasure so deep it bordered on pain.

"Dominic, please," she pleaded. "I need . . ."

Me. You need me.

The words reverberated in her mind. He lifted his head and his eyes glittered, almost ruby red, a feral, dark promise nearly stopping her heart. Then he bent his head and sucked once more on her most sensitive spot, his tongue flicking hard and fast. Two fingers penetrated her and she choked, screaming as her body clamped down like a vise, the orgasm rolling over her fast and hard, so that her back arched and her hips ground against his hand.

Tears rolled down her face, and when she lifted her hand to wipe them away, he moved over her. He brushed the sweat from her skin as if it had never been there, tasting her tears as if they were a fine wine, stroking back her damp hair while she came down from the earth-shattering ripples of pure bliss. He was infinitely gentle, so tender she felt wrapped in a cocoon of love when she had long ago forgotten there was such a thing. He was giving her something beyond price, and it wasn't the rapture of his lovemaking. He made her feel hope again.

His soothing voice whispered to her, telling her how beautiful she was. When she found the energy she lifted her hand and traced the lines in his face, the small webbing of scars that ran down to his shoulder.

"I feel like I'm in the middle of one of those fairy tales my aunt used to tell us." Her voice trembled, her lashes were wet and spiky and her mouth quivered. "Are you real, Dominic? Do I dare believe in you?"

He lifted her into his arms, cradling her close to his chest. "Yes."

She stared into his compelling eyes. He didn't move or speak. Just waited. She was coming to know him now. He didn't mind the time it took for her to figure things out. If she needed time, he provided it. Something inside her shifted. She felt a little exposed; that small nugget of trust was taking hold, and it made her so vulnerable to him. She'd never allowed herself to need anyone; it was too easy for death to take them. She'd learned that lesson at a very early age. No one was safe. Not parents, not baby brothers. Not best friends. No one. If she dared to love them, they soon were torn from her.

"You didn't let me give back to you," she whispered.

"You have given me more than you can know, *kessake*. You are exhausted. We will rest now, and tomorrow you will eat properly."

She smiled at him, too tired to point out that he sounded like he was giving orders. And maybe he was. But right now, she desperately needed to go to sleep. She didn't even care that he opened the ground and floated them down into it, holding her close.

13

My dream lover and lifemate,
You know every part of me.
We're bound forever, soul to soul.
You hold the very heart of me.

DOMINIC TO SOLANGE

Dominic lay without breath one moment, and then the next his heart began a strong rhythm, air pushed through his lungs and his eyes snapped open. Fully alert, he dropped his fingers into the soft thick fur covering him. Sometime during the day Solange had shifted to her jaguar form. Something had disturbed her enough that she felt she might need her animal form to protect them while he slept.

Minan, are you awake? He poured love into his voice. The sun had not yet set, but it was close. His body felt the prickle of awareness that told him the night sky had not yet descended to keep his skin protected.

Do you hear them? Is that what woke you? They have been working around the cave entrance for some time, but your safeguards are holding. Brodrick is not with them.

The female jaguar lifted her muzzle and stretched languidly, as only a cat could do, but she unsheathed her claws, testing them as well. The ropes of sleek muscles rippled beneath her luxurious pelt of rich tawny color and dark rosettes.

There is no need for you to rise yet, she added. *I can lead them away if they get too close. I've been thinking the situation over and I know where I'll take them.*

That was his woman. Calm. Matter-of-fact when it came to facing death. She could handle a fearsome battle with such ease, and yet when she faced him as a woman, she was shy and vulnerable. The contrast between her two sides was one of the many things he found intriguing about her. She was his woman alone. No other man would ever see her body, sexy and soft and flushed with color, so aroused, just for him alone. She would never get that confused, dazed look in her eyes for anyone else. The Solange the world saw was only one side of her; he had both, and that pleased him immensely.

"I was hoping to wake you with a kiss this morning." His amusement spilled over into his voice.

The jaguar turned her head toward him, mischief in her brilliant green eyes. Her long tongue came out and rasped over his face. He burst out laughing. The jaguar grinned at him, very pleased with her work. Dominic shoved her off him, using his enormous strength, tumbling the cat off of his body and into the rich soil, and then he dove on top of her.

Solange twisted out of his way so that he landed in a crouch a foot from her. She kept rolling, came to her feet and sprang at him. He dissolved into vapor.

That is so cheating, she accused, her cat's eyes watching

the vapor stream out of the deep pit up to the cavern floor. He knew she didn't mind: She had her own skills. She could leap a good twenty feet and run up to thirty miles an hour. She had a flexible spine and radar that said he was . . . His soft laughter taunted her. She was looking in the wrong spot.

She leapt to the surface after him, looking around for him. She could smell him but not see him. She looked up. Dominic dropped from the ceiling and landed astride her back, wrapping his legs around her belly and his arms tightly around her neck. She rolled instantly, over and over, felt his hold loosen. Using her enormous strength, she sprang a good ten feet straight into the air, came down with her head toward the ground and threw him over her muzzle. He landed on his back, and before he could dissolve again, she pounced on his chest.

Laughing, he literally lifted her, tossing her through the air, somersaulting and coming up onto his feet. She was fast and strong and he could feel joy bursting through him at their rough-and-tumble play. He had all but forgotten playing.

Solange twisted in midair, landed across the room and charged, standing up on her hind legs at the last moment as they came together, her large front paws on his broad shoulders, his hands on hers. They danced in a circle, each exerting force on the other, trying to push the other over. Dominic suddenly went in close, belly to belly, wrapping his arms around her, aching for her unexpectedly.

Shift. I want to feel you shifting into my arms. He knew there was seduction in his voice. His body was unrelenting in its need of hers, and the urgent demands were becoming more difficult to ignore, even with his centuries of discipline. He wanted to wake up to her soft lush curves, even if he couldn't have her yet. It was necessary to kiss the perfection of her mouth, and if he'd unconsciously used his hypnotic voice—which had little effect on her royal . . . bloodline—he couldn't help it.

She laughed softly, the sound shimmering through every nerve ending in his body. He felt her mind slide against his. *You were thinking "royal pain in the ass," but changed your mind just in case I was listening in, didn't you?*

He rubbed his head against the thick, rich fur of the jaguar's muzzle. *I was thinking about your beautiful bottom, that much is true. Shift, right now, while I am holding you.* It was an extremely difficult maneuver, just as shifting on the run was.

Are you challenging me? I could do it, you know.

He felt her glow at his certainty. Her mind turned softer, more intimate, and she opened more to him, as if his approval of her allowed her to relax in his company just a little more.

I'll be of more help hunting in this form.

True, and you can shift back when we go, but right now I would like to hold my woman and tell her good evening. Which was all true, although he wanted to map her body with his hands—and his mouth—and commit every curve and valley to memory for all time.

He felt the movement in her mind first, that initial breathtaking moment when the woman reached for her form; the quick, intelligent mind; the soft, almost shy beginnings of sensuality; of awareness; the hesitation of finding herself naked in his arms; the quick summoning of courage to do as he asked—because she loved pleasing him. She craved the approval in his eyes, in his mind, and that small smile he always gave her when she did something he asked. That was not only humbling, but a tremendous responsibility.

He felt the wrench in her bones, heard the popping and

cracking of a shifter in transformation. Fur slid along his arms and chest and then receded. The muzzle retracted. The jaguar turned her head away from him, dropping her chin to protect her exposed throat.

Look at me. Look into my eyes. He could not lose the intensity of the moment. Seeing her come to him. He *needed* this moment. He had to look into her cat's eyes and see his woman coming to him. Emerging for him alone. She would never do such a thing near anyone else, let someone witness the total vulnerability of such a moment when she was completely at his mercy, unable to protect herself as jaguar or human.

Those amazing green eyes glittered at him. All intelligence. Seeing him—inside of him. He locked gazes with her, holding her to him in her most defenseless moment, seeing the wrenching fear, drinking in her fight to trust him with her life, with the very essence of who she really was. He knew she was fighting her own nature, that elusive, wild nature that insisted she remain secretive, hidden from the world. But for him, she fought to expose herself in her weakest position. Her eyes changed subtly, still tilted, still enormous, but far more human. She looked almost terrified, but she didn't look away, nor did she flinch from him as her much more petite shape slid against his.

Dominic held her silky soft curves tight against the hardness of his body, watching the expression in her eyes change from fear to joy. Her long lashes fluttered, and that sweet shyness slipped into those brilliant green eyes, a look that sent every protective instinct he had rushing to the surface. Still holding her gaze, he bent his head to hers, taking his time, inch by slow inch, waiting to see her find her natural sensuality. He needed her to want him just as much as he needed the soil that each day rejuvenated him.

Her eyes went slumberous, sexy. Her lips parted in

anticipation. He took her breath as his lips settled over hers. His hands slid down to the curves of her very royal bottom and he lifted her up around his waist, all while his mouth kept possession of hers.

He was very hard, his erection full and painful, and for a moment he rested her heated entrance right over the throbbing, mushroom head of his cock, the temptation almost more than he could bear. But she had to know for certain he was what she wanted, and as much as he didn't want to admit it to himself, she still didn't have full trust in him. She hadn't given herself over completely to him.

He set her back on the woven rug, his hands skimming her body as he kissed her. When he lifted his head, she looked a little dazed, confused and even disappointed.

"Good evening, Solange," he greeted.

Her half-smile turned to a frown when her gaze dropped to the heavy erection grazing her stomach. "I don't understand. You clearly want me."

"Yes." He smiled down at her, his thumb tracing that little frown on her face.

"I want you."

"A little. Not enough. You have doubts, Solange."

Her gaze shifted from his, just a small flick, but it was enough to tell him he was right. She shook her head. "I do want you. My body is in a constant state of arousal."

That had been difficult for her to admit. He could tell she had to make a tremendous effort to tell him the truth, but he felt triumphant that she had. She was far closer to accepting him than he had realized.

"As is mine," he agreed. "The difference, *kessake*, is that I *need* to take care of your needs. You want to take care of your own needs as well."

She opened her mouth to protest and then abruptly

closed it, her frown deepening. She studied his face and then her gaze drifted back to his very large, unashamed erection. "Isn't it supposed to be mutual?"

"Not for me. I need to feel your acceptance, Solange. In your mind, in your heart. In your very soul. When you burn to please me, when it is the only thing that matters to you, then I will know you accept me."

"I do accept you, Dominic." Her lashes lowered and her bottom lip trembled slightly.

He stroked his fingers down her cheek, infinitely gentle. "When I take your body, Solange, there can be no room for doubt in your mind. No matter what I ask of you, you will trust me enough to do it without question because you will know every single thought I have is for you. Your safety. Your health. Your comfort. If I made love to you now, it would satisfy your body, but you would still question whether I love you for yourself or because I have to."

She flinched. He'd definitely read her correctly. She was worried about that. She didn't understand how he could fall in love with her. She didn't even believe it was possible.

"I'm not a nice person, Dominic."

He caught her chin in his hand and forced her head up until her green gaze met his. "Neither am I, Solange. Not in the way polite society would view me. I take lives just as you do. I make life-and-death decisions every day and have for centuries. I do not doubt myself in the way you do, perhaps because I have been chasing the undead for so long."

"It isn't the same thing. Jaguar-men are my own people."

"I killed my best friend while I still had my emotions, Solange. And I would have killed Zacarias had you not interfered. You saved his life."

She sighed. "I just don't want you to have a false impression of who I am."

He laughed softly. "I look into your mind and see a beautiful soul. You shine for me. Now get dressed in one of your robes and eat something. We will be hunting later."

She took a deep breath and let it out. Just as she turned, she brushed her fingers over his heavy erection. His cock jerked. Every nerve ending fired. She gave him a sassy smile and walked to the small alcove, and her hips held a definite enticing sway. He couldn't stop the predatory smile.

He watched as she pulled out the long red metallic duster. "The green one. I want to see if it matches your eyes."

"The green one?"

There was a little hiccup in her voice. She wasn't quite ready to put on a micromini and parade around in front of him with nothing else but the formfitting, ultra-revealing sheath. He was pushing her comfort zone, hard, but he wasn't certain how much longer he could hold out. He had gone from wanting her trust to *needing* it.

Solange moistened her lips, but didn't turn around. She hesitated, but managed to force herself to put the red duster back and pull the green ladder dress out. It took a little wiggling to get it over her hips. The stretchy material clung to every curve. The ladder, made of thin strips, crept down the front and back, leaving much of her skin bare. The spaghetti straps settled onto her shoulders as if made for her, which, she realized, it had been. That gave her a little more confidence.

She brushed out her thick, wavy hair before really looking at herself in the full-length mirror. The dress not only brought out her eyes but showed off her body. The ladder bared her breasts, the fabric barely covering her nipples. As it was nearly see-through, she could see how beaded her nipples were right through the material. The ladder formed a V down to the hem of the dress so that her belly button showed through the thin slats and she even caught glimpses of her mound when she moved. She turned to look over her shoulder. Her back and bottom were covered only with the thin strips as well. She could just see the bottom half of her cheeks peeking out at her.

She stared at herself, shocked at how aroused just dressing in such a revealing sheath made her feel. It was sexy, and knowing Dominic had made it for her gave her the confidence to wear it. She wanted him to be in such a state of urgent need that the next time she found an opportunity, he wouldn't be able to resist her.

When she walked into the cavern, the soft lights played over the walls, the flame burned in the pool and a table was set with candles. He was dressed in a suit. Tall. Handsome. *Gorgeous.* He was heart-stopping with his long hair pulled back with a leather cord and his ever-changing eyes a vivid turquoise. His broad shoulders and narrow hips were made for an elegant suit. He appeared more Old World than ever. Very gallantly he took her hand, and with a small half-bow, kissed her knuckles, tucked her fingers into the crook of his elbow and walked her to the table. He pulled out her chair and waited for her to sit.

"I can hear your heart beat," he whispered as he leaned down, his mouth by her ear as he pushed in her chair. "It follows the rhythm of mine."

To Dominic's surprise and pleasure, Solange smiled up at him, and there was seduction in her smile. She shifted just an inch, but her breasts strained against the small thin strips of material, drawing his attention. His fingers drifted over the stretchy fabric to linger for a moment on her nipples.

"You please me, Solange, doing what I asked of you. Thank you."

"I wanted to see that look in your eyes," she admitted, lowering her gaze.

He opened his hand and showed her the two dangling earrings, the rubies and emeralds matching her bracelet. "May I?"

"Please." She held very still while he put them in her ears. She expected it to hurt, but it didn't. She touched one. "The green matches the dress."

"The stones match your eyes," he corrected gently. "And what look in my eyes?"

He walked around to the other side of the small table and sat down in the chair opposite her. He reached for a bottle and poured a sparkling liquid into her wineglass and a much darker one into his. The candlelight played over her face, caressing her soft skin and illuminating her cat's eyes. Need punched low and wicked, an instant and rather brutal assault on his body. She was so beautiful to him, inside and out, whether she thought so or not.

"I like the way you look at me," she said, "like you're pleased with me when I do something so simple as to wear what you ask." She ran her hand along her thigh. "It's a beautiful dress. But aren't you worried about the jaguars hunting close by?"

His gaze followed the nervous progression of her palm as it smoothed over her bare thigh. The dress was very sexy, her body breathtaking in the soft flickering lights. He loved how the light played over her face. She wasn't adept at hiding her thoughts from him, and he found himself nearly flying when he touched her mind and saw her desire to please him—that making him happy made her excited. She was beginning to see herself as he saw her: feminine and sexy and wholly his.

He indicated for her to take a bite of her steak. He waited for her to do as he requested before answering. "Actually, I doubt they are hunting us. They seem more nervous, not actually hunting. Too many vampires in one area means anyone with warm blood is going to be in danger."

She pushed around the small bites on her plate. "How you managed all this, I'll never know."

"I have never sat down to a table and shared a meal," he said. "This is a new and very pleasant experience for me."

He found he couldn't take his eyes from her. Everything she did delighted him. The way she chewed and swallowed. Her nervous little glances. The hand that drifted down to tug at the impossibly short hem of her dress. Each time she shifted in her chair, her bare bottom slid over the polished wood and he caught a glimpse of the enthralling temptation between her legs.

He leaned across the table and waited until she raised her lashes. "I dream of taking your body over and over, while you are slick and hot with your sweet-tasting nectar. I love to hear the way you moan and whimper, such beautiful music, my little cat. I want to hear you beg me never to leave your body."

He kept his tone the same, as if they were discussing jaguars and vampires. Her eyes went wide. Her body flushed and she shifted restlessly in her chair. He caught the scent of arousal. Her small tongue darted out to lick nervously at her lips. Beneath the thin green fabric, her nipples grew harder.

"You can't say things like that to me."

"It is true." He nodded toward the bowl of fruit. "You need to eat some of that as well."

"I can't eat when you say things like that." She pushed her hair from where it tumbled around her face. Her hands trembled. "I think, since we've been home, I've been in a constant state of arousal."

"Is that a bad thing?" Her eyes intrigued him, but it was

that little reprimand in her voice that sent a wave of heat through his body.

"It is when we're supposed to be concentrating on planning out how you're going to survive walking into a meeting with who knows how many vampires, all of whom would love to tear you apart and feast on your blood."

"Before I consider trying to survive vampires, I have to figure out a way to survive this relentless ache you have put here. It refuses to go away, Solange." His hand deliberately dropped to his immaculate trousers, calling attention to the thick bulge there. "And you put it there."

Her eyes changed. The almost painfully shy woman disappeared, only to be replaced by a temptress. She flashed a small, rather smug smile as she picked up the glass of sparkling champagne even as she shifted again in her chair, drawing his attention to her lush breasts. "It's very gratifying to know I'm not the only one suffering."

His voice dropped an octave. "Are you suffering?"

She licked the drops of champagne from her lips. "You know I am."

"Why?"

"I've had a few dreams of my own," she pointed out. "While you sleep, I am thinking of all the things I'd like to do to you."

"Now you have my full attention." He sat back in his chair, his heart beginning to thunder. At last. She was thinking of *him* and how best to give him pleasure. He could see the determination in her expression and that sexy, intriguing tilt to her mouth.

"Actually," she corrected, playing with the stem of her glass, "I *always* have your full attention, your complete, absolute focus. You make me feel not only beautiful, but important and sexy and everything you need. You make me feel important."

"You are all of those things."

She ate another bite of her steak, a small frown of concentration on her face. "I've had a lot of time to think about things while you were sleeping, and I realized it's really all about courage. I have to find the courage to put myself totally into your hands." She looked up at him then, her eyes showing that same determination, but this time mixed with fear. "That's what you're saying to me, isn't it?"

He nodded. In that moment of self-discovery, she was more beautiful than ever to him.

"You want me to recognize this side of me is every bit as important as the fighter in me."

"Important not only to me, Solange," he agreed, "but to you as well."

"It's much easier to contemplate all of this when I'm in my jaguar form. I feel safe."

"I want you to feel safe with me."

Her eyebrow shot up. "Yes and no," she pointed out, proving to him that she was every bit as shrewd and intelligent as he'd suspected. "You like me a little off balance with you. I get the feeling that tangling with you is a bit like trying to play with fire." The pulse in the side of her neck fluttered. "I don't want to get burned."

He flashed a predatory smile at her. "Only you can decide if it is worthwhile to give yourself into my care. Only you can decide to trust me with your heart, Solange."

She took a bite of apple, her expression thoughtful. "If we do this, Dominic—"

"When," he corrected. "When we do this. Because, *kessake*, there is no question that you belong to me. You will come to accept me eventually." She was so close. He could feel her reaching for him in her mind, wanting to give herself to him, but fear of betrayal held her paralyzed. He loved that she was working it out, analyzing each step cautiously, just as her cat would. Her reticence endeared her to him even more.

She took a breath. "*When* we do this, we'll have a future. What does that mean to you?"

"I would bind you to me, of course," he said, locking his gaze with hers so she was unable to look away.

She swallowed almost convulsively. "Okay, I get that. But then what?"

"I will take your blood—and your body—and make you wholly mine." There was no compromise in his voice, or in his eyes.

Her breasts heaved as she drew in a ragged breath. She put down her fork and once again picked up the crystal flute. "You always make everything sound so simple."

"It is very simple, Solange. When we are in a battle, you trust me with your life, as I do you. Here, when we are alone, you need to give me that same trust. I already have your complete honesty, and you are more loyal than anyone I have ever known. I give those same things back to you at all times."

She moistened her lips again. "I trust you," she said. There was hesitation in her voice.

He smiled at her. "You are beginning to trust me, and I find that an amazing gift. I thank you for your belief in me. You sit there wearing a dress I made for you because you want to please me. And you do, very, very much."

She flushed a soft pink, the color enhancing the green of her eyes. "Dominic, what about after? Juliette was converted. MaryAnn, too. Are all lifemates converted?"

"As a rule, but it is a choice. If you chose not to, you would grow old and die, and then, of course, I would choose to age and die when you left this life for the next."

The flame in the candle leapt, throwing a dark shadow across the wall. Dominic was on his feet immediately. No enemy could penetrate his safeguards. He knew that. Yet . . . He turned slowly, tracking the dark shadow.

I caught sight of him for just a moment. He blends into the dark when he ceases all movement.

Solange pulled the dress from over her head and laid it carefully over the back of her chair as if it was precious to her. There was no panic in her movements, and he wanted to smile at her. She was the right woman for him, no question about it. All business. Everything else set aside, all doubts and fears gone so that his strong warrior went back-to-back with him against any adversary.

Vampire? Jaguar? He couldn't scent an enemy, but every instinct told him they were no longer alone.

I don't think so. My jaguar may be of more use.

She shifted without asking him if she should, trusting her own instincts as she always had in battle. In spite of the danger, he felt the first whisper of unease at the idea of losing her. *She* had been the one to worry about what would happen should something happen to him, but in that oddest of moments, he knew he wouldn't want to face life without Solange. Without her fierce fighting spirit and the sensual, shy woman he was coming to know.

Let me in front of you.

Every muscle in his belly tied itself into a tight knot of protest. He didn't know what they were dealing with. She hadn't really asked him, so much as told him she needed to get closer and the warrior said yes while the man said no. He found he was at war with his own instincts.

My cat is raging already. She knows we have company.

She made no demands, simply waited. Dominic couldn't bring himself to step behind the large animal, but he glided to the side of her. She crouched low and raised her muzzle.

He likes the dark. Light the room.

Dominic did so without hesitation and caught a glimpse

of something skittering across the walls into the crack of the nearest pool, where the water streamed in. He couldn't identify it, but now that he was merged with Solange, his senses tuned differently and he could "feel" the creature. He didn't have the same sense of it as Solange. She and the cat were one and the same, and she could make sense of the pattern in the jaguar's mind.

I've never encountered anything like it.

Tell me.

It seems very small, much like a house cat, but shadowy, as if it might not be all substance. It came in through the water, so it swims.

He had seen four distinct legs, so it was an animal, or at least had been. *Claws? Webbed feet perhaps?*

Dominic inhaled sharply and noted the jaguar relied on her hearing and sight. There was little scent to betray the creature, so he couldn't identify it that way.

Maybe both. It moved into the dark before I could really get a sense of it. I heard fur slide along the wall of the cave. A whisper only, she informed him.

Is it hunting us?

It is hunting something. I don't scent fear. Do you?

He didn't. Now that he knew where the creature was hiding, he dissolved into vapor, streaking across the room to pour into the crack. A howl filled the cavern, and the thing launched itself into the center of the room, clearing a good twenty feet, growing in size as it soared through the air, claws outstretched, aiming for the jaguar's eyes.

Solange twisted away at the last second, and the claws raked deep furrows across her neck and down her side as it dropped to the floor. Dominic, merged as he was with Solange, felt the burst of raw, burning pain as the shadow cat attacked. She whipped around and slashed at the intruder.

Her huge paw went right through the insubstantial creature. It took a second bound and scurried into the shadows near the boulders and the entrance to the chamber, once more diminished into a small, almost house cat size.

Are you all right? He kept the worry out of his voice. It would do neither of them any good. She could handle herself in a fight—even against vampires. This—*thing*—would not ruffle her.

She gave the mental equivalent of a shrug, reinforcing his belief in her. *What is it?*

Something very dangerous. Dominic emerged once again by her side. *Move away from me, but give yourself plenty of room if it attacks again.*

You think it's hunting me? Again, her voice was very calm.

We will test that theory. I will give it a shot at me.

He heard her catch her breath, but she didn't protest, trusting that he knew what he was doing. He moved to block the creature's vision of the jaguar, filling the cave with his power and presence, growing in stature. Solange remained very small behind him, crouching close to the ground but, he noted, out away from the walls where she had room to maneuver.

Dominic concentrated on trying to reach the creature with his mind. There was nothing at all. Not blank, like the undead, an abomination of nature, might leave, but truly nothing, as if the creature wasn't real. He considered that. A hallucination he shared with Solange? He knew that would be possible, though unlikely. He was an ancient and difficult to trick. And the blood staining the jaguar's coat was very real.

The sound of dirt trickling down the cavern wall was his only warning. He turned his head and caught a glimpse of a shadow scurrying across the ceiling above his head, look-ing like a streak of black, lengthening with each bound.

Coming at you, he warned as he leapt into the air to try to get his hands on the thing.

His palms met, going right through the shadow cat, but he felt hot breath, and just as the creature sprang past him, the brush of rough fur.

Solange met the cat in midair, this time driving with her broad muzzle and a mouthful of teeth deep into its chest wall. Again, she passed through the cat, but it whirled as she began to drop, gripping her back with his claws and sinking teeth into her neck, driving her down to the floor. She rolled, roaring, as the teeth drove deeper, finding her vein.

Dominic struck hard, tearing the cat from Solange's back and dragging it away from her. He felt the fur, the heavy muscles and the spray of blood across his face, and then the creature was insubstantial again, sliding through his grip to once more become nothing but a shadow.

Solange! Talk to me.

Her breath hissed out in a quiet agony. She shifted, clamping a hand to her neck. Blood poured between her fingers. Dominic whirled around and pulled her to him, pressing his palm to the wound to cauterize and stop the flow of precious blood.

The creature sprang to the floor, once more emerging into substance, lapping ferociously at the blood on the ground.

Close your eyes. As a precaution he shielded her eyes himself, clapping his hand over her face.

Flames leapt from the candle on the table, joining with one rising from the bottom of the basin. White-light radi-ated throughout the cave, a blinding beam of heat that struck the creature before it could slip away. It shrieked and burst into blue-purple flames, spreading across the room, growing into a giant shape with a huge gaping mouth filled with spiked teeth. The legs went stiff and the spine bent.

Dominic could see small tube-like appendages inside the mouth filled with blood—Solange's blood—and his heart skipped a beat as realization dawned instantly. The shadow cat had been sent by someone to collect her blood. Someone else knew about her royal blood and wanted it for their own evil purposes.

The creature's eyes turned on Dominic for the first time, seemingly just noticing him. The eyes whirled, black to red, vague and empty. Suddenly, for one heart-stopping moment, they went a glittering silver, cunning intelligence staring into the room, searching.

Before those eyes could focus on them, Dominic took Solange straight to the ground, covering her body with his, his hand still over her eyes as the mouth grotesquely opened wider and the silver eyes quartered the room.

Dominic flicked his hand at the fire, fanning the air into a turbulent whirlwind that sent the flames into a wild burning ball. The silver eyes turned back to the vacant blue-purple. The mouth yawned wider, emitting a harrowing scream of horror as the flames consumed the creature. In the midst of the flames Dominic could see a tiny black sliver of a shadow desperately trying to separate and slink toward the water. Dominic directed a fireball at it, watching with satisfaction as the last remnant turned to ash, completely incinerated. A foul stench permeated the air, and again he sent the wind crashing through the cavern to air it out.

Beneath him, Solange was utterly still. He lifted his hand away from her eyes and swept back her hair, his heart thundering hard.

"Talk to me, *minan*."

She stirred, blinked up at him—and smiled. His heart stuttered. There was blood covering his hand, coating her neck and shoulder, there were deep furrows torn from her skin along her ribs and down her left hip, but she smiled at him. Her green eyes were totally clear. He could see pain reflected there, but she pushed herself into a sitting position, one hand coming up to touch his face.

"Don't look at me like that. I'm fine. I've had worse. Thanks for stopping the bleeding. I might not have been able to do that myself."

She shivered and he instantly wrapped a blanket around her, the comforter with all the healing symbols on it. Solange shook her head. "I don't want to get blood on this. It's so beautiful and I'd hate to ruin it."

"Leave it," he commanded, holding the blanket in place. "I can get blood out. Just sit there for a minute, Solange, while I clean you up. You are in shock."

"No, just shocked that that thing was able to get past your safeguards and come in right under our noses. He should have killed me. He was sucking my blood out fast, rather than trying to finish me off. What was it?" Her voice was low and husky, as if her throat had been damaged in the attack. She cleared her throat several times and coughed, bringing her hand up to her mouth to cover it.

Dominic pulled her hand down. Her palm was smeared with blood. He lifted her and opened the earth, floating them down into the rich soil. He wrapped her in the comforter. "I'm going to heal you, *kessake*. Just rest. We will discuss this next rising. In the meantime, I will safeguard even our water and the very cracks in the rocks."

She touched his face again. "I'm really okay, Dominic." Her lashes fluttered and drifted down.

Dominic felt the soft whisper of fear creeping down his

spine, a whisper that grew into fingers of terror when her breathing became labored. *Solange. Do not leave me!* The pain was sharp and terrible and so unexpected. She was wound tight in his heart. He gave her the command with every ounce of strength he had and set about working frantically on her. It took him three times going outside himself and into her before he spotted the tiny venom drops left behind by the murderous shadow cat.

14

My dream lover and lifemate,
You know every part of me.
We're bound forever, soul to soul.
You hold the very heart of me.

SOLANGE TO DOMINIC

Solange became aware slowly, inch by inch, rather than all at once as she normally did. She could hear her heart slamming hard in her chest and her pulse roaring in her ears. Her mind felt slow and hazy and her body sore. She was very disoriented and couldn't quite get her eyes to open, which terrified her. She began to struggle, trying to fight her way out of sleep, knowing she was never safe and that waking was one of her most vulnerable moments.

"I am with you, Solange."

Dominic's voice penetrated the layers of fear she felt at not being able to function properly, and she subsided, aware she was in his arms. At once she felt safe and protected, a feeling she was entirely unfamiliar with. She could smell his masculine scent and she inhaled to draw him deeper into her lungs. The tension receded even more.

She moistened her dry lips and reached for her voice. "What happened?" Her throat was very sore and she was very thirsty.

"You were attacked by a shadow creature." His hands swept back her hair. "Try to open your eyes for me, *hän sívamak*—beloved. You have given me a little bit of a scare and I have to tell you, that does not make me happy."

She couldn't help the smile at the edge to his voice. She had scared him, that was obvious, and he didn't like it. Somehow that warmed her even more.

He leaned close, his lips against her ear. "Do not look pleased after I have been fighting for your life these two risings. I am not above punishing you for scaring me."

Her lashes fluttered and she clamped down hard on the surge of laughter at the male irritation in his voice that was so unlike Dominic. She had apparently driven him to the edge of his patience and she hadn't even been conscious. "If I get punished every time I scare you, I think we're going to be in trouble."

She found the energy to lift her lashes. His face came into focus. All those hard, tough edges. That gorgeous face. His eyes, midnight blue, dark with worry. She could see strain where there never had been. He actually looked exhausted. The hours of trying to save her had taken their toll, and it didn't look as if the soil had rejuvenated him much.

"I'm sorry, Dominic."

He kissed her, a long, slow, incredibly tender kiss. Tears welled up in her eyes and she blinked them away. She could feel his body trembling against hers.

"I really am sorry. The injury didn't seem like a big

deal," she reiterated. "I knew you could stop the bleeding so I wasn't worried."

"The creature injected three drops of venom into your bloodstream. It took me several healing sessions to find them. I knew something was wrong, you were slipping further and further from me."

"Poison?"

He shook his head. "I do not think the intent was to kill you. You had a reaction to the venom. If the intent had been to kill you, the shadow cat would have injected a lethal dose."

She indicated she wanted to sit up. He moved, retaining his hold on her, allowing her to sit up very cautiously. She felt slightly nauseated, but after taking a few deep breaths, managed to maintain. "What was it?"

"If I had to guess, I'd say it was very much like the high mage's familiars. Xavier has been destroyed, I know that to be true, but I studied him for years. He used creatures to do his spying. In all of my centuries, I have never encountered anything quite like it, but I have had time to consider it. The safeguards did not stop it because it came through the water as a shadow. They must have gotten a blood sample, some way to track you specifically."

She inhaled sharply. "Brodrick. His jaguar bit and clawed me. My blood would have been all over him. I haven't seen mages too often in this area, but once in a while, one shows up. He must have used one to track me."

"The creature was taking more of your blood back to whoever sent it. I think the venom was to paralyze you so you would be unable to resist should they return to take you prisoner."

Dominic's voice was grim and she flicked him a quick, under-the-lashes glance. She rubbed her hand over his set jaw where a muscle ticked, giving away his underlying mood of suppressed fury.

"Dominic, no matter where we are, we are going to have enemies. Both of us. You must have made many in your centuries of existence, and I certainly have here. Whatever they intended to do with me isn't going to happen. You prevented that."

"They attacked you in our home, right under my nose."

"*Our* noses," she corrected gently. She locked gazes with him. "What is really upsetting you, Dominic?"

His breath hissed out between his teeth and his eyes spun into a glacier green. "I gave you my word that you would be safe with me when we were alone. Someone nearly killed you and not only did it scare the hell out of me—all those hours of desperately trying to find what was hiding from me while you slipped, inch by inch, away from me—but I had to face the fact that I failed you."

A slow smile lit her eyes and she leaned into him to nuzzle his neck. "My God, Dominic, you're not perfect. How very shocking is that?" She laughed softly. "You kept me safe. I'm not dead, am I? If the situation had been reversed, I doubt I could have saved you. I don't have your ability to heal."

He wrapped his arms around her, crushing her to him. For a moment she thought she was in danger of every rib cracking, but she melted against him, unresisting, recognizing he needed to hold her as close as possible. When his strength gentled and allowed an inch between them, she tilted her head to look up at his face.

The night had taken a toll on him. Her unflappable, calm-under-every-circumstance man had been extremely distraught over her. "Let's track the thing back to the sender," she suggested. "My jaguar won't be too much help at first, not through the water. I'll have to go around to the source, but you can follow through the cracks where the water came in."

"How does one track a shadow?" he asked aloud.

"It's a mage trick, right?" she asked. "So there's a foot-print. We just have to find it. You know that better than I do. You're just a little shaken up right now. We were look-ing at smell and sight to go after it, but you can lock on to a mage illusion." She poured her confidence in him into her voice and mind. "Can't you?"

His smile was slow in coming. The green in his eyes blazed into turquoise. "I believe that would be possible. It looked at me, right before we destroyed it."

She didn't point out that she had had nothing to do with destroying the shadow cat, that it had all been him. She would have lost her life had it not been for him.

"The eyes were vacant, and then, just for a moment, they changed, grew intelligent, and the eyes were silver."

She felt worry in his mind, although there seemed to be only that same speculation in his voice. "What does that mean?"

"Some mages, a very few, can possesses another body, leaving fragments of themselves behind. It is not the same as a blood bond, which Carpathians use to track those who may betray us. Once inside the host, the mage can force the body to do its bidding. As far as I am aware, no vampire has ever achieved it. And no Carpathian would choose to do such a foul thing."

Everything in her stilled. Even the breath in her lungs. "Could someone like me do it? A jaguar?" She could hear her own heart roaring in her ears.

"Brodrick?"

She chewed nervously on her lip. "I told him I was his daughter. He didn't deliver a killing bite to my skull when he landed on my back, and he could have. I was very vul-nerable for just that one moment, and that was all it would have taken, but he hesitated. He bit me, and he had my blood on him. Maybe he wasn't certain I was telling the truth, but his jaguar should have known, so that doesn't make sense."

"He would have to be mage-trained to accomplish such a feat. It would not be easy, and I doubt he would have taken the time for such complex training," Dominic said.

She heaved a sigh of relief. "But they got the blood from him to track me, so he at least has knowledge of the mage— and it must be a mage—who sent the familiar. Brodrick would have knowledge of his cooperation. He exchanged the blood for something of value."

"We know he has an alliance with the vampires."

Solange pushed back the heavy fall of her hair as she sighed. "The other jaguar-men are not protected from the vampires or mages by their blood."

"We know you have something extraordinary in your blood," Dominic agreed. "I had a lot of time to study what was happening in my body as well as your own. Maybe the mages have need of it for some reason—and anyone willing to force another's body to his bidding should not have access to your blood."

"Let's do this, then. He'll never expect us to be able to track his familiar back to him. Anyone arrogant enough to take possession of someone's body will believe he's too powerful to be caught."

She was suddenly aware of her body. She'd been so comfortable with him, she hadn't realized she'd awoken naked. It felt good not to be worried about what he might think of her. She already knew. She wasn't ashamed or wanting to hide herself from him. If anything, she felt a little sexy and very cared for. He'd given her a confidence in herself she never believed she'd have. She didn't hate her scars anymore. She didn't mind that she was too curvy by modern society's standards. Most of all she appreciated that no matter if she was in jeans and a T-shirt, ready to fight battles with him, or naked from shifting, or together alone face-to-face as a man and a woman, she didn't have to hide who she was from him.

He had given her the gift of freedom, of acceptance, and, looking up at his face, her heart opened to him and took him in. Her moment of revelation was waking up in his arms to see him beating himself up over what he thought was imperfection.

"Why are you looking at me like that, *kessake*?" he asked.

She could see the dawning knowledge in his eyes and she smiled. "I think I'm madly in love with you, my Dragonseeker friend."

"Lover," he corrected.

She gave a small smirk. "Not yet." She stretched languidly as only a cat could do. She stretched sensuously as only a woman sure of herself could do. "Let's go hunting."

He groaned. "That was just mean."

Her smirk turned into a full cocky grin. "*Now* you're finally seeing the real Solange."

"I like the real Solange."

"Well, no one has ever certified you as sane, have they? Get us out of here."

He wrapped his arms around her and floated them from the deep earth. "You are becoming a bossy little thing. I can see I have given you far too much scope, woman."

She wasn't about to test the threat in his voice. He had a decidedly wicked side to him, definitely very sexual, and she wasn't going to get herself in trouble. Her confidence was growing with every minute spent in his company, but she had the feeling he knew a lot more about her body than she did, and would use his knowledge to his advantage. She nuzzled his neck. "You always smell so good."

"I should not let you get away with distracting me."

She circled his neck with her arms and turned her mouth up to his, her first daring risk of initiating any real physical contact between them. She felt very brave, and her heart nearly exploded when his lips moved under hers, parting to draw her tongue into his mouth. There was no hesitation, only the same heated eagerness she felt. His kisses thrilled her, sent her into another world of pure sensation where she lost herself, her body going up in flames.

She pressed tightly against him. Her breasts ached, and as always, she was wet and welcoming for him. It didn't bother her that he knew. She *wanted* him to know. She took pride in her reaction to his hot, inflaming kisses. "You're so beautiful," she murmured against his mouth. "Really, truly beautiful, Dominic. Thank you for saving my life."

His fingers bunched in her hair and pulled her head back. Her womb clenched in reaction to his sudden aggression. "You are more than welcome. But I meant what I said. *Never* scare me like that again. I will be putting you in an impenetrable bubble if you do."

She laughed out loud. "You probably could really do that. Come on. I'm a little worried that if this mage saw you, he could identify you to the vampires. If he's in league with Brodrick, he could very well be in tight with the vampires as well and he'd blow your cover."

"Protecting me again, I see."

She shrugged. "It works both ways. I might not be able to come up with an impenetrable bubble, but I can find something else."

He ruffled her hair, massaging her scalp where he'd been so rough before. "I bet you could, too, my little warrior woman. When we have children, make them all boys. Little girls running around with no fear in them will be too much for my heart."

Solange stepped away from him, hastily turning her head. She knew she would never be able to hide the shock his teasing had produced. Her heart pounded so hard she feared it might crash through her chest. *Children?* Plural? A family. She bit her lip hard. She supposed that was the natural progression of a committed relationship. Dominic was always five steps ahead of her. She was still tiptoeing around having him inside of her and he was already at *children*.

"You're hyperventilating." There was amusement in his voice. Purring, satisfied male amusement.

Solange glared at him. "You said that on purpose."

He definitely kept her off balance, and in a way it was exhilarating. She could never be with a man she could walk on, let alone be with one who didn't stimulate her intelligence. She liked that he played. She'd forgotten laughter and teasing. She'd certainly forgotten playing, and it was just plain fun with him. She even missed wearing her sexy clothes. That was a new experience for her, one she would treasure and never *ever* tell her cousins.

Dominic shrugged. "Nevertheless, it is true."

"For that, I'm producing ten daughters. Two at a time. And since I have no idea about raising children and you're so knowledgeable, I will let you do the raising." She managed to sound as if she was doing him a big favor, but the "true" part had definitely sent another somersault rolling through her stomach.

He laughed and nudged her. "I will accept your terms. Mostly because you will never hold to them. You are very opinionated."

"I've been very quiet these last few days."

"Risings," he corrected automatically. "I am in your mind, never forget that."

She tried not to blush. If he was in her mind, he would be seeing quite a few shocking things, especially the last couple of risings. "We should go before the trail gets too faint."

His grin told her he knew she was deliberately changing the subject. "I suppose you are right, although I find this conversation very interesting. Once I remove the safeguards, wait for me to scan the area and make certain it is clear before you leave the chamber."

She rolled her eyes. "I think I'm perfectly capable of determining when it's safe to emerge. It isn't like this is my first time."

"You nearly died. Whether you like it or not, you are going to have to put up with me being a little on the protective side for a bit."

She secretly didn't mind his protective side because she was going to do whatever it took to win each battle, and hopefully they'd always be thinking alike, but it was nice to have someone worried about her.

She blew him a kiss and shifted, shocked that she did so easily, certain of him now. She liked that—being so certain of him. He did trust her at his side in a fight, and she found she could tap into his battle experiences, which gave her insight to the way he worked and also valuable information when facing his enemies.

"I will follow the water to the source and see if I can pick up any 'footprints.' "

I'll be waiting in the forest by the stream where I think it is most likely he found a way in. At some point he had to be more than shadow. Each time he attacked, he had to become his flesh and blood self, so there will be tracks. In this form, I can track anything substantial.

She waited, crouched at Dominic's feet, taking the chance to look over his magnificent body. He was really quite gorgeous, although she found his hard-edged masculinity a little intimidating. He was well endowed and she had to admit she found herself looking at that one part of his anatomy more than any other, absorbing the shape of him, the girth and length. She'd never been intrigued by the male phallus, certainly never the real thing. Now she felt almost obsessed, wanting to touch him, to taste him, to know him as intimately as he knew her.

Hidden deep inside the jaguar where she was safe, she sighed, recognizing that now it was essential to please him. She craved bringing him pleasure. Her. No other woman. She wanted to be the one to send him soaring, and she didn't know the first thing about making love to a man. She didn't do that sort of thing. Mostly she killed them.

Dominic dropped his hand on top of the jaguar's head. "It has been said that the sun hides inside the jaguar at night. After meeting you, Solange, I believe that could be true. I look at you, in either form you choose to show yourself, and I see that bright light leading me through a labyrinth of darkness. I know our union has been difficult for you, and I thank you for being open to me."

Solange felt a curious melting in the region of her heart. He was so good at making her feel beautiful and important to him. She wanted to give that back to him and was determined to learn how.

I wouldn't have missed being with you for the world, she admitted shyly. Safe within the jaguar's body, where she'd often hidden to tell her dream lover her deepest secrets, she found it easier to admit the truth to him.

He rubbed his fingers in her fur for a few more moments. "There is no one close, *kessake*. Be safe."

You, too. She sprang past him, eager to get on with the hunt. Dwelling on whether she was going to be good in bed was depressing—and scary. Hunting something—or someone—dangerous was invigorating and natural.

She crawled through the twisting maze of tunnels to

emerge in the forest. The moment she felt the night air on her muzzle she shook herself, happiness bursting through her. She loved the forest. On the floor, the air was rich and still, the oxygen levels so high she felt energized. The rain forest was vibrant and alive, ever changing and yet always the same. She could count on the life cycle of the forest, everything living, breathing, growing and then falling. Death and decay came next, sometimes fast, sometimes slow, but always feeding and enriching the cycle of life.

She loved the rain forest during the day, but the night always seemed special to her. This was her world. She might want to travel, but mostly she wanted to see other worlds like her own while they were still in existence. The jaguar-people's time was over. There was no way to save them, not anymore. Not with Brodrick's leadership honing the men into brutes who chose to live with violence toward women, who took part in the slaughter of women and children they deemed unacceptable to them.

As few knew of their species, there had been no law down through the centuries to protect their women, and with no leadership to recognize their importance, the species had been doomed. She sighed and began to wind her way through the trees toward the small stream that was up above her chosen cave, feeding her small waterfall. She listened to the murmurs of the animals in the canopy above her head. She heard the flutter of wings and the slide of monkeys as they slipped from one limb to another, not yet ready to settle completely for the night. Bats wheeled and dipped, chasing insects, while small frogs hopped along the tree branches.

Already the songs of the many bird species were giving away to the call of the cicadas. The frogs began their nightly chorus, singing to one another from the various puddles on the forest floor, while the tree frogs chirped much more gently and harmoniously. Moths as big as dinner plates scattered across the sky. Fruit bats clung to the succulent fruit. Fireflies signaled to one another in brief flashes like neon signs.

Solange took it all in as she padded through thick vegetation, occasionally coming upon a porcupine feasting on fallen fruit. A snake struck at a mouse, detecting the heat as the small creature scampered too close to the silent predator. She startled a gecko as it emerged from its hiding place to hunt. The hungry creature raced up the tree, its eyes shining red in the night through the leaves as it looked down at her.

The jaguar ignored the nocturnal animals and kept to her course, moving a little faster now that she was away from the cave system. Above her head, fluorescent mushrooms appeared suspended in midair, growing on the trunks of trees that blended in with the night. A faint light glowed here and there from luminous fungi dotting the forest floor.

She kept to a brisk pace for several miles, working her way up the steeper slopes, leaping over decaying trunks and skirting termite mounds. The sound of water running over rocks was constant. She startled a small family of tapirs. The herbivore, related to horses and elephants, looked like a pig with a longer snout. The adults were darker-skinned with white-tipped ears and a yellow throat, but the single baby running with them had red fur with stripes and spots. At home in the water, the tapir often grazed in the rivers and streams.

She was getting close to her destination and she began to quarter the area, taking her time, looking for traces of anything large passing the same way. The shadow cat had to have arrived in its true form. Whatever the creature was, even a hybrid, it must have left behind evidence of its passing.

She was careful to examine trees, certain the creature was a cat and would sharpen his claws often. He would leave scent marks behind. Someone might have bred him, but there were certain characteristics imprinted in a cat's nature that could never be stamped out. She searched for signs of scattered leaves, of rake marks, casting back and forth along trails.

The tapir path was well-traveled and led to the stream. She crossed the worn trail several times, marking a new, very faint scent already fading. Rain was ever present, nearly every day at this time of the year, and helped to remove traces of animals passing along the animal routes, but this scent was distinct because she'd never run across it before.

She followed the smell and found crushed mushrooms where a large cat had stepped on the fragile fungi, the head imprinted with a partial track. She found rake marks high on a fig tree and a scratch on a buttress root where the cat had hunted a kinkajou, a small animal that looked a bit like a ferret but was of the raccoon family, a favorite of jaguars to hunt. The shadow cat had liberally sprayed a fern where a male jaguar had scent marked, challenging the other male for the territory. The shadow cat appeared to be in his prime and unafraid to challenge any males, clearly aggressive even in foreign territory.

She followed the small bits of information—crushed leaves, an overturned stone, a rip on a tree branch and another partial print beside the ribbons of water that flowed into the small stream that fed her underground basin. She was positive she had found the trail of the shadow cat. She sank down near the bank of the stream and waited, her head on her paws, her body still, the rosettes hiding her in the dappled brush and leaves.

A branch cracked. The crickets ceased their chorus for a

brief moment. She stayed very still, wishing she'd chosen a spot in the trees where she could see what—or who—was coming at her. Not Dominic. She knew where he was at any time. Not a vampire. There was no feel of the dread the undead brought with them. The forest hadn't shrunk back, appalled at the foul abomination of nature.

There was a sudden scattering of monkeys overhead. A jaguar, then—and he'd taken to the trees. He had probably caught the scent of the shadow cat, and had come hunting the male who had been aggressive enough to challenge him. She needed to pinpoint his exact location without giving away that she was anywhere near.

Dominic. If you can hear me, don't come out into the open when you emerge from the rocks. There's a jaguar here. I don't know if he's harmless or hunting.

I can hear you. Dominic's voice came immediately, sliding into her mind intimately. *Are you in danger?* There was a grim edge to his voice, as if, had she once again put herself in danger, he was going to have to carry out his promise to put her in a bubble.

Solange struggled to keep amusement out of her mind, knowing he didn't find the situation fraught with humor. She'd been in danger her entire life. Today was no different. That was what living in the rain forest and being jaguar meant. *I am perfectly fine for the moment. What did you find?*

She inched her way into a better position, watching the trees. He would have chosen one with lower branches so he could easily spring on his prey. That narrowed his choices somewhat. He would want branches nearest the stream. There were tapir paths clearly marking the frequent trips from forest to water. The banks were muddy and hoofprints indicated several tapir had come to feed in the water recently.

The shadow cat definitely came this way. I have not seen the imprint of this mage before; each is unique to the user. But I will know it should I come across it.

Are you close?

Right behind you. I am drifting with the steam coming off the forest floor. Have you spotted his location yet?

She caught the tip of a tail twitching in the tree just to her right. One limb swept out over the water and the jaguar crouched, very still, other than the tail that often betrayed excitement, eyes glued to some prey in the water she couldn't see.

I'm not close enough to tell if he's fully animal or my species. I can't scent the man in him. Either way, it was going to be dangerous to move. She was in his territory, and regardless of whether he was animal or jaguar-man, he would be interested in a female.

The steam on the forest floor began to widen and drift upward, slowly obscuring vision as the gray vapor spread, a thick mist that stayed along the bank and the surrounding trees. Layer after layer deepened until the forest floor and the stream were no longer visible. The thick mist wound around the fig tree, crawling up the trunk like the liana vines. The jaguar began to cough. Solange heard a series of grunts and the whisper of fur along the trunk. A high-pitched call came from the far bank—a tapir calling to a family member sounded much like a bird.

She heard the crash of the heavy male as he dropped to earth, not more than thirty feet from her. She stayed very still, letting him pass by her in the thick mist. Layers of the fog surrounded her, and deep inside the jaguar's body, Solange smiled. Dominic had managed to wrap her in a bubble. The male jaguar was not going to scent, see or hear her.

He wouldn't have found me.

I am not taking chances until the sight of your pale face, your body without breath, leaves me. And that may take some time.

You do have a tendency to harp, don't you? The woman inside the jaguar stretched, smiled, a hint at her hidden sensual nature. She couldn't help teasing him, especially when she was safe, deep in the jaguar where he couldn't find a way to retaliate.

I have a tendency to keep my word, and you might remember that, kessake, when you are feeling all snug and warm there in your safe little den.

Her soft laughter washed over him. She felt his reaction, and for a moment her heart beat faster and her mind warmed. The first tentative merging of Solange the woman and Solange the warrior had been exhilarating and made her feel very brave—which, considering she had been ready to fight a jaguar, was vaguely amusing to her.

She waited while Dominic pushed the jaguar out of their path using a mixture of heavy fog and a slight compulsive push. *Which is cheating. I'm not certain that qualifies as a fair battle. There might be a moral issue here.*

His mind flooded hers with warmth, a teasing, sexy amusement that sent heat surging through her veins. Hunting was a lot more fun with a partner. She felt a little bit safer, and it helped that he was intelligent and experienced. She didn't feel as if she had to protect him. She could even acknowledge he might feel the need to protect her. He had quite the arsenal to draw on, and truthfully, in battle, as far as she was concerned, whatever it took to win was fair.

He is clear now, Dominic informed her. *I will get rid of the fog.*

Solange worked her way to the bank of the stream as the mist slowly evaporated and Dominic stood beside her, one hand in her fur, his fingers massaging her neck. Her jaguar loved it, rubbing her head against his thigh in response.

He went this way. Solange took a couple of steps, certain now of the cat's tracks. Even with the male jaguar in the area, his prints overlaying the shadow cat's in places, she easily could distinguish between the two. The shadow cat had gone into the water right at the very entrance to the limestone labyrinth. *Why did he risk being tracked when he could take the shape of a shadow?*

"That is an excellent question," Dominic murmured aloud. "Did his master have to be close to keep him a shadow? If so, we should be able to find where his master waited for him."

He came from that direction. Solange took him back through the forest to where she'd first come across the tracks. *We know he went into the water and never came back out, but his handler must have gotten him close enough to pick up my blood scent.*

She could feel Dominic frown, and his fingers bunched in her fur, but he didn't react, simply stepped back to allow her to lead him through the forest, backtracking now. Once she was on the shadow cat's trail, she grew more certain of herself, moving faster, winding in and out of the trees away from the stream and yet away from the interior.

No cat would go in this direction unless he was feeding on cattle. This area is patrolled heavily by men with guns. They protect the cattle fiercely, and unless a jaguar is old or injured, it will stick to the game here in the forest. Maybe he was looking for an easy meal.

She didn't like getting too close to the enormous cattle ranch that lay just on the outer edges of the forest. The men fired a warning shot as a rule, trying to drive a wandering cat back into the forest, but just as often, one might be trigger-happy. She'd noted Cesaro's reaction to her cat. It was almost instinctual. The cattlemen considered it their duty to keep the cattle safe, and cats were predators they didn't want near the ranches.

"We are on De La Cruz property." Dominic sounded grim.

Yes. It is quite large. All of their places are enormous. They are very wealthy. They employ a lot of people who are very loyal to them. They take good care of their workers and the families who stay with them throughout the years seem to grow wealthy as well. Many of the locals are fiercely loyal to them.

"Solange, whoever is handling the cat has to be on this ranch."

Her heart jumped. *Maybe not. Maybe it was looking for a meal.* But she knew he was right. It made sense. The tracks led straight to a road. And on the road there were tire tracks. She'd seen them often in her wanderings. The trucks the De La Cruz workers used were all the same, as were the tire tracks so clear there in the mud. The heavy cat had leapt from the back of the truck. The tracks were deep behind where the vehicle had been parked.

Dominic crouched low to examine the ground. "There are boot prints here. There must have been a cage of some kind in the back of the truck and he let it out."

Not vampire.

"Definitely not vampire. What do you think is going on here, Solange?"

A silly fluttery feeling in the pit of her stomach told her just how much it mattered that he'd asked her opinion. She turned the small bit of information they'd collected over and over in her head. *Maybe we aren't the target at all here, Dominic. They don't know about you yet. And what threat would they consider me? Zacarias is the biggest*

*threat they have in this part of the world. He's the one most
feared of all the De La Cruz brothers. He carries the most
power and is the most influential with the leaders here.*

"All true, but why would they need your blood? What
would that have to do with Zacarias?"

*Whatever it is, I'll bet they didn't count on me giving my
blood to Zacarias. I'm not known for my generosity in that
area.*

"So it if isn't a vampire"—Dominic was already following the tracks of the truck in the mud, knowing it would
lead them back to the De La Cruz ranch—"then who would
send a cat after you? And who has that kind of black magic
ability to possess another's body now that Xavier is dead?"

*Are all mages in league with the vampires? Did they all
follow Xavier?*

"No, the mages have scattered to the four corners of the
world. Many were experimented on. Xavier held Razvan for
centuries, and in that time he saw many terrible things done
to young mage women and men. A few fanatical mages wor-
shiped him and followed his teachings. They hate Carpathians and want them wiped off the earth just as much as the
vampires do."

*So we know whoever sent the cat has to be mage, and
not necessarily in league with the vampires. He may have
his own agenda. And he's using someone at Zacarias's
ranch. If he's been there for some time, getting established,
he must have been very distressed when Zacarias showed
up. He rarely comes here.*

They stood at the edge of the forest, staring down at the
cleared barrier between the forest and the extensive cattle
ranch. The truck tracks followed the road straight into the
De La Cruz property.

Solange shifted and stood naked beside Dominic, smiling a little at his body's instant response to her.

"You could give me a little warning so I would be ready with clothes," he said.

She lifted an eyebrow. "I think you're a little off your game, Dragonseeker. I expected clothes. Maybe I should be going to visit our neighbors just like this. It would definitely get us in the door."

Instantly her body was clad in familiar jeans and tee. She laughed at him. Even her hair was pulled back in a high ponytail. "Yeah, that's what I thought. Let's go see who wants my blood."

Dominic held out his hand. Solange only hesitated for a second before she put her hand in his and walked with him up the muddy road toward the sprawling De La Cruz ranch house.

15

I can never betray you.
You can never part from me.
In love forever, this life and next.
You are the very heart of me.

DOMINIC TO SOLANGE

Cesaro saw Dominic and Solange coming and rode out to greet them on a dark horse. In full gaucho gear, he was an impressive sight. The horse all but pranced under him. He flashed a wary smile in greeting. "All is well?" he called.

Dominic shook his head. "We may have discovered a plot against Zacarias, Cesaro. We are not certain, but would like to discuss matters with you. You know more about this ranch and the people on it than anyone else, I would imagine."

Cesaro slipped easily from the horse's back, retaining the reins. "Of course. You have only to tell me what you need."

"The undead are gathering near this place and your people are all in danger. The undead will be seeking blood each night. Because there are many, they will take many lives. They can take any form, man or creature, including bats. How prepared are you should they come?"

"Each house is protected, but we must guard the cattle," Cesaro replied.

They got into the house the other night, Solange pointed out to Dominic, not wanting to disprove Cesaro's statement and hurt his pride. As a woman, he wouldn't like the protest coming from her.

"Forgive me," Dominic bowed slightly, "but how did the vampire get into the main house the other evening? He attacked young Marguarita. Did you make inquiries?"

Cesaro frowned, swept off his hat and scratched his head. "I can't think how such a thing happened. She would never invite anyone inside the house, and she would know she was safe inside. *Don* Zacarias has given precise instructions and we all follow them *exactly*. Each family residing here knows it is life-or-death. No one would open the door for the undead. For *anyone*."

Zacarias would have protected all of them from compulsion as well, Solange reasoned. *All the brothers protect their families that way. Someone opened the door and let the vampire inside. Someone here is working for the vampires.*

Dominic turned Solange's statement over and over in his mind. It still didn't feel right to him. He was missing something. "I would like to check on Marguarita, and discuss this further with you, Cesaro. Perhaps you could introduce me to those working here."

Cesaro's eyebrow shot up. He was responsible for the men and women working for the De La Cruz brothers. "Do you believe we have a traitor?"

Dominic chose his words carefully. Most of those working on the De La Cruz ranches were related in some way. "I just want to make certain that everyone is safe."

Cesaro turned his head and whistled. At once a younger teen bounded up and took the horse's reins, his eyes curious, but he didn't ask questions. When Cesaro waved him away, he looked disappointed but he took the horse back toward the corrals.

Dominic glanced down at Solange's upturned face and the question in her eyes. She'd been in his mind when he'd touched the boy. He could see Zacarias's barrier firmly in place. If a mage had managed somehow to take over one of the workers, he would have had to go through that barrier.

Marguarita? Could she have been possessed and opened the door for him?

Dominic shook his head. *The undead tried to get into her head and was unsuccessful. He questioned her, and even though I felt the strength of the compulsion in his voice, she refused to give him information.*

They followed Cesaro to the house. Dominic glided rather than walked, although he appeared to be walking with his easy, fluid, graceful stride and paying attention to Cesaro as he identified workers they passed. He didn't want to take a chance of making it appear as if he was examining the mind of every person within range. Everyone appeared protected.

The house rippled when they walked in. Dominic stopped abruptly. "Has Zacarias been here?"

"He would not leave with the undead walking the night. The cattle are restless and last night we lost several to the bloodsuckers. They dropped down from the sky. Two of my men barely escaped with their lives. Zacarias returned right after that and strengthened the protection in each house. He told us the cattle were not worth dying for and he wanted his men inside at night."

"And yet, it is night and you are watching the cattle."

Cesaro frowned. "We cannot just let them be slaughtered. This is what we do. Who we are. We are taking precautions. If there is a disturbance, we all go inside immediately. We have shelters set up for our protection."

Dominic exchanged a long look with Solange. These men were feudal in their own way. They had a job they took great pride in, and they weren't about to abandon their cattle to the vampires rampaging near their homes.

"Marguarita took a turn for the worse," Cesaro said. "She ran a high temperature and could barely breathe. *Don* Zacarias must have sensed she was dying and came to try to heal her again. He spent much time with her and then left. He is not resting here. He said it would be too dangerous for all of us."

"Perhaps he is right," Dominic acknowledged. There had been a touch of guilt in Cesaro's voice, as if he was ashamed that Zacarias would think they could not protect him while he slept. "He is feared by the undead and they do not know I am here. They believe he is the only one between them and what they want. They will try any means to kill him." He looked Cesaro in the eye. "Do you understand what I am telling you? He does this because you are his family. He will go to any lengths to protect you, even from himself."

Cesaro heaved a sigh. "I understand. It is our duty to serve and protect him as well. This does not feel right to me."

"He is lucky to have you," Dominic said with another small bow.

Ask him if anyone visits regularly that maybe doesn't work for Zacarias but borrows his vehicles once in a while, Solange prompted.

Dominic pushed a smile into her mind. Of course she would hit on the right question. He loved her all the more that she understood the way these men thought and acted, and it didn't bother her. They would feel much less inhibited discussing the workings of the ranch with a male than with her. He was Carpathian, like the family they worked for, and they knew he was Zacarias's friend. She was a shifter—a cat they equated with being an enemy. Cesaro was respectful but uneasy in her presence.

I do not care what others think of me, Solange said. *Only you.*

He could feel the truth of her words and it warmed him. She belonged to him—she *wanted* to be his alone. *You know I value you above all else.* Her opinion, her skills, most of all the love that was beginning to show in her cat's eyes.

His heart tripped a little over that shy, very new look. Sometimes when she looked at him, her expression sent his body into a violent, almost brutal state of arousal. She was so new to the idea of actually sharing her life with someone, and yet she was trying very hard to find a way around absolute terror to come to him whole. He loved the experience of watching her struggle to accept not just him, but her growing love for him. It was an unexpected journey he'd never thought he'd take, and he found himself loving her all the more for it.

"Cesaro." Dominic halted just outside of Marguarita's room. "Do you have a neighbor who is allowed to use the De La Cruz vehicles? Perhaps someone who was here the day of the attack, and two nights ago?"

Cesaro froze with his hand on Marguarita's door. He turned slowly, a wash of color in his face. His eyes went diamond hard. "There is such a man, he has been trying to court Marguarita. The De La Cruz family has been good to him. He bought the ranch that borders ours about a year ago. He had little left after the purchase and we have helped him several times."

"You say he is courting Marguarita."

"*Trying*. We all found it amusing. Marguarita, as you have seen, is quite beautiful, but she is young and a little wild. Not with men, do not get me wrong. She is a good girl. But she likes her independence. She cooked and cleaned for her father and has the pick of the horses. She loves horses and is a good rider. This man, he can't tame her. Her father and I had many nights of amusement over this courtship. Marguarita has not even appeared to notice what he's doing with his flowers and candy. She smiles at him, as she does with all the workers, and thanks him on behalf of her father and all who would get joy from his offerings. She acts as though he brings things because he is allowed to borrow equipment."

"Has he shown anger over her rejection of him?"

"No one can be angry with Marguarita. She is a joy."

Dominic indicated to open the door. The moment he stepped through, he knew death had been very close. Had Zacarias not risen, this young, once vibrant woman would have died. She looked so pale she was nearly translucent. Dominic approached the bed. He glanced at Solange. She nodded, understanding. He would leave his body and go into Marguarita's to examine her, ensure she survived and check, this time, for splinters of possession. Solange would have to watch his back for him.

"It would be best," she said softly, "if you could leave us alone for a moment, Cesaro. And then we would very much like the name of this man who has visited and used one of your trucks."

Cesaro nodded and left the room. Dominic knew he stood beside the door with a hand on his weapon. Whether to protect them or Marguarita, it mattered little. The man had a duty as he saw it, and was prepared to defend the De La Cruz property and everyone in it.

"Very loyal people," Solange said.

Loyalty, Dominic knew, was a quality Solange very much admired. He glanced at her face. Cesaro was a handsome man.

Solange laughed. "You're such a *male*."

He wrapped his arm around her waist and drew her tight against him. "*Very* male," he confirmed. "And I keep what is mine."

She rolled her eyes at him. "Evidently you're feeling a little insecure this evening. Have I done something to make you think I'm looking at another man?"

"You were not looking at me."

Her soft laughter was like an aphrodisiac to him, sexy and teasing and all woman. "I'm always looking at you, Dominic." Her voice changed, dropped the teasing note, and was pure, raw honesty. "You fill my vision so much there's no room for me to see another man—ever. I only see you, Dominic."

His hand curled around the nape of her neck and he bent his head to taste her again. She was like the finest mixture of honey and spice and he could never get enough of her. "I could kiss you forever," he whispered against her lips. He tasted both warrior and woman, and it was a potent mixture.

"I had no idea kissing could be so addictive," she said. For a brief moment her body melted into his, soft and pliant and accepting. She glanced down at the pale woman. "Do you think the neighbor deliberately marked her for death at the hands of a vampire because she wouldn't cooperate with him?"

He saw the shift in her mind, the depravities of the jaguar-men, and knew her thoughts sickened her. His hand moved to her ponytail, playing gently with the thick strands. "There are good men and bad men in every race and species, Solange. Living here, doing the work you do, has made you see all men in a bad light. Cesaro would never strike his woman. Once you are able to scan minds you will be able to see for yourself that many good men exist in the world."

She shivered slightly and he knew his reference to her being fully Carpathian disturbed her a little. She had brought the subject up once in a roundabout way, but he knew she wasn't allowing herself to go there yet, and he respected her need to come to terms, very slowly, with what their life would be like together.

Dominic turned back to Marguarita and shed his physical body to become wholly spirit. He had no doubts that Solange would guard his body from harm while he worked at healing the young woman whose throat was so mangled. Zacarias had given her blood, more than he probably could have spared. The interesting thing was, he found traces of Solange's pure royal blood. The Carpathian blood was usually predominant, and here it was, but her strain was very distinct and it had somehow attached to the Carpathian blood, fully compatible, but not taken over. Her blood was very unique and had definite healing properties.

There was no way to repair the vocal cords fully. The undead had used razor-sharp talons, shredding through the cords. Both Dominic and Zacarias had concentrated on the muscles in her throat used for breathing and swallowing. She would live, be as beautiful as ever, but she probably would never speak again, or if she did, in no more than a husky whisper. But she would live. They had done their best for her.

He examined her mind, her memories, but there were no dark slivers of possession. She had not opened the door to the vampire. She'd heard her father's dying warning and she'd obeyed him, backing into her room and waiting for the workers to come. She had been crying for her father, knowing he was dead, but she had not gone to the door.

And that meant someone else had been in the house

without her knowledge. That someone had been familiar enough to enter without detection, and the safeguards didn't affect him. He was not considered an intruder.

Dominic pulled back to reenter his body, swaying a little with no idea of time passage. Solange paced like a restless cat from window to window. She glanced over her shoulder at him. "You okay? You look pale. Do you need blood?"

"Not yours. You are killing the parasites and we need them. I will ask Cesaro which man is strongest here."

"He will insist you take his blood."

Dominic smiled at her. "I know."

She covered Marguarita gently and brushed tendrils of hair from her pale face. "She'll be traumatized by this. And if a friend betrayed her, it will be all the worse. Maybe we should ask MaryAnn to come visit." She looked up at him and there was trust in her eyes. "Perhaps you could suggest to Cesaro they send for her."

Knowing her need to help women abused by men, he nodded. "I think that would be a good idea."

Dominic led her to the door. They still needed to add to the protection of these people, as well as track down the neighbor. And the undead were out in force. Likely encounters meant he had to be at his strongest.

Cesaro whipped his head around as they came through the door.

"She is sleeping as peacefully as possible," Dominic said. "I believe she has survived the crisis and is on the road to recovery. Do you know all the De La Cruz brothers?"

Cesaro nodded. "They come here from time to time. The brothers share the ranches."

"Manolito's wife, MaryAnn, would be a very good choice to help Marguarita through this. Perhaps if you sent for her, she would come."

"It would give us another man to defend the ranch,"

Cesaro acknowledged, knowing Manolito would come with his lifemate. "Thank you." He bowed slightly toward Solange, as if knowing just whose idea it had been. "I will do so immediately."

"Tell us about your neighbor."

"His name is Santiago Vazquez. He's about thirty and has only three men working for him. I rarely see anyone around his house. The ranch is very run down. He needs money to build it up, and there is little money to be made on a ranch just starting up."

"Do you have a very healthy, strong man working for you who might be willing to donate blood tonight? I have much to do and cannot go hunting."

"I am in good health," Cesaro said. "Please, it is an honor. You are doing so much to help us, and I am no longer afraid of the giving."

"I accept with gratitude," Dominic said, and stepped up to the man immediately, again not wanting to give him time to become afraid.

Solange looked down at her hands and he touched her mind even as his body felt the rush of energy the hot blood provided. She was upset that he wasn't taking her blood, and it fed her silly anxiety of inadequacies. He reached out and brushed the pad of his thumb down her cheek. Her gaze jumped to his. He slid his mind intimately against hers.

Your blood is superior to his, kessake. And I would much rather take from my woman, but I have yet to walk into the camp of the enemy.

I know. It's just that I haven't met any of your needs. Not one. And you are always doing for me. I want to be the one who gives you whatever you need. Another woman . . .

Would never please me the way you do.

He felt the brief flicker of a smile, although she didn't change expression. He politely closed the two puncture wounds and bowed slightly before beginning the intricate web of safeguards to add to Zacarias's work. The ranch would be doubly protected against the undead.

"Do not let strangers approach you. Often the undead appear beautiful. If they are very powerful, they can control how they look and talk, and will often take on the form of someone you know. They cannot pick anything from your mind, but they will study those who live here and try to appear as one of them. Their eyes can give them away, and often, when they walk upon the grass, it shrivels or withers. Nature will recoil from them. The animals will be uneasy when they are near and no dog can stand them."

Cesaro nodded his understanding. Feeling he could do no more to protect them, Dominic indicated to Solange it was safe to leave the house. They went out into the night, inhaling deeply to get the stench of fear, sickness and near death from their lungs.

They walked until they were out of sight and back under cover of the trees. Dominic took Solange into his arms and rose into the sky. She lifted her face so the wind blew over her. She was completely relaxed in his arms, trusting him to keep her safe no matter how fast or high they flew.

I love this, she confided. *There is something very freeing in flying, like running along the branches in jaguar mode.* She laughed softly and nuzzled his neck. *You've given me some of the best experiences of my life.*

I want to give you many more, Solange.

He loved the happiness in her voice. Whether she knew it or not, her trust in him was growing every moment they spent together. She had fully aligned herself with him. The woman and the warrior were merging. Her confidence in her appeal for him was also gaining strength. He bent his head and bit down gently on her neck, right over her tempting pulse. He was definitely going to the meeting the next rising so he could finally rid his blood permanently of the parasites and have no worries joining with her—if he could hold out.

He circled above the small ranch that lay sprawled across the rolling hills just meeting the southern tip of the De La Cruz property. Where the fields had been clean and well tended, the fences sturdy and the cattle in good shape at the De La Cruz ranch, it was the opposite here. The water hole was filthy and the cattle stood in thick mud, heads down in misery. The forest had begun to encroach, heavy vines taking down the fences in several spots. There hadn't been any attempt to repair the fences recently, although Dominic spotted several places where the grazing land had been cleared some time earlier.

He bought land that had been worked, he pointed out.

But he hasn't improved it at all.

Dominic dropped to earth inside the tree line. "Shift, Solange. I will go in first."

"I've got a stash of weapons close by. I'll cover you with a gun. He's human, not jaguar, and I've just got this strange feeling. I think I'm going to need my intellect to be sharper than my claws this time."

His dark gaze drifted over her. She wasn't really asking him, just stating her opinion. It didn't occur to her he might decide to overrule her. He loved that confidence in her when she read a dangerous scenario.

"Hurry, Solange. We are losing too much of the night."

She nodded and dashed away. It took a good five minutes, but she returned with a small case covered in dirt. "I think I'll do best in the trees just above his house. Try to keep him centered in the windows or better yet, keep him outside. I should be able to cover you if he's got company. Are you picking up more than one person?"

"Not in the house. He is alone at the moment, but there

is someone in the smaller building behind the main house, and a third man seems to be in the barn."

"I should be able to cover all three locations. My jaguar is uneasy, Dominic. There is something very disturbing to her in this place. Be careful."

He knew it would embarrass her, but he leaned down, framed her face with his hands and kissed her thoroughly. "Remember what I said about scaring me."

She rubbed her cheek against his like the cat she was. "No worries. Take me up to that tree branch. It will be faster than if I climb."

He glanced up. The branch was a good fifty feet above-ground. Most people would be terrified of the height, let alone at night with little moon. The rain had begun to fall again, just a drizzle, but it would be enough to make the branch slippery. Without a word he wrapped his arm around her waist and took her up to her perch.

It was more difficult leaving her than he'd thought it would be. He *did* trust her judgment and if her cat was uneasy, something was off at the ranch. He was expecting to find a man who had been possessed, but he knew Solange expected something else as well, and for the first time he had no real clue to what they faced—or why. There was something in Solange's blood that made it special, and he was beginning to think *they* were the ones being hunted now—and for her blood. But who was after her? The vampires? Brodrick? Someone else?

He let his breath out in a long, slow hiss of frustration.

Does it really matter? Her voice was soft in his head, almost tender, brushing along nerve endings that felt almost raw. *It is my way of life and I chose it long ago, just as you chose your life. They are not expecting two of us. They believe they are facing a female jaguar only, and they will make a mistake—if they haven't already.*

He thought of those silver eyes. Possessing another's body, taking over without consent and forcing the body to do one's bidding was such a foul, vile crime. Even with all he'd seen in his long centuries, he couldn't imagine why anyone would be willing to cross that line of humanity other than Xavier, the head mage who had started the war with the Carpathian people so many centuries earlier.

Solange's response was reassuring. She was matter-of-fact about facing death and her calm acceptance of their way of life allowed his mind to settle to the task at hand. She was not a woman who would panic, or worse, throw herself into unnecessary danger to prove some point. She was experienced and read situations correctly, had endless patience and knew when to retreat without her ego being involved. She was a good partner to have. When there was need, she would be at his back—or his side—without hesitation. There was something appealing about having a partner he could count on.

She knew his protective instincts would come into play and she accepted that as she did everything else about their life together. Somehow, his Solange had become his world and she'd enhanced everything in it, including going into battle.

Whoever was in the barn is now in the house with Santiago Vazquez. I got a good look at him, and didn't recognize him. I know most of the humans working at the laboratory as well as most of the jaguar-men. This man isn't from around here.

He gained the porch without alerting anyone to his presence. Someone moved around inside and he could hear a voice coming from the back of the house. The man he assumed was Vazquez answered in a louder, much angrier voice.

"She's alive. I was just there and she's still alive."

Dominic stood on the porch, listening. They had to be talking about Marguarita.

"You promised he would kill her if I did what you said. I've done everything. The slutty little cock-tease is still alive and there's no fun to be had in this hellhole."

The man with the lower voice murmured very softly, but his tone carried command. "She is of no importance to us now."

"She was important to me. She was my in with the De La Cruz family. I tried to get her alone to compromise her, but she wouldn't even go riding with me."

The man with the low voice sighed. "Her family would have killed you had you done such a stupid thing, and then everything we worked for would be gone. She's nothing, Santiago. There are many women, and we can ensnare any of them once we are in possession of the book and the blood of the royal jaguar. Focus on what's important here. If we get those two things, we have it all. Power. Women. Wealth beyond dreams. And the vampires, Carpathians and the jaguar-men will bow before us. We can rule where we want to rule."

Did you hear them, Solange? Dominic had repeated the conversation in his mind so she could follow along.

"Damn Brodrick. He's so fucking evil his blood is tainted now. He's ruined everything with his sickness," Santiago complained. "His mind is rotted as is everything in his body."

"We will find her," the second voice soothed.

They are mage then, she said. *And they have an agenda of their own. What is so darn special about my blood? And why wouldn't Brodrick's blood do? They obviously have to have some kind of connection to him, and they must know he has the same bloodline.*

Somehow his depraved lifestyle of murder and rape has

ruined the purity of his blood, Dominic answered. He had no idea how, but there could be no other explanation.

The two men inside the house were obviously in on their plot together. One wanted the life of a wealthy rancher and the other wanted power. Santiago was more likely the weaker link, and the one whose body was possessed by the other, although Dominic was certain they were related. The two smelled like siblings.

I will go around to the shed to see who is out there. They would not have anyone here that was not part of their plan.

I can't cover you from this angle, Solange objected. *I can see both men in the house through the large windows, but from here I can't see inside the shed.*

I will be in another form. He found himself smiling as he moved around the verandah toward the back of the house, a very faint stream of vapor.

As he approached the shed, he slowed into a fine stream, nearly floating around the small wooden building. He could feel the force of energy pulsing from inside. The warped walls could barely contain the pulsing power trapped inside. *Do you feel this?*

He felt Solange's sharp intake of breath. *Get out of there, Dominic. Don't get too close.*

Where there had been no breeze, the rain forest floor so still beneath the canopy, without warning, the wind whipped into a frenzy, rushing at the line of trees surrounding the ranch on three sides and right toward Solange. A roar burst from the shed. Inside something blazed white-orange, shining through the cracks of old warped wood.

Something large hit the door of the shed hard enough to shake the entire building. The door splintered halfway up, bulging out.

Get out of there, Solange, Dominic commanded.

Do I have stupid written on my forehead? Half laughter,

half exasperation and a dash of very healthy fear edged her voice. She knew whatever was in that shed had scented blood—*her* blood—and it was coming for her.

Dominic countered the direction of the wind, pushing it away from Solange so the creature—whatever it was—couldn't find her by scent. The shed shook a second time as the large animal hit the door. This time the wood gave in the middle, breaking and pushing jagged shards outward.

Two men burst from the back of the house, running across the uneven, muddy ground toward the shed. The two looked exactly alike—and neither had silver eyes. Both stopped abruptly about halfway to the shed, spinning around, going back-to-back, hands raised. One spotted the tendrils of fog and immediately hissed something to his twin.

"Alistair!" Santiago yelled as the huge creature in the shed slammed into the door a third time, blasting through it. An enormous black cat leapt out, rushing straight for the forest.

Dominic recognized Santiago's voice, knew he was in trouble and began to streak across the yard. *Shoot the cat, Solange.*

The back door of the shed burst open and a third man rushed out, his hands up as well. Santiago whirled around, shoulder to shoulder with his brother, and simultaneously both men slammed their hands straight at the mist. Behind them, the silver-eyed Alistair added his powerful energy to the other two. For a moment they looked as if they'd merged into one being.

Light burst from their fingertips, exploding outward directly into the vapor streaking away from them. The sound of a gunshot reverberated through the forest. A hole blossomed in the center of Santiago's forehead. The second man hit the ground, rolling toward cover. The force of the blast struck Dominic and blew him out of the sky.

A second shot sounded and the man on the ground

screamed. Dominic hit a tree hard and barely managed to
land in a crouch on his feet. His entire body burned and he
took a moment to assess the damage. Solange sprayed
the ground in front of him, driving back any attack from
the mage brothers.

The cat was out of his sight, but running flat out for Solange. Dominic had to make the choice between destroying
the mages and protecting Solange. There really was no
choice. He went after the enormous cat. Built like a saber-
toothed tiger with enormous muscles, the black cat could
become an insubstantial shadow and could only be killed
when it was in substance form.

As he raced after the cat, Dominic took command of the
skies. Thunder rolled, dark ominous clouds boiled out of
nowhere. Rain poured down. Lightning forked across the
sky, building electricity and energy into a frightening mass.
Lightning bolts slammed the earth over and over, striking
all around the yard between the house and shed. One hit
the shed and it burst into blackened splinters of wood, spilling the contents into the open.

Inside were small cubs in various stages of misery, some
half formed, some screaming in pain as their twisted bodies
were half solid and half shadow. Their pitiful mewling and
growls could be heard over the thunder shaking the ground.
The uninjured mage raced toward one of the escaping cats,
calling out a command. About half-grown, with part of its
body transparent and eyes glowing a hot red, the cat whirled
around, hissing and spitting, fighting the compulsion to return
to the mage.

Lightning slammed to earth again, and large, white-hot
explosions burst around the mutilated cats, incinerating
them so fast they couldn't feel the blast of heat. Only the
half-grown one remained, cowering, trying to slink away
from the mage.

Don't kill it! Solange sounded shattered. He could hear her weeping deep in her mind. Her female jaguar was outraged and struggling to surface. *We can save that one, Dominic. Please. Please don't kill it.*

Dominic kept the bolts of lightning up, driving the mage away from the cat even as he tuned his mind to the cat's. He wasn't at all certain it was a good idea to try to save a mutated cub programmed to go after Solange's blood, but he couldn't resist the plea in her voice or the tears in her mind.

Run! he commanded the cub. *Try for the river and I will help you if possible.*

The cat, with the added help of Dominic, broke free of the mage's restraining spell, spun around and ran into the forest.

Solange fired off several rounds as the large black cat tore up the tree trunk, shredding bark as it scrambled to get to her. The thing was heavy, and she climbed higher, into the thinner branches, but they were covered with leaves and Dominic lost sight of her. He could see the cat though, a huge animal, the muscles straining as he clawed his way slowly up the tree, his eyes fixed on Solange. If Dominic blasted the animal, it would take out the tree—and Solange—unless his timing was perfect.

The cat shimmered, nearly translucent, and made one huge jump onto the heavier lower branches. His growls rumbled hideous and loud, so that the forest creatures went silent, cowering in dens. Even the ever-present very vocal cicadas went silent. The forest seemed to hold its breath as the cat dragged its body up to the next level.

Are you ready? Dominic asked, his heart in his throat.

Was it possible for her to shed her clothes and shift in time if the tree went? He knew she was fast, but . . . He pushed the thought away. He needed a clear strike zone.

Solange was waiting, intent on getting a clear shot through the dense foliage. She didn't have room to maneuver and her perch was precarious. Not only was the limb flimsy, but the weight of the cat sent the tops of the trees swaying.

Dominic moved swiftly, trying to cover the distance to catch her if needed, but all of his senses were focused on the cat. The large animal continued to stare straight up at Solange, growling and slobbering.

Can you reach its mind? Solange still sounded calm— much calmer than he felt with the huge animal ripping through the trees to get at his lifemate.

The other cat had been protected by the mage with a strong barrier. Dominic pushed hard into this cat's mind. The creature existed for one purpose only—to bring its master Solange's blood. The mutated animal's senses were all programmed for one scent, for one person. There would be no stopping it from dragging her from the trees and hauling her to the mage.

He took a breath and narrowed his vision, centering on the space just below Solange. It was the only true open space.

Be ready, beloved.

The cat leapt at her. Dominic blasted it, catching it in the air, but the lightning bolt crashed through the huge body, slamming into the tree. The cat disintegrated into ash and the tree toppled with a terrible splintering crash.

Solange timed her jump using Dominic's mind. She vaulted from the tree as the bolt passed through the cat, leaping out and away from the falling tree. Still clutching the rifle in her hands, she made no attempt to shift, simply trusting him to catch her. He managed to get his arms around her as she fell about two-thirds of the way. At no time did he feel panic in her.

But he felt panic-stricken, his heart thundering in his chest as he held her tight enough that she could barely breathe. She didn't try to squirm away, simply allowing him his moment of relief.

He swooped over the ranch. Santiago's dead body was still lying on the ground. A blood trail led to where a vehicle had been parked. The silver-eyed mage and his sibling were long gone. Dominic changed direction, heading to the river. The smaller cub paced up and down the bank, yowling in distress. He snagged the creature and shoved it into Solange's waiting arms.

She caught it below its front legs, holding it out away from her, face out, rocking gently. The cat's head drooped to one side and it fell instantly to sleep.

Great. Now we have a friendly little kitten. What are we going to do with that? Dominic asked in disgust.

Solange's soft laughter warmed him as nothing else could. He had the feeling that in their lifetime together, rescuing animals, children and possibly adults was going to become commonplace.

16

I can never betray you.
You can never part from me.
In love forever, this life and next.
You are the very heart of me.

SOLANGE TO DOMINIC

Solange woke with her body wrapped tightly around Dominic's. For the first time she hadn't slept in the form of her jaguar. She wanted to lie beside him, skin to skin, and wake up looking at his face, touching his body. She dreamt of him, sometimes at night, sometimes during the day, but Dominic always filled her mind now. At times he seemed the center of her world and she didn't even know how—or when—he had so taken over her thoughts.

Sometimes, like now, she felt like she was drifting in a sea of need, craving the way his beautiful eyes moved over her with that look of such intense desire she could barely breathe. This evening, on waking, she felt almost possessed in her need to be with him, as if he truly did own one half of her soul. She'd spent her life alone, independent, and it was strange to wake up with Dominic as her first thought. She wanted to be everything he needed just as he was everything she needed.

Dominic had awakened the woman in her. For the first time in her life she felt sexy and alive. She enjoyed the way he looked at her when she was wandering around their lair in the clothes he'd asked her to wear. She found she liked to dress for him, to see the dark lust building as his gaze followed her around the chamber.

She sat up slowly and looked him over. His lashes had lifted the moment she moved, his arms coming up to halt her progress. Her bare breasts brushed his hard chest as he held her in place. He had impossibly long lashes that would have looked feminine on anyone else, but the very black crescents only served to bring out the colors in his eyes. His slow, sexy smile melted her heart and slightly mesmerized her.

"Kiss me, *kessake*. Kiss me now before that little ball of fur-trouble bounces down on top of us and spoils my good mood," he growled. His hand slid up to bunch in her hair, giving her no choice but to comply.

Solange leaned over his body, unconsciously sensuous, sliding her skin against his just for the sheer luxury of touching him. He was so physically beautiful to her, his body honed by battle, a warrior in his prime, everything that appealed to her cat. But the unexpected sweetness in him, the way he saw to her every need, the way he focused so completely on her, as if everything she said and did mattered to him—that appealed to the woman.

She took her time lowering her head toward his, savoring the way she felt, that hot, delicious, restless need pouring over her, mixing with a terrible, frightening, overwhelming love that stole her sanity. The moment her lips brushed against him, the fire started, rolling over her, burning hot and out of control. His hand kept steady pressure on the back of her head as he took his time exploring her mouth, long, drugging kisses that melted her bones.

His hands stroked caresses over every curve, inflaming nerve endings even more, until her body shuddered with need. One hand drifted lower, his thumb brushing gentle, almost tender strokes over her mound and down to her sex. He caught her ragged breath in his mouth, holding her captive there while he took his time kissing her until she sagged against him, so boneless she couldn't move.

Dominic wrapped his arms around her, and with his mouth welded to hers, floated them up from the rich earth to the floor of the chamber. He left the little cub curled into a small ball of fur, still asleep on top of the healing soil.

Solange felt the woven rug under her bare feet as he put her down, but her body was no longer her own. Mostly she felt hot and needy and so in love she could barely find words. She could only look at him with her heart in her eyes. Dominic Dragonseeker. The legend. The man. *Hers.*

His smile was slow and certain. "Bath or food?"

She crushed her need to say *you*. He utterly bemused her and she couldn't speak. She glanced at the inviting hot water and smiled up at him, hoping he would join her.

"You love a bath," he said, his gaze burning hot over her.

Solange nodded. She was very conscious of him behind her as she made her way to the steaming pool. The water closed over her skin, tingling, bubbles rising, frothing over the raw nerve endings so that her breath caught in her throat and she closed her eyes, allowing the sensation to rush over her.

Dominic followed her into the bath, finding a niche in the smooth rock so that only his chest and head were above water. Solange ducked her head under the water and allowed him to pull her back against him so he could wash her hair. She loved the feel of his strong fingers massaging her scalp. The water lapped at her chin as he rinsed out her hair.

"I've been thinking about the little cub," she ventured, trying not to sound shy. Her newfound realization of how much he was wrapped up inside of her made her feel more vulnerable than ever. "If you give him Carpathian blood, do you think you can put him right? He's such a sweet-heart, Dominic. Is that even possible? Giving him your blood once the parasites are removed?"

The cub was solid in front and back, but his middle was shadow, which made it difficult, if not impossible, for the cat to eat.

"Maybe. I honestly do not know what can be done for the little guy." He ducked his head beneath the water to wash out the long silken mass.

There was regret in his voice and Solange frowned. She waited until he was finished and then brushed the palm of her hand over the heavy muscles of his chest. "I thought the blood of Carpathians could heal almost anything."

"This is twisted magic, Solange," he said, catching her hand and pressing her palm tight over his heart. "I want to help, but I do not yet see how we can undo this damage."

She sighed and leaned forward without thinking to lick at a drop of water running down his chest. "They didn't have time to program him to need my blood. He's such a sweet little thing, but we're going to have to find a solution fast or he's going to starve. What were they thinking?"

"I doubt they cared whether the cat was hungry, as long as it did what they wanted."

"We have to do something for it. Keeping it asleep is the only way to keep it from starving, but that's a temporary fix."

He smiled down at her and her stomach did a little flip. "If it is at all possible, we will find a solution."

She believed him. He had said he wanted to help but didn't *yet* know how. She knew Dominic deep down now, at the core of who he was, what he stood for, and he would not allow the kitten to suffer. He paid attention to details, no matter what they were.

She turned more fully into his arms and tentatively reached for him to explore. He was so sacred to her, she almost felt as if she should ask his permission to touch him. She felt very daring running her palms over his chest. He made no move to stop her, and her reticence vanished. She followed the sculpted contours, memorizing each defined muscle, trying to absorb the shape and feel of him through her fingertips as she stroked caresses over his body. She heard his breathing change, felt the stirring in his body, the rising need. He stayed quiet, just watching her with the approval she craved in his eyes.

Her fingers traced every rib, his tapered waist, splayed over his flat, hard belly. She felt the muscles bunch beneath her hand in reaction. Already he was hard, very aroused, thick and long and straining toward her hands, but he moved then, sighing softly.

"We have to be careful, Solange. You need to eat."

His voice was firm and she allowed her protest to die in her throat. She did need to eat, but she needed him more. She touched her tongue to her lips and nodded, hardly daring to breathe in case the wrong thing came out. Like a protest.

This evening wasn't supposed to be about her and what she needed—she wanted it to be about him, but she was uncertain how to proceed.

He dried her off with a soft, warm towel, as always taking care to make certain she was completely buffed and rosy before he did the same for himself. Solange didn't move, watching him without blinking, afraid she might miss the smallest sign from him. He donned his usual elegant clothes with that easy wave of his hand she found so breathtaking.

"Which robe?" His voice was low and husky, taking for granted that she would want one of the gowns he'd made for her—the gowns he preferred her to wear when they were alone.

"The dragon robe," she said, unable to meet his eyes. She *loved* that gown. Her heart pounded and she tasted fear and excitement in her mouth. When she wore the Dragon-seeker robe, she felt not only beautiful, but as if she truly belonged to him.

Dominic held out his hand, and the exquisite stretchy lace lay over his palm. Gallantly he held the robe so she could slip her arms into it. He cinched the waist himself, so that it was tight in the middle, flaring over her hips, but leaving the front open. The fabric clung to the sides of her breasts, leaving them bare of even the star-strewn lace.

He cupped her breasts in his hands, lifting the soft weight, his eyes going hot. Her breath exploded from her lungs as he bent and sucked one nipple deep into his mouth, tugging and rolling with his tongue and teeth until it was a hard little bead. His mouth moved to her left breast to repeat the same attention, taking his time, teasing and stroking until her soft moans became mewling whimpers of need.

Her breath came in ragged gasps as he continued to lavish attention on her sensitive nipples. Her breasts felt swollen and hot and her body tightened into a restless, familiar ache. She shook her head, her gaze cloudy, her hair spilling around her shoulders in complete disarray.

"This is supposed to be for you," she whispered.

He smiled and tipped up her face. "This *is* for me." His hand slipped down her open robe to find her sex. He slipped his finger inside of her. "You are so hot and wet for me, Solange. So ready. For me."

She shuddered, gasping at the shocking heat racing through her body.

"This is definitely for *my* pleasure," he whispered. "All for me. I want to touch you, Solange. And I need to know you welcome my touch anytime." He pushed two fingers into her and made a sound of appreciation deep in his throat.

She felt that sound resonate through her entire body. Everything in her settled. She would do anything for his pleasure. If it was important to him that she was aroused, she would take pride in being ready for him.

"I love how you feel," he whispered, his eyes darkening more. "Soft like silk." He brought his fingers to his mouth. "But even more, I love the way you taste."

Her heart lurched. She got lost in his eyes, in the dark, heated depths, just melted until the violent world around her fell away and she thought of nothing but him. A tremor ran through her body as Dominic sucked at his fingers, his eyes dark and hot. A small whimper escaped as a bolt of lust shook her entire body.

He smiled, male satisfaction very evident. "Come with me, Solange. You need to eat."

Eat? Had he actually said *eat*? Her body was hot and needy and he wanted her to eat? She licked her lips and took his outstretched hand. He led her to the candlelit table and held out the high-backed chair for her. This small cavern was their world, and he liked elegance and finery. The dishes on the table were beautiful, as was the silverware. Everything Dominic did had an elegant touch to it. He was Old World and courtly and made her feel special beyond anything she could ever have fantasized. Solange pushed down the uncomfortable feeling of not belonging. She *did* belong—here, with Dominic.

She put the woven napkin in her lap, her fingers sliding over the soft material. Beneath the table she twisted her fingers together in an agony of need. He had given her all of this. A home. A man who treated her as an equal. A man who listened to her and addressed her fears with respect and love. She had never imagined a relationship could be so good, and it made her sad for the loss of her people. All the women who had been brutally used and thrown aside because Brodrick refused to acknowledge they were good for anything but breeding.

Dominic was the opposite of everything she despised in a male. He fed her meat, one small bite at a time, *meat*, which he found repulsive and yet knew the cat in her needed. She could see the effort he had taken to study what foods would best suit her body, and the balance was all there. Dominic cared for her health and comfort. He cared for her peace of mind.

Solange bit down hard on her lip, tears glittering in her eyes. She blinked them away, hoping he hadn't seen, but Dominic saw everything when it came to her, every small detail.

"What is it?" He took her chin in his hand and tipped her face up to his. "Tell me."

He could have easily looked into her mind, but she loved that he didn't. That he waited. It allowed her to gather the courage needed when she was too shy or embarrassed. Eventually, she knew, she would get over that and realize fully that everything she felt and said was important to him.

"You move me." She couldn't find better words. "The way you love me, it—moves me." She struggled to get the words past the thick lump in her throat. She wasn't like him. She couldn't find easy compliments, but it didn't mean she didn't feel emotions every bit as deep and intense as his.

His smile made her tilting world come right again. Her heart fluttered and she found herself smiling back, breathing easier, as if her lungs followed the rhythm of his.

"I want to discuss the conversion with you, Solange. We need to look at it from every angle before we make a decision. We have no idea what it will do to your blood—or to you—and that worries me. Your jaguar is strong and there may be repercussions."

She continued eating, watching his face in the flickering candlelight while she turned the idea over and over in her mind. Conversion. Becoming Carpathian. Living in the ground. Drinking blood instead of eating. She could do all those things as long as she was with him—but she couldn't give up the other half of who she was. She was jaguar. She would always be jaguar. Her cat was *her*.

"What happens if I don't convert?"

He shrugged, the movement easy and casual. "I told you. We would both grow old and die together."

"You would stay with me?"

"You are my lifemate. You are the woman I love. There is no other answer. And, Solange," he leaned in to her, so that her gaze was held by his, "there would never be regrets."

She believed him. That changed things instantly for her. He would give it all up for her without regret. Everything in her loved him, yearned for him, wanted desperately to give him back all the things he'd given to her. She felt a little helpless not knowing what women did for their men, but even if she didn't know, she would forge her own path, just as he seemed to be doing with her.

She picked up a slice of mango. "Would my jaguar be destroyed?"

"I do not have the answer for that. What happened with your cousin?"

"She said her jaguar made the conversion difficult, but she feels her cat with her, yet not in the same way."

"Your blood is different from your cousin's?"

She nodded. "Her mother was a royal, but not her father. The lineage is all but wiped out now. There is only Brodrick and me. I know I am the last of my kind. I can't save our people. I've known that for some time, and as sad as that is, it is the truth. Our time is over." She took a breath. "I want to protect my jaguar. She's as much me as the warrior and the woman. Is there a way to ease in to the Carpathian world and see if she is accepting?"

"Once I am able to gather the information we need, we can try one blood exchange to see how she takes it. Right now, if I took your blood, it would kill the remaining parasites in my body, and I need them to gain entrance into the vampire conclave taking place this next rising."

She tried to breathe evenly, to keep her heart from pounding. "We should test how far I have to be away from you in order for the parasites not to react to my presence. I'm a good marksman and can make shots over a good distance, but not with the crossbow. I need that to kill the vampires."

He nodded. "I thought your crossbow was ingenious."

"I'd like to take credit, but Riordan, Juliette's lifemate, helped me come up with it. He mixed this great accelerant for me because vampires seemed to be showing up more and more in this area. We knew Brodrick had made some kind of an alliance with them. It took a while to figure out why. Everyone thought he was controlled by the vampires, but I knew differently. I knew they couldn't influence him."

"I have a difficult time fathoming why a man would sell out his entire species without a vampire controlling his mind, because he has to know the vampires are influencing his fellow jaguar-men who do not have his particular brand of protection."

"He's wholly evil," Solange said, unconsciously lowering her voice. She shivered, remembering the look in Brodrick's eyes as he slashed the throat of her six-year-old friend because she couldn't shift. "He enjoys his power over women. My aunt told me how he dragged my mother out of the house by her hair after he killed her parents, then held her captive for months. She was very broken when he let her go. She was only seventeen at the time, and he was terribly cruel. He enjoys hurting women, and in his position as leader of the people, the men embraced his philosophy that the women were to serve their every desire and they could treat them however they wanted. Brodrick believes all women are less than he is, and that he has every right to hurt them for his own entertainment."

Dominic took a slice of mango and held it to her mouth until she took a bite. She knew he was worried about her not eating enough; she could read it in his mind. So she ate the fruit and felt a silly little glow when the sheen of approval lit his eyes.

"His father before him was the same way, as was his father. Something happened long ago to prompt this, whether he was born sick and twisted, or whether some event made him that way, we will probably never know, but Brodrick was raised by his father to enjoy hurting women.

"He didn't have to follow what went before. In the end, we're all responsible for the choices we make," she argued. "He's allowed the extinction of an entire species in order to pursue his depraved proclivities. I hate that his blood flows in my veins."

He stroked his hand down her hair, to comfort her. "You are an incredible woman, Solange, and not any part of him."

She felt the flutter in her heart and looked up at him, uncaring that he would see the stars in her eyes. He made her feel like a fairy-tale princess, beautiful when she knew she wasn't, special when she was ordinary, sexy when she hadn't the first clue about being a woman. Dominic was her Prince Charming and always would be. Every day with him seemed a gift to her, a fantasy she could never have conjured up on her own.

All those days when she made up a fantasy companion, her "perfect, ideal man," she had never realized just how perfect he could be for her. He was a man, and she had never been able to bring herself to trust a man. After meeting Riordan and Manolito De La Cruz, watching the two men with her cousins and her friend MaryAnn, she had wanted to trust in them and come to love them for who they were, but . . . She sighed. It had been Dominic who had allowed her to find faith in men again.

"He wants the database of psychic women the vampires have compiled," Solange said. "They are finding every woman who tests high for psychic ability, and by asking questions about their backgrounds, they're able to provide enough information to trace those who are descendents of the jaguar people. Essentially, Brodrick uses the database as a hit list to kill those he thinks can't produce a shifter and breed those who can."

"We will get the data, Solange, protect the women and destroy the laboratory and all of their computers," he assured.

It sounded like an impossible task. She'd tried for several years to figure out how to do it, but had been unable to come up with a plan.

"I'm not good with computers," she admitted. "I have no idea how to copy the information. In the end, I just figured it was better to blow the entire thing up and hope the data went up as well. I mapped out a blueprint of the building so I could plant explosives and bring it down."

Dominic leaned over and licked the mango juice from her lips. Her womb clenched and her stomach muscles bunched. "I think we can get the information. I have a friend standing by to help with the computer problem. He gave me very precise instructions."

That sensuous lick had caused her temperature to soar, and she became acutely aware of her body all over again. He seemed all too aware of her, too.

"What friend?" she asked, trying to stay on task.

The pad of his thumb traced a slow line from her collarbone to the tip of her breast. She sucked in her breath sharply. His thumb continued to smooth over her bare stomach to slide lower.

A small smile tugged at Dominic's mouth. "He is considered a punk kid, although he is not much younger in human years than you are, but he is very gifted with computers. He wanted to come, but I could not take a chance that he might think himself capable of fighting a vampire. His name is Josef, and at times I think most male Carpathians, myself included, have considered sending him to the vampires just to stop his antics. The boy is very modern and runs a little wild. He is waiting by his computer to take over the ones in the laboratory as well as their network."

She laughed. "I never considered that Carpathians might have trouble with their children. And that one sounds intelligent."

"You would be surprised. I was a very wild boy myself. Once I almost shifted inside the middle of a huge boulder just to show off."

Her eyebrow arched. "Wild? How wild?"

His smile bordered on a smirk. "Not as wild as I intend to be."

Her body shuddered as he cupped her sex, one long finger stroking and caressing. His gaze had dropped to her breasts, making her very aware of her body all over again. He could do that so easily, just brush her with his gaze, and every cell responded. The blush started somewhere near her toes and crept up. She forgot what they were talking about, everything falling out of her brain to leave her wide open for him.

She took a deep breath and admitted the truth to him. "I can't think with wanting you."

His gaze jumped to hers. "Do you trust me enough, Solange? I do not just want your body. I want you to give yourself to me completely. Anything I ask. Anything I need. Even if it scares you a little, if you trust me, we can have everything. There is no going back once we commit. I will bind us together and there is no retreat from that position. Our souls will be bound and there is no way out for either of us. You cannot make a mistake. My needs must be yours. Every moment of your life will be dedicated to me. To my pleasure and comfort. You will be giving yourself into my care, your health and happiness, everything to me."

She swallowed the fear that was rising. She refused to be defeated in this, her one chance at happiness. "Because your care is in my hands." She wanted him to see that she understood what he was trying to tell her. Everything she thought, everything that mattered to her, was important to him—and he wanted to be just as important to her.

He nodded slowly. The room seemed very still and utterly silent, as if even their lair held its breath. His gaze remained steady on hers.

Solange took a breath and smiled, the pounding in her heart settling as it found the rhythm of his. She'd never felt so sure of anything. "I want you with all my heart, Dominic. I might be afraid now and then, but I trust that you'll see me through. And I promise you, I will do everything in my power to make you happy."

His eyes went a deep, piercing blue. His voice dropped to the low, seductive note she had become familiar with. "I have waited a long time to hear you say that." His fingers stroked over her breast. Her nipple peaked and he leaned forward and captured her breast in the scalding cauldron of his mouth.

She cried out, arching her back, her hands coming up to cradle his head to her. His silken hair flowed over her arms and she threw her head back as the fire rushed over and into her. He had a magic mouth, burning hot and so talented.

She was a little bemused as he drew her up and out of the chair and into the middle of the chamber. A wave of his hand changed the entire room. Candles sprang to life along the walls, up high so that only a soft glow cast light across the room. The woven rug seemed thicker beneath her bare feet, but really, all she saw was the man standing in front of her.

Very gently he slipped the gossamer dragon robe from her shoulders, letting the stretchy fabric pool around her feet. Her breath caught in her throat as she felt the slide of the lace down her bare skin. He cupped her shoulders, looking down into her upturned face. Her heart thundered in her chest, almost hypnotized by his absolute control, his enormous strength, but most of all the heat in his eyes. She shivered beneath his touch, unable to look away from the gathering intensity in his eyes. He slid his hands down her arms to her wrists, watching her with his complete focus.

He stared into her eyes for a few more moments, holding her gaze captive while he gently entwined his fingers with hers and pulled her arms out away from her body. Very slowly his gaze dropped for a long inspection of her body.

She felt her color rising and her nipples peaking under his hungry gaze. Where before she might have been embarrassed, now she could see the appreciation in his eyes, the absolute desire, and she felt more sensual than ever. So much more of a woman than a warrior. She took pride in the fact that he was aroused by her.

"I love the way your body grows so wet for me," he said, inhaling her welcoming scent.

He had told her that many times before, but this time she felt different, knowing he was telling her a simple truth. She blushed a deeper shade of pink. She was wet for him. Welcoming. He hadn't touched her and her body had responded with an urgent need, coiling tight, her nerve endings burning and raw. She found she also took pride in how aroused he could make her body when she was close to him. He needed her to respond—and she did.

"I can't help it," she answered. "Looking at you makes me that way."

He smiled down at her, a slow, sexy smile that made her heart clench hard in her chest. He pulled her naked body slowly, inexorably, into his fully clothed one.

"Undress me, *kessake.*"

There it was, everything she'd been waiting for—hoping for. His eyes had gone dark with a potent, very intense mixture of love and lust. She felt the instant response of her body, already so completely focused on him. She could count the beats of his heart. She knew the ebb and flow of the blood in his veins. She knew his mind, and his heart. At last she had the opportunity to know his body, to memorize every muscle, every erogenous zone.

She slipped the elegant jacket from his shoulders, folded it carefully and placed it almost reverently on the small bench seat beside the pool. A rush of heat colored her skin as her hands smoothed over his shirt and then went to the buttons. She could barely breathe as she slipped each one open to reveal his bare chest. Again she slid the material from his shoulders. She held the white silk shirt to her face, inhaling his scent deep into her lungs before she folded the silk and placed it neatly on the bench.

Heat exploded through her body as she ran her hands over his chest and down his flat belly before dropping to the front of his neatly creased trousers. He stood barefoot, his shoes arranged under the bench as if she'd put them there herself, allowing her to kneel in front of him as she drew the trousers down his long legs. He placed his hand gently on her shoulder as he stepped out, one leg at a time.

Solange's breath caught in her throat as his heavy erection sprang free. He was thick and full, every bit as mesmerizing as the rest of him. She folded his trousers almost absently, her gaze focused on him. She was barely aware of the fabric leaving her hands to join the pile of clothing on the bench. She could only stare, hypnotized, irresistibly drawn by the evidence of his arousal for her.

She cupped his heavy sac in her palms and bent forward to lick almost helplessly at the small pearly drop glistening on the broad, mushroom head. His breath left his lungs in an explosive rush as his cock jerked with the fiery sensations shooting through it. She leaned forward and drew him deeper into her mouth, feeling satisfaction as his entire body shuddered with pleasure.

She loved how incredibly hot and smooth he felt against her tongue, the heavy weight of him filling her mouth, sliding oh so slow, a little farther each time. He allowed her to control everything, let her get used to the size and feel of him. Velvet over steel, filling her mouth with the heat and fire of him, with his desire for her. She took her time, wanting to know him intimately, every pulse of his hard flesh.

He groaned deep in his throat when she swiped her tongue over the broad head and proceeded to pull back to lick delicately once again. Her gaze flicked to his and satisfaction soared through her at the strained arousal etched into his face. His hand fisted in her hair, and red light flickered in the depths of his eyes as he pushed his pulsing cock against her mouth. She stroked his bare hip with one hand while the other circled the base of his heavy erection, and she deliberately curled her tongue around the base of the broad head.

He jerked against her mouth and his breath left his body in a harsh burst. A warning growl rumbled in his chest and throat. Again, satisfaction soared through her. She had always paid attention to detail. She could get this right. It wasn't about her, it was about him and his pleasure, and she was coming to know that she could deliver pleasure to him.

She watched his eyes, watched the muscles bunch in her jaw as, with infinite slowness, she took the sensitive head of his cock into the scalding heat of her mouth. His hips jerked involuntarily, desperate for her to take him deeper. She felt the erotic bite of pain in her scalp where his fingers tightened in reflex, and she moaned. The vibration went through her mouth straight to the hard flesh and she felt the answering throb. She allowed the hard length of him to sink into her mouth and was rewarded with a jerk of his hips and the sound of his harsh breathing filling the chamber.

Candles flickered, the soft light casting shadows along the deep lines carved into his face. His chest rose and fell, gleaming bronze in the dancing light. He adjusted the angle of her head so he could slide a little deeper, using small, almost helpless thrusts. She knew he controlled his movements, but she loved the way he couldn't stay still, needing the hot clasp of her mouth.

He pulsed against her tongue, and she loved the raw feel of him, the smooth texture and hot, sexy heat. He tasted all male, a spicy, erotic, very masculine flavor she knew she would be addicted to forever. He tasted like Dominic, passion and desire, love and acceptance. She stroked over and around, growing bolder as she felt his reaction. She kept her gaze locked with his, watching for every sign of pleasure, and when she saw his eyes glittered, the lids drooping heavy, she flattened her tongue and rubbed over the sensitive spot just underneath the crown, which she'd discovered by sheer accident.

She moved her head, a slow withdrawal, all the while watching the heat in his eyes, judging his pleasure while her tongue stroked and caressed along that sweet spot. She paused for a moment with just the tip between her lips, watching him catch his breath, his eyes go deeper blue, almost midnight black, and very slowly she took him in again. She burned with the need to please him, to give him the exquisite pleasure he'd given her, the same focused care.

To watch his body, his eyes, to feel his heightening sensation, was such an aphrodisiac to her. She felt her body's response, the burning pressure between her legs, the ache in her breasts and the need rising so urgently for him. There was acute satisfaction in her own response, but she kept her focus solely on pleasing him.

She increased suction, slow and then fast. Hard and then soft, all the while her tongue teasing and dancing. His husky, musical voice turned guttural, thrilling her. His thrust became a little deeper as he skated the edge of his control. She took him a little deeper and sucked harder, eliciting a harsh groan.

Solange was burning alive, inside and out. Her mouth felt scorching hot, but between her legs she was on fire with urgent need. She wanted—*needed*—his body inside of hers. Her body ached for his, the craving so overwhelming that she wanted the taste of him forever in her mouth, his body imprinted on hers for all time.

His gaze locked with hers, holding her captive as he began to take over the rhythm, thrusting a little deeper. She tightened her mouth around him, increasing the suction, desperate for him. The quick, hard thrust took her breath, but as he penetrated deeper, she learned quickly how to take a breath when she could because she didn't want to stop—not now, not ever. She loved what she was doing to him, loved that she could take his control and replace it with such mindless pleasure he couldn't focus on anything else.

He moaned, his breathing harsh. "Stop, *kessake*, I cannot hold on." The hand in her hair began to pull her head back, although his hips refused to cooperate, using quick, hard thrusts to push deeper into her tight mouth.

She danced her tongue over him, stroking and caressing, bringing him to the very edge of his control. He set his jaw and forced her head back farther.

"This is too dangerous, Solange."

She slowly, reluctantly relinquished him, breathing hard, confused. "I don't understand. You wanted this. You wanted me . . ."

"*Want*," he corrected through his clenched teeth. "I want you. But I cannot endanger you. I have parasites in my blood that I might pass to you."

"They can't hurt me," she pointed out, frustrated and growing more annoyed by the moment. She sank down onto the floor and glared at him. "You started this."

"I thought I could stay in control enough to separate the parasites and keep them from contact with you, but they go still when you are close and I cannot think straight. I am sorry, Solange. I had thought I would make love to you this rising."

She reached up, her fingers caressing the hard, thick length of him, watching with a heated gaze the shudder that ran through his body. "Have you ever heard of a condom? Don't Carpathians have condoms? Because I'm thinking that if you're all that worried, a condom might be just the thing."

His smile was slow in coming. "I had not thought of that. As a rule, Carpathians do not need such things."

17

Look at me—now see yourself through my eyes.
Look at you: the most beautiful on this earth.

DOMINIC TO SOLANGE

Dominic reached for Solange. His body burned for her. He could barely reason with needing her touch, needing her soft skin sliding against him. Needing desperately to be inside of her. His soul raged at him to bind her to him, to claim what belonged to him. To unite them for all time. His discipline was at an end and nothing stood between him and the woman he loved.

He lifted her into his arms, cradling her to him. Beloved Solange. She looked excited, sexy and fearful all at the same time. His every protective instinct surged to the forefront. The mixture of sensual woman, as desperate for him as he was for her, combined with innocent inexperience only added to his need to be tender. He had expected, with the intensity of her cat's heat, that she would be very experienced in her lovemaking, but it was clear that she wasn't.

Love was nearly overwhelming, threatening to drive him to his knees. She had no idea of her beauty or her appeal to him. Carpathians saw what was inside. The body was simply a shell. Perhaps because they could shift into any form they chose, the outside mattered little to them. But he could see into her heart and mind, and he'd fallen deeply in love. Solange was exactly the woman for him, with her fierce loyalty, her unfailing courage and her natural sensuality.

He had waited for so long, so many centuries, until all hope for this one woman had faded. He held her cradled against his bare chest, hardly able to comprehend that she was his at last. His body ached for her, hot blood pounding through his groin, his cock a constant, heavy ache that refused to go away. Her skin, all that soft expanse of silk and satin, drove him to the brink of madness. He'd been patient, waiting for her to give herself to him, to trust him enough, but the demons raging in Carpathian males had never quieted, never given him peace, demanding he bind her to him, claim her for his own.

Her hands smoothed over his chest, small, just a whisper of a touch as he laid her gently on the bed. He was so shaken with need, he'd nearly forgotten a bed. He caught her small moan in his mouth as he kissed her, her silken hair bunched in his hand. He allowed himself the luxury of getting lost in the sensations of Solange as he kissed her again and again. Hot silk, a promise of things to come. Her fantastic mouth, moving against his, all honey and spice and uniquely her.

A fever of love and desire raged in his body. Dominic Dragonseeker, perfectly controlled and disciplined, could no longer control his own temperature. He wanted her so much he could barely breathe. Discipline and control were his way of life. It was a unique experience to burn inside and out, to have his heart pounding in his chest and cock, to tremble from sheer need of a woman—need of a lifemate.

He loved the way she looked beneath him, her eyes so dazed and hungry, desire naked on her face. The flush that spread over her body delighted him. Her breasts were beautiful in the candlelight, a temptation he couldn't resist. He lowered his head, his hair sliding over her body so that she writhed beneath him, her nerve endings already inflamed.

Her breathy little whimpers drove him mad, and he wanted—needed—more. His mouth closed around the soft swell of her breast and drew her nipple inside. A tremor ran through her and she cried out, a soft, broken little sound that nearly shattered his last remnants of control. He loved her soft, inviting breasts, and mostly he loved her reaction when he tugged and rolled her nipple with his teeth and fingers. Her body strained toward him, writhed under his assault, and he couldn't help but merge minds so he could feel every sensation pouring through her body. Beneath him, her stomach muscles bunched and her head tossed wildly on the pillow. Her hips bucked, seeking his body.

He suckled, encouraging her soft little moans of helpless pleasure. Heat rushed through her veins and he actually felt the spasm in her womb.

"Dominic." She whispered his name, over and over, her hands fisting in his hair, holding him to her.

The needy sound in her voice drove his temperature up a few more degrees until he thought it might be possible to burn from the inside out. He took his time, lovingly lavishing attention on her breasts, teasing and tugging, his tongue dancing, pulling strongly with his mouth and gently laving, giving tiny nips and easing the sting with a caressing stroke of his tongue.

One hand slid over her flat stomach, feeling the muscles

there rippling and bunching in arousal. Her heart drummed beneath his mouth, a frantic, rhythmic beat that called to his blood. Fangs filled his mouth unbidden, the temptation overriding every discipline. He licked along the creamy swell of her breast and bit gently. She went utterly still.

He raised his head to capture her gaze with his. Her cat's eyes had gone from green to golden. His hand covered her sex, the moist heat calling to him as strongly as the beat of her heart. He exposed his fangs, letting her see, knowing the demon in him was close to the surface; his eyes were glowing. Nothing mattered but her acceptance—her total trust.

Solange's breath came out in an explosive rush as he pushed two fingers deep into her hot channel. Her mouth opened, her eyes went wide.

Dominic!

Stay with me, kessake. *This will be good for you.* He soothed her gently, feeling the tremors running through her body. He bent his head and licked at her creamy breast, just along the sweet swell.

His thumb found her clit as he sank his fangs deep. Her body nearly convulsed. He felt the explosion rocking her, her muscles clamping down on his fingers. Her body nearly bowed. The pain of the bite gave way to the erotic ecstasy. He knew he couldn't take much, but he wanted to feast on her in every way. She was delicious, her honeyed, spicy taste filling his senses. His cock throbbed and burned. She writhed beneath him, and the urgent need burned white-hot and bright, raging through his veins like a firestorm. She moaned softly, and his body reacted with savage aggression, filling so full, the ache turning brutally painful.

He swept his tongue across the small pinpricks and kissed his way down her belly, an almost frenzied rush. He wanted control and tried for it, but the moment he gripped her bottom and lifted her hips to his mouth, all he could think was to feast. He forced himself to check her state of mind just once, his gaze locking with hers. Her eyes gleamed with shocked excitement.

Solange drew in her breath at the pure sensuality carved into his face and the hunger in his glittering, ever-changing eyes. There was no denying he was losing control, and although she was scared, her body was thrilled. She felt as if she'd been waiting for this moment forever. He paused, staring at her, his lids half-closed, the thick lashes intensifying the vivid blue of his eyes.

Gaze locked with hers, his tongue slowly swiped through the velvet-soft folds. Her entire body shuddered. Her gasp was loud in the silence of the room. She clutched at his broad shoulders, trying to find an anchor when it was already far too late. He made a sound, a low, primitive growl, before he indulged himself. And it was an indulgence. He feasted on her, drawing the hot liquid from her center with strokes of his tongue. He licked and caressed. He suckled and nipped. His hands controlled her hips as she bucked helplessly, crying for release, pleading with him to stop—to never stop—as he drove her higher and higher until she felt on the very brink of insanity.

The fever raged hot and strong, yet she couldn't quite reach the release she needed no matter how high the pressure built. She couldn't stop from pushing into him, writhing, head tossing, hips bucking, as out of control as he seemed to be. He was making sounds, deep, animalistic growls as he devoured her, licking and sucking, so that her womb spasmed, wept and clenched, spilling more of the hot cream he needed to try to sate the ferocious hunger.

Pleasure rippled through her belly, spread down her thighs and centered in her deepest core, hard, curling waves that shook her entire body and rippled through every muscle and cell. She heard her own desperate cry as he suckled her sensitive clit one last time before kneeling up and over her.

"Wait." She could barely get the hissing command out. Her body still shuddered with aftershocks and her mind refused to clear.

Even so, Dominic, always aware of her needs, stilled, his eyes glittering nearly ruby red, lust and impatience stamped on his sensual face. But he didn't move, his breath coming in ragged, harsh gasps as he watched her struggle to speak.

Solange drew a deep breath, trying to clear her mind enough to confess. It was necessary. She should have days earlier.

"Dominic." She was barely able to get his name out, but she had to tell him. He had to know. "I've never been with a man." She couldn't still her restless hips from seeking him, as he knelt so close, only an inch from her hungry body.

He frowned. "Of course you have. You are jaguar. I have seen the images. The man undressed, you . . ." His frown deepened. He obviously didn't want to discuss her past sexual history. "It doesn't matter."

"It *does*. I'm trying to tell you."

"I do not need to know. I saw the images in your mind, Solange. Each time a different man when your cat was in heat. You were with them . . ."

She closed her eyes, ashamed. "I'm sorry, I know I let you think that, everyone thinks that, even Juliette and Jasmine, but it isn't true. I tried. My cat drove me with her needs, but I couldn't ever let them touch me. Each time, I panicked. The thought of allowing a man to touch me sickened me. It's amazing how vomiting kills the mood for men."

"Tell me you are certain, Solange."

"You know I am. I want you. I want this."

"I need to hear you say it."

She didn't look away from his gaze, her own steady, but she could barely get the words out, her breathing harsh and uneven. She was on fire with need and more than desperate for him. A part of her wanted to yank his hips to hers and just impale herself on him. "More than anything, Dominic, I trust you. I want us to be together in your way. I *am* afraid, but only of the unknown, not of you or us. I'm certain."

His hands dropped to her thighs and spread them farther, lifting them over his arms. He leaned over her, forcing her legs higher, giving him better access. His erection brushed against her sensitive, pulsing entrance, and she cried out as darts of fire raced through her body. She closed her eyes, afraid of what was to come, but so frantic for him to relieve the terrible building hunger that couldn't seem to be sated. She feared she would never get enough of his pleasure. His hands and mouth were so incredible, she couldn't imagine what his body was capable of doing.

"Solange, keep looking at me." His eyes glittered with purpose and resolve. "*Te avio päläfertiilam*—you are my lifemate."

He didn't just say the words to her; he chanted them. The musicality of his voice had always appealed to her. She felt each word as he uttered it in his native language and then repeated it in her language so she could understand what the words meant. Her heart began to beat even faster as she felt the broad mushroom head of him pushing into her.

"*Éntölam kuulua, avio päläfertiilam*—I claim you as my lifemate."

The words came from somewhere deep inside of him and resonated deep inside of her. She loved being claimed,

belonging solely to him. She wanted him with every breath
she drew into her lungs. She *needed* his pleasure more than
she needed her own. And belonging to him was so right.

His hands gripped hers tighter, forcing her to keep eye
contact with him. She had never been so excited—or
turned on—in her life. She loved looking up at him, feeling
the thick, hard heat of him stretching her as he invaded.
She felt empty inside and needed to be filled with him—
with his essence.

"*Ted kuuluak, kacad, kojed*—I belong to you."

Her body flooded once again with a tidal wave of pure
heat. She felt the slick moisture pooling between her thighs,
arousal bunching her stomach muscles. He did belong to
her. Every inch of him. And she would see to his care—his
happiness and his pleasure. He pushed into her tight folds
just another inch, stretching her until she burned, just on the
edge of discomfort.

"*Élidamet andam*—I offer my life for you."

She would give her life for his, but that wasn't entirely
what those words meant—it was so much more. Every
aspect of his life was in her hands. She couldn't stop her
hips from moving, trying to draw him deeper, even when
he felt too big to fit. He seemed to know how desperate she
was, but also how stretched she felt. He held still, waiting
for her body to adjust to his size.

"*Pesämet andam*—I give you my protection."

She knew he would always—*always*—have her protection in return, and she could live with that. He didn't treat
her as if she couldn't take care of herself. He respected her
ability to fight an enemy. He protected her always, including waiting for her body to adjust to the invasion of his.

"*Uskolfertiilamet andam*—I give you my allegiance."

Tears burned. Most of her life she had felt alone, fighting
for a cause that couldn't be won. She'd taken care of Juliette

and Jasmine, and a hundred other women. This man would always be on her side, no matter what, his first allegiance to her. He pushed deeper and stopped when she cried out in shock at the tremendous burning. He felt huge, impossible to accommodate in her tight channel. But still, her body didn't seem to know that, desperate for his invasion.

Once again he waited, breathing deep, fighting for control. His fingers tightened around hers. His eyes were incredible, glowing, changing, beautiful.

Breathe for me. Relax.

She took a breath, following the rhythm of his lungs, making a conscious effort to relax her straining muscles. She'd been more afraid than she'd realized, locking down on him. The moment her body accepted him, he slipped another inch into her.

"*Sívamet andam*—I give you my heart. *Sielamet andam*—I give you my soul. *Ainamet andam*—I give you my body. *Sívamet kuuluak kaik että a ted*—I take into my keeping the same that is yours."

Solange felt the difference deep inside her, tiny threads weaving them together, as if her heart and soul were one with his. He had reached her barrier, the thin strip protecting her, that line no one had ever been allowed to cross to possess her. Tears ran down her face. She was no longer afraid to trust him; she'd made that leap of faith and she'd given herself into his care with no reservations.

"*Ainaak olenszal sívambin*—your life will be cherished by me for all time. *Te élidet ainaak pide minan*—your life will be placed above my own for all time." His voice deepened. Firmed.

The intensity of his declaration made her shiver. His eyes glowed a hot turquoise. He bent his head, licked at her pulse and sank his teeth into her as his hips surged, breaching the barrier. The pain was a sharp burning nearly covered by the shock of his fangs. He paused again while she breathed away the stretched, burning feeling. Very slowly he lifted his head again to look into her eyes with their bodies locked together.

"*Te avio päläfertiilam*—you are my lifemate. *Ainaak sívamet jutta oleny*—you are bound to me for all eternity. *Ainaak terád vigyázak*—you are always in my care."

He bent and took her mouth for a brief, heart-stopping moment, and then he released her hands and began to move, a slow, long slide that had every nerve ending rippling with sensation. Fire streaked through her. Solange gasped, her eyes widening in shock.

He pulled back and surged forward, harder, faster, the friction sending lightning arcing over her. She had never dreamt anyone could fly so high or feel so much pleasure. It was frightening, the loss of control, and yet exhilarating. She dug her nails into his biceps, attempting to find a way to anchor herself in the building maelstrom of burning heat.

His body moved again and she tightened her muscles, hearing him gasp.

"You are so tight, Solange, scorching hot."

Was that a good thing? She didn't know, but he shuddered against her, his breathing even harsher than before, and each time she rose to meet him, his hard hands encouraged her. It felt so good, those long, deep strokes of searing fire. She didn't want them to stop, yet she feared burning alive if they didn't. He didn't stop. His first gentle strokes gave way to a harder, faster, pounding rhythm that took her breath and sent her climbing higher than she imagined possible.

He plunged deep and she cried out, a low, almost mewling sound. The pressure grew and grew, never letting up as he merged more deeply and he lost all control. Fire spread through her body. Blazing heat rushed through her veins.

Tension stretched her nerves to a breaking point—and beyond—until she strained for release, tears running down her face, a firestorm consuming her. Always he drove into her, velvet over steel, between her thighs, riding her hard, penetrating so deep.

The fierce pace continued over and over until she could only gasp, apprehension filling her, her body no longer her own. She twisted helplessly, writhing beneath him, her head tossing wildly, while he held her pinned, his body taking her higher and higher. She opened her mouth to scream but no sound emerged. Every one of her senses was concentrated between her thighs, centered on the thick, hard force driving deep into her body over and over.

Streaks of fire grew into fiery flames and the tension coiled tighter as the frenzied pounding drove deeper still. *Dominic.* His name was a keening cry in her chaotic mind.

Let go for me, he coaxed.

Could she fly that high and not die? She opened her eyes and looked at his beloved face. The lines of lust and love carved so deep, the sensuality and fierce intent in his eyes, the perfect mouth, and those hard hands gripping her so firmly. The long hair falling around his face was like that of a fallen angel.

He moved just slightly and the friction against her most sensitive spot sent her mind reeling with pleasure. She gasped, stiffened, her gaze locking with his as her entire body tightened around his cock, clamping down almost violently, gripping and milking while sensation after sensation tore through her body. Her orgasm burned through her core, a firestorm out of control, flaming through her stomach, spreading up to her breasts and down her thighs. She screamed as his cock swelled even more, and he emptied himself, the condom keeping her safe. She could feel the scorching heat, every nerve ending alive with pleasure.

Dominic collapsed over the top of her, struggling for breath, holding her tight, her legs still trapped over his arms, his body still locked with hers. He didn't want to ever leave her. The moment he had the strength, he gathered Solange in his arms and rolled over, bringing her on top of him like a blanket, her head on his chest, ear over his pounding heart.

For the first time in his life he felt complete. So many centuries he had felt utterly alone, and now he would never be alone. Holding her felt right. He allowed his hand to slide down the curve of her back to the rounded curve of her buttocks. She was his, and she'd given herself freely, without reservation, opening her mind and heart to him. She'd taken him into her body, his private haven, his sanctuary.

His other hand tangled in her wealth of hair. He loved the feel of her, all silk and satin. Her soft skin seemed to melt into him, become part of him. He moved slightly, feeling the instant reaction of her inner muscles, how they gripped and pulsed around him, clamping down as if she didn't want him to leave her body.

His feelings for her were so overwhelming he couldn't speak for a moment. *You know that I love you, Solange.* He made it a statement, because there was no way she couldn't know.

He felt her smile. She made an effort to lift her head enough to lap at his pulse, a slow, languid movement a life-mate would make naturally. His body responded with a jerk of his cock. He wanted—no, needed—to feel her bite, to exchange blood in the Carpathian way.

She pressed a kiss over the pounding beat. *Yes, I can feel that you love me.* Her voice turned shy. *I hope you feel how much I love you.*

He wrapped his arms around her and held her to him, waiting until she snuggled into him. *Thank you for your trust. I will always hold it as a precious gift from you.*

She rubbed her chin along his chest, and then nuzzled against his throat. "You say things that turn me inside out, Dominic." She swallowed hard. "I didn't know a man could be like you."

"I am perfectly fine with you thinking that." And he was. His woman was his alone, and he liked that no one else ever saw this side of her. She reserved her trust and faith for him.

"I don't think I'll ever be able to move again," she said, one hand sliding up his chest to curl around his throat. "Does it get better than this? Because if it does, I won't live through it."

He laughed softly. "You will live. I will see to that. Because I intend to repeat this experience as often as possible."

"Of course you do."

"But without the condom. I want to feel every inch of you surrounding me." He allowed his body to slip from hers.

"I told you the parasites would avoid contact with me."

"I refuse to take a chance."

Silence greeted his statement, although he detected a slight moue with her lips.

"Did you just roll your eyes?" he demanded.

She laughed softly. "It could have happened," she admitted.

He rolled her over abruptly, pinning her body beneath his, his expression stern as he looked down into her laughing face. His hands framed her face and he kissed her. It wasn't what he meant to do, but he couldn't help himself. She was so beautiful to him, so miraculous. Solange Sangria Dragonseeker. *His.*

He loved her mouth, the taste of her, the heat of her, the long, drugging kisses she never pulled away from. She opened herself to him, kissing him back over and over until they both ran out of breath and he collapsed on top of her again.

Her laughter bubbled up and she pushed at his heavy body. "You're crushing me."

"I know, but I cannot move."

She tried to shove him, but laughter rumbled in his chest and he didn't budge. He nuzzled her neck. "Were you trying to move?"

"I'm waking the kitten and he's going to pounce on your bare butt."

He rolled again, with more haste than grace. The thought of the shadow cat's claws getting anywhere near certain parts of his anatomy were enough to scare any man, even a Carpathian warrior.

She smirked. "You're such a baby. Let me up. We really have to wake him and figure out how we're going to feed him."

He reluctantly allowed his arms to slide away, releasing her. Solange stood up on shaky legs, smiling down at him. She robbed him of breath. Her body gleamed with a fine sheen from their lovemaking. He loved that she didn't attempt to cover herself. Her breasts stood out proudly, and he could see the marks left by his teeth and mouth and hands. Her hair was wildly disheveled and her mouth a bit swollen from his kisses. She looked like she'd been thoroughly made love to, but he wanted to see his seed running down the inside of her thighs.

"I love looking at you," he said, sitting up.

"I know," she answered, a satisfactory purr in her voice. She stepped into the pool and rinsed off.

Dominic, fully clothed, waited for her with a warm towel. "I will have to go hunt," he said. "And do some scouting."

"I'll go with you, but I want to take care of the cub first."

"There is no need this evening," he countered. "I can look and figure out the distance you will need to be away from the vampires in order to keep the parasites silent." He rubbed the water drops from her skin, wanting to lick them off. Already his body was stirring. The tight clasp of her body combined with her scorching heat was addicting, and he would never be sated, no matter how many times he took her. And he intended to take her a million times.

Solange dressed in the short emerald green ladder dress. He loved the way the slinky material clung to the outsides of her breasts yet bared them to him. He couldn't resist caressing the light weight just to feel her softness against his palm. His fingers rolled and tugged her nipples until they were hard little beads.

"You're going to make me damp and needy all over again," she warned.

"I want you that way. If I could, I would have you in a continual state of arousal. When this is all over, be prepared to spend a long time that way." His hand crept beneath the short hem to cup her bare mound. His thumb circled her clit with a languid expertise. Her breath hitched in her throat and he leaned over to capture the breathy moan in his mouth. "I love the way you sound," he confided. "You please me, Solange. So much."

"I'm glad, Dominic. Wanting you is very easy."

When she began to ride his hand, he abruptly pulled his fingers away, licking them, his eyes on her face. "Keep wanting me."

"I don't think that's going to be a problem."

He seated himself across the room from her, wanting to watch her with the cub. Its yowl was loud as he waved his hand and removed the sleeping spell. The kitten stretched before lifting his head, its gaze darting around the room.

until he found Solange. He ran to her fast and rubbed up and down her leg.

She dropped her hand into the fur and knelt to nuzzle the mewling creature. "We need to call him something."

Dominic cringed inwardly. "It is probably best to stay detached," he advised.

"He needs a name," Solange insisted.

Dominic sighed. He didn't want to give the animal a name, not when he doubted if he could save the creature. How did one make shadow into substance? She was already half in love with the little bundle of fur and claws, and he couldn't bear to break her heart. She'd had enough heartbreak in her life. He'd healed terrible wounds, some even mortal, but this . . . He sighed again.

"*Hän sívamak*, if you get attached and I cannot save him, you will mourn the loss."

"Naming him isn't going to make a difference, Dominic," she answered, her eyes betraying sadness. "I'm already in love with him."

The kitten bounced across the room, the strange, purring growl rumbling in its chest. The shadow cat probably weighed around forty pounds, all muscle, but it couldn't keep its solid form. Dominic could see the evidence of rosettes in the sleek black fur, proof that the mages had used a jaguar in their experiments to produce the shadow cat.

"Shadow," he said.

She laughed softly. "Very inventive."

"What would you name him?" he challenged.

"Shadow, of course," she said.

The kitten shoved his face into Dominic's and licked his head, retreated, and then bounced back to bat at him playfully with a paw. He could see why Solange wanted to save the little thing. The cub's face was so cute. He winced at the word.

Her soft laughter rippled through his mind as the kitten gave up on him and bounded across the floor to her. "Adorable. He's adorable."

"You are going to collect all sorts of creatures throughout this life together." He groaned aloud, but deep inside he found he was laughing. He should have known she had a soft little heart. She'd spent a lifetime protecting women and caring for her cousins. Gruff, dangerous Solange melted at the sight of puppies and kittens.

She scratched the cub's ears. "I am dangerous, Dragonseeker, and you'd best not forget it. And don't go telling my cousins your little theories about me."

"I have not had the pleasure of meeting them yet," he said, keeping his tone speculative. "I think we will have many long conversations."

She flicked a warning gaze at him. "I've worked *very* hard at being surly. You are *not* going to ruin my reputation, *especially* with my cousin's lifemate."

He raised his eyebrow. "You do not want them to see you all girly?"

She winced openly, gritting her teeth. "I am not girly." The shadow cat nudged her so hard she nearly fell over backward. She had to catch it around the neck to steady herself. Immediately the kitten laid its head on her shoulder and gave his growling purr.

"You are girly, all soft and mushy inside," he teased.

She looked horrified, even as she soothed the shadow cat, unaware of the picture she made, the look of concern on her face as she babied the animal. His heart felt as stupidly soft and mushy as he'd just labeled her. She was so beautiful to him, as complex and mysterious as the most beautiful flower he'd ever seen.

The cat wiggled free and raced around the room, pouncing on anything that looked as if it might be moving. Solange's laughter filled the chamber, soft and musical, her eyes following the kitten's antics as it rushed around the cavern. Shadow widened his eyes and pressed his ears forward, inviting play. He stalked her across the room, with the slow freeze-frame of a cat, and then pounced on her. But she sprang to one side, avoiding the rush. The kitten rolled over and over, his momentum carrying him past her. He stood up a few feet away, shaking his head.

Dominic saw the look building in Solange's eyes, and before he could protest, she had raced across the chamber and ambushed the cat. They rolled together, over and over, Solange in her barely there dress and the cat with lethal claws and teeth.

Heart in his throat, Dominic waved his hand, building the image of clothing, thick and protective, around Solange— heavy cotton jeans and a long-sleeved top with a vest as a shield. The two rolled across the floor, snarling, spitting, rearing up, breaking apart and then coming together in a fierce mock battle, rolling once again.

The kitten backed off, arching its back. With his long tail curled, he sidestepped around Solange and then rolled over onto his side. He kept his tail in a hooked position, indicating he wanted to play. Laughing, she obliged.

Dominic realized she was feeling the kitten out, learning his strengths and weaknesses, trying to get a feeling for what had gone wrong inside of him. Why the middle part of his body was caught in shadow form. He took a chance and went outside his own body, knowing the animal was important to her and that she wanted to save him from a slow starvation.

The sibling mages had obviously been present when Xavier had mutated species for his own twisted purpose. Two of the teeth in the cat's mouth were tubes to draw and store blood. The cat had been bred for one purpose—to retrieve blood for the mages. The digestive tract and stomach were scored and lumpy, as if the combination of cat DNA and black magic had fought and scar tissue had built up. The shadow encased the middle of the cat, keeping the insides from working. He couldn't see how it was possible, but if the cat could wait, he could try to give it blood after he had pushed out the parasites.

He felt the cat's muscles bunching, ready for another spring, and exited quickly to reenter his own body. He caught the blur of motion as the cat sprang into the air, over Solange's head. His back claw caught her temple, ripping open her skin and driving her backward into the rocky basin. Dominic's heart nearly stopped when he heard the loud, ominous crack.

Solange slipped to the floor, her eyes glazed over. He was at her side instantly. Blood poured from the back of her skull. He was immediately in her body, not caring that the cat could easily attack his defenseless body. There was no skull fracture, just a very deep and nasty head wound. He repaired it from the inside out before returning to his own body. Lifting her, he made a halfhearted attempt to move the cat with his foot, but when it didn't budge, he took her to the bed.

"Talk to me."

Humor glittered in her eyes. "Ow. *Major* ow."

Relief flooded. "You took a few years off my life."

"Good thing you're immortal. I must be getting slow. I should have moved my head out of the way. He's clumsy but he's fast—and strong." She looked over at the cat and her smiled turned upside down. "Shadow! Stop that. He's lapping up the blood fast, Dominic."

Dominic turned to stop the kitten, nearly waving his hand to remove the blood, but he noticed a solid spot, right in the middle of the cat, where none had ever been. His heart rate accelerated. "Solange." He stood a short distance

away from the cub, making no attempt to stop it from licking up the blood. "Look."

She sat up gingerly. "What am I looking at?" Dominic
had already cleaned the blood from her hair and skin and
taken away her headache. When he said he would see to
her care, he took that literally.

"Your blood acts like some kind of weapon against
black magic." Dominic could barely take in the revelation.
No wonder Xavier had been searching for her. "Your blood
doesn't just kill the parasites. Xavier created the parasites
with black magic, and here they are unraveled and rendered harmless, back to their original form."

"That's impossible." She stood up, shaking her head.
"Check inside of him, Dominic. Make certain my blood isn't
going to harm him."

Instantly Dominic was at her side, wrapping a steadying
arm around her waist, but his eyes were on the cat's body.
He had heard whispers of a blood—royal blood—that
could defeat black magic, but in all his centuries and all his
travels, the rumor had never been substantiated. Slowly,
Brodrick and his ancestors had killed the very thing that
could have protected them.

Dominic did as she asked. The massive scar tissue was
slowly repairing and the layers of shadow were giving way
to the tissue and cells that belonged inside of the cat. He
merged his mind with hers so she could see the evidence
for herself.

"That doesn't make sense." Solange took a step toward
the kitten. Already a good portion of its left side was substance. The fur was thinner and there were still gaping
spots where the shadow showed through, but her blood was
forcing the magic out.

"Xavier needed your blood to open the book because it
was the only thing that could after he put the spell on it. No

one understood that," Dominic murmured, more to himself than to her. "Xavier was too clever even for himself. He sealed his book so no other mage could use his spells. He was growing paranoid, already sick and trying desperately to stay alive using Carpathian blood to sustain him. But there had to be younger mages coming up, growing more powerful, so he sealed his book of spells. Then he couldn't open it either. That is why your blood became so important."

Solange shivered. Dominic rubbed his hands up and down her arms to warm her. "Xavier is gone from this world, Solange. He cannot harm you. The mages who created this one"—he waved his hand toward Shadow—"are long gone. They abandoned the ranch next to the De La Cruz property."

She frowned at him. "How do you know that?"

"Carpathians send news to one another upon rising. Zacarias sent word."

Solange knelt beside the kitten, circling his head with her arms, and smiled up at Dominic. "If my blood did this, then I'm happy. I've never been particularly proud of my lineage, but if it can do this much good, then I'll keep it."

Dominic frowned, but didn't say a word. He wouldn't take this moment away from her for anything, not even to explain what would happen during conversion.

18

Look at me—now see yourself through my eyes.
Look at you: the perfect man of my dreams.

SOLANGE TO DOMINIC

Solange held her breath as she watched Dominic stride across the open ground toward the laboratory with his confident, superior air. She had no choice but to stay hidden in the trees, at least a hundred and thirty yards from him. Even then, the parasites quieted. They didn't go still, but they definitely ceased their tempting, painful whispers. She wanted to be closer, where she felt she had a chance to protect him, but once inside, he could only share with her by merging.

Her heart in her throat, she kept her gaze fixed on him. There were three human guards that she could see. Two were at the door of the lab and one near the southern corner. The guards watched him uneasily, but no one challenged him. They fell back under the shocking gaze of Dominic's piercing eyes.

She recognized the two jaguar-men off by themselves, keeping a wary eye on the group of vampires milling around the open yard. Both stayed close to the forest where they could easily shift and disappear into the canopy should they have need. They were heavily armed, something she rarely saw in the jaguar-men. They mostly relied on their cat for protection, but they were obviously not taking any chances meeting with vampires and humans.

A small group of immaculately dressed vampires stood to the right of the door, talking, trying to appear human, but the guards had sensed their unnaturalness and kept as far from them as possible. Occasionally one of the vampires would look toward a human and smirk, eyes feasting and saliva dribbling. It was deliberate provocation and told Solange that even the vampires were on edge. A meeting of this type was unheard-of. Representatives of several master vampires had arrived, but hunger was the most prevalent emotion she could read. There were few people to donate blood and if they wanted their meeting kept quiet, they couldn't have a massacre. The vampires had gone without feeding, and the smell of human blood had to be driving them crazy.

A sliver of moonlight fell across Dominic's face, highlighting the dark edges, the strong lines of his jaw and the gleaming, flowing hair. He looked exactly like what he was—a dangerous predator—and everyone and everything moved out of his way. She had seen him many ways: as the warrior prepared to go into battle; as a man, helping her learn to appreciate being a woman; and as a lover, fiercely passionate and infinitely tender. But she had never seen the legend in action.

Everyone gave him a wide berth, especially the vampires

who recognized the legend striding into their midst. They
scattered as he deliberately walked through their circle. No
one spoke to him, but they didn't take their eyes off him,
even as he walked straight up to the door. The guards actually held it open. He disappeared inside and the vampires
closed ranks and began to whisper.

I don't like this, Solange protested. *Couldn't you have
gone in unseen?*

Dominic had the blueprint of the laboratory in his head
from the drawings Solange had made for him. She had
spent hours hiding inside the facility and she paid attention
to detail. He had to get inside the area housing the computers, and they had security codes for that.

This is what I do best, kessake. *I will be fine. Just be ready
and keep alert. They cannot spot you or our plan fails.*

She hissed at him, and deep inside he smiled at his spitting little cat. *I love you, too.*

She subsided and he moved through the first entryway
into the hall leading to the experiment rooms. She had said
there were at least five scientists working on various experiments. They were human and involved with the society to
stop vampires. Unfortunately for them, they were in league
with the very ones they sought to stamp out. The vampires
pointed them at Carpathians, and the human society members did their best to kill as many as possible.

He opened the door and the scent of blood assailed his
senses. He had fed from Zacarias's workers, building his
strength for the long night to come. He was going to be in
two places at one time, a difficult feat for anyone. He was
adept at it, but still, cloning oneself drained strength fast
and he would need to be at the top of his game to do battle.

No one looked up when he entered. There were four
men in lab coats surrounding a fifth man who was not
human. He was dressed in combat clothes and his face was

handsome, the dark eyes compelling, every hair in place in spite of the humidity and heat. He was having a difficult time maintaining, with the scent of blood so heavy in the room.

Dominic paid little attention to any of them, his attention caught by the sixth man in the room. This was the one who kept the vampire in line, kept him from falling on the lab techs and devouring their blood. He was the one in charge, the one who made certain the vampire in the chair allowed the humans to take the blood from his veins. Twice this one had narrowly missed being killed by Dominic. His name was Flaviu, and they had detested one another as youths. Flaviu had shown a proclivity toward harming animals even before he lost his emotions. Dominic had not been surprised to see him choose to betray the Carpathian way of honor very early.

Flaviu stood up abruptly, exposing his fangs in a threat, yet backing away slightly to give himself more room. His gaze shifted surreptitiously toward the door. "You are—unexpected."

Dominic ignored him, treating him as he might a lesser vampire—with contempt, as if he were beneath Dominic's notice.

The fangs slipped again, betraying the egotistical characteristic so prevalent in vampires. When he spoke, Flaviu's voice was raspy, as if he couldn't get his voice to work around his fangs. The vampire in the chair moved restlessly, earning him a reprimand from one of the surly lab techs.

"What are you doing here, Dragonseeker?" Flaviu demanded, his tone high-pitched. "No one is supposed to be in here. You have to leave."

Dominic stopped moving around the room, examining each of the experiments and checking the slides under the

lens of the microscope. The silence stretched and lengthened. He let the vampire squirm under his piercing gaze.
Several more heartbeats went by and even the techs looked
up from their work.

"Do you really think I will obey a worm like you? I have
come at the call, but I will not walk blindly into a trap for
anyone. Stand aside or challenge me, but think carefully
before you do." His tone dripped contempt.

The room darkened. The tension stretched to a taut, thin
margin. Hissing, Flaviu backed away from Dominic. The
vampire sitting in the chair jumped to his feet, knocking
the techs out of his way.

"Henric," Flaviu snapped sharply.

Instantly the lesser vampire stopped his forward motion,
but his eyes glowed red with hatred. Without another word,
the two vampires left the room. Dominic allowed a brief
flare of satisfaction.

*They're going to be waiting for you. The first chance
they get, they'll ambush you.*

I am well aware of that. I will lead them straight to you.

*Good idea. I'm getting bored while you're having all the
fun. Work your magic, Dominic, and get into the main room.*

*I scanned the techs as I came in, and none of them
knows the security code to the room.*

He glanced at the men, who immediately looked away
and went back to their respective workstations, each clutching a vial of blood. He moved closer to one of the stations.
Several vials of blood were labeled with various names,
Brodrick's most prominent. Someone wanted to see if the
jaguar-men had an effect on parasites. He moved closer
and tested the nearest tech for resistance.

His brain was wide open, which made sense. The vampires would want men they could easily influence working

the computers in the laboratory. He attacked swiftly, piercing the man's mind to search for the experiments. He shared his findings with Solange.

The techs believe the men working in this region have all been infected with an unknown parasite and they are working on a solution. It was suggested to them that the men who live and work here—meaning the shifters, although it is clear the techs do not understand they are shifters— might have built up an immunity against the parasites. So they are testing their blood against the infected blood. They had some results with Brodrick's blood.

Solange brushed against his mind, a gentle, loving slide that shook him with the intensity of feeling in that small, tender gesture.

"What are you doing in here?" The voice was harsh and commanding.

Dominic turned slowly, his gaze falling on the guard. The gun was pointed firmly at his chest and the eyes were flat and cold. He nudged the brain of the tech closest to him.

The tech responded immediately. "He's consulting with me, Felipe."

"Sorry, man," Felipe said, shaking his head. "They've got people coming in from all over and they don't seem right. I thought maybe you were one of them."

Dominic smiled easily. "Yeah, I got the vibe, too. They all seem a little arrogant, like we're beneath them or something." He held out his hand. "Dominic. Hopefully I won't be here that long."

"Felipe," the guard said, taking the extended hand.

Dominic tested his resistance. This man would have the security code to get into the room where the computers were housed. "I can see why everyone is on edge. Who are these people? Why are they here?"

Felipe shrugged. "Brodrick tells us who is coming and when they're going."

Dominic sent him a wave of camaraderie, a subtle testing of the man's acceptance. Felipe grinned at him and clapped him on the shoulder.

"Are you keeping count?"

Felipe nodded. "Damn straight. I want them all gone as soon as Brodrick gives the word. They make everyone nervous. Sooner or later one of the boys is going to accidentally shoot one of them."

"Yeah, that would be terrible," Dominic said, sarcasm dripping from his voice. He pushed a little deeper into the guard's brain. The man really didn't like the visitors, and that could be used to Dominic's advantage. Felipe was head of security and the vampires hadn't thought to protect his brain—of course, none believed a Carpathian hunter would infiltrate their meeting.

"Brodrick's got a couple of his men guarding him. He calls them the 'elite' and they certainly think that entitles to them to do whatever they want. Every time a woman gets brought in, they're all over her. And they like to hurt her. They're cruel bastards. We just keep away from that side of the lab when they've got one here."

Dominic felt Solange's reaction, her sick, churning stomach, her racing heart, and the sorrow that she couldn't prevent the jaguar-men from kidnapping women and bringing them to a place where others allowed their atrocities. *We will make certain Brodrick cannot continue.* He sent her the reassurance even as he pushed deeper into the guard, planting more seeds of friendship. Felipe would come to believe they'd known one another a long while and that he could confide in him.

"Brodrick's got a lot of men coming in," Dominic said, pushing uneasiness into the guard's mind. "Something big must be going on." He amplified the uneasiness, glancing toward the room where the computers were housed.

Felipe's gaze followed and he frowned, rubbing at the bridge of his nose. "I counted seventeen big shots, and a few that seem to be serving the others." The guard took a few steps toward the door, obviously growing worried enough to check on what was likely his main responsibility.

Dominic gleaned from his mind that three computer techs worked around the clock on their research, finding psychic women and tracking lineage. Now was his moment. The guard was going to open the door, and he would have to be in two places at one time. Dominic separated himself from his own body, leaving his clone to step away from Felipe, to stand across the room in plain sight of all the researchers and Felipe, lifting his hand as the guard glanced around to make certain that when he punched in his code, no one else could see the complicated numbers.

Dominic allowed his real form to dissolve into molecules, lighter than air, floating around Felipe like dust particles as the guard punched in his code and opened the door to peer into the main room. Dominic simply floated inside. Satisfied that the tech was working and no one had disturbed him, Felipe closed the door. Dominic heard his footsteps receding.

Josef was a young Carpathian, considered a wild teenager, although he was in his early twenties, and he was obsessed with computers. Dominic had contacted the boy for aid, knowing the information in the computers would be vital to the Carpathians. These women were potential lifemates. They were also in need of protection. Before the entire operation could be destroyed, they needed that information. Josef had developed a virus that would destroy the entire network the jaguars and vampires were using. Once uploaded, the virus would spread like wildfire and destroy everything, filtering from one computer to another without detection until it was far too late for anything to be saved.

Dominic floated across the room until he was hovering around the tech. The man was engrossed in his work, uncaring that the woman he was gathering information about might end up kidnapped and raped, or dead and thrown away like garbage by the men employing him. Dominic probed the tech's mind. Again, he was astonished that the man wasn't protected.

He shimmered into substance, standing behind the tech, burying his fangs in the man's neck. The blood was energizing, and he took enough to exchange, so he could monitor the tech from a distance as well. He allowed a small amount of his own blood to drip into the tech's mouth. The exchange gave him complete control. It mattered little that the tech would ingest parasites, as he wouldn't be alive that long. The tech took the tiny drive from his hand with the program that would allow Josef to take over the computers from a distance. He could download all the data they needed, and when he was done, upload the vicious virus.

Once Josef's program was in the computer, Dominic took back the drive and had the tech open the door. He floated out to reconnect with his body. The computers were now in Josef's more than capable hands. Dominic had other work to do.

You're certain the boy will be able to retrieve all the data and really destroy their network? Solange sounded anxious.

He knows what he is doing, Dominic reassured, sending up a silent prayer that he was right. Josef was wild, but he was highly intelligent and programming was his first love.

Reconnecting with his body sent a tremor running through him, and for a moment his legs shook. He stored that reaction in his mind. He couldn't afford the couple of seconds it took to readjust when he was in the midst of the vampires. One moment of weakness, of vulnerability, and he would be torn to shreds. He was one of the most feared—and therefore the most hated—of Carpathian warriors. And vampires had long memories. They existed on a steady diet of hatred and revenge.

Dominic made his way through the laboratory. It was actually smaller than it appeared from the outside because the walls were thick to withstand an assault as well as to keep the inside cooler. There were sleeping quarters for the men who lived there, five scientists and three computer techs. The barracks were attached, housing seventeen guards. There was no evidence that the jaguar-men stayed, which fit with their personalities. They would want to sleep in the forest where they could see or feel an enemy coming at them.

One room had several barred cells. There were blood-stains on the cell floor as well as blood spatter on the wall from the women slaughtered there. No one had bothered to clean up, and the stains were piled on top of one another. Any prisoner would have to endure lying in the cell knowing others had been murdered there. The sight sickened Solange and he felt her silent weeping.

There was no way to save them all, kessake ku toro sívamak—*beloved little wildcat. In this life we can only do our best.* He sent her warmth and comfort.

I know, it's just that they needed someone, and the thought of them dying like that, all alone, scared, with no one to help them . . . She trailed off.

His heart melted a little. His Solange. Tenderhearted. Who would ever believe the truth of her? *I cannot be late for this meeting, Solange. Are you up to this?*

He felt her instant reaction, the steel spine, the unfailing courage. Her need to protect him. *Of course I am.* There was a bite to her voice, a definite reprimand, the implication that he had no need to ask.

Dominic knew she was ready, but he wanted her to know it. The sight of the cells had really shaken her. He strode boldly from the laboratory into the open yard. The vampires had gathered just beyond the open area around the building, far enough away that no one else had the opportunity to hear them.

Giles held court, with at least twenty vampires around him, while his own lesser vampires guarded his back. Dominic had to admit it was an amazing sight, one he had never dreamt he'd witness. Vampires' egos were too big, and they didn't stay for long in the company of other vampires. And food sources would eventually disappear. As it was, the hunger radiating from the group was so overwhelming that, even though he'd fed well, he still felt a ravenous appetite.

The heartbeats of the human guards patrolling around the building were overly loud, a thundering drum calling to them all. Dominic subtly fed the hunger, increasing the need as he slipped into the group. His parasites leapt and rejoiced, answering the call of the others in the bodies of the surrounding vampires.

Solange had gone very still, afraid for him, but he knew her hands were rock steady on her weapon. She had them in her sight now and a part of her settled in spite of the danger.

"Dragonseeker." Giles's voice cut through the whispers of the parasites and the hissing and growling of the vampires.

He had known the master vampire would single him out. He was legend among them. The murmurs started, and he stayed standing while they all turned to look. Black hatred added to the crushing hunger emanating from the group. He took a step and they parted immediately, stepping back away from him as he moved toward Giles. He didn't look right or left, but kept his challenging gaze on the master vampire. He walked with utter confidence, his expression holding both superiority and contempt.

Giles looked him up and down, as if Dominic were beneath him, but the lesser vampires moved closer as if he'd given them direction. "I heard rumors that you had joined our ranks, but did not believe them."

Flaviu stepped away from Giles, revealing exactly who had told the *master* the Dragonseeker was among them. *Take a good look at him, Solange. I will be sending both him and his friend, the one off to his left, after you. Tell me before you kill them so I can shield the sounds and flash.*

No problem.

The confidence in her voice reassured him. She could handle the pair. He gave Giles a cocky, mock salute as he shrugged his shoulders. "Ruslan used to make sense. Whether he does now, we shall see."

"You have sworn allegiance."

Again Dominic shrugged. "If he has found a way to take down the Dubrinsky family, I will aid him. Draven Dubrinsky started this entire mess by selling out my sister's lifemate to Xavier. His father should have destroyed him, but he allowed him to continue while the rest of us were required to defend our people. We need a strong leader."

Giles nodded slowly, looking a bit relieved. It was clear he didn't want to have to try to defeat Dominic in battle. His relief was apparent to the other vampires as well, and they moved back as Dominic returned to the rear of the group. He didn't want any of them behind him. He could easily spot the ones who had been followers for some time. They were far more comfortable within the group, while others, like him, stayed slightly apart.

Giles stood and everyone went silent. "We have come

together for one purpose—to see to the destruction of the
Dubrinsky family. All over, envoys for the five are meeting
with our members to let them know the time is near for us
to rise up and take over ruling."

A roar went up. Under cover of the energy, Dominic
fed the hunger cravings. He needed the scent of blood to
enhance the effect, and stared hard at the guard who was
keeping an eye on them, his gun close, and his knife in his
hand as he carved a stick of wood. His hand slipped and he
yelped, jerking his blade from his grip. Blood welled up.
Dominic sent a small breeze building behind him, pushing
the aroma straight into the mass of hungry vampires.

Giles held up his hand and waited for the crowd to quiet.
Several turned their heads toward the bleeding guard. The
guard paid them no attention, not realizing their appearances covered monsters and he was in grave danger. He
walked several steps, calling out to his companion, blood
dripping onto the ground. Dominic fanned the breeze just
enough to send another burst of scent into the air.

"Dubrinsky lives as in the old days. We have gone to
modern technology, and in the end that will defeat him. He
rules his little corner of the world and forgets the larger
picture. We have acquired wealth and used it wisely. Our
company owns a satellite and we have pinpointed Mikhail
Dubrinsky's favorite resting place."

The roar went up again, a thunderous shout that covered
the subliminal message Dominic sent into the conclave. *Hunger.* Gnawing, biting hunger that refused to leave. *Starved for
blood.* Wonderful, aromatic, adrenaline-laced blood. *Human
guards walking around thinking they were in charge, holding their pitiful weapons.* Humans were so fragile, one tearing bite of the flesh and the delicious hot blood pumped out
like a fountain. *So many of them, enough that with just a few
moments of heady work the conclave could indulge.* Open a

few arteries and the blood would spray everywhere, enough to feed everyone.

More heads turned toward the guard. Two of the vampires licked their lips and one's disguise slipped just a bit, his dark, thick hair, disappearing to reveal his true nature, the graying wisps that were left covering his scalp.

Solange, the two vampires, Faviu and his buddy Henric, are getting very hungry. I am going to send them your way.

About time, she responded. *I was thinking about taking a nap.*

"We have a three-point attack planned, but first we will hit Dubrinsky where it hurts. He has a weakness for the people in the village near where he lives. We will attack the humans, his women and children. They will believe the main attack will be centered there, but in fact we will follow his movements by satellite. He will not expect an attack from the air, from the ground and from beneath the ground simultaneously. He will be destroyed."

The guard had disappeared around the corner of the laboratory, but Dominic replicated an image of him, blood dripping, heading into the forest, and he projected that image into the heads of Henric and Flaviu. The two vampires looked at each other and then at the others. Saliva dripped from Henric's mouth and Flaviu exposed his fangs twice. Dominic simply waited, allowing the image of the guard to replay in their heads.

"We will, of course, have a few practice runs. We will try such an attack first on a couple of our greatest enemies in order to perfect the attack on the prince."

Dominic's heart lurched. *Zacarias! Are you getting this? They have to mean your family. Your people are in danger.*

Power flowed into his mind. Zacarias. There was no edge, as if the continual call of the vampire had been pushed away by sheer will. Zacarias had more will—more heart and courage—than any other warrior Dominic had known. He would do his duty, protect his family, and there would be no worry of turning until after the job was done.

I hear. I have sent the news to my family and it is being sent to the prince as we speak. Josef is nearly finished copying the data from the computers. Get out of there.

Dominic smiled a little at the absolute authority in Zacarias's voice. He would expect obedience. Everyone obeyed Zacarias. They always had. Zacarias was swift and deadly, and held tremendous power. He didn't have patience for those who didn't follow his word. He didn't speak lightly, and if he said something, that something became law.

Will do as soon as my task is complete.

Dominic broke off, needing his attention centered on Solange. She was in the trees, moving fast, drawing the two vampires away from the safety of the conclave. He moved a little deeper into the circle of vampires, wanting to make certain he was seen and couldn't later be blamed for the disappearance of the two. More than anything, he wanted to destroy Giles. The vampire had grown powerful and arrogant.

Solange. Can you kill them?

Solange sighed. Of course she could kill them. Dominic persisted in worrying. Before it would have aggravated her, but now she knew loving someone meant you fretted about their safety. She was certainly apprehensive about Dominic surrounded by a crowd of very hungry undead.

Henric dissolved into vapor, searching through the trees for the missing guard or the blood trail that would lead to him. Solange positioned her arrows over her shoulder, the crossbow behind her back, and used a liana to slip from the canopy to the ground. She did her best to look helpless, fluffing out her hair and humming, trying to look like a lost tourist. She wandered aimlessly, leaving tracks an amateur could find, but all the while making her way toward the second vampire, the one Dominic had called Flaviu.

Flaviu stepped out from behind a tree and bowed low. "You look lost."

Solange sent him a tentative smile. She had practiced a million times with the crossbow, now she had to get it right. "I am lost. My friends and I are backpacking and I got separated from them." As she talked she moved into position. Now or never. Henric wouldn't be gone long. *Now, Dominic.*

Solange didn't wait for an acknowledgment. The crossbow slid into her hand, the arrow fitting smoothly as she brought it up and shot almost in one continuous motion. The head of the arrow pierced Flaviu's chest and ignited, the flash white-hot. He opened his mouth but his heart had incinerated in his chest and his body slowly crumbled to the ground, the fire spreading from the inside out. The vampire burst into flame and rolled, his grotesque mouth stretched thin over long, stained fangs. He snapped at her, clawing the earth, trying to drag himself across the vegetation to reach her. The smoke rose, a blackish red, strange shapes with open mouths appearing and then subsiding.

Solange backed away from the undead as the remaining flames burst into a bright fireball and ashes rained down.

Get out of there, Dominic hissed. *Run.*

She sprinted away from the evidence of a burned vampire. There was no wind below the canopy, but thunder rumbled in the distance and the heavy layer of mist that had developed began to turn to a steady drizzle. That might help remove her scent, but she doubted it. Henric would be coming after her.

She leapt over a rotting log, sprinting for the small cache of weapons she'd hidden a hundred yards ahead in the huge sprawling tangle of roots. Her cat suddenly leapt, slamming hard against her bones, frantic to get out. Instinctively

Solange changed directions. Behind her she heard a high-pitched yell.

"Stop, woman!" Henric sent the order, pushing hard at her brain.

Solange stopped abruptly and turned to face him, her movements uncoordinated, like a jerky puppet. She blinked at him, shaking her head, fear stamped into her expression.

Henric smirked, now that he had her under his control. He wanted her terror, wanted the adrenaline flowing, lacing the blood. The high he got was better than sex to him. He crooked his little finger at her.

Solange didn't feel the pressure in her brain. She shook her head violently and let out a little squeak. What did most women do when they were terrified? When she was terrified—and she was fairly scared—her mind raced with every weapon possible she had at her disposal. Long ago, she'd learned that her intellect and her ability to stay calm were her two most powerful weapons. In this situation, she was certain a gun, knife and definitely her crossbow would be more helpful.

She made a move as if to run, but her feet refused to move. "What do you want?"

"Are you having trouble running?" Henric taunted. Deliberately he allowed his civilized mask to slip, showing her the skin stretched taut over his skull, his bloodred, glowing eyes and his dark, bloodstained teeth revealed by a parody of a smile.

"Help!" Solange twisted and turned frantically. "Someone please help."

"No one is coming to help you." Henric took a step toward her and watched as tears swam in her eyes. "No one is going to come. No one can save you."

"What are you?" Deliberately she recoiled, wringing her hands together.

Henric shuffled a few steps closer, drawing out her fear, feeding on it. He looked down at his hand. His fingernails lengthened into long, razor-sharp talons. Smiling, he looked back up at her.

Solange held her crossbow and now she was smiling. *Now, Dominic.* "Then I guess I'd better save myself," she said aloud as she shot the arrow.

Henric tried to dissolve, but she was close, almost too close. The arrow shot him through the heart and nearly pushed out the back when it ignited. Henric, half substance and half mist, shrieked and howled. He spat curses at her as he tried to dislodge the arrow burning white-hot from his back to his heart. The arrow had gone through the center of the withered heart, impaling the organ and holding it to form.

Solange calmly fit another arrow into her crossbow and shot him a second time, watching with cool detachment as he burned to ash. She took a breath and let it out.

They're dead, Dominic. Where do you want me?

No injuries? Not even a scratch from running through the forest?

She heard the concern in his voice and carefully inspected her body to ensure she had no cuts or scratches. *I'm good.*

Make your way back to your original position. I will get things going here. Everything is in place. When all hell breaks loose, these are the leaders I want you to try to take out.

Solange studied the images in his mind. She recognized Giles and his lesser vampires. Dominic had paid attention to four others. One looked older, unusual for a vampire to make that choice, a distinguished, silver-haired man wearing, of all things, a business suit.

He goes by the name Carlo. He has been living in Sicily so long he thinks he is part of the mob.

She could see that. He certainly looked intimidating. The second man was slender with the cold, flat eyes of a killer. He wore casual clothes and he made her shiver for no reason at all. His hair was longer and drawn back in the usual Carpathian style. His jaw was pronounced and he idly swung a chain. He stood a distance from the others, and his gaze was watchful.

Akos. He used to travel with a falcon. I would not be surprised if he uses a harpy eagle to watch the skies, Dominic warned. *Wherever he goes, there is a bloodbath.*

Great. He and Brodrick are probably friends.

Men like Brodrick and Akos have no friends, only those they use as pawns. Do not underestimate him. If you have the shot, take it when the frenzy starts.

Solange was a little uneasy with the word *frenzy. What are you going to do?*

Turn them on one another. As soon as Josef gives me the word that the virus has had a chance to work through the computers and destroy the data and spread into the network, I will destroy the laboratory as well.

"He's going to turn them on one another," she muttered aloud. She had a picture of vampires devouring one another in her head.

She climbed back up the tree and found her favorite resting place. Two boughs made a nice little cradle for her to stretch out in, her weapons close. Her favorite sniper rifle lay waiting, and she checked it out of habit. No one had disturbed her blind, but she cast around for tracks, always careful of the jaguar-men.

I'm in position. She used the scope to take a better look at her targets.

The third image he sent her was of a short, stocky man who could easily have passed for a jaguar male. He had thick, ropy muscles on the frame of a serious body builder.

*His name is Milan. He will try to outdo all of them for
viciousness just to prove a point. If you cannot get him, get
clear. If you only have three shots, Solange, make him one
of them.*

Will do. I know what I'm doing.

They can take to the air, he reminded.

She flooded his mind with warmth. It was strange to
have someone concerned about her well-being. *I'm not the
one in the lion's den. Show me the last one.*

This is Kiral. The man had chosen the form of a young,
virile man. He wore skintight jeans, and she doubted seriously if the bulge in the front was really his. She was fairly
certain he'd stuffed his pants.

He can choose his form, Dominic reminded.

She could hear the humor in his voice. *That is just obscene.
He scares me with that package. I think I'm shooting him first.*

Dominic's soft laughter soothed her nerves.

She took her time studying each potential target. The
vampires were all talking at once, but she could feel the
tension in the air, in spite of the distance. The rain fell
steadily, making her cradle a little slippery, and she tied off
a couple of vines for added safety. Thunder rumbled, and
twice, in the distance, lightning forked.

The air felt charged, as if violence would erupt at any
moment. She realized she wasn't the only one feeling it. There
was movement on the roof of the laboratory. Guards crawled
across the flat rooftop, staying low, getting in position. They
were heavily armed and Felipe led them. Solange was fairly
certain Dominic had prompted him somehow to gather his
men to defend themselves from a potential threat—but she
knew they were the bait.

Giles continued to stir up the vampires, pitching the
plans to them and emphasizing technology and how
Mikhail Dubrinsky, the prince of the Carpathian people,

lived in the dark ages and refused to change with the times. Solange could see the crowd had grown restless and many of them were having trouble keeping up the illusion of their appearance. Hunger beat at them and the scent of blood was heavy in the air. She didn't know how Dominic was amplifying the smell with the rain falling, but he managed.

With businesslike precision she fit her scope to her weapon and the rifle to her shoulder. She was certain the frenzy was about to start.

19

I'll wait for you to see it, forever if it takes . . .
Solange, my very own, amazing gift beyond worth.

DOMINIC TO SOLANGE

When Dubrinsky leaves his lair to rush to the aid of the village, it will be far too late, we will have turned his people into the dead. Blood will run in rivers down the streets. Ours will be a feast beyond all imagining, celebrating our new world order," Giles, the master vampire continued.

The vampires roared again, but this time the sound wasn't quite as loud. More moved from the inner circle to look hungrily toward the laboratory where the humans lived and worked. Dominic pushed their need for blood up as far as he dared. He wanted more information, and Giles's control over his conclave was beginning to unravel rapidly.

"Our puppet awaits our orders. He will be programmed to drive a truck with the bomb into the prince's home. His lifemate is with child. We will get every one of them. From beneath the ground, two of our best will destroy everything above them. And from the air we will destroy everything below. Once he is gone, the vessel will cease to exist."

Dominic waited for the roar of approval to quiet. "What of his daughter?" he asked, keeping his voice pitched low so the vampires had to strain to hear.

Giles looked annoyed. "She is of no consequence. She is female."

He's been too long in Brodrick's company. Solange's sarcasm filled his mind. *The jaguar-men are slinking into the forest. They sense something is going to happen and they don't want any part of it,* she added.

Are they coming toward you?

The idea that the jaguar-men might go after her while he was otherwise busy shook him. He should have been prepared for them to abandon the site. Wild animals had sharp senses, reading emotions. They couldn't fail to read the ravenous hunger and the discontent of the vampires. It was even possible the hunger had gotten to them as well and they had gone hunting.

No. But I'll stay alert. You just worry about being in a nest of very dangerous killers.

And you remember that where those two are, Brodrick is not far behind.

He felt her uneasiness and knew she was concentrating on protecting him rather than herself. He bit back his inclination to give her the order to retreat. She wouldn't do it. He wouldn't have done it if their positions were reversed. He had to trust in her skills.

I love you.

Three little words. Her soothing, tender tone. He took a breath. She would be careful for his sake. He needed her, and she knew that.

His orchestra was in place; all he had to do was start conducting. He sent the pieces of the plan to Zacarias. They didn't have a timeline, but Giles wasn't going to give one, not when they wanted to test their plan first. It was now or never. He had to destroy as many of the undead as possible. He didn't want anyone escaping to know that their plan had been compromised, so that feeding frenzy had to start with someone else. He looked at Giles's trusted vampires.

You're smiling.

Am I? Maybe I am feeling just a little mean.

He felt her take a steadying breath. He did the same and reached for the technician inside the laboratory. *Take the guard's gun and wound the researchers inside the building. Force them to come outside.*

The overwhelming sight and smell of blood would send the vampires spiraling out of control. All it would take was for one to go after the wounded humans and the dam would break. The others would follow suit. He was certain Giles would try to assert his authority and send in his lesser vampires to control the mob, and that would open them up for attack. The guards on the roof would begin firing in an effort to protect their colleagues from the undead, and in the ensuing mayhem, he and Solange would be able to kill at will—he hoped.

The sounds of gunshots were muffled by the thick walls of the laboratory, but distinct nevertheless. Giles gave up holding the attention of the crowd, stopping abruptly as they all turned toward the commotion. Lightning forked across the sky, sizzling, blinding with white-hot heat, very close. One bolt slammed into a tree just to the edge of their group. The tree exploded, branches splintering, the trunk blackened. Flames rushed through the network of limbs.

Men poured out of the laboratory, running into the cleared ground between the forest and the building. White coats and guard shirts were splattered in bright red, inviting blood. A few of the men, obviously just awakened and without wounds, shouted for the guards. The computer tech rushed outside brandishing a gun, firing into the chaotic crowd.

A shot rang out from the roof as a guard fired. The sound echoed through the forest. The computer tech staggered, and on the fringe of the vampires, the one called Milan fell to the ground.

Done.

Solange's voice whispered in his mind and he directed a series of strikes at the shocked vampire group. He incinerated the fallen Milan as well as two others who had been close. Even as he did so, a group of vampires rushed the bloody techs. Giles shouted to his lesser vampires to intercede, to form a wall between the humans and the hungry vampires, even as the master vampire began to retreat.

The first of the undead ripped the nearest wounded tech open, falling on him, gulping the rich, hot blood. Guards on the roof opened fire. The sound once again reverberated through the forest and Kiral jerked, spinning around. He glanced up toward the canopy, exposing his fangs. A volley of shots rang out. Men screamed in horror. Blood spattered across the yard. Vampires tore into one another, ripping through Giles's guard to get to the feast.

Lightning pounded the ground, striking Kiral, incinerating him on the spot. One vampire caught in the crossfire between the guards and the lightning strikes went down, bullet holes in his head, while the other half of his body burned. He dragged himself blindly across the ground toward the pooling blood while the others trampled him to get to the humans who had huddled together in an effort to protect themselves.

Dominic's clone pushed, shoved and clawed his way

with the frenzied pack of the undead, eager to get at the blood spraying into the air and over the terrorized humans. The guards fired into the mass, adding to the chaos. Lightning forked and struck and thunder rolled, adding to the terrible din.

Dominic flowed across the ground, slamming his fist into the heart of the nearest vampire, his speed so fast he was a mere blur. He took the heart, and just that fast incinerated it before switching directions and rushing Giles. The lesser vampires were torn to shreds, desperately trying to join the feast and get to the well of blood to repair their torn bodies. He caught Giles just inside the line of massive trees.

Dominic struck hard, slamming his fist deep, fingers seeking the ultimate prize. The master vampire twisted away, raking his talons across Dominic's face, digging furrows down his jaw and to his neck. He leaned down and sank his teeth deep, forcing Dominic to retreat. The two stared at one another, blood dripping from Giles's mouth and hands and running black down his chest. Dominic's neck and face bled freely.

Giles licked his lips. "How can this be? You are one of us."

"I am Dragonseeker, you fool," Dominic said, contempt in his voice. "Did you really believe I would choose to give up my soul and join your despicable ranks?"

Giles snarled, revealing his bloodstained teeth. "You are responsible for this mess."

Dominic shrugged. "Of course. But you will be blamed." Deliberately the vampire sucked Dominic's blood from his fingers. "You have the parasites. They answered my call." As he spoke he took a step to his left.

Dominic didn't wait for the attack; he struck fast and hard, slamming a bolt of lightning at the spot where Giles's next step would take him. The master vampire shrieked as the white-hot energy burned through his shoulder and down his side, hip and leg, a laser beam sheering one quarter of the body completely off, cauterizing as it burned through the rotting flesh.

Giles went down, rolled, reaching for his severed body, clawing at it, trying to drag it to him as Dominic leapt on him, driving his fist deep once again, fingers burrowing through decomposed flesh and tissue to reach the withered heart. An ominous crack was his only warning. A spear slammed through his back, impaling him, driving him down to the ground and pinning him there. Roots burst through the vegetation to wrap around his throat and tangle around his body, holding him.

Dominic exploded energy outward, burning through the woody roots. Even as he did so, root structures formed a caged of finned, thick wood, holding him prisoner. It was a delaying tactic only, a chance for Giles to repair his rotting body. Dominic braced himself and shoved the spear through his body, cauterizing the wound as he did so. The pain washed over and through him. He heard the echo of Solange's shattered cry and pushed her out of his mind, afraid she would feel the mind-numbing pain.

He forced his body under control, rolling, seeing the multitude of bats staring at him with hungry eyes. They dropped, covering his face and head, biting ferociously as he exploded the cage of roots outward to allow his release. He managed to get to his knees, flinging the biting creatures aside and staggering a little as he got his legs under him.

Giles pushed himself up, his body stitched haphazardly together, one quarter of his body blackened and grotesque. He growled, spittle running down his face, his eyes blazing bloodred. "My body is dead, Dragonseeker. I can take being cut into a million pieces and still defeat you. Your body is flesh and blood. You feel pain."

Dominic's eyebrow shot up. He was weakened from using energy to sustain the storm, and keeping his clone where the other vampires could clearly see him. He didn't want the information compromised. He knew some of the emissaries would escape and he couldn't afford the plan to be changed. That meant being visible so there was no chance that anyone would discover he had brought about the destruction of the laboratory and everyone in it.

"You flatter yourself, Giles. You always did. You seem to be stalling for time. Do you believe your pawns will come to protect you?" He kept his tone a low taunt. Giles had believed himself invincible, but he was shaken. Dominic knew his reputation was legendary and the master vampire would much rather his minions battle the Dragonseeker than himself. He also was well aware that the undead had huge egos and, although true, the taunt was insulting.

I'm working my way to you. Solange had a sob in her voice.

No, stay away from here. I will defeat him.

I'm not in a position to help you.

Take out as many as possible, but fire only when the guards do. I will not be there to finish them, so they may detect your presence.

Dominic kept his attention centered on Giles. The vampire's face twisted into a mask of pure hatred. Dominic prodded him more. "You lost control of them, didn't you? Instead of protecting the humans, they are ripping them to pieces, gulping blood. And somehow I think even if you'd managed to escape, Ruslan would be very, *very* angry. He is not the most forgiving man I ever met."

The red eyes began to burn, but the vampire held his

temper in check. "This incident will only make the humans much more eager to join with us to hunt the undead. We will point them to Dubrinsky's precious village."

Dominic had managed to push the pain far enough away that he could breathe again. Solange was trying to do it for him, matching the rhythm of his burning lungs to her breathing.

Dominic bowed slightly and waved his hand, making certain that Giles followed the gesture with his furious gaze while Dominic gathered the powerful energy sizzling and crackling in the sky overhead. He let the power fill his exhausted body and, leaving a second clone behind, moved away from his body, leaving the clone exposed and open.

Standing just in front of it, insubstantial and transparent, he waited for Giles to make his move. His clone hunched a little and pressed his palm to the blackened hole in his chest, just to the left of his heart. He could feel his strength ebbing. Two clones and a storm drained his energy fast, but he held his transparent form.

Giles charged, rushing full force and with preternatural speed, going for the kill. Dominic stepped forward to meet the rush, using Giles's momentum and his own incredible strength to punch forward. In the split second before the vampire got to his fist, Dominic materialized, his clone dissolving. Giles impaled himself on the extended fist. Dominic seized the heart before the undead knew what was happening. He extracted the withered, blackened organ and tossed it a distance from the master vampire, directing the lightning to the putrid object.

Giles screamed hideously, the cry reverberating through the forest. He staggered across the ground, his hands seeking his missing heart. Slowly crumpling to the ground, he spat at Dominic before his body succumbed to the loss. Lightning jumped to the body, incinerating it. The vampire writhed and twisted in the searing flames, as if a part of him still lived. The fire hissed and spluttered in protest, but burned quickly, reducing the undead to ash.

Dominic dropped to one knee, his head down, dragging air into his lungs. He still had to wait for Josef to signal it was safe to destroy the laboratory and get Solange to safety.

Dominic! Her voice gave him the necessary incentive to move.

Giles is dead. I am returning to the battle.

I can hear the weariness in your voice. Do you need blood? I can come to you.

When we are finished here. The idea of her blood, that incredible healing force flowing into this body, energized him. He strode back through the trees to the laboratory as he allowed his clone to dissolve.

Solange breathed a sigh of relief and turned her attention back to the chaotic scene at the laboratory. Screams of terror filled the air and the scent of blood permeated everything. Bullet after bullet rained down from the roof. The undead, now riddled with bullet holes, looked up to mark the guards as prey. She had wanted these men dead, but not like this, not in such a horrific manner. The vampires had lost all control, devouring everything with blood. She couldn't spot either of the jaguar-men. They had definitely made themselves scarce at the first sign of trouble.

She fit the rifle to her shoulder again and squeezed the trigger a split second after a guard fired. A volley of shots drowned out hers. Lightning slammed into the downed vampire. She searched through her scope to try to find one of the vampires Dominic had wanted destroyed. It was difficult to identify any of them now. The images had faded, leaving them as rotting corpses, skin peeling away, sunken eyes with tufts of gray or white hair sticking to their skulls.

Blood was everywhere, on their clothing and faces; their

hands were slick with it. She went by clothes recognition, hoping she had it right. She spotted the one she thought was Carlo standing at the foot of the building, under the eaves, out of sight of the guards. He went up the side of the building fast, skittering up the wall like a lizard, leaping onto Felipe's back, teeth tearing at his neck. The first shot got him through the back of his skull, the second through his back and straight through his heart. His form shattered, he spun around, face covered with blood, eyes blazing madly, looking toward the forest. He leapt into the air, beginning to shift when the lightning struck him, incinerating him so that ashes rained down into the mass of frenzied vampires ripping and tearing, gulping bright, hot blood.

Solange wiped the sweat from her face, her stomach lurching. She'd never seen anything like the chaotic bloodbath taking place. The undead devoured everything in sight, tearing at each other, snapping and biting like a wild pack of starved animals. She was used to the laws of the forest, but this was something altogether different. Sweat dripped into her eyes and she reached again to wipe it away. Her cat leapt just as the muffled sound of powerful wings from above registered. She rolled from the cradle of the tree, catching a liana and using her forward momentum to carry her to the next tree. She'd lost the rifle, but her crossbow and arrows were around her neck and she had a knife strapped to her thigh.

The harpy eagle screamed as it missed, the huge talons snatching empty air. Razor-sharp, the size of a grizzly bear's claws, she would have been seriously injured had the large bird managed to sink those talons into her.

Solange, talk to me.

Dominic's calmness steadied her. She fit an arrow into her crossbow and studied the night sky. The eagle was circling, preparing for another attack. Lightning forked the sky, allowing her to see the huge bird coming closer.

A little glitch. Your friend Akos sent the harpy eagle after me. He's directing the attack. You might want to take him out for me so I don't have to shoot this beautiful bird.

Do not take chances, Solange. Shoot it if you have to.

Solange timed the bird's attack, allowing her cat to guide her reflexes. As the eagle approached, soaring low in the canopy, dropping rapidly, the heavy wingbeats were a warning in her head. She waited, counting silently to herself. She didn't want to kill the magnificent creature, not when she knew a vampire was using it to attack her. Ordinarily the bird would never have done such a thing—unless she was too near a nest.

The talons nearly raked her face as she ducked back, but the bird had no way to turn, the branches too close and severely limiting the maneuverability of the eagle. The wings used powerful strokes to gain enough height to clear the branches and rise once more into the roiling sky. Heavy black clouds lit up around the edges with the sizzling lightning, revealing the eagle as it circled around toward her once more.

She tracked the bird with the crossbow, but something in her refused to kill it. There'd been too much killing today. She could still hear the screams, the terror, the sound of gunfire, and knew the remaining men were being slaughtered. All of those working at the laboratory had been fully aware that they were targeting women for kidnap, rape and death. She didn't have to like the manner in which they were dying, but at least they had chosen their own path. The harpy eagle was being forced into unnatural behavior.

Dominic hissed at her. *I cannot find Akos. Kill the eagle and get to safety quickly. I will track him.*

A warning. A command. Worry. Dominic thought the vampire was coming after her. She thought it more than likely the undead was using the opportunity to escape.

She braced herself to obey, watching as the eagle made its approach and then dropped fast out of the sky, talons extended for the grab. She timed the dodge a second time, realized those claws were larger than she had thought, and hurled herself out of the way. She flung her hand out, expecting to catch the liana she had marked for her safety rope, but she missed it, her palm scooping empty air.

There was no shifting in midair; all she could do was make herself as limp as possible and try to find soft vegetation. She landed hard, her air whooshing from her lungs, leaving her gasping for breath and unable to move. Stars exploded behind her eyelids. She lay in the thick vegetation, desperate to breathe, her body aching in a million places. Eyes closed, she let a small groan escape, considering just going to sleep right there. It seemed too much of an effort to get up.

Tell me you are alive and well, Solange, Dominic demanded. *Akos is coming after you and I have to stop him.*

Be my guest. I'll just lie here and rest.

~

Dominic took to the air, following the faint blood scent Akos had left. The vampire was vicious, with a streak of cruelty he'd had since childhood. In shredding the humans he had gotten blood all over him. He hadn't bothered to take the time to clean himself, probably reliving the experience and basking in the memory of the bloodbath. He enjoyed the suffering and terror of his victims, and the scent of their blood permeating his clothing would heighten the memory.

Dominic heard the eagle scream and abruptly changed

direction. Akos was fleeing, calling the harpy to him as he streamed through the forest, winding his way in and out of the trees, unaware he was leaving droplets of blood behind. Dominic didn't want to get too far from Solange, not with all the vampires in the area. At this point, they had fed well and would disperse rapidly, fearing Giles's wrath. None but his lesser vampires would be aware that he'd been destroyed and they would leave immediately. Still . . .

He caught up with the mist a few minutes later. Droplets of blood scattered through the gray vapor trail identified the vampire instantly. Dominic used a rare Carpathian command. Vampires had been born Carpathian and therefore were still subject to the law of blood.

"*Veriak ot en Karpatiiak*—by the blood of the Prince, *muonìak te avoisz te*—I command you to reveal yourself." His voice boomed through the forest, shaking the trees. The ground rolled beneath his feet, and above him lightning split the dark clouds.

Monkeys howled and rushed through the canopy, agitated. The harpy eagle screamed again, his flight stuttering in the sky before he recovered and settled into the branches of a tree, slowly folding his great expanse of wings. Rustling in the underbrush betrayed a multitude of wildlife. A snake lifted its head and lizards skittered across boughs and trunks.

The vapor wavered, grew substance until Akos, transparent, fighting the command, landed hard on the ground and staggered quickly to his feet. His clothes were drenched in fresh blood and his mouth, teeth and jaw were smeared. Blood spatter caught in his hair appeared as shiny black dots when a burst of lightning lit up the darkened forest. He grinned, showing his spiked teeth. "Dragonseeker. I should have known."

Dominic circled to the right, keeping a wary eye on the

sky. Akos would use the harpy eagle for distraction and he would try to end the battle fast. A vicious fighter, he only chose the battles he could win. His eyes had taken on a glowing red, but they were darting back and forth, as if Akos thought he could still escape.

"There is no escaping justice," Dominic said quietly, watching the shifting eyes.

The gaze went up just for a split second and Dominic used his blurring speed, slamming into Akos as the harpy eagle dropped from the sky. His fist penetrated the chest wall as the talons reached for his eyes. He whirled them both around, the vampire shrieking, the black blood pouring over his fist and arm, burning through to the bone. The eagle's claws wrapped around the back of Akos's skull, ripping and tearing for a purchase.

~

Solange didn't really dare rest, lying there unprotected, afraid the vampire would send the eagle after her. She cautiously opened her eyes to look up at the darkened canopy. Three pairs of cat's eyes glowed back at her, staring with a predator's intense focus. Her heart jumped in her chest and began to pound. Jaguar-men. They hadn't gone far from the laboratory, had probably found a safe haven in the canopy and watched the bloody massacre. Her first instinct was to try to run, or to shift and run, but these were strong males, fast and ferocious, used to hunting. She didn't have a chance so she stayed still, willing herself not to panic.

Dominic. She kept her voice very calm. *How far away are you?*

Tell me, beloved.

She savored the sound of his voice, so calm, so confident. Her heart settled. This time she wasn't alone. These men would never take her alive. She had vowed that a long time ago. She knew Dominic would come for her. She just had to hold them here.

Brodrick and two of his soldiers. Give me an estimate. I can keep them distracted. She felt the crossbow in her hand. She hadn't dropped it. And she had the knife.

She felt his hesitation. *I must destroy Akos. Can you manage until I get there? Tell me the truth.*

Her fingers tightened around the bow. She brought it up and fired. The arrow went straight and true, streaking through the sky, up through the leaves and branches to drive into one of those glowing cat's eyes. On impact the arrow ignited, burning through the skull. She heard the thud as something heavy dropped from the branches. She rolled over and over toward the slope that would take her into some semblance of cover.

I've got this covered.

She got a mouthful of leaves and ants as she tumbled down the ravine and skidded through the mud to land in a small creek that was pouring into a larger stream. She hastily crawled into the cage of one of the larger trees on the embankment. It offered a little protection. They couldn't come at her from behind, and she was armed and ready for them. It was only a matter of time before they figured out how to get her, but she just needed to buy time. They expected her to shift and run, but she wasn't playing their game.

Akos is just ahead, I am circling around behind him.

His eagle may be with him now, Solange warned. She could hear swearing. One of the two jaguar-men had shifted, probably to check on their companion. He was dead. There was no way he could have lived through that shot. *Pay attention to the sky.*

As if answering her, lightning forked in a spectacular display, streaks stretching àcross the sky. The dark clouds went purple, laced with fire. She wiped the sweat from her face with her sleeve. A twig snapped and her entire body tensed.

"Clever girl."

Her heart sank. She'd known all along it would be him. Brodrick. She clenched her teeth to keep them from chattering. The wind rose suddenly, completely unexpected, and unexplained, howling through the trees, carrying the voices of all the women this man had murdered, calling on her to bring them justice. The rain beat steadily, a mournful sound accompanying the moaning wind.

"Do you hear them?" she asked, her voice surprisingly steady. Keep him talking. Maybe, if she was lucky, he would get into her line of fire.

"Who?" Brodrick asked.

"The dead." The howling rose to a fever pitch. "They're calling you." She kept her voice pitched low, hoping he would have to come a little closer to hear her. And where was the other one?

"You're the one they're calling," he corrected with a growl. "Come out of there and throw your weapon away."

"I may have your blood running in my veins, but I managed to get my mother's intelligence. You want me, come and get me."

She heard another twig snap off to her left. The other man was working his way around, trying to come in while she was distracted by Brodrick. She whispered to her cat, making certain she was alert.

"Solange, you have to know our race is dying out," Brodrick said in a reasonable tone, as if they were old friends discussing a long familiar topic.

She could barely make him out, a good distance from her, pulling on a pair of jeans. She averted her eyes. He was smart enough to keep out of her line of fire, although . . .

She wiggled, pushing with her feet until she had enough room to lie prone. She went to her belly inch by slow inch, using her cat's freeze-frame ability so as not to alert him to a change of position.

The thick, twisted, finlike root coiled as it rose up to join the tangle of roots supporting the tree and forming her cage. She slowly slid her crossbow to the very edge, under the root. There were only a couple of inches of clearance, but enough for an arrow to shoot through. It was a tricky angle, and she couldn't use one of the special vampire arrows, but the smaller, more traditional one would do.

"Of course I know, Brodrick. You did that and you did it with deliberate malice. You knew exactly what you were doing so spare me the 'you need to save our species' speech. Who is your friend? The one sneaking around louder than the cicadas? You'd think if he was supposed to be your guard, he'd learn how to be silent." Sarcasm dripped.

She adjusted her angle slightly as he faded back into the shadows. He would move. A foot. A hand. It didn't matter what part of his anatomy he exposed; she would have him.

Brodrick sighed overly loud. "Reggie, you may as well come away from there."

Annoyance edged his voice. Fingers of alarm tracked down her spine. She shivered, frowning. He was up to something. Her one advantage was that they wanted her alive. Brodrick would never kill her and certainly neither would his companion. She was far too valuable alive. She was a full shifter with royal blood. Brodrick wanted an heir. As disgusting and despicable as that sounded, she knew his intent. She tasted bile in her mouth, but her gaze never left the shadowy figure moving back and forth behind the veil of dense brush.

Brodrick moved again and she fired from where she lay on the ground, the arrow rocketing through the brush. He screamed. Cursed. She heard the heavy fall of his body as he went down, crashing into brush. She sent up a silent prayer there were nettles growing there.

"I'm fucking going to make your life hell, you little bitch," he raged, his snarls reverberating through the forest. "Every day you live will be nothing but pain. I know more ways to cause pain to a bitch in heat than you ever imagined."

In the small confines of the root cage, Solange found it difficult to fit another arrow into the crossbow. She wiggled around, trying to stay quiet. Her leg brushed against the thick wood on her right side as she tried to get her arm in position. Something grabbed her ankle, pinning her hard to the ground. She felt the jab, a sharp sting, even as she abandoned the crossbow, pulled the knife on her thigh from its sheath and in one motion rolled and stabbed, driving the blade deep in the side of the man holding her down.

Come now! She sent the frantic call to Dominic. *They got me with a needle.*

She'd known Brodrick was up to something. They'd misled her by snapping twigs, making her think Reggie was to her left. Stupid, stupid mistake. She tried to stay calm, breathing evenly, not wanting whatever they injected into her to move too fast through her system. They thought they had time. She'd go to sleep and they'd drag her out and have her at their mercy. They were unaware of Dominic.

Reggie spat curses as he staggered back away from the roots. He made it about seven feet, staggered and went down to his hands and knees. "Brodrick. Get over here and help me."

He was out in the open where she could shoot him at will with an arrow. Using slow, careful movements, Solange fit another arrow into her bow and waited, this time as far back in the cage as she could get. They wouldn't be able to fit through the tangle of roots easily with their stocky bodies, and she wasn't going to make it easy for them.

Sweat beaded on her forehead. Her vision blurred. Around her, the twisted roots moved slightly, as if they might be coming alive.

"Brodrick," Reggie wailed. He had his hands clamped tight against his side. Blood dripped steadily through his fingers.

"Stop whining," Brodrick snapped. "You let the little bitch stick you. I told you she was lethal. You underestimated her."

"Why is it," Solange asked, her voice sounding tinny and far away, "that the man who attacks the woman always gets upset when she fights back? I've never understood that."

"I don't mind a little fight. It adds to the enjoyment when a woman fights, all that delicious fear," Brodrick said, ignoring Reggie's increasing distress. His partner began to drag himself toward the brush. "I love to watch their faces as they beg and plead, so willing to do anything for me, endure anything for me, just to live." His laughter was taunting, filled with contempt. "Believe me, you'll do the same."

She had a good direction on him now, if he stayed put, but she had to hurry. Her arms were beginning to feel like lead. She wiped the sweat from her eyes with her elbow, building the picture of him in her mind. His size. His shape. He was standing behind the fern and brush, his shadowy outline becoming distorted.

"You should have killed me when you had the chance," she said, wanting his response, wanting one more reassurance of his position. Her vision was astonishingly blurry.

"When you give me a son, it will be my pleasure, and

you'll take a long time dying," he replied, supreme confidence in his voice. "Just like old Reggie."

Reggie slumped on the ground, moaning, but his strength had run out with his blood.

Solange drew a deep breath, and as she exhaled, she fired the arrow. Brodrick grunted. She waited, heart beating fast. The ground shook as Brodrick went insane, breaking through the brush, destroying everything in his path, his rage boiling over. Roaring, he rushed her shelter, smashing through the roots, driving right through the splinters of wood to grab her hair. He jerked hard. Solange sprawled on the ground, releasing the crossbow from her numb hand. He dragged her out of what was left of the root cage and threw her to the ground.

Look at him. Keep looking at him. Dominic's voice was calm.

She felt that same calm. *I have to do this.*

In a detached way, she heard the fists hitting her body, saw the snarling, twisted mask of hatred rising over her, but she didn't feel anything other than a sense of purpose. This monster had killed nearly everyone she'd ever loved. He'd destroyed countless lives as well as an entire species. She watched him with an indifferent, impassive look that enraged him further. He bent over her, his hand on her shirt. Before he could rip it from her body, she poured every ounce of energy and will into the hand holding the knife.

She slammed the blade home, right into his black heart. She didn't have enough strength to push it as deep as she would have liked, but judging from the eruption of blood pouring around the blade, she was certain it would be enough to kill him. His eyes widened in complete shock. She could see he had never entertained the idea that a mere woman would be able to defeat him. Rage replaced shock and his hands dropped from the hilt of the knife to her throat.

Before he could wrap his fingers around her neck, a blast of white-hot energy knocked him back and away from her. Dominic knelt beside her, his hands running gently over her body. Everywhere he touched, bruises healed.

"I have to push the sedative from your body, Solange," he said and proceeded to do so.

He helped her into a sitting position. Solange rested her head against his chest for a moment. "Thanks. I'm still shaky."

Sensing movement, Dominic whipped around, his body shielding Solange as he faced Brodrick. The man ripped the knife from his chest, and using his last strength, went to throw it at Solange. Dominic spewed fire, a Dragonseeker trait rarely used. The flames engulfed the shapeshifter, burning bright red-orange.

Solange raised her eyebrow. "I didn't know you could do that. It's kind of freaky."

He kissed her. "Just do not make me angry and you will never have to see it again."

She laughed softly. "I want to go home."

"Josef is finally finished. I can take down the laboratory," he told her. "And then we can go home."

With her eyes on the fiery conflagration, and Brodrick's screams filling the air, she sighed softly. "Get it done, then. I want to sleep for a month." Her nightmare was finally over. The other shifters would scatter and they'd be someone else's problem. Hopefully they would go where the law could reach them.

Dominic concentrated on the laboratory itself, building the image in his mind. He had paid attention to every structural point. Beneath the earth he pushed the first wave up directly beneath the building. The earth shook. Brodrick crumbled and writhed on the ground. In the distance they could hear the loud thunder as the laboratory shook apart.

Dominic didn't stop until the last block was smashed and there was nothing left.

He turned and looked through the falling rain toward the sky, bringing down the lightning one last time. The bolt slammed into Brodrick's writhing body, incinerating it completely. The white-hot energy jumped to Reggie and turned him to ash.

He held out his hand to Solange. "Home, my own. We have that little bundle of fur and claws to feed."

Solange put her hand in his and without a glance toward the blackened ashes, she walked side by side with her life-mate toward home.

20

You're the calm in the storm, the most gentle power.
In your hands, I'm a flower. Near you, my heart beams.

SOLANGE TO DOMINIC

The smallest of sounds woke Dominic. Soft weeping. His heart stuttered awake, his eyes snapped open and he turned his head to find Solange. She huddled a foot from him, knees drawn up, head down, the fall of her sable, sun-kissed hair hiding her face from him. But she wept, His Solange. His heart and soul.

For a moment he could barely breathe, anxiety rushing through him. They had exchanged blood for the first time before going to sleep. He had waited several risings to ensure all the parasites were gone from his body before they had tried their first exchange. She didn't appear to have experienced any ill effects, but . . . The process itself had been difficult when it should have been erotic. Solange could not be put under compulsion. She had to voluntarily take his blood on her own, and she had struggled, but she'd trusted him enough to see it through.

"Solange." His voice was infinitely tender. "What is wrong, my own?" He couldn't help merging with her, afraid the exchange had injured her in some way.

Instead of physical pain he felt the remnants of her nightmare, the child desperate to hold her mother, and he wanted to weep for her. There would always be moments of sorrow in her life he couldn't prevent, couldn't heal no matter how much he wanted to. He crossed the short distance between them and sank down beside her, drawing her into his arms, cradling her on his lap, his face buried in her shoulder. He rocked her gently until she calmed and grew silent.

She pressed her hands over her ears. "I dreamt of my mother, and when I woke up, I couldn't stop crying. The sounds are so loud, Dominic, everything, even my own tears. The sound of water, of small animals and insects. I can hear what is happening outside the cave and I can't turn it down. My head hurts from all the noise. And the sounds were so amplified, and you were so utterly silent . . ." She trailed off. She pressed a hand to her heart. "And now I can hear the sound of my heart pounding. I was so afraid even though I knew *intellectually* you were safe."

His hand went to the nape of her neck, massaging the tense muscles. "I am so sorry about your mother, beloved. We will meet her again in the next life and she will welcome you with open arms. And I am sorry I frightened you." He tightened his hold in an effort to comfort her. He wasn't her mother, but he loved her fiercely. "Let me see about your hearing," he added gently.

Carpathians could hear the beat of wings in the distance, the smallest of stones rolling down a hillside. Dominic and

Solange had exchanged blood and the conversion was beginning, but she should have been able to turn her hearing to an acceptable volume. Dominic left his body, sending his spirit into hers, examining her carefully, trying to determine what his Carpathian blood had done to her.

His blood should have begun the process of conversion, yet the cells were distinct, her cells bonding with his, separate yet together. It didn't make sense. Her jaguar seemed perfectly intact, other than the Carpathian blood cells piggybacking on hers. There was no chaos, no antibodies rushing to thwart the process at all. It was as if their bloodlines had merged, one on top of the other, coexisting rather than competing for dominance.

Her hearing was a different matter. Already acute due to her jaguar, the Carpathian blood had amplified her abilities until sounds were overwhelming. He moved through her, checking for other differences. There were subtle changes, nothing like he expected would happen. Puzzled, he returned to his own body.

"Is that better? It is a matter of turning down the volume. When something is not quite right, think of how it works and you can fix it just as I have done for you. If it is not enough, you can try it yourself to see if it works."

She turned her tear-wet face against his throat and sighed. "Yes, that's much better, thank you. I'm sorry I woke you. You shouldn't be up yet."

Everything in him went utterly still. She was right. His body knew the exact time of each rising. He had lived centuries and there was no doubt that he could tell the time of night when it was safe to rise. He had no doubts that the sun was still high. This time of day his body should be leaden, impossible to move. He was at his most vulnerable with the sun so high. Even beneath the earth he would feel the prickly sensation that threatened to burn his skin, yet he was perfectly comfortable. Uneasiness stirred. Every Carpathian needed a built-in warning system, and his seemed to be missing.

"The sun has not yet set." He made it a statement, but his mind was shocked at the realization. The sun was still in the sky and yet just minutes ago, he had walked over to her, sat down, pulled her into his lap. He had moved with no difficulty, no lethargy. Impossible! He was an ancient, and the sun, still in the sky, should have rendered him helpless.

She bit her lip, her eyes going wide, the shock betraying her comprehension. "If the sun is still out, Dominic, should you be awake? Can that hurt you? To be awakened while the sun is still up?" Anxiety was in her voice.

"Waking is not the problem." Very gently he put her from him and stood. "*This* is the problem. I should not be able to move right now."

He studied her face. She had changed very subtly. Her cat's eyes were still direct and glowed there in the dark, giving evidence of her excellent night vision, but not in the same way as before.

"What?" She touched her face. Sudden panic crossed her expression. She shifted without hesitation, ensuring her jaguar was safe.

Dominic had seen her shift so many times and she'd been incredibly fast, but this time he barely blinked and she was fully jaguar. The cat stretched languidly and nudged him with her head, clearly unaffected by the Carpathian blood. He was more puzzled than ever.

"This makes no sense, Solange."

The conversion was always painful, some less than others, but still difficult. Her jaguar should be reacting adversely, but instead she looked at him sleepily and yawned. Solange shifted back, laughing. "She's annoyed at me for disturbing her. She's not at all upset with the first blood exchange—in fact, she likes it. She feels stronger and faster." The laughter faded from her eyes and anxiety crept back in. "Check your body, Dominic. Maybe my blood is doing something to you."

There was worry in her voice. He was already assessing his body. His hearing, like hers, seemed more acute, although he'd automatically turned down the volume. His night vision was just a little bit clearer. He didn't feel the sun's warning on his skin, and his body, although heavy, hadn't gone leaden as it should have.

"*Minan*, I can detect no harm done to me. I am still fully Carpathian. Our blood does not mix. Mine does not take over yours; rather, the two strains connect. It is odd." He sighed, frowning a little. "We know that your blood can remove any spell cast with the blood sacrifice of black magic, and it heals damage done by black magic, but I do not understand why, when I give you my blood, the cells seem mated, yet one does not take over the other."

"I feel the worry in you."

"I do not like anything I do not understand. It makes no sense that I can move now or that I do not feel the warning prickling beneath my skin that tells me the sun is high."

"I actually feel rejuvenated," Solange admitted. "I was looking forward to another blood exchange, but if you think my blood is somehow affecting you adversely, I suppose we shouldn't try another until we figure out what is going on."

The wistful note in her voice touched his heart. She was fully committed to him, to the Carpathian way of life. Her one fear—her jaguar—was taking the whole conversion process in stride as if nothing at all was happening. Did he dare try to bring Solange more fully into his world? Yet even as he wondered, his hand was already, of its own volition, curling around the nape of her neck, drawing her to him. He craved the essence of her, pure Solange, the taste and rush unlike any other. She was an addiction he would never get over, the craving for her deep in his bones and seared irrevocably into his heart.

She shook her head. "Not yet. First go up to the cavern floor and see if your alarm system works from there," she insisted.

Heat flared. His Solange. Protecting him again, this time from himself, from his own needs. He floated easily toward the surface. Nearing the cavern floor, he began to feel the uneasiness of a Carpathian when the sun was high in the sky. The sensation wasn't particularly strong, but the warning was there. He realized his strength was waning, his hovering body beginning to feel clumsy and foreign. Deep inside the earth, he was able to move with a Carpathian's fluid grace even though the sun was high. But the closer to the surface he rose, or perhaps the longer he remained awake during the day, he was losing strength. He returned to Solange.

"If your blood is doing anything to me, it is allowing me to be alert during the day. I have no problems with that."

His smile dispelled the anxiousness in her eyes. She returned his smile and leaned into him in a blatant invitation. "Then we should keep going. Take my blood, Dominic. Bring me closer to your world."

His heart leapt. More than anything he wanted her to be part of his world. He wanted many lifetimes with her, not just one. He had gone so long without anyone, and now that he'd found her, he didn't want to give her up so fast. More important, she'd never had joy in her life, and he wanted centuries to give her as much joy as possible. "You are certain, Solange?" he whispered, nuzzling her neck. He kissed his way down to the swell of her breasts.

She arched into him, her body soft and pliant. "I think we should give it a second chance. My jaguar is sleepy and annoyed that I keep asking if she is all right. She would have protested if she was hurt." Her arms crept around his neck and she pressed her body to his.

He loved how she did that—gave herself to him without reservation. *Solange.* He whispered her name, shocked at the overwhelming love pouring through him. He sank his teeth into her tempting pulse. She cried out, a breathy little sound that sent a lash of erotic heat rushing through his body. He swept his tongue over that sweet spot and sank his teeth deep.

Her entire body shuddered. He felt the ripples starting deep in her core and spreading like a wildfire throughout her body. Her hot, sweet nectar poured into him, filling his cells with crackling energy. He fed, devouring her, taking her very life force into his body, feasting until her moan snapped him from the enthrallment. He swept his tongue across the pinpricks and, gently repositioning her, opened a line in his chest for her. He cradled her head, encouraging her, his body already shuddering with the need to feel her feeding.

Again she was tentative, but his Carpathian blood had made some changes in her. This time she licked at him with languid, sensual sweeps of her tongue. She lapped like the cat she was. Each stroke of her tongue sent shimmering fire dancing through his veins. Her mouth opened, moved over his chest, her lips soft and tender. She bit down and his entire body tightened, the rush close to an orgasm. Her teeth had extended enough to take his blood in the way Carpathians were meant to. She didn't seem to notice, her mind hazing with passion.

It was difficult for him to give up the amazing, sensual experience of his lifemate exchanging blood, but his strength was definitely waning. When she had taken enough blood for a true exchange, he pressed his hand to her mouth and she instantly pulled back, lapping again with her tongue. He had to close the wound, but he discovered the edges were already seamlessly repairing themselves.

He kissed her again with passionate thoroughness and took her back to earth with him, tucking the comforter around her, watching carefully for signs of distress. She pulled the comforter closer around her and fell to sleep long before he allowed himself to follow suit.

~

Dominic woke before Solange, determined to check her health. She lay sprawled across him, her legs over his thighs, beneath the blanket of rich earth. The comforter was bunched in her hand to the side of her, but sometime during their sleep she had burrowed instinctively beneath the soil. The dark loam covered her nearly to her neck. He took that as a good sign.

The moon was high; he felt the welcoming beams even below the earth as he did each rising. He allowed himself a brief sigh of relief. That hadn't changed. His body was completely tuned to the night. He could hear insects and even the soft rustle of mice. Outside the cave, something splashed in the stream. The kitten gave a small mewling sigh in its compulsion-induced sleep.

Dominic lay still, aware Solange had spent a lifetime in danger. She would know if he moved. He barely allowed his breath to rise and fall in his lungs as he left his body to examine hers. There were far more Carpathian cells attached to her cells now than there had been prior to their last exchange. The change was also more pronounced now. Organs were definitely reshaping. He was both satisfied and afraid. He needed to find her jaguar. So far, Solange had not experienced any discomfort and neither had her cat.

Her jaguar was completely intact, although when he studied her carefully, the organs she shared with Solange were reshaping as well. His heart beat harder, just for a moment, at his finding. The change in his rhythm was enough to awaken Solange. She was fully alert in moments, lifting her head, eyes moving quickly around them to search out any threat.

"What is it?"

"We are safe, Solange. I woke a little early to make certain you were suffering no adverse effects." He waved his hand to clean them both before she could really process that she'd been sleeping *under* a blanket of soil.

Solange nuzzled his chest, inhaling his scent. "I love how you smell, Dominic." She gazed up at him and smiled. "There are definite advantages to being Carpathian."

His fingers tangled in her hair. She looked at him with stars in her eyes. He found it amazing to have a woman look at him as if he were her entire world. And maybe he was—she certainly was his.

She stroked a hand over his chest, pleasure showing openly on her face at the simple act of touching him. "Did you check to make certain my blood wasn't doing anything freaky to you?"

He laughed softly, already caught in her spell. "Our blood together is doing something a little freaky, but I am still fully Carpathian. And your jaguar still seems to be wholly jaguar."

"Then really, there's no reason to wait, is there?" she asked.

He shook his head. "We should be cautious, Solange. I do not want to rush you into a decision you may regret."

Solange sprawled across his thighs, her hair spreading like so much silk over his skin, one hand caressing the velvet sac between his legs. She propped her chin on his thigh, mouth inches from his burgeoning cock.

"I feel incredible."

As she spoke he could feel the warmth of her breath teasing the head of his cock. It jerked in anticipation. She leaned a little closer and licked from the base of his shaft to the very sensitive spot just beneath the broad head. Every nerve ending went on alert. His entire body shuddered. He had fantasized about waking up to her mouth on him, but the reality far exceeded his fantasy.

"I see no reason not to finish the conversion, Dominic." She licked up his long shaft a second time, engulfed the entire head for one long, heart-stopping moment, and then pulled back. "I feel great. You do, too. I think we should just make the exchange and see what happens."

He swallowed hard, watching her every movement. She was going to seduce him into getting anything she wanted and right now, it looked as though she wanted him.

I do. I do want you so very much.

Her cat's eyes gleamed a deep emerald green as she took him deep inside the scalding heat of her mouth. He lay back, savoring the feel of her soft mouth. She formed a tight ring with her index finger and thumb as she drew him deep, pulled back to balance him on her full lips and then completely engulfed him again.

His breath exploded out of his lungs. He tangled his fingers in her hair. "I could wake up to this forever." As seductions went, she found the way to get anything she wanted.

That's what I'm trying to say here. This would be a great way to start every rising for the next few centuries.

Her tongue stroked and teased, curling along the underside of the head. His hips bucked as she took him deeper with each stroke. He could already feel the explosion building. It was amazing how quickly she'd learned how to please him with an expertise he could hardly believe. She watched him with such intensity, paying complete attention to his every gasp and groan, learning from every reaction how best to drive him wild.

And she was an incredibly quick study.

"Solange . . . oh, God." He nearly exploded when she began humming, the sound vibrating through his cock and spreading heat through his veins.

I love how this makes you feel, she purred in his mind. *I love your scent, how soft your skin is here. Like velvet.*

His stomach muscles bunched as her fingernails lightly scraped along his sac and her fingers stroked and caressed, rolling the velvety balls very gently. She was good at detail, and very focused on his pleasure. Searing fire spread through his body and took his breath.

She began to move her head to the rhythm of his hips, taking him deeper, constricting him tightly before allowing his cock to slide along the velvet rasp of her tongue. He bunched her hair in tight fists, and pushed her head down, closing his eyes as her throat opened.

"You are so beautiful, Solange. So incredibly sexy. Oh, God, that's right, *minan*, I love when you do that with your tongue."

You make me feel sexy.

He loved the confidence in her voice. The hunger in her, the way she enjoyed what she was doing, wanting his pleasure, learning every hot spot, using her knowledge to push him beyond his control—it all made him hotter than ever. He filled her mouth, eyes half-closed now, watching, her hair bunched in his fists, holding her while his hips thrust in and out, stretching her lips, each surge taking him farther into the hot, constricting depths.

As if reading his mind—and she probably was—she began to suck harder as he tugged her closer. His cock swelled and pulsed with wild need. Her mouth tightened around him as the quick, hard thrusts penetrated deeper. She drew each breath fast as he pulled out. He held each thrust for a longer period of time in her hot, wet mouth, the fire racing through him. He could feel his body drawing tight.

She moaned, and the sound vibrated straight through his heavy erection, sending the fire racing through his body. He realized he was pulling on her scalp, yet she was on the edge of her own orgasm, the bite of pain only adding to her drenching desire. His cock tightened, burned. He thrust hard and deep. The explosion seemed to start in his toes and rocket through his body as he emptied himself in her.

He couldn't think or breathe with the mind-numbing pleasure, yet he was still hard and aching, needing more, needing the solace of her body. His hands in her hair tugged insistently until she moved up and over him. He caught her hips and guided her until she straddled him. Already he could feel the scorching heat of her feminine channel as, with infinite slowness, she began to impale herself on his thick, pulsing length.

The breath hissed out of his already burning lungs. She was so tight, grasping him, clamping down as she slowly opened for him and allowed his invasion. He loved the feel of all that hot silk gripping so tightly. When she tightened her muscles around him and he slid through those hot folds, the friction was incredible along his shaft.

Dominic watched her face, the dazed wonder in her eyes, the expression of shock as her desire built. Her full breasts swayed gently, and a flush spread over her body as her hips rose and fell with a steady, slow rhythm. He flexed his fingers on her hips, gripped and thrust up as she came down, all the while gazing at her face. Her breath caught as pleasure crashed through her. Her eyes went wide, almost completely cat. He watched her register the myriad of sensations as his thick, diamond-hard cock pushed through her tight, silken folds.

Dominic. She breathed his name in a kind of awed wonder.

The look in her glowing eyes, the absolute adulation, the glittering excitement building, her need urgent and unashamed, made his heart clench. Love washed over him.

He lifted her again, hands urging her to a little faster pace. She did a small spiral with her hips on her downward path that took his breath away. Her muscles gripped, biting down so that pleasure ripped through him. She made a small, inarticulate sound, throwing her head back as he thrust deep, driving upward as she came down. The broad mushroom head, filled with nerve endings, bumped her womb, lodged tight, scalding him with heat. Locking them together, he rolled her under him, blanketing her body with his own. The action sent fire racing up into his belly and down his thighs.

Solange closed her eyes, allowing the fire to wash over her. She'd never felt so sensuous or beautiful in her life. *He* had done that. Dominic. He had made her aware of how wonderful it was to be a woman. He showed her how giving could be just as perfect as receiving. He showed her love.

He leaned over her, looking into her eyes, his expression making her pulse race. His eyes were turquoise, hot, intense, burning into her with such hungry desire and unashamed adoration that she wanted to give him everything.

Deep inside her, she felt his hard, thick shaft stretching her, filling her, sending sensation after sensation rippling through her body. He set a hard, fast rhythm that left her gasping, the friction intensifying with each deep stroke. She tightened her muscles around him, attempting to match his fierce rhythm. The streaks of fire threatened to engulf her, consume her, burn her clean until there was nothing left of her.

This was Dominic, driving her into a frenzy of need and passion, taking her so far past what she ever thought possible, her body belonging to him, claiming his for her own. She let the haze take her, let her mind just go, flying into subspace as the building inferno began to engulf her. She writhed under him, her hips bucking, meeting his hips in frenzied need. Her orgasm washed through her like a tidal wave, building higher and higher, stronger and stronger, until she heard his hoarse shout. His hands gripped her tight as he surged into her one more time, driving her up so high the explosion was fast and hard, ripping through her, taking her breath, so that her muscles clamped down like a vise, taking him soaring with her. She fell over the top with him, struggling for breath.

They lay for some time, just breathing hard. Solange kept her hand tangled in his long hair. When she could find it in her to move, she brushed kisses along his jaw. "I think you wore me out."

He kissed her forehead. "I think it was the other way around."

She looked up at him, wanting him to see that she meant what she said. "I want us to complete the ritual, Dominic. I want to come wholly into your world."

Dominic drew in his breath. This was the moment. He locked gazes with her, brushing back stray strands of her hair. "You have to be certain, *kessake*. Once this is done, there is no way to undo it." Very tenderly he kissed her mouth, noting she was beginning to tremble. The enormity of her decision was sinking in. "I will love you with all my heart and soul just as we are. You do *not* have to do this for me."

Solange took a breath, let it out and smiled up at him. She trailed the pads of her fingers over the lines etched into his face. "There is no one I would rather be with, in this life or the next. I have thought about this and I feel the rightness of it."

"It may be incredibly painful. I can help you through the pain if it comes to that, but I have heard it is a terrible thing to go through." He knew he was the one hesitating, not her, and yet he longed for this.

Her cat's eyes stared straight into his. "I'm not afraid, Dominic, and no matter what happens, I will have no regrets."

"Even if I cannot guarantee your jaguar?"

Her tongue touched her lips. "She will survive."

Joy surged through him. Dominic trailed fire from her lips to the swell of her breast. His teeth tugged gently at her nipple and his tongue lapped before he suckled strongly. She gasped and arched into him. He kissed his way to the pulse beating at the creamy swell, licked once, twice, and then sank his teeth deep. She cried out, her body going soft and pliant. She tangled her hands in his hair, cradling his head while he drank, her body shuddering through a second orgasm.

She tasted like heaven. Like Solange—his lifemate. The woman he loved above all else. Spice burst over his tongue. Every cell in his body reacted, soaking up the honeyed nectar, filling him with energy. His body responded with urgent need, wanting to claim her, to join with her and be one. He slid his tongue over the pinpricks and lifted his head.

"You are absolutely certain, Solange?"

Her eyes were glazed, her lips swollen from his kisses. She smiled up at him and touched his face with gentle fingers. "More certain than I've ever been about anything."

She had come so far, trusting him to do this. His heart swelled, nearly bursting with his love for her. It was such a precious gift—her trust. Her desire to please him. That she could take such a risk, that she *would* take such a risk for him, was humbling.

Dominic drew a line across his chest and cradled her head. *Come into my world, my own,* he invited. *Drink.*

Solange didn't hesitate. She wanted this. All reservations were gone. She had never truly belonged anywhere, and now she had found a home in Dominic. Her lashes drifted down and she snuggled deeper into his arms, her tongue sliding over the seam of the wound in tentative exploration. She felt Dominic's entire body clench and shudder with pleasure, and rejoiced that she could give that to him. She was acutely aware of his shaft once more growing hard and stretching and filling her.

She felt along her teeth with her tongue, a little surprised to feel two had lengthened. Already the need was on her, a terrible craving she couldn't resist even had she wanted to. Dominic—her own. She sank her teeth deep. He cried out hoarsely, and her body clamped down hard on his. His essence flowed into her. Hot. Powerful. Rich. She felt the connection between them, the sharing of mind and body, the very blood flowing in their veins.

Her body moved against his, soft, made for him, fitting perfectly to him. His hips thrust deep and the now-familiar fire took her. He took command so easily, his hips surging into hers, penetrating deep, dragging over inflamed nerve endings over and over. Each stroke was more powerful than the last, pushing her higher until she hovered right on the edge of great precipice.

Dominic shared her mind, stole her heart and completed her soul. With the taste of him filling her, his breath moving in and out of her lungs, she lifted her hips to meet his, tightening every muscle around his hardened length, dragging another explosive release from him as her own took her high.

She swept her tongue over the laceration and watched it close, a little awed by what she had done. The taste of him was in her mouth and she leaned in to kiss him, to share with him the very life force he had shared with her.

"I love you, Solange," Dominic said.

She settled into his arms, knowing he was far more nervous about what was to come than she was. "It's going to be all right," she murmured, a little sleepily. "Making love is tiring business."

"Your body is changing, *kessake ku toro sívamak—* beloved little wildcat. As soon as I know it is safe, I will put you to sleep in the ground so Mother Earth can do the rest."

"You will have to watch over our kitten and feed him," she said drowsily. "And make certain you play with him. He's just a cub and he needs lots of attention."

Dominic nuzzled the top of her head. Every muscle was bunched tight in anticipation of seeing her writhing in pain. "I will, Solange. Have no worries."

"Check my cat now. Make certain she's all right."

He took a breath, allowed his spirit the freedom to leave his physical self behind to enter her body. Her organs were reshaping at a fast rate, both hers and the jaguar's. She should have already been in pain, but somehow her blood was still intact and seemed to heal the organs as fast as his blood changed them.

He returned to his body. "Your jaguar is not paying any attention to what is happening."

She turned up her face to his. "I knew she'd be fine. I'm tired, Dominic. I'm going to sleep now."

Her lashes drifted down and she was out, trusting him to look after her and the cub. Heart pounding, mouth dry, he held her for hours, just waiting for the pain to start. She simply slept. Her jaguar slept. He kept vigil through the night and finally, when he was certain he could do so, he put her in the earth with him and closed the soil over their heads.

⁓

Dominic allowed Solange to sleep for three risings. He checked her carefully, ensuring she was healing properly. He played with the kitten, making certain it had enough food, but each rising, he awakened earlier and earlier just to see if he would feel the warning that the sun was out. He didn't. Mostly he worried about Solange. He found, as silly as it was, that he missed her. He was used to sharing her mind, watching for her laughter, and enjoying just being with her. The world seemed far less bright without her beside him.

On the third rising he chose to wake her before the sun went down. He wanted to see the effect it had on her. He woke her gently and, cradling her against his chest, floated her out of the earth to her bath. She wrapped her arms around his neck and hugged him.

"I want to check my cat," she protested as he placed her in the hot water.

"Bath first," he said firmly. Her care had to come first.

She smirked and shifted right there in the water. Solange. His miracle. Her cat chuffed her disgust and shook her head, those green eyes gleaming with mischief. His warning radar went off, but he was too entranced with the laughter building in the jaguar's eyes. She gathered herself, her muscles rippling beneath the tawny fur, and sprang, hitting him in the chest and knocking him over. He tried to catch her, but she took him down to the ground, standing on him, her tongue rasping over his face.

He caught her muzzle in his hands and looked into her laughing eyes. "I knew you were going to be trouble from the first moment I laid eyes on you."

She shifted in his arms, kissing him. "No, you didn't. You thought I was going to be docile and sweet." She jumped up. "Come on, I want to fly on my own."

Dominic caught her arm, restraining her. "The sun is up. We need to be a little cautious."

She ran her hand down her arm, frowning. "I don't feel any different, Dominic. Shouldn't I? I slept beneath the earth. I am fully Carpathian, aren't I?"

He swept his arm around her, cleaning the water from both of them as he did so. "We are both Carpathian, *kessake*, but we are also something more."

"I don't understand."

"Neither do I. Your blood is unique and remains intact. I think, somehow, although you are fully Carpathian, we both retain all the properties of your blood."

She bit her lip. "I don't know how I feel about that."

"Because of Brodrick?"

She nodded.

"Your blood also comes from your mother."

Her cat's eyes blinked once and a slow smile curved her mouth. "I should have known you'd say the right thing, Dominic. Thank you."

He took her hand, waving his other one to cover her body in her jeans and tee, her warrior armor. They made their way up toward the surface of the cave, maneuvering through the narrow tunnel. As they reached the entrance, light spilled in, dappled from the surrounding trees shading the area. He remembered emerging from a cave not so long ago, the sun burning his skin in spite of the cover, burning through the feathers of the harpy eagle. Now there was no reaction whatsoever. It had been centuries since he walked in the sun.

"Stay here, *hän sívamak*." It was an order, nothing less,

and he looked down at her upturned face, letting her see he meant it.

Her protest died in her throat. She nodded.

Dominic slowly approached the entrance. The light grew stronger, reached for him. His heart pounded in anticipation. He took a few more cautious steps out of the cave. The sun fell across his body. Every muscle tensed. Nothing happened. There was no burning. No blisters. No terrible repercussions, just the feel of the sun on his skin.

He turned and looked at Solange. His miracle. She took his breath away. He held out his hand to her. Solange walked slowly toward him, reaching for his hand, smiling up at him with love shining in her eyes. He threaded his fingers through hers and called silently to awaken their kitten. They waited together until the little cat joined them, before walking together out in the sunshine.

"You Are the Very Heart of Me"

Dominic to Solange:

Dreams

I was half-alive for a thousand years.
I'd given up hope that we'd meet in this time.
Too many the centuries. All disappears
As time and the darkness steal color and rhyme.

But then beyond hope, you came into my dream . . .
Glowing eyes like a cat, but fierce need like a child.
Your warrior heart, loyal. Your anguished, "Don't leave me."
Your head in my lap: *Csitri!* Strong and wild.

Questions

Can you come to trust a man once again?
Can you come to love an old one like me?

Let my strong arms protect you, let me sing you to sleep.
Let my song bring you healing, like the earth and the sea.

Look at me—now see yourself through my eyes.
Look at you: the most beautiful on this earth.

I'll wait for you to see it, forever if it takes . . .
Solange, my very own, amazing gift beyond worth.

Lifemates

When you meet me,
You complete me.
You bring me back to life again.

You reveal me. Then you heal me
Of all the scars and strife.
And when my life was spinning downward,
You caught me.
I'd forgotten how to smile, but
You re-taught me.

My dream lover and lifemate,
You know every part of me.
We're bound forever, soul to soul.
You hold the very heart of me.

I can never betray you.
You can never part from me.
In love forever, this life and next.
You are the very heart of me.

SOLANGE TO DOMINIC:

Dreams

My life was an anguish, my family ripped from me.
My rage had sustained me. I'd given up hope.

Tears fell in rain forest, heart bled in the blood-ground.
My father betrayed me. I barely could cope.

But then beyond hope, you came into my dream . . .
Your melody haunting, your gentle voice healing.
The soul of a poet, great heart of a warrior.
You gave all for your people. Let me give you feeling!

Questions

Can you find beauty in this rough-hewn woman?
Can you come to love a shapeshifter like me?
Let my soft arms caress you, let our songs blend together.
Let me stand by your side—let me set your heart free!
Look at me—now see yourself through my eyes.
Look at you: the perfect man of my dreams.
You're the calm in the storm, the most gentle power.
In your hands, I'm a flower. Near you, my heart beams.

Lifemates

When you meet me,
You complete me.
You bring me back to life again.

You reveal me. Then you heal me
Of all the scars and strife.
And when my life was spinning downward,
You caught me.
I'd forgotten how to smile, but
You re-taught me.

My dream lover and lifemate,
You know every part of me.

We're bound forever, soul to soul.
You hold the very heart of me.

I can never betray you.
You can never part from me.
In love forever, this life and next.
You are the very heart of me.

MUSIC AND LYRICS BY DR. CHRISTOPHER TONG
TO HEAR THIS SONG, GO TO WWW.CHRISTINEFEEHAN.COM

And now for a preview of

Spirit Bound
a Sea Haven novel

by Christine Feehan.

Available January 2012 from Jove Books.

~

Be sure to continue reading for
special deleted scenes from *Dark Peril*.

Stefan Prakenskii paced up and down the small cell. He knew exactly how many steps he could take before he leapt to catch the bars and do pull-ups. A dozen more pull-ups before pacing to the end of the cell and dropping down for push-ups. There was no getting used to the smell of the prison, or the slime on the walls or the way the showers didn't work or the constant vigilance to stay alive, but he didn't mind any of that. He could endure anything—he had endured much worse.

He was a patient man, but once he had determined it was useless for him to remain in the cell, that his mission was a complete bust, he wanted out. It was a waste of time for him to stay, yet a month earlier his boss hadn't agreed to pull him out. Every day was increasingly dangerous and irritating, his mind becoming consumed with the only decent thing in the prison.

Swearing under his breath, Stefan took the latest photograph from the wall of the woman his cell mate was obsessed with. She stood on a beach, the ocean waves rising behind her, a little turbulent, and it was obviously windy, but there were no landmarks Stefan had a chance of identifying. She was undoubtedly beautiful with her long black hair blowing in the wind. Dressed in jeans and a tee, she still managed to look elegant and sexy at the same time. If he was a man who was interested in relationships, no doubt he would understand his cell mate's fixation with her. And the idiot was totally obsessed with her. There were hundreds of photographs of just this one woman, taken over a period of years, taped all over the walls.

It didn't seem to matter how intelligent a man was, or what he did for a living; in the end, it seemed, a woman often brought even the greatest of criminals tumbling down. And this particular woman was no exception. Stefan planned to use her to take down Jean-Claude La Roux's international empire for good, if need be.

He glanced down at the picture in his hand. She looked pensive—no, sad. What had put that look on her face? Surely a woman like her was not pining away for a man like Jean-Claude. A small band of inviting skin peeked out temptingly between her tee and her jeans. His thumb slid over that little strip as if he might feel just how warm and soft she truly was.

No doubt Jean-Claude was a man of untold wealth. Stefan supposed a woman might find his good looks attractive, if she liked oozing charm. His charm covered a multitude of sins, but then women might find that edge of danger exciting as well. Women could be just as easily swayed by the wrong things as men could be by beauty.

"What the hell are you doing with that?" Glaring at Stefan, trying to intimidate someone impossible to intimidate, Jean-Claude La Roux snatched the small photograph from the hands of his cell mate. "You have no idea who I am."

Deliberately Stefan showed his teeth and then spit on the floor of the cell. "That refrain is getting old, Rolex." He infused total contempt into his tone, calling the man the hated name he'd given him.

A man like Jean-Claude, the head of a vast crime empire, would detest a common criminal taunting him. It was an affront the man couldn't accept. In the two months Stefan had been undercover, trying to collect information, he'd had to defend his life on several occasions—a tribute to La Roux's authority even there in the prison. La Roux hated him, and one word from the man had sent several prisoners trying to curry favor by attempting to get rid of Stefan, the thorn in his side.

There was no doubt that Jean-Claude was every bit as powerful in prison as he was out of it. On the surface, sentencing him for his international crimes in France seemed good. The French prison system wasn't considered a place to coddle prisoners, but even with mold on the walls and slime trailing from the ceiling, Jean-Claude managed to look wealthy and powerful. Every other prisoner gave him a wide berth until Stefan had come along. Stefan goaded him at every opportunity, and not one of the men paid to teach Stefan a lesson or kill him had succeeded.

There was no doubt in Stefan's mind that, given an hour with the Jean-Claude, if he was free to interrogate him in his own way, he would have all the information they needed. But here, in this French prison, with guards watching day and night and the government all too aware of their prisoner, he didn't have a chance to extract what he needed from the man. That only left one possibility. Jean-Claude La Roux had to escape. Stefan sighed. He'd told his boss that same thing many times over the last two months.

Stefan indicated the walls, covered with photographs of the same woman. "You have a lot of pictures, Rolex, but you sure don't have any letters. I think your woman is on that beach with another man, laughing her ass off."

Jean-Claude replaced the photograph, his hand smoothing over the glossy paper. Stefan noticed, with some satisfaction, that the crime lord's fingers trembled when he touched the woman's face.

"You do not see a man in any of these photographs, do you?" Jean-Claude looked him over with obvious contempt.

Stefan knew he wasn't much to look at. He was tall, with wide, axe-handle shoulders, a thick muscular chest and large arms with bulging muscles. He didn't look suave or wealthy, or charming. He looked a brute, not very smart, with longish hair and lots of scruff. Scars webbed his skin and his knuckles were callused and shiny. He had a square jaw and dark blue eyes that looked straight into other men's souls and found them guilty. Stefan exuded raw power through sheer physical strength, and men like Jean-Claude automatically dismissed them as muscle and brawn—never looking beneath that surface to see if there was any intelligence behind the mask of a brute.

In his mind he used his own name—*Stefan Prakenskii*—as often as possible because, truthfully, he was so often using another name, he was afraid of forgetting who he was. And maybe he had already lost his identity, long ago. What was he? Who was he? And who really gave a damn anyway. There wasn't a beautiful woman standing on a beach looking sad and pining away for him—and there never would be. He was successful at his job because he refused to let women like the one Jean-Claude obsessed over, into his realm of consciousness.

He glanced again at the pictures covering the stained wall. There were hundreds of them. Jean-Claude had the woman under surveillance for a long time. She had changed little over the years the man had spent in prison, but he was right—there was no man ever photographed with her. Stefan cursed under his breath and turned away from the pictures.

The woman would get under anyone's skin if you stared at her long enough. And in a tiny prison cell, really, what else was there to do but notice her lips and her eyes and all that long, glossy hair? Jean-Claude was feeding his own addiction, growing it into a monster, and Stefan had uncovered that weakness immediately and used it against the man, making him ripe for an escape. He didn't see other men with her in the photographs, but who could stand thinking about another man touching all that soft skin?

"I will say this for you, Rolex. She's beautiful. Where the hell did you ever meet a woman like that?" It was time to change tactics.

For the first time Stefan allowed a little admiration to creep into his voice. Just as he suspected, Jean-Claude couldn't resist the need to talk about his woman or respond to the first sign that a man such as Stefan, who only seemed to admire obvious strength, might respect the crime lord at least for his ability to attract a beautiful woman.

"She was an art student, studying in Paris," Jean-Claude said. "She stood outside the Louvre, all that long hair flying around her face and she paused to scrape it back away from her face and for just a moment . . ." He trailed off.

Stefan didn't need him to say it. The crime lord had probably lost his breath just as Stefan had the first time he'd looked at her photograph. She could easily have been a model on the cover of magazine—yet more. There was something undefined, a quality he couldn't put his finger on, something innocent and sensual at the same time. Something mysterious, remote, just out of reach. Something terribly elusive and yet made a man want to reach out and grab her, to hold her for himself alone.

Oh, yeah, the woman definitely had an impact on a man,

especially one locked in a cell without a companion. Stefan had endless patience when he was on the job, but seriously, this was a bust. Jean-Claude would make a beeline for the woman and for the microchip he'd stolen from the Russian government—a microchip worth a fortune on the black market. That chip contained information that would set their defense system back fifty years if it got out.

"She any good at painting?" Stefan asked.

Jean-Claude nodded. "She's good at everything she does."

Stefan remained silent, waiting for more. He knew it would come. Jean-Claude wouldn't have said anything at all if he didn't want to talk.

"She's already made a name for herself in the art world. Her kaleidoscopes have won international awards. Her paintings are sold for a fortune, and she's a conservator of old artwork for private collectors. They fly the paintings to her under heavy guard."

Jean-Claude sounded proud of her. Conservators were rare, responsible for restoring the health of paintings hundreds of years old. It was difficult work and a somewhat small community. He doubted if there were many award-winning kaleidoscope artists. The information that would be very helpful in finding her identity. Stefan had already sent several pictures back to his people in order to start the investigation into just who the mystery woman actually was.

"I have to hand it to you, having a woman like that willing to wait for you."

Jean-Claude didn't say anything, but stared down at the quiet, pensive face. Stefan knew the words would eat him, the idea that maybe she wasn't waiting for him. La Roux had a better cell than most inmates. He wasn't like the majority, suicidal and depressed with the conditions which told Stefan that guards were smuggling him items and doing their best to curry his favor right along with the prisoners. It hadn't taken long for word to get around that if a guard displeased Jean-Claude, one of his men retaliated against the guard's family.

Stefan had been in this disgusting place long enough. There was nothing more to be gotten from the crime lord. He had told his government to break the man out of prison and either snatch him as he came out or let him lead them to the microchip. Either way, it was better than rotting in the small confines of the cell staring at a woman whose name he didn't even know. Obsessing over her right along with Jean-Claude. He was leaving tonight before he lost his mind staring at a woman who would never look at him twice.

"I hate saying anything nice to you, Rolex, but she's got the face of an angel. I can't imagine that any woman lives up to that." He needed to find a way to keep the man talking. After two months, he still didn't even know her name, Jean-Claude was that tight-lipped.

Jean-Claude glanced at him and then at the picture. He smiled for the first time since Stefan had been shoved into his cell. "I'm sure you can't. She speaks seven languages. Seven." A snide lip curl told Stefan that Jean-Claude was certain he could never learn more than one language.

Stefan spoke French fluently, with a perfect accent, and his undercover persona—John Bastille—certainly didn't appear as if he was an educated man, other than in criminal pursuits. If truth was told, Stefan could match the dream woman language for language, which meant she was educated and all the more alluring. He was a bit surprised that Jean-Claude liked intelligent women.

"She's the type that would argue," Stefan pointed out, staying in character. His type of muscle man wouldn't want a lowly woman arguing with him. It said something that Jean-Claude wanted a smart woman.

"She definitely speaks her mind," Jean-Claude agreed,

a small half-smile creeping into his eyes as if remembering a moment he found particularly amusing. "You wouldn't understand."

Stefan pushed down the hundred and one crude things his undercover persona would have said, knowing it would end the conversation immediately. Jean-Claude hadn't said more than three or four sentences in the two months they'd shared a cell. Instead, he looked down at the floor as if in sad reflection.

"I had a woman once. One worthwhile, not a prostitute. I should have been a little nicer to her and maybe she would have stuck around." He flashed a quick, envious grin at Jean-Claude. "She didn't look like that one. What's her name?"

Never once in all the months had Jean-Claude referred to the woman by her name, or said where she was. He was very close-mouthed when it came to the angel on the wall. It bothered Stefan that he secretly thought of her like that. *Angel.* Mysterious. Elusive. So out of reach of the ordinary man. Out of reach of a man who lived completely in the shadows. A man without a real identity.

"Judith." Jean-Claude's voice was clipped and warned Stefan not to push any further on the woman's identity.

Triumph surged through Stefan. Jean-Claude was as bored as he was in the cell. And he wanted to talk about his woman. He *needed* to talk about her. Stefan wanted him to crave her, to take the opportunity to escape when it was presented to him—not by Stefan of course, but by one of the guards. It wouldn't be that difficult to arrange. Having Jean-Claude La Roux owe a favor would be like hitting the lottery. At the same time, Jean-Claude didn't give anything away for free. What was he after?

"Pretty name. She looks exotic, but that name is American, isn't it?" Actually the name was of Hebrew origin, but

Stefan doubted very much if the crime lord was aware of that fact or even cared. It was a stab in the dark, a calculated feeler.

Jean-Claude eyed him warily. "What the hell difference does it make?"

Stefan allowed a surge of anger to show, more triumphant than ever. He'd struck a nerve. The mystery woman could very well be from the United States, not Japan as he'd first thought. "Not a bit. Just makin' conversation. The hell with it." He turned his back on the crime lord—a calculated risk. Showing indifference was the only way Jean-Claude might keep talking. If he thought Stefan was too interested, the man wouldn't say a word. Stefan had to hand it to him, he was intelligent enough to play his cards close to his chest.

Turning away from La Roux, only had him staring at another wall of photos. He was surrounded by the mysterious woman. She definitely looked of Japanese descent, but not entirely—she appeared tall. It was possible she had an American parent. The coastline where she appeared to live could be one in the United States rather than Europe. He hadn't considered that possibility before.

One of the pictures he loved the most was of Judith—he had her name now—walking barefoot in the sand. The wind was blowing hard and her long, silky looking hair streamed behind her. He could see small footprints in the wet sand. For some strange reason, that photograph got to him. She seemed so alone. So sad. Waiting for someone. Jean-Claude? His stomach knotted at the thought.

"You married to her?" He didn't look at Jean-Claude when he asked, preferring to listen to the tone of the voice, rather than the answer.

"Engaged," Jean-Claude replied after a long pause.

"She know it?" he asked slyly. Stefan hadn't seen a ring

on her finger in any of the photographs, and he'd looked for one.

Jean-Claude shrugged. "It doesn't much matter what she thinks. She's my fiancée and when the time comes, she'll be with me one way or another." He picked up one of his many books and held it out to Stefan. "You ever hear of this crap?"

Stefan pushed down the little twinge of pleasure in knowing the woman wasn't quite as taken with Jean-Claude as the man was with her. He took the book, one he'd looked at a couple of times, shocked at the subject matter. He feigned ignorance. "Aura? What is that supposed to be? I never heard of it."

"Can you believe this crap? Do you see colors around people's bodies? New Age bullshit, is what it is." There was such anger, such bitterness in Jean-Claude, a suppressed rage that for the first time made Stefan worry a little about Judith.

"Your woman believes this stuff?" Stefan asked, keeping vague puzzlement in his voice.

"Damn right, she does. Takes it very seriously. I've read all about it, but I've never met a single person who believes in it or can see colors surrounding people other than her."

"So she's a little bit crazy." Stefan flashed a lecherous grin. "Don't you think her body sort of makes up for all that? Keep her mouth busy and you don't have a problem." His stomach knotted tighter. His gut actually hurt.

Jean-Claude shot him a furious look. He snatched the book out of Stefan's hand and threw it against the wall of the cell. "I don't know why I would expect someone like you to understand."

Stefan didn't want to understand. He wanted out of this stinking cell, away from the man whose soul was rotten. There was no mercy in his world. No soft skin. No dark eyes a man could get lost in. He wasn't even real, no more than a dark shadow sliding in and out of places others called home and leaving behind death and chaos. He didn't know what a home was and he no longer cared. He had lost his humanity long ago in places like this, surrounded by corrupt men who traded in human flesh and wreaked havoc on the world for money.

He'd been in the business too long when he started to fixate on a woman just because she was the only thing that remotely resembled innocence in a stinking prison cell.

"You know, Bastille," Jean-Claude began.

Stefan went on alert. For the first time Jean-Claude sounded different. They were getting to the business of why the crime lord had deigned to speak to him about his woman. Jean-Claude had been steadfastly silent and it just wasn't in him to have a friendly conversation, no matter how much he might want to talk to someone about Judith and the photographs. He'd given to get something.

Stefan turned around, leaned one hip lazily against the cot and raised an eyebrow.

"Why didn't you kill me? You knew I ordered the beatings and the hits."

Stefan kept his expression carefully blank. He shrugged. "No money in it. I want out of here. I came to do a job and once it's done I'll get out."

Jean-Claude's eyebrow shot up. "A job?" he echoed.

"Relax, Rolex, you aren't the mark." Stefan allowed a small smile to creep into his eyes. "I won't say it didn't cross my mind a time or two, but there's no percentage in it."

"But you would kill me if someone paid you to do it."

"We're not exactly friends." This time amusement reached his voice.

"I underestimated you," Jean-Claude admitted.

Stefan noted with satisfaction that the crime lord realized just how close he had been to death. All those nights with Stefan lurking like a lethal viper just feet from him. "Everyone does." Again, Stefan showed no malice.

Jean-Claude studied the scarred face. "I could use a man like you."

"I'm not sticking around. I'll be out of here by tomorrow." Stefan spoke with supreme confidence.

"How?"

Stefan shrugged again and stayed mysteriously silent.

"You have a way to escape?"

Oh yeah, there was interest in the crime lord's voice. He wanted out. Once out, he'd have the money to buy a new identity and face. Stefan did it all the time.

Stefan turned away from the man and sank down onto his cot, silently declaring the conversation was over. When they went to dinner, a man would be found dead in his cell. As the prison locked down, John Bastille would be absent and Jean-Claude La Roux would know there was a way out. When he was approached by a guard to help him escape in a couple of weeks, he would jump at the chance.

The prisoner, already dead in his cell, was a Russian traitor, one in for arm's dealing, but he was guilty of so much more than that. He worked for Jean-Claude and was responsible for giving the crime lord the location of one of their top engineers, Theodotus Solovyov, who had designed their current defense system. The attack on Solovyov had left Stefan's brother, Gavriil, with a permanent injury, placing his life in danger.

Gavriil, undoubtedly one of the government's top agents, had been appointed bodyguard to Solovyov. He had managed, in spite of superior forces and being outgunned, in spite of being stabbed seven times, to keep Solovyov from being kidnapped and to drive off the kidnappers, but the microchip Solovyov had sewn into his coat had been taken. Only Solovyov and his wife had known the microchip had been placed there. Solovyov had been sold out by his own wife, and Gavriil's mission had been considered a failure.

A man like Gavriil Prakenskii was not forgiven failures, nor was he retired gracefully. He was simply retired. Gavriil had managed to escape from the hospital and had disappeared. He would never be safe again, not bearing the Prakenskii name. The only Prakenskii truly safe was their youngest brother, Ilya, who had been groomed to be an Interpol agent. He had worked for the secret assassination squad for a short time, and his services had been required on and off, but he hadn't been given the life of living in the shadows the way his older brothers had.

Stefan had helped Gavriil escape, carrying him through the darkened streets to a waiting car where he smuggled him out of Russia. It had been a very narrow escape, and without a doctor, Gavriil would have died. But he was gone now, using another identity, and Stefan doubted if he'd be lucky enough to ever see his brother again. Once he'd learned from Gavriil that only Theodotus Solovyov and his wife, Elena, had known about the microchip sewn into the coat, they both had known Elena had been the one to sell out their country.

As soon as Gavriil was out of danger, Stefan followed the money trail and found not only Elena's guilt, but the tie back to Jean-Claude La Roux. Elena died after providing the name of her lover. Her lover had given up the rest of the hit squad before he had died. One by one Stefan had hunted every participant who had destroyed his brother's career and put his life in jeopardy, killing them all except for the one in the French prison. That last detail had been attended to earlier in the evening.

Stefan lay down on his cot, ignoring Jean-Claude's puzzled look. The man wanted more information and was probably regretting that he'd set the tone for their rocky relationship. There was immense satisfaction in knowing Jean-Claude was going to regret a lot of things—ending Gavriil's career not the least of those regrets.

~

Four days later, Stefan took his time in the hot shower, grateful for a decent room, clean bathroom and comfortable bed. He wrapped a towel around his hips and stepped out onto the cool tiles. Setting his gun down on the sink, he dried his hair, staring at the fogged image in the mirror. John Bastille was no more and Stefan Prakenskii was back. He wasn't any better looking than Bastille had been, even cleaned up. His body was in shape, every muscle loose and ready, his waist tapered, hips narrow and his core strength absolutely solid. His body was a machine, trained for any possibility. He knew a thousand ways to kill someone. He could seduce any woman out of her clothes, her sensibilities and her secrets— and had done so more times than he could count. He could hit a target a mile away in a high wind without a problem. He could deliver a needle as he brushed past his target without them feeling anything more than an annoying insect bite. He had no idea how to be anything else.

Picking up his gun, he went into the small room, his home for the night. He had the door primed—he wasn't a trusting man and never would be. The windows looked out over the river, his last resort should he be attacked and there was no other way out. He had set an escape route over the roof and one through the hotel as well. He had four exit strategies, and an arsenal in his room. Still, he never felt safe.

There was a restless feeling in him that hadn't been there before. Maybe it was time to get out. He'd lost too much humanity. His senses were going numb, or maybe they had been gone all along and he hadn't noticed—or cared.

In spite of his determination not to look, he found himself standing in front of the dresser where the photograph he'd lifted from the wall—his favorite of Judith on the beach—lay right where he'd put it. He'd tossed it there, trying to tell himself he would turn it over in order to better help with finding her identity. A little mistake like that could blow everything. Blow the entire two months of living in a dirty cell with a monster. What was he thinking? He didn't make mistakes.

He picked up the photograph and stared down at that pensive face. His thumb slid over the band of soft skin revealed between her jeans and tee. What was it about her that got to him? She was a mistake, and yet, knowing it, he'd taken the photograph anyway. It wasn't her striking looks—and he did think she was beautiful. He was inexplicably drawn to something inside her that shown through in this picture.

He forced himself to toss the photograph back onto the dresser. He would never see her, never know what happened to her, but if he was making mistakes, regretting who he was, then it was time to employ his exit strategy. Every man in his business had one because, in the end, they all knew too much about the secret project that had developed them in the first place.

He dressed carefully, slipping into his weapons as easily as the suit that had a casual elegance when his wide shoulders filled it out. His face was subtly different, his eye color a striking blue, a few of the scars gone. He'd trimmed his dark blonde hair into a much neater style and shaved all facial hair. His watch was in place, an equally elegant piece without being too showy. He looked like a wealthy businessman, but the kind who had fought his way to the top. Cursing his own stupidity, he dropped the photograph back onto the dresser.

"You're going to get yourself killed over a woman," he said aloud.

As if on cue his pager buzzed. Puzzled, he opened his

computer and signed in. At once text spread across the screen. The woman had been identified with the clues he'd given them. Judith Henderson—an artist on the rise. She'd made quite a name for herself as an expert conservator restoring damaged paintings. Private collectors sought her out and entrusted paintings worth millions to her care. In addition to her restoration work, she was an acclaimed artist in her own right, both as the creator of international award-winning kaleidoscopes and as a painter whose original works commanded hefty sums. She lived in a small village on the Northern California coast called Sea Haven.

Everything in him stilled. Sea Haven. How often would that little village touch his family? His youngest brother, Ilya, had settled there. Another younger brother, Lev, had disappeared there, declared dead, going down with a yacht in the ocean. He didn't believe Lev could be killed so easily. Was this a trap of some kind—a trap for him? Or maybe for Lev. Maybe they were using him to try to find his brother. A man like Lev, with all his abilities, didn't die easily. He didn't panic, not in the worst of circumstances.

Petr Ivanov, a man with no human feelings whatsoever, had been sent to find and eliminate Lev should he still be alive. He had reported back that Lev had indeed died in the yacht accident. The body had never been found, but the investigation had been thorough. If Ivanov hadn't been convinced of Lev's death, he wouldn't have risked his reputation on his report. Everyone had supposedly stopped looking for his brother. Did that mean they really believed Lev was dead? Or were they setting up Stefan to lead them to his brother?

He didn't react to the news scrolling across his screen. Like Lev, he was not a man given to panic. He waited in silence. In stillness. A new message appeared on the computer screen, and his heart jumped before it settled.

There was a gallery for sale in Sea Haven. He was to go undercover and establish a relationship with Judith Henderson, who managed the place for the owner, a man by the name of Frank Warner. Files would follow detailing the mission. He felt himself go still. He was to interrogate Jean-Claude when they broke him out of prison. He would get the information from La Roux—his handlers knew he would. Traveling to Sea Haven, as much as he wanted to go find out about his brother, would be stepping into a minefield.

He waited another heartbeat and sent back his reply. *I do not understand. I am to interrogate Jean-Claude.*

The anonymous orders continued to scroll across the screen. The plan had been changed. If anything went wrong and they missed their chance to pick up Jean-Claude when he escaped from prison, they wanted to make certain they could acquire him should he go to Sea Haven. Stefan needed to get there well ahead of him and establish his cover with Judith Henderson. If necessary, should the crime lord show up, he would interrogate both Jean-Claude and the woman once he had both of them in his custody. Stefan's gut reacted, lurching sickeningly. He actually tasted bile in his mouth. Extracting information from La Roux was one thing, but the woman too? He opened his eyes to look at the text a second time, willing the orders to magically change. He must be damn tired to have such a physical reaction to the order.

He closed his eyes briefly, shaking his head. This mission was definitely something other than what he was being told. It made no sense to think agents would break Jean-Claude from prison and then lose him. He was being sent to Sea Haven not because they thought they'd lose the crime lord, but because he was bait to lure his brother, Lev, out into the open. They hadn't accepted Petr Ivanov's report on his brother's death after all. The orders served a twofold purpose: revealing Lev's whereabouts, and if by some miracle La Roux slipped away from the other agents, Stefan would be in place to extract the information they needed and then kill him.

Swallowing his absolute repugnance of the orders, he typed in his agreement. Moments later, he received a down-loadable file containing his cover and everything they had on Judith Henderson. He signed off and poured himself a cup of coffee, then sank down into a chair, rubbing his temples. He'd been getting blinding headaches lately, an-other sign he was crashing. This assignment had just gone south fast. He couldn't afford to be crashing, not if they were sending him to Sea Haven.

A part of him wanted to go, and that sent concern through him. He didn't want to lead Petr Ivanov to Lev, and if Lev was in Sea Haven, he would find Stefan, no matter how solid the cover was. He swore in three languages and took a sip of his coffee. Judith. Damn the woman. She'd gotten under his skin in that prison cell. He hadn't known it was possible for anyone to do that, let alone a woman he'd never met.

He opened the file, reading about her life. Japanese mother. American father. Both deceased in a car accident. She got her height from her father. Those long, beautiful legs. He forced his mind back to data, committing her life to memory. She had one brother, older, who had raised her after the death of her parents.

Paul Henderson, now deceased, executed, with a single gunshot to the forehead, but not before he'd been tortured. He had gone to Paris and left with his sister. They both dis-appeared and Paul resurfaced in Sicily. He was killed there. Judith turned up *after* Jean-Claude was imprisoned and took her brother's body home to the States. What did that mean?

Had Jean-Claude been looking for Judith? He turned the

thought over and over in his mind. It fit. It was possible she'd run from the man with her brother's help. She was intelligent, and men like La Roux couldn't afford intelligent women. They figured things out. Once she figured out La Roux was dirty, Judith might have not been able to live with it. On the other hand, she may have taken something valuable from him.

The thought didn't sit well with Stefan, but either scenario could explain both the death of her brother and Jean-Claude's continued interest in her. As did the fact that she'd dropped out of sight until Jean-Claude had been imprisoned. Because she had surfaced suggested she truly didn't know just how dangerous La Roux really was, or just how far and expertly he could wield his considerable power from his prison cell.

Stefan continued to scroll through the downloaded dossier. The file included several images of Judith's paintings, both the ones she'd painted before she left Paris and the ones she'd painted after. The moment his gaze touched the first painting he felt a hard one-two punch to his gut. Her drive and passion literally robbed his lungs of air. He couldn't take his eyes from the series, studying each painting carefully. They were intriguing and beautiful, deep, three-dimensional colors, amazing lines, all passion and fire. Her drive and passion.

"There you are," he whispered. "I see you."

She poured herself into the painting, holding nothing back, breathing life into her work so that every seascape, every tree, cloud or bush had movement and sang or sobbed. Color was a musical instrument in her hand, wielded by an expert; her courage was astounding. She understood colors and their meaning. She drew her strokes like caresses, both bold and shy, sensual and innocent. She was a seductress with her colors, a dream within reach, yet unattainable.

Stefan ran both hands through his hair. She was out there for the entire world to see. She had bared her soul in these paintings. God, she was breathtaking. He felt his body stir, a shock beyond imagining. He was always in command of himself, physically and mentally. He'd been trained since he was a child. His body came to life at his command and performed when and where he needed it to. What the hell was this woman doing to him with her paintings and her photographs?

There was more of the real woman in the paintings than in the mysterious photograph he'd stolen from the crime lord. She'd hidden herself, drawn inward, held herself aloof from the world. But here, in every bold stroke, he could see her fire and passion.

Stefan forced himself to move on. Her time with Jean-Claude was well documented. The rumors about La Roux had begun to surface and there were a few pictures of a young Judith smiling up at Jean-Claude, wearing happiness like a second skin in all the surveillance photos. His reaction to seeing the crime lord with her was primeval, visceral, even animalistic. He wanted to kill the man with his bare hands. He flexed his fingers and slowed his breathing, pushing all emotion from his mind.

Stefan studied Jean-Claude's expression. The arm around Judith's narrow waist was possession, as was his expression, but there was something more. If a man like La Roux was capable of love, it was there. Whatever it was, obsession—Stefan was beginning to understand the word—the look on Jean-Claude's face as he stared down at the laughing Judith, said it all. He would pay any price to keep her. For certain, if the man eluded the other agents, he would be going to Sea Haven to collect whatever he thought of as his—and that included Judith.

Stefan read the file carefully, committing it to memory

before examining the few photographs of Judith's work after her escape from La Roux. Each painting was good, no doubt about it, but her later work was much different from her originals. She was very restrained, showing the absolute beauty of the piece she worked on. Flawless color schemes; bold, courageous strokes; but for him, the paintings themselves were flat. They were still beautiful, but she—Judith, the essence of the woman—wasn't there anymore. All her passion and fire was restrained, gone, replaced by a mask that was good, brilliant even, but not real.

"Too late to cover up now. I see you," he whispered again. "I'm coming for you."

He pressed his fingers hard just above his eyes where a headache was beginning. Damn it all. He didn't want another life. He didn't dream about another life. He played the cards dealt to him like the automaton he'd taught himself to become. He didn't feel. He didn't even want to feel. He no longer thought about his parents and how, in the darkness of their home, guns had been put to his mother and father's heads and the triggers pulled. There was no safety inside four walls. There would be no safety for him anywhere—ever. And anyone with him would be at risk. Anyone he loved would be taken from him. Better not to ever take the chance, so never feel.

He repeated the mantra softly aloud. His steps whispered on the carpet before he even knew his own intention. He crossed to the dresser and picked up the photograph of Judith Henderson again, drawn by some force greater than he could resist. A woman who spoke seven languages. Intelligent. Beautiful. An artist. He didn't even know what that would be like, to have the freedom to paint, to pour your heart and soul onto a canvas.

He knew languages. He was intelligent. And he knew paintings. Everything about them. It was all necessary to his business. His temples throbbed and he sank back into his chair, the photograph in his hand. What was it about her? That lost, lonely look? The wind in her hair? The sun shining on the water. His imagination, so long repressed, leapt forward in spite of his desire to suppress. She was waiting for someone to come and unlock that passion and fire. She was waiting for the right man to give it to.

What the hell was he thinking?

In this special section,
you'll get an exclusive look at
three deleted scenes from
Dark Peril

The "little" kitten crept silently through the dense foliage, eyes fixed on the back of his prey. Learning to hunt was more fun than work. He used the freeze-frame stalk, one slow inch at a time, his body flexible and strong, forty pounds of sheer muscle, growing nearly visibly at each rising. When he was excited, he couldn't always keep his substance, slipping more and more into the shadow cat that he was.

The woman moved silently through the rain forest, seemingly with no destination, ambling along in that strange, fluid, silent way she had. Her heartbeat resounded through his body. He heard the way her blood flowed like the greatest temptation running through her veins, a call to the hunger that wouldn't subside. She paused. His chance. He crouched, prepared to pounce.

Dominic leapt between the shadow kitten and Solange, cuffing the cat as it attacked. "He still has instincts, Solange, and he is dangerous, no matter how much you want to save him."

Solange swung around at the sound of the kitten hissing his displeasure. Instantly the hiss turned to a purr and he rushed to her, rubbing her so hard along her legs he nearly knocked her over. She gave a little sigh as she reached down to scratch between his ears. "Only to me, Dominic. He's never gone after you or anyone in close proximity to us. I've deliberately brought him in close to others as we've passed them and he hasn't shown the slightest interest."

Dominic turned away from her. She could easily touch his thoughts, but she was too wrapped up in trying to puzzle out how best to combat the kitten's need for her blood to be concerned with Dominic's reaction—and that was what she should have been most worried about. The cat was going to grow quite large, and as it did, the ability to turn shadow at will would surely improve and the animal would be lethal—to Solange. He couldn't take chances with her life. No matter how much she was falling in love with the kitten, her life was far more important.

"Solange . . ." he began.

She shook her head. "I know what you're going to say, Dominic. I've thought of the dangers as well."

"Sooner or later, if he's separated from you, he may decide to take someone else's blood and he may kill them."

"*We* take blood. We need it to survive just as he does. But you've gone inside him, just as I have, in order to try to repair all the damage to him. My blood is filling in all those empty spaces, and maybe he's needy because of that. In the meantime, we'll train him."

"You know better, Solange," Dominic corrected gently. "He was bred to find you, to take *your* blood specifically. He is a definite threat to you and he is growing fast."

She was silent a few moments, petting the purring kitten. "Dominic, at this point, I can give him blood and we can keep him with us. I'll work with him. We just can't make a decision until he's a little older and much more solid through the middle. He'll at least have a chance at a normal existence."

"Sivamet." He kept his voice as tender as possible. "You know there will never be normal for him."

"I know. You're right." She ducked her head again, biting at her lower lip. "We're not normal. Either one of us. I'll watch out for him, Dominic, and if he gets out of hand, I'll step aside if that time should come."

"Look at me, Solange," he said. This time there was no gentleness in his voice, only soft, implacable authority. "If the time comes when I deem this animal too dangerous for you, I will destroy it without consulting you again. I do not want you to ever say I did not warn you."

She flicked her gaze at him, her expression closed, although when he touched her mind, she didn't flinch away. He was skating the edge of her ability to recognize his authority. It mattered little to him other than he disliked making her uncomfortable. Solange was definitely his partner in all ways, but when it came to her safety, he wasn't willing to compromise. Traveling with an animal as potentially dangerous as the shadow cat, when it was created specifically to take her blood, was pushing his own comfort zone.

She moistened her lips and he wanted to lean down and kiss her. She was trying to find a middle ground, he could see it on her transparent face, and he had to give her credit for wanting to meet him halfway.

"I know it's worrisome, Dominic. I wouldn't be trying to heal him if I didn't think I could. Look at him, he's so affectionate. He has the ability to learn."

He nodded. "That is true, *sivamet*, but he is still an animal with instincts."

Solange dropped to her knees beside the large kitten, still rubbing his head between his ears. The cat purred until the forest seemed to ring with his pleasure. He put his head down and bumped against her over and over, trying to get closer. Dominic sighed. He was going to have to wait and see. He knew it would only be harder on Solange if the kitten didn't make it. She was already so enamored with the little creature.

"I will keep trying to get him to accept my blood as well," he said, by way of concession.

Her eyes met his. She smiled at him. "Have I told you that I love you? Because I do."

His heart leapt along with his pulse. He had to be very careful because the woman could disarm him with just her smile.

~

Dominic glanced down at Solange as they approached the De La Cruz main home. He sent his call ahead to the brothers and, like Solange, he knew they were being carefully scrutinized as they neared their destination. She moved just a little away from him, giving him room to fight should there be need. She was dressed in her fighter armor, blue jeans and a T-shirt, her hair pulled back into a severe braid. She looked totally serious, her eyes restless, constantly searching for hidden traps. Dominic thought her absolutely beautiful.

She moved over every obstacle with fluid grace, flowing over the ground in absolute silence. The contrast between his warrior and his woman was absolute—and the sexiest thing in the world to him. Solange was dependable in a fight, as dependable as any Carpathian hunter he had run across. Her power might not be the same, but her courage and her determination were.

You are nervous. He used their more intimate form of communication. She didn't even glance at him. Didn't betray that he had spoken to her by so much as a change of expression.

You have no idea the ribbing I'm going to get from my cousins. Juliette and Jasmine will be laughing their heads off that I've got a man. And that MaryAnn, she's a counselor for women who has been working with Jasmine, and a girly girl if I ever saw one. She wanted me to paint my fingernails—and toenails. Can you imagine?

Mmm, he speculated in a darkly velvet voice. *The possibilities are astounding.*

That earned him a flick of censure out of the corner of her eyes. *You had better not egg them on, Dominic. You will find yourself on the ground crying like a girl.*

I can only look forward to that event. Rein in your kitten. He thinks he is going to stalk Manolito who just might get the wrong impression of him.

Solange's gaze sought out her kitten. *Shadow, come to me now.*

"Whoa! Uncle Manolito, check it out," a young man's voice called out.

A slender boyish male of undetermined age rushed out of the bushes straight at Shadow. The kitten leapt into the air, growling a warning, his body going insubstantial. One moment he was solid and then next he was nothing but a shadow slinking through the brush back toward Solange and Dominic.

"*Veriak ot en Karpatiiak*—by the blood of the Prince," Manolito swore. "Josef, get back here where I can protect you."

It was too late, the boy was already out in the open and then vanishing after the shadow cat. "Did you see it? Really, Uncle Manny, it was a seriously sick kind of cat."

Solange glared at the boy, her hand sliding to her weapon as his head bobbed in and out of the brush, obviously following her kitten. "My cat isn't sick," she called out. "Leave him alone before you scare him into injuring you. Don't you know better than to chase a poor little kitten through the brush?"

Take your hand off your weapon, Solange, Dominic counseled.

She sniffed her utter contempt of that idea. "Manolito," her voice changed, "Uncle *Manny*, you know me very well. If that idiot touches my baby, I'll retaliate and it will be bloody. Call him back."

"Like I have any authority over him," Manolito muttered. "I would pin his ears back myself, but MaryAnn says he needs to find himself. Go ahead and wing him, Solange. I am all for it."

"This is your genius, Dominic?" Solange demanded as a grayish-black blur rushed her, hiding behind her, his body going from transparency to substance and back again, ears flat and tail swishing, indicating his agitation. "This thoughtless *boy* who chases my kitten?"

Josef halted abruptly in front of her, picking leaves off his shirt. He grinned at her, his eyes bright, darting past her to look at the hissing, spitting kitten. "Totally sick. Awesome, Dominic. Where did you find that?"

"He is not sick," Solange reiterated. "He happens to be a shadow cat and is supposed to look like that."

"Sick is good, kind of like cool, you know," Josef said, waving his hand dismissively. He tried to step around Solange but she glided with him, easily blocking his path. He blinked up at her as if really seeing her for the first time. He flashed her a disarming smile.

Solange had never seen anyone quite like him. His hair

was spiked, his eyes mischievous and he had a pierced ear, a spiked collar and bracelet. She narrowed her eyes at him, giving him her most intimidating stare, ignoring Dominic, who had moved slightly to insert his larger frame between her and the boy. She guessed him to be in his early twenties, but looked very young. Despite his strange appearance, he had a look of innocence about him. "What exactly are you?" she asked.

Manolito made a snorting sound. Dominic's lips twitched. She snapped a glare at both of them and put a calming hand on Shadow's head. The cat rubbed her leg, nudging her hard enough to shove her forward a step.

Josef didn't look in the least upset at her question. "I'm a Carpathian male. What are you?"

Dominic growled a low warning. "Mind your manners, boy."

"I suppose it's a legitimate question, since I asked him," Solange said. "I'm his lifemate. Who would have thought."

Manolito looked startled. More than startled. Shocked. "Are you kidding, Solange? You with a man?"

Here it comes. Prepare yourself, Solange warned Dominic.

Sure enough her cousins, Jasmine and Juliette rushed from the house. Juliette was Riordan De La Cruz's lifemate.

"Tattletale," Solange hissed at Manolito.

He smirked at her.

"You see what they're all like, Dominic," Solange confided aloud so Manolito couldn't fail to hear her complaint.

"Now who's tattling?" Manolito teased.

Solange braced herself as Juliette flung herself at her cousin, propelling her backward. Solange took a step back with one leg to keep them both from falling, knocked into the hissing kitten and tripped, clutching at her cousin. They

both went down together, Solange landing on her butt.
Juliette landed on top of her and the kitten leapt on her head.

Solange glared at Dominic, who didn't change expression,
but she could hear him laughing in her mind. *You could
have helped,* she accused.

True, but I have never seen you this way.

What way? She narrowed her eyes at him.

Flustered.

You do remember I'm armed, she warned.

He flashed a grin at her and pulled the kitten off Juliette
so they both could get to their feet. Solange rose reluctantly
to look around her at her gathering extended family. They
were all grinning like idiots—just like Dominic. She wished
the earth could open up and swallow her, and it wasn't until
several minutes later that she remembered she could actually make it happen.

~

Solange placed her hand over Jasmine's rounded stomach.
"Not long now at all, Jasmine. Have you had any problems?
I should have been checking in more often. I swear, time
gets away from a person in the rain forest."

Her youngest cousin smiled at her and shook her head.
"I've been fine. No more being sick, thank heavens. Everyone's been very helpful, but we were worried about you."

Solange ducked her head. Juliette and Jasmine had
spent their lives worrying about her just as she had them.
Perhaps having Dominic for a lifemate made her more
aware of the people who loved her and how it had to be for
them when she disappeared for long periods of time with
no word at all and no way to know if she was alive or dead.
"I'm sorry, Jasmine, I should have tried to find a way to get
word to you that I was safe."

Jasmine's smile widened into a teasing grin. "Or at least that you found yourself a handsome hottie out there in the jungle."

Solange glanced at Dominic, wishing she had the time to tease and visit with her cousins. She would always be a little uneasy inside a house, always uneasy in the presence of men. Even with her cousin's family, which technically made them hers. But she wanted to spend a little downtime with these women she loved. She looked around at all of them, pressing her lips together tightly. It seemed she never came bearing good news. Jasmine was close to her term, and yet, even now, she couldn't rest and feel safe.

"What is it?" Nicolas asked. He came up quietly behind his lifemate, Lara, one hand settling gently on the nape of her neck.

The atmosphere in the room changed from joyous celebration to somber in an instant. Solange shook her head and squeezed Jasmine's hand, remaining close to her. Juliette came up on the other side of her very pregnant sister. Juliette's lifemate, Riordan, put a hand on either of their shoulders in a gesture of comfort.

"We bring news of an attack, a large-scale, well-planned attack on your home and that of your people working here. This is to be the practice run before Malinov sends his army against the Prince. Zacarias will be out there"— Dominic gestured toward the rain forest—"where he will do the most good. They will come soon and you must prepare those loyal to you for the fight, because they are certain to be on our heels."

"You used the word, 'army,' Dominic," Rafael said. "How many are coming at us? You have any idea of the numbers?"

Dominic shook his head. "My sense is, we have a problem on our hands. We need to be prepared for waves of vampires and perhaps human puppets during the day if we do not defeat them immediately. The good news is, they have no idea we are aware of their plot."

"Jasmine can't stay here," Juliette said. "Solange, you have to take her somewhere safe."

Jasmine shook her head. "No. I'm tired of being the weak link, Juliette. Solange is always the one who faces our enemies. I can fight just as well as anyone else if I have to. I'm capable of using some of the weapons Riordan has developed for the workers to use to kill vampires. We do drills all the time. I know what to do."

"But . . ." Juliette turned her face toward Riordan, who immediately pulled her closer to him. "Are you certain, Jasmine? Solange can get you out of here, you know she can."

Solange wasn't as certain as Juliette. "Here we have all six Carpathian males and six Carpathian females. I haven't lost my ability completely to face the day, and Dominic is able to as well."

Nicolas frowned at her. "How is that possible?"

"It has something to do with Solange's blood," Dominic answered, aware Solange was very uncomfortable in the spotlight. "I cannot stay as long as Solange. We have done a little experimenting, and in truth, we are still struck by the Carpathian weakness, our body going leaden when the sun is at its highest peak. But we have more hours in the morning and evening. That may aid us."

Nicolas continued to frown, his expression turning thoughtful. "Can this be shared by all of us, if we exchange blood with you?"

Solange tried not to squirm at the idea. She forced herself to stand straight, never changing expression. No matter how much she wanted to be comfortable in the presence of such overwhelming, powerful men, she knew she never would be.

I would give them my blood rather than have you distressed.

Every knot coiling so hard in her stomach eased, settled. There it was, that velvet tone that stroked her deep inside where no one could see. Dominic. Her lifemate. She tasted him on her tongue. He stood with her, shoulder to shoulder. In front of her or behind her, he was always going to be there with her.

"We are more than willing to share blood, with you, Nicolas," Solange said, knowing that with Dominic she could do whatever had to be done, including sharing her strange blood with the other males. "But you can't count on it to serve you without first testing it for limitations."

"And the effects seem to be cumulative. Zacarias was given blood, but there seemed little effect on him," Dominic added. "So we do not know who it will work on and just what they may be able to do with it."

Nicolas caught Lara's hand. "We will talk to the workers and give them the option of deciding for themselves whether they stay or go, with no repercussions later. This is not a human fight, and even with all the training we have given them, they will be at a terrible disadvantage. In any case, they should move their women and children out of harm's way. Rafael, you and Dominic work out a battle plan. Manolito, get the structures protected. Riordan, you do your best with the livestock." He turned his head, his eyes meeting Jasmine's. "Little sister, you will do as you are told. You are precious to everyone in this room. You have a child to protect."

Jasmine shook her head, tears in her eyes. "Don't send me away from everyone I love, Nicolas. That's happened too many times in my life and everything is destroyed, everyone I care about dead or injured. I need to be here. I can handle weapons. I'm not a baby."

"No one said anything about you being a baby," Solange

said gently. "He's saying we need to know what we're fighting for and you are our reason."

"Luiz and Josef will take Jasmine to the inside vault room the moment we are under attack. No vampire can get inside," Nicolas commanded. "No hesitation, Luiz. If you have to, carry her in and hold her there. Josef, I expect you to obey me in this. You are to guard her."

Josef looked rebellious. "I'm Carpathian and skilled in battle. You're letting humans battle vampires and yet expect me to hide. I may look like a boy to you . . ."

"I said you will obey me in this and I meant it. Just the fact that you would argue with me while everyone else is rushing to secure the compound is enough to show me you are too young to engage in actual battle."

Josef flushed and ducked his head. Even the tips of his ears were red.

Dominic stepped closer to him. "Have you forgotten you are the only one of us able to decipher the encryption we retrieved from the Morrison laboratory? We need that material to protect those innocent women—to ensure that not a single man who has a potential lifemate among those women is lost. That is a huge responsibility, Josef, and it lies solely with you. Do not *ever* forget your importance to your people. Playing hero and getting yourself killed would be foolish under the circumstances. Do you not agree?"

Josef shrugged his thin shoulders but he looked much happier. "Yeah. I forgot for a moment how important that was. I'm on it, Dominic, you can count on me."

"We are all counting on you, Josef," Dominic said.

The boy puffed out his chest. Solange found herself smiling. Where the De La Cruz brothers were more like her, annoyed at the boy for having to explain, Dominic was patient and had bolstered the boy's confidence with a few simple words. She really needed to learn such tricks from him.

Obviously you will make the better parent, Dominic, she conceded. *That was nice of you.*

Everything I said was true. He wants to be a hunter, but his true weapon is his brain and the fact that he embraces the modern world as none of us truly do. We need him. He needs to know he is needed.

Solange loved him all the more for that observation.

A MUCH-ABRIDGED CARPATHIAN
DICTIONARY

This very much abridged Carpathian dictionary contains most of the Carpathian words used in these Dark books. Of course, a full Carpathian dictionary would be as large as the usual dictionary for an entire language (typically more than a hundred thousand words).

Note: The Carpathian nouns and verbs below are word stems. They generally do not appear in their isolated, "stem" form, as below. Instead, they usually appear with suffixes (e.g., "*andam*"—"I give," rather than just the root, "*and*").

agba—to be seemly or proper.
ai—oh.
aina—body.
ainaak—forever.
ak—suffix added after a noun ending in a consonant to make it plural.

aka—to give heed; to hearken; to listen.

akarat—mind; will.

ál—to bless; to attach to.

alatt—through.

aldyn—under; underneath.

alə—to lift; to raise.

alte—to bless; to curse.

and—to give.

andasz éntölem irgalomet!—have mercy!

arvo—value (*noun*).

arwa—praise (*noun*).

arwa-arvo—honor (*noun*).

arwa-arvo olen gæidnod, ekäm—honor guide you, my brother (*greeting*).

arwa-arvo olen isäntä, ekäm—honor keep you, my brother (*greeting*).

arwa-arvo pile sívadet—may honor light your heart (*greeting*).

arwa-arvod mäne me ködak—may your honor hold back the dark (*greeting*).

asti—until.

avaa—to open.

avio—wedded.

avio päläfertiil—lifemate.

belső—within; inside.

bur—good; well.

bur tule ekämet kuntamak—well met brother-kin (*greeting*).

ćaδa—to flee; to run; to escape.

ćoro—to flow; to run like rain.

csecsemő—baby (*noun*).

csitri—little one (*female*).

diutal—triumph; victory.

eći—to fall.

ek—suffix added after a noun ending in a consonant to make it plural.

ekä—brother.

elä—to live.

eläsz arwa-arvoval—may you live with honor, live nobly (*greeting*).

eläsz jeläbam ainaak—long may you live in the light (*greeting*).

elävä—alive.

elävä ainak majaknak—land of the living.

elid—life.

emä—mother (noun).

Emä Maγe—Mother Nature.

én—I.

en—great; many; big.

én jutta félet és ekämet—I greet a friend and brother (*greeting*).

En Puwe—The Great Tree. Related to the legends of Ygddrasil, the *axis mundi*, Mount Meru, heaven and hell, etc.

engem—me.

és—and.

että—that.

fáz—to feel cold or chilly.

fél—fellow; friend.

fél ku kuuluaak sívam belső—beloved.

fél ku vigyázak—dear one.

feldolgaz—prepare.

fertiil—fertile one.

fesztelen—airy.

fü—herbs; grass.

gæidno—road; way.

gond—care; worry; love (*noun*).

hän—he; she; it.

hän agba—it is so.
hän ku—prefix: one who; that which.
hän ku agba—truth.
hän ku kaśwa o numamet—sky-owner.
hän ku kuulua sívamet—keeper of my heart.
hän ku meke pirämet—defender.
hän ku pesä—protector.
hän ku saa kuć3aket—star-reacher.
hän ku tappa—deadly.
hän ku tuulmahl elidet—vampire (*literally: life-stealer*).
hän ku vie elidet—vampire (*literally: thief of life*).
hän ku vigyáz sielamet—keeper of my soul.
hän ku vigyáz sívamet és sielamet—keeper of my heart and soul.
hany—clod; lump of earth.
hisz—to believe; to trust.
ida—east.
igazág—justice.
irgalom—compassion; pity; mercy.
isä—father (*noun*).
isäntä—master of the house.
it—now.
jälleen—again.
jama—to be sick, wounded or dying; to be near death.
jelä—sunlight; day; sun; light.
jelä keje terád—light sear you (*Carpathian swear words*).
o jelä peje terád—sun scorch you (*Carpathian swear words*).
o jelä sielamak—light of my soul.
joma—to be under way; to go.
joɲe—to come; to return.
joɲesz arwa-arvoval—return with honor (*greeting*).
jörem—to forget; to lose one's way; to make a mistake.
juo—to drink.

juosz és eläsz—drink and live (*greeting*).

juosz és olen ainaak sielamet jutta—drink and become one with me (*greeting*).

juta—to go; to wander.

jüti—night; evening.

jutta—connected; fixed (*adj.*). To connect; to fix; to bind (*verb*).

k—suffix added after a noun ending in a vowel to make it plural.

kaca—male lover.

kaik—all.

kalma—corpse; death; grave.

kaŋa—to call; to invite; to request; to beg.

kaŋk—windpipe; Adam's apple; throat.

kaδa—to abandon; to leave; to remain.

kaδa wäkeva óv o köd—stand fast against the dark (*greeting*).

Karpatii—Carpathian.

Karpatii ku köd—liar.

käsi—hand (*noun*).

kaśwa—to own.

keje—to cook; to burn; to sear.

kepä—lesser; small; easy; few.

kidü—to wake up; to arise (*intransitive verb*).

kim—to cover an entire object with some sort of covering.

kinn—out; outdoors; outside; without.

kinta—fog; mist; smoke.

köd—fog; mist; darkness.

köd alte hän—darkness curse it (*Carpathian swear words*).

o köd belső—darkness take it (*Carpathian swear words*).

köd jutasz belső—shadow take you (*Carpathian swear words*).

koje—man; husband; drone.

kola—to die.

kolasz arwa-arvoval—may you die with honor (*greeting*).

koma—empty hand; bare hand; palm of the hand; hollow of the hand.

kond—all of a family's or clan's children.

kont—warrior.

kont o sívanak—strong heart (*literally: heart of the warrior*).

ku—who; which; that.

kuć3—star.

kuć3ak!—stars! (exclamation)

kule—to hear.

kulke—to go or to travel (on land or water).

kulkesz arwa-arvoval, ekäm—walk with honor, my brother (*greeting*).

kulkesz arwaval, joŋesz arwa arvoval—go with glory, return with honor (*greeting*).

kuly—intestinal worm; tapeworm; demon who possesses and devours souls.

kumpa—wave (*noun*).

kuńa—to lie as if asleep; to close or cover the eyes in a game of hide-and-seek; to die.

kune—moon.

kunta—band; clan; tribe; family.

kuras—sword; large knife.

kure—bind; tie.

kutni—to be able to bear, carry, endure, stand or take.

kutnisz ainaak—long may you endure (*greeting*).

kuulua—to belong; to hold.

lääs—west.

lamti (or lamt3)—lowland; meadow; deep; depth.

lamti ból jüti, kinta, ja szelem—the netherworld (*literally: the meadow of night, mists and ghosts*).

lańa—daughter.

lejkka—crack; fissure; split (*noun*). To cut; to hit; to strike forcefully (*verb*).

lewl—spirit (*noun*).

lewl ma—the other world (*literally: spirit land*). *Lewl ma* includes *lamti ból jüti, kinta, ja szelem:* the netherworld, but also includes the worlds higher up *En Puwe*, the Great Tree.

liha—flesh.

lõuna—south.

löyly—breath; steam (*related to* lewl: *spirit*).

ma—land; forest.

magköszun—thank.

mana—to abuse; to curse; to ruin.

mäne—to rescue; to save.

maγe—land; earth; territory; place; nature.

me—we.

meke—deed; work (*noun*). To do; to make; to work (*verb*).

minan—mine.

minden—every; all (*adj.*).

möért?—what for? (*exclamation*).

molanâ—to crumble; to fall apart.

molo—to crush; to break into bits.

mozdul—to begin to move; to enter into movement.

muonì—appoint; order; prescribe; command.

musta—memory.

myös—also.

nä—for.

naman—this; this one here.

nélkül—without.

nenä—anger.

nó—like; in the same way as; as.

numa—god; sky; top; upper part; highest (*related to the English word:* numinous).

numatorkuld—thunder (*literally: sky struggle*).

nyál—saliva; spit (*related to* nyelv: *tongue*).

nyelv—tongue.

o—the (*used before a noun beginning with a consonant*).

odam—to dream; to sleep.

odam-sarna kondak—lullaby (*literally: sleep-song of children*).

olen—to be.

oma—old; ancient.

omas—stand.

omboće—other; second (*adj.*).

ot—the (*used before a noun beginning with a vowel*).

otti—to look; to see; to find.

óv—to protect against.

owe—door.

päämoro—aim; target.

pajna—to press.

pälä—half; side.

päläfertiil—mate or wife.

peje—to burn.

peje terád—get burned (*Carpathian swear words*).

pél—to be afraid; to be scared of.

pesä—nest (*literal*); protection (*figurative*).

pesäsz jeläbam ainaak—long may you stay in the light (*greeting*).

pide—above.

pile—to ignite; to light up.

pirä—circle; ring (*noun*). To surround; to enclose (*verb*).

piros—red.

pitä—to keep; to hold.

pitäam mustaakad sielpesäambam—I hold your memories safe in my soul.

pitäsz baszú, piwtäsz igazáget—no vengeance, only justice.

piwtä—to follow; to follow the track of game.

poår—bit; piece.

põhi—north.

pukta—to drive away; to persecute; to put to flight.

pus—healthy; healing.

pusm—to be restored to health.

puwe—tree; wood.

rauho—peace.

reka—ecstasy; trance.

rituaali—ritual.

sa—sinew; tendon; cord.

sa4—to call; to name.

saa—arrive, come; become; get, receive.

saasz hän ku andam szabadon—take what I freely offer.

salama—lightning; lightning bolt.

sarna—words; speech; magic incantation (*noun*). To chant; to sing; to celebrate (*verb*).

sarna kontakawk—warriors' chant.

śaro—frozen snow.

sas—shoosh (*to a child or baby*).

saγe—to arrive; to come; to reach.

siel—soul.

sisar—sister.

sív—heart.

sív pide köd—love transcends evil.

sívad olen wäkeva, hän ku piwtä—may your heart stay strong, hunter (*greeting*).

sivamés sielam—my heart and soul.

sívamet—my love of my heart to my heart.

sívdobbanás—heartbeat (*literal*); rhythm (*figurative*).

sokta—to mix; to stir around.

soŋe—to enter; to penetrate; to compensate; to replace.

susu—home; birthplace (*noun*). At home (*adv.*).

szabadon—freely.

szelem—ghost.

tappa—to dance; to stamp with the feet; to kill.

te—you.

ted—yours.

terád keje—get scorched (*Carpathian swear words*).

tõdhän—knowledge.

tõdhän lõ kuraset agbapäämoroam—knowledge flies the sword true to its aim.

toja—to bend; to bow; to break.

toro—to fight; to quarrel.

torosz wäkeval—fight fiercely (*greeting*).

totello—obey.

tuhanos—thousand.

tuhanos löylyak türelamak saγe diutalet—a thousand patient breaths bring victory.

tule—to meet; to come.

tumte—to feel; to touch; to touch upon.

türe—full; satiated; accomplished.

türelam—patience.

türelam agba kontsalamaval—patience is the warrior's true weapon.

tyvi—stem; base; trunk.

uskol—faithful.

uskolfertiil—allegiance; loyalty.

veri—blood.

veri ekäakank—blood of our brothers.

veri-elidet—blood-life.

veri isäakank—blood of our fathers.

veri olen piros, ekäm—blood be red, my brother (*literal*); find your lifemate (*figurative: greeting*).

veriak ot en Karpatiiak—by the blood of the prince (*literally: by the blood of the great Carpathian; Carpathian swear words*).

veridet peje—may your blood burn (*Carpathian swear words*).

vigyáz—to love; to care for; to take care of.

vii—last; at last; finally.

wäke—power; strength.

wäke kaδa—steadfastness.

wäke kutni—endurance.

wäke-sarna—vow; curse; blessing (*literally: power words*).

wäkeva—powerful.

wara—bird; crow.

weńća—complete; whole.

wete—water (*noun*).

From #1 *New York Times* Bestselling Author
CHRISTINE FEEHAN

DARK PREDATOR
A CARPATHIAN NOVEL

As brutal as the undead he hunted, Zacarias De La Cruz was a master executioner. Over the long, dark centuries, he plunged into so many battles they blurred into an endless lifetime of evil that hardened the soul of this merciless, ruthless and implacable dark predator.

Now his stark and savage journey is over. After a thousand years in a gray world, he has accomplished everything he set out to do. His brothers are safeguarded. Each has found a woman who completes him. And they are at peace. For his brothers, Zacarias has walked the edge of madness, but with centuries as a killing machine now left to the past, and without a hunt to define him, Zacarias wonders, for the first time in his life, who he really is.

The answer awaits him back home in Peru, in an unexpected betrayal, in the vengeance of an old enemy, in the inevitable consequences of a bloody family legacy, and in the deliverance of a lifemate he never could have imagined.

"After Bram Stoker, Anne Rice and Joss Whedon (who created the venerated *Buffy the Vampire Slayer*), Feehan is the person most credited with popularizing the neck gripper."   —*Time*

"The queen of paranormal romance."   —*USA Today*

"Feehan has a knack for bringing vampiric Carpathians to vivid, virile life in her Dark Carpathian novels."   —*Publishers Weekly*

penguin.com

THE CARPATHIAN NOVELS FROM
#1 *NEW YORK TIMES* BESTSELLING AUTHOR

Christine Feehan

DARK PREDATOR

DARK PERIL

DARK SLAYER

DARK CURSE

DARK HUNGER

DARK POSSESSION

DARK CELEBRATION

DARK DEMON

DARK SECRET

DARK DESTINY

DARK MELODY

DARK SYMPHONY

"Feehan...finds more readers
with every title."
—*Time*

penguin.com